BORN
BROTHERS

BORN
BROTHERS

LARRY
WOIWODE

MICHAEL DI CAPUA BOOKS

FARRAR, STRAUS AND GIROUX

NEW YORK

Portions of this book first appeared,
in substantially different form, in *Antaeus, Harper's,*
The New Yorker, and *The Paris Review*

With special gratitude to Bob Shapiro,
a brother

FOR WILLIAM MAXWELL

who always saw it as complete

AND FOR MY CHILDREN

God Be With You

Contents

Morning Light

Living

Leaving

Death: History

Losing

Learning

Last Light

A friend loveth at all times,

and a brother is born for adversity.

PROVERBS 17:17

MORNING
LIGHT

Dear Charles,

I had put off writing you for a few days because I wasn't sure of your address; that is, if you were still there. You may well have sent me a letter I didn't get, due to my own recent move.

I still have no definite plans for a vacation, other than knowing I'm going to take one. At present I work during the days at Pres-St Luke's, then do my extern emergency-room duties two nights a week out here. I plan a hiatus around the middle of Sept—I'll see what I can do as far as influencing my cell mate to drive to NY City. Let's just say that nothing is definite at present and leave it at that.

Last Friday (17th July) I was informed that I had been promoted to the Junior year. That almost certainly means that I will graduate from Med School, and the why bother? what next? is it worth it? and what is it? type feelings come flying faster all the time. But then nothing but drabness would result if I knew all the answers.

Next time I'll tell you about all the lives I've saved out here at Garfield. Right now I must catch the 6:00 AM bus for work.

Commuting is so much fun.

                                                        Fraternally yours,
                                                                    Jay

Garfield Park Hospital
Chicago, Ill   7/64

+

At the sight of his letter I'm back on my back in that room in the Chesro, on a bedspread with chenille waves worn away in the shape of a body. From the valley of the bed I can watch my patch of Manhattan sunlight, parted by a window sash, climb up the wall toward the ceiling, past the sink that doubles as urinal and bathtub. The tinny-dim sheet of greenish mirror above: the medicine chest. I picture myself at the sink, with a black line popping up, stinging, above my palm and turning pink under the faucet as a jolt goes through the cords that control my knees. A slice across the other starts a brownish gout down the drain . . .

I go over the speech I imagine myself giving when my brother arrives: At the beginning, I was sure I could see the end to this shining through from the other side. Please sit down. Do you prefer Jay now, or Jerome? No, you use the chair. I'm used to this bed. I feel I've been in this room for twenty-five years. Actually, it's closer to twenty, and the room hasn't always been the same, or even the place, but the identical events keep unfolding out from it, so it feels that way. Now, you and I know it isn't difficult to make a pilgrimage, and I'd like you to listen to how this one began with the arrival on the air of those sounds that I at first thought were mere internal noise.

Born beginning being better but—

Hn?

Daddy blew his smoke into me in breaths that were blue.

Hn?

Daddy blew blue smoke into my ear in a way that opened up inside rooms.

"Hn?"

"I know you're going to be feeling better, but you're going to have to sleep soon."

His words came down long tunnels of blue he drew away behind. Earache. The pain of it like a needle inside my head, deeper than the rooms and hallways that his smoke went traveling through.

I was four, at home in our big bed, which was as white and cold as snow, if I moved, from the fever that burned both eyes and laid me out in shivering lines—my head high on pillows, the light like ice when I looked out toward him through the air dividing my temperature in panes of different-colored shapes of light across the room.

He sat on a red stool, close, the rolls in his robe bulging over his lap, while his cigar, wedged fat in his fingers, lofted smoke above his black curly hair. He turned the cigar in his mouth, his cheeks going out like balloons, and smoke snagged along his face, frosty and dark against the window behind, huge. He leaned and a stream nipped at the hole in my ear, and then his lips connected with a kiss, and sudden smoke burned my eyes worse. Ow! I wanted to say.

My hands on the snowbanks, closed and neat.

"Are you feeling better now, Charlie?"

The sound of his voice set me on a slide toward sleep. "Oh."

"Smoke hurts?"

"Mmm."

"I hope you're going to be feeling better so you can sleep soon. I'm praying for you."

+

This room is so small that its two windows, with a narrow wall between, mist at their edges when I try to take them both in— no profile now to cover them, no wide dark face bending near, no voice with its slide toward sleep, or the shuffle of hoarse breath, tuneless, when he sang:

Pony boy, pony boy, won't you be my pony boy?
Don't say no, here we go, right across the plain!

The windows here are hung with dark-green plastic drapes I've pinned back, and a set of gauzy sheers, gray from city grime, renders every outside color pastel. I turn from the sheers as they sway in with the wind and brush a leg, and then I turn again, over and over, on into the night as I think, and sometimes say out loud, "I'm waiting here to be saved."

This is for him.

+

Memory alters the shape of the past—giving that uncle the chin he always needed, repainting a room in the shade it should have been—but it never alters the emotion that each shape has the power to evoke.

To remember is to admit loss and make ready for death.

+

There is a white picket fence as high as my eyes where I sit. Flowers sway and bend across its painted laths, which look damp with paint, as the ground is damp—a cold greasiness of clay. My white shoes on the grass beyond, on its spears and sheaves, are lumps of truth. I reach out to put one in my mouth but the light is so brilliant the moment burns through, and then I'm pulling up flowers and piling them in my lap.

+

Dark and light across a room. Most of the time it stays where it is, or, if it travels, it travels slowly—those slats taking most of the day to get to the top, the ceiling—but sometimes the light and shadow switch, and there is something that bumps. "It hurts," hard instead of soft, a door banged shut. I feel that a part of me has gone into hiding, a half I can't put my hands on, like the white shoe, and although I sit silent, listening (in a crib, I think), that half is moving in another room in a way I can't move, and is doing something I wouldn't do.

+

A white windmill on wheels, with a blade that turns, rolls between my knees. Uncle Elling's gift. I spin the blade and it windmills away. I pull it back. It wheels away again. I reach for it and a hand like mine hits my reaching hand. I look into the same face I see when Mom holds me above the sink to show me a pouting child. It's my brother, so they say, and he is the missing half. I start hitting him back.

Our house has three rooms. Ein, Zwei, Drei, his big voice goes counting, all coated in blue. The other one, my brother, is everywhere I want to go, hinging every which way, except in this room I crawl into. His name is like a car taking off, jurrr-*ohm!* There. He just stuck his head in the door to check on me.

Amber ampules clotted in a moving mass.

+

Inside the splintery boards of an orange crate, I watch the rope ahead, held in her glove, spring and hum as she trots in front of the sled the crate is on. I've never traveled so fast this close to the ground, and snow from her boots, which are busy in their run up the street, hits my face in clumps and ticks. And then a voice, in close warm breath, arrives with the reason I'm so imprisoned and warm; these are his elbows and knees. He cries out, "There's our old house!"

The white front with two windows, the door in between, four gray boards going in steps to a platform I could crawl beneath and watch shoes come scraping up. Ants winding in a ribbon through bars of light touched each other's ears when they met. "An ant is an insect that lives down a hole," Mom said then. "An *auhnt* is your relative." Off to the side, away from the steps, now almost buried under banks as white as the pickets, is the fence where I sat. And in the middle of winter I have flowers piled over my lap again.

Can something happen more than once?

Why did we move?

+

He travels below as I'm carried to a table where a woman in white, with a white hat like wings, stands in sun from high windows. A struggle with clothes and then an iciness streaks down my arm, starting a sweet thickness in my throat. A favorite smell. Rubbed with it through fever. Now so strong the light turns silver, as I hope I can have the white wad reeking of it, and then there is a flash that I'm sure is inside me—how could she do this?—and the sound that comes from my mouth is as glassy as the thing I see sticking in my arm.

Our yard and sidewalk, paths and streets and blocks widen out at this, and I'm standing in spring sun at our new place, next to the red-gray barn by the alley—Scott Haig's barn, we call it, as we call the house, which he owns, Scott Haig's house— and for the first time I understand, from the shadow and light on the boards beside me, what it means to have a brother. We're in the box that holds our "land pile," as he calls it, and so I do, to imitate him. Here Daddy drove down stakes, nailed boards across them to the barn, and filled the box with sand hauled home in gunnysacks. "A place for boys," he said.

My brother is in the center of a tractor tire inside the box, the place to be, and now he smiles and holds up a spoonful of sand—but then that is replaced by this room so far removed in time, with its dim ceiling covered with spatters I don't care to inspect, and I turn away, trying to wrest that moment from memory, subdue it, stop this, in the way that I tried to subdue him from that time on, although he was never mine to begin with, of course, and was here before I ever began.

+

Now, nothing is simple, but you and I know it isn't difficult to make a pilgrimage. All you have to do is pick up a suitcase or two, whether they're packed with clothes or not—in order to establish your identity—and set off. You have to have a place to head for, of course, and once you arrive you'll want a room that will hold a bed, a chair, and you. The pilgrimage, or the room itself, can also be called a retreat, and what you expect to happen on a retreat is a change. The change, you have decided, can take place only in isolation, but once you've settled into your room, with its bed and chair, there will be moments when you'll wonder whether you aren't waiting to hear a knock on the door—that auspicious visit. And if you incline too far in that direction, the knock will come, like it or not.

From the day that I moved into this room, I felt threatened. At the first sight of it, I slammed the door shut, trotted down to the super's apartment, put the key in his hand, and made for the street. But a week later, when I had looked at worse places for twice the rent— I was living in a hotel off Broadway while I looked, and one morning I opened the paper and saw that a man had been shot in the head the day before in the vacant lot beside my hotel (from a rooftop, it was conjectured, with a high-powered rifle) only about an hour after I had walked through the lot myself. It was the spring after J.F.K. had been assassinated, with everything under a tarnish, so that even colors looked off, and as I walked through the lot I felt sought out and bracketed, as if enameled on the air—the glitter of broken glass in the gravel about to fly into a kaleidoscopic fix—and now I left the hotel, numb, keeping close to buildings, and ended up in a thunderstorm, shocked by its mechanistic roar, with no grass or trees to muffle the rain driving over sidewalks and streets and cartops, washing up oil, filling gutters, causing their contents to float (all the windows around closed tight, with great traceries of water sliding down them), a section of the *Times* drooping in soggy wings over my head.

I stepped into an entry, and saw a man assembling umbrellas under a floodlight. He signaled me into a long room that smelled of fabric and varnish—bare except for rows of umbrellas resting open on the floor, and racks of their skeletons. He showed me how the covering was sewn in wedges and then fitted over the metal ribs, and it was the dexterity of his fingers that held me. The rain hadn't stopped, and heat waves rippled above a taut umbrella under the floodlight. I bought it for four dollars; my passport in the city, and probably partly a gift.

But when I went out with it opened, I was more aware of my soaked clothes, and my feet soaked worse, from the holes in my shoes after days of walking pavement, and then I saw, near Avenue A, the sign on its chains, creaking in a wind: THE CHESRO *Transient Hotel   Rooms by night   week, month, year*

The cramped vestibule with its wainscotting of dirty marble—shelter from the storm, at least. A smudged card above the buzzer read *Super Apt.* I pressed the button and waited, hearing the rain let up, and was about to leave when the lock responded with a rattle like a rale.

Up the steps, shedding drops like wrung-out vestiges of my remaining self-respect; into sight of the super, standing outside his door in slacks and bedroom slippers, bare from the waist up, scratching at his hair, then at his belly, brown as a loaf of bread. His hands went to his eyes—"Ah ya-*ha!*"—and twisted there like a child's.

"I'm sorry I woke you," I said. "Is that room still for rent?"

He stared at me in incomprehension, then looked down at my shoes, which gave off a bubbly hiss. "Room?" he asked. "Who you?"

"On the top floor. I looked at it last week."

"5-A?"

"Pardon?" I said.

"You sell mareewanna?"

" 'Pardon?' I said."

"Mah-ree-*wan*-na," he said, his tongue bulging from the effort to enunciate with his dentures out. "Pot."

I looked down, along the angle of his stare, to my attaché case and the dripping black umbrella I was leaning on.

"The Go'ment Man, yesterday, clapped him up, selling here," he said.

"I don't have a thing to do with it!" I said, appalled that he would think I dealt in dope.

A hand went to his chest, where tufts of hair, the color and texture of steel wool, grew in patches from enlarged pores, and then he placed the hand over his heart, an oath. "We eating!"

By now I was nearly overcome by an oily, garlicky, tomato-and-meaty smell gnawing the doorway behind him; I hadn't eaten all day.

"I'm sorry," I said. "I'll come back later."

"You got money for a munt?"

"I thought I didn't have to pay a security deposit." This promise had remained with me throughout my looking. "It's what you said before."

He shouted over his shoulder and a girl came running up and collided with his rump, then peered out from behind it. Seven, eleven, nine—I couldn't tell which, it had been so long since I had spent time among children. But her eyes were as shiny as her shoeblack hair: an intelligence I could trust.

"You got the bucks?" she asked, and laughed, half hiding behind his butt and baggy slacks again.

"I thought—"

"Show him some," she said. "Some dirty 'em and go, one day."

"Maybe I'd like to try it for tonight," I said.

"No overnight!" the super cried, suddenly angry. "No more!"

"But the sign says—"

The girl had a finger to her lips.

"No more wee-men up! No cathouse!"

I took out my billfold and unfolded it—forty-some dollars— and with a whistle the girl was gone. The super motioned me through the door, then through another, into a room so yellow it was like a cube of saffron, all brilliance and smell. His wife, stringy-thin, was at a stove that seemed the source of the yellow light, holding a child on a hip and stirring whatever it was that added the density of steam to it all. At the table was a fiftyish man, as thin as she was, whose features had floated through my consciousness for days without any connection—the long thin nose that looked stretched from mock weeping, watery eyes to go with it, and the grin of a man about to ask for a handout toward a jug of wine. It was here that I had seen him, the first day I'd looked at the room.

Now he pointed to his empty breast pocket, his ambiguous grin going off, and put a pair of fingers to his lips, so I shook out a cigarette. The super took a ledger from the top of a refrigerator painted aqua, shoved plates and silverware aside with it, and sat beside the mock weeper, who now needed a match. I lit him up and he seemed to exhale from every opening as he stared at the cigarette like a connoisseur.

The super had slipped on a pair of horn-rimmed glasses and was peering over them as he thumbed through the ledger's clothlike, greasy pages. I noticed graying coils in his hair, and then his lower lip slid out, crimson and fleshy, and I thought: A Negro. Suddenly they started to talk—the woman with her back to me at the stove, the girl popping her head in and out of a doorway, the sly-comic smoker from Cervantes, and the super, who went thumbing on. I could catch a few of the words but there was a Castilian slur to some, along with a slangy level of mispronounced English, all in rhythms that shook the sense out of my schoolbook Spanish. Puerto Rican. This is my pilgrimage, I thought; this is why I've come. The gullible and fanciful side of me had me living here for years, learning their language, eating their food, and then the super came to a page and ran his finger down a list of names, crossed out with a red pencil, under *Room 5-A*, and the other side of me went: I can take it for maybe a week.

+

"The Jethro (as I'll call the Chesro) is layered like the levels of Dante's Hell," I wrote a week later, in a sentence that took about that long to formulate. First thoughts come hardest; after that, things flow.

On the first floor, the super, Tony, lives in three steam-filled rooms, each of which has a kitchen stove in it, it seems. Something is always cooking. One or another of his extended family is usually at the table in his front room, which is also the kitchen, and the place where everybody pays the rent. (I have three hundred dollars of my savings hidden, in the form of a check only I can cash.) These people are older men and women he might be giving refuge; I won't say harboring, not yet. Tony and his wife have two children of their own, the only family here.

I should add that on the ground floor, beyond the narrow stairwell, huge printing presses groan and wallop and shake the building most of the day, turning out tracts and pamphlets in Cyrillic. This is a Spanish enclave in Little Russia—Ukrainian bars on both sides. On Tony's floor are the enfeebled, the palsied, the broken-down (on crutches and canes), the ones with bad hearts or the bulge of pacemaker batteries under their shirts, or those who can't be trusted far from Tony. They stand outside their doors or lie on their cots with their doors open, watching in hostile silence as I go by—my youth, I guess. On the next floor up are the elderly who can navigate better and are less vocal, along with the only young women in the building, a Negress and a Puerto Rican, who live above Tony's rooms—so they can pound on the floor if there's trouble?

On the next level are the alcoholics who get violent or noisy, or the troublesome, like the grandfatherly man with white hair who sits on his bed with the door open and argues in Russian with a person

*nobody can see, and then takes his head in his hands and cries, "Oh,
yo ho ho-ho-ho!" in a pattern like a formal lament, over and over.
And on the last floor, where I am, are the leftovers, the misfits, and
the young. The fellow beside me, who affects a Mexican poncho (he's
my age), sells mareewanna, I believe. I hear visitors whispering about
"nickels" and "bags," and on the first night when I moved in . . .*

I leaned back. I was in the health of youth and from that
vantage had the habit of assessment. I knew that these people
would have an effect on the change that would appear in me,
and I was happy for their diversity; I was happy to be among
them. I had come to the conclusion that there were no absolutes,
at least not for me. The only truth that was valid was the truth
that originated in me, without presuppositions, and all I needed
was the time to prove that.

*No single system or entity, such as God—if He exists—can contain
anybody's personal truth, I'm convinced, from the many facets I find
struggling in myself for expression—which the Jethro seems a picture
of. Whenever I step into the atrium outside my door, at the end of a
deserted hall, I'm filled with intimations of the lives on every side, not
to mention the layers below. This keeps me breathing light and on my
toes. Something unnameable is headed my way.*

*I'm upbeat and basically good, like most everybody when given a
chance. The only thing that bothers me is the smell of cooking from
Tony's rooms. Every part of this building and every person is subordi-
nate to that. You get a whiff of it from people's looks, or when you
put your hand on a stair rail. You can't get free of it, no matter how
often you wash your hair—it must be the protein in hair that smells
adhere to. I make few trips out, almost exclusively for food. I'm eating
less. Sometimes so many people are leaving, slamming doors, it's like a
shooting match. I went to a store today and bought a paperback
dictionary—all I'm going to allow myself. It maybe should have been
a Bible (I've searched through the drawers; no Gideon's here), but this
was the best I could do, given the neighborhood, and anyhow, I have
to stick to open-endedness and strict definitions. No givens. Facts.*

+

MAY 9. *The fellow beside me (Mexican poncho) and I opened our doors to head downstairs at the same time, and after some embarrassed business with keys at our locks, I tried to make friends. He looked put off, perhaps because I was in a suit jacket and carrying my suitcase— or attaché case, actually. I carry these notes out when I leave, so they aren't peeked at; Tony and the maid have passkeys. I suppose I could be envious of Mr. Poncho—I mean, of the visitors he has. There. See. He could read this and construe that to mean something. Or somebody could.*

+

MAY 17. *This spring at last feels summer-bound. I pried open both windows, which are so close together they look cross-eyed, to let in air. Then I sat on the sill of the window to the right (it opens onto a fire escape) and soaked up the late-morning sun. Been sleeping a lot. Bells from the neighborhood churches were bonging in the blocks around. I felt restored, ready for the change in me, and then I noticed, at the other end of the fire escape, a pigeon lying on its back on the metal slats, flattened—dead for so long its bones were poking through matted feathers. It could get you down if you let it.*

+

To start. The rent (to abbreviate matters) was nine dollars a week. No deposit, as promised. Could the super's daughter be nearer thirteen? I received a smile from her as I peeled off the bills and laid them on the table, light piling over them in a yellow sheen. "No di-ning!" the super said, meaning in the room, and I thought, Who could? I knocked back some drinks at a bar next door, where everybody was rumbling in that extra-ordinarily low octave Ukrainian has, and then hailed a cab to the hotel, picked up my suitcases and guitar, and told the driver I was delivering these to a singer who preferred to live in flophouses. "Bob Dylan," I said, suggesting by my winks and nods that I was Dylan, as if it were necessary to explain our destination, given my clothes. The alcohol.

Then dripping again, in the fan-shaped atrium. Three doors with pea-green panels, their numbers painted over. A bare light bulb above, suspended from the ceiling on a greasy, twisted cord, its bulge speckled brown by generations of flies, as if emerging from the filth of a surrounding squeeze as light. It sways in a wind. Or I sway with concentration, drawing its burning heat closer to my forehead, which gives off scattering coils at its center like sparks. The membranous present. Pity for the world and the way we've left it. No, built our way up from it with the materials it has yielded, now petrified into mistakes we take for the truth. Babel. Everybody running chickenshit away toward any door of comfort. Or those at the edges scabbing on additions to keep the killing light from exposing it all as a sham.

Then to work the tricky lock.

Not as bad as I remembered, except for the stink: death down wet holes. Over to the windows, which won't raise at first, then bang wide. Out the right one, green metal slats of a fire escape, with a clump resembling a rag in the corner, about to sift through like ash. A flop back onto the bed, too giving to provide an overview. The present so thin, with the past burning away the future at a point like a welding spot—held in its bead of consuming bubbling heat. The fuel of the past feeding the future—or the future as it's perceived, open-ended, although it must be as structured as the past to remain in balance, no collapse.

The ceiling covered with paper printed with bricks, the lines of mortar silver. Whoever put them up unable to match the rows of bricks from sheet to sheet at the seams—and who'd put bricks, even paper ones, on a ceiling? Another paper meant to resemble knotty pine pasted over the walls in generally vertical swaths, except under the windows: crosswise there. A wardrobe at the foot of the bed, covered with marbleized paper, brushes the ceiling, a string of yellow fringe around its top.

This gets me up. I open its door. A sweet smell of aging wood sending the last of its resin toward light. I put my suitcases and guitar inside and knock on it—not veneer—and then poke my head inside, down on my hands and knees, and breathe its scent, like a spring in the woods, and imagine crawling inside to sleep. Or living in it. My real room within this representation around, telescoped down a degree to throw people off. I sniff it and put my tongue to the wood. Mahogany.

And then I'm scrambling away with chills kneading my

back. It's the first place a thief would look, and there's no lock on it. A face like Hopalong Cassidy's is smiling up from the linoleum. Something in its pattern. My one eye able to focus beams in on a suitcase on the floor of the wardrobe, to the approximate spot where my three hundred dollars are stashed, under the innersole of one of those worn-out shoes, and I feel, as if tripping an alarm by my attention, a seismic change in the neighboring rooms. From the wall behind the wardrobe, where the fellow in the poncho lives, a smell like burning leaves filters through, with a double-voiced straining over tokes, and then a woman's near knee starts knocking the wall as they strive together with their senses pried open to the explosive end, a clattering melee of growls and shrieks—his Levi's around his sneakers, poncho on, and the woman trying to chew her way through it, from the frothy sounds.

And then from a door across the room, which I hadn't noticed, with a shelf like a bar spanning it, a moan seems to rise in response, but then a stream goes tinkling into a container of tin—prostatic groans.

I sit, and then have to stand to get my bearings. No bathroom. I go out the door, into the atrium, and down a short hall to another door, its upper glass panel stamped with translucent stars. The door swings over miniature hexagonal tile (those gangland slayings in barbershops) dirtied by bilious feces drying, considering the reek. A stool with a repainted seat, the cover missing from its tank, water circulating through it: a floating milk carton bobbing above its top. Bear-claw legs of a tub gripping the tile, as if tearing the cracks in it; a plastic curtain, with scum caked in its folds, hooked to a hoop of pipe, where a brass shower head, as large as the head on a sprinkling can, drips past a window that looks onto a dirty shaftway.

Back in the room, on the bed, displaced, I figure I might as well be Dylan, though nobody would recognize him in this place, and then my flesh takes on the contours it does when his music invades me at its highest decibels—bare stick figure of existence that I'm able to get by on. No indebtedness. No dues. Don't think twice; it's all right.

There's a slap and rattle at my door and the sly-comic sidekick from Cervantes is inside by the time I'm on my feet (I must have forgotten to slip the bolt), smiling as if to remind me of the forty-odd dollars I've flashed. He has a hammer in one hand. He surveys the room in a slick-eyed roll and homes in on the wardrobe. He asks for a cigarette and I have it in his mouth and lit fast as a wingbeat, a check on him. Using both languages, he lets me understand that if I pay him a dollar a week he'll give my room special attention.

I hand him my pocket change, and say, "Let's give it a try."

He gets down on his knees and I get down on mine again, a pushover to suggestibility, and we lean and look up at the sink trap, encrusted with layers of paint, largely dark-green, cracking away from its U. He taps it with the hammer, sending down a shower of flakes, and goes into an explanation I can't understand, pointing and crooking one finger, then turns to me, his ambiguous grin going awry, and puts a hot hand on my shoulder. "Pobre Jorge," he says, and rolls his eyes, then nods at the bed, an invitation. "Pobre Jorge." It is wine.

If I walked out tonight, I wonder, what could they do?

+

MAY 22. *Terrible dream. One so awful you don't want to wake, because that means claiming it, and then you're never quite the same. I'm still shaking and have to pant to get my breath, reliving parts of it—that real. Apocalyptic nuclear destruction of the spot where I stood, beside a park like Union Square. I have to— There the ballpoint flew from my hand and hit the floor like fallout from it. I have to put it down in some form so I can walk away from it.*

> *Warning spirits or familiars aren't*
> *Supposed to appear anymore, I was*
> *Assured, but one did, in a dream,*
> *In the shape of a man, laughing.*
> *He threw himself on the street and*
> *An orange wave spread from him. I ran.*
> *Buildings of steel and brick were knocked*
> *Back off their foundations and dissolved.*
> *Pavement rose like pages in a book, printed*
> *With bodies, automobiles—and then pieces*
> *Of it all came past in a sucking silence*

Until the collapsing boom formed
A mushroom overhead, blowing even
The wind away in an ashy silence that
Put out the light of the world.
When the wave reached me, I—

*Same day. Continuing later. When I got to this point, I shoved
back the chair, not sure I could take this alone, feeling last night's
coffee (all these cardboard containers in my wastebasket) about to come
gargling up. I grabbed my towel from the sink and threw it over an
arm like a maniple, which I do so anybody in the hall will know
where I'm headed, and heard somebody tapping on the door.*

"Cleanin lady," a voice said. "You need cleaned up in there?"

*I looked around the room in wildness, as if there had been an
actual holocaust, and then I believe I said it wasn't so bad.*

*"Bed?" she asked. She asked if it was made, or if I wanted it
made, and I opened the door. Her eyes with their yellowy whites were
rolling so much I checked to see if my pants were on, and then draped
the towel over my shoulders and let her in. What a relief to have her
in this room.*

+

MAY 27. *This street is unlike any other in the city. Doors and
storefront trim are painted in primary colors, and there is a musical
pattern to the colors that you feel you will catch if you learn the
sequence of variations. The street has its own smell, of stew and wine,
mingled with a heavy Latin saffron underbubbling, so that I could say
if I was near it, even blindfolded. When I walked down the block the
first time, before I knew I would move here, I started singing "On the
Street Where You Live," and felt the way I used to feel when I ran
across town and got my first glimpse of our property—that
breathtaking knowledge that I had a home. The mystery is that the
mystery keeps growing. It appears wherever it wishes, in whatever
guise it adopts, and beams out of a face or a cornice with the power to
confound. So I have to start over with no assumptions, or the premise
that experience can teach. Nothing remains under the jolt of the new.
Nothing relates to what I see now.*

*Old men walk up and down the street as if they're running
errands, wearing hats and old overcoats in this heat, and seldom*

deign to stop and talk to one another, though they're friends. Mostly foreign languages are spoken, and the contrast between the two most common, Latin and Slavic, is like hornets in an iron drum. Up the block is an old people's home, where patients worse than the ones here are brought out to the sidewalk each day for an airing, always when I'm walking by, it seems. Or a hearse is parked at the curb and a body on a stretcher, draped with velvet, goes wheeling across my path.

One bald man with trembling hands and a single glistening eye (the other is a grayish globe contained in its rolling by a spiderwork of tissue) always stops me, grabs hold of my shirt, and begs a cigarette with scissor fingers. I know I shouldn't give in, but he grabs hold and rolls his horrible eye until I do, and then stuffs the cigarette in a pocket, clacking his teeth, winking the good eye, and sends eruptions out of the ragged hole in his throat where a voice box should be.

Bums from the Bowery go by, sucking the nipples of their twisted paper bags, blank and stunned, as if they're trying to find their way back to familiar ground, and now and then the anonymous man in front of me, always in a suit and tie, it seems, dips at the waist and goes for the curb, throwing out his arms in a swan dive, and releases rattly puke in the gutter. A gang of adolescents rules the block at night, or terrorizes it; there are street fights with other gangs, both sides armed with knives and chains, and the worst of the casualties are carried off in city vans. One night a pedestrian, a well-dressed man who shook a fist at the gang leader, was attacked in a flurry and lay on the sidewalk, blood spreading beyond his rumpled body, while the windows on all sides banged down. Some of the gang, along with their teenage girls (made up like tarts), usually sit along the well of the three steps that lead down to the door of the Jethro—my personal gauntlet to run.

The street is unnumbered and ends at Tompkins Park, and every time I come to the avenue where it begins, walking east from the subway, the corner sign sends my breath bulging into my throat, and three heartbeats thock there like marbles pressed into my windpipe:
St. Marks Place.

In my room I have the missal Dad got me at the start of high school, as if I had reached my majority then; and there was a sense that evening, at the church sale in the basement of the parochial school, of being singled out, when he touched the missal I'd been leafing through—large as a priest's and with a half-dozen colored

ribbons dangling from it—and said, "You like this?" Then bought it
as I stared up at him like a four-year-old. Now in the missal I see:
"Sts. Mark & Marcellianus, Martyrs, Red, Simple: These two
brothers were pierced with arrows, after a day and night of suffering,
A.D. 286." And feel it refers to Jerome and me—a heart-stopping bolt
of grief. What is happening to him?

+

Today, when I see the sign *St. Marks Place*, after another empty
session of tryouts and rounds to agents, and step up on the
curb, I, he, we, the entire corpus of us lift into an atmosphere
of anxious possibility, where the first concussion of the ultimate
bomb might come, or snipers find the right position behind
open windows, breathing on oiled stocks, while mica in the
sidewalk hovers like suspended specks about to fly into place,
sending my legs into the numb wallow they have at night on
unknown ground.

Which is how I approach the Chesro, terrified that the
sidewalk is littered with eight-by-ten glossies of me flung out
my window, and when I start down the three steps, walking
over facsimiles of my face, the teenage thugs jump up and say,
"There he is! That's the guy!" One grabs my hair and jerks my
head back while another makes a sparkling sweep through my
throat with a switchblade—not to kill but to cut my windpipe to
silence me—and then slices through my shirt to my belt and
saws away at that, the knife point punching deep as my throat
blows blood like the bald cigarette bummer, and then rips down
my pants and has others hold me as he uses the dulled blade
to gouge open my sack and saw off my parts, one two three.

But the teenagers remain sitting, deferential—their attention picking me over to such a degree it seems to loosen cells
in my stomach as I step past with my attaché case. And then
the leader, with his T-shirt sleeves rolled up over the rolls of
his arms, and one sleeve cubed by a cigarette pack, says, "Yo,
bittio." I mean, what the hell is *that*?

In the vestibule, I shake in a night pisser's ammoniac reek,
sending steam over the door panes, it feels, as I fumble out the
keys I keep clutched in my pocket to stab with. And realize,

from the half-dozen portraits of me in glass, pale from poor food, that the thugs believe I'm an addict—a role they probably revere in its downhill dive toward self-destruction.

Cooler air, the edge of being inside: that queasy superiority of sudden relief. The amplified rasp of my shoes on the stair's sandy treads, like locomotive's chuffs, echo off the stairwell as I see, in a flickering series, the scale I stepped up onto in the subway wavering at 122; the dimness of a distant club car and the faggy-acting Okie with his Elvis cut mirrored beyond blackish glass, along with the tabletop and bottles and my own face, as if a quartet of us were projected through space and engaged in maneuvers manipulated from the outside, satanic and condign, with pinpoints of light in the distant countryside shivering through our reflections—this on the train to Chicago last spring to see Jerome, on the first part of my pilgrimage; while in a more physical measure of memory I encounter the different shapes and weights of bodies I've inhabited, and recall how, just before I left for Chicago from a cushy booth-announcing job, I put on so many pounds so fast that when I hurried up or down a flight of stairs like this my breasts performed under my shirt like a fifty-year-old woman's who has forgotten her bra.

On the molding outside the super's door, where the mail is wedged, one letter, mine, with a return address that sets up a trembling in me. *Him.*

The old people are in their doorways, watching, and my ears twitch toward them for a warning of anything amiss. The second flight—wooden steps with clattering chromium strips affixed to them—leans to the left in an incline that increases with every floor, so that when I reach the final landing (or start up to the roof as I've done), I'm off-kilter, unbalanced; and now to hold myself plumb I shift the attaché case to the other hand and let my shoulder slide along the wall.

"Featherdusting, they call it in the theater, he thought," I whisper, as the wall skids away under my jacket with a tearing sound. I pause on a creaking tread; a chink.

We are less than a year and a half apart in age and in the style that is in fashion at the time we are dressed in matching—

I shake free of this and step on.

Featherdusting, they call it in the theater, he thought. You take a featherduster and dip it into a bucket whose bottom is covered with water-base paint, and then slap it against the inside of the bucket until most of the paint flies free, and then dab it over a painted flat so the flat takes on, from the aspect of the audience, the dimensional texture of plaster or stucco or, with additional work, knobby stone. Crenellated castle keep. Stairs up to the dungeon; a life of walking these.

A similar technique employed here, to apply ivory enamel over the dark green of the stairwell, but the effect is of moldy cheese, or an eroding disease of the flesh in its final stages of corruption. I'm panting outside my door. There is always the possibility that it will be off its hinges. Or somebody will be behind it, waiting—a teenager up the fire escape, the handyman on an inside job, or my personal assassin, wandering the other half of the world, here for his or her final rendezvous. Or worse, I'll see myself turn from the bed, startled, as I say from the door, "What are *you* doing here?"

Then to work the tricky—

Did I put my keys away when I picked up the letter? I set the case down, scissor the letter and *Backstage* between my thighs to free both hands for the pocket of these pants, too tight; bought when my others grew baggy, in a Broadway shop where shiny stacks of them were the mainstay of a place going out of business, according to its sign, and a cheery Puerto Rican seemed to sense my unease, as if seeing through to this place, and worked his sale on that. Laughing with him at the feel of them under his love pats. "Keep the others, ha-ha," I said, as in a cheap shoe store, and walked out wearing the new. Worth it for his look. Like feelings that storm out of the past and have to be integrated, leaving the moment that they rose from coldly sovereign, unaffected by you.

Then to work its tricky lock.

I knee the door open so it hits the sink with a crash, and feel another door open off the back of my mind onto a black freeze that the odor of the room enters—something of a goat, or curds turning—which passes from my feet to my stockings and is beginning to gather in the wardrobe and appear, I'm afraid, on my breath. I hit the switch. The fluorescent tube flashes its night lightning, slamming nothing unexpected into the frame, and then goes on for good in a dim buzzing drone. The bureau mirror. The eight-by-ten glossies; a single full face and four character shots on their low shelf—the board like a bar over that door.

I won't check the dust lines on them, as I've promised myself I would not do again, and then I see my real image flickering in the big tilted bureau mirror that trembles whenever I move in the room or the presses below begin to wallop and quake as if running off misdeeds of mine that multiply with such dimension I keep leaping out of my outlines.

I shut off the light, throw my case onto the bed, shut the door, put the letter on the bureau, then go around the bed and raise the roller shades and stop, overtaken by the sensation of the wait with Jerome at this hour for the evening meal, in our assurance that it would appear—the past heaving up peeling landscapes. The hovering line of light over snowbanks at noon, like a force rising from them, and how a short walk down a plowed road could seem days in length in that brilliant suffusion of sameness, light on snow, white on both sides, and then this heavily rolled bulge of ice, earth-streaked, at our boots. But the firmness of his walk kept insisting, Only a day, only an hour, only a second of one season of the year, while the shuttering of time through the moment as through branches overhead made the opening onto spring more apparent. Green steps going from a melting landscape into greenery.

The pinned-back drapes let light through the sheers, but the grime in the weave of the sheers, or its glaze on the glass beyond, tints the air, so that the marbleized wardrobe and the rest—the bureau painted red-brown, the bedside table, the gray chair next to the bed occupying most of the room—take on the aspect of a stage set before it is struck for the last time. I go for the sink, unzipping, unstuck from the past. There is no escape from a pilgrim's cell.

I shake off the last yellow-orange drops, like food coloring down the sink, hit the faucet, step around the bed, and shove up both windows, sash weights rumbling inside the walls in phlegmatic Slavic. Across the street, in the window opposite, is my huge neighbor in her gray bathrobe. She sits on a pillow on her sill and rests one arm, Juliet-like, on a piece of metal grillwork that curves out from her window in a mock balcony—the only person in sight, closer than the teenagers below, and at this level she seems touchable, if I let my limits extend—and then she raises her eyes in a look that lets me understand she's seen me at the sink and is sickened. A virago, able to eviscerate with her abusiveness. She and her son shout to each other up and down, and she's yet to be bested in her battering obscenities; the son calls her Mama Balls.

I step behind the narrow wall between the windows and stare down the block; greenery of a corner of the park, where the crowns of trees, in their mediated foliage among brick, have the look of stilled explosions. The dream that woke me. I ease around, and out the other window the buildings up the street, with a yellow exception, are orange and gray, like the row of a chessboard in that diabolical Russian story being serialized in the city's weekly magazine: rooftop ventilators, water towers, stairway hoods with their single metal doors, skylights, chimney pots, and, thrusting up everywhere in a bristling fretwork, television antennas—bare frozen pergolas of a less substantial time and design.

I reach and grab a sack off the fire escape, hurry to the other side of the bed, and hunch over. Amplified crackle of greasy paper, along with a scratching noise. Minuscule pinkish pinheads, insects, move in swirls through the French bread, its holes their caves or labyrinths, all of them alive to a pattern of motion that never takes the least of them by surprise. Now they peel back in waves from my attention, aware of a face. The sound is the faucet, not them.

Toss of the sack and bread back out, for the pigeons, but the salami under the faucet. The bugs go down like a stain. On the bed, my back to her, I tear the casing away and take great bites, barely chewing, and get down chunks that claw as if to climb. Taste of juniper, perhaps the black spots spices, keep going, Agh-*gawk*! Gagging bite of— Dimwit! Horse-ache! Squiggly walls of knotty pine and bricks aswim. Argh! Think of three windows, with mullions like— Others live on worse. No memory quite enough to nourish; none you can escape so fully into that you vanish. Youth as death, the voice of machine guns.

Bodies paying the price up front. Thanks to you I'm alone. Thank you for that.

The letter, hope of pleasure, next on the dresser top. Unless I have to clean *uch!* up this sordid tangle it takes to exist. Save the letter for after a shower, a reward, although the vision of that place sends heated clots untangling through the bloat in my craw. The sight of Jerome's name comes down through corridors of green more secure in their placement than the one outside, and sets my hair bristling like the network of antennas on the buildings, and already I'm composing an answer, *I haven't mentioned this to you because I know how you worry about my well-being, but there's no desk in this room and to write I have to mount one of the knobs of a dresser and sitting sidesaddle write at shoulder level,* as I tear open the envelope:

> *Dear Charles,*
>   *I had put off writing you for a few days because I wasn't sure of your address; that is, if you were still there. You may well have sent me a letter I didn't get . . .*

+

We are a year apart and are dressed in matching sailor suits, bib overalls, knitted tams and plaids, and from the time we begin appearing in town we are taken for twins. "Let me see, now. You're Jerome."

"No, *I* am," he says, and I look at his grownup-sized head, with its silky whitish hair, which parts by nature on "the girl's side" and has to be trained in place with liquid hair set that comes in a comb-length jar. The bulge of bone at the back of his head is huge, and its domed front forces his eyes into slits, Oriental-shaped, with faint downsloping eyebrows that lift in sad bands when he smiles. His eyes, lit from behind, with a probe in them—now on me, now off—sometimes mourn like a mistreated dog's. His lips, so full that the upper folds over the lower at each corner when he smiles, droop—the lower with a weighty plumpness that seems to say, *This is the way it is. This is the way it will be.*

While I think, *Dear me, do I look like that?*

I turn to the bureau and see his letter, held in my hands at the mirror's top, shaking with the presses in this shaking and wonder at these phantoms of our youth. Rainy days on the Great Plains, our eyes on one far hill as if it were truth—though my version might seem to him a monstrous image magnified out of praise, or the opposite, considering the years I have to travel through. I had no words for it then.

+

Through the door of our bedroom, past the dining table, are three windows that let in light. When we look up from the floor where toys and shadow lie, it's like looking out a ship. The sun is so bright beyond the tied-back curtains we can hardly see our neighbor's house, which is a wall of white without windows. The dining-room table, in the windows' alcove, is glazed with sun that trembles on the ceiling in three panels if we bump it, or purposely shake it to watch the panels rock, which drives Mom "wild," as she says. Us, too. The shadows of the table legs, moving in separate blacknesses and lengths through seasons of the sun, turn like solid bars.

We shake it now, laughing, then crawl in a thumping race to our room over a blooming like mountains underneath. The rug going in a downhill plunge, the slide of earth's skin pulling free. Over the hump of wood at our door, banging my knee, we grab two creatures made of Crazy Ikes, and gallop them toward one another in the crash of a fight. A giraffelike head goes spinning off.

"I did not!"

"You're a liar!"

"Thief!"

"Say!" we hear, in the low voice that comes to us from another height. He is in the door, a tall man in a white shirt and green suspenders, taller than our mother here, his curly hair nearly at the door's height, with the sun from the windows sending silvery worms weaving in and out of his shirt. We three. He stands as he does after a warning: The Superintendent. At school he teaches math, science, history, and English, each one a finger he unfolds from his hand and then extends all four fingers flat, his thumb bent at the joint like a pistol cocked—a trick I can do but Jerome can't—and then lays his other hand across the fingers, grips them, and gives a shake. Now he speaks:

"Dad always said to us on the farm that you could pretty much tell how a man would treat people from the way he treated his horses. And anybody who would treat toys like that would probably treat horses the same way. And for brothers, how you two talk! Do you hear?"

Then we're blinking at sunlight as his footsteps go out to the kitchen, where we hear him say in the voice he usually uses at home, "Good evening, dear. I'm back already. Here, let me help you."

+

Dad is talking to a Father with a shiny head who sits in a chair at the window where the sun comes up: *front room*. Jerome and I are beside him on the couch, half faint from being forbidden to move. The Father can do this. He says words funny and is all in black, with a white ring around his neck: Schimmelpfennig. Dad's ring is on Jerome's side, I see, as great a loss to me as when Dad hangs his hat up high; I could smell the aroma of his head in it all day.

I take the hand next to me and put it, huge and dark, over my shorts. He pulls it away, to point something out while he talks, and when it returns I spread it over my legs again. It's bigger than both my hands and as wide as my lap. Blue bulges run in rivers under the wrinkles, and black hairs lift from it in curls. The inside is pink, with paths over it, and yellow bumps up where his fingers start. These fingers are tough. I hold one in my hand as I do when we're walking, wishing we were, and its rough curved nail is like a turtle's shell. I want a turtle, and this is the hand that could give it to me. *My pet.*

I lean to look into the room where they sleep, and on the end of the bed I see her legs and shoes: *lying down to rest*. The start of her dress is there and then the door ends, or the wall is, so I bend over, pulling Dad's arm around my back, and his fingers squeeze my shoulder in a grip that hurts. I stick the end of one in my mouth and bite the turtle's back.

"All right, now, Chuck," he says, and slaps my leg. "That's enough."

+

Enough, yes, as I hear another voice say: In every life there is a need to learn about mercy, which first must be learned from a parent. So why the pain like a hole in my heart here? Because of my impatience with my own son, now at this most trusting age, four? Or from another of the scars along the wounds in anyone who imagines he can heal himself, and then you?

Where were we?—am I?

It's difficult for us to fit a word to something it doesn't sound like, especially for him. If the word won't match the part of the thing it's meant for, or the thing itself, it slips off the, ah, whatyoumaycallit, you know, that shiny bending thing, wide at the end but flat, for slipping under and lifting—and we learn to use the names that others do, when we do (spatula, for that, for instance, now in Daddy's big hand, turning over eggs crinkled at their edges), out of habit. There are times when this won't work for Jerome. He'll stare at something, his face set, and mouth its word over and over, to tame it to its sound, or vice versa, and there are times when this won't work, either.

I rise on my haunches from the floor, my head cocked, hearing a car on our corner take off, and say, "Jerome. What was that?"

"A cow."

"A what?" I have him.

He bows his head and says, "A co-ow."

And later, exchanging farms formed by squares in the linoleum, where implements and hard rubber animals stand, he says, "That's my car."

"What?" I have a black-and-white Holstein in my hand.

"That's my car."

" 'Cow,' you dumb nut."

A further problem arrives when I adjust to his confusion, and ask one day where Dad is going, and Jerome says, "To fill the *car* up with gas."

Consider this the brief for a case to be presented later.

+

Spring. Out our front porch is the neighboring wall of white. Deke Frieze's place. We wear our caps. Past the skinny tree we hammer nails into, like a catch in memory, each bleeding a long golden tear. Past the front of Deke's, where a door without steps is nailed shut and screens in gray frames hang like tattered orange cloth, then down Deke's drive to his weed patch. One day at a time and one time, this day.

We lie on our bellies, altered in this growth that shields us from people (and the sun, even, in some of the burrows we've hollowed beside a huge fallen tree), and engage in snake-crawling, as Jerome calls it, bending sideways at the waist and shoving with the opposite knee, our arms tight at our sides, no fair to use, going deeper into Deke as our eyes narrow to beads in the thickly twined grass with its sickening yellows and greens.

Old Deke might be on his porch on this side with a cat in his lap, combing his hair in the sun, or might walk to his door with a scrape of carpet slippers—the rims of filthy winter underwear at his ankles and wrists, a cat in each hand—watching us with eyes that purr. Or we walk right in. The cats on the table leap away from us among tins of food and start complaining, over and over, like porch swings set screeching up and down the block, and keep this up until Deke rises from the quilts and blankets on his cot across the room. Cats gather so close to his slippers that he picks up the one that suits his mood and drapes it down his front as he sits in the rocker and stares at us with a look like a shrine to a saint inside, and sometimes goes *hoo hoo hoo*, crying so hard he can't stop.

Mister Man, we call him, but only between us, our name for everybody strange, and then laugh at the sound of it, but not here. Here we call him Deke, as he tells us to. Our mother doesn't like this, so to her we say Mr. Deke Frieze—too much to remember some hot afternoons.

"So," he says, in his voice that has a noise in it like singing gnats. "So, have you boys been good today? Have you listened to your ma and obeyed her rules? Or your dad, if he's laid some down?"

We dip in the deep nods he enjoys, since we look the same, he says, while I narrow my eyes and Jerome narrows his lips. Twins. On Deke's walls, in yellow light with clouds of sparkling pinpoints drifting through, are posters of a blue I've seen only here. Letters in gold and silver glitter, branching into scrolls, or with glittery rays shining out from curlicues, speak from the posters in the dim hoarse voice Deke adopts when he reads them:

JESUS IS GOD   BLESS THIS HOUSE
FOR YOU CHRIST DIED

He rises from his rocker, letting it rock for the cats to paw and bat, and serves us store-bought cookies from a tin. We flap our hands to keep off the flies ("In case you dare eat there, which I'm sure you do, keep the flies off your food!" our mother has said), a performance Deke believes is our wave of goodbye.

"Yes, I know, but don't forget and go out till you finish up," he says, hoarse notes. "Your ma mayn't like you having such sweets between meals, I suppose, hoo hoo." He's crying. "But I can't help it! I know that's why you come here, *hoo*, ain't it? Oh, yes, and here's yours, kitties, cats, a hoo hoo!" The same cookies, crumbled over the floor. He pulls out a handkerchief and wipes his eyes. "Now you boys, a hoo, run and play while you got the *hoo!* freedom, a hoo."

Around a branch of the fallen tree, the smell of weeds and crushed grass like perfume leading to the place where she gathers us to tell a story—stems and leaves shaking spears and sharp saber tips at our eyes—while dew from the grass that the sun doesn't reach (how chilly, even at noon, over our overalls) passes up our thighs as we slither under the trunk of the tree and see a real snake, jaws wide, wiggling its tongue at us.

We're up into light and back, panting, at the tree, where droplets from the nails attract ants, yellow jackets, and bees.

Most people have statues.

Most people are Catholics.

Son of real tears, man of sorrows.

+

We go over the crossroad to Mrs. Glick's ditch, through her lilac bushes, to her hedge at the back, and through it to the road that runs along the blank difference our town has from others: The Lake. Its high ledge looks down on a spread of water that pulls in waves through our legs and giving knees.

"Would you jump from here?" I ask, in one of the dares that get more dangerous each day.

"Would you?" he asks, and his eyes enlarge, saying, *I'm ready to.*

We take off on a run, scared, hurry through Mrs. Glick's side door, and yell, "Potato pancakes!"

She drops her sewing and goes to the bin at the bottom of her stairs and takes out a potato, peels it in one long curl (for her chickens to fight over), and grates it into a bowl among the clutter on her table, kindling up odors of sweat and kerosene.

"Well, Jerry!" she says. "How's it with Jerry today, ay?"

She always uses his name; it's her grandson's, and she thinks Jerome was named for him, because Mom and Dad lived here, on her front porch, when Jerome was born, six months after *her* Jerome, but— Here Jerome rolls his eyes and wrinkles his lips (he was named after an uncle), as if he has no teeth, like her, and I try not to laugh as she looks past the back of his head at me, apparently Jerome to her. Her glasses are off.

"Yes, Jerry, all you have to do is ask, like I say, and here they are, fried the way your dad liked them so much when you three lived here—crinkly at the edges. Oh, I miss you all a lot! Forks! Why do I always forget forks when forks is what you need to eat? Your ma once called me a scatterbrain right to my face, God bless that baby doll of a gal. All right, eat up there, Jerry, and you, too, mister." We smile at her mistaken switch of us, as if Jerome is Mister Man to her. "I'll fix you some more, if you want, when you finish up them," she says, and shakes her head at our house. "Just don't tell her."

+

Father's car smells of candy canes and wet cigars. Through blue smoke from one in Dad's hand, a farm goes past. I slide down from behind him, where I usually like to lean, and put my face on the bristly floor mat. Heated air blows under the seat over my eyes, and I close them and see a blue dot beyond my forehead. The car sways and the dot slips over a tunnel of blue I could enter again. *Last Chance.* Then a door opens and Dad leans down his head, smelling of hair oil, and says, "You boys stay back here. Guns can be dangerous."

Father raises the trunk and they pull out long brown socks and open them on steel darker than the car, then shove in red and green tubes and pump them up. They walk over stubble to a square of cornstalks, barrels down. A rag jerks up and both guns rise and punch their shoulders back.

> *Fwup!*   *Thwat! Thut!*   *Ka-thock!*

It's hard to tell if they walk or run, they're so small, and a hill in the field takes their legs and then the rest of them until they're gone. A racket arrives from above and we lean against the windows and stare up. Vs of geese, wider than clouds, float and quaver and rain down cries like glass being scratched. Then Father is saying, "Ach, a vaste of ammoonition, dem." The door opens on a smell of matches from their guns, and Father reaches to a bag on his back and dangles a bird from its claws. "One fessent," he says. "Your dot's."

Dad's, I think, and see Dad smile, then watch the head of the pheasant wobble on a sliver of skin.

"Perfect shot, Martin!" Father says.

+

Now to sit and simmer in the summer shine. Fling both windows wide? *No, no, no* comes down to me like a litany from another time—my mother's voice. I'm in a different city now, in a room with one window, under fluorescents that hum in the pitch of an overhead sun, and my thigh hurts. Ahead again. No matter how far I travel from events, portions of them remain at my edges, more durable than that table I ran into. My thigh aches, but the ache remains inside a knot pulling me outward with an even greater force. I always felt I was close to those years, but while I looked away the world around them changed, and then I was an old man.

+

Hot summer, and a sky with no limit to its lift of blue. We're in the back yard, at the top of the stepladder Dad keeps out for his work on Scott Haig's barn. A jar as tall as hair set stands on the ladder's top, and we stick wire rings in it and blow through them to see whose bubbles will float farthest out. A few make it to the road and go up in silent explosions that send off flying spray. We can see the lake from here, its sunken-blue surface as still as the sky, with dark strips sliding below—not shadows or swaying weeds, but catfish we'll catch, we hope. Our height is immense. There isn't a curve to the sky, it's so clear, and then I sway and see, at the side of our house, the slant of the gray cellar door, and think: An airplane.

We sail paper planes from the ladder, in a contest to outdo our bubbles. It seems there is a birthday party going on below, or the yard is crowded with friends around tables covered with paper tablecloths, or it's the beginning of a rattling hail, but no. We get the garden hose and drag it up, firemen now, and spray it toward the house—a cone of fizzing mist that sets off a rainbow—spray it toward the road and Mrs. Glick's; then Scott Haig's barn, whose roof is gaping now, after Dad began to tear it down for lumber to give to Grandpa Jones; toward the outhouse, with wires running to the ground from the corners of its roof.

"Watch out for those clothes on the line!" our mother calls. She's in the back porch, behind a row of windows I see her through in smaller shapes, as if the windows are on top of one another instead of side by side, running back through different days to the rooms of other houses that open backward to— We turn the hose straight up and I'm walking beneath the fluttering clothes on the line, imagining a row of diapers, with a letter on each, spelling TIMOTHY, our new brother's name, as I sing to a radio song the words an uncle has taught us: "I'm lookin under a two-legged wonder, that I've underlooked before! First come the ankles, *second come the knees*, third come the panties that blow in the breeze! No use explainin the thing remainin is some-thing that I a-dore! I'm lookin under a . . . !"

I see myself in the loft of Scott Haig's barn, like the loft at Grandpa Jones's, where you can peer through a nail hole and watch yellow light film everything over like a screen—I'm walking under the half-open roof, keeping clear of the broken glass scattered on boards, among nests of hay so old they look like string, and see a jar with nails in it, a muddy Prince Albert can, Dad's toolbox, and then the shock of sky above; the shriek as he wrests old nails out of the roof with the nail puller, and the crisp rap, coming back from the lake, when he sets its jaws around another; the daze I feel with each nail pulled—eee-yah!—while I stand in the loft as we did at Grandpa's and watched Grandpa saw a cow's horn off with a handsaw; the awful smell and then a spout of blood from the cow's head running over an eye; and feel those days rise through this moment at the stepladder's top.

Jerome and I come down in a clunking rush and go to the lawn mower, one on each side of its handle, and push it over the lawn in lines as straight as we can, with our heads down and arms out straight, avoiding the hoops and balls of our croquet set, which we've left out again, and shouldn't have. Mowing is our job. We have to keep at it with our extra energy over the summer, Dad has said, and because we haven't remembered this, with the ladder and the rest, the day feels as quakingly spun as the whirring reel scattering clippings back over our feet.

"It's a heck of a time for that!" she cries, still in the porch. "Now that you've got the grass all wet with the hose! From your piddling around! With my clothes still on the line! It's getting dark out!"

We straighten from our pushing and see, in the curve of light above the lake, the darker band of night coming down, as if called by her, and feel afraid. What will Dad say? And then the frog catcher's son, who is walking beside the cables strung from posts along the lake, waves to us. He has appeared over the summer with his father, and they've moved into a deserted house out by the dam. For a living they sell frogs (and anything else they catch) to restaurants, Dad has said, where people pay money to eat them.

We run to the edge of the road, and stare at the gunnysack over his shoulder, at his dirty face and uncut hair, his patched shirt and raggedy pants rolled above dusty ankles, and figure if anybody would know what a pecker is—a word we're trying to figure out—he would.

We begin: "Do you know—" "How much do you—"

And he says that his pop gets ten cents a frog, market price, and for every one *he* catches, he gets that. His pop's fair. No, he says, holding the gunnysack up like an old man, no, these here weren't frogs in here, these were bullheads, for a catfish dinner for the priest.

"Father Schimmelpfennig?"

"That's the guy."

The thing to catch, he says, is turtles. They can bite a finger off, or claw like a she-bear, and you have to deliver the suckers alive, but— He shoves a grimy paw in his pocket and pulls out a handful of change. That's why you don't care about losing a fingernail or even drownding in the lake, he says, and lobs the coins up and snatches them from the air with the magic of catching a turtle, and is off.

We stare after him and I think, Oh, for a fair pop, who pays you money instead of saying if you mow the lawn you might get a scooter later, maybe, and lets you stay in a house you never have to clean up! To be a frog catcher's son, free to live in filth and catch as many turtles as you please!

"No, no, no!" she calls from the porch. "Not that now. The lawn!"

+

The streetlamp at our corner has a switch that Dad turns on at night. When he isn't here, Jerome and I boost one another up the pole and push the switch with a stick. Moths carom down into its cone of light, and if we move back we can watch each one on wobbling wings following certain lines that singly or as a whole make sense, never touching or colliding with another, all of them swaying and folding in along the edges while every individual keeps striving in its separated pattern toward the globe of light, where other, smaller insects swarm and gather near or at the center of their tremulous formations but never interfere; and then one night we draw into darkness under the tree in our yard and watch a man in a uniform tilt back his cap beneath their fluttery agitation in the cone of light and turn to Dad (whose shirtsleeves are rolled up) and shove his hands into his trouser pockets, lifting his tunic out, and look up. He has married our mother's sister, our auhnt, and all day his voice has been so loud that the piano in our house has hummed inside its wooden case. Now Mom and her sister sit at it, singing a song we can hardly hear above the insects, and then Dad's voice changes; he looks up at the lit and trembling cloud, down at the glass scattered in the gravel at their feet, and just as Jerome steps closer, our uncle speaks:

"It's damn serious business, Martin. It's serious as the dickens. Who in God's name wants to get his butt shot off?"

+

Down the street a house, pulled by a tractor, rolls on wheels out of the trees where it stood. We run past Deke's and Mary Liffert's to the Congregational church on the corner we're not supposed to go beyond, and then do, looking back like thieves. The house, with its rear windows facing us, goes trundling around the corner, rocking, and heads for the highway. We go to the bricked and earthy hole where it was and crawl inside and find, in a landslide of dirt, colored capsules that smell like the winter vitamins we're forced to take. We lick at them and I picture the two of us at the town dump, standing on broken cement, ready to fight over something we've found. Can that be right?

I look into Jerome's eyes and he shrugs. Then we discover that we can't get the vitamin smell from our hands. What will our mother say?

We run to Mary Liffert's and bang on her door and see her screen tremble as if from the mountain of water we'll need to wash with.

"So. It's you two little stinkers again. Now what are you up to?"

What is she? Picking cork out of bottle caps and storing it in a shoebox, or peeling tinfoil from gum wrappers and balling it up big as a grapefruit, or cutting the bottoms off tin cans and stomping them flat, or sorting through ration coupons on the wobbly table in the porch she calls her office—or writing a letter there to one of her sons who are "in the War," as she says.

"In the War, and you don't know how they'll get out, though D-Day's past, if they ever will, which is up to the Lord, of course. It's them dang Rooshins I worry about, a savage herd—no matter what side they say they're on. They claim some ancestors of theirs ate babies once. Oh, it was a long time ago and they'd be a lot littler than you two squirts—I'd say one of your thighbones'd be the devil itself to snap—but it's that mentality of theirs that makes your blood creep. I can't comprehend anything like sense about them Japs. Those dirty little stinkers are all some kind of pagan worshippers, and you can't never trust what no pagan will do. Worse'n Protestants. Now the Germans, like we are, are clear."

She's beside the table in her rocker, where she rocks most of the time as she works, her plants in the porch awobble, so that we can see, when we go by, the white of her hair rising and falling behind glass to a trembling of blossoms and vines. She fixes us with the eye of a priest and tilts her rocker to the table and takes a deck of cards from her apron pocket, then kneads them together with a clattery purr. She deals, shifting her big arms around the table while the skin curving from her chin to her chest like the pouchy throat of a frog quivers and draws us near. We play Old Maid, then Hearts.

She holds her cards against her bosom and stares over her glasses at Jerome. "Who's the Virgin Mary?"

"God's mom," Jerome says.

"That's right, the mother of Our Saviour, the Lord Jesus Christ." She takes a trick. "How was He born?"

"Virgin birth," he says.

"That's right! And she's the most dear and sweetest mother that ever walked this earth, bar none! Hail to her! Praise her womb! Whoop." She snaps up another trick. "How come we have a Pope?"

"To guide us in all matters that we do," Jerome says.

"That's right! Even what he prints in *The Register* is the Gospel truth. He can't be wrong or there's no ghost of a church, not a real one, and don't let your mother tell you no different on that. He's the Ambassador of God Hisself!"

When she wins, as usual, she pulls out a rosary from her apron pocket and Jerome and I kneel at the table. "We're on the Sorrowful Mysteries this week. The Second Sorrowful Mystery is . . ." Then the prayer we seem to have always known, repeated ten times, followed by a "Glory Be." We go with her through her dim living room, where pictures of her sons rest among thick plants in stillness, on into the pantry off her kitchen. She gives us our choice of Rice Krispies squares or sugar cookies today, and we choose the sugar cookies, three each.

"If I could bless you legally, I would," she says. "At least you're baptized, and when you get to school the Sisters'll straighten you out on the rest. But you, mister," she says to me, and unlike Mrs. Glick she has me right. "You're going to have to bone up more on your catechism answers, you. Now, let's see you both make the Sign of the Cross."

All this doubling of every action, and then we're back home, where we remember at the same time, as we step into the porch, that we forgot to wash our hands. The doorknob above us rolls, the wood swings in, and our mother is above us. She scowls to hide a grin, as if amused at the Eisenhower jackets and field caps (she once slapped me for calling the cap a name our uncle did) we both have on.

"You two have been someplace you don't usually go and probably shouldn't have been," she says. "I can smell it on you."

+

There is a blurring of her and her perfume in the crush and wash of covers as she sits on the edge of our bed.

"Obadiah!" I cry out.

"All right," she says. "Obadiah it is. For tonight."

The pinup lamp burns on the wall behind her, a yellow-white moon. She pushes back her hair, and her face, directly on us, is too much to take close up. Bulges of shadow shed her personal color, and then a flash of a laugh, as she bends to scratch at an ear, confuses that. Smooth eyelids, with a shine on their curves, shield whatever it is that blinds yet draws us near, and when she wets her lips we push up on our pillows to prepare for the glimpses we'll get of this in her voice. It arrives from different areas of warmth at first, while we watch her teeth and lips, enveloped in sound.

There's a catch as her shoulders lift, and it's her head that rocks, not the room. The cardboard cover of our big bedtime book, worn raggedy along its edge, rustles up, touching my chest. I rise in a fever and see over its top to a black-lined picture of yellow and blue, a pooling geography like the one from a nail hole in Grandpa's loft, and below that the ranks of the words that she reads:

"The pride of thine heart hath deceived thee, thou that dwellest in the clefts of the rock, whose habitation is high; that saith in his heart, Who shall bring me down to the ground? Though thou exalt thyself as the eagle, and though thou set thy nest among the stars, thence will I bring thee down, saith the Lord."

A trembling sensation enters my ears and leaves me deaf, in a fall through dark, tasting my teeth to find a way out, with only the pulse of her voice to see me through. Then my brother moves and yellow light slips over her cheek like a shield.

"But thou shouldest not have looked on the day of thy brother in the day that he became a stranger; neither shouldest thou have . . ."

And I'm sorry for the times he has been a stranger to me, when I've laughed at his backward words or pointed to him in his trouble, to show others how he looks when he's caught.

"For the day of the Lord is near upon all the heathen: as thou hast done, it shall be done unto thee; thy reward shall return upon thine own head."

An ache, not a reward, lifts in a swirl from mine as she captures a breath—the shock of her face and hair overhead. Then I'm gone, a speck outside myself, circulating in the currents spreading from her throat, near her source, until I feel her gather for the end, which arrives in a higher voice: "And saviours shall come up on mount Zion to judge the mount of Esau; and the kingdom shall be the Lord's." Thumped book shut. "None of ours, boys, none of any man's, but the Lord's."

She rises, drawing the wash of sound back into her, and I rock where I lie. My brother stretches out, he yawns; he sighs "Good night" as she goes to the wall; he turns his back. She reaches out and drops darkness down and the door shines around her in beams that travel through the windows of my days to that room where Daddy still sits blowing breath into me that is blue. Too far off. That hope in the house on our sled. So hushed and dim now: *Why move?*

Boards creak and there's a breeze that sends her perfume over us in a wrap; she leans. I want to hold her neck and swing. But she bends over him, he reaches up, and then her lips are on my face with a sound that sears. She draws up, her face near the ceiling, pale hands at her waist, and whispers, "Good night, you two. Sleep tight." I cover my head. I plug up my ears. *Don't let the bedbugs bite.* And then I don't know if she's said it. I unplug them. I listen again.

"Good night, Chuck," the mound beside me murmurs.

I can't speak. I drift through time that seems to widen into hours, and then I swoop down and wake to a new morning under new morning light.

+

One night after she's left us, when the wind and the boards of the house are silent, I form into a cave of listening:

"All that that one wants to hear is Obadiah, Obadiah."

And in the shuttle of stillness that travels between them, I imagine her sewing at something in her lap while he turns the pages of a book, across from her in his chair, the two weaving together a pattern I won't be able to avoid—a spiderweb in sun, before I've noticed its sparkle, clinging to an eye.

"It's the only piece in the whole book that's from the Bible."

"Hmmm." This sets the pattern stretched between them trembling.

"Well, once in a while he wants to hear 'Billy Goats Gruff.' " Her low laughter sends a shine through the pattern's filaments, one of which is speeding toward my forehead, while a darker wash of sleep starts closing in. I fall.

I'm back.

"To hear, I think, how that old troll catches his in the end."

Then my hand comes down, covering this, and I'm snapped into the flat light around. Fluorescents hum. The pipes in their basement network bang, and I feel cursed by my kind of memory, which turns on narrowing variations around a single point until the point gives; or shepherds these voices to a concluding seal that jolts me out of their presence. And by the revelations that family relationships, in their silences that reveal as much as speech, can often unexpectedly bring.

I would rather settle inside that day so quakingly spun, with the whirring reel scattering clippings back over our feet. Those revolutions. Revelations. Which sometimes mark a day as clearly as if lines are drawn, and sometimes merge most from one year into a dot. That child pulling up flowers, his outward reach toward beauty (compared to the shoe), which at the same time destroys it—he's very much with me now. Not in that collusion with my brother, both pushing the mower as one, sprinkled with the grass we've wrongly watered, and borne on its freshness over the lawn we covered hundreds of times throughout the years we spent under the power of those two.

Then the phone rings. Who, at this hour? *Her* voice answering it. An illusion, it seems, until the same voice, coming from the foot of the stairs, calls out in my mother's intonations the badge and the signifier of my everlasting name.

The footbridge across the center of the lake, with boards nailed in Xs down its sides, is all white. From the swimming area on this side of it, I hand-walk over the graveled bottom, which feels spongy with bloodsuckers, and watch the Red Cross lifeguard lean over the rail at the center of the bridge with Eve Ianaccona, a high-school girl with long black hair, and stare down at the tinny patch of them both mirrored, standing on the bridge, in the water below.

High above them, higher than the trees on the bank across the lake, is the silver water tower with the name of our town painted across it. We live in a place like nowhere else, from the way people talk about it: North Dakota. The water tower is a block from the back of our house, and as if from its catwalk I see our back porch, on the inside, with its row of windows squaring light over our nakedness as we undress and pull on our trunks and grab our swimming towels—too young for the bathhouse until next year, Mom says—and I want to say to the lifeguard, "I looked at you in the water, and then up at the water tower, and—" And I blush. I'm supposed to be one of his favorites, he has said; he comes to town once a week and I've half drowned myself to earn a card from him that certifies me as a Beginner in Swimming.

Jerome didn't receive his. He's afraid of the water this summer, and if he can't touch bottom, he flaps in panic like a duck taking off.

I dog-paddle out, coughing, to the dock and sit on its edge with my back to the lifeguard and Eve, so they won't know I'm trying to listen, but I can't hear them. I do a splashing kick I hope will bother their talk. And then I see Jerome, in water up to his waist, grip his shoulders with crossed arms, shivering, his lips blue, and stare at me from dark sockets filled with shadow, as if to say, *How could you leave me?*

My feet come to rest and I think: What are we going to do?

+

An older girl is sitting on the Army cot in our dining room, with both hands back on the canvas stretched above crosses of wood. Jerome and I, below the legs of older people, sit in the middle of the furnace grate, where we float, no floor beneath, on rising heat. *The Register.* It's dark out, and the door to the attic, usually closed, is opened wide behind the girl, the doorknob above her as big as a globe to steer by. Brown light on the cold scary steps—so high we have to crawl up them one by one, afraid they'll work on us like teeth at the dark top, where storm windows are heaped. Legs move, the girl moves the things like pipes, with curved bands for her wrists, which she thumped into the room on, and stands them beside the cot. She shakes back long hair and looks out from glasses that her eyes seem to touch, bulging blue.

"I'm sure glad you decided against me being upstairs," she says, and laughs a deep laugh as pretty as Mom's—a surprise.

"Oh, we didn't know!" Mom cries. She looks around for help: to Dad, the others here; the cot's been hurried down, as it was hurried upstairs, when Mom said to Dad, "Your sister-in-law mentioned this cousin of hers is practically a saint—or was it a nun? I'll have to check the letter. We better make provision for her, don't you think? How about doing something with that corner of the attic?"

Jerome and I nudge to the edge of the grate as the girl

reaches to her knee, unlocks something, and lets a leg swing down.

"Oh, goodness!" Mom cries. "We never would have thought of having you sleep up there, if we'd known!" She leans to somebody and whispers, "Why didn't you tell me?"

"Oh, that's okay, dearie!" a woman says in a high voice that sings inside her nose. "Hardly anybody's heard yet. It come on so sudden." She shakes her quivering chin and her lips purse. "Polio."

"Polio!" Dad says.

"Polio" goes around the room on different tongues (Jerome repeating the word to match it somewhere), and I hope that Mom never gets it, and then I turn to Jerome, whose look says, *This will happen to you.*

+

A woman in a suit as red as Santa Claus's stands inside the front door, one hand on the knob, stomping her feet so hard that snow takes the shape of her shoes on the throw rug—a teacher from high school.

"Children!" she says, in a voice almost as low as Dad's but with a pleasing girlish lilt to it. "What are you busying yourselves with?"

We're lying on the floor with a coloring book, and point with our crayons, feeling the slice of air she's admitted travel across the linoleum and slide up our arms as Dad and Mom appear from the kitchen.

"Mom, what's for white?" I ask.

"Oh, don't be a fool!" she says. "Just because Inez is here."

"It's for snow," I say.

"What can I do for you, Inez?" Dad asks.

"My coat got caught in the door. I mean, my sleeve's in."

"Your coat?"

She grips her arms as we do, when we stand naked outside the washtub on a cold Saturday night, and gives a low sudden laugh. "That is, my sleeve is pinched between the school doors. I was flinging my coat on—in too much of a hurry, of course— and had to leave it there."

"Don't move," Dad says, and pulls his own coat and hat down from the hook where they hang. "Sit and have a cup of coffee. Alpha? I'll be right back!" He goes toward the door and he and Inez do a dance around the extra pair of feet in white, and then he swings back around with a hand over her shoulder, and says, "But what's the hurry? You're here." He throws his other hand wide and says in his acting voice, "Tomorrow, and tomorrow, and tomorrow, creeps in this pet-ty pace from day to day, to the last syllable of recorded time!" He hugs her close. "If anybody's made off with your coat, we'll know one of two things." He holds up a finger. "Either the person's a thief"— the other—"or has a coat caught somewhere else and is colder than you! I'm off!"

+

Now when I pace this house and turn at angles that seem to parallel other angles, I know that I'm describing angles inside the broader ones that have been paced out far beyond me, long before, by my father.

+

We're at the corner of our front lawn, where the sidewalk gives onto the crossroad below the streetlamp, sitting on a blanket. Kitty-corner from us, past a pair of trees across the street, a rise of mowed lawn leads to the biggest building in town—orange brick with white letters at the center of it: HIGH SCHOOL. The glory of the lines and curves of those letters in the sun! I stare at the window to the right, where Dad's office is, and see sky shining from it. Then, up high in a steeple above the roof, the dim bell creaks and then clangs against the clouds that show through the arches of the steeple on all sides.

Two students come down the concrete steps, and then the double doors swing wide and the rest begin to leave. Public schoolers from the first grade up, who also attend here and have classes on the bottom floor, appear in brighter colors and go off in every direction, while we wait between two different times. Across our street and two houses down, the square white church with its pointed steeple hides part of the parochial school. *St. Mary Margaret's.* The crush of bodies in the packed pews, people kneeling under the choir balcony of dark boards, others standing, Dad with his knees apart in spite of the squeeze, pressing me on one side and Jerome on the other. On the back of the pew ahead, white buttons with clips to hold up hats; if you press one down and let your finger slip, it goes off like a gun. Just sit still; you have to be quiet here. Dad. When other children say "our father," I think:

> Our Father who art in Heaven,
> Hallow would be thy . . .

The prayer we say there. Amen. Windows with colored leaves and rings in them, white frames holding them in an arch (how do you bend boards?)—the one of Joseph with a sprouting staff my favorite, in the middle of tall panes of blue, a weight of carrying around his shoulders, light leaning on him. Hairy fluff under the kneeler. Father Schimmelpfennig chanting to the highest arch above the altar, the choir chanting back, the altar bells chiming, and Dad with his head down pounding his suit to his chest with a fist. They all go up to take Hosts and Jerome makes a face that has me after him. We know how to get to each other here without letting it show. This is a sin.

Now the bell in the cupola of the parochial school, a silver dome with a cross on it, goes off. Jerome should be there; Catholics have to go, and most people are Catholics. From our blanket on the lawn we see the students start home, turning on routes away from us. Two of Jerome's buddies, Douglas Kuntz and Leo Rimsky, call to him from down the block. We have chicken pox. Dad is the only one it doesn't bother. *Immune.*

I tell Jerome that if he hadn't gone down the block with Sandy Pinkerton—the nine-year-old he's always with, whose long blond hair seems to pull her chin high—we wouldn't have chicken pox. I tease him about following her tall tricycle with our little squeaky one, her front tire at the height of his head, and do a copycat of him bent over, his legs winding into a blur as he tries to keep up with the way she pulls herself ahead in the strides she takes when she walks, except that her knees, when she rides, rise through her hair and part it the way Mom's hands part hers when it's washed.

Actually, I say, he likes Mary Ann McClure—because nobody would want her as a girlfriend. She has pigtails tied with rags, no front teeth, and wets her pants so much she smells like ammonia, and just then Mary Ann walks by, heading toward her house at the edge of town, and waves a wrinkled handkerchief. "See," I say. "She likes you." Then I sing, to the tune his buddy Kuntz sometimes thumps on our piano:

Doc-tor, Doc-tor, can you tell?
What will make poor Jer-ry well?
He is sick and about to cry!
That will make poor Mary A-ann die!

"About to die," he says. "You dumb nut! And she's the one that's supposed to cra—ka-rue, ker a— *Cry*-y!"

He covers his chicken-pocked face with his hands, and doesn't see the white doors swing wide and Dad start his first steps down.

+

We get the scooter for his birthday, for both of us.

It's of maroon-and-ivory metal, a grief to people up and down our sidewalk—especially noisy if we lift the squared kickstand up from the rear of the riding platform, out of the groove around the metal tongue that you stomp on with your heel in order to stop, and let it scrape behind. The handlebars are at the level of our eyes when we propel it, and anyway, it's better to look down at the ribs of the riding platform, where your left foot rests, while you pump away with your right, seeing concrete and the cottonwood fuzz on the tilted slabs flying past underneath and, farther back, the frazzle of sparks ignited by the clattering kickstand. Only occasionally do we hear "Hey, there" or "Whoops" from an adult who has to step aside to avoid a crash (traffic is light, to say the least), as we stand with both feet on the platform to look out, coast, and catch our breath.

We ride double, one pair of arms crossed over the other's at the handlebars and the person on the off-side pumping with his left foot—he's better at this—but none of our buddies can get the swing of how to do it double with either of us. Somebody behind, with hands at my waist, pushes me up to top speed and then hops on behind with a dangerous sway to work the brake while I attempt to steer.

"It's like a chariot ride!" I cry, and the newly gathered group at our house has another theme: Let's go for a chariot ride. The waits get too long, since Jerome and I have to alternate between being one of the pair ("Well, it's ours"), and arguments take up about as much time as the rides. For us a day is measured by the number of times we've gone down the block and back, multiplied by any crossings of the road at the Congregational church, which we still shouldn't do, and we speculate whether giving somebody a push as he stands and steers is really only half a ride, which our buddies claim, since we're aware of what it's like to have our heads down toward that racket and flurry of flying sparks—and how are we going to count it, between us?

It gets worse. Buddies leave and aren't friendly when they see us. Dad is away from sunrise until night, doing spring's work for a farmer, so we can't ask him for advice, and he might only say, as he does, "Well, what do you two think you should do?"

One morning we go to the porch to check on the scooter before breakfast—which we've started to do for fear somebody might steal a ride before we're there to supervise—and find that it's gone. We run all over, searching, and Mom comes up and says, "In a town this size, it can't disappear for long." And then, in a jagged afterthought that rocks us on our feet: "Unless somebody got so fed up with the thing they threw it in the lake."

We walk along our side of the lake, looking, in fear, until the cable in its regular swoops has us dazed. We pray in bed that night, as she suggests, and the next morning it's back!

We celebrate with a trial run before breakfast, get paddled for that, and turn grim as Mom says it'll be necessary, from now on, to keep it inside the front porch, with the screen door hooked. It's possible some high-school boys stole it as a prank, she says.

One morning it's not in the porch again, and from the screen door we see it on the dew-covered grass, next to the tree with nails, mangled so badly we carry on as if it's Dad himself. She comes up and puts a hand on each of our heads, and says, "I know, it's terrible. Did you bring it in last night?"

This scatters my thought so much I can't remember for sure. "I can't remember!" I cry, and turn to him.

"Neither can I!" He puts his hands to his hair in an awful look.

"Did you lock the screen door?"

"I don't know!" we both shout, and howl like hounds.

"Hush. Your dad left when it was still dark, and was backing around that way, like he usually does, he said, when he heard a crunch."

"Oh, no!"

"He doesn't understand how it could have got damaged so badly from that, he said, but maybe it did. He doesn't think he saw it when he came home last night. He's almost certain it wasn't in the porch. He's sure he didn't hook the screen door, not that he ever does. He comes in the back way, and drops his clothes in a pile there. Now it's a mystery."

"Bull-loney! It's ruined!"

"It's a pile of junk now!"

"He'll fix it, I'm sure."

Dad takes it apart and hammers the pieces of it over a rock in the alley (where the now demolished barn is merely stacks of boards of different lengths tied with twine), trying to straighten out the worst of it while paint chips fly. It's never really right afterward; a wheel rubs, the handlebars feel off-center, and its balance is gone. It rests against the back of the house, beside the slanting cellar door, and turns orange at the places where it was bent and then hammered upon. Rust streaks run down the siding from its handlebars.

+

We can be anywhere we want to be, Dad says. All we have to do is close our eyes, or turn on the radio, or both. It's true, we've decided, and both is best. If we don't look at the cloth with silver threads in it, behind wooden bars at the radio's front, the voice that vibrates and bobs and travels in different directions, caroming off the walls until the walls disappear, could be a person. *The Speaker.* When the walls go, the speaker takes on flesh and is present with us, and then, in a strange shift, we are where the speaker is, in a cave under a mountain or inside a castle— A peek at the knobs, arches that control this; or the *inside* of arches, solid, rather than the other way around, and pointed like the fingernails of certain women; when we ask Mom why hers aren't that way, she says, "I have to work."

She's beside the bookshelves the radio is on, looking out the window toward the sun, her arms crossed, and has us on the couch; her witnesses, she's said. A program called *The Stump-Us Boys* is on. One of the boys starts out on an instrument, as if finding his way through the corridors we travel when music is playing, then another joins in, and finally a whole band is playing the same song—one that the speaker announced. The idea is to trick them, as she's told us, by naming a song they don't know, and now that I've opened my eyes I hear the music that plays when the program begins, and the speaker saying ". . . the song of your choice and your name and address on a penny postcard to the Stump-Us Boys, care of this station. And remember, it's been a long time since anybody's stumped us— the Stump-Us Boys!"

"And you know why," she says, "you loathsome hypocrites. You're in cahoots! 'Stump-Us Boys,' my foot!" She turns to the radio with her hands on her hips and stomps a shoe. "He won't read off anything you don't know! I've sent you 'Sweet Betsy from Pike' seven times now, you harebrained idiots, you hypocrites, and you haven't attempted it once! You cheat, that's what you do, and you know it, you hear? You cheat!"

+

I follow Jerome's buddy, Douglas Kuntz, across the low-mowed lawn of Dad's school. I want to learn Kuntz's "secret trick," as he's called it, although I'm afraid. It's cold, Jerome is sick, and his absence is like a lagging balloon, putting even my walk off, both feet thick. Kuntz has me lie on the merry-go-round platform, with my head touching a pipe, then has me grip the pipe with both hands, to hold my head tight against it, and suddenly the merry-go-round is going so fast in its squeaking circle that I feel my feet, rubbing another pipe, lift up.

"Shut your eyes!" he shouts, from his pounding run ahead of me. I do and a trembling grating enters my skull and, with a shock that wipes away my sense, enters my stomach, traveling in varying directions with pressures that shift to different speeds, and then Kuntz cries, "You're Superman flying to another planet, faster than speeding lights! Eeeee!"

With the rub and strum of steel and wood going through my bones, no up or down, I fly instead to Kuntz's house, a yellow railroad car with printing on the side and pass through it, seeing him on a covered hassock at his radio, in the orangy stain of a kerosene lamp, listening to *The Lone Ranger*, his mouth open wide, pulling at his mussed-up hair, as I saw him once (when we came to help him deliver an issue of *Grit*, or those tin containers of White Rose petroleum jelly?), while his mother, cooking at a steamy cookstove in a corner, bulks as big as the voices Kuntz keeps turned up high, as if she's fashioned out of silence from their craggy weight, and now she steps on stump-thick legs with fleshy stockings rolled to her shoes to look toward Kuntz, who is still listening—her mouth open, too, with brown moles around it, her steps setting up a shaking in the curtain across the door to the other half of the car, where Kuntz's older sister prowls, sometimes in her tittycups, as Kuntz says, and cats pad under beds and leap where they please in the way I—

"Okay, let *go*!" Kuntz yells, with a last-ditch shove, scraping past, but I'm wise to this and keep diving to see if I can't enter again the room where I saw his sister on her back on her bed with her legs up and stomach bare as she paged through the magazine she held to the light, and then with a tearing pull I'm down in a cartwheeling jumble over the grass beyond the merry-go-round. Its platform keeps on pulsing past in curves above my eyes, and below it I can see along the back of the school to the football field across the road, a few yellowing trees at its end. Beyond that, the open countryside—mingled with a smell of grass and dirt, and the revolving shadow above slicing at the sky—is like a strip of my life set out for me to see in a way I never have: two colors lying together, blue above green.

"Okay, Chuckie, now for the secret trick."

Then what was that?

He runs to the high slide with the hump at its center and

climbs its ladder toward the platform it feels I can't lift my eyes to see. "Come on up, Chuckie! You got to watch!"

My stomach gives with inner sweepings as I rise on legs three times their weight, swaying and stabbing to find the center of the merry-go-round still whirling inside me, and make it to the ladder, steps scrolled like the treadle of our sewing machine: one of her feet on the treadle, the other back and bent as at the start of a race, in a brown shoe to her ankle, the leather of it worn, nicked, dark with oil, with woodlike layers down the heel higher than a man's, and laced up its center with neat brown lace. Her thick stocking forms and re-forms folds above her shoe on the treadle as it rocks and the big black spoked wheel beside it blurringly spins. There's a whir in the wood that holds and gobbles the cloth, and then the rocking stops and her foot comes off.

"Fixed," she says. "Done. Now you both have these to wear to church tomorrow." She holds up a new shirt.

I seize my glazed reflection in the slide's polished platform, my sweaty hands squeaking, and look from the reflection to the worn soles and frayed cuffs of Kuntz. He's kneeling. A rib I've somehow bumped presses against the breaths I try to take.

"Look at this," he says, and turns on his knees. His pecker is out.

"I know."

"No, this." He grabs the looped curve of pipe handrail above his head, leans out, and directs the beginning stutter of his stream toward the top of one of the slide's tall legs. "You got to go in that hole at the top of that pipe," he says, shaking. "Maybe we can get Jerry and some of the other guys to help. Hee! We'll do it every day until it's full to the top and then some girl'll see it and think, Hmm, what's in this here, and taste of it—hee!—and prollolly have a baby coon."

His stream goes off in lifts and spurts, and curves of it lash and spatter the dirt. "Don't, haw, make me laugh, you dope!"

This is so far beyond me I can't speak.

"Your turn," he says, and pushes off and gives a whoop as the rattly hump below resounds. "Leave it hang out when you slide down!" he calls through cupped hands. "That's the secret trick!"

There are beads of yellow on the silvery platform. I crawl up and kneel, the ground a sudden shock of green as I grab the pipe. The merry-go-round's effects have shriveled me.

"What's the matter?" Kuntz cries. "Can't you find it?"

I baby-step on my knees, both hurting, out farther, pull on the skin at its end to stretch it, and try to aim, realizing I have to be careful so I don't get any on my shorts where Mom can see it, and my dribble misses the top of the pipe. I let go of the curved hoop, freeing the other hand for help, and then have to grab back—

And there's not even time for fear as I go headlong into the green.

+

A bar sings between my ears where my eyes should be and a duck with feet like a horse is on my chest sucking up my breath. I try to scream and a *whoooan* of wind goes through winter trees. My edges are gone and prickles of the last of me go speeding off in numbing streams. The bar between my ears is part of a slide, I see, and start to sit, but lines over my head and chest draw me liquidly down.

"Ahh!" I cry, and air enters the empty space in me like flame.

Kuntz is quacking. "Look at me, Chuckie!" he yells. He's waddling beside me with his butt slung down, so close I can see his face shake, his hair up in a plume, eyes bugged, his flat hands flapping at his shoulders and his lips stiffened into a bill: "Quack! Quack!"

There's a breaking open inside of noisy alleyways with my laugh, and the flame enters and forces a *whoooan* through my head. Humming whiteness underneath slow weight. He pulls at me but my edges are loose, voice out, chest wrong, and then in a dimming struggle his arms are underneath. My hurt side cracks and spills buckets as I try to say, No, don't walk.

Then the blue bar swings back down on me.

+

A hum like static travels to a place behind my nose, bleeding over the last of this. *Hey, hey* echoes in an emptiness too huge for the town. His voice, hot breath, close: "I already buttoned your pants. So don't worry. Your ma won't know what you did."

Wood, distant rasps, his arms sliding to leave a hardness like boards underneath, which the pieces of me settle on. The sound our front door makes. I scream and the *whoooan* is the porch screen.

"Goodness," she says. "Two of a kind. What sort of a stunt—"

"He fell off the slide," Kuntz cries. "I don't know what to do!" Then he leaps off the porch with the squeaking noise he makes when he cries.

+

I'm on a table at the head of a flight of stairs, in shadow. Doors of metal cabinets ring around with a hint of my favorite smell, and then the blur in me parts to admit the new doctor from McCallister, Hogelvode. He runs chilly fingers along the tape over my chest, and his breath and scent fall over my shoulders.

"Don't let it upset you, Mrs. Neumiller," he says. "Kids fracture ribs all the time. Once you've seen enough of these, you figure it's a normal part of childhood."

"None of my children has."

"One has now." He pulls me up to sit and turns into rain. The bulge of a shot in my hip forms a clotted welt. He leans through the rain with fingertips that touch the tape again, and I see my brother's hands, mature, with the delicacy of training in them, travel across the edge of the tape, over my skin, and feel my eyes smart from staring down at this perspective, or from the touch that sends shafts of healing in. Then he takes my hands in his, gripping my fingers with his thumbs, and lowers his face closer to me than Dad does, and I see that his eyes are brown, with greenish radiating slivers in them, and skip a breath. His thumbs grip. "Anyway, you're a tough little shaver, aren't you?"

This enters like further rain to be seen through; I can't speak.

"You're going to be well in a few weeks. You'll heal fast. Are you going into the Navy when you grow up?"

"No," I say, through a mouth that feels full of old socks.

"The Army?"

"No."

His back with a cross of suspenders over it is toward me with his turn, my hands free, and he says to her, "Well, there's the Air Force."

"One uncle there is enough."

"The Marines."

"Ha!" she cries, and at the sound of her voice I look up and see her through Hogelvode—her pretty mouth open as if to take something in, lips puffy, her eyelashes uneven and weighted from tears, moisture starting down one nostril, and her stare so steady on him I know she won't give. So I crawl down from the hard-topped table, among shining fixtures in the white-tiled room, and float to her and take her hand in mine, ready to go.

+

Now my favorite character in the funny papers—which Jerome reads as we sit on the couch—is Rex Morgan, M.D. There is another strip, not a regular one, which I like nearly as well, of a misshapen beast the color of a pickle, with bristles over his body and a cigar in his teeth, who hits people with a hammer or pick, or twists iron around their arms or heads, and causes lightning flashes of pain to spring up. His name is Peter Pain. After he has done his work, a hand like Hogelvode's holds out a tube, and then something from the tube is rubbed in—naked limbs and backs with fingers over them, sheets and open clothes giving off hints of Kuntz's sister—a stamp of earnestness across the frames, and then the beast, at the last, running off, crying, "Curses! Foiled again!"

"What does this mean, Mom?"

She's at the sink in sunlight that divides her face when she turns. She wipes her hands on her apron before she takes the colored pages, but dark edges form around her fingers through the printing.

"Here, this," I say, pointing for her.

"Oh, that silly thing. It's an advertisement. It's for an ointment called Ben-Gay."

"Yes, we know," Jerome says. "But what does this mean, here, when he says, 'Curses. Foiled again'?"

She turns further, so that her whole face is darkened, and says, "You act as if it meant the world to you."

I look at Jerome, his plump lips sober, and then up at her; she's put it into words. "What does it mean, Mom?"

"Just that. Foiled. Stopped. Frustrated in questionable designs." The newspaper comes back into my hands with a clash. "Just like you."

+

Jerome and I sit under the dining-room table, partly tented by cloth draped from it, and feel showers of sensation fall through us as she cuts with growling scissors across the tabletop. A scent like the scorch of a hot iron pressing a shirt arrives, and I imagine burning leaves, cigarettes, Dad's cigar when it's first lit, and picture the box of matches in the kitchen cupboard—an oily, old-wood smell sliding out with the cardboard drawer where they rest in packed rows: the poison tang of their red or blue bulbs with white tips. My pants feel full.

I sneak past her legs to the kitchen, get one of our chairs made of shiny pipes bent under its seat down to another bend that rests in a U on the floor, slide it to the cupboard, get up on it with twinges of blood erupting in my ears, and grab the box. Then I'm on the back-porch steps—old wood worn like fur—under a sky the blue of Dad's eyes, and sense a tang of burning leaves. The outhouse looks stripped in the empty space where the barn once stood, with wires running from its roof to steel stakes to keep Halloweeners from pushing it over.

I take off for the back of Deke's, panting at the marching sound of matches in the box, go through his weeds the opposite way, past his side porch and the fallen tree, around to the front. I lean against the ledge of his nailed-shut door and try to quiet the throwing-up of my breath. Then I take out a match and draw it across the strip on the box—explosiveness of pure heat— and suck in the sooty coil that climbs from its tip: cap smoke and cloth scorched, drawing ashy edges around like a freeze. I blow it out and suck in the darker smoke, but it's not the same, and then stick the match in my mouth—the sizzle of its crusty coal like a knife's salty *wheet* on stone.

I slip to the ground and poke the match into the dirt beside

Deke's house. Then think better of that and put it on the door ledge, where I can keep it in sight. Now I'm as huge as when I wake. The scrape and flare of another's ripe streak, a smell I'm already able to cough up and taste in sticky threads on my tongue. Then such a pile of matches on the ledge I know I must have drifted off. The missed time balloons inside my stomach as I dizzily try to count the pile. Miniature black tadpoles of smoke drift past my eyes and draw the corners of them down in watery lines. I feel I've grown warm puffy gills, and plutter and vleep, eee.

+

And then, in a bending of events like the pipes of the chair, we are at the dinner table, all of us, in four of the chairs that match. I've been caught by her, and can't keep from crying. The first part isn't clear, but next we were in our porch, she had me by a wrist, she grabbed a bundle of matches, struck them, and held them under my hand. A bite at my fingers, fiery nails for teeth, with a shock that snapped me like a whip. I hit a wall and cried, "My rib!" though it didn't hurt, to make her stop. But she had. She was down on her knees, crying, with ointment and gauze, wrapping my fingers up. Now I stare at the bandage beside my plate, hoping to hear Dad say, "I appreciated the meal, dear," as he usually does, so this will be over.

But the thought of his hand gets me going again, and she jumps up and rummages at the stove, her back to us, and I see Jerome start to give. Dad tells me to explain what I was up to, with all those matches on Deke's door ledge, or give him some idea of what I had in mind when I did that, and I start crying at his attempt to understand. I wasn't going to burn anything, I want to say. The smell, the smell. But he won't believe me, I'm sure. He says I have to answer the question, or be quiet, or leave the table.

I wish I could do all three! I want to shout, but I can't, and gulp to get at my voice, down below food I've swallowed, now swelling in a lump, until I want to slide to the floor and pull the tablecloth with me.

So he tells me to go to bed, into dark where I feel they'll get their wish; I'll disappear. I'll wet the bed again, I want to scream, and then I'll rip it up! *I'll do worse!* Then I hear, through the covers I've crawled to the bottom of, to smother myself, "I don't know that you needed to be so severe, Alpha."

"Oh, I know, I know." This deeper voice is different, and doesn't seem hers. "Let me be, please. Just let me be."

Blankness. Which Jerome comes crawling into, feet toward my face. He pulls me up with a hand around the one not burned, then flops on his pillow, so all I can see is a big bulging hump, the back of his head. He snuffles and says into his pillow, "S'all yer fall." Then turns his face to me—silveriness with holes in it. "Now are you happy?"

I remember the song that Mom and her sister were singing the night Dad and our uncle stood under the cone of moths

> *Oh! Mairzy doats!*
> *And dozy doats!*
> *And liddle lamzy divey!*

and see them singing under the piano light, Mom's hands on the keys, and the way they turn and wink and wag their heads when we walk in. She has the same silly look on her face that other people have when she calls them dumb as sin. No matter how much we don't like her singing the song, she sings it still and gets the same look. It's not fair. She cheats.

> *A kiddley divey too,*
> *Wouldn't you?*

Ha! Ha! Ha! Their laughter and then the *Hoo-WAH! Hoo-WAH!* of our uncle echoing through the night.

Out the window I can see the branches of Mrs. Glick's lilacs, bare in the light of the streetlamp—and then a round moon, as wide as the lake, bows up over the water. It sets her house and the lilacs into harder lines as it rises, drawing me toward it, through the window, and parts the lake with a path I walk upon.

This wonder from summer still with me, like the eagle's swoop into morning light, now rising from the path the moon places under my feet. To walk off on it then, a frog catcher's son, carrying only a sack of fish. West or east? There are directions. My hand stretches toward a rock—wrapped in gauze and curled to keep the pain from pulsing worse—a silver-screened paw on the other shore, now pulling me up. From far off the who! who! *whooooo* of a mourning dove starts. This small opening through which I've been let back into the world. Things as they always were, swaying in silence, perfect and beautiful.

+

MAY 29. *(Continuing May 22 from notes) The maid is in her sixties, with a seamed face she keeps pink with powder, and cupid lips outlined in red; a hairnet. Her legs, in beige stockings, are so thin they remind me of Minnie Mouse in those old cartoons. She comes twice a week from "Up in Ha'l'm"—as she says it, with an air of elegance, in one syllable. Her radar is tuned to everything in the building. She cleans at least thirty rooms, by my count—swirls her mop over the floor, dusts a bit, and changes linen—and is always talking about the "messes" left by drunks, in her circular way of talking. She'll give an opening statement, elaborate on it, return to her statement, elaborate a bit more, and so on, all the while cleaning, and as she turns to leave she'll repeat her start—as if tying the tag of a refrain—once more. Today it was "We got a troublemaker in the builden."*

Why should I imagine it was me? No, it's the guy next door, it turns out—the one in the poncho, I assumed. But no, after a return to her statement, and some elaborations, I learned that Ponchito was taken away earlier in the week by the narcs. I thought I'd heard some cursing and scuffling in there, and maybe a yelp, but with all the rest going on, who could say? "Yup, they got onto his sellin that Mary Ann," she said. But the troublemaker *is the new guy. He's young, apparently a Puerto Rican, and "He's sittin in there, not here hardly mourn a week, and he got three, four TVs, them tape recorders, a stare-yo-phonic or two— No, we got a troublemaker in the builden." Another thing of interest along the way was "No, Tony the super, he got a real good heart, but maybe too good. He take too many this type in." It's what I thought at the first!*

So she interrupted my recording the dream, which I'll never get back to, and don't regret. But I've been troubled ever since by a terrific reversal, which I wish I could chart. After she left, I thought of the two or three times I'd seen her, in such different dress, on the street; she wears a swank coat and a pillbox hat with bobbing berries on it. Her makeup is more carefully applied, and she carries herself like a sorority queen, with hardly a trace of the limp she has in the shoes she wears here. Shiny heels in the street.

Anyway, each time we've passed, I've said hello and she's gone past without a hitch, head up, as if I don't exist. So I can't figure whether she doesn't want to acknowledge me, a spook (she mentions her "man"), in the street, or doesn't want to associate with anybody from the Jethro, as if that would place her here, or what. From the way she talks in my room, I sense that she views me as her ears. Or mouth. "A man one builden down—he used to live here—you should hear his tale, he said. Go see him!" Or: "What you do with all this paper?" she asked once, hitting it with a dustrag. I've stopped carrying this out, in an attempt to befriend the neighbor who is now gone.

After she left, I envisioned her solitary beauty in the street. Here, wearing patched clothes, she has messes to clean. At this point, the dream reappeared, and all went blank. An outside force seemed to invade me and suggest that I was the troublemaker of her story, and I felt another person emerge in the blankness to think for me. It's impossible to trace the branches of my thought then, but once the tenor of it became clear, I recognized the person. My brother. He was so much with me I didn't know who was who, and we were thinking together as we used to when we were younger, although then it was often wordless—a pictorial sense we shared, so that we could glance at something and then back at one another and laugh—and now our thought, as it went tumbling in place, was this: In many instances you've been dishonest and tried to get retribution, sometimes in such petty ways only you could recognize them; these ways might seem "minor" to you, since they're the methods others use all the time (here one branch, which I think was mine, went off into how one person can commit an awful act and not only get away with it but be applauded or cheered on, while another can do exactly the same thing but try to soft-pedal it, and be considered a dirty, sneaking, low-down . . .), but to an objective observer some of your acts would be inexcusable. And if you say this or that one is "minor," then you also must admit to a few that aren't (the particulars here weren't important, although landslides of these, from different viewpoints, *came tumbling into place), so how could you trust yourself outside your sphere, in a position of unlimited power? Worse, if there had been a button handy at certain points that would have removed me, you would have pushed it.*

Now, who was this?

My own fantasies of revenge are never detached, but have me getting the person to admit his smugness, or the cowardice under his cruelty, and then beg forgiveness on his knees, and so forth, before I slug him.

All of this reaffirmed the dream. I sat on the bed feeling foreign, part frozen, yet sweaty as a clam. It's taken this long to even try to get some of it down. Now I can leave, I hope. 3:00 a.m. Such a session causes you to pray there is plenty of bureaucratic tangle in the place where the real button is, in order to keep anxious hands from it. But it's something I can't dwell on, or this will start all over again.

+

Dad's hand, the only one able to perform such a feat, opens on a turtle, a miniature one, and Jerome and I grab at each other at the sight of it pawing up his fingers as if they're logs. My birthday. Dad has also brought home a pair of goldfish in a cardboard container, where they flit until their bowl is ready, as Jerome's half of my gift.

He and I kneel on chairs at the dining-room table—sunlight lying with the weighted heat of fall on our arms—and watch the turtle pull himself out of water onto the rock at the center of his circular cake pan, the home I've constructed for him, into the realm where two giants lean. He cranes his head back, above the grooves that outline the squares in his shell when it's wet, one eye like a yellow pinhead on me, gold and green stripes shining in his snakelike neck, and when I merely blink he flips into the water with a splash.

"Tiny," I whisper, my name for him, and hear the scratch of his claws on tin as he attempts to swim off.

"Why not take it along?" Her voice, which comes from the kitchen, where Dad is pacing, judging by the squeaking boards.

"That means the fish, too," Dad says.

I turn to Jerome, who nods, his head so near I know how the turtle must feel to see me blink.

"I don't see how we can manage all that, and them, too," Dad says, "if it turns cold on the way back. Bill said he'd watch the pets."

"Can he see them?"

"Oh, Alpha, goodness. He'll check on them every time he comes to stoke the furnace, he said."

Bill Faber, our neighbor across the street, is the blacksmith. He has a purple birthmark under one eye and wears a black patch over the other, with cotton often stuffed under the patch, and glasses over that. He's going blind. "It's from looking at that fire that the electrizity makes when he welds," my buddy Brian Rimsky has said. "Don't ever look at it or it can burn holes inside your brain the same size as these here little ones in the middle of your eyes!"

I turn to Jerome and wonder why it is, then, that Bill's wife is blinder than Bill. Jerome's eyebrows rise in their sad bands: *Who knows?* She doesn't even go to his shop. She never leaves the house, except for church, clinging to Bill's arm past Father Schimmelpfennig's porch and then up the steps fitted with pipe railings to the church's double doors, where the man who rings the bell takes her arm below heavy white flesh that sways. When we visit her at home, she sits at the table under a noisy clock with her head high, smiling her pretty smile while she looks at a wall and talks, and then asks us to crawl under the table, please, or over the living-room floor, to look for something she's lost. There are hundreds of things on the floor, except where she sits, and some of the pictures on her piano aren't right. I close my eyes and imagine I'm her, inside her darkness in her house, and hear Tiny clawing on tin.

Then their voices in the kitchen rise as if through static from my turtle's narrow slice of— *The Speaker.* The turtle and the fish will stay, I hear. We're going to Grandma and Grandpa Jones's for Thanksgiving.

+

The trip begins as usual, with Dad and Mom in the front and the two of us in back—Dad waving to every person we pass, saying, "Frank. Joe. Howard. Bill." Jerome and I turn to one another and frown: Does Dad think they can hear him? We check to see if his gloved hand, when it comes down, slaps the steering wheel so the horn ring wobbles, which means he isn't pleased with how long it took us to pack. It comes down lightly and, out on the highway, lifts to cars and trucks, fewer names coming as we pass the blue-creased rise of Hawk's Nest, our only hill. Jerome and I scramble on our knees to the other side of the car, to stare at it, rocking, Mom's perfume clearer here, and Jerome turns sober at the sight of snow on its side. Will we get another sled this winter? Our new brother, Tim, lies on Mom's lap, below her open coat, asleep.

Now two fingers or a single finger lift in Dad's silence, as they will to anyone who passes us the rest of the trip, or until Fargo, where traffic bothers him, and will lift after that until the turnoff in Minnesota to Grandma and Grandpa's farm. In McCallister, I see the brick building with Hogelvode's office at the top, and cry "Calfie!"

"What?" Dad says. *"Calf?"*—as if we've jumped ahead to the farm—and Jerome and I are thrown against their seat back. "Where?" Dad asks.

"Up there," I say, and point at Hogelvode's.

"Oh, my stars and little fishes!" Mom says, and turns so she can see Jerome. "You there, first-grader," she says. "Doesn't that say 'cafe'?"

He looks out. "It sure does!"

She laughs so hard I can see the fancy pointed tooth at the side of her mouth, gray and gold-rimmed—a pearl we try to bring out with her laughter—and my face heats up.

" 'Calfie,' " Jerome says. "Ha!"

Her eyes widen with her silly look as she laughs louder— *Damn fool*, as I've heard Dad say about somebody, although I don't know who.

"Calfie, indeed!" she says. "That's one on him, for his teasing about your 'car and cow' and 'shoulders and soldiers,' right, Jerome?"

"Oh, come now, Alpha. You can be about as bad as they are, when you're in one of your holiday moods. Goodness, it means he can read!"

He looks back and his eyes roll on me in a tug at their red edges, as if he's afraid. I'm sure he's going to add a compliment, or run inside and buy us ice-cream cones, but he restarts the car and pulls away. His fingers lift, his gloved hand reaches to wipe at the fogging windshield, his window rolls down and we receive a peppering of ice as he sticks out his arm to signal for a turn, and then we're out of town.

The countryside grows more unfamiliar with each far-spaced farm, and just as I feel groggy, I see Jerome nod. I raise hands that feel slowed and weighted to my eyes, to rub myself awake. Our shoulders bump, and we turn on our knees to face the rear. How could we forget the trailer? It's right behind, loaded with bundles of barn boards, pushing at us with a jerky busyness that causes a chatter, now that I notice it.

"Row-der grader," Jerome whispers. "No, rocket bombers! *how*itzers!"

We put our elbows on the shelf behind the seat to support our weapons—gunners out a turret window—and scatter ammunition at haystacks hiding the enemy; at fence posts, farm buildings, cows, birds that might be passenger pigeons; and then a car comes crawling up. If we don't keep it back, the Germans will win, and Germans will be in America, chopping people up. We make a secret adjustment of our guns.

"Boom. Brrrat-a-tat-tat! Ka-thock! Brrr-eh!-eh!-eh!-eh!"

Jerome is jumping with the force of the kickbacks, and I sight in until I see the driver, wearing round glasses—Germans!—and send a ratcheting volley into each lens. Their car swerves. Or the trailer does. The back window is dotted with spit from our barrage. I aim at a woman beside the driver, and two heads appear around her from behind.

"Please, you two," Mom says in the front. "Can't you find something constructive to do?"

"We've got him on the run! He can't pass!"

"Stop that! Both of you! Sit in your seat!"

We do, and soon the car comes whining alongside, with a pair of kids in the back seat letting us have it. They understand. I raise a finger with my thumb cocked back, a .45, and get them both with silent blasts.

"I saw that," Mom says, rising and twisting in the seat, Tim gripped in one arm, and slaps my hand. "Behave!" She's kneeling now, about to say there is violence enough, and those who live by the sword will die by it; but instead she bites her lower lip. Her eyes mist, and she sinks and sits.

"Say, you two!" Dad cries, as though jolted. "Do you always have to be shooting at one another?"

Why can't she let us be American heroes, like the soldiers in the Saturday-night movies, or in the song she sings: "Soldier boy, soldier boy, where are you a-going, waving so proudly the Red, White, and Blue?" She hardly lets us play with other children (kids are goats, she says), as though they'll give us a disease, or change who we are.

"Sleep!" Dad says.

I sink down and close my eyes and picture my turtle dreaming away on his circular beach, safe from the frog catcher and his son (who have moved out of town over the fall) and from every hand or animal that might harm him—his sparkling head lifted from his rock. Then I see Mrs. Bill Faber in her kitchen, smiling at the wall she's talking to, the skin under her chin astir, and imagine a turtle with a head her size at the door. How she would feel hemmed in! I'd grab a gun—guns are good to have in the night—and shoot it; I'd save her.

I get on my knees to look out the rear window, knowing I can do this now that I've been slapped, and see a sudden change. It's more than night coming down, although night has begun. Snow is descending grayly across a countryside that widens out so flat behind the speeding car it feels we're flying, and the shifting flakes turn pastures here and there among the open fields so gray they start to rise to meet the snow, while yellow squares of stubble caught between them tremble: kites ready to lift off.

The trailer jogging in its separate sort of pant behind, powering the car from the looks of it, reminds me I can read, almost, with those bundles of different lengths of boards like parts of letters ready to be used by Grandpa Jones—and I'm glad Jerome helped me learn their sounds. The barbs and bars and wiggly letters in a line were as familiar from the first as these fences everywhere across the fields, with a pulse to the words like the swoops of telephone wire beside the car, and I'm happy Jerome is here, with Mom and Dad, and we have grandparents to go to.

Now the sounds of the trailer and the motor enter my thoughts, bringing down a band of blue on the fields beneath the falling snow, and it will always be like this, I see. It will be like this today, and be like this tomorrow, only tomorrow will be better, because it's always better the next day.

I fall asleep on my knees.

+

Mom is at Grandma's kitchen table, in a wooden chair with a leather seat, in the corner where the windows join. These are silver from sun off snow, and press silver edges past her outline. Her hands are on her stomach. "What a beautiful bird!" she says, and sighs.

In light that Jerome and I have to squint against, so that at first it appears that there is something blue (like the turkey he has colored at school and brought for Grandma to tape to a window), we see a real turkey pace along the snowy driveway, past implements buried in a bank beside the fence, and then fan out its tail and wings, so they drag, while a red-blue balloon blows up below its wrinkled head.

"Yes," Grandma says. "I'm afraid that poor devil's on his way to our Thanksgiving table."

"Mother! How could you?"

"What do you mean? What do you expect us to eat? You used to do it yourself, Alpha."

"But it seems so—I don't know. Sordid."

"Goodness, Alpha, we have to eat! It's traditional! I mean, the turkey. The eating itself, as we well know, is a necessity."

"Something else, then, Mother, please."

"It's all butchered, dear, you know that, no matter what we eat."

"What an awful thought!" This is said so quietly I wonder if she's falling asleep. "It seems so—" She covers her silvered face and Grandma comes up behind, tall and black, and grips her shoulders so hard her body appears to give at every joint.

"Oh, Alpha, you were always too sensitive for your own good! I always maintained that and I still do. Or you tried to prove you weren't by braving it. Oh, Lord, Lord, what life and the rest will lead us to! You were my dearest hope, the 'bestest of the bunch,' I used to say. You always suffered something special, and now another child, yet. What, oh, Lord, will we do?"

Jerome and I turn to one another. *What?* And then slip in silence out of the room, since we aren't present for them anyhow.

+

And then to watch, with its head whacked free, the turkey stagger and flutter in the snow, its neck spouting blood over banks of white, but all in silence—only a clash of feathers on snow, a pulsing germ of gray at its butthole, and then one claw clawing at the cold; shivering stiff; clawing, and then curling closed.

+

Back home, the turtle is gone. Bill noticed it wasn't there the first day, he says, and gives a left-handed look in my direction from the eye without the patch, and I notice a bathroom smell about him that isn't nice. The goldfish, though, they're all right, he says, nodding toward the bowl on the corner cupboard, where fish food is scattered like cracker crumbs. The biggest fish floats belly up. I point, about to speak, but Mom pins me with a look, and when Bill leaves, Dad takes the fish by its tail to the back porch and gives it a fling that sends it flying into the drifts climbing the outhouse. I feel the cold and sudden shock, and imagine my turtle there, mouth gaping wide.

We look for him, the four of us, all day. Jerome and I cover the floors while Mom and Dad move the furniture back and forth, first in one room, then the next, through the whole house. I step into the back porch and see only the potty chair, once ours, which Tim uses now. Another on the way, according to Grandma Jones. "It's a mystery," I say to Mom.

She sweeps and dusts, then pushes back her hair: "There's more soot and corruption than if a bunch of high schoolers were carousing here for a week. Does he wipe his feet?"

"Alpha, hush."

Then she's at the three windows in the dining room, and when she looks up she sees that I've seen what she has.

"Could it?" she asks me.

"What?"

"Fit down here?"

I stare at her brown-laced shoes over the furnace grate.

"Well?"

I kneel and stick three fingers through a slot of the metal scrollwork, not even the widest, and see Jerome looking from around the table as if it's his fault; his hands go to his hair.

"Yes," I whisper.

"Dammit!" She stamps a heel so hard the grate rings. "All I can say is I hope old Bill had the blame thing going full blast"—she stomps again—"when that miserable creature took his last dive!"

+

Oh, oranges, the mere color of them, coming in crates at Christmas from our grandparents in Illinois, with purple tissue covering them (as if purple is the only color that can contain their nestled populations), and filling the depot, where pews sit back to back, with a springtime acidity! Pebbled suns in a bowl on the dining-room table, glowing as if giving off the warmth that comes through the windows from the real winter sun, with a rainbow-edged reflection of the glass bowl traveling its course across the table every time we climb onto the chairs to check on them—orange lights stamped with blue-purple names as foreign as the place they grew in; the packed heft and texture of one in our hands; the smell as a knife slides through the skin so perfect for slicing, the gaseous spray which can be lit with a match, if there is a chance to hide alone with a match and a piece of the peel. The eruption in our mouths of the slivers of watery meat, eaten in sections, halves, or whole—rolled into a spongy pulp and then poked with a pencil, if she isn't watching, and sucked upon, and then, once the juice is gone, torn apart and feasted upon down to the white inside peel, which scours the coating from our teeth and makes our numbing lips and tongues tingle and swell up from behind, until, in the light from the three windows (shining in rainbow tints through an empty glass bowl) we see orange again from the inside.

+

Then it's time to move. We've gained a sister (besides our brother) below the level where Jerome and I contend, and three people in each bedroom is too much, as Mom says.

I see our younger brother, Tim, at the other end of the dining-room table, his nose barely above it, blond hair up in a tuft, and it's the clearest I see myself here. I've just walked in from McCallister with Dad, and I'm wearing a green tweed topcoat that was once Jerome's. The cold between the car and the house has stripped my senses raw and there are faint edges, like a skin of light, around every person here, besides a raked emptiness behind my nose, which adds to the illusion. My tonsils and adenoids have been removed.

The table is a slab of sun my little brother looks across, and when his hands come up and grip its edge, I feel they'll dissolve. A new weight of age, which includes a pang for my turtle, fills me with concern for Tim, and his hands remind me of how I held on in the hospital, swallowing blood, and gargling salt water over that.

I hurry over and hug Jerome, then sit on the couch to steady myself for the rush of sensations that arrive: first the gauze mask soaked with ether coming down—voices hurrying off in garbled chimes. Then my body pressing through the hard-topped table until all that's left in the room, now white, is an eye above a mask, Hogelvode's, with slivers of green in it, pressing me inside a separate space within the smell that's melting me. With a hiss, I start into a circle of whirling, from the high dive at the lake down into water past the rocks at its bottom, through weeds that sway and take on a deeper whir than the weeds outside Deke's—never quite hitting in the dim murk against rocks or bloodsucker mush, and never rising high enough, in the curve at the circle's top, to grab the diving board, and after several revolutions underwater and into the air and around again (half dark and half light, as on a huge wheel whose sound overpowers everything), I realize I haven't been holding my breath. Then in an echolike sucking which could be my drowning but seems a mouth moving near, the spinning speeds up and in a crush I fly free.

Gone, but not. I remain in a space that seems reversed, enormous now. A speck of light is a star traveling to a distant one, while further dots and circles lift into voices arguing their way into me.

And still I wheel, then rise up, bodiless, and feel my tongue buzz to the cries. There are other naked bodies, mingled with flashes of fish and flying seaweed, caught in the whirling, too: Brian Rimsky, Douglas Kuntz—somebody who has had a hand on me—and I search for Jerome, for any help or sign from him, but a cold wind rises out of his absence, and the arguing swells until my selves are joined together with a blow.

I'm back in a hospital bed with Mom's face so close I can feel her breath on my eyelids.

I'll never be the same, I realize, as the current of cold from Jerome's absence covers me now, and I'll never tell anybody about this. I'm still inside the separate space, and know that there is something other than living: it could come as it did to my turtle, and is the opposite of sitting on a couch.

I bounce up and down, happy that Jerome is here, as he always has been, actually, and that it's the beginning of a new season—signified by the cards beside us on the couch: hearts trimmed with lace, cats holding up hearts, hearts plain and pierced, plus some that say "Get Well."

"Stop that!" she cries. "Sit still! Do you want to start up some new complication? Why, you could—" Her face streaks white as I finish for her, from the vantage of my new perspective: *bleed to death.*

+

The man who comes to move us, while Dad is at work, has an iron hook for one hand. There is a hard rap at the front door, and when Mom opens it, he draws back. His shirt pocket, shaped by a cigarette pack, has *Rick* above it, and the look of his rough apologetic face isn't right. Mister Man in the flesh.

"I know, ma'am. You're probably thinking, 'Like a one-armed paperhanger.' That's a reaction a lot of folks have. But, you see, I wrap a towel here around the end of it, so it don't scratch up your furniture none, and I can lift more with it than

I could do with my good hand. Some dirty little Jap blew it off. Didn't feel a thing."

His eyes fasten on us in a look like anger as she steps back.

"Well," he says, and gestures with the hook toward their room off the entry. "Do you want me to start in here in your little bedroom?"

LIVING

There's a knock at the door, where every knock to me now is his.

"It's me, son. Cleanin lady. You need cleaned up in there?"

I look down on a square of linoleum like the linoleum in an upstairs room of our next house—its border printed with pictures of Hopalong Cassidy and his cohorts, their faces framed by horseshoes and coils of rope—and though I lie in this cubicle among the maze of others in the ranks of buildings rooted to this rock, I smell the tarry reek of linoleum from that other room, whose walls hover near.

"You in there, boy?"

She has her passkey.

"Cleanin lady! You want me to give you time you get tidied up in there? I can do some of these others, hey?"

She either smells me or can see through doors. I turn and sit on the edge of the bed and try to decide. Finally I say, "Yes."

"You want to wait till next week?"

I go barefoot across the linoleum I'm sure will dissolve, step off it, as weighted as in a rising elevator, and twist the bolt. I step back to the sink.

She pokes her head inside, nostrils aquiver, casing the room, and then comes in pulling on a mop handle, her narrow shoulders broadening into hips so big she might be wearing a bustle, her oversized shoes below her stockinged legs moving in an ungainly agility akin to dance, and drags a clattering bucket on wheels with a bang over the threshold.

"How you?"

She studies me as if to discern the level I'm surfacing from—her cheekbones gold under pink powder. A scattering of freckles across them seems the source of the perfume entering me in walnut sheets. "No, we got a real troublemaker here."

All my possible troublemaking acts pass through me with the shock of spilling intestines. "I'm okay." I actually say this.

"No." She drags out the mop and performs some swirls with it over the linoleum and I see, from the heightened way in which the faces shine back, that at least the rug is real. "No, he had him this woman in, and raised such a ruckus half the builden was up. He's a troublemaker, all right. He drug this woman in, I don't know if she wants to be with him no more—shouldn't be, not in this builden—and the next thing she screamin and carryin on and he screamin back. Then she out and down the stairs by Tony's, still at it—she was cut somethin bad, the fellow says, the one hangin out by his door all the time—and Mr. Troublemaker, he run after, screamin he going to kill her! You didn't hear that?"

I'm looking for a place to rest.

"His room's all tore up, and now I ain't sure if it the two of them together, or him after she leave. No, he's a mean one, that one, and there's mess there, all over the floor—one of the two. She might be his wife. He's a troublemaker, yup. They been divorced before and then she come to visit—they got five children, he says, most of em growed—and they get all drunked up and one gets sick at the gut and be laid out all day. No, he's a troublemaker, that one. Wouldn't talk."

She's at the window, where paint spatters and flecks of soot project spots of shadow over her apron, staring at the woman in the bathrobe. "No, you got about the nicest room in the builden." She produces a cloth from a pocket and slaps the window as if to wipe the woman away. "Air's fresher here and you don't get nobody's pacin, or whatever, up above. A nice old gent, he lived here and he did the fixin up—that nice decorator wallpaper all around, your shelf across Stinkpot's door, and the bitty one in yon corner." Above the door, to the right; I hadn't noticed it. "He kept a statue there. He painted the furniture and such, and put down this lumoleum, yup. One day, no answer. So I think, Gone to see his boy, then. He had him a boy up to Poughkeepsie he gone on the train to see a lot. I used my key and here he was, on top of the covers, dressed like always, necktie on, peaceful as a doll. Heart attack. In his sleep, they said. Suicide, I figger, but my thoughts go kinky a lot. Suicide, when you lay here and pray God take you off?"

With a wet rag she grabs from the wringer of the bucket she wipes the sink, then the mirror above, and I see a crucifix reflected below the hollow of her throat and have to squint as if she's bearing it toward me.

"No, we got a real troublemaker here. Haul him a woman up, his wife, I suppose, and get drunked up on a gummunt check, then start beggin her to come back, cryin about the kids. You got to take what you get, and let the rest go, or you carryin too much. You know the one. His door open wide and that old TV playin all hours. Oh, that room, *ah!*"

The cloth splashes home and she throws up tiny palms, pink as her powder, and pinches her nose. "Such mess you wonder what they eat! I tried to get the most of it—some under the bed even, like they crawlin around playin hide-and-seek— but I had to leave for the stink. Phewy! 'You sit in it awhile an see what it's like,' I say, 'then hope I be back.' It's worse cleanin mess when the boo made it layin there, watchin you like he all froze up. How your bed be?"

She goes to it and flips back the chenille spread, the blanket, the top sheet, then studies me as her lips, outlined in their cupid shape, wrinkle up. "You need clean sheets? You want some?" She flaps the covers on the bed like sails. "Ah, you can go another week."

She plumps the pillows, jerks the sheet, heaves the blanket and bedspread in waves that draw them flat, smooths out the remaining wrinkles, then chops a fold below the pillows that she draws to both sides, military neat. I feel I'm already on the bed, fading, drifting off to North Dakota, heading further back than I've ever been before.

"No, I'm grateful for them like you in this builden—no

trouble, clear mind, and not up to anything you can see. I thank the Lord for that. Thank you, Lord. No, we got us a trouble-maker here."

The bucket wheels out behind her, bangs, and swings another way, hazy in the shadow of light from the bulb, like a solid curve of pottery. I go to the door and press a button that fires the bolt home, and on the bed feel as insubstantial as a hurried written version of my name—as if the ledger is opening below for a red line to run me through.

"Yes," I say, and turn and sit on the edge of the bed as I was sitting when I first said "Yes."

"Cleanin lady! You need cleaned up in there?"

+

Then I'm back in the basement of the most recent place I've moved to, grappling for a hold on things as if I've fallen through. North Dakota, indeed. Here behind a deep freeze, in a cubbyhole hardly wide enough for this door that doubles as a desk, with unpacked boxes and crates stacked pell-mell like parts of the past closing in. I focus through this to a bare living room, as big as half of Scott Haig's house, but with similar windows, three of them, bowed out in a bay toward the sun, as if reframing the patterns already laid down in the other place. Bare dark corners turn us back to the tripled windows over windows, as they appear, and all opening onto light.

We must be seeing the room for the first time with her, without our father measuring and testing its walls and floors, giving them substance, because the coolness of unlived-in space climbs to our knees. Dots of dust drift toward the windows, in the direction of Hawk's Nest. She grips our hands as if to hold us in place, in an airiness like clouds glimpsed through rafters. She might be singing. She cries "The space, the space!" in her singing voice, which these walls return to me when I stop to listen. Behind this deep freeze, the walls are of concrete, and echo everything flatly back, reaffirming an earlier intuition: that I'd never be able to say what I wanted unless I was in prison.

"Hey," Jerome cries across the room, from a swinging door whose motion parts the air in panels like the panels of light on the floor. "There's an upstairs here! It's got a banister!"

+

It travels straight down the flight of stairs, except for a curled knob that hooks to the right (as you slide) at the last step—the kind of banister we've always hoped for. It takes practice to develop the timing to press and spring with parted legs at the knob, and then land with our feet on the floor, without doing damage to our butt bone or jewels. With a free hand we can strum the balusters to produce different tones and know the moment we have to spring, but when our buddies come to visit they can't get the hang of this, and she says we'll have to stop before somebody gets hurt. We slide down it anyway, drying our hands first, so our palms don't squeak with the braking and leverage for the spring, but there is always the noise of hitting down, which we explain by saying we were jumping from a step—though this wears thin, especially after she says not to jump anymore—and she is so seldom out of the house we hardly have a chance to practice how to slide down it frontward, which is what we've wanted to do since Kuntz tried it his first time here and hit the front door so hard the key shot out of its lock. "Cuckoo," he said. "I hear cuckoos, Jay and Chuckie. Do you?"

+

Jerome and I rig a string over the rail in the upstairs hall, run it in a loop down to a knob of Dad's business desk (set into a slanted cubby under the stairs), and have a pulley to raise and lower notes. First it's war reports, then "3 cows," and then— after I sketch at it a while, lying on my stomach in the upstairs hall, my dispatch point—a drawing of the tangle I see, bulging and hairy, when Dad's bathrobe parts.

There's a noise and I look over the rail to see Jerome, with his hands over his head, bouncing around on his stomach. I lie down on my back (carved balusters on one side, an open door on the other), and the corners where the walls meet the ceiling surge, pressing toward me until I'm tempted to take out my own thing and shake it up to the tingling buzz that ends with me in shock, solid but smaller, my eyes bugged. Through the open door, most of the wall I see is covered by a roll-top desk. This is where Dad is going to write a book, he says, now that he isn't teaching, and has time. The desk downstairs, for his insurance business, holds policies and notepads, with a picture of the Holy Family at the top.

One edge of a metal cot runs like a pointer to the roll-top desk, and it was on the cot that we learned how confusing Davey is; he is Dad's brother, so he's an uncle, but he's only eleven. He says to call him Uncle Ajax. Why? He was here in the summer, with Grandpa and two uncles who built an addition onto the parochial school, for the Sisters—two stories high, with three bedrooms upstairs, one down, plus a kitchen and a chapel. Father Schimmelpfennig was there each day, in a white straw hat and the tan suit he wears in the summer, supervising too much, Grandpa said. When the addition was done, the Sisters' old house, at the edge of the parochial-school playground, was carted off by a tractor, like the other house we saw—to the country, where farmers need houses, Dad says. And then Grandpa and Dad and our uncles poured cement at the back of our house, from a porch next to the bay windows around to the edge of the coal shed at the back door, and troweled it at night, holding up a lamp, so we'd have a place to play.

Dad set up the Army cot, and pulled a trundle bed from under the metal cot, "For you boys," he said, and at night Davey sat on top of the cot, with the two of us on the floor, and recited poems with words worse than "pecker" in them. One night, when the only sounds in the house were in the room where our uncles, Jay and Fred, seemed to be passing a ball back and forth on the spouts of their snores, Davey leaned to us and whispered, "Say, do you guys jack off?" I looked at Jerome, who still seemed to be trying to figure out the "critch finger" Davey showed us ("It means up your rosy rectum with my rusty ramrod," Davey claimed), and Jerome said, "We've watched Dad."

"What! Right in front of you?"

"A couple times. In the car."

"*Jack off!*"

"When a tire's flat."

"Oh, whew, I was thinkin old Martin might be slippin a cog or so. No, no, I mean—" So he poked up a finger, to demonstrate on it, then leaned against the wall and put his hands behind his head. "Now, I'm not so sure how it works if you have one of them Coke-bottle affairs."

"What's that?"

"Well, I tell you. I'd heard of it but never seen such a thing till one time at school. A dinky kid from this real poor family out by the State Forest, well, he pulled his out beside me at the urinator one day and there it was, this great big glob of wrinkled skin over the end of it, so it looks like a Coke bottle's top—no purple head that you could see, like your honest-to-goodness, normal, everyday one. Why, I couldn't tell where there was a hole the pee could come out of, but here it come, whistlin Dixie like a girl's. What a sight to see!"

I was about ready to tell him how it came out, and then realized he would know that Jerome and I had the problem he was talking about.

"It's probably best," he said, "if you start out just rubbin it, bein you're young and all. But, boy, don't let yourself get caught!" He dropped on his back and stiffened his legs and kicked them up and down as he pretended to do what he had demonstrated, and cried, "Oo, I got der tingle in der bingle down to der dingleberries! Wheeee!"

Now the string slides over the wooden rail with a note on its way up, and pauses above the step, held by a paper clip. I pull it loose and see a flat pecker, like our sister's, but so wrinkly with skin I have to laugh. I send him down my version of it with his attached. There's another shaking attack from him, then there are sweeps of shifting air around my ears as the swinging door below swats in its frame. Her heeled footsteps stop beside the business desk.

"What's that?" she asks. "No, let me see! Hand me those!"

I peek over and see the drawings in her hands, under the curve of her hair, and then she looks up. "You there. Who drew these?"

I stare at her raised eyes and open mouth, a face of a different shape from my height, and wonder why Jerome won't speak. "Both," I say.

"Both what?"

"Both of us did them."

"Who drew this one of me?"

Her? I seem to rise to the ceiling, unable to see her in my fear, and feel I'll not only wet my pants but my loose knees, too, will take a pee.

"I'm not sure," I say.

"Not sure!" She holds up a sheet and rattles it. "This!" Then her face is gone and her hair dashes where the white width of it was as she shakes her head. "Your dad will have to see these when he gets home. I was positive that attitudes like yours would lead to this." Does she laugh? I try to read this from Jerome, to know if we'll be let off. "He'll have to spend some time again on biology," she says. "Here at home. I've never seen anything so misinformed in my life! Now, both of you get into the bedroom here, and take your licking from me!"

+

"I'll yank you into line!" she cries, or "Yank him into line," Dad says, when he's home. This is done by grabbing a handful of hair, or an ear, or a pinch of upper arm, and giving a jerk up to a line we can't see. When I hear the words, the hair over my scalp bristles, as if I'm blushing there, and I duck and cover my head with both hands. We're not only yanked but pinched, paddled with branches, books, cooking pots, a flyswatter, and (most often) her metal-backed hairbrush, as we lie draped over her lap at the bench of her vanity. She is usually in tears herself and keeps saying, as she does now, after tearing our drawings up, "Won't you ever, ever learn," over and over, in a beat that falls so strongly on each whack I'm afraid she won't stop.

+

Relativity has been viewed as the way in which two people schedule a lunch for Wednesday, say, and from that point on, but particularly on Wednesday, begin to move in relationship to one another, through their own schedules, in order to arrive at the restaurant where they have a table reserved for Wednesday at 1:00. The trouble with using people as examples for relativity is that other people tend to transfer this scientific theory, so far unproven, into the realm of human relationships, or worse, theology.

Relativity has no relevance to morals.

+

Jerome has a new problem with his speech now. Whenever he is spoken to, no matter what is said, he'll say, "Huh?" Which becomes so predictable she beats him to it: "Are you two ready to practice your duet? *Huh?*"

"That's the cereal we'll be trying this winter, if that's what your wondering look is about. *Huh?*"

+

Our playroom is at the head of the stairs, next to the room housing Dad's roll-top desk, and we lie in the center of our tarry-smelling linoleum, with its smiling cowboys who flatten toward the edges, and face each other with toys and guns. When we pound at our pegboard, which has a bench at each side, we take whacks at each other's fingers, as if to prove we're always fighting, as she claims. She says he doesn't listen, maybe because of me, and I'm so often at the center of trouble when it starts, or found running away once it's begun, that I understand what she means when she says, in the midst of one of my pleas (which ends with me in her lap at the vanity bench), "The Great Arbitrator of His Own Cause!"

+

My favorite cowboy is Gene Autry, whom we see in serials at the Saturday-night movies, where all the children chant the upside-down numbers "Five! Four! Three!" and then watch a scattering of dots unfold to a lion turning its head to roar. So now Jerome says that Gene Autry isn't a real cowboy, because he sings, and women do that. His favorite is Roy Rogers, and then Hopalong Cassidy, after our linoleum arrives, and then he decides that Hopalong, who has white hair, won't last long, so now it's Lash La Rue. And I know why. I can't stand noise, especially when I'm building with our Lincoln Logs, and all I have to do is start on a serious project and—

"Keh! Keh!" Jerome cries, dancing across the linoleum and cracking an imaginary whip around my ears. "Keh! Keh! Lash La Rue!"

+

My flat and scary dead-blue eyes, sending currents through me in a circulation of iciness, slide away as I pull open the medicine chest. I paw around in it for the quickest tool. The straight-edge razor I've carried from place to place for years? No, a new one, a double-edge fresh from its slippery pack, the pressured slice and sting of splitting flesh, wrist numb, a surge of blood burying white cords, and then its pink froth under the faucet.

"Ah!"

+

"What a lovely Indian summer," Mom says, staring out the bay windows with a box in her hands. They're still unpacking. Jerome and I run out whooping, playing Indian, and in the shallow ditch beside the house we find a piece of hose large enough to roll a kittenball through. It's made of canvas and could be a wind sock, if it weren't so long and round, and then we look up, for some reason, at the sky, and I hear in my head a song we thump out in duet at the piano:

> Down at the airport, the wind sock is blowing;
> It tells which way the wind should be going.

A wire coiled inside the hose holds it in its circular shape. We get a rope from the coal shed, tie its ends to the outer coil of wire, and step inside the loop, a team of horses. We trot down the road beside our new neighbors, the Heatons. We horse fart with flapping tongues, prance past the parochial school and the Congregational church, and from there can see, far down the block, the stores and buildings of Main Street. I turn and notice the front of the hose digging into the road— dust pouring out its snaking end like tan exhaust. Powdered horsepower! I can feel our flanks, the flies over our hooves, the flash of our teeth when we neigh as we travel from block to block, moving together under harness in a perfect match. We want to show everybody how happy we are at the new house; Mom, too! But our buddies seem to be gone for the day, or else the houses are hiding everything. There's our old place!

Now I feel we've gone too far, although the lake is there under a sheet of summer light, and I turn and tug him toward home. But as we pass the front of the parochial school, where hundreds of anthills rise in reddish cones and scraps of cellophane swirl, the horse beside me screams, drops his harness, and heads across the playground on a run.

For a long time afterward, whenever Jerome gets excited, or can't sit still, Mom says, "What's the matter, Jerry? Have you got the Saint Vitus' dance, or are those red ants back in your pants, dear? *Huh?*"

And if I happen to laugh, she says, "You needn't be so smug, you there, with that 'What?' I've been hearing from you. That'll be the next thing, I suppose, 'What.' *'Huh?' 'What?'* I expect to be hearing some brilliant conversations from you two."

+

Though it isn't spring, in order to test everything before we have our buddies over, Jerome draws a circle in the driveway with a nail and we pat down the fuzzy ridge of it. I put my cheek to the ground, to sight the lay of the land, and the dirt stings my skin with its strength. Has it been buried for a winter? Where have I been? The ground smells like life, and the big fresh circle, with twigs and pebbles lying outside the mark left by the nail, draws me down in sudden dizziness.

We count out marbles into the circle, pack them in a ring, and I sway on my knees. My shooter is a clear beauty with fizzlike bubbles in it, his a dull blue—no steelies allowed in our game. I win the lag, sway, then shoot and see the pack jar with a marbly crack that sends two flying loose, and as they speed outside the line, I picture myself in the house when it's still bare, crawling into the living room, away from a conversation about Dad's new job that is so weighted it drives me, down on my knees, onto the square of tin the oil heater sits on—padded underneath with something that causes it to crackle—back to where the tin gives way to boards, and specks of dust are doubled in the varnished sheen, to a marble against the baseboard. Who left it? I lie down and touch it with my tongue. I roll it out and try to pick it up by pinching an eyelid around it. I experiment with its fit up a nostril. It sticks against the bone with a burning whine and I picture myself as Donny Ennis, the brain-damaged idiot twice my size who clumps around town, and cry out, astonished at the pain.

Vaseline, a bobby pin, and the hollow tone in her voice that tears bring on: "How could you do such a thing? After choking on that other one?" I feel the solid circle of the other in my craw, wiry squeezers tightening on it—gagging for air until my hands are blue—and then her slap on my back that sends it flying with a scream. Then an aching core of warmth, like circular bleeding, which I now feel up my nose—the burn of water sucked up in the salty pinch that can drown.

"Can't you learn! Do you want to end up having another operation?"

+

"The one day in a month when I don't feel well," she says, "and do you think you two can behave? No!"

Her voice is hoarse. This is similar to the newest warning we've received: "Behave, you two, and *leave things alone that aren't yours!*"

Or "Behave! I'm not raising a bunch of wild Indians to exhibit at a sideshow."

We have to laugh at this.

"Stop that giggling! I'm raising human beings! And I want you two to act like one. Some. I want you to act like a pair of them, you hear?"

+

When we are upstairs and hear the front door open, followed by footsteps, we listen for the briefcase Dad carries on his trips to clash down under the stairs on its metal studs. Then he calls her name and is gone by the time the two of us, in a thumping run down the stairs, are at the briefcase, beside his downstairs desk, on polished boards, magical in its placement in a shaft of sunlight from the door—handles drooping from either side of the clasp at its top, which we hurry to work.

Its black, alligatory leather scuffs at our impatience until we get the full-width jaws open, then its accordion sides expand as we dig around, searching through compartments filled with insurance policies in paper sleeves fitted with cellophane. Sometimes we tip it over, each fighting for his half, and its businesslike insides release, in a feat like magic, red-and-blue-stamped balsa airplanes driven by rubber bands, plastic peashooters, popguns you cock like a rifle, with a cork on a string; a book, the card game Authors, tubes of pink plastic you can blow into bubbles that won't break and that spin down from the head of the stairs to hit with a plop, or a box of candy, for Mom—gifts as if it's Christmas, winter in June.

+

"Everybody has to work," she says, so we have chores. We go down to the basement, where planks are laid in paths over the dirt floor and mice peek from between stones and a salamander's tail slaps as it dives, and carry out ashes from the furnace in an old coal bucket we lug paired up. Or carry up the pail from the chemical toilet we use on cold nights, or go to the shelves lined with canning jars and choose our dessert for the evening, bothered by the jars of bulging pickles with their sprigs of dill that curl against the glass and send up her voice faintly singing "Lavender blue, dilly dilly, lavender green," as she was singing in the kitchen when she canned.

Our only other duty, besides taking care of our bedroom and the playroom, is doing the dishes. She goes into the living room with the little ones after the meal and listens to the radio (with Dad, if he's home) and we take turns washing and wiping. There's an argument every night about whose turn it is to do which, since washing is worse, until she writes out a schedule on a calendar above the sink, giving us each a week at a stretch. A week! Our fingers will turn to prunes and all our buddies will know. Better not to argue.

Whoever is washing stands on a four-legged stool, so the slop of oily water doesn't run down (or up) his arms past the elbows. The stool is the size of a chair seat, and low, and will tip if you stand with both feet at an edge, so you could slip and hit your chin on the sink and bite your tongue off, as we've done, or almost. Bleeding teeth marks. Then the stool goes under the sink in the bathroom afterward, so it's there in the morning for brushing our teeth. *Don't forget.* It's the perfect perch from which to hit the drier on the head with a spatula. He strikes back with a ladle across the ribs. I break a plate on his forehead. He upsets the stool and dumps the dishpan and its contents—greasy water, chunks of food, and the silverware that's left—over my school clothes. We overturn the kitchen table, where dried dishes are stacked, and block the door with the table and chairs we smash. We toss forks and spoons at her when she tries to get at us and the dishes we're emptying from the cupboards and breaking against a wall.

Or this is what we'd like to do.

I take a cup from the steaming rinse water and wipe it dry, holding it with the towel covering my left hand, as she has demonstrated, so our fingers never touch the dishes (though we have to scrub our hands before we even begin), and it's so hot it hurts my fingers where they've already been scorched. "What'd you rinse this with?" I ask. "Kerosene?"

"Shut up and wipe."

"I want to listen to *The Shadow*. It's supposed to be the best program on the radio."

"You listened to it once."

"Sure. When I was two."

"Last week."

"That was our hundredth anniversary of washing dishes."

He holds up a butcher knife. "Shut up."

We go back to doing the dishes as we are supposed to.

I have to find a place to escape from him, or leave him behind, although even when I hide and try not to think of him, I do. I feel off-balance because of him, and keep getting drawn away or turned aside from things, like the pair of dogs—one black, one white—with magnets in them, that spin away from each other and the red hydrant you slide them toward, unless you first rap them on something hard.

I've fallen off the roof of the coal shed and out of the tree beside the driveway, and was able, after the last fall, to wheeze out to the dim face above me I knew was his, "Don't tell Ma-om," just as there was a crackle in the driveway of a car pulling up. Dad. Next week, as we lie in a hush on our stomachs in our playroom, sighting up a tower to get a feel of the height we've reached by using up all of the red and white plastic bricks that were part of another gift from Dad, the front door opens and closes, we hear his heavy steps, and then his voice in their room: "Well, how many trees did he fall out of this time?"

His briefcase strikes down in a new spot on its metal studs, and there is a chuckle of springs as he sits on their bed, where she's lying down to rest. "I'm tired of this life," he says.

"Yes, dear, I know. Lie down here with me, please."

The statues in church are draped with purple on my birthday. As I stare around at them from the front pew, where I sit with the rest of the first-grade class, I feel a darkness enter of another year closed off. Jerome and I carve jack-o'-lanterns with her help and leave a soggy mess of seeds across the kitchen. Then the smell of scorched pumpkin and smoking wax as the candles burn down in the glowing heads we've set up on stools at the windows. For trick-or-treating this year, she has ordered costumes from a catalogue; Jerome is a pirate, with scars and a black patch like Bill's over one eye of his bearded mask, oilcloth boots, and a sword made from a wood lath, painted silver. I'm a skeleton. My suit is black, with glowing bones over its front, and my mask a skull.

I look in the medicine-chest mirror, and at first the bony stranger reminds me of the doctor's kit I want for Christmas. Then a coldness gathers at my shoulders, where the suit is entirely black, and enters in a current through my hair. The pirate and I carry papier-mâché pumpkins with candles inside, shining through the cellophane over their smiles, and after our first stop across the street at the Heatons', out of sight of home, I blow out my candle.

"Hey," Jerome says. Car headlights come around a corner and I turn my back until they're close and then spin around and start dancing in the ditch toward the beams. The car sounds its horn and swerves with a gravelly crunch. "Hey!" Jerome cries.

I run, part blind, to the bushes at the end of the parochial-school playing field, and get behind a tree trunk, hearing voices from the car talk to Jerome. I'm panting, in danger, a real skeleton, as bare as the branches of this tree against the moon. Ridges of bark press through my mask as I hold on to hide, and then the car pulls away and I see Jerome's pumpkin flickering above a sidewalk. He runs at a pair of girls in sheets, swinging his sword like his whip, crying, "Keh! I got you!"

I'm already headed in a backward dash in his direction when I hear a girl say to him, "I know who you are. You're—"

I swing around and release the scream that sent the marble flying, and even Jerome jumps. One girl sits where she is, on the sidewalk, her sack of candy spilled, her mouth gaping as she tries to breathe, and the other runs down the road, noisy as a chicken, and tosses off her sheet.

"You're going to get it from Mom," Jerome says.

I do. When we've finished our tour and return, the mother of the girls has been by, and Jerome also tells Mom about the car. I feel shrunken beneath her in the kitchen light, sweating under the suit and mask, which I've chewed around the mouth—painty gauze damp.

"Get that crap off," she says. "Then get into our bedroom."

"You got it for me!"

"Don't contradict me. Do what I say!"

But before the suit is off, she has me over her lap at the kitchen table, using her hand, saying through her teeth, Won't you *ever, ever* . . . and it's one of the times I'm sure she won't stop. She must feel my sweat, because her song changes to, You'll get *ill, ill,* through the rhythm she keeps up, and below I see her brown-laced shoes in a dance, my broken-open bag between, and candy corn spilled like beads. I grab at her legs to get her to quit and then a coldness covers me as I think: *There is worse to come.*

She steps into our room after we're in bed, with her hands at her waist, looking worn out, and reaches to the pinup lamp on the wall. The circle on the ceiling goes. In the darkness I can still see her face, a ghost patch at the lamp, and then the mattress on my side gives, I roll into her, and she's holding my hand. "Forgive me," she whispers. "I lost my temper. It's something I have to— 'Do unto others as you'd have them do unto you,' right? There are those who like to be scared and those who don't, and those who can be scared seriously. I mean, for good. If you enjoyed yourself tonight, there's a trait in you you're going to have to watch out for."

I can partly see her now, blue in the dimness, and then she lets go of my hand and reaches to arrange the hair that falls the wrong way over Jerome's forehead, and in the darkness above me I understand: The worse to come will happen to her.

"As for you, mister," she says to him, "I don't worry about you the way I used to. Help keep an eye on him for me from now on, will you?"

+

Now when we go outside the air chills us to the waist, rising above the ground like a shadow of the snow we want to be wading through—and in the cubbyhole of this basement the same chill grips me to my knees. The trees are bare except for a few shaking leaves, and the land beyond looks stripped under a sky so pure it brings out colors I can't remember seeing. Reds and shades of pink and orange and yellow appear over the fields and in the creases of Hawk's Nest, along with dozens of varieties of brown and violet. But it's the air itself that foretells the change more explicitly than any calendar, when the heat of the land starts leaving, as the same air signifies the change now, in this cold country I've chosen to return to, where I wake these cold fall mornings from yet another dream of everlasting snow.

+

Grandma Jones is coming to visit. There's a granular sound to her voice that grates words clear, like the finer dust that floats down from the window screen Jerome and I are using to sift sand for a project of ours on a suddenly warm, Indian-summer day. Or this is in my mind as we sift sand in the sandpile we've found, fringed with weeds, beside the outhouse, when we hear from the direction of the house, "Heigh-ho, out there, you two young brutes! Don't you know your grandma's here? Didn't you hear the train come in ten minutes ago? Don't you care? Here I am, all tuckered out from the walk—I'm getting old!—carrying a suitcase and a shopping bag full of presents, plus a fat turkey for your Thanksgiving feast, and when I walk up to your place"—by now we're on the cement slab, tugging at her coat, and she dips away and lifts the bags higher, fighting us off and laughing her high girlish laugh—"ha! When I get here I have to holler my fool head off before you say hello!"

"Hello! Hello!"

"I ought to bop you on your behinders, your big hind ends, you scalawags you!"

She drops her bags and twirls Jerome around and then my feet are off the cement and the house and shed and hedge go by in parting streaks, and next we are each in an arm, at her shoulders, the height of Dad here, swaying, and I receive, from the face I've watched in the whirl, a kiss that resounds off the siding. "How I love you both," she cries, and Jerome gets his. "How I love this new house you're living in!"

Mom, who is outside by now, says, "Mother, we didn't think you were coming till the weekend. Martin—"

"How I love it that you're settled into a real house at last, Alpha!" She lets us slide to the ground and says in the voice from her silvered kitchen, "Come hug me, dear."

Tim comes out and stands beside the coal-shed door, and then Mom and Grandma let each other go, both brushing their cheeks with the backs of their hands in the same way, and Grandma whispers, "Good Lord, Alpha, you're not expecting again, are you? Why didn't you tell me, dear? What is that man trying to do? You'll end up like me!"

+

"I'm that fat, Mother," Mom says. "The truth is, I haven't recovered from Marie yet." Our new sister. Grandma has brought us shirts she has made for my birthday, and an alphabet book of occupations: A for astronomer, B for barber, D for doctor, down to zebra trainer. She had me read it twice before she said, "By jing, Alpha, he can read, like you said. Do you think he learned how from those building blocks we—"

"The funny papers," I say, and turn to Jerome to tell how he helped, but they're busy with the questions that make up most of their talk. So we sit alone, though not alone, below voices that go on like the coffee on the stove they seem to have forgotten until it stomps in its pot. As they sip it from Mom's Fiesta Ware and continue to talk, Grandma pats my head, her hands never still—patting, smoothing, picking at threads, crimping a seam—except when she's asleep, perhaps, though once when I watched I got tired myself at the sight of her stretched out, her hair undone and down to her waist, a hand at her throat, and her chest sinking as it does when she says, as she often does, "This eternal work."

Now as her hand keeps up its *pat pat pat*, I stare across the room at the tabletop, white-silver in the sun, and feel them hover with its radiance above Jerome and me, although they're also here with us, and understand: it's the two of them who direct us, not Dad. This idea swells in me until I can't feel her hand. I am who I am, and think the way I do because of them. And my brother—

"What?" I ask. Grandma has said something, after all, to me.

"That's what it'll be next, I tell them," Mom says. *"What?"*

"Oh, Alpha, stop." This comes out so kind I look up. Grandma's eyes behind gold-wire glasses are the blue of Jerome's, but with darker layers drawing me in to discover where the blue ends, and I remember an afternoon like this on her farm, when the sun shed an orange as orange as orange crayon across the stubble where lavender flowers of flax once waved and— What? It was fall, but the warmest day I've felt, and the same warmth is over me now. Her stare comes from the other side of all the years our mother has lived, and now, in a tone of voice for both of them, she says, "I said, 'Which one do you want to be, Charles?' Which one of the men in your book do you most want to be when you grow up?"

I'm afraid to say "doctor," which might lead to mention of a doctor's kit, because if anybody knows how much I want one, I'm sure I won't get it.

"The junk collector," I say.

"Mister *Man!*" Jerome says. "Fwee!"

Grandma's face turns strange and suddenly she's laughing so hard she has to slap a knee to get herself to stop, gasping like a girl, and I'm afraid she'll have to ask for the glass of water she needs when she's upset, or after she finishes a meal, so her food stays put, as she says; she gulps it down and then places a hand on her chest, below her neck, and lifts her head like a bird, her mouth opening and closing while her Adam's apple climbs and falls to force the water past the food her hand appears to be holding in place until this is through.

"A junk collector!" she cries. "Ha! Oh, hoo, Alpha, do you hear that? Of all the lordly professions in that miserable book, this one wants to be a junk collector yet!"

"Sometimes he talks before he thinks," Jerome says.

"*What?*"

Grandma and I say this at the same time, so I'm okay.

"Oh?" Grandma asks. "Is that so?"

"Or he says things just to surprise people."

"Well, now, who's this serious little old man here?" Grandma says. "I don't believe I've met him yet. He sounds about thirty-seven! Oh, Alpha! where did this pair of comedians come from, anyway, dear? The Katzenjammer Kids! No, *worse*. Alpha, Alpha, how are you ever going to handle the likes of these two?"

+

Then Grandma is at the depot, beside the hissing train we watch with fear as the engine's biggest wheel begins to give, *chuff*, and here is Dad, who has made it back before the weekend from his trip after all, looking tired as he tries to hurry Grandma on. The biggest wheel sticks, then spins, sending sparks spraying back with a ringing like a bell, its shiny plunger whisking in and out and then slowing to push, and we hear Grandma saying above this, "Lord, time to go before I had time to sit!"

I feel as out of breath as she sounds, seeing the wheels under the cars begin to roll.

"Come now, Mother, *please*," Dad says, taking her arm in his hands in impatience; he can't stand being late. "Please get on, Mother, dear."

Jerome turns to me, surprised that Dad has called her this, which doesn't sound right, and in their searching looks (including some from Mom, who has a grip on Tim and Marie), it seems as if they're trying to decide what to do to set this right—that note of Pul-*eees*, *Ma*-thur, like Jerome or me trying to get a hand between our butts and Mom's hairbrush.

"Goodbye," I yell.

"Goodbye, all!" she cries. Her granular voice, sifting each word clear. She leaps up on the lowest of the three steps leading to where Dad has set her suitcase, in the open air, on the platform between two cars, and is already skimming away, her hand at her throat and her Adam's apple struggling above it in her need for a glass of water as her eyes run, her look above us, on Mom or Dad, and then it's on me in a flash that approaches faster than the mass of metallic hammering carrying her away, and she cries, "Charles! I love your choice, dear! I hope you're a junk collector yet! They're *rich*! Goodbye, birthday boy! Goodbye, Jerry dear! Grandpa sends his love, too! I forgot! *Goodbye!*"

+

At home, Jerome gets out an orange crate but we find we no longer fit in it, so I start lining up kitchen chairs as I've seen in a book, and then Jerome slaps his forehead and I follow him to the storage closet behind our bedroom door. We grab two chairs and stand on them, then take down our Lionel electric train, which we seldom use, because there wasn't room to set it up in the other house, and when it came as a Christmas present it was so far beyond what we expected, it didn't seem ours. Now we fit together the oval track on the linoleum of the living room, and his fingers shake with an excitement I can feel. He plugs in the transformer and we hear its hum spread through the floor in vibrations and smell its electrical stink as I hook up the wires running from its terminals to the board with contacts on it that he clamps under the track. I take the cars out of the oil-stained compartments of the cardboard carton and set them, one by one, on the tracks, hooking them up. Then he lifts out the heavy engine and hands it across.

"Trial run," he says, and I elevate the engine's rear from the track and watch its biggest wheels set the plunger pumping.

"Okay!"

I hook it to the cars and he sits with the transformer next to him, turning the knob that increases its hum, and then the train begins around the oval with thumps we can feel through our knees. He speeds it up around its route, the engine rocking and the cars clacking at the corners in a kind of count, and now there's another smell, oily and electrical, that the engine sends like a signal to me, and I move beside Jerome, feeling the hair on my arms stand up like his, and study the cunning careful stubbornness in his fingers on the knob as he keeps it below the level where the engine will tip over and cars go peeling from the track.

"Going home!" he yells.

"Going home!" I cry, and then, both in the same voice: "Hope you have a safe ride!" Then we sing, from the blue plastic record Mom has bought us, along with a crank-up record player, because the other side of the record is "Sweet Betsy from Pike":

Casey Jones, mounted to the cabin!
Casey Jones, with his orders in his hand!
Casey Jones, mounted to the cabin!
And he took his farewell tr-ip to the Promised Land!

Then the transformer goes and I see his hands, with the same cunning stubbornness in them but a fine-boned delicacy, move below my vision as he sketches a floor plan of the house in which our electric train is circling. "This is the living room, here," he says, and puts a forefinger down. "Big. With the bay windows over here, facing south. Our bedroom was opposite the bay windows, here—the same as at Scott Haig's house, but so far across the room we didn't get the same light. Mom and Dad's bedroom was off this far end, here, with hardwood rolling doors between their room and the living room—those enormous double doors that went rumbling back inside the walls, remember? Their room had a good-sized window, like a picture window, looking out on the front porch, there, which had to face east, and to this side of the window, the right, was a door; out it, you were in the front hall. The front door here, the stairs going up— Well, we know what was up there."

He keeps his head bowed over the floor plan and his hair is so close I pick up not only his scent but faint sensations from it. "Down the hall, through that swinging door, across the living room, out here"—he draws in the lines—"was the kitchen, not bad-sized. Windows in the corner where we ate; Mom's pantry at the other side—a sort of hall, like so, lined with cupboards, with a window at the end, and a sink here where we did the dishes, ugh. The john was behind the sink, if you saw through walls, off this part of the kitchen. No running water, but a tub, so we didn't have as many baths in washtubs after that, though enough, still. You had to pour a bucket of water, lugged all the way from the town pump, down the stool to flush it—there was a septic tank—and unless we were sick, or it was a dire emergency, or the night of a blizzard, we used the outhouse. There was a chemical toilet down the basement for a while but that had to go because of, pardon me"—he holds his nose—"*der schtinck.*

"Dad kept a path dug to the outhouse in the winter, and the last winter we were there the snow drifted above the outhouse door. We put pieces of wood and cardboard over the path, piled snow on them, and had a tunnel. Less cold, but more work, I'm sure, for Dad when it collapsed. The inside john also had a door to our bedroom, through this big closet, here, besides the door from the kitchen. Straight across the kitchen from that door was another that led out onto the enclosed porch where Mom did the washing. That's where our rabbits died."

"Rabbits died?"

His head goes back and his eyes squint so that I can hardly see them through the reflections of wood grain and brick over the lenses of his glasses. The face is more familiar than mine, since it has always been outside me to observe, and what I notice now is the scar to the left of his heavy lips, and then he shifts his glasses and I'm enwrapped in blue. Who would have thought that he'd be here, with his New York itinerary arriving the same day on three-by-five cards, and then come up with this?

"I believe Dad got us a rabbit for Easter the first year there. We kept it in a box on that porch. It was early spring and too cold, I suppose, even inside the porch. The rabbit had babies and they died—all of them, I think. They looked like mice. It seems there were dozens."

"I remember! They were all pink!"

"Right. Their eyes weren't open, and there was hardly any fur on them. Maybe they were premature."

We both blink. Then, from our vantage of that porch, stepping down its steps, I'm in our yard; the driveway beside the coal shed leading to the road, a hedge there, and our blue car parked next to the shed, underneath the tree I fell from. Lilacs to the left, the garden beyond. A worn path past the lilacs to the outhouse, whose roof is gray against a hedge higher than it; caragana around the house had grown up that tall. On the other side of the lawn, in a corner of the hedge, rabbit hutches on the planks of a cistern—long pens made of chicken wire stretched over frames, but with board floors that had to be cleaned by Jerome and me. The start of these must have been that doe, which I'd forgotten.

"What happened to the rabbits?" I ask. "Remember? We had all those cages of them."

"Maybe Dad sold them. I don't know. Another of those 'projects.' "

I see Dad at the pens, filling jar lids with rabbit pellets, bulking above us as he performs these miniature chores as handily as we do—speaking to the rabbits in the teasing voice he reserves for animals and children under four. Then I see Dad's best friend, Hank Kauter-Haupt, the janitor of the parochial school, standing at the back door, holding a hand over an eye that's dripping blood, saying, "Martin, you must take me to da dochtor." We try not to stare at the glass eye Hank receives to replace his real one (steel from a chisel pierced it) as we see him cleaning up at school, or holding out the collection basket in church on its long wooden pole; and I notice Dad's excited nervousness whenever Hank comes by, as he often does, to buy one of our rabbits.

"Pretty soon, Hank is going to have as many as us," I say.

"Oh, he doesn't breed them," Dad says, and turns to conceal the curved-up half grin that appears when he tries not to smile.

"Oh?"

"Oh, no."

"What, then?"

"Why, he and his wife and kids"—he shows his teeth and clacks them in a way that reminds me of the shears he has been using to trim down the hedge, all of it, he hopes, before the freeze—"they *eat* them!"

Jerome straightens the sheet of his plans along the edge of my bedside table in his careful way, and it occurs to me that most people fall into two divisions: those who love day-to-day domestic life (whose order seems disorder at times) and those who don't. He and I appear to have both sides in us, and to trade the sides back and forth—another of the widening solo flights he has me circling on in every direction I've been wanting to test, and can now, with him here. I knew everything would be all right when he walked into the room, which I was embarrassed about, and stopped with his first step onto the linoleum and held up a hand as he rocked back and said, "Hey, our playroom."

"Please," I said. "Sit down. No, you use the chair. I'm used to this bed . . . I feel I've been in this room for twenty-five years."

And when we were bicycling through Central Park (he loved this ruggedness at the heart of the city), and he jumped off his bike and ran onto an outcropping of rock where two black teenagers were having a fistfight—*staging it,* I thought, to entrap us and steal a bike, but it was too late to warn him—ran up and pulled them apart, speaking to them in a tone that allowed no quarter, as a father might, I understood, as the pair walked away without any dirty back-looks and Jerome started down the rock, the principled strength of our father, and thought: He went into medicine for me.

Then we were on a narrow street near Astor Place, after a matinee of *After the Fall,* when he said, "By the way, the play was on Dad."

"Dad?"

"Well, I didn't have too much to come here on, you know."

"Oh?" Jerome was usually handing me money, so I always assumed he had enough.

"Yeah, I had to take out a loan this year to stay in school."

"Goodness." I had been at the point of asking him for some cash.

"So, when I told Dad I was coming out, he slipped me a twenty and said, 'Take Chuck to a good play. I know he'd like that.' "

I turned to the window beside me, to conceal my feelings, and faced the green-painted plate glass of a commercial building, a mirror.

"He didn't mention to say it was on him. Laura keeps close tabs on the purse strings now, you know."

"You're telling me?" Our stepmother; I refused to turn to him.

"You'll have to try to forgive her for that. It's something in her nature, or character—nothing against us. It took me a while to realize that." In the glass I saw him raise his head, jut out his jaw, and scratch at it with his fingernails. "Say," he said, "I think I'm going to have to pull me a shave job at your place."

Below my perch on the bed now, he turns the enameled chair to me, leans his elbows on his knees, and puts his steepled fingers to his lips. What? This breathing presence from his eyes, which have become more almond-shaped with age; then the orange landscape of our grandmother's farm opens in me, and I see acres of wheat stir in a wind.

"Well," he says. "Are you ready now?"

"What do you mean?"

"To read that diary?"

A blush colors my vision. When he arrived, I kept asking what he wanted to do, and he said each time, like Dad, "No, what do *you* want to do?" until I finally said, "Read you some of this notebook I kept."

"What notebook?"

"Actually, sort of a diary. I kept it for the part I played." The only role I've done in the city, a blind street beggar—an alcoholic, as I envisioned him—in an off-off-Broadway show.

"You don't really want to hear any of that," I say.

"Sure." There's an urging lilt to this, and his eyebrows, once faint sad bands, now tangled and coarse, rise above his glasses. "Read it. Please."

So I pull it from under the bed and lie back, flipping pages, and it occurs to me, as if from under the shade of a close-lying thought, that men should give their form to the family before they move into the world to form it in their way, since they usually leave it to women to work out that form in everyday life, which makes me— Or leaves us—

"Here," I say, and read: "An old man, fifty or sixty, emaciated, with a massive, protruding chin, was walking down the street—a cigarette clamped in one corner of his jaw. He was wearing the Bowery costume. A dark jacket with padded shoulders. Gray gabardine slacks. A white shirt open at the collar. He was arguing with someone, invisible, in a voice that wasn't human or animal. The closest thing I can compare it to is a yipping litter of pups. He had no language."

I'm so nervous the page is a spangled drift:

Earlier, a man in the same costume but with the addition of a felt hat, somewhat better dressed. He was standing on the sidewalk talking with a friend (invisible) about his woman—the pipe of a street sign he held with one hand: NO PARKING. *His talk was quiet and logical, accompanied by the greatest tact and with constant deference to the woman. At a certain point in the conversation he turned and kissed the sign. Immediately he turned to his friend to make sure the gesture wasn't misinterpreted: Nothing personal, nothing personal. Mere affection for* her.

"Ha!" Jerome says, and socks his thigh as if to keep from cracking up. My eyes shine and sting, near tears, and the air takes on a pitch of tension that numbs my hearing. I flip backward. "Here," I say.

I need very little sleep actually, can revitalize my mind and body with three to five hours of it, and have gone for more than three days without any at all. Nevertheless, I usually sleep ten to twelve hours a day, and have slept for as many as twenty, simply because my dreams are more real, more compelling, more major *than my acting, or my life.*

We both begin laughing at the same second. It grows to the laughter of hysteria and won't let up. There's a dangerous mist in the air of uncontrollable sneezing or a seizure, and then both of us freeze at full stop. My other or oracular self, which doesn't need hospital ether to make itself known, slips out to observe this moment in its entirety. Silence. His face is back and his mouth open, baring his pointed eyeteeth, and a hand is rising to slap his forehead. My shoulders are drawn in and my head going down, as though I'll bury my face in the notebook, and the maroon bedcover gives with my weight coming down. By a trick of the fluorescent fixture above, our faces look struck across by the morning light we used to wake to, in the house sketched on the paper under his hand, and in the houses before that, all the way back to the narrowing point where memory encounters mere blank numb nerves.

And now sensations come: the constriction of the laugh, his warmth and the scent of his hair, the gentle press of healing he is applying across this moment, as he has applied it through his visit, while time has held its breath. And holds it still, as we face each other free of those years, and then gives with a grating dislocation, so that I'm back inside myself, laughing, while behind closed eyes I see flickers of light appear and break through me in waves that increase in brightness until their amber amplitude rises from us both out of a source like the source of all that first and early, lasting morning light.

Then everything we knew to be is turned upside down in one night. A new pressure or pattern of coldness forces us farther down in bed, deeper under the covers, where I feel I'll have to turn inside out to get away from whatever is there. Deep in my dark cave, I think how good it is to have Jerome beside me, though these are his feet. No matter the time I wake, morning or night, he is there. And then in the stillness that spreads from the room in every direction, I know what the change is: snow.

We're up and at our window and have to hug one another at the sight of it. We never realize that snow is what we've waited for until it's here. The only color in the countryside is in the sky. I want to walk over the sky, the way I walk down roads in other seasons, like somebody walking on his hands, but that isn't the same, quite. I want to crawl across it the way spiders and flies crawl across our ceiling.

"Be happy you're boys," Dad says. He's in the doorway in his Indian-blanket bathrobe, with the darkness of the living room behind him, his hands in his pockets and ovals of light sitting on his cheeks from his glasses—so brilliant in the brilliance from the snow that the stripes in his robe are like rainbows. "Don't boys like sleds? Isn't this snow about right for one?"

I'm struck by the winter daze that cold and then too much

heat can cause, before I've even been outside, and by the time I start to answer, he's gone. Jerome and I run to the pantry in the kitchen to look out its window toward the Heatons' house. Mr. Heaton is the mailman for the farmers in the area, and his snow treader stands beside their house. Or we call it a snow treader. It's Army surplus, Dad has said, gray-green, with numbers stenciled on its side, and probably used to pull a gun, but now it's home from "the War," like Mrs. Liffert's sons—a tiny cab on wheels as tall as tractor tires, with a slant to its back that has it leaning into action. Mr. Heaton comes out the door, across the porch, and looks up at it, testing his whiskers for their winter growth, and then walks to his car and drives off. Not today.

The pantry is as dark as midnight when we turn, and only partly there, to my eyes, and then the light in the kitchen divides me so much I'm not sure it's the same morning that we're having breakfast at the table. The corner across from me looks sawed off by light, and the radio is turned up high. We listen for news about school, but everything in winter is good to listen to. On Friday nights I like to hear:

> To look sharp and be on the ball!
> To feel sharp, on the ball indeed!
> Then be sharp, use Gillette Blue Blades!
> For the slickest, smoothest shave of all!
> Ding! Ding! Ding!
> "The Friday-night fights are on the air!"

My hero is Joe Louis. I pray that I'll meet him soon, and know that one day he'll come up our walk in his white boxing trunks (the way I always picture him), even if it's snowing, so there'll be the dancing in your eyes you get when you stare at dominoes, but so tremendous your head will hurt, and he'll step up our front steps, shaking the whole squeaking porch, then thump the door with a boxing mitt. Somebody else will have to answer; I'll be too shy. I'll look around the corner of the hall and see him above whoever is there, even Dad, with streamers of snow from the roof of the porch sailing behind his shoulders like the paper ribbons in newsreels of a parade, and he'll say,

"Hello, there. I'm Joe Louis. I understand there's a boy named Charles who's been praying he'd like to meet me. You tell that boy I'm here."

What a way to meet him, with snow sparkling in streamers over his oiled skin! Every time the picture appears, I cry, "Joe Louis! The number-one champ-peen!" and swing at Jerome to start a boxing match.

"Maybe if you two had a punching bag," Dad says, "you'd leave one another alone. It'd certainly save wear and tear on the furniture. Now stop that!"

It's not Cream of Wheat we are eating, with its rubbery scum on top, or Malt-O-Meal, with a picture of a man like Joe Louis on its front, or even oatmeal or cornmeal or any other kind of winter mush, not yet, but breakfast food from boxes. I stare at the one in the center of the table, still in a daze, reading the printing to locate myself. There are wiry lines of Niagara Falls, pictures of an Indian, and the dark-gray cards Jerome has taken from between the biscuits and fanned out beside his bowl: "Injun Uities is a bastardization," Mom has said, "but you can use such a word if it's accurate, as it is in this case—it's a bastardization of ingenuity, a quick-thinking kind of horse sense."

Jerome says the ideas on the cards would be perfect for our club, if we had one, and then a hollow voice calls from the back of a cave *"Straight Arrow!"* and echoing hoofbeats start up, until I feel the box in front of me has come alive. But it's the radio; it's Saturday.

Then the speaker says that the following schools will be closed, and the school where Dad once taught is mentioned. We cheer. There's a sound outside like a machine gun chattering, and we run to the pantry window and see, through fuzzy parting streaks, Mr. Heaton up in the cab of the snow treader and smoke spouting out of the pipe above its back. Gears grind, he wipes at its windows with a mitten, waves to us, and the snow treader trundles into the gathering lines of gray with tires crying. We run back to the kitchen and start pulling on our bulky clothes to go to the farmhouse at the edge of town, Bendemeers', for our daily milk, hurrying to start off on this chore that we usually complain about, when Dad walks into the kitchen and says, "You boys wait."

He takes down his brown canvas coat lined with sheepskin the color of butter, which can warm our faces in a second if we stand inside it where it hangs, and unsnaps its brown-stained collar. He pulls the coat on over his suit jacket, pulls on his floppy overshoes (which Jerome and I bend to buckle, knowing how good it feels to have overshoes buckled up over your feet by somebody else), and then puts on his cap with the furry earflaps like half-moons on each side, turns the flaps down and ties them with a cord under his chin, pulls on his mittens lined with gloves, rolls up the collar of the coat so it arches above his head, and says, "All right, now let's go."

This is it, this is what winter is for, I think, struggling through air so thick I can hardly see the hedge around our house or, after we've gone a ways, the house itself. The grayish streaks cross in streams that plunge and groan around us, and it's only when the wind sends them to one side and makes us feel the ice is slipping under our feet that we're sure this is snow, spiraling into our sight, over our foreheads, tightening the skin there, stitching it with needles headed toward an inner ache above an eyebrow, dripping from our lashes, along with real tears from the force of it, and gathering in furrows on the scarves Dad has tied under our eyes so that a gust of this doesn't get us gagging, which can lead to a cough, which can lead, through throat and chest diseases, down to a hospital room, or worse—spitting up blackish clots of blood from a gouged emptiness where your tonsils were. And though the scarves smell like dirty wet dogs and sprout bristles where our nostrils and open mouths are gasping behind, giving me glimpses of the monsters I imagine under a bed, they block the worst of the wind and deaden the sound that's been beneath this morning from the moment we woke—of a huge and moving river going by in a current so constant and deep we've hardly noticed we were hearing a blizzard—and now each flake seems to vibrate with a separate voice within the larger tones of the streams that are breaking against us with a force that gets my scarf fluttering so wildly I feel the end of it is flapping its last, way back by the coal-shed door.

As Dad walks ahead he drags his feet, plowing the snow aside in a path that's still difficult to manage, knee-deep, so we grab a tail of his coat to keep in touch with him and his direction through this wind-blown morning that has turned into night.

"It looks like it's going to be a real blizzard," he calls over his shoulder, and we shake the tails of his coat in excitement. If this keeps up, Mr. Heaton will drive the snow treader to the edge of the lake one day when he is back from delivering the mail, stop across from the water tower, near our old house, and then swing the machine down the steep bank. *That's it, folks*, you'd think, but soon it will appear on the ice of the lake and turn and start back up, chugging and bucking against the climb until it gets close to the top with the last of its steam, and then leap over the lip of the bank, its front wheels slamming down, while everybody cheers. Then the volunteer firemen will roll out a pair of wooden wagon wheels with canvas hose wound on an axle—the steel rims shrieking over the icy road, with perhaps a knit green mitten stuck to one rim and circling, like last time, with each turn of the wheel—and soak the trail the treader has left, shaping it with shovels into a trough of solid ice, and then we'll wish we had a new sled, or one apiece, so we can get our fill of sledding before the icy lines around our wrists, like aching fire tightening there, seem the only portions of us alive as we clump home crying on frozen feet.

A blizzard will deposit too much snow for Fox and Geese, but if the crust freezes we can press peach crates upside down into it and then pull the cut cubes free and use them to build igloos, or snow forts for our serious snowball fights—the worst of them between the kids from this side of Main Street and the town kids, as they're called, from the other side. High schoolers and fathers join in, fastening slingshots of inner tubes to the branches of trees behind banks left by the plow along our street, and high schoolers and oddballers will drive their cars onto the lake (someone in a sputting Model T) and send them into rumbling skids, spinning end-to-end halfway across the width of ice, underneath the bridge, so that when you come down the frozen trough with a crash of your sled and go speeding out across the ice farther than you thought you'd go, the front of the sled slapping over the rippled surface with strips of cracked blue swept clean by the wind, you sometimes have to twist the cross brace and pull yourself into a sudden sideways slide to avoid a car, sending up a showering fan that takes tints along its edges from the sun, so low now its light is like a highway rather than a path on the lake.

"There!" Dad calls, and we look around his sides and see the gray buildings of Bendemeers' appear and disappear among the blowing sheets, the bristles on our scarves icicles by now. My stiffened boots take on a freezing grip as we go up the steps to their enclosed back porch, and creak over linoleum in a new stillness. No wind. But it's colder here, with a chillier version of the salty manure smell that we hate. Dad's breath steams blue clouds as he pushes his glasses up on his forehead and bends to our quarts of milk. Columns of crystals, crowned by paper caps, rise above the bottle necks like three hats tipped in different directions. *So cold.* He takes the empties out of the carrier he has built for us and drops the full ones into its wooden sockets, and then steps to the door and with a backhand of his mitten sends the hats flying into the crisscrossing whitenesses.

"Let's get back before this gets worse," he says.

+

I raise the window shade an inch, wide enough to look out from the bed: the gray-bathrobed woman is gone and blue light reflects off brick. Yellow windows shine from rooms where people stir, and there is a shimmer over the woman's windowsill, as there is over mine, I see, below the sash. Snow. I fall back on the covers over the shape of the man here before me, and sink down in it, dead myself. Or as good as. Then the afterimage of the snow on the sill, in crystals as rounded as BBs (sugar snow, we called it), rises through me in filaments and I'm in the basement of the parochial school, in the room where the first and second grades meet, at my desk a row over from Jerome's, staring up at the sky divided into diamonds by the wavy wire mesh that we wade up to from the playground, grab with our mittens, and touch with our tongue tips to see if we can lift them free without leaving a strip of skin. From outside now, I shake the wire mesh at the boy staring past me, to shake his confidence that God protects him like the mesh over the windows. But the wire works both ways; the shaking of this rebel can't get through.

+

"If this keeps up," Dad says, and lays his frosted glasses on the kitchen table, "the country roads are going to be blocked till spring." This is the third day of the storm.

"Oh, boy!" we cry, and start to hang our stiffened clothes on the hooks behind the oil heater. "Sleds and sleighs!"

"No, don't get undressed. I'll lead you to school. I have to see Father anyway, about some contacts, and if I have to, I'll lead you back." Then in his acting voice: "And all our yesterdays have light-ed fools the way to dusty death!"

"You're not selling insurance in this weather!" Mom says.

"Just talking to Father about some contacts."

"Should those two go? I thought school was called off."

"Parochial school never is, especially now, with that nice warm addition Dad built for the Sisters attached to it, right?" He smiles down at us. "So, 'Once more unto the breach, dear friends,' huh?"

+

Jerome and I are the only ones in school, other than the Sisters of the Presentation Order, who teach us. Sister Mary Benedict sits at her desk at the front of the room, one elbow up, the full black sleeve of her gown drooping from its tight inner one, her forehead resting in her hand. She tells us we may read, but I've read all the books in our library (three wooden shelves behind the piano) and I stare past the snow on the high sills, in the direction of our house, at pale sky, cleared of blue by the snow that's fallen and finally stopped—pale-gray, partitioned by the mesh that protects the windows.

I raise my hand and ask if I may check the steps. Sister nods yes, without looking up. The steps, at the side of the room, lead to the main library, and books are stacked on them as if set off on a race to where they belong. Because I was five when school began, I felt I should work hard to keep up, but once I finished the shelves of books, and Jerome said that he hadn't, I haven't. There's a table next to the steps, with a hectograph on it, and I press my finger into its slab of jelly to see if any printing comes up on it purple-blue. No. Jerome and I share something that others here don't, which I can't name, although I see it in the Sisters when they call on us. But whenever Sister Benedict or Sister Colette tells us something that Mom or Dad wouldn't, I'm less sure of what it is that we share, which is confusing.

Each step takes me into a higher level of heat, and I feel the warm cocoon that winter puts me in, not just from heat, although it's hotter in most buildings in the winter than at any other time, but from the inside out. *Heat rises,* Dad says, and the thing to learn is how everything works, I've found. I sit, high enough to see to the end of the street, and turn over a book, then stare down at Jerome, bent at his desk, and wonder how far ahead he is. Sister sometimes warns him I'll catch up, and at other times says that I'll never be like him.

My best friend is Brian Rimsky, and Jerome's is Brian's brother, Leo. We're the same ages, or the oldest and youngest two are . . . Jerome is so much better at arithmetic, I'm ready to give up. Mr. Rimsky owns the grocery store, and Brian swipes us candy and gum, and says, "Don't swallow bubble gum. It'll get in your appendix-cytus. That's where gum goes, and it's too big a gob to get in at once. When too much is there, it explodes. You can die from it. Really, really," he says, grabbing my shirt, "that's the *truth.*" Or, "Most cantaloupes got worms in them. Every kind of raisin bran does, too. Once I got so sick on some, my puke was all wiggly with them. Really, it's true!" I see him saying this at the back of Scott Haig's house, or I see his head, as big as Dad's, against the boards of that house as he says this, and then his eyes close as his head pops forward from a slap across its back—his brother.

"Shut up," Leo says. "You probably got sick drinking that fruit jar full of your own pee."

"What?" I say to Brian, and then the others move off from us—there's a birthday party going on, or our buddies are here for some sort of celebration—and Kuntz calls from the ditch, "Come on, you guys, break it up! Let's play ball."

"Play ball!" Buddy Schoenbeck yells, backing out in line with the water tower above, toward the skeleton of the last wall of the barn.

"My grandma's a better ballplayer than you guys," Arno Litwak says, and slides his hands into his shorts, which are so new and neatly pressed, like most of his clothes, they look starched; he lives with his mother and grandmother at the edge of town, and his dark hair is always neatly barbered, although it swings over an eye like a broken wing, no matter how often he pushes it back.

"Okay!" Jerome cries, and hits a patch of dirt with a bat he holds choked up so high its end scrapes his ribs.

"I have to go," I say, and head on a run for the outhouse.

"Oh, come on!"

"Start without him!" Kuntz yells. "The outfield for you, buddy, when you're done with the old peanut-butter squeeze, wawk!"

The shut-in echoing sound of the outhouse, with dozens of granddaddy longlegs gliding over rough boards, past pinpoints of light, toward the eaves, and three mounds glistening below like monster heads. In a corner, behind a bag of lime and corncobs kept in reserve, is a soup can filled with lime. There's a clean can beside it. I pee in it and it heats up; I swirl it, sip and cough at the salty iodine wash, then drink it down, throw the can into a hole, bang open the door onto sunlight, flushed and about to heave, and cry, "Okay, I'm ready!"

Then we are playing kittenball on the playground here, using a tree near the school as home base—a dead tree, about to be chopped down, causing the school to look outlined from my left-field post: two stories of yellow brick with dark trim; the Sisters' new house, covered with "shingle material," as Grandpa called it, clinging to its back. As we play, Albert Mitchell, a seventh-grader, walks past me and the pitcher, lost in his own world, as Mom says, and stops in front of the tree. "Oh, tree," he says.

He spreads his arms, then bends to the initials on its bark as if to find a special set, and suddenly jumps up and grabs a big branch. It breaks off and almost hits him over the head. He leans on it like a staff, and says, "I think that I shall never see *this* tree next Saturdee. Too bad. There are birds in it."

"Where?" Leo Rimsky asks.

"There's a nest right above that fork."

"Boost me up to it, Albert," Leo says. "Please."

Albert drops the branch and holds out his hands in a stirrup. A bird goes flying off as Leo's black tennis shoes, with circles on the ankles, paw their way up, chunks of bark flying, and Albert walks off around the corner of the school, back in his world again.

"They're speckly ones!" Leo says, and two hit at our feet in plops; triangular beaks, rubberlike, bigger than the heads, and the heads hooded on both sides by dark globes—closed eyes.

"Bombs over Tokyo!" Leo cries, and I see him apply a pinch, and with a flip of his wrist send one spattering over Brian's head.

"Leo!" he screams, scrabbling at his hair. "Damn you! I don't want no damn dead bird guts on me!" He picks up the branch, crying, and slams it to the ground. "I'm going to kill you!" He licks at the tears beside his mouth as if to salt his anger. "I'll kill your ass the second you crawl down!"

+

Sister hasn't noticed that I'm all the way up to the library landing. I step inside. As many books as Mom's and Dad's line the shelves on every wall, behind glass doors. Should I start on these? Reflected in the glass is a plaster-white statue of the Infant of Prague, standing on a table in the center of the room, with one hand raised and the other supporting a white globe with a cross at its top. On this end of the table there is a real globe, with colored countries spanning it, and I spin it as I pass, then wish I hadn't. A gurgling sound goes up from it as it rolls in a wobbly circle before it squeaks to a halt. I listen for Sister. Not a sound. I should start back down, but instead I go to the doors constructed of tiny panes of glass, at the front of the room, and swing them in. Is this how Dad felt at his school? I see a font of holy water to one side of the door, and I reach up and make the Sign of the Cross before I walk through. The second-story hall.

To the right, through the doorway to the third-fourth-fifth-grade room, the black tent of Sister Colette's back shifts as she leans over her desk and scribbles on some paper. She wouldn't tell on me. The door across the hall leads to the rest rooms, and I could go there, so I would have an excuse for being away, but I hear water sloshing in that direction and imagine opening the door of a stall on Hank Kauter-Haupt, down on his knees, with a brush in a bowl. I turn to go down the stairs to our basement cloakroom and see Sister Mary Michael, the principal, older and crabbier than the others (sometimes we can hear her, from the basement, scolding students up here—"the head chewer," Kuntz calls her), at her desk to the side of the upper grades' room, staring at me. No. Her head is raised but her eyes are closed, and now she puts her fingers to them, underneath her silver-wire glasses, and rubs.

I hurry down the steps, missing the squeaking ones I've learned about on my trips to handle the business I've announced by raising one or two fingers, or to shake my Coke bottle until it's ready to explode, and stop at the edge of the cloakroom—wooden benches surrounding a gray-enameled floor. I ease ahead as the Injun Uities teach, and peer toward the light falling from the door: there is Sister Benedict, still at her desk with her head in her hand. I tiptoe across the cloakroom to the chapel-auditorium, which smells of incense and varnish, and if I go any farther I'll have to genuflect; a candle is burning in a red globe above the tiny altar where Father says daily Mass in the winter so that the furnace in the church will have to be fired up only once a week. I genuflect before I leave. I could walk into our room, where Sister continues to hold her head in winter light, but I sneak all the way back around, closing the library doors behind me, and when I start down the steps toward Jerome, I see a team of horses, a brown and a gray, turn the corner and highstep down the street in my direction, nodding against the harness and the load behind.

The horses are hitched to a hayrack mounted on wood runners which skim along at the level where I stand. Their driver is covered with a blanket to his fur cap, and steadies himself on the load of straw with a boot held out against the rack's front upright. The gold mound stops outside the front windows, rocking, the rack giving, the horses steaming and blowing frost past icicles hanging in the shaggy hair under their lips, and then the straw begins to tremble and give as mittens and overshoes and then faces appear through the black and wavy diamonds of protective, metal-wire mesh. Farm kids. A dozen run toward the schoolhouse doors, and some tromp on up the stairs. The ones who finally enter our room, smelling of Bendemeers' porch, tell us they dig caves to keep warm on the way in, and the rest of the day they're scratching themselves and picking straw out of long underwear.

And when the sky outside our windows starts to turn dark blue, the horses appear again, pulling the hayrack, and stomp and steam so much the mist blurs them. There's a rumbling of feet in the cloakroom and everybody except Jerome and me, it seems, crawls or dives into the straw until it looks like a load of straw again. Then the hayrack glides out of town, giving off after-school talk while Jerome and I run in its wake to the road we're not supposed to cross, then follow it farther out, and finally stand and watch it travel so far off it wavers like ice on a stove against the plain.

"I wouldn't care if I froze to death," I say, "if I could ride home in a hayrack once."

"Just be happy you live in town," Jerome says.

+

On a day when we are the only ones in school again, Sister says I might have a gift for penmanship, so I examine the condition of the nib on my stick pen, check the level of the inkwell in my desk, and take out my satchel. Its front is stamped with a cowboy clinging to a bucking bronc—Gene Autry, I figure—and in the fall its smell of oilcloth was so heady I could open it and be in Grandma Jones's kitchen, under silver windows. Now my tablet's bitter reek of bleach and strawy wood is a stronger scent. I get out my pencil case, whose sliding top is a ruler with a pencil sharpener at one end, take out a pencil redolent of Christmas trees, and then my Palmer penmanship book. I begin with designs, moving my whole arm and not my fingertips, and create a row of ovals so perfect a bumblebee could crawl down them. Then a line of the up-and-down strokes that, hooked to a screen door, would bring it shut with a bang.

I fill the rest of the page with capital As and take it up to Sister. She is still reading—her winter mood. I try to discover a way to see into her wimple, as she calls it. I want to know if she has any hair (Brian says no) and what color it is, and how she keeps it hidden under this hood with its shinily starched white band. She runs a finger over the red welt the band leaves in her forehead. The black pleated sides of the hood are too tight at her cheeks and under her chin for a peek, so I go back to my desk. I'll have a better chance with Sister Colette, I figure. She's new this year and looks loose at the seams. Her downy face, with round gold glasses, reminds me of the girl on metal crutches, and her mouth opens on teeth bent back toward her tongue when she smiles. She comes down from her classroom if nobody's there, and sits at our cutting and pasting table, in a child-sized chair, with her shoes showing beyond her long skirt, winding and unwinding a crumpled handkerchief she keeps in her sleeve, and Sister Benedict excuses us to visit her.

Today she reads another poem she has written; these are about trees and hills, difficult to understand, and I stare at the cutting table, which is divided into squares across its top, and feel that she measures her rhymes the way we measure paper with its squares. She tells stories about Michael the Archangel and the Dragon, evil spirits, saints—gripping the big beads of the rosary that loops through her belt in her lap as she talks—and about boys who displease their parents by teasing animals, fighting with one another, or receiving First Communion in a state of mortal sin. Some are struck by lightning the second they step out of church, she whispers, or evaporated out of their parents' arms. Her furry eyebrows rise above her glasses and her downy mouth opens on her bent-back teeth and bright tongue.

Gone to hell, of course.

+

The Sisters give us seeds and crumbs to scatter over the snowbanks for birds, and the birds' cries against the brick building are wilder than in spring. Inside, we wipe and wash the classroom slates, clean the erasers on a revolving brush in Hank Kauter-Haupt's furnace room, which is as scary as hell, with the big rumbling furnace about to blow, and a lost eye rolling toward us from the shadows. Then we empty the pencil sharpeners and scrape the Crayola wax from their metal spirals, and Sister Colette gives us our fifth piano lesson that week.

Sister Mary Michael and Sister Stanislaus, the housekeeper, come down the stairs, and Sister Benedict puts away her book, and then all of them, like black fluttering birds themselves, kneel around us on the floor of the chapel-auditorium and pray for the safety of those who can't be with us, and for better weather. Then they help us on with our coats and boots, smelling of hand cream and the pink Lifebuoy soap they pass out at the beginning of the school year, and take us to the front doors and send us off through the towering whiteness, where dark is already coming down (flapping between flakes like their dresses and hoods), and we step into a brightness that hurts, inside smells of supper rising from the stove where Mom stands, and the oldest Sister seems a girl who could learn as much in an hour, here, as we do in a day at school.

+

The wall behind the oil heater is where we hang our winter clothes. The walls of our bedroom, which is also our playroom, now that the upstairs has been closed off, hold school papers and holy cards from the Sisters. On the top of the dresser is a shrine—a cardboard box I've pulled a pillowcase over and pushed in at the front to form a niche; here I've placed the statue of the Blessed Virgin that used to be in Mom and Dad's bedroom. "He has a natural sense of reverence," I heard Dad whisper. I genuflect to the shrine on my way to the window.

I sit beside Jerome and stare out at the snow. The drift at this corner of the house has climbed over the outside sill and started up the lowest pane of glass, so that we can look down it from the inside like looking out a cockpit.

"Let's get out the sled and go sliding," I say.

"That clunker'd sink three feet in this stuff."

"What happened to the hedge?"

"What do you mean?"

"It's gone."

"Dad trimmed it."

"Really?" Since we've been in school together I keep trying

to push him past what he has learned to where we used to be. "Then where is it?"

"Underneath all this."

"Maybe it went down South," I say, and elbow him in the ribs.

"Don't be a dummkopf. It has roots in the ground."

"It must be dead, then."

"Hibernating."

I scratch into the spangled ice at the edge of the pane, furry near the wood, and say, "Did Jack Frost do this?"

"There's no such animal."

"Sister Colette said he lives at the North Pole, has a suit like Santa Claus, and icicles in his beard."

"If Sister Colette really said that, she was making it up."

"I left out cookies one night and the next morning they were gone. There was water beside the plate!"

"Dad ate them."

"Oh, shut up."

I shove his chest, he falls back on the bed, and I'm on top of him before he can move, trying like the devil-to-beat-anything to club that big bulging hump at the back of his head.

"Stop that!" Mom says from the doorway. She pushes a blackish swirl of hair from her face. "How many times do I have to tell you two how angry it makes me to see you fight! Shame on you, both of you! It's wrong and you know it. It's a sin! And it's even worse when brothers engage in it. It's—"

"Well, he started it," I say.

"No, I didn't! He pushed me down and then we were, ah . . ." We're not to roughhouse on the bed. He covers his face.

"You're not to roughhouse on your new bed, you know."

It's not new, I want to say, but the one they used until *they* got a new one. Ours is upstairs, probably shaking on its legs in the cold.

"And if you lie," she says, "Santa might hear of it."

From somewhere in the living room, Dad clears his throat.

We know enough to understand what this means, and drop on the bed and start rolling around on the covers.

"Stop!" she says. Then in a different voice, "Up off the bed, okay?" Now that she has been our mother, she's free to be herself. "It's stopped snowing, did you see?"

"Yes!" we say, and run to the window.

"It'd be lovely to be out in, wouldn't it? Well, now anyway. The way it was coming down, it sounded like brooms across the ceiling!"

"This winter will be the best ever for sledding," Jerome says. "And all we've got—"

"Is that old clunker that'd sink three feet in this stuff."

"Hey, I just told him that and now he's saying it! Tell him to quit being so pesky and so *ob*-stinate."

Hearing her criticism of me come in his voice narrows my vision to the back of his head.

"And now we're back to where we began," she says. *"No fighting."*

+

Jerome wades ahead, holding his elbows high, and a glowing halo trembles at his edges as he moves with the plunges of the figures in my dreams. There is only him and the snow and, above, the beautiful bitter winter bite of blue. He stops at a snowbank as high as Dad and turns, blinking, and above his scarf I see: *Why are we here?* The big bare tree at the edge of the yard, with limbs branching over us, cracks like a shot, and ice scatters down on our red-and-blue knitted sledding caps.

"Are you afraid?" he asks—a blue wisp through his scarf.

"Yes." Sister Colette has said that God and Mary and the angels are watching over everything we do, and that's exactly how it feels now.

" 'Although God is everywhere,' " he says in a hushed voice, " 'we do not see Him because He is a spirit and cannot be seen with our eyes.' That's what the Baltimore Catechism says."

"Let's build a snowman."

"We can't until the snow packs," he says.

"Let's dig a cave, then, and hide in it."

"Not till the crust freezes."

"What should we do, then?"

"Get in out of it."

I struggle over to a white swelling, get up on it, feeling my feet shake on the hidden hedge, and then rise and throw out my arms and dive. I'm in darkness with blue light at my sides, sinking, I feel, through the sky I've been crawling across.

I hear his voice and then, closer, he cries, "How is it?"

I turn and rest my cheek on the snow with my eyes closed, trying to hold on to the feeling of falling, which is about to reach the crazy-bone lightness that arrives when Dad takes the car at high speed over a dip in a country road. I look up and blink through the sparkling fringe on my eyes, and see Jerome staring down at me. "It's as good as the runway down to the lake," I say, and crawl up into sunlight. "Try it!"

He does, I do, we do it together holding hands, until the snow that gets packed into our overshoes and around our collars and cuffs has melted and started to freeze again in aching bands, and the pink sun, flat at its bottom, is going down behind the grain elevators. We start for the house, and I turn and see a row of slashes along the hedge, as if dozens of us have been diving to prove that we can fall, too, like this cold and yielding snow, and not suffer loss; and then I turn and sit on the edge of the grape chenille spread, faint and displaced, and feel sweat run down the curve of my rib cage—afraid to move.

+

Some of these mornings I wake to the special silence that spreads through the house after a noise, light lying on the ceiling like a cover over me, and listen for our parents. Sometimes voices rise from their bedroom, but I've never heard them argue—a blessing. Now it's night. What has awakened me? I believe in Santa Claus about as much as I believe in Jack Frost, but I want to know what our parents do on Christmas Eve. *Honor your father and mother* means "obey," so I shouldn't stay up, but if I knew what they did at night, maybe I would understand them better.

The yard looks varnished by the moon, all gold, shining at the edges of banks and drifts. The lights at the Pflagers', across the corner of the block from us, go out, sealing them behind blackness, and the wind starts to rise. The frame of our window rocks in and out and its panes begin to hum with a sound the room picks up. I kneel and stare at the drift climbing the glass, as if underneath it, and feel the shadow of Joe Louis over me. "Charles," he says. "You and I . . ." There is a movement inside me like prayer, but no words for it. I'm asleep on my knees.

+

In the morning the window is covered with a crust that forms white continents, except at its center. Did my forehead rest there, I wonder, from the covers where I lie, with no memory of how I got here. It's wonderful to have a brother, in this otherworld that winter is, and I crawl toward his heat and feel sleigh runners beneath us as horses pull us home under hayracks of snow.

+

Mom is bringing in the bed sheets that she left too long on the line. She leans them, like enormous flakes, against a wall of the porch, while the tubs beside the slogging machine steam gray when the door opens wide. I steady the sheets, which I love to smell in this state, or suck on for their cottony ice, and Jerome, who has been called here to help, stands in a coat, holding the door for her.

"Get inside," she says. "Or get something on if you're going to stand there and watch."

This is to me. I say, "You've just got on that—"

"Hush! Get indoors!"

I go in, to the hooks behind the stove, pull on a sweater, and step back out. One of the sheets is starting to melt and I dash over and catch it as she carries in the final one.

"Did you hear what I said?" she asks.

I pull a pinch of the sweater out from me. "I put this on."

"Good Lord."

Her own fraying sweater is held at its center with a safety pin, and it chills me to see it. She moves Jerome aside and slams the door, stomps snow from her shoes, bends and brushes at icy burrs clinging to her anklets, and then jerks the gearshift at the side of the washing machine. Its slogging stops and with another push and grinding pull she gets the wringers rolling in a steady purr.

"Oh, God, those sheets," she says, and steps to me. "Here."

She grabs the one giving the worst, clips it to a rope overhead with a clothespin she has moved from the pocket of her sweater to her mouth like a cigar, and continues this, getting the rest of them hung before they double over with a sound like gritting teeth. She takes the cover off the machine and hands it to Jerome, who holds it like a shield, then raises a finger at me and makes the motions of a clashing sword.

"Oh, God, ouch, *help!*" she cries, and I see her fingers, with twisted cloth attached, start through the wringers.

"*Ahhh!*" she screams. "Help! Goddamn!"

The assembly above her hand blows apart, a white piece hits the wall, and the top wringer thumps down on the floor and rolls to my feet.

"Oooo, that woolly nightie of hers got caught on my en*gage*-ment ring! Oh, it hurts!" She squeezes her ring finger and then covers her face, one hand gray, the other red. "Ooo, Mama," she wails, in a voice I've never heard. "Oh, Mama, help!"

Or Jerome, either, from his look—as if he's letting out the awful gas the steamy air is suddenly loaded with.

"Mom," I say. "You cursed. You took the name of God in vain."

"Yes!" she cries. "Yes, I have before, and I've done worse!"

+

It's vacation, and we clump home on frozen feet from sledding, our faces stiff as masks, numb except for an itch where our ears were. The nuggety ice tightens at our wrists like rope burns and travels down the inside of our arms in a pain that's connected to the rope of the sled we pull. The clatter of its runners on the ice cheers us past the red and green lights in the windows of the darkening homes, and our own kitchen is so warm I feel asleep on my feet. Loaves of bread, on the floor beside the oil heater, are rising—the spots on some, raisins; the red and green chunks, bitter fruit—and Gabriel Heatter is on the radio hurrying to the end of the evening news. Then Yogi Yorgesson comes on, singing:

> *Oh, I yust go nuts at Christmas,*
> *On dot yolly holiday!*

while I sink to the floor, dazed and melting, my ears setting the sides of my head on fire. Yogi ends his song with "While on duh radio Gabriel Heatter vas saying, 'Peace on Eart, Good Vill tovard men!' " which is what Gabriel Heatter was just saying, and then I hear a sound from the sink and I look up and see Mom leaning against the pantry wall. "This is crazy," she whispers, wiping her face with a hand. "Crazy!"

She pours water for our bath from a teakettle into a washtub, and we both crawl in and are embarrassed by the way she sits on the floor, with her face so close, and washes us everywhere. I yell, "I want oranges and pecans and candy canes and raspberry candy with jelly in it for my Christmas stocking!" and notice her reddened face and eyes, and add, "And a handkerchief."

"Yes!" Jerome says. "And marshmallow Santa Clauses, and almonds—a whole bucket of them—and balloons and, oh boy, candy cigarettes!"

We slosh around and shake with laughter at this.

"Quit!" she says. "You're splashing. My clean waxed floor will be ruined! Step on that rug when you get out. Out!"

She towels us until we're raw, and then rubs us everywhere with olive oil. I stand close to the stove under a towel and dream of green olives, bowls of them at picnics, and how they surround their red plugs like the warm wrap winter places us in.

Then Jerome snitches a pinch from one of her loaves, now deflating, and she leans and puts her arms on the edge of the tub. "Oh, *oh!*" she cries, and the water below her vibrates and rings. "There isn't one thing I can keep nice anymore! There isn't anything I can call my own! I don't know if I can live like this! I wasn't meant to!"

+

I lie on my stomach in the living room and try to draw the headache I have. It streams out one eye and bends back through the touchy part of my temple—a register stuck behind the eye it's pouring from, and should go down on the paper in crossing beams. I scratch some scribbly lines and feel my focus pull the room through the paper toward me. I shove the sheet aside and swing my legs around, to get the shadow of my head out of the way, and then decide to trace the shadow itself.

I look up for Jerome, and Marie, taller from where I lie, toddles up and plops down beside me. Her cheeks are as fat as a baby's and her eyes huge in her bald, pudgy head. Something in her pushes at me, and I crane to one side like the dog with the magnet in it. She reaches over to pat my paper, then jerks back her hand and screams.

She barely bumped her head on mine, if that, and when I try to remember if she did, the headache hurts so much my eyes cross. A bubble blows from her mouth, then her face darkens as she fights for breath. I hold her, and feel the floor shake as Mom and Dad come running up.

"What did you do?" Mom asks.

I look up through my headache, squinting an eye, at a giant, her dark hair mussed. "Nothing. I wasn't doing anything."

"Why are you acting so funny? What's that paper and pencil for?"

"I was—" I'm embarrassed to admit what I was doing.

She grabs Marie and carries her into the kitchen, and Dad, with a startled look at me, follows them in.

"Aren't you going to find out what it was?" she says from there.

"Is Marie hurt?"

"He could have poked her eye with that pencil."

"Are her diaper pins all right? Do you see anything?"

"Diaper pins are always all right. There isn't a thing."

"What could it be, then?"

"Why don't you find out from him? What's the use of hemming and hawing around about it? He acts guilty as sin to me."

"But he said he didn't do anything."

"Martin, please."

I head on airy skates for our bedroom just as he steps through the door. "Charles."

"I didn't do anything. She sat down by me and started screaming."

"Now, you know and I know that nobody starts screaming for no reason. What happened?"

"I just told you. She—"

"I want you to tell me the truth!"

"I'm telling you the truth!"

This is too loud. His hands, at his sides, rise up, his fingers curl around his thumbs, and Jerome and Tim hurry through the doorway from behind and seem to drive him toward me. He takes a side step to get his balance. "Tell me what you did."

"Nothing!"

"Answer in a civil tone! Did you poke her with that pencil or not?"

"I said I didn't!"

"Don't yell, and don't lie to me!"

"I'm not, dammit!"

His fists pump once, changing his color, and his hair goes swimming up. I dive through the door before he can grab me, and crawl to the other side of our bedroom. The thumping of his run is like thunder, and shakes the house, affecting the dresser I try to crawl behind. He comes around the corner, a jack-in-the-box, eyes bulging, lips out, holes for his nose, then flies apart like her washing machine. There's a growling in the room as I see the dresser won't do, and go for the bed.

He slaps my face. I cover it and he hits my hands so hard I'm on the floor with a nosebleed. Or it feels like it, in the ringing through my broken ears. He grabs an arm, jerks it from its socket, tosses me on the bed, and pounds my behind so hard I spring up and down. "Now stay here till it's time to sleep!" he yells. "Don't come out again tonight! And quit crying or you'll get worse!"

There is a wallop of air as he slams the door. I get up and limp, hurt and stiff, to the dresser, knock the shrine over, unable to stop wailing, then lean on the wall and slide down it. I can't sit. I roll on my stomach. I don't want to live in this house, I try to yell as I kick the floor. There can't be a God or He wouldn't let this happen. It's not fair! I'd like Joe Louis to come and knock them all apart, and then I look up at the window and see that it's overgrown with frost. There must be some troll or an awful cold monster who never forgets, because if I don't get even with them for this someday, he will.

+

The next day is Christmas Eve. Jerome and I follow Dad out the shoveled drive, alongside the car in Indian file, me last. The banked street is a channel for the wind we woke to, and I can feel the fuzz in my nostrils freeze. Zero. We step up the bank on the other side, over snow piled higher than Dad, past the buried teeter-totter and the slide with half its steps rising from a drifted bank, across the corrugated playing field, and step around the corner of the parochial school just as a wind caroms off its front with such a crack we walk in place. I can't breathe. The harder I try, the tighter the cold closes on my throat.

I'm swung around and my back slammed, and then Dad, who is behind me, blocking the wind, strikes me on one side. My face is aflame. He guides me around the corner of the school, next to the metal-wire mesh that it scalds my tongue to see, and slaps my back again.

"Are you okay?" he asks.

"Yes, I believe."

His hands are still on me; thumbs circle between my shoulder blades. I want to say, Forgive me, but he doesn't know what I've thought. I nod.

We step around the school and several men wrestle out of the church vestibule, dragging a man whose face is green.

"My Lord, it's N. J. Ludvig," Dad says, and takes off in strides we have to run fast to keep up with.

The men are getting Mr. Ludvig into a car's back seat, all panting steam, and before we have a chance to see him close, the car doors slam and with a whirring of tires, stinky streaks on ice, the car slides toward us, and Dad and Bill Faber give it a shove that sends it down the street. One of the vestibule doors closes and Hank Kauter-Haupt snaps its locks into place above and below as the men file in the open one, and then the bell in the steeple above begins to clang.

Inside, Hank Kauter-Haupt, dressed in his blue suit, short at the sleeves and shoes, reaches his arms overhead, his hands around the rope, head back, going up on his toes, and then comes down with a neat bend to his knees as the bell clangs in a dimmer chime—still in shape, Dad says, from that other war, the First, a man of history with heavy silver hair sheared to his ears, his face a bony mask—and goes up again with the rope, head back, his eyeglasses like coins, and then steps up to us as the rope climbs above his head and snaps, and, in a delicate gesture, gives Dad a stiff bow. "Herr P'fesser," he says, and his nervous grin, worse today, draws back on false teeth, his fixed eye catching the light as he repeats his slight bow, then shakes Dad's hand. "Martin."

"What happened to him, Hank?"

"Ach, his heart's kaput. He fell in his pew. He vohries too much."

"Money. Such worries, Hank." Dad pulls off his hat and shakes his head, and scattered curls spring up from his hair, now turning straight.

"Ja, not good. Fodder unnointed hem."

There is an uneasy stir, coughing, a rearrangement of bodies beyond the open inner doors, and I turn and see the backs of people and feel the smell and pull of them as a crowd, then get my first whiff of incense burning in the thurible as the gold bell above the sacristy door clanks. There is a rustle of clothes, the clomp of kneelers, and a wash like applause as everybody rises for the procession of altar boys, then Father. He steps with the covered chalice to the center of the altar, which climbs in arches to the ceiling, with candles flickering at every level on it for Christmas, then steps back down with his hands inside his sleeves, and we join the crowd at the rear of the church as Hank closes the doors behind us and Father bows at his waist toward the altar, then stretches out both arms, and cries in his chanting voice, "In nomine Patris, et Filii, et Spir-i-tu *Sanc*ti!"

+

Jerome and I put on our heavy clothes for the walk to Bendemeers', and it's so cold that after we've gone a ways my butt hurts again. At the football field across from the high school, I stop and stare at the window where Dad's office was, and then hear a sound of hooves on the road, and a team of horses comes jogging up with a noisy clashing of harnesses, pulling a shed mounted on hayrack runners.

"Hup!" a man shouts from inside, behind a glass window at the front, with a slit below for the reins, which he shakes with a leathery clatter over the horses' rumps. Their speed picks up and the sleeve of smoke from the stovepipe curls in tatters over the shingled roof where snow has started to melt. These are the rigs used by farmers, now that winter is here for good, and country kids say that the stoves inside, which burn coal, are perfect for making toast and popping popcorn during their long rides in, which seem to take hours, the way the horses move.

"Hie-up!" the man cries, and the team cuts across the football field as if it's a pasture, breaking wind in the freezing air, probably hauling a load of presents for children we know.

"I wish I could ride in one of those," I say.

"You'd have to be a farmer."

"I will."

"Tell me another, Corly McCrother."

"What if winter lasted all year?"

"The farmers couldn't raise crops and we'd starve."

"I wish we didn't have to wait so long for it." I'm thinking of the upset of the last few days. "Or it came more often."

"Christmas is when Jesus Christ was born."

"I know that."

"Even Jesus has only one birthday, my dear."

"Jesus can do whatever he wants!" Sister has told us to bow our heads when we mention him, because the Bible says every head shall bow at his name, so it seems we're nodding a lot. "Jesus could have a hundred!"

"Huh-uh. He had to be obedient."

"Who to?"

"God."

"He is God!"

"But he had a special mission to do. He had to die on the cross."

"That's the other one! There are three."

"Three persons in one God, goofball. One *He*."

"Not *him*."

"I see you haven't been paying attention in catechism lately."

"I have, too!"

"What do you mean, 'I have, too,' " he says, in his way of mimicking me that makes me feel my fly is unsnapped. "That's how it is. He died on the cross. You know that or you don't."

He turns and goes toward Bendemeers', singing Christmas

carols, his breath forming fans of different shapes in front of his scarf. I want to yell that I know all this, but it's difficult to believe that the infant in the manger is the old man nailed to the crucifix above our living-room door. I know that he died for everything I did, or didn't do, and he has become a greater hero to me than Joe Louis, whom I love more than anybody, except for Dad.

Jerome comes back with the bottles in the carrier and sets them at my feet. It's my turn to carry them, his gesture says, but we stand in the tracks of the sled and watch it narrow into a wavering sliver on the plain. The snow everywhere across the plain is turning golden from the sun, and the rack crosses the point where gold rests against the far-off edge of sky like a line at the end of our world, gone.

+

At the Heatons' I set down the carrier and take off as if skating on air. Dad has come out of the coal shed to the car, and when I get to him he is trying to rearrange an old Army blanket over a carton in the trunk. I ask him if Jerome is right about Jesus. He turns to me, surprised, and blue vapor fumes past his face and frosted earflaps as he thinks.

He says, "I guess I'd have to say he was."

"So why have Christmas? Why celebrate?"

His eyes move over my face as they have when I've been ill. "Because Christ, who was the son of God and also God Himself, became a man and suffered in our place, to be our Saviour."

I hear Jerome coming from behind on a run that has the bottles jingling, and then the trunk lid slams down with a windy thump.

I go in and talk to Mom, who was raised in a different church. She is at the stove stirring syrup about to candy, so she can't take time to explain, she says, but as I pull my way out of my layers of clothes, on the floor in front of the stove, she tells me that Christ was born in a manger in Bethlehem, yes, and was crucified. "But that's a reason to rejoice," she says. "Look at his precepts."

So there.

I go to bed early that night, crawling between sheets so newly washed they smell of snow. Jerome arrives, pulls the covers over our heads, and whispers, "I bet that box in the trunk is a sled. Did you see a label? It was just the right size. Well, maybe too long. But not if it's a real long one, huh? We could ride double on it! Even if it's a regular one, we'll each have our own. We can . . . We won't have to do those breath-squashing belly flops on each other's backs. We could . . ." He's on a downhill course himself, from the way his voice grows faint, and then the sound of his breathing settles into sleep.

I uncover my head, pull the covers from his, and turn to the window. It is bare at its center now, and I pass through it into the library, under the white arms of the Infant of Prague, go to the first bookcase, reach through the reflections on glass, and take out a book and sit on the floor and start to read as Mom covers her face and says, "It's crazy!" A blurring sensation, as if the winter daze has overtaken me for good, upsets this, and then the window is there once more. But the room has changed. I've been asleep.

I hear singing and get out of bed and go to the window. . . . *angelic hosts proclaim, Christ is born in Bethlehem!* Loudspeakers have been hung outside the church's vestibule, and the choir is singing Christmas hymns into a microphone. They'll sing until Midnight Mass, like last year. Their voices spread a silver haze, heavier than the snow, over my senses and the area of our yard that my sight controls:

> *It came upon the midnight clear,*
> *That glorious song of old . . .*

I move my lips along with the words I remember. Soon it will be Epiphany and I'm not sure what the feast celebrates. I'll never get it right.

> *Joy to the world, the Lord is come!*
> *Let earth receive her King!*

A different kind of cold rises from the floor and I can't hear singing. If everything happened to Jesus that they say, and he is God, then what will become of me—a dreamy sinful boy from a tiny town in this frozen Northern state on the turning world? The wind comes up and a lightning-rod cable at the corner of the house slaps against the siding in the cold air, and then the shade on the streetlamp swings, tipping its cone of light over banks and drifts, and sudden snowflakes appear against the window, tapping there as if to signal me.

I go to the door, closed now, and the knob looks as big as doorknobs used to be, a globe to turn. I get it open. The Christmas-tree lights are lit, and from the height of the tree in the bay window they shine in a firelight of interconnected beams—such an array of color across the air I feel the season enter me. Chairs with our names on them are set around the oil heater, and stockings hang from their backs. I go toward mine, and something, like a head gone soft, brushes my arm, then wobbles on a rod when I step back. Light shining through the isinglass in the door of the heater touches the sunken head in spots, and I see nubbles—a basketball. No, a punching bag. "Now maybe you won't have to use each other for one," I can hear Dad saying.

There are new socks on my chair, packages, sacks of candy, and a dark box I pick up and shake. Not a doctor's kit. Clothes. I hear voices and set it back. But then there's such a hush, sending up further blurs through my daze, that I'm sure I imagined them. I go to the tree. Past the mound of packages that Jerome and I have helped heap up is an addition smelling of paint. The slat down its center reads *American Flyer*—a sled long enough to seat three our size. Three, I think, and feel again the tug of Jerome being right.

A dark square leans against one runner. I pick it up and feel the alligatory surface of Dad's briefcase before I read through the light reflected across its cellophane: *Junior Doctor's Kit.* The one I've wanted, with a miniature X-ray machine. I have to sit on the sled with weakness. I don't deserve this.

On cotton rolls under the boughs is a stable, with cattle, sheep, and camels, the Night Visitors. Joseph and Mary beside a manger, where the infant lies on straw, his arms outstretched, with rainbow-colored constellations over his stomach. The blur overtakes me and I see layers of flakes like curtains unrolled, frosted panes going past like shuffled cards, icicles as big as Dad that run from the coal-shed roof to the ground and chime from their bubbly insides when he shoulders them down.

The bell at the church is ringing for Midnight Mass. Christmas.

I put down the kit, and the tree lights gutter around my vision in a colored swim. Why Jesus? Couldn't they let him be?

Do people always do whatever they want with children?

I walk to the kitchen and look at the coats hung behind the stove, and figure I might as well start dressing up to go out into the cold.

"Charles?"

I turn. A man in silver robes stands in the living room. He moves, darkness and shadow falling from him, and then Dad is in the door in his Indian-blanket bathrobe.

"What are you doing up at this hour?"

The bulk of him looks black in the doorway, with colored light from the living room shining past his mussed, upright hair. Somebody else is in the room behind him. "What are you doing out here? Are you all right?"

"Yes, I believe."

He comes and puts a hand over my forehead. *"Mmm,"* he says, and corners of the room hum in response. "You're probably troubled or worried about what you asked me and Mom today, is that it?"

"Yes."

"You needn't worry about anybody as willing as he was to accept his role in life. If he had any doubts, it wasn't more than once. 'Father, Father, why hast thou forsaken me?' *What a marvel it must have been to hear his voice!*"

These last words, a whisper, ring back from the walls, and the person behind him enters the room.

He rubs my shoulders and back, and says in a different voice, "Get into your pajamas now. I'll come in and say good night."

"I have them on, Dad."

"Oh, of course, of course you do."

I'm at the center of a feeling I've only sensed before—every area of my skin parting into specks that vibrate like snowflakes in the wind. Dad is composed of these, and the house, and the ringing of his voice has opened further spaces between them, so that now it feels the wind is blowing through us both. It travels through his fingers into me, as the hem of his bathrobe lifts, toward the other person present with us.

"Charles, Charles." These words come down the corridor they travel when I have a fever.

"Hn?"

"Forgive me."

"What for?"

"If I've disappointed you, or been unfair, or let you down."

I know you didn't mean to, I want to say, but my voice is so thin it won't work. No, I start to say, and then I rise above his shoulders and feel his hands gather me in, then there is the stride of his feet underneath me, and I hardly have time before I'm headed down to sleep in that North Dakota night, in the house where I feel I was born, in the warmth of the wide white bed where he tucks me in next to my brother, to thank Jesus (my head nods, nudging me closer to sleep), or is it God?—to thank whoever it is who has given me—given Jerome and—given us— To thank Him for our father.

My daughter walks into the room. She is eight, back from school, wearing a shine of work accomplished, and her stare sets my eyes dancing to find a level in hers to adhere to. She seems to study me to determine the depth I'm rising from this day, and then shrugs and looks down at the toe of the shoe she's twisting into the carpet. "Hi, Dad."

"How was school?"

"Oh, fine."

Her hair, which is in braids, reveals even through its plaits the blond thickness it has hanging loose, and picks up highlights from the window. She walks to the desk at my side in this narrow alley where I work, between the desk and a table that holds my recording equipment, and looks at a letter, taps her finger across it, picks up a paperweight—a bee on a thistle sealed in a lens of synthetic amber—sets it down, turns a matchbook square to the recording equipment, and sighs. I let my weight lower into the chair with a sigh of my own. She comes upstairs nearly every evening, after her long trip in from the suburb where she goes to school, and lately she has been making noise on the stairs, or at the door at its head, or across the pair of rooms to here, after being reprimanded several times for sneaking up on me. She loved to appear with a *"Boo!"* and

I had to force myself to be calm, in order to explain to her how being surprised could ruin my concentration, and might ruin a recording, and on the positive side said that with some warning I would have a chance to draw away from my work to prepare for her (I managed not to mention a recent fear of heart attacks), because I've come to look forward to her visits. At dinner, if she hasn't been up, I'll say, "I missed you; I missed our talk," and she'll stare down at the table and blush.

"What did you do—or what came up today?"

"Oh—" From the desk, she checks me over a shoulder, and then is back to spinning a paper clip. "I studied, worked, played. The usual."

I wait. "It went okay, then." And feel myself drifting back until my attention plummets to a phrase in my script, grappling with its turn—

I wheel my chair backward, to see her better, then slide down in it and stretch my legs, trying to relax, fretful that the bulging demons in me, if not visible, can be sensed. I pick at a hair above my temple, isolate it between my thumb and forefinger and find that it reaches to my crown, and want to pull it out—the pop of it going, and then the itchy buzz where its root was, follicle raw to the air. She goes to the door, always swung in, leans against the edge of it with a shoulder, and rattles its noisy knob—spattered with a dozen shades of paint—until I want to take her hand.

"I guess nothing special happened, really," she says.

"Oh?"

I draw up in my chair a bit, crossing my arms, and think: It's Leslie again. Leslie, her girlfriend, has been giving her trouble over the past month, and a few days ago, when my daughter pointed out to Leslie that something she said wasn't true, Leslie slapped her face.

"Well, I did have kind of a problem with Kim."

Kim is the other one. My daughter has had a trying relationship with her, from the time she started attending this suburban Christian school, and Kim appears to be a problem to others, too; she *causes* her problems, as the teachers say. She's from the East, strung with piano wire, as I imagine, in the way that she bears down on each situation as if her existence depends on its going in her favor. From the stories I've heard, I can see her sweeping from moment to moment in the imperious attitude that eight-year-olds can have, wise to weaknesses, autocratic, and then putting her finger on the exact spot that causes contention to ring in everybody else. It's a disposition I'm not unfamiliar with.

"What was the problem about?"

"She pushed me real hard, and then she wouldn't talk to me all day. She'd turn away every time I looked at her."

"How come?"

"Well, I was pulling her around and—"

"Wait a minute. You were pulling her around?"

"On her roller skates. In the gym at noon, when we have permission to roller-skate if we want to."

I know, I want to say, since we've had to invest in fancy skates for this. "You were skating, too?"

"No, I was in my shoes."

So much for the investment.

"That's why she wanted me to pull her."

"Oh."

"Well, anyway, I was pulling her around, and these boys kept coming along and bumping into us, going lickety-split on their skates, trying to knock us down—I fell down flat once—and she kept asking me to run as fast as I could all the time. 'Go faster,' she'd yell. 'Come on, *run*! You can keep ahead—' "

She catches herself and stares beyond me, blank.

"Of the boys?"

"Yes." She glances down at her turning shoe; the boys might be another matter, but not the main point of this one. "Then all at once she acted like she didn't *approve* of how I was pulling her or something, besides always saying how slow I was, and then she gave me a real hard push. I fell down."

"Did you do anything back?"

"No."

"Good. Why didn't you tell her you were tired, which you probably were, if you'd been pulling her around so long, before it came to that?"

"Boy, I was! And then she went around all day, you know, like she was something special, and kept talking to everybody else, like Leslie for about *fifteen minutes*, but wouldn't say boo to me."

"Well, what do you do in such a situation?"

Her hands start up on a flight as if for the doorknob and I rise from the chair, about to take them in mine, trying to slow this so I can thread my way through it. Her energy is catching, and my small room, with the door down for a desk and the table nearly as big, shrinks even more, so that I have to take a step to keep my balance. I say, "There's one sure rule: Never return evil for evil, if evil it was. As soon as you do anything, she's got that to go against, and then you come back with yours, and that can go on forever."

"What should I do?"

"Walk away, or ignore her, which isn't the best, or be nice to her, which is better."

"I tried to! She wouldn't talk! She stuck up her nose at me! And you know that ring? The ring with the little cross on it that I got at Leslie's birthday party?"

"Yes." She won this in a potato-sack race; she loves to race.

"Well, when I was pulling her, she was jerking on my hand, and squeezing and pinching so hard the ring dug way down into my finger here. It hurt bad! You can see."

By now we're engaged in a kind of dance, and I take her hand as if to formalize this, surprised again by the stout strength in it, and see a red welt at the base of a finger. "Well, you should have stopped and said, 'Look, Kim, if you want me to pull you, don't squeeze my hand so hard, or let me take my ring off first' "—I lean and kiss the spot—"and been clear about your reasons why, before—"

"I didn't feel it then!"

I'm talking so much our dancing keeps up, although it's too unpredictable to be called a dance. "Well, you could have said, 'I've been pulling you around about X amount of time, and if you want me to pull you faster, you'll have to let me stop and rest awhile,' so there'd be no question that it had to do with her personally—just that you'd had it. You were worn out."

"Well, I was! I was pulling Angeline around for about the first ten minutes of the hour, and—"

"Oh!" I say, and our movement stops. "No wonder Kim

was so angry. She wanted you to pull her as fast as you'd been pulling Angeline."

A hiss starts to one side of us, as if the radiator is leaking steam, and goes off in the air above my head. I blink at the change in the room and stare down at a young woman below me. She's looking down, too, chafing at a welt on a finger.

"Mom said to say dinner is ready when you are," she whispers.

Now that I've said as much as I have, I don't know what direction to take. "Are you all right?"

"Sure."

"Tell her I'll be down in fifteen minutes."

"That's what you always say."

"I do?"

"Yes. Sometimes it's so long I get tired. The food's all cold."

"I'm sorry." Should I add only a word or two to encourage her when she talks, so that her path to me is always clear? I resolve to do this. But as she goes to the door, her head still down, fragments of me are already in the chair, and other vital ones are even further back, picking through the words of that phrase, which, with the—

"I'll see you at dinner, Dad."

I hardly hear this, or I hear the echo of it after she's gone.

"I'll be right down!" comes back so loudly from the walls I hear my father's voice. Are those her footsteps going so slowly down the stairs, or have I missed her footsteps, too? I sit and sense my consciousness turn, and I find I'm facing what I should have before: if parents were always present, or merely available to their children, then childhood wouldn't be spent in mourning, as most of it is. As hers is, I think, and get up to leave, then look down at the street, where insects billow beneath a lamp, and underneath this I see myself in a T-shirt at a window of the Chesro, in the gaudy room my brother will never enter again, staring out at falling snow.

+

I'm beside a young woman at another window in New York, in light so dim that when I draw back I can see her only in silhouette, but with the tinted contours of her face showing through. She is not a daughter of mine, although I treat her in ways that cause us to act as if she were, and so wring from her a daughterly tone. She leans farther forward on the sill, and now the window is more than a wall's opening on the scene—like a corridor she is staring down to the brick wall of the courtyard across the way. "Know what?" she says, her profile outlined by a pink sky above the buildings, and I see that out of the density of pink, snow is coming down in a counter-turbulence of shifting flails, and then she raises her face so that it takes on tones of the sky in the eerie light, and says, "It's nothing at all like rain. It turns around and it also climbs."

+

Don't know date. There's a new atmosphere in the building, as if the science of mechanics is overtaking it. More TVs are present, with their tendency toward poor reception in the context of this place; the Slavic presses wallop at a higher speed, and I've heard a metallic rattling in the hall late at night. Illusion, or something gravely wrong with me?

+

Aspirin and a smell of oranges in a downpour from rafters, the taste of cod-liver oil with ice cream on top—a crib across the room that shouldn't be there, with somebody crawling in it, strips of shadow higher, dark and light. Tim? The noise of springs like amplified breathing through my hearing opened wide, no stoppers on it. Striped curtains, once a bedspread where Mom's legs lay, hanging over our window now. That time of life or this wall tipped up, all meaning bleached from it yet hovering an inch above in a yellowed shine.

Blew blue smoke into me in breaths that were blue.

Hn?

Dad's smoke in me opened up all those rooms.

"Do you want to eat now, Charlie?"

A grate of grinding teeth, a sound I wake to that assures me I exist. Raw passageways from the back of my nose down my throat, which is swollen closed, except for this pad of ice cream going past my chest (at every parting river in me an aching clot or lump), down to feet that are like paddles attached. Swinging them, covers sway. The bed tips from my head—held in the aching lines that held it after I fell from the slide, like the cords holding Gulliver in a book, but these aren't silken cords or simple cords but *sing*le cords, since each is a sin.

"Have you committed uder sins, Chals?" Father asks.

Dad above me on the stool, a face below black hair, mounting a white shirt, huge. The clink of the spoon like a pipe down a well. *Eilring!*

"Please, Charles, have some more."

"No," I moan, the back of my nose abuzz with sorrow for myself.

"You're sure?"

His voice draws cords from the corners of my mouth toward my ribs, and tears transform everything to glass and roll.

The blue behind his glasses turns down toward the dish, a heap of white, with the spoon revolving it, and when I wake the dish sits liquid, the spoon submerged in white, on the top of a red-painted stool.

He's back and takes my hand and holds it, then puts his other hand on my forehead. I slide down the cords into sleep, and when I wake he says, "Why don't you try to sleep now. I'm praying for you."

I wake on the couch and see the oval of the oil heater sail through an eye. I pant in wet pajamas, and then a voice like Grandma Jones's says in a far room, "Father Schimmelpfennig is here." This quavers like cellophane. "They say it's time."

+

Then I'm back, not sure how long I was away, or how I got pneumonia, or got out of it, my chest narrower in shallow air. Jerome walks in with a clashing of clothes that smell of the cold, and sits on the end of the bed. The shifting versions of his face, tinged from the yellow shine, narrow to one as he stares at me.

"How do you feel now?"

"Pretty good."

"Do you want to learn Latin?"

"What?"

"The Latin of the Mass. We're learning it in second grade."

"What else are you doing?" A burr in my nose. Since the classes meet in the same room, I've always been able to participate in either, and feel I've advanced to his now—older.

"Nothing too interesting. History, geography, multiplication tables, drawing woodpeckers. And *singing*, ugh."

He can't sing, I understand in a new catch inside. Can I?

"Would you like to learn the Latin?"

"Yes."

"Okay, here's what we had today. After you procession in with the priest and make the Sign of the Cross, he says, *Introibo ad altare Dei*, and then you go, *Ad Deum qui laetificat juventutem meam*. Try it."

"*Ad*, ah . . ."

"It means 'To God who giveth joy to my youth.' You pronounce the words distinctly, but not so loud you disturb any worshippers. It's probably really hard if you can't look at the Latin. I'll say it again."

It makes as much sense as English in my state. Over the waking sleep of my recovery, I memorize the lines and watch his face. He smiles more, and when Mom says from another room, "Don't overtire him now, he needs his rest," he winks. Jerome? Later, if I want to serve, he says I'll have to learn the motions to go with the words, but he can teach me those, too, and by the time we're through with the Confiteor, the Latin that's entered forms an eye in me. Flecks of illness filter out my head through its iris. I see the priest and the altar boys, in their red cassocks and white surplices with embroidered yokes and sleeves, moving over the steps of the altar during Mass, and see myself among them. Then I'm alone. I pull myself onto the altar, crawl over the stone holding the relics Father kisses during Mass, turn the key on the tabernacle, pull open its door, push back the curtains and—

Are those the glowing bones of Christ in the dark?

+

Jerome comes into the room, looking over his shoulder like a thief, and sits on the bed, which gives in a way that sends my illness sliding off. He looks toward the door, then whispers, "We've got a new club."

"Where?"

"In Benny Ennis's barn."

I'm confused again; the barn is across the street from

Pflagers', behind Ianacconas'. I say, "It's always been in their barn."

"That was the old one. This is a new club. We elected officers. It's more exclusive, Benny said. You have to pay a dime to join."

"Is Brian in it?"

"He's going to join when he swipes one. Leo joined the town kids' club—Dickie Sill's. He's the only parochial schooler in it, except Dickie, so we'll have to rock Leo. You can't have mercy. They didn't."

"Rock him?"

"We had a rock fight after school with Dickie Sill's guys, starting uptown, and they drove us past here to our clubhouse."

"I heard something, I thought."

"Everybody got beaned." He rubs a hand over the bulge at the back of his head that I used to hate. "I have bumps and Kuntz got a bloody nose none of us could stop. But everybody was safe, once we were in our clubhouse and pulled the ladder up—that's new—then broke out Alan Pflager's and Benny's BB guns." He leans in with a fainter whisper. "We have weapons now. Dickie and his guys retreated and kept yelling they'd get us back. We're playing for keeps this year."

From the kitchen Mom says, "Does the sudden secret you two seem to be sharing have anything to do with that hubbub I heard outdoors? You know I won't tolerate fighting, especially of the organized sort."

Our eyes slide and meet and I try to enter his, to learn how he feels about this warning, and discover that he won't let me in. His eyelids bulge with his eyes' upward roll.

"Jerome, come here and tell me what you've been up to."

He leans again and whispers, "I'm not going to lie, but I might commit some sins of omission."

The bed rocks and he's gone. I strain to hear what he says with my newly sharpened senses, and hear her; she whispers, "Don't you realize if you keep him in a state of excitement he'll never get well?"

+

She dresses me in clothes that are too hot, then bundles me in blankets that press the illness close, and Dad comes in, wearing his fur cap and sheepskin coat, and picks me up. She tosses another blanket over my face. No air. He strides through the house, and I hope he'll get a hold that doesn't pinch, which he does when I'm about to slip. A different feel comes into his walk, and the blanket above me glows so bright I can see blue fuzz. There's a wind and he bends close, forming shadow above me. "Just a ways more," he whispers, and his words vibrate the blanket like a drum.

I'm uncovered in the brightness of the chapel-auditorium, afraid I'll unwind from his arms at its size. All the people move to an altar rail hammered together out of the wood left from the Sisters' house. First Communion? Dad carries me to the rail and kneels, and Father Schimmelpfennig walks up in a white cassock with a stole crossed at its front, carrying something on fire that reflects off his balding head, and stops at me. "Chals," he whispers, and lays a hand on my hair. He looks older, with purplish lips brown in one corner from his cigar, his cheeks as dark as Dad's before a shave, and gold in his teeth. Over my shoulders he slides a pair of candles bent like prongs, and I glance back and forth at the flames behind my ears. "It's da feast of St. Blaize," he whispers. "Dis is to bless your troat. I'll pray for da rest, too."

He sketches a Sign of the Cross in the air, murmuring in Latin, and closes his eyes. As Dad turns to carry me away, I see Mrs. Welsh, the widow whose eighth-grade son is a school problem, touch a lacy, crumpled handkerchief to her nose, and then Sister Colette is there, with her smiling teeth bent back toward her tongue, as if she's panting: a kiss.

Then the blanket is over me in blackness again.

+

There are days when church seems as dark, with the choir chanting, "At the Cross her station keeping, stood the mournful Mother weeping . . ." The clash of chains as Father elevates and swings the censer in the aisle toward the next Station of the Cross—all in plaques on the walls. Older altar boys march forward first, the tallest carrying a crucifix on a pole, a pair with candles on poles, and then Father, in his embroidered cape and purple biretta, looking pale, with younger altar boys behind, one carrying the censer until it's time to use it again, another the boat of incense. My need to serve overtakes me, and then there's an elbow at my side, and Jerome registers the same thought. *Together*, his look says. He winks, a corner of his eye drips, and I'm sure I'll never get well.

+

On Good Friday, purple shrouds cover the statues in church once more, as if the saints the Sisters speak about had died. At the head of the church, a crucifix, reaching from the steps at the Communion rail into the aisle, rests on a cushion. I'm frightened by it as we move closer—Dad behind with hands steering my shoulders, unaware of how he keeps bumping me into Jerome. The bony body arches up in a color like cream, every rib a bow, the drops of blood on His side and down His face, from the crown of thorns, brilliant as fingernail polish. Jerome keeps looking back at me the way animals do, eyes rolled to the corners, showing red. The person in front of him steps up, kneels on the floor, puts his hands on the sides of the cushion, and leans and kisses the feet. When he rises, an altar boy wipes the spot with a cloth. Jerome steps up, gets down like a dog, and does it. Dad's hands guide me forward and let go. There are glittering drops on the feet, too, I see as I lower myself, and realize that the hospital smell I like is rising from where the altar boy has wiped, and I'm back in a bed there, in a white room, weak, with a crucifix above the door, my scalp so tight my hair feels knotted, and then through that I see a pen start across a sheet of paper in a phrase that will smell, once it's set down and finished, ink-fresh forever, better than alcohol.

My illness is gone.

+

Our Easter egg hunt is held inside the house this year, for me and the little ones. It seems another one was born while I was ill. Jerome and I plan to add everything from the hunt to the quart jars of gum and candy we've been saving during Lent—not that I've been hungry for candy this year. I wander around and find the chocolate rabbit and colored eggs left for me, in a nest of paper grass behind the oil heater. There are two more eggs in shredded purple cellophane on a bookshelf below the radio. I step through the swinging door into the hall and see, in the same shaft of sunlight from another life, Dad's briefcase, and I know, without opening it, that the largest collection of candy is inside.

I go back through the door and leave it for the little ones.

+

I'm allowed outside only when Jerome is with me, and then can't go far, and for our own celebration of Easter he promises to take me to the clubhouse. I follow him toward the Ennises'—along the hedge where the last dull snow, speckled with black, is crusted in the caragana stems—wearing a corduroy jacket like his, the last of our matching clothes. In my weakened state, with my mind light as smoke, I see a block away, at the end of the street, the fence at the edge of town, and it seems a triple horizon. The gray and brown plain, rising in slanting lines to the point where the horses and the shed became a mirage, is too much to take in, and the sky all around us elevates me into its violet, queasy, so I have to stare at the ground to remain beside Jerome. At the Ennises' barn, a two-story shed that's actually a garage, we slip into a darkness that smells of used oil, and I can make out curled fibers from shipping crates on the coal-black floor.

A rope ladder hangs from a hole of yellow light.

"Why don't you use these," Jerome whispers, and touches one of the boards nailed in a ladder across a pair of uprights; it's the way we used to climb to the hole, bending around from there to pull ourselves onto the floor of the loft.

"No," I say. I want to use the rope.

He starts up and I follow, swaying with his climbing weight as if from the web of our dishonesty (we said we'd stay on our block), and then I hear his thump on the floor above, and a hand takes my wrist.

I swing where I hang, trembling, then look up at him.

"No," I say.

I pull myself into light, over the hump of wood, and reach out and paw at the floor until he grabs me. I'm up. Out a door at the front of the loft, the budding branches of a tree are framed against a gable of the Pflagers' house, a brighter tan than ours. Jerome opens a box of comic books beside a mattress. He points out a hiding place under a board where BBs are kept, their jar of Russian peanuts, a bushel basket of empty pop bottles to return for deposit, a bucket of rocks, and slingshots along a rafter.

"Where are the BB guns?"

"They'd get stolen, probably. Benny and Alan take them home when they leave. They have special dispensations to quit a fight if we're losing, so they can run back and get them up here. Are you ready to go?"

He steps around as if he's new here, uneasy; he pulls the rope ladder up.

"Is somebody from the other club coming?"

"We'll probably be the last ones up. This is how I have to leave it, or I'll get kicked out. I don't know who left it hanging."

"So we go back down the boards like we used to?"

"You better. I have to leave the club-member way. It's supposed to be so spies won't know if anybody's up here, but it's silly; people can still come up the boards. It's neater this way, though. Also, we don't want Donny Ennis messing with the rope. He could get hurt."

"How do members have to go?"

"Down the tree. It's not so bad. It's part of our initiation."

He goes to the open door, leaps out, and grabs a limb of the tree, setting the buds quaking, then hand-walks over to the trunk, scissors it with his legs, hugs it, and slides out of sight. I go over and look down. He's on a patch of muddy ground, beside squares that could be car batteries, staring up, his eyes so narrowed I can only see shadow in their sockets. "Use the ladder," he says. "You're not a member yet."

"I want to be."

"Come on. I said it was silly. Really."

I look out and can see where hands have worn the bark of

the branch. I leap and grab it, and as my weight jolts my arms and my legs swing up, I think: This is too hard for me now. Then at the same moment, from the way my feet keep rising, I realize my grip is gone, and the green world I head toward now is fouled with greasy mud and widening squares of black.

LEAVING

"What's the effect of this commitment on you?" Jerome asks, after I've read from my journal and after our laughter, and I turn to the black slab of the window, assuming he means my commitment to acting, and see us reflected there in miniature. But he could as well mean my commitment to this room, or . . .

"Well, I'm scared," I say, and he laughs a gentler laugh. "But also free in a way I never expected to be."

+

Now I go over and raise the shade, then try the window itself, and finally have to hit its top sash with the heels of my hands to break it free; it's frozen to the frame. I raise it to my forehead, the sash weights rumbling down, and brush the snow from the sill onto the fire escape—clumps strike the narrow drifts on the platform like splashes across their parallel regularity. I sit on the sill and breathe the frigid air, which is rinsed cleaner than when I walked this street in a downpour. I shut off the light and sit on the sill again. Snow is falling in lumpy, hazy flakes, and mist is rising toward it from the melting street (besides columns of steam climbing from the manhole covers at the intersection, under the shine of a streetlamp) and frosting the cars and lampposts and bricks with a fur of hoarfrost.

The city below could as well be in Russia. I've only imagined where I am. Cornices and window ledges are heaped in bulging Slavonic style, like Gothic or medieval gingerbread, and sounds and voices down the block take on the slowed and muffled basso of an Eastern Orthodox chant. A corridor behind me leads to the interrogation room, but for now I have this moment to look out one more time on Moscow.

A window opens a ways down the street, and a man places his elbows on the ledge, sending down a silent shower, and then props his chin in his hands. It's a holiday and he has had too many vodkas. He needs the activity of these falling flakes and the fresh air to steady him. He has a brother he would like to see, but the bureaucracy, or a series of interrogations, or his lack of rubles, or a combination of these, has kept them apart too long. He sighs gray plumes. His hope for them is that they will travel to America this year, to New York, as they've planned to since childhood, and he will open a window on a scene like this, and see him in that window there, a brother in the city.

+

One scientist's picture of relativity is this: as the earth spins on its axis, a man walks down the aisle of a speeding train with a fly crawling on his jacket. A conjunction like this occurs in a fall, as you become observer and participant, and even if you're knocked unconscious, you might recapture some of the freezing focus that enters as you fall (with a clarity, it seems, in proportion to what you'll suffer), while chains of imagery connected to the second before start unreeling and draw days and then years past in a speeded-up flashing that lets you know you've left this life—everything rushing backward through that corridor where a man sits breathing smoke into the blue remains of you that multiply into all the rooms of every house you've ever seen, as time turns into the cells that send up pictures intact, so that they're viewed as they're stored, and ultimately are—simultaneous—and then there is a jolt as the chains are overtaken by voices and colors in a concussive crush, and you realize the uselessness of trying to breathe, your brain pulled out like a drawer, and your thighs, bunched umbrellas of weakness as wide as the world, supporting the wail going out your eyes.

Then you understand that it's your brother you're leaning on, a block from where you hit down.

Into the driveway, along the coal shed, up one step. He reaches through cottony plasma to hammer on the green-reinforced winterizing over the screen door, sending shaking sensations over my chest. A sticky weighted heat like syrup covers my shoulders in a rearward pull at my only remaining point of light—an eye turned backward on pain.

She opens the door. Her legs.

I try to look up and voices enter from every direction, grappling at my jacket, while the end of a day of snake-crawling at Deke's, that sickening slide of green, goes up in white.

The bathroom, lights sprawling from fixtures, the worst whiteness to see, my jacket peeling back as her wiggly voice tells him to get his off, too, water cascading into the sink, which my face heads toward. A cloth at my head, dabbing, and then hair parted from a numbing pole.

"Run and get Mrs. Heaton! Hurry! Tell her Mr. Heaton has to get us to the hospital right away! Run!"

Then I'm in a rocking car, in her lap like a nursing baby, my face pressed to where Marie sucks and butts for food, the nerves in my belly button raw to the bottom of my stomach. Then her distant voice, hollow in its threat of weeping up her substance: "Why does this always happen when your dad isn't here? Why did you have to do this now?"

+

Dr. Hogelvode's hands steady me as he steps back from the table where I sit, and I look out of the dazzle of my state, brightened further by the gauze above my eyes, and sense him moving off for good.

"Well, you've weathered another tough situation, old friend. Only five stitches. It's a blessing your brother was there."

His steady look is meant to measure the effect of his words.

"Yes," I say. "He helped me."

He turns and I turn my lopsided, liquidy skull enough to see Mom's hands at her waist, her fingers interwound and squeezing. The hands start to rise, and I can't look higher, after the way she held me during the drive, dripping tears over my head and the front of her dress.

"He's suffered a concussion, Alpha. You'll have to keep an eye on him for the symptoms I've mentioned."

"Oh, Doctor!"

"It's not as bad as you might think. I checked the X-rays again. The concussion is what to watch for. There's a hairline fracture, but—"

"Oh, Lord, what a cross!"

"Calm yourself, Alpha."

"First— And then— Just recovered, and now this!"

"He seems fine."

"What if I get home and he's not?"

"Do you want us to keep him in the hospital overnight?"

"No," I say, and the room gathers in a whir at my throat.

"If any of the symptoms develop, call me. Take him gently along now. Get some rest."

"I saw gray stuff!"

"The scalp is fatty and gray-blue."

"I saw it, Doctor! You can't deny that!"

+

I wake to Dad's footsteps coming down the hall, past the swatting swinging door, into the living room. "Well, Alpha, I looked," he says. "It must have been one of those dead-celled old tractor batteries beside the Ennises' garage that he hit."

"There's a rusty old disc harrow down there, too. I saw it."

"Yes, I know, Alpha. But he didn't fall anywhere near that, from what Jerome said. Jerome is awfully upset. Frankly, Alpha, if he would have hit that disc, I don't think he'd be with us."

Springs settle as he sits in his chair and says under his breath, "Eeeh! Should we have disciplined him when he started climbing things and falling? Instead of being kind, because we were afraid?"

"I don't know, but would you check on him for me now? I'm afraid he won't wake up."

+

I walk along our hedge in my plaid jacket, with a bandage taped over the shaved island at the back of my head, and remember how I walked beside it like this before, seeing dust-brindled snow among its stems, but without this cold and numbing portion of my senses added, or missing, or filled in from the distance in a different way, and wonder: Am I the one who was a brother to Jerome?

+

Dad is sharpening a knife with the long steel sharpener, *whit*, whait, *wheaty*, in a noise like whistling. The meat grinder is clamped to the table, and I turn its crank as Mom presses pieces of roast beef and potatoes and onions into the grinder's top, all crackling as they catch in its screw. Jerome's turn is next. We want to feed it for each other but she says we'll get a finger in too far and grind it off. Then I'm done and I dance to the whistle of Dad's sharpening, imagining the broiling brownness of the hash on the stove, and chant as I dance, "Mmm, Mom, burn it, mmm, so it has a crust on it, mmm, boy!"

"Calm yourself," she says, in a new tone that seems part of my unrest. "Settle down before you hurt yourself again!"

+

I roll over to the gray-silver ceiling of bricks, and through it see another ceiling, on the afternoon when I lay beside the railing of the stairs, waiting for Jerome's note, and then I turn and see Jerome at the roll-top desk, kneeling on a chair in sun that bleaches his blond hair white, and I reach beside my bed and pick up the microphone of the recorder I've bought with the last of my savings, and turn it on:

"What is it?" I ask, beside him at the desk, where he's drawing with Dad's ink eradicator.

"A picture," he says.

"I can't see any picture."

"Naturally. It's invisible."

"Why do you want it invisible?"

"Because it's mine!"

+

When there are still gray-ridged patches of snow here and there, I go around the coal shed to the pantry window, swing up the wooden slat from the opening at the bottom of the storm window (cut into it for winter ventilation), and create a microphone. I step up on the wooden box I've carried here and sing into the mouthlike opening:

Hair of gold, eyes of blue,
Lips like cherry wine;
Prettiest gal I ever knew
And I'm gonna make her mine!

and figure I'll be a radio singer, or news announcer, although I would rather save people, the way doctors do. I sing the verse with all the feeling I can summon and picture Ginny Bower, a blond country girl with plump lips "like cherry wine," and a scar down one cheek, who wears skirts that show her dimpled knees and the cords in the hollows behind them (good to follow up the steps of the slide), and sense the song travel through my picture of her into her real self, and think: Dear God, let her know I'm singing this. Let me kiss her.

I pray and sing with greater fervor, as Sister tells us to, and a darkness rises above me, almost touchable. An answer. I close my eyes, imagining the microphone hooked to Ginny's ears, and see her turn, and then the darkness bends around my head to the touchy pole at its back.

"That's nice," a tiny voice says.

This can't be. I step back, blinking, and through the glaze of both windows I see my mother staring down at me.

"I said that's very nice. Was it for me?" From her look, she's talking loud, but her voice barely comes through. "Was it?" she asks.

"Your hair isn't gold."

"What?"

"Your hair's not gold!"

"But was it?"

Shoots of new grass pierce a piece of snow beside the foundation in a pattern I should recognize. "No!" I say, looking up. I shake my head.

"Oh." Her lips form the word. She draws a strand of hair from her forehead behind an ear. "Well, it was nice"—her mouth moves—"even if you aren't always"—her volume goes up—"quite on key."

Sparks of understanding go pinging into half-remembered outer spheres, and I wonder whether what I realized about Jerome doesn't apply to me.

"But you're young yet," she says. "Your voice hasn't settled. There was real feeling in it."

I blush, ashamed, and then hear something, and see her eyebrows arch to their highest and her eyelids flutter as if she's fainting.

"Mom! What's the matter?"

"Oh, I . . ." This fades behind the panes.

"What?"

"I'm tired!"

"What of?" Now I'm sorry I was so insistent my song wasn't for her.

"From." Her face colors with the force of this. "Work. Talking through a window like this. If you want to talk to me, come inside."

She turns and is gone. Jerome comes around the corner of the coal shed, pushing the mangled scooter, and backs away with surprise at the sight of me. He leans the scooter against the siding, and says, "I think I got it fixed so it works right." He brushes off the front of his jacket and puts his hands under its waistband and rolls them up in it. "Not that it makes much difference, I guess. I mean, we're older now."

+

Outside the granary where I record, one of our Northern winters is either nearly over or has just begun, and cracks and mouseholes in the granary walls let in drafts—drifts rising in the lees of some—that invade this lenten space in the way that the landscape invades and spans all time, so that there is no place to return to, not even the present, riding ahead on a future wearing thin, as a cold wind blows through the thought that every fashion of attempted escape always ends in regret.

Sun squint. I'm with Brian and others on the steps of the parochial school, wearing the brown-tweed suit Jerome wore for his First Communion, with a white flower pinned to my lapel—like hospital gauze when I glance down, a shock. The girls, in white dresses and veils, grip baskets of flowers. May Day, the day of First Communion, with Dad on the lawn in front of the steps, pointing a camera at me, and Jerome at his side, his hands in his pockets, smiling as if the picture is of him. Other cameras clatter, and then Sister Benedict forms us in lines, two by two, and we fold our hands and begin singing:

O Mary, we crown thee with blossoms today!
Queen of the Angels, Queen of the May!

Our voices ascending, as the song says, above our footsteps on the sidewalk, where flower petals are scattered. Sins unconfessed, coming in a rush, set the sides of my head itching with sweat. Those boys struck by lightning. But wouldn't it be worse for Sister if I dropped out of line? Or Dad and Jerome? If I missed some sins, I'll confess them next time, I decide. Into the vestibule of the church, past Hank Kauter-Haupt standing in shadow, grinning, we pause and rock in time, then begin:

Ah-on this day, O beau-ti-ful Mo-ther,
Ah-on this day, we give thee our love!

Down the aisle, singing still, toward the front pews, where Father Schimmelpfennig is at the Communion rail in white vestments, his arms outspread, smiling happily at us. Mary Angelica Schoenbeck walks up the bed-sheet-draped steps to the statue of Mary and places the crown of flowers on her head. They slip at a slant. Mass begins and then it's time for Communion, my hands under the starchy altar cloth, and when I open my mouth to receive the Host (with Father staring down to check how this will go), it feels like a sticky flat hole open to my toes. My shoes are absent or made of air and won't move.

I've closed my eyes too long—afloat, the bandage reversed, bumping the high arch of the altar; no, bumping Brian's head as I try to get down to my knees in the pew.

Down now. All new.

+

Waking, I hear a splash and heaving of water in the bathroom beyond our closet—a liquid heaviness that enters the dream moving in honeyed electricity up my legs to a center brighter than any bone viewed through an X-ray machine. I take hold down there, and the bedcovers spank and flap at the speed of the gallop I have to develop to—

There is an impact of wood on wood and Dad is through the closet door, staring at me with the blankness he has without his glasses, startled, his hair damp, one hand still on the knob, bulky in his bathrobe, while the tailings of my dream seep away, and the room drops in place as solid as shelves in a grocery store. Jerome stirs.

"What's—" Dad looks confused, as if he'll go back the way he came and start over. Then he shakes his head, his blank eyes blurred, and says, "Excuse me, I—" *Was in a hurry*, his look seems to say, and then he puts his hands in the pockets of his robe, draws in his chin, and walks past the end of the bed, bull-like, out our bedroom door. Streams of the dream enter again, and I feel I won't have to worry for a while that he'll chew it off with his shouting, as I'm afraid she will.

+

Rocks crash into the hedge at the front of our house, a hail of them, and one hits a car parked in front of the Ianacconas'. Jerome and I have hid behind it. He's panting with fear. We've all been hit, some so hard that I can hear whining and crying as we throw, and my head feels as if it's bleeding from its touchy pole. The town-kids' club has two high schoolers from out of state on its side—Dennis Russell, who used to live in our house, and a friend of his from South Dakota, Lenny Roos. They're big and mean, the cause of this, and have helped drive us toward our clubhouse, where most of the members now are, from the stomping noises in the loft—preparing a surprise barrage these guys are going to catch.

It started beside the Town Hall, with Russell claiming South Dakota was better than North Dakota, *in*-finitely better, he said, so that the pale sky seemed to crackle, while Dickie Sill signaled for his town kids to step back, and then Russell said that the Lone Ranger lived in South Dakota, in a cave in the Black Hills, which everybody knew, and would never visit a flat platter of a state like this, or such a piss-ant of a town—and here Kuntz came charging forward and tackled Russell so hard you could hear his shins crack. Kuntz, though younger, held his own as they rolled around in the ditch, and even got on top, and then Russell's friend stepped up and raised his joined fists and brought them down in a hammer blow on Kuntz's back. A sound like a drum struck. And then Roos, at the side of the road, reached down and somebody yelled "Rock fight!" and the ground rules, set up by past battles, took hold: Anything Goes. Some of the first rocks went spattering off the tin-covered Town Hall, and a younger Sill, Dougie, put a hand to his face, took a couple of wobbling steps, and sat down.

Now Brian is at the center of our crossroad, with his arms over his head, whooping and howling, and Leo—sided with the town kids—directs rocks at him to keep him pinned; Jerome and I were trying to keep Leo away when we were cut off. I run in a crouch to the rear of the car and see Russell come around the hedge at the head of our garden, on familiar ground, and fling a rock at him. He starts one off in sidearm surprise, seeing mine already sailing toward him, and, before he can dodge it, it catches him in the chest with a *thup*. "Oooo," he says, stepping back.

"That's for Kuntz!" I yell.

A pair of Schoenbecks run up and join Russell and I dive behind the car as a rattling volley strikes its rear, and front, too, where Jerome is trying to hold off Roos and some others I don't want to know about. We're going to get it soon, I figure, and then glass beside me breaks. I start to crawl under the car, seeing legs coming toward us from three sides, and hear "Stop that!"

"Stop that! Do you *hear*?" At the center of the slice of light

I look out from, as dizzied as when I fell from the merry-go-round and watched it turn above, I see our mother heading in our direction down the front walk.

"Stop it, every one of you! You've run across my garden and broken a light on that car. Stop that, I say, stop!"

There's a clack and clatter of dropping rocks and the legs go off like a scattering of birds. Even Brian leaves the crossroad, limping and holding one ear, cursing Leo.

"All right, you two, under the car there, get out! Get over in this house, this minute, and get yours! Then get it again from your dad when he gets back, by George! Besides the week of work you're going to do to pay for that taillight! Get in here!"

Down the block somebody caws like a crow, then high hard voices bark and laugh as Jerome thumps up the porch steps, dodging her first trial swat, and I hold up a hand as if to say, Just a minute. My head!

+

The briefcase clacks down on its metal studs and we're beside it on our knees as usual, but this time there's nothing in it but policies and the smell of leather. We wander out to the kitchen, where Dad is talking to Mom, who's looking out a window, her arms crossed.

"In the trunk of the car," he says over his shoulder, before we have a chance to ask, and then he pulls out his keys and hands them to Jerome.

At the car, Jerome cries, "Another sled!" and works a key into the sun-heated trunk, which is worn orange over its curve. Inside are two baseball gloves, more pungent than the briefcase, which we've begged for so much it feels as if we've stolen them.

We go back in, guiltily silent, and Mom says, "I wonder how our finances can bear such an extravagance."

"Well, it's almost his birthday," Dad says. Jerome's. "They can be for that." He smiles at her but she doesn't smile back.

Finally we tell him we can't find a baseball. "Well, I'll get you that next," he says. "I thought we had one."

We take a colored wooden ball from our croquet set, unable to wait any longer, and after a few excited pegs, with our bones under the gloves swelling in an ache, have to roll the ball back and forth on the ground. Dad walks out with a blue sponge-rubber ball chewed by Marie and begins to pitch to us, rocking off his foot with a startled look when his weight comes down, as if treading on a nerve, but it's his arm. He pitched when he was younger for a team from Courtenay, and hurt his arm throwing too hard one afternoon; at the high school he was the coach of every sport.

Now he throws the ball to us in a single hard hop we're afraid to field, even with the gloves, for fear of our jewels. "Here, then," he says. "Throw it to me that way. See, get in a crouch, like this."

Jerome returns a grounder underhanded and Dad rolls an easy one that I grab up and toss back.

"Where'd you learn that?" he asks.

"What?"

"To throw like that. Throwing rocks?"

Jerome and I blush. "I've seen you pitch," I say.

"Well, yes, but." He glances at Jerome, and then up to the side; Mom is staring at us from the bay window, her face set. "That could be true, but generally it takes a little practice. Try it again."

I grab up another grounder and whip it back into his bare hands.

"That's it! Why, you— You're a natural athlete! That's just—"

He looks up at her as if to get this straight, studies Jerome, and then goes over to him and adjusts the glove on his hand. "Now, first, hold your fingers like . . ."

+

Rice pudding with raisins in it, whipped egg whites like foam for tapioca, marble cake, peach cobbler, angel-food soaked in lemon sauce, apples cored and filled with brown sugar and then stewed, cinnamon rolls with walnuts in them and white frosting on top, sliced bananas with sugar going gray from cream drawn up, Rice Krispies squares, brownies, divinity fudge—there's always something on the kitchen table for us after school, and our friends follow us home, welcome to come in and eat. But this afternoon when Jerome and I hurry in alone (I'm hungry in a way I haven't been since my First Communion) and see the table empty, I say, "Hey, Mom, isn't there anything to eat?"

She is at the ironing board across the room, with the confused look of concern she gets when she irons, and now she tips the iron back on its metal holder, makes wide eyes, and covers her chest with both hands. She sings in a loud voice: "If I knew you were comin, I'd have baked a cake!" She grabs the iron by the handle and stomps it up and down on the board as she prances where she stands in her brown heels.

"Baked a cake, baked a cake! If I knew you were comin, I'd have baked a cake, how'd ja do! how'd ja do! how'd ja do!"

+

Ill again. My throat. From not wearing my jacket, she says.

Jerome walks in with the look of joining another club, sits and tilts the bed in his direction (as I open my eyes on this grape-chenille island, expecting him here, and see the shades drawn), and then goes over and closes our door. He flops his arithmetic book back and forth and takes out a card. On the front is a picture of the Virgin holding the Christ Child, and below, in scrolled golden print, "To Mother Dear," which my eyes hook on. He opens it to a verse about mothers, and across from that I see, with the blanks filled in in pencil:

SPIRITUAL BOUQUET

Visits to the Blessed Sacrament	7
Holy Communion	2
Rosaries	3
Masses	5
Ejaculations	26

"What's this last one?" I ask. I have my finger on it.

"A fleeting prayer like a thought." This sounds like Sister Colette. " 'Jesus, Mary, Joseph, be with Mom today.' That's one. The 'Glory Be' is another." He smiles at me. "It's for Mother's Day."

"What's that?"

"Dummkopf, the day when every child lets his mother know

how much he loves her—usually with a gift. Don't you appreciate what Mom does? Don't you love her? Sister Colette talked about it. All of us at school are giving these."

"When is Mother's Day?"

"The second Sunday in May, you dope."

I study him to discover whether he's going to return to the phase of calling me names, and he looks away at the window.

"I know," he says. "You haven't been in school. You're sick." A brightness like a band of sun gathers in his eyes at this, and I'm sure he's about to laugh.

"You're giving her this on Sunday?"

"No, after supper tonight—a surprise. Before Dad gives her anything, or the other guys give their cards first. It'll get around fast."

In my fever I see Kuntz's mother turn from the steaming stove in the railroad car, reaching— Jerome slips the card back in the book and puts the book in our storage closet. Then he's out the door, and I hear Mom say in the kitchen, "Is he well enough to eat with us tonight?"

I go to the closet and see his book, beside our oily-smelling train set, shine back from the darkness. Other toys are here from winter, along with the jars we've filled with candy over Lent again. I've stuffed some waxy Easter grass into the mouth of my jar, to keep it separate from Jerome's: mine is fuller. I wriggle my fingers through the grass, get out a purple egg almost the size of a real one, and shove the whole thing into my mouth. I pull down paper and a box of crayons, trying to get the egg past my swollen throat, about to choke, and bump shut the door to the living room.

I go to the walk-in closet off our bedroom and open the door at its other side, into the bathroom; the door there, to the kitchen, is closed. I lock the closet door behind me and sneak over and lock the bathroom door, hearing them talking in the kitchen—and realize my sense of smell is back: tuna casserole, with green beans. I fold a sheet of paper into quarters on the toilet seat and write in my most careful Palmer style, on the outside, "To Dearest Mother." I open it and print across its doubly large inside, "I Love You," and with the final word the walls draw away while I shrink, as if viewing myself at the start of my fall, dwarfed by the fixtures and shining snaky pipes below the sink, where old washcloths hang, while the etherized part of me attains the ceiling. I hover and watch a boy, dozens of times smaller, draw a border of flowers and color them and their leaves, and then fold another sheet of paper into an envelope (I'll need tape for this, he thinks, from a cramped area inside his illness) with the assurance that his mother will like his card better than his brother's.

And then he sees, on top of the toilet tank, almost out of reach, the bottle that always stands there, and now notices what it is—flat, squared at the top, and pinched in at the middle, with a blue diagonal band running from a shoulder down to the belt at its waist, the bottom half narrowing into legs: a soldier. The red belt reads *Bon Marché*. Perfume. The boy is sure he understands why his mother never uses it—too nice. He screws off the cap, and a part of his brain, sensitized since his fall from the loft of a garage, absorbs the womanly haze in a yellow fiber that makes contact with the scar at the back of his head, and with a wallop I'm myself again.

I'm hungry for more candy, starving for food; I'm well.

I unroll a strip of toilet paper, here since Grandma Jones's visit, fold it into a square on the toilet seat, and sprinkle out the perfume—gold droplets striking gray-black—on the tissue, then put the soldier's hat on, the soldier back, and the soaked tissue between the folds of my card. No tape in the storage closet. Mom and Jerome are talking now in the living room. His book is still here. I chew some gum and use a bit of it on a corner she won't notice, and, when I'm called for dinner, swallow the rest. From the dim living room I see them, struck in light at the kitchen table, and feel I'm walking down a hall out of my illness.

Dad talks less lately, and dinner is a loop that leads me back to the storage closet. Has Jerome been here? The book seems moved. I check my envelope and card; okay. A trial whiff, the smell faint, most of its yellow fiber gone, but there. I step out the door. She is on the couch, studying his card in her lap, her hair swinging over her face, saying something I don't catch. Then, "It's so thoughtful of you!"

A chair scrapes back in the kitchen as I hand her mine. She unfolds the envelope, and I see her smile confirm the experience in the bathroom: she likes mine better.

"You made this," she says. "Goodness. What an amount of thought and care. You—" And then she wrinkles her nose. "Oh, but, oof-da, did you have to go and use that awful perfume? Haven't I said how much I dislike its stink? And what's this? Is this *gum*? Good Lord! You know I can't bear to see that stuff chewed up and stuck somewhere. Why did you do this?"

+

On Sunday, when the rest are taking naps, Dad ushers Jerome and me into the kitchen, nudging at our backs in the way we dislike. He pulls out his billfold, places a dollar bill on the tray of the high chair, and says, "It's Mother's Day, boys. Run uptown and see if you can't find Mom something nice, just from the two of you."

We don't speak. The spring sunlight has drawn out buds along the hedge we walk beside, no snow now, and then I see his new baseball cap, pulled forward from the bulge at the back of his head, and realize mine is on. Gifts after the gift of the baseball. I can't see the caps in the puddles reflecting this pair of twins, betrayers of one another with their cards. A frog hops across the Eichelburgers' lawn, which steams after a Sunday watering. Across the street, at a house where sheep wire is nailed on two-by-four frames to form a fence, Bernie Coulter, the son of the new high-school superintendent, starts windmilling his arms, going into a clackety run on his roller skates, and hits on his butt.

Sill's Cafe is the only place open. Dickie isn't around. We glance through the glass showcase that holds candy bars, cap guns, and painted plates, and I look around at the ice-cream tables and booths that Jerome and I used to crawl beneath to see if gum was stuck to their undersides. Sometimes there were gobs that were almost fresh. Mrs. Sill comes over behind the case and her flowered dress is the background against which we view our possible gift. "Yes, Mother's Day," she says, and sighs, then goes back to the stool where she always sits, at the end of the counter ("Don't spin those stools!" Dad has to remind us, whenever we walk past), and I feel that Jerome and I are always between Mom and Dad, or they're between us; or one or another of them is between us and the other parent.

Jerome wants me to decide, and I don't want anything to do with it; the dollar is his. But I don't like what he picks, so finally we settle on a box of chocolate-covered cherries and a plaster-of-Paris wall plaque. The plaque is in the shape of a keystone of the sort we've seen in our schoolbook on Rome, with four shining yellow tulips on pea-green stems, and curling leaves of the same green raised from a white background. We have money left, and spend the rest of it, fifteen cents, on a card with a padded silk heart that has *Mother* painted across it.

At home we hand it all to her and want to run and hide.

But we sit on the couch until she opens it, the card first. We receive a full-eyed, nervous look and a thank you for the plaque, and, with the candy, "Umm, yum, I'll sure eat this." In the sunlight the cellophane comes off the box with a noise of fire, and she pops a piece in her mouth. "Hurr," she says, chewing, and holds out the box for us; we each take one and I see the crinkled paper cups inside trembling.

We go into our room and sit on opposite sides of the bed. Dad is absent, as he's always absent on Sunday afternoons—"for a nap," he says, although we know he can't sleep during the day. It's lonelier in the house with him here and off in another room, in bed. I notice that Jerome's baseball cap is still on and pull mine off. His comes off then. What's happening, I want to ask him. What's wrong? Footsteps go into their bedroom. I step to our doorway and see, in the alcove of the bay window, in the seat of the chair she was in, the wall plaque, lying in a shaft of sun that looks artificial, and see it with her eyes, ashamed.

The sliding oak doors to their bedroom are closed and I'm at a remove from them, under this silver-brick ceiling that seems it has lowered a foot. They've become the worst that they can become for me—not there, when they are there. A sheet of silence covers the doors of all their Sunday afternoons, and I won't presume to know what they say, or presume to undress them, although I know by now what happens there, as we all do, and if it happens more than once too often to any of us, then we are the ones who are to blame—those of us who arose from such bedrooms.

And then to wake in the morning to the same light, and to look over the edge of the bed at a ball beside the baseboard, with dust gathering in clumps at its sides and teeth marks over it—as round and blue as the beginning of time—and never to want to leave that room again.

The lilacs, the delicacy of the lilacs, and their spicy, bee-laden scent that comes mustily from sachets during the winter, hinting at this unfolding from bushes everywhere in town—at front and back doors, around outhouses and in clumps at the edge of alleys, bordering yards and gardens—of pink and purple or blue, besides every shade of white, in a furring of blossoms. Their incense renews the need to walk over bare dirt, where new shoots are opening the ground with two-leaved beginnings of lavender-green.

"La-aa-avender blue," I sing in the style of another hero, smelling the conelike, packed lilac clumps. "Dilly dilly, lavender green!"

I lie down on the ground, where even the smell of earth doesn't diminish their smell, cupping a two-leaved shoot between my palms. "If I were king, dilly dilly, you'd be my queen!" Then I realize that Jerome isn't with me, and that I'm singing this to my mother.

+

Jerome knocks on the screen door of the Sisters' house and Sister Colette peers from the window inside, her hands up, and then her mouth opens on her bent-back teeth and she unlocks and opens both doors. "Ah," she says, "our boys are here early this week." We go down the hall, through a door on the left, into their tiny chapel, past the altar with its single step, and through another door to a room like a closet, and take off our coats. Cassocks are here, black rather than red, and have the feel of clothes seldom worn; we help each other button bottom buttons and then pull on our surplices and flap their short sleeves like butterflies, and smile. Father walks in, bearing his cigar smell, and ruffles our hair so hard Jerome has to pull out a comb through the slit at the side of his cassock for us to use.

"Goot dat you're orrly," Father says. "You can help me tress."

We've studied how to vest our priest: the amice that ties over his shoulders, then the alb, like a cassock, but white, embroidered with gold at its hem. He ties the ties at its neck and holds out the cincture for us to pass around him; then the maniple, green today, over his arm, the stole that crosses his chest and is held in loops of the cincture (he murmurs in Latin through all this and kisses the crosses sewn on each piece); and as he lowers the yoke of the chasuble over his head, with cold air coming down on us from the green silk and turning the air itself green, I picture the large cape he wears to grip the base of the ciborium when he elevates it at Benediction, as if the Host behind glass at the center of its sunburst of gold prongs has turned the metal electric, and then Father blesses the air above us with a whispering of green and places a hand on our heads, pressing the electricity into us.

We follow him with our heads down and hands together—fingers pointing upward, as they should—into the sunlit chapel. Only the Sisters and Mary Liffert and Father's housekeeper, Wilhomena, are present on wooden folding chairs for this Saturday-morning service, and after Father's *Introibo*, the days of my recovery return with our first response: "*Ad Deum qui laetificat juventutem meam . . .*"

And then the formal pattern of the Mass, complicated yet rendered transparent by the Latin, until we are following Father into the closet, where I notice now the spatter of unhealthy colors in the tile, and scuffs along the rubber baseboard—our other life over too soon. When Father is unvested, he hands us a fifty-cent piece and leans so close we can see chapped wrinkles in his lips; he looks over his glasses with eyes as blue as Dad's, and whispers, "Da ladies here"—an eyebrow rises—"dey appreciate your help but can't pay you. Dey are penniless"—this hisses in the room—"by dint of dere vows. As children, we should respect more dere dedication, den, no?"

Don't we? He reaches to his black overcoat and holds out in the fingertips of each hand, as he holds out our report cards at the front of the classroom every six weeks, two Hershey bars. On our way out, Sister Mary Michael gives us lemon drops, and Wilhomena peppermints twisted in cellophane (Mary Liffert is gone), and we're at the door when Sister Stanislaus hands us a box of cookies for the family and Sister Benedict puts her book down on the kitchen table and comes over, smiling, and gives us each a Mars bar. "So you have something for yourselves," she says. Then Sister Colette whispers, "Boys, I want to see how you've progressed." So we go to the piano at the back of the chapel, where she slips a handful of lemon drops into our coat pockets, and then raises her arms, surrounding us with the black of her gown, and counts to start us off: "*Down* at the *air*port the *wind* sock is *blow*ing . . ."

+

All Jerome gets for his birthday is a card with a dollar in it. The next day Dad leaves on a trip to Canada, his longest, and is away a week. Jerome won't let me come near him, and one morning I wake to him throwing up in bed. Or I figure he is and move fast, after the night I woke to a reek of slippery beans and hot-dog pieces and didn't know which of us they came from, because both of us were heaving and had them over our faces and hair, besides a slick mess on the bedclothes, and were bringing up more—I scramble free and see that he's crying. I put a hand on his back but he shakes it off. "Go away!"

"What's wrong?"

"Dad's home!"

He has been in an accident; I can see the car mangled like our scooter, Dad's face cut, an eye gone, blood in his hair, and know that I won't be able to stand seeing him hurt. "What happened?"

"Go out in the living room."

"I'm afraid to."

"Look!"

I slide to the end of the bed and see it from there: a new bicycle, a Hiawatha, the blue of the lake, like the one Jerome has been looking at in a catalogue—a girl's model, minus the crossbar, so he can reach the pedals without sawing himself off. I start toward its shiny, cheerful handlebars, and see the sliding oak doors to their bedroom closed.

Behind me, Jerome cries, "It's for both of us, Dad said!"

+

Dad trots alongside, holding the seat, so that when we sway to the right, trying to push that pedal down full power, he swings us back plumb, and once we've advanced to wobbles that cause twists of the handlebars, and one of us is able to hold the other up, we're on our own.

We find out that the back wheel isn't "properly aligned," as Dad says; the chain keeps coming off. Finally, he has to take two links out of it, and we stand on each side of him at his tool bench in the coal shed and watch, to make sure we know how to do this. When he isn't selling insurance, he's driving tractor for a farmer again, Evan Savitsky ("Evan, Skavitsy, Skavaar!" we sing), and he has on an engineer's cap with the bill a bit crooked and a pipe in one corner of his mouth—all of which complicates the pressure and turn of his tools. He's been painting the bathroom and spatters of white on his face bring out the shades baked there from fieldwork: copper, rose, gold, Indian-red, with red-black across his cheekbones (his glasses also spattered), and the sockets of his eyes yellow—colors that please us so much we march in step, chanting, "I'm my own grampa! I'm my own grampa! It sounds funny, I know, but it really is so, oh, I'm my own grampa!"

"Well, he might be able to put up with this noise," Dad says. "Grandpa, that is. But it's not easy for me. I see what your mom means." He turns with grease on his face, holding up a wrench, and recites in his acting voice, "Life's but a walking shadow, a poor player that struts and frets his hour upon the stage, and then is *heard no more*."

+

Being a mechanic is almost as good as being a pilot, and when we're not riding the bike we turn it upside down, to get at the chain—plucking the spokes or holding our fingers to them, for the musical notes, as we crank the pedals with our hands in a crawl until the rear tire picks up so much speed it puts out a rubbery hum, then reversing the pedals to hear the ratchet and screech of its "coaster brake." And whether it's from our fixing or not, the chain keeps coming off, especially when Dad's away, so we have to fix it even more. Finally we take off the chain guard and have a bike closer to the kind we want—fenders next.

We fight about sharing it, but not every hour. We can't wait until one of us can manage it well enough to ride the other around on the carrier, when we put the carrier back on. We've tried to jump up on the fender, holding on to the seat, but always tip, and have bruises and scabs on our elbows and knees. The pairs of our pants that weren't patched before are now. One day as he is fighting to get me off, he insists the bike is his, so I give him a shove and pedal away. He can't keep up. I glide by the Eichelburgers', watching pebbles go popping from under the tires, then settle into my pump again, the point of the seat scraping my spine above its middle—can't even sit. Now a wobbly turn at the crossroad in front of the Eichelburgers', past the place on the other side of the street with the sheep-wire fence where Bernie Coulter, still trying to learn to roller-skate, is slipping backward and spinning and flailing his arms as though he'll take off, then is on his butt, scowling at me. I breeze by, so happy to be free of Jerome I wonder if I don't actually hate him. I'm never apart from him enough to even think this.

On the right is the lot where the house was moved so long ago it seems a stranger found the vitamins—or was that at the town dump? The open hole of the basement has been filled in, and weeds and bushes grow there over a mound of dirt.

Yes, I do hate him, I think, as the lilacs at the far side of the lot give way to a wall of Pflager's Hardware—especially his lumpy head and his tendency to get special gifts, and then the chain slips, my foot flies from the turning pedal, and I look quick and see a sprocket of the big front gear punch into the cord behind my ankle.

My feet hit down on both sides and I stumble to a limping stop. I look over at Pflager's, as if somebody there has caused this, then back at Bernie Coulter. Gone. The sensation in the cord isn't yet pain, though I've swallowed my breath in a clot my heart raps upon. It isn't like anything I've felt, this spangling jab of ice, and then there's an easing and ache as the warmth of blood starts down. I can't look. I stare at Pflager's, the lot again, and realize that I've seen this exact view, in the same light, on another day: I was standing here, with a bicycle between my knees, its handlebars at my eyes, feeling this spangling ache loosen with the heat of blood. Can I walk out of this, I wonder, or even try?

I shuffle ahead, the bike still maneuverable between my legs. I can. Who else would have an accident like this? There's oil around the bleeding hole. The sight of it sends dim trills through the scar at the back of my head. I step from the bike, wheel it home, limping, and lean it against the coal-shed wall. Jerome? The hole is sending aching branches down like cramps; I have to curl my toes when I walk. I go to the hedge and wipe at the wound with some grass, a bullet hole, paste grass over it, and then limp into the house and put on socks and shoes.

+

She still oversees our Saturday baths, a burning shame, scraping us with a damn washrag, fighting our hands, until our skin heats up—a feeling Dad has confirmed by saying, in a whisper, when we were sent to him for inspection, "You should be clean, you're both beet-red."

I ignore her by picturing the barber, who never talks, and seems to know we are mostly there to have our heads massaged and the tingles clipped off those few hairs that are growing wild; then to have it combed besides, wet down, stroked, and talcum shaken— I sneeze into the tub.

"Now what? Sick?" she asks. "And what's this?"—holding my unwashed foot so high I have to cover my Coke bottle with both hands.

"I hurt the back of it there. Cut it out!"

"How did you hurt it?"

"Playing around. *Don't!* Don't wash it that way!"

"Playing around how, is what I'd like to know."

"Don't! Can't you leave me alone?"

Her face, close up, is reddened and running from the heat, and her stare moves in on me. "You mean you're not going to tell your own mother how you hurt your foot?"

"Why?" I ask, afraid of her hollow tone.

She drops my foot into the water and her face takes on the look it must have had when she examined my split-open head. She throws down the washrag with a slosh. "Well, when I get done! with you here! you can go in and see your dad! He'll cut your hair! He'll give you both haircuts! We can't even afford thirty-five cents apiece to send you to the barber! now that he's—gone and bought you that damnable *bike!*"

+

I turn on the tape recorder. "That desk. Its writing surface remains palely blue-and-black-stained still, aromatic of casein glue and the astringent tannin of that Skrip ink that came in chunky bottles with a membrane-thin well of glass at the top to dip your pen point in . . ."

I turn and hold myself on the edge of the bed, yawing with anxiety, sure that if I step into the outside air I'll vanish. Then I swell until I fill the room, turning ancient with size, and the tickling over my ribs is a beard, white. Tears run from it, because no corner is left where I can turn on myself and repent.

+

Dad takes us on an insurance trip to Devils Lake. "Jake, Jake, from Devils Lake!" we chant for miles, hoping to visit Dad's friend of that name, who lays linoleum and allowed us to ride on his rumbling metal roller as he pushed it over the floor of the Sisters' house. Outside New Rockford, driving up the ruler of the road, we see more water in the ditches than is in our lake. I look past it, over the flatlands on every side, to the shapes of trees that mark distant farms—tufts against the sky. Ducks paddle through patches of weeds and flap away from the car, feathers dripping. There's a stretch where the road has been built up into a ridge, and I shy from the water widening away on both sides in silvery reflecting sheets, with fence posts showing above waves that give off glancing light like millions of tiny mirrors shaken by a wind.

There is no end to this blue beneath the blue of the sky, as if land has turned to water, and I feel a wateriness as huge ready to enter me and drive who I am out a spangled opening.

"Come on!" I say, from between Dad and Jerome, wanting to get past this, and afraid to stop until we do.

Then I see Dad's grim face, all the reds and browns gone from it, as he steers with both hands clamped to the wheel. I slide down below the windows, sick to my stomach, and Jerome elbows me away. I kneel on the hump and press my head into the seat, with my hands over it, and feel we are swaying and sinking into water, which the sounds of the car confirm, and then a picture springs up: Tim nursing at her, or me, with sun on my face, a glow of heated light through the orange-yellow heaviness about to smother me. I look past this to her face, the center of her in my mouth, sweet strings raying over my tongue, and then her voice, vibrating through a membrane like fever: "This is the last of this for you. You're old enough to talk now. Enough's enough. Here."

"Mmm!" Dad says, in his noise of absent-minded pleasure. "You can see the outskirts of Devils Lake! Chuck, are you asleep down there?"

I push up in the seat just as a semitrailer smacks past. My neck feels swollen with leaden gills. There is a concrete abutment, a metal shed, then a cracking at the door as Jerome's legs go up past me in a suck of wind and Dad cries "What the!" and his arm is across my chest, knocking me back, his fingers around the ankle of Jerome's leg. The car sways off the road onto a ragged bumpiness, shaking a sweaty smell from Dad's shirt into my face. Jerome is lying on his stomach, his arms out, both hands holding the padded armrest of the door, which is wide open, his face down over flashing gravel and patches of oil.

The car slides to a stop, the door sways wider, and Dad jerks Jerome's foot and cries, "Let go now! Let go so I can get you back in!"

Jerome does, his hands striking the gravel, beside scattered pieces of glass, and he scrambles in backward over the sill.

"What the—*heck* were you doing, anyway?" Dad asks. "What kind of a stunt is that?"

Jerome isn't crying. He stares straight ahead, as if seeing somebody he doesn't want to. "I leaned on the door handle," he says.

"Good Lord!"

"But I caught hold of the big door-closer when it came open."

"Right on this curve. Lord! Well, we should thank the Lord that your reflexes are fast."

"And you got hold of his foot," I say.

"Yes."

The engine is off. In the breadth of silence above, I sense him praying. The strongest words I've heard him use are "Gol blame" or "Son of a gun" or "What the Sam Hill!"—though now that we're older he will say "Damn!" or "Hell!" and watch us, his face shying from the word while his lips, held in a tight smile, take on the pinched look of tasting alum (her cure for canker sores), and he has said to us, "I never once saw Dad drink, and I doubt that *I* ever will. I figure I can make a big enough ass of myself sober." Now a noisy drilling of insects sends pinpoints of sensation into my back where the bicycle seat scrapes. Then I'm outside myself, fuzzy as the car's interior, overseeing an arrangement take place among us, as if we're shifting positions in the car.

This time it's Jerome's turn, I think, grateful that Mom isn't here.

"Are you all right?"

It's Dad's voice, fainter; he's turned to his window, away from us, as though to look over the land. He cranks his window down.

"Yes," we say.

He reaches to the key and there's a metallic chattering before the engine catches. "We'd better get going," he says. "I'm already late for my appointment. At this rate, there won't be time to see Jake."

I groan, Jerome punches down his door lock, and Dad

pulls the car unsteadily onto the road as a semitrailer comes barreling around from behind, its horn blaring into a terrible shape. The wallop of air rocks our car and wrests my hair around as if I'm at the wheel.

"By golly, I don't know," Dad says, and hits the hand shift so hard the horn ring wobbles, then pulls off the road. "I really don't know." He shakes his head. "If they offer me that job of principal, even though it's a step down from where I was, I might take it."

+

He does. He trims down the remaining hedge and piles the branches, as if to end matters, in a back corner of the yard. We learn to climb on the pile without our feet falling through, and then we pull off some of the larger branches, carry them to the tree by the driveway, lean their tops against a low limb, and have a lean-to. Mom gives us a patched and reripped sheet, perhaps from our roughhousing, and we hang it from the limb, in front of the lean-to, and invite our buddies into the yard for a home-town carnival; admission, two cents. They drop this into a coffee can as they come through the gate of the flat-topped hedge, and we settle them in front of the sheet, feeling as henlike as Sister Colette.

Jerome steps from behind the sheet in an Indian headdress, with Dad's bathrobe tied around him and trailing, and recites the opening verse of *Hiawatha* to their boos. I waddle out in a pair of goatskin chaps that once belonged to Grandpa Jones and try to twirl a piece of twine, which goes over worse.

"You could at least use a rope," Leo complains.

"Get a horse!" Kuntz cries.

I do a cowboy on a bucking bronc, jumping and arching in front of the sheet, and then groan and grab at my jewels.

"I've got a love-el-ly pair of co-co-nuts," Jerome starts to croon, and everybody yells, "You can't sing!"

So he turns his headdress backward and recites the rest of the verse our Uncle Davey taught us: "A beeg one, a leetle one, one as big as my head! It got that way when I ruptured it on the corner of my bed! Yah!"

We pass out the Kool-Aid and cookies Mom has made, and everybody is satisfied with that and getting a penny back.

"Well, we tried," I say to Jerome, and he rolls up his eyes.

"Did you see the way I slipped my whistling tackle into Russell when he lied about the Lone Ranger?" Kuntz cries. "Oh, my back!"

Kuntz is maneuvering over the brush pile as though on top of Russell again, and now he cups his hands around his eyes and bends his head down to the branches. "Holy gosh," he says. "This is another world down here. Imagine if we had a hidden cave at the bottom of it!"

+

Jerome and I sit on bare ground that is cool from the branches piled here as the hedge came down—so cool it feels winter is at the surface, rising again. We stare at each other, our faces divided into patterns of shadow by the branches overhead. The sky is more somber seen from here, past the branches—a canopy of a thousand windows. Kuntz found a loose patch at one edge of the pile, and we were able to burrow from there to the center of it; then we formed a line and pulled limbs out from inside and piled them over its top, propping shorter ones upright inside, until an open area grew, and one final post at the center was all that was needed to hold it up, like a Mandan Indian lodge. It can seat all seven of us.

A bushel basket to one side of Jerome is half full of the pop bottles we've collected for deposit. The pennies from our carnival are in a Prince Albert can of Dad's, buried under the basket. None of us ever really liked Benny's or Dickie's club, and now we have our own.

"I remember once I had a dream like this," Jerome says, and moves, and his right eye is covered by a patch of sunlight that turns its center into a planet.

"What should we plan for tomorrow?" I ask.

The blue world turns down, back up, and is directed at me. He sighs. "Something peaceful."

"We could have lictors carrying fossks." *Fasces*, a word from our book on Rome. "We could use those old doorposts by the outhouse for the fossks. I'll wear the torn sheet Mom gave us for a toga."

We've decided, with our friends, that our club won't be like others and have a leader or ruler; we'll have a monarch, and elect a new one each week. The first election is over. Everybody wrote his choice on a piece of paper and dropped it into the coffee can, and Leo, who was counting the votes and knew our handwriting, said everybody voted for himself—except Jerome, who voted for me. I'm the monarch.

"We were sitting down like this, on ground or something that was cold, and I could only see the pieces of your face I see now."

"What do you mean?"

"In that dream."

I weave my head around.

"Well, you know, about the same pieces I see now. I was looking through broken glass, or something that was cracked, and it was just about like it is now."

"My head?"

His lips compress and there's a rapid shuttering of light as he blinks and bows. Then both eyes look out from a mask, the one still lit, at the distant sky his planet seems traveling to, toward something perhaps as complicated as the Milky Way.

"What else?"

His head shakes once. His lips are firm. He won't speak.

+

"All right," I say. "You see, lictors walked ahead carrying these fossks." I point to the doorposts lying on the ground, grooved, with carved medallions at their tops. "They made sure everybody paid respect. You other guys should bow or something when we come past."

"Oh, great," Brian says.

"This is one of the rules of our kingdom now, and you have to follow the rules and do what I say. You can't break the rules or the lictors—I hereby nominate Kuntz and Leo—will throw you out."

"Oh, good!" Kuntz says. "Bowing hurts my back."

"Dope," Brian murmurs.

I have on the Indian headdress with its feathers removed and stars pasted to it, and the sheet over my shoulders. Leo and Kuntz bear the fasces as we march around the back yard and I try not to smile, attempting to imitate Father at Benediction. I want to walk like a king but the sheet keeps jerking at my neck. Then I see Brian pounding his chest in a *Mea culpa* when he bows, groaning, "Oh, great me!"

"All right," I say. "This is my decree. Now, before next week, right today, we're going to see who will be the next monarch."

This is something Jerome has thought up. I take the sheet and drape it over Kuntz's shoulders.

"I knew it!" Brian cries.

Kuntz smiles, showing yellow horsey teeth, and says with the buzz in his nose that sounds like waxed paper over a comb, "Good gosh, guys, it's like I thought all along. Thanks."

"No," I say, "I am yet the monarch. This is your test." I hand him a croquet mallet from the concrete slab and grab a handful of Popsicle sticks that Jerome has marked, then lead Kuntz over to the driveway. "Okay, this is my proclamation. Everybody wears the cape and strikes with this same mallet three times, trying to hit in the same spot, and the cape can't fall off when you hit. You have to hit right around here"—I rake a circle with my heel—"where the driveway is hardest. Whoever's hole is deepest after three hits, he's the monarch. This is my decree."

"Thanks loads, guy," Kuntz says. "But this silly thing's going to fall off with my first wham."

"That's the idea," Jerome says, and winks at me.

Kuntz takes his three taps gently, bent over, trying to keep the sheet on his back. Arno takes his, then Buddy; Leo bends lower, choking up on the mallet, and hits so hard on his second try that the sheet slips away.

"He's out!" Kuntz cries.

"I caught it before it fell all the way off!"

"But you lose your last turn," I say, and place the Popsicle stick marked "Leo" beside his hole. "We'll see how deep it is soon."

Jerome does three one-armed taps, holding the sheet tight at his neck with his free hand.

"Look at that fruit!" Brian says, but he notices Jerome's technique. Brian is last. He tests the mallet—"No warming up!" Leo yells—tests the sheet around his shoulders, his neck, clamps it to his chest with his pointed chin, and delivers three overhand blows.

"He cheated!" Leo cries.

Jerome and I almost laugh. "No," I say, "I didn't put any rules in that you couldn't do that. You could have."

"Well, mine's deeper anyhow!"

Jerome puts a marked Popsicle stick down each hole and draws a line at ground level with a pencil; Jerome is the only one everybody trusts. He gathers up the sticks and compares. "Hmm," he says.

"What?" Leo asks.

"That's strange," Jerome says, and smiles at him. "Brian won."

They won't stand for this, whatever the rules, as we thought, so Jerome gets the Mirro-Matic timer from our kitchen and draws a line across the driveway. They have to keep the toe of their left shoe there, I tell them, and then I hand them each a croquet mallet. "The idea is to see who can chop the biggest hole," I say. "Ready, set, proceed!"

They start swinging, their heads nodding and wagging in the speeded-up chatter of old newsreel clips, a rhythm I conduct, and then I picture Jerome's fuzzy circle drawn in the dirt for marbles, and seize the power of memory, stronger than their clobbering, and see my mother appear in the door of our schoolroom, where I've been kept after hours, and then I watch myself, in the dimness of the gray-enameled cloakroom where Sister has sent me, sneak back to hear her say to Mom that I need to develop responsibility, so I can direct my energies, and then, "He has a marvelous sense of counting, from the piano, I suppose, and he used to have such a nice voice, too, but it's suddenly gone, maybe from having his tonsils out. I noticed it rehearsing for the Christmas program . . ."

That unfolds, with the gray risers set beside the piano, and the first and second grades lined up on them, Jerome behind,

singing with breath I can feel over my ear "Toyland, Toyland"
to a tune nobody else is singing, which makes me wonder if I'm
singing his tune, so that when Sister asks each of us to come to
the piano and sing separately, I'm frightened. Then I'm back
in the cloakroom as Sister says, "So he has that experience
behind him." What experience? "And he has a dramatic flair
we might nurture. What's your thinking on this?"

"I think it would be wonderful!"

"Would you make him the tails?"

"I'd love to!"

Her foot pumping the scrolled treadle, the big black spoked
wheel blurring at her knee as her stocking forms folds to the
whir in the wood that gobbles up cloth, and then her foot comes
off—a coat of tails, bright blue, with gold piping around the
lapels and rickrack on the sleeves, which I wear when I work
with Sister, learning how to use her baton (and carry it home
for practice, angling it back under my arm, as in a picture she
has shown me of Mozart) in the sketched-out patterns for four-
four, two-four, and three-quarter time; Hank Kauter-Haupt
building a smaller set of steps in the boiler room, with a platform
on top, and then the dim cloakroom again as I look into the
lighted chapel-auditorium at Sister, seated at her piano, and at
her nod I march in with the baton gripped under my arm and
my head enshrined in Mozart's, my senses dinning with "The
Stars and Stripes Forever," but hear no applause, which Sister
has said might happen—"since people here probably aren't so
aware of the niceties." But somebody is, or else my mother has a
lot of hands, because a scattering of clapping arrives as I mount
my dais, another word from Sister—who is, I see as I turn to
bow to her, partly the source of the pounding hands. I do a
hop and pirouette I'm not supposed to, spinning too far, so I
have to unwind a ways to face the audience for my bow, and
then I draw out my baton like a sword and hold it horizontal,
holding Sister, too, at my mercy: *the conductor.* I raise my arms
and up come the sticks, cymbals, triangles, and tambourines—
Kuntz at the bass drum—and St. Mary Margaret's Rhythm Band
is off with the clatter and jangling of "Turkey in the Straw."
And in a rush of reverse unreeling, I'm back through those
speeded-up newsreels—of marching soldiers swinging their

arms too far as their heads go nodding and wagging like marionettes'—to this hacking going on at my feet.

"Time's up!" Jerome cries, as the dinger on the timer dings. The mallets stop, he takes out a pad and then hands me Dad's folding carpentry rule. I throw my toga across a shoulder, bend to measure the first hole, and announce how deep it is.

"How wide?" Leo asks. It's his hole; we placed him at a hard spot.

"What do you mean?"

"How wide, how long? You said biggest. It's got to be the whole square area of the circumference of the place you dug, not?"

I look at Jerome, who is looking at the pad, his lips compressed.

"It can't just go by *deep*ness," Leo insists. "You got to have the volume it holds by body and weight, with what you're measuring there."

"Geez," Brian says. "Next he'll be making change."

Leo slams his mallet down. "Shut up! You can't go just by how deep! Some of these here ain't big enough to hold a pint of piss in!"

With a flurry of flying mallets and fasces, the club disbands in that moment. Except for Jerome and me. And Brian. And then Brian, so angry his chin is trembling, doesn't want to be a monarch over two people who are practically the same, he yells, and leaves.

So it's only Jerome and me, under the crosshatch of shadow that seems the underside of a weave holding together scraps of the years we've spent together. The light is dim, supper near, neither of us monarch now. But the blue of his eye, bared in the light, looks into me and then off at that gathering constellation, and in its silence something rules.

"They'll be back," he says.

"Oh, no."

"Sure."

Has he planned this?

"But I wish it was the same as before," he says.

"How?"

"In that dream."

"How?"

"This time. Just you and me."

+

On a day in early fall we walk with Dad up the low-mowed lawn of the high school, under shady trees, on the other side of the block from where we used to live, and step beneath his arm through the white front doors into an empty hall that smells of varnish and the oily red sawdust used for sweeping up. Stinging light returns from every surface under the fall sun. We go down to the basement, with low basketball hoops at each end bent down a bit from their backboards, to a stack of cartons in the center of the floor. Sunlight slants beside them in wavering rectangles, where newly applied gray enamel appears to be melting under wiggly patterns of the same protective wire mesh we have at our school.

Dad opens the cartons with explosive rips and takes out books and smells them. He opens a book on top of a stack, turning pages, testing the feel of them between a finger and thumb, then pauses to read. The aroma of the books and bindings, of gluey iodine and wet paint, dizzies me. Dad reads on, leaning his elbows on the cartons, one hand in his hair, with his polished shoes in a patch of sunlight that climbs the cartons and lights the trousers of his suit below the knees a burning blue. Jerome and I sit on the floor at his feet, with our backs against the books, and he stands for so long, with one foot cocked behind the other, resting on its toe in perfect relaxation, that the school itself, with its shining squares and surfaces, seems him.

Jerome's head falls onto my shoulder, and I support him, half asleep myself. Then I'm in a dim locker room in the basement, watching Dad open a fishing-tackle case on an exercise table—drowsy as I was in the hospital; since my fall, warm weather has me feeling like a fly falling asleep on a windowpane. The windows above front on the playground—the slide, our other house—all their panes so reddened by the sun it hurts to look at them, and I imagine myself crawling from pane to pane, as if each were a warmer bed. The scrabbling of his hand in the first-aid kit, as he calls it, sends up such a stink of medicine I'm sure we walked a hall of the hospital in light like this.

"I was sure they wouldn't use it," he says, and takes out a jar, edged in gold from the light. "It's amazing how things stay the same. I got it for the football boys years back. 'Instant Energy,' it says. Ha. It was supposed to supply them with the needed desire to run and tackle as they should. Full of sugar and protein."

He opens the lid and shakes one into his hand, a gray-brown lump, and throws it into his mouth, head back, as he tosses down popcorn, and chews. "Tastes all right. Do you want one? Chuck, you look asleep. Jerome is. I laid him out." He pulls a watch from his vest pocket. "Goodness, that late. Your mother will want an explanation. My fault." He slides the case under a bench. "Come on, let's get home."

No, I think, I want you to talk in this way in which you used to talk, words merely words, to me alone, and below the spattered ceiling I'm surprised not only by the pattern but by the mechanics and the limits of the loom, while the perfect cloth of which I get mere glimpses goes on in its continuum of silent speed, and all of these moments, along with thousands of others once so unmanageable and individually dispersed, now shift interchangeably within the same framework of time, whenever I close my eyes to watch them in the weave of their travel above where I lie.

+

The dining-room table and chairs are near the bay window, and a man sits with his hands inside a sack of black cloth on the tabletop, rummaging with a bulk that rattles and clicks from whatever it is that he's up to. He says, "No, you aren't going to see a rabbit jump out of here, boys. There's nothing magic about this. It's to keep light off my film, that's all. If light hits it, it's done for. Then your dad wouldn't have pictures of his high-school kids and you wouldn't have one of your dad. Then what would we do?"

+

This case looks like the first-aid kit but is painted green. Dad sets it on a table in the Town Hall, lifts me up beside it, and opens the case on alcohol and talcum, and something so powerful that when I locate the sticky bottle he calls it "spirit gum."

"No, don't play with it," he says, and taps my hand so I drop it. "Leave the makeup kit alone."

He takes a pink ball from a compartment and rolls it between his palms, shoves it against my nose, and then shapes and molds it to fit my nostrils. I can look down, cross-eyed, and see its pink hump. He pulls out a tube like toothpaste, squeezes orange into his palm, where shades of other colors lie in streaks, and rubs some across my forehead with his thumbs. "Grease-paint," he says, passing his thumbs under my eyes, over my cheekbones, under my nose, down the new pink knob of it, then across my chin and down my cheeks. He works this over my face in a massage, with his fingertips, picking up drops from his palm, and the pressure of his fingers and his nearness, as he moves between my knees, with Jerome to one side, send up feelings I wasn't aware were in my face toward my thumping Coke bottle, and when his breath, which he holds in reserve, heaves over me, the ends of my hair light up.

He wipes tissue above my eyebrows, dabs spirit gum there, takes a braid of gray hair from the kit, unwinds an end of it, and snips this off with shears. He rolls it into fluffs with his fingers and presses it to the spots where the spirit gum burns worse than iodine. He holds a mirror up and I see an old goof with a big nose tinted red, and fuzzy eyebrows up in startled surprise. The sight of this sends me farther behind my own face, which I can never really see, and when the curtains on the Town Hall stage, pulled by Dad, draw back on us as elves in Santa's Workshop, I assume the giggling is at me. I strike the shoe I'm supposed to be mending in high overhead blows, then pretend to hit my thumb. I suck on it and waggle my eyebrows at the laughter.

By the time the superintendent's son walks on as Santa Claus, tall and sure off his roller skates, I've found that I can wiggle the blob of my nose as well, and nobody can hear what he's saying. His mouth opens as it does when he's forgotten his lines, and beneath his makeup I can see his eyes: scared.

This is serious, I know, and then Jerome, hammering beside Leo, gives off a warning, and I follow his look to a shape that moves over the auditorium floor to the stage: Mom, appearing from the waist up, like a reflection on water. "Straighten up"—can a whisper carry like this?—"or I'll yank you out of there!"

+

I receive the blow she hit the stage with at home, and lie in bed that night feeling ill again. "Hamming," she called it. Now I hear her voice in the living room rise with his above the radio, sending that shuttle back and forth, and I know that something is being decided about me. No, they're talking about Christmas. I don't care if it comes. Then her voice is a line of light that connects: "Why did you put so much makeup on him in the first place? That was what started it. No, don't wave me away, or act the shrinking innocent. Even the Sisters are aware of his nature. If you're not teaching him, you should be. I should. We might as well admit we're the cause of this."

+

The illness of wrongdoing is with me until spring, when she coaches me in a monologue for the Amateur Hour. The training is so trying that when Brian and Kuntz start laughing (though I'm not hamming it up) at the goatskin chaps I did my bucking in, I think: These people are *hicks*. They don't know what Mom and Sister know, and at the end of the speech, to shut them out, I pull my hat over my eyes. Mom calls this "slapstick," and for days it feels I'm being struck by the word.

+

The shame of the hat is with me when I turn in my desk on the second floor of the parochial school, in the middle-school classroom, to look at the miniature statue of the Infant of Prague, on a shelf against the back wall, and feel I've moved so far from under his arm (in and out of a grade I hardly remember without Jerome present) that the Infant now stands this reduced, and then I chant with the rest of the third-grade class:

Thirty days hath September,
April, June, and November.

Sister Stanislaus is teaching the middle grades this year. Sister Colette is gone.

All the rest have thirty-one,
Except for February;
It alone hath twenty-eight,
Except when leap year rolls around,
Then it has twenty-nine.

Sister faces the fourth grade, at the center of the room, where Jerome sits, and I hear again the story of the Tower of Babel. She turns to the fifth grade, farthest off from her, and holds up a tablet colored like a comic book at the front of her desk. Its pages flip over and reveal, one at a time, the forty-eight states. She asks a fifth-grader to name the state, from its shape and the emblems and products pictured, and then another names the capital. It's difficult to see all the pictures from where I sit, but I know the capitals by now. I can sense the spread of the states across the continent, and when Sister pulls the map at her back like a window shade down over the blackboard, their blues and pinks and yellows call in the same voice, *Come.*

+

The maid is in front of the marbleized wardrobe, with both hands on her mop handle, staring down at me in bed, the shining curls under her hairnet askew, like a wig. I'm merely an eye, that marble I swallowed, rolling and rendering everything my own, impervious to reason, while my remaining self rises farther north than I've been before. She says, "No, I'm gibbeted up in sadness at that man. It ain't Jesus done it, I tell him, it the unkindness of his heart, the cancer there, the nastiness of you. No, if he come back he ain't gettin none from me. He ain't gettin in that door. He can weep and pray and moan and I be quiet as a spleck on the glass there. Even he boompity-boomps it with his shoulder, he ain't gettin in. He gonna have to break it down to see me, and he break it down this time, he liable to arrest, he know that. I tell him. That scare that man. He's a troublemaker. No, he start that boompity-boompin, I call him on it that minute. Ain't no way he gettin home this time. No, I'm all gibbeted up because of him now. Ain't Jesus or you people here. It that man. A troublemaker true."

+

The makeup kit is on the seat of the toilet stool in our bathroom. Dress rehearsal. Jerome and I are entered in the Amateur Hour with Mom and Dad this year, in the adult division, and we know why the prize of twenty silver dollars is a goal; the last time we looked for our U.S. Savings Bonds, in the pigeonholes of the desk upstairs, they were gone.

Mom is the prologue and sets the scene in the kitchen: a bank of the Ohio River—a milk crate to represent a log, another a rock, newspapers for the water. "A real pastoral effect, eh?" she whispers to us in the bathroom, where we wait with Dad. Then her speech: "You are a little boy once more, lying on your belly on the cool, damp sands beside the river. It could as well be the Pipestone," she adds, in one of the lines she and Dad have rewritten—our local creek. "Play to them!" they've both said.

Dad is Lut'er, or *Looter* in our pronunciation, a bum so backward he can barely speak, as he enacts it (which is so real I have to control myself to keep from laughing), and I'm Giz, about as ignorant but eager to show it. I talk all the time. I'm his age and have shavings of crepe hair glued in an itchy grizzle to my cheeks, and now I make faces to free my mouth enough from the gripping net of spirit gum to be able to speak, and turn to Jerome, or Dr. Stephen Van Dexter. He frowns and plucks at his goatee, trimmed to look like a goat's beard, and at first I figure he suspects I'm acting up, but all he's interested in, with that fast-talking spiel of his, is quack cures and a quick buck and she . . .

+

She spreads the newspapers over the spotlighted stage of the Town Hall, where dust specks sparkle, while I watch from the darkened wing on weak legs, beside Jerome, and experience such pressure after the weeks of rehearsal that a drop of pee squeezes out in my pants. Her prologue goes on: "You are still young enough to see the wonder that everywhere touches the world; and *men* are in the world—" She has finished with the props, and stares at the milk crates as if sizing them up, her knuckles on her hips, and then out at the audience. "—*all sorts* of men." There are some giggles. She dips and unfurls a hand in their direction. "But you can still look on them with the shining eyes of brotherhood!" Now stepping toward our wing. "Everywhere about you, men and things are reaching for the infinite"—hands up—"each in his own way, be it big or little, be it the moon or the medicine show"—this is her voice of waxing rhapsodic, as she puts it—"and you yourself are not yet decided whether to reach for the stars or go fishing!" She lets this hang and then rolls her eyes and says in her everyday voice, "Brother!" A few people laugh. ("If they laugh here," she has said, "we're close to getting them, and if there's any applause, we could be home safe, but don't count on it, *act*.")

The laughter grows as she does a twist on her feet and then raises her hands and flings them out as if shooing the audience ("Too bad Susan was born a month too soon," she said, "or I could play off that"), and steps off. The rising response sets off a spatter of applause that goes through me like rifle shots. I'm done, I think, not sure if it's more pee that I've let go or if it's my legs that are water now.

Then from the back wing at the other corner of the stage, Dad, with a cane pole over one shoulder and with a week's growth of stubble tinted gray (more daring for him, as a teacher, to let a real beard grow, they've decided), comes shuffling out in bare feet with long, probing, turtlelike extensions of his neck that make it seem his head is pulling his loping body forward— and barely has enough wits in it to do that. Some high-school girls squeal. Now portions of what Mom has stated in her prologue make sense, considering the way this filthy man with broken-down bib overalls (one suspender unsnapped) bears the shambles of himself across the stage, and there's a burst of applause above the squeals. It's how they want to see him, I think, and get a glimpse of the ingenuity they've put into this.

He walks and walks, it seems, until he gets to the first crate, decides it's too heavy to move with his foot, since it's the rock, and drags the other to the river and sits.

When he takes the angleworm out of his shirt pocket, there are shrieks and excited clapping, and then he juts his chin out so far it seems his neck will break, rolls his lower lip fleshily out, and lets go of his first spattering spit of chaw. I start enjoying him myself, when hands grip the roll of nerves in my shoulders.

I might yell if she didn't whisper hotly in an ear, "Get yourself in line, Giz. You're next."

Looter casts out his worm and begins to drop off with a rattling snore that jerks him awake, my cue. I put the crooked branch over my shoulder, check its safety-pin hook, bow out my legs and drop my butt, and shuffle out whistling a tune nobody can hear (which I'm grateful for), the way he keeps dropping off. The stage spots spiral down in separate suns, each with sparkling panes of different brightnesses between, and a rush of feeling goes out of her nail marks in my nerves. The floor is ice. I could fall through. A freeze enters my legs, past my sliding insides, and lifts off my head. What's this? At the rock I find a milk crate. The tricky sight of it drives a headache through my scar out an ear. *What?* Dad's real eyes, red-rimmed, roll to me from beneath greasepaint, checking my state, and order me to sit, pinning me inside Giz and the tempo we've worked out over our weeks of rehearsal.

I get off my first spattering spit (it's licorice we chew; the newspapers aren't just props, and the sight of everything Dad's let go sickens me) and feel the whoops and cries will push me backward off the rock. I lean into the noise and with wiggling fingers work the worm dug up from our basement (they were down too deep in the cold garden) onto my safety pin, and cast off and see the worm coil and uncoil as if heading for Dad's. I arch out my bare right foot, dirtied with lampblack worse than the frog catcher's son's, toward the papers, and lower my big toe with a peck of a tap, avoiding the coiling, shiny mess.

Why am I the first to speak?

"Tiz warm as fraish melk." It comes out right, in a creaky voice thinned by fear, with a broadening of the accent our

Illinois relatives have—hicklike and coated with fur, the "fraish" dragged out and "melk" dropped like a pea in a bucket.

Looter's head moves around in half-witted slowness, like an ape's, as if he can't quite understand human speech.

Twice, I have to speak first: "*Hattie Brown* come in yet?"

His look catches me from falling as my voice gives. He spits.

Three times: "She's a mighty fine little st*eee*amboat!"

And then, in the profound and hollow croak that always seems to take him a minute to get out, he finally says, doing whatever it is he does to his Ss: "*Sh*he's-sha wo-ter-logged!"

We wait, as I've been warned, until they quiet, for the fast part.

"She ain't waterlogged!" I say.

"She is."

"She ain't."

"She is."

"She ain't?"

The argument dies of malnutrition, the script reads here.

Then me again: "River raisin?"

A consideration that sends his entire self crawling back into the corner that contains his remaining BB of mental capacity; then he says with a frog-eyed conviction that used to crack me up, "Nup!"

And now, with his new stage power, it nearly cracks me up again, but I get out on the downslide, "Fallin?"

"Nup." Secretive and self-satisfied; his prissy half smile.

Then in the wheedling impatience I've hardly had to work at: "Ah, standin *still?*"

Looter's moment, when he is permitted his only smile, a goofy half-cracked gawk that causes his eyes to look even more blank: "Yah!"

After a mosquito bites me ("Gawrsh! A yaller nipper at noonday! An look at that whelp!"), Dr. Stephen Van Dexter walks on, whittling a piece of wood with a jackknife and poking his yellowish goatee at every point of the compass. He sees there is no place to sit and chaws and spits at this, his goatee jiggling with the vigor of his chew, looks back and forth at us, jutting his beard both ways, then sets a foot up on my box and says in his hyped-up wheeze, "What gits me is how they done it!"

Looter and I draw into ourselves further; then, bit by bit, I emerge like an animal coming into view, curious.

H I M : I traded a two-pound catfish for a bit of that salve and I don't know how they *done* it!

M E : Kickapoo?

H I M : Yess, Kickapoo Indian salve. I don't think no, uh . . . *Indian* . . . ever seen it!

M E : You ain't never sure about nothin, these days.

H I M : I smelled it and it smelled like kerosene, I biled it and it biled and *burnt* like kerosene. [The effect of this is like a freight train going by, in comparison to us dimwits.] I don't think it was nothin *but* kerosene . . . [the beard at me] an *lard*.

M E : Reckon twas common kirsene.

H I M : Now I don't know if it was *common* kerosene, but I know twas kerosene, an I bet kerosene'd cure a heap of troubles, if ya'd *use* it right!

M E : That air doctor said the salve'd cure most anythan.

D A D : [*As though a voice from the grave, long dead*, the script reads, which is how it comes out] Which doctor?

M E : The man doctor [angry at him], the one with the pinted mustache!

D A D : Ho, I seen him take an egg outa Brian Rimsky's ear, and Brian, he, huh, uh—he swore he didn't have no hen in his haid!

H I M : But the lady doctor said . . . [Jerome's jumped in too soon; it sounds like people are pedaling paddleboats out there.] But the *lady* doctor said it warn't so good—effie-cacious, she called it, withouten ya took two bottles of the builden-up medicine, a box ah the pills, and a bottle of the *hair fluid*!

He screeches this and goes into a gobbling laughter like Grandma Jones, then tucks their response away like a coin, and heads on. It turns out that this lady doctor, who feels that I— Giz—should take the medicine like the Indians did for my "ainternal trouble," has given me a box of the liver pills. Doc wants to know if I have them with me. Uh-huh. If I've taken any? Nup, I'm savin em. What fur? Fur the day when I'm feelin sicker'n I am today. Doc goes into a long speech about kerosene and camphor and lard, and how he would have saved his second wife "if the winder hadn't a-blowed in and she got all kivered with snow," and about his third wife and how he took a stitch in time and told her about his remedies, which is why she's so healthy now—his eyes always on my pocket—and then he cries, "Giz, let me see em!"

I do, and he says they smell like kerosene. He wants one. Looter does, too, so I trade them each a pill for a bite of their chaw, which Looter measures off with his big hand across the licorice plug.

The taste of the pill convinces Doc that it's kerosene, and he has a proposition: why don't the three of us start up a Medicine Show.

Here the steamboat Hattie Brown *comes in,* the script reads— Mom in the wings hollering in hoots.

HIM: I'll make the salve and do the talkin, Giz'll whop things up, and Looter here'll git cured of lumbago, a crick in the back, and tizic.

DAD: [Feeling his back for the crick] But who'll take an egg outer somebody's ear?

HIM: Giz'll do that. An my daughter Lavinia'll play the pianny.

Looter asks where we'll go with it first and Doc says Bowdon, so Looter wants to know how we'll get there and Doc says walk, unless somebody gives us a ride, and I say we can use my johnboat—which I figure must be a part of the bathroom humor Mom keeps claiming is in the script—and Looter wants to know who'll row. We'll take turns, I say, and then Looter asks how *fur* it is. Three and a half miles, I tell him, as Doc keeps repeating, every other line, "Will ye go, Looter?"

DAD: Uhhhhhhhhh.

HIM: Huh?

ME: He said uh-huh.

HIM: I thought he said *uh*-uh.

ME: He said uh-*huh.*

HIM: He didn't say anything of the sort. He said *uh*-uh!

DAD: How fur— [this difficulty he has putting a complete thought together] uh, didja say it was?

HIM: Three and a half mile.

DAD: [Who swallows his chaw, eyes bugging] —!

ME: We'll each take an oar!

MOM: [Crying from the wing] Stephen! Stephen! [And from the way Doc hops up, you know this is his third wife, and that he's in for it.]

HIM: We kin come back on the *current.*

DAD: [Rebaiting and throwing his hook back in the river, where his worm slides into a pool of licorice puckering the paper] I'll think it over . . . but I ain't givin no hope. Three and a half mile is purty fur one way . . . but *two* ways . . . well, it's [shaking his head so hard his cheeks go into a moist flapping] . . . it's *turrible!*

MOM: Stephen!

HIM: Come on, Giz, we'll talk it over.

I'm hurried off by him as fast as I can manage in my walk and, once in the wing, shed Giz and turn quick, to see the ending Dad has saved each night until now. Out in the sparkling arena, looking small, he says, "Three and a half mile . . ." He gives his wagging headshake and his lips take on their expression of tasting alum; this is serious business. He begins a breath-holding business of pulling in his hook, removing the worm, and returning it to his overalls bib. He stands, his big head wagging as he attempts to take in all that has happened this afternoon. He turns a bit toward us, then back, groaning internally, it appears, his eyes enlarging with a blank earnestness in which the first bit of light appears, and then he says in a whisper that cuts through their amusement like the sound of him sharpening a knife, "*Two! ways!*"

His new headshaking is against anybody who would try to talk him into such foolishness, and there is a rise and swing of his weight back on one leg—a noble stance; nobody's fool now, about to head in his own direction—and then his weight comes down forward so fast it seems he'll fall, but he catches himself with a quick glide, poised, facing them with the clarity of his decision, and says in a firm rush that pours into the doubts that everybody has about our village, especially on an evening like this, away from our radios, gathered at such an event:

"Hyatt, North Dakota, is fur enough for me."

And then that neck-extending, probing walk, quicker now, which is covered in its endlessness across the stage toward us by their applause. In the wing he turns with a smile, himself again, and grabs Mom up, revolving her as her hands rub and slap his back in an upward grip. Back down on her feet, she rises on tiptoe and whispers something to him. He looks over at us, still smiling, but his eyes begin to well with shadow, as if he's watching our weeks of work gather to this end, and finally he says, "Well, dear, it might be my swan song, you know."

"What?" she says, and steps back, startled and pale, her hands on his chest. "What do you mean by that?"

He shrugs; he won't explain. At the end of the evening he insists that we all walk out to the center of the stage to receive the applause of the people and our twenty silver dollars, and Jerome's startled look at me seems to say, *I'm leaving.*

Or else he's afraid that Dad might be, as I am.

+

Leo and Brian keep saying, "Is this place fur enough for you, Tiz?"

"Giz," I say, "*Giz.* Can't you guys get anything right?"

"It was our applause that won you that first prize, old Tizzer, don't forget that," Leo says. "But is it *fur* enough? Or should we ask old Jerome to check on that, like he does everything for you?"

"Go on. Get out of our yard."

Easter vacation, like winter in a way, with zigzagging ice fringing the puddles in the road. All of us walk close to Mom as she carries Susan at the head of our parade—off to show her to Grandma Jones. Marie toddles between Jerome and me, with a hand in each of ours, dressed in her best, trying to stomp in every puddle with her white shoes. The big brown metal suitcase with clothes for the three of them swings from its handle in Dad's hand, the sheen on its side tipping sliding panels of the puddled road, along with a bending miniature of Tim. The end of the road, then, and across rusty frozen grass, like a gritty kind of candy underfoot, up the embankment to the shining railroad tracks—Dad grabbing Marie, who is squealing, and lifting her by one arm over each rail. We walk across the ties of the platform and into the depot, where our breath steams and the open rafters, about to release a storm of oranges, ring.

Mom sits on a slatted bench and uncovers Susan's face as Dad goes to the ticket window of prison bars. Jerome and I slip back through the doors, outside, where it isn't any colder (our noses red and dripping, if my dripping nose is as red as his), and step onto the ties and look away from the rising sun that gilds the rails in copper spines. A metal whittling rises from the tracks and then, far to the west, the cry of the whistle is an arrow pointing to the engine trailing smoke. Now everybody is outside and there's a dim happiness to the turn of Mom's lips as she stands beside the depot door, with Susan in a pink-blanketed lump—smiling down at her, up at Dad, reminding him of the things he shouldn't forget, like the two of us using our handkerchiefs—the green plume of her green hat trembling as she agrees with her advice. Then the engine sounds its warning at the outer edge of town and both of them shout to us to get hold of Marie, *Oooo-hooooo!*

We watch the big black locomotive, head-on, pass the elevators, swaying back and forth in growing size across the cars behind, causing the rails below to creak and give, its weighty power driving thumping earthquakes through the platform ties (a flash from the bolted boiler over the cowcatcher's iron bars) as the air thickens and steam hits us in its racketing passage with a stink of oil and clinkers—the shining piston slowing in its watery sleeve—then the explosive hiss that sends us back screaming, knowing nobody can hear, our hands over our ears, as it shrieks to a halt. And then rocks, sending a clanging back to the caboose, which appears to hop—sprays of steam pouring at us from underneath in clouds that gag us when we try to breathe.

The fireman, with his striped cap turned backward and a leather apron laced to his legs, climbs down a ladder from the cab of the engine, and salutes Jerome and me. Tim runs up, grabbing my coat, and the engineer waves from his window, in a holiday mood, and calls something to the fireman that opens a smile across his crusted face. The fireman beckons to us. Dad is beside the set of metal steps, handing Marie by the waist to the conductor, and then he takes Mom's hand and leads her up the steps and places her hand in the conductor's, a minuet against the metal backdrop of the train. He picks up her suitcase.

"Hey, boys!" the fireman yells. "The boss says do you want to come and visit him?"

We're at the ladder so fast it feels we've flown—Tim, too —and go clambering up with Tim between us, no time for permission, shins hitting the metal bars in our haste, hands from behind helping at my hips. The engineer, tossing aside his gauntleted gloves, pulls Jerome up by an arm, then Tim;

then me. He kicks a metal door shut over an orangy-white stew of heat, and the oily-carbon smell affects my tongue. The door has holes that throw out flames and beams, and there are levers and glass-covered dials with needles that jiggle and swim in the racket of noise. The engineer stands Tim up on a pedestal like a stool, its seat covered with pieces of carpet, and tells him to pull a handle hanging from a metal rod. At the blast of the whistle we duck and hold our ears and the man's black-seamed face goes back in a laugh.

Then he cries, "Give her two toots! Time to go!"

Tim does, and his frightened laughing face against the metal looks like cream. The engineer squeezes the handle of a lever set in notches, and yells, "This makes her go!" He shoves the lever ahead, flips another that fires out plumes of steam, and I see slats and cracks of light shift beneath the metal floor. The jerk rings back to the caboose again and big sudden tears roll down Tim's cheeks.

"I want to stay home with Dad!" he cries. "I don't want to go!"

"Don't worry, young scamp, here's your dad, right here."

He's far below us, looking stricken, his face as white as Tim's. He holds out both arms as if he'll catch us when we're thrown. But we're handed down, through the fireman on the ladder, to Dad, whose grip is rough and angry across my ribs—Tim last, still crying. Dad holds him as Tim barks out the solid welts he can leave on the air and our ears. There's another hissing release that drowns even this and then a rumbling of weighty steel as the train gets going. Mom comes gliding up slowly in a doorway, and yells, "Can't you two behave even once! You scared us half to death! Getting Tim to disobey, too! Shame!"

"The engineer asked us to!"

She glances in that direction with a frown, which is overtaken by a darkening fear, and then back at us. "That doesn't mean you had to! Say goodbye before I'm halfway to Grandma's—miles off!"

We're trotting alongside the train by now. She throws kisses with both hands and the flurry of this brings out her tooth outlined in gold. We cheer. "Goodbye, you all!" she cries.

"Goodbye!"

"Mind your dad, now!"

"We will!" A chorus.

She stares above us, and the darkening fear, which before was only a flash, alters her face. "Goodbye, Martin dear! I *love—*" Her voice breaks. Her gloved hand goes to her forehead and we stop in bumps against one another at the sight of tears dropping below the glove.

"Goodbye!" his loud bass roars over us from behind. He calls again and I turn and see him raising the tail of his overcoat with his free hand, to get at his handkerchief. The stumpy thunder of the freight cars starts, fracturing the ground, each car faster than the last, with a slice of air between, giving on implements across the street in a vacant lot a dozen times, until the caboose comes grinding by, red lanterns swaying from the corners of its rear platform, and erases the noises left in the rails with a metal whirring like an iron over clothes, as the train bends and unbends in a smart quick way to escape the caboose shoving it ahead, away from us across the plain.

We're able to hear once again. Which allows us to see the unclouded, picture-postcard sky filling with morning light in degrees that the faintly ticking train clicks off. I turn to Jerome.

We're the same, or so I see in his look.

And then: *But we'll never be the same again in this life.*

+

"Well, I guess we're going to be batching for a while, boys."

"Batching?"

"Bachelors. Men alone." Dad turns from the stove, with a dish towel around his waist, holding up like a holy-water shaker the spatula he has used to turn our eggs—crinkled brown at the edges—over with, and the spatula keeps turning in memory, an emptiness inside the time before she gave it its name. "Fun, huh? Or how does it strike you so far?"

Not so hot, I want to say; but none of us says anything, so he turns back to the eggs he is trying to prepare differently this morning, by placing a slice of cheese and mustard on top. "Bachelor's eggs," he says. The name is like her absence in the house, so touchable it seems she's here—especially in the evening, when none of us wants to stay up—so that a chilliness covers us like new clothes. I lie in bed unable to sleep, feeling Jerome turn down his own cold halls through a place that must be as complicated as the growing route of newly discovered tunnels opening in the colored map of my ice-cold dreams.

+

There is a shuttering of shadow and light as we try our chilly, shrunken lodge, and I sense the reflections on the storm and inside windows slip away to reveal her stare on me.

What? I want to say, but see that Jerome won't speak.

The sky above, with limbs across it, is like the lake when you rise from its bottom toward the shadow of the bridge in sunlight, and I close my eyes and imagine that I'm dying, and know that if I do Jerome will remember the chrysalis we found in the tree by the drive after I fell from it, the crackle of Mary Liffert's rocker, the smell of Deke's, and the airplane landing in the field beside the lake and taking people up for rides on the Fourth of July; the cross we drew with chalk on the crumbling steps of the Congregational church, and our talk there about "Eeny, meeny, miney, mo" and whether the game was gambling, or its words proper to speak; the ride we stole on Jerry Klucke's pony, and all the other things that nobody else knows about; and though he wasn't with me when Hank Kauter-Haupt caught me in a bathroom stall with my Coke bottle shaking, or in the room when Sister had me sit at the front of the class to help others with words and I kicked up Mary Angelica Schoenbeck's skirt as she turned from me; or last summer in Grandma Jones's kitchen when I saw RUSSIAN A-BOMB THREAT across the newspaper and asked Grandma what it meant and she said, "Oh, more about the cold war," and I walked out to the alfalfa field beside her house, where blossoms were bending under bees, toward the evergreens, and then sat and was covered by a freeze over my shoulders, like the one that must be covering the warring part of the world, and saw Jerome and me joined by a rope, circling one another, pulling, testing, but always keeping our distance—

I open my eyes to his planet centered on me. There is a sensation like the shower of sparks falling over us when we were tented under the table where Mom cut, and I feel his agreement with my decision since she left: life will never change us, as it does others. We're silent, but words rise in the way they must have before the Tower of Babel.

This is living.

We'll never leave this life.

Or light.

It shines down every day.

It's always over us.

Even when we're inside.

It's always over the lake.

Whether it's water or ice.

And on this land and us.

What light.

+

Then there's a shift. School is out and we're driving down the roads we've memorized toward Grandma and Grandpa's farm, when there's a blast from outside like a shotgun. Jerome and I stand up in the well between the seats, and Marie, sitting in Mom's lap in the front, screams as the car plunges toward the ditch with a flapping sound. We slide to a halt, finally, on the shoulder, next to the deep ditch.

"Blowout," Dad says.

"Oh," Mom says, and moves Marie next to the door and bends over Susan, lying asleep on the front seat, and holds up a hand to shade her face from the silhouettes of crushed red-and-yellow bugs, drying across the windshield, that the sun projects over them all. "It scared me. There's no spare, I suppose."

"Dear, is there ever a spare when you need one?"

"What about that place up ahead?"

On every side, early-planted fields shimmer in the heat, each one tilting at a different angle until the curve of sky, bright blue, rests against them at the end of sight. It's the kind of view I imagine when Dad mentions that our Great-grandfather Neumiller homesteaded in the state, as if a home steadied the lay of this land like an anchor. A distance ahead, at a slight curve, a barn with a fence angling out to the highway stands so red against the sky it smells of paint; and across the road from it a gray-weathered house, with gables facing in four directions, rests on the only rise for miles.

"Deserted, I'm sure," Dad says. "I've never seen a soul there."

"Nor I."

There's a rustle behind us, and Jerome and I let Tim push his way between us, to see out.

"Somebody probably rents the fields, and the barn and pasture."

"I assume," she says.

He strikes the steering wheel so hard it quivers in the dappled light. "This is exactly why I want to move to Illinois!"

"Oh?" she says, and Jerome and I look at one another over Tim, and the sad bands of Jerome's eyebrows rise high. "Why is that?"

"Something like this is always happening."

"It wouldn't in Illinois?"

"Well . . ." We wait to hear more about Illinois, and then I move to a side window, only now afraid that the car went wild, and stare out; I always felt we would stay in North Dakota until we were buried here, like our great-granddad. "There would be family there," Dad says.

"There isn't here?" Mom says. "My folks don't count?"

He sighs and takes hold of the wheel. "Of course they do. But they're not quite next door, Alpha."

"You'd want that? You'd want to live next door to your folks?"

Dad shrugs and raises his hands beside the steering wheel and the silhouettes of shadow darken over his palms as if drawn there. "I don't suppose anybody will be coming down this road in a while."

"Not at noon."

"There's a gas station in that piddley-dink town up ahead."

"How far is that?"

"Three to four miles, I'd guess."

"You'd better go, then."

He gets out, and then all of us do, the doors creaking open like the sides of an insect about to take off. We walk down the ditch with her, into yellow-blossoming mustard, while he gets the jack from the trunk. She carries Susan bundled in a blanket, although the sun is as noisy in its own way as the ratchet of the jack. Marie holds to the back of her dress, keeping close, and Mom goes up along the pasture, which is cropped low and covered with cow pies, toward the barn. Its red bulk returns the noise of the jack past us in an echo. She walks up the ditch and across the road, with all of us following, to a two-track lane, not the one to the house, where the hill begins to rise.

She spreads out the blanket, down on her hands and knees, and lays Susan on it, then lies down beside her, her head on an outstretched arm. Her eyes are closed. We seat Marie beside her and Jerome stretches out on the grass with his head on the blanket. "Oh, for something to read," Mom says, and rolls on her back, with a wrist over her forehead, and then rolls again, now with her arm lying full-length over the grass. Tim and I sit near her hand; he rearranges himself and lays his head in my lap. There's a pattering sound and Dad comes past in a trot, rolling the tire like a hoop beside him. His tie is loosened, his sleeves rolled up, and there are stains under the arms of his shirt. "An hour or so, I hope!" he calls, and the tire wobbles to one side as he looks at us; then he has it back under his bent-over control.

Mom doesn't even stir. Her eyelashes look spangled in the sun, but shadows as black as they are quiver in wiry tension over her cheeks. Her lips are set. Dad grows smaller down the highway and then his tie climbs up over a shoulder, flapping, and I picture it flapping like this while the fat over his chest goes shuddering in his run to first base during a Sunday baseball game—Jerome and I nudging one another at the busyness of his flesh, after the joy of seeing the ball he hit rise into the blue like a loop of song; and I felt then, for the first time, that he wasn't so old; that he might do even better if he lost some extra pounds, as he calls them, and that he could join the Army still, as Jerome and I keep hoping he'll do. He held up on second and had a high-school boy come out and run for him. He was pitching for the town team and came off in heavy strides, massaging his arm, his head down—serious; even his hit hadn't lightened his mood.

I lie down. My head is barely on the blanket, but near hers. I close my eyes and the sun is like a heated moon printed under both lids. Dad is worse coaching basketball. He slams a fist into a hand, or slams both hands onto his legs, or springs from the bench and runs up and down the court with a fist in the air, or cups his hands and yells at the refs. They tossed him out of a game in the state tournament last winter. Hyatt's team reached the state, and Mom and Marie and Susan and I went to Valley City with Dad and the team on the train, and stayed at the Albert Hotel; Jerome and Tim were at the Heatons'. The bellhop who brought our suitcases up to the room had on a red jacket and a flat red hat like the fellow on the radio and in magazines who yells "Philip More *Ray*-s!" His name was Johnny also, and I pulled on Mom's coat and asked if it was him. He kept smiling as he showed us the room; there was one bed.

"It's the best we could do," he said. "State tournament, you know."

"I know," Dad said. "That's why I—"

"Didn't you say your reservations were for a larger room, Martin?"

"That's what I was saying." Then Dad wondered if maybe Marie and Susan couldn't sleep with the two of them; I could sleep on the floor.

"But, *Martin.*"

"I guess I won't wait for that," the bellboy said, and walked out.

"Martin! Where's your mind?"

"What do you mean?"

"You didn't tip him!"

"I was thinking about the game, I guess."

"Oh, what an embarrassing state of affairs. He thinks we're hicks."

"I'll pay him later."

"That's what I mean!"

Basketball boys are running up and down the hall, and some stick their heads in the door and holler, "Hey, coach!" or "Let's go get em, Pops!" They won't be quiet. She slams the door. He pulls off his hat and unbuckles his belt and sits on the bed. His stomach is so big his clothes don't fit anymore. He had to buy a new suit for the tournament and now even it looks tight. He takes his head in his hands.

The first game goes well, an easy win, and the next morning, in the bathroom, where I wander when I hear the noise of water running, I see Dad with a towel around his waist, his big belly the pale white of winter flesh, with wormlike moles in the hair over it but not in the hair across his chest, though there are different-sized globs of them, like putty, on his fatty sides and over his shoulders, in a dotted array of every color from white-pink and gray to purple and black, with one huge one rising out of the hair behind his ear, besides two or three others I can't see but know about, because he warns the barber about them when he has a haircut. The barber here has cut one, and Dad is dabbing at it now with tissue and coming away with blood. He leans toward the mirror above the sink and presses his fingernails into his cheeks, so that white threads spring up and go whirling into coils; some fat ones strike the mirror like stumps and stick where they hit. When he lies back down on the bed, on his stomach, I see brown-red moles with straggly hairs sprawled out from them like spiders attached, and want to pick them off his back—or at least touch them, to see how they feel.

That night the team loses its closest game, the one he gets thrown out of, and at breakfast in the hotel the next morning everybody seems to be staring at us. When a radio announcer interviewed Dad after the game, he said into the microphone that he wanted to apologize to everybody, "especially the folks back home. Forgive me." I see the bellboy walk across the doorway of the restaurant, whistling, while Dad asks the waitress about something on the menu—a smaller portion for Marie.

"Yeah," she says, and sniffs the air. "If that's the way you want it, guy. The customer's the boss."

He sits with his overcoat still on, his shoulders hunched and hands clenched on the tabletop, looking twice his size, his face a clotted mass of shame. A man behind the counter, beside a cash register or adding machine, is chewing on a wad of gum and licking his thumb as he counts a pile of dollar bills, and a cheerleader in the corner pulls her glasses off, covers her wrinkling face, and cries. The waitress dashes from table to booth to counter, as if to spread the gossip, *That's the guy.* The news must have appeared over radios everywhere when he spoke into the microphone. Instead of looking underneath the table, as Mom has warned me not to do, I run my hands along its bottom to feel for gum attached; there are always fresh gobs in a large restaurant. Gum is everywhere under this one, and so thick in front of me it forms a bulge. The waitress comes past and I stick out a leg and send her into a foot-slapping stumble. She turns, red-faced, and says, "Why, you little son of a—" So Mom takes me to our room, without any breakfast, saying, "What's wrong with you. She could have been. This is the last. Must you always. Can't you?" I don't want to hear this again and try to pull away. She jerks and spanks me, saying, "Is this ever going to stop? Is it? Is it? Is it?" until I'm sure this is the time she won't stop.

Doesn't she know how she hurts me?

Doesn't she remember my tonsils being out?

Doesn't she remember my strep throat and pneumonia?

Doesn't she remember holding my head to her after I fell?

I fall to the floor, where I've been sleeping beside a radiator, and imagine pipes connecting the radiators and sinks and stools in the rooms around. In this whole town. Now everybody knows about me—a broadcast of moans. I try to turn my feelings toward Dad, but his body as I've just seen it is so big they slide off. I imagine my funeral, with them both at my coffin, wailing about how they wished they would have treated me better, and roll my face on the bristly rug, wishing for this.

In the evening a fresh fall of snow is colored by the city's neon lights. We walk across the tints of it, over a wooden footbridge painted white, with crisscrossed boards below its rails, like the bridge in Hyatt but fastened above by cables it seems to swing from. Lines of light bulbs, strung along the cables and smoking in the cold, are like stars below in the frozen creek. My butt feels as if it's had fifty penicillin shots, when the biggest needles are used. I wonder if Mom's hand hurts, and look up to find her staring down at me over Susan's blanket, under the smoking electric bulbs. Her lips are pressed together to keep them from trembling and tears jerk in sprays down her nose.

"I love Valley City!" she cries, and her eyes, too, are smoking, it appears, and then she stares out over the campus, where lampposts hold globes of light above shoveled walks, and whispers, "I wish I could live here for good!"

The inside of the gym, with its noisy crowd, is like a heated box a storm keeps passing through. The game is as close as the other, and when Dad jumps up, two boys on the bench pull him down. People boo. Our cheerleaders hurry out to the middle of the floor, in maroon-and-gold skirts down to their anklets, and swing their arms as they cry:

Chickery chick cha-la cha-la,
Bollika wollika inna bananika

whatever that means, as if it's magic, and are so excited by saying it their faces, dotted with pimples, turn red from their eyes to the roots of their hair. Everybody is standing at the end of the game, so I'm unable to see, but Dad's team wins. They take third place. At the hotel, nobody can sleep—people are running in the halls—and then at last the lights in our room go out. Mom and Dad undress in the dark and get into bed. I was asleep, wasn't I?

He says, "I wanted so bad for them to win first."

"Oh, Martin."

Slats of light from the venetian blinds lie over the side of their covers like cooler edges of the radiator at my back. "That technical foul against me in the second game did it."

"Our boys were simply too inexperienced."

"The foul, you know, goes down in the state records."

"Oh, please. It only shows how much you wanted them to win."

"For their sake, yes. For me it doesn't matter. I've come farther than I ever expected. I have nothing higher to attain to."

"Oh, stop being false-modest."

"I'm not."

"Then subservient, or whatever. It doesn't become a resourceful, strong, clever man like you."

"I should be the one my children look up to. I've let that slip."

"Only when you were selling that awful insurance."

"It was good for the people who bought it, for the price. I still believe that. Their families are protected."

"But it wasn't a job for somebody with your gifts. Just see!"

"Please."

"Who's still young yet, and has just gotten a little out of shape. *Look at me.* You're not even thirty-five, dear."

"It's only this week that I've felt I'm no longer a child leading children."

"Bask in your reflected glory."

"Don't be facetious."

"That's the most distant thought from me. Those boys think so much of you, they'd give up their lives if they had to."

"I've never known a better bunch. The whole male high-school population, literally, all seven of it, when you count little Alf, the freshman, as a whole and not a half."

"I'm so glad you got him into the last minutes of the game. He's set up for life, to hear him talk."

"Well, this is my zenith."

"Oh, stop. You certainly—"

"No, now, listen. I've come to think a bit less of my supposed talents this year, especially after that foul. No, I think this is important. I have more than I ever hoped for—besides you and the children. The Lord knows I'm content. This is it."

There is movement of the covers, clothes sliding, and she says, "Well, I still don't know what we're going to do about—" A fuller wash of sheets, as though she has risen in bed toward me, and her next words, though barely whispered, strike at my back like spears. "That one." She drops back down. "I don't know what possesses him at times. Here we thought we could keep an extra-close eye on him, having him along, and it turns out that he's even more unpredictable away from Jerome."

I fall asleep. We all must, because she is saying, "Come on, now. You've been resting for over an hour, and that looks like your dad."

I sit up with a sun headache, my hair damp from sweat, and see Dad's white shirt down the road, glowing against the green fields and bannering and weaving like a flag through heat waves.

"Look at that!" Jerome says. He has gone a few steps up the lane and is pointing to something above. I walk up beside him and see a car the same age as ours, facing away, its hood jackknifed up. It rests over flattened tires, on rusted rims, with furrows leading to the place where it sits. Tim joins us and we tiptoe to it as if it might wake. The grass all around it, or what's left of the grass, is low and clumped in brownish bunches, as though scorched by fire. The car's paint is nearly gone and rust furs the dents and scrapes in it. The scorched ground has erupted with anthills, and ants are wavering over its hull in chains of patterns like hurried handwriting gone wrong.

Mom comes up carrying Susan, with Marie gripping her dress again, and the car diminishes under her height. We move closer. The top of the steering wheel is bent down to the dash and sausage-like chips cling to each side of the bend. The webwork of the windshield is finest where three bulges protrude, and there are rusty lines imbedded in the near bulge—stains down the crumpled dashboard, flaking continents over the seats. Half of the front seat is shoved ahead, and a greasy flattened glove lies on the floor behind it; a crescent wrench beside that, spattered with brown drops. A torn grocery bag has spilled bars of honey-colored, homemade soap, and pieces of the bars lie crushed on the floor, among a scattering of pennies I would never touch, and a torn rag doll shedding its stuffing of nylon stockings.

"Get away from there!" she whispers. "Don't go near it! God! Dear Lord Jesus, what a— Oh, but for your grace!"

Her tortured eyes go to each of us, as if measuring us against the car and herself at the height of the hilltop. And then she draws up into the center of herself, from the way her shoulders rise and her head goes back in her dramatic stance, her neck broadening and the cords in her throat showing white as if she's about to sing, with tears like rivers of water holding reflections of the sky over her face, and wails in her hollow voice, "An entire family of living souls must have perished here!"

JULY 3. *I have to get this down while I have a chance. I woke late, drugged from the heat, with a feeling that my tongue was stitched to the roof of my mouth—a pain behind an eye like an open hinge. There was a smelly sheen of the building on my skin, my clothes over it like molasses. I thought I heard a fluttery knocking at the door, then a telephone ringing down the hall. A telephone here? An alarm?*

I got my soap and towel and opened the door. The new neighbor stood there, backing away in a hunched feinting, as if I had caught him at the keyhole. Veins pulsed in his forehead as he gestured in spidery jerks with a beer can, spilling out a curve of foam that hit the floor with a flop. He grinned and sucked at the can, then held it up. "Wan some?" His eyes were glazed and so direct they looked lidless (there is a scar under the left one), staring past me as the skin of his face twitched with his hangdog grin. His teeth chattered in an attempt to explain something, but all I could make out was "Puerto Rico."

"Fahgive!" he said, which I took as an embarrassed apology for his use of the language. Then I realized he was asking me into his room for a beer. He is new in the city; his language is terribly broken. I threw my stuff in the sink and followed him (thin neck; bony shoulders under one of those shiny sweater-shirts with metallic threads in it) into a room half the size of mine—like a corridor with a door at this end and a window at the other. He has moved his cot to the far

side, which is why I haven't heard thudding knees, if that still goes on. The shade was down. One of those half tables that usually stand against a wall was under the window, and a six-pack sat on it in gold light. Three or four cans were open, with triangles of foam wilting above their tops. The place is so full of the electronic equipment I had heard about from the maid there was no room to turn. He put a heated hand on my shoulder and levered me down on the cot, then held out the hand for me to shake—damp as cheese, difficult not to react to—and when I started to let go, he gave a sudden grip. He kept shaking hands with such a glazed and dreamy, direct look I wanted to yell, "You've got the wrong guy!"

"Raul," he said. "Can you thay?" When I did, he said, "Think it's funny?" He dropped my hand in a move that sent out the first warnings to me. I said of course not.

"Better not, mahn," he said, and sat next to me. He handed me an opened beer, which was as hot as the room and flat, day-old—burp or gag. I burped and tried to get it down fast, so I could leave, and barely heard what he was saying—did I want a radio, as I took it. I said I didn't have any money, to cover myself, in case everything was hot.

"No, mahn, listen at a radio!" he cried, and with his sudden anger the equipment looked haloed. He turned the volume of a tiny whispering radio at the head of his bed up to a blare; a Spanish pop station. Entertaining me, I assessed—a cheap shot. Then he started saying his name over and over, which is what I want to get to: Raul Vega. He made great emphasis of this and tapped his fingernails, long and blue-rimmed, under his throat. The din of the radio pressed more of the glaze into his eyes. They looked purple now. He asked me if I liked him, and right away asked if I liked this place, and then said that he didn't; he said he had only been in the country a year and wanted to go back to Puerto Rico, but the cops wouldn't let him. He asked if I spoke Spanish.

I said, "A little," and he went into a tirade in the Puerto Rican I can barely understand under the best conditions. His yellow face— the scar on its left has the curved, jagged look of half a bottle cap— stayed stiff as a dead man's, and only his eyes remained alive, as if wired to the inner sense that keeps jerking his limbs around, but there were sudden levels of expression in him that convinced me a genius was trying to speak. He was explaining something similar to my sense

*of the smell in the building, but taking it further; everybody
unfamiliar was the enemy. He put a heated hand on my shoulder, and
I said that I didn't understand Spanish (I found the textbook phrases
for this) as well as he understood English—not to mention how he
spoke it. This seemed to please rather than anger him, as I was at first
afraid it might, and then he said something about a park I couldn't
catch, and more concerning the <u>policía</u> I had heard about in his
tirade. Now his theme was "Inna park."*

*"That one?" I started to swing my can toward Tompkins Square
and stopped at his look.*

*"No, odder." His hand came down on my leg. "I don't like
somebody don't like me. You like me?"*

"Sure."

"You know Tony?"

"The super? Sure."

"You like?"

"Sure."

"Wha you do."

"What?"

"<u>Whacha</u> do?"

"Sleep."

He smiled a foxy queer's grin. "No. Inna city."

"Look it over. I'm looking for work."

"You like marijuana?"

*"Oh . . ." I couldn't see him getting higher than he was. He
stared at the sighing radio so long the music seemed to penetrate
him—skullbone sympathy; I felt sorry for him. I had finished the beer.*

"Bahsteed inna park say, 'Get home, runt!' "

He is my height, 5'6", about 110; I asked if he meant a cop.

*"Some mahder homper. He fren, too— <u>My</u> fren. You see down
by bottom at the steps?"*

*None of this, I see, conveys the way he talks; I doubt if all of his
tape recorders could, without his looks and gestures, but it's necessary
to convey some sense of it, so there is no doubt that this is the man. I
asked him what he meant.*

"Hey, mahn, I shoo dis black mahder homper."

"You shot him?"

*"Hey, look." He reached from the cot to his equipment-laden
dresser, pulled open a drawer, dug in a tangle of clothes, and came*

up with a nickel-plated pistol, squared like a miniature .45, with white plastic grips, and slapped it into my hand. I pretended to examine it through a crystalline terror that silenced the radio. He asked if I liked it and I think I shrugged; there were tears in my eyes. He said to watch it, because there were "bullets in him"—the pistol, which I'm sure is a .22. "I shoo dis black mahder homper wis him."

"In the park?" This came out in a croak; my fingerprints were on the thing. "Down by bottom at the steps," he said, and indeed, about a week ago I saw what looked like caked blood on the barbershop tile of the vestibule, smears on the panes of the door and the ceramic walls, which seemed to bear new nicks, and maybe even some drops in the direction of the steps, but I had thought: No, it can't be . . . Then Tony and his sly-comic sidekick repainted the vestibule green, tiles and all.

Here Raul went into the important speech: "He say, 'Go home, Puerto Rico, wetback runt.' I say, 'Shut up, I hurt you bad.' He say, 'You inna park, I cut you heart out.' Two big guys wis him inna park. They say, 'Beat your ass!' Boy, I'm get mad. Odder day, he's inna park. He say, 'I tought I say I cut you heart out, runt.' He come after me. I run back. Big homper run fast. He's cotches me atta door. See." He pulled down the neck of his shiny shirt and bent his chin toward a greenish cut across his chest, above the nipples. "I say, 'Leave me go! Leave me go! I hurt you bad!' He say, 'Hurt me? Oh, baby, baby, baby,' he say, 'I hurt you. I break your back.' He got his knife. See?" He showed me the green cut again. "I take this," he said, and grabbed the pistol from me. "I shoo him, bang, bang, bang!—six times inna guts. He cryin like a baby. I run tell Tony. He say, 'Get inna room!' I come up and amblunce take him black mahder homper off. Still cryin like a baby."

"Still alive?" I was shaking. He said it was good he didn't have this, and tossed the .22 in the drawer and dug out a stiff sock and pulled a chunky revolver out of it—a service .38. If I could have been sure it wasn't loaded, I might have gone for the other. It was loaded. He broke it open and started picking at the cartridges with his blue-rimmed nails, swinging the barrel past my face, which sent a wallop through me that dimmed the room, and then colors reappeared with such clarity I felt as I do when light is reflected off dusty car chrome, that I would sneeze and set him off. He banged the gun butt on the table, the shade swung in, and the room belled around us in a broad expanse. A voice was nattering on the radio in Spanish, and then a translation came, flooded with static: *People aren't basically good; they're the opposite.*

Then he remembered to press the ejector, and had to grab in his twitchy way at showering cartridges. *I figured this was probably my last chance, and visualized a cowboy-movie scene as I went for the .22— But what then? Shoot him?* He picked up a cartridge from the cot and held it out in his palm, nearly at my nose, while I tried to keep the pistol, though broken open and empty, in view below. It was gripped between his legs, and with his other hand he was finding cartridges and poking them into the holes of its cylinder. "Tear you guts out," he said, and closed the thing with a click. He said nobody should say that to him, and his head, skinnier against the gold shade, revolved to me. He asked if I liked him. I said yes. He asked if I liked Puerto Ricans. I said yes.

He freed a hand and we shook on that, in the drawn-out cheesy way that started this, and he asked again if I wanted some marijuana.

"No," I said. "But I'll have another beer."

He stood quick and turned and then slowed, his head down, shoulders drawing in, over the table, and then he reached out, picked something up, and laid the pistol down. I was about to jump him from behind when he turned and held out a Polaroid of a honey-skinned woman, with dark hair bleached in streaks, lying on her back on a bed with a knee up, in green bikini underpants and a shiny green bra. He asked if I liked her. I believe I said "Nice," trying to avoid any leering erotic interest.

"I kill her ass. She an my fren. I shoo hor!"

I needed to get this straight, now that I was involved in it, so I said, "You shot your friend?"

"No, black mahder homper. Shoo my fren, too. I can' ever see her, can' go out, the cops— Ayy, Tony!"

He rocked back, startled, his face yellow-gray, and I eased up from the cot, seeing his eyes start into their jerky sequence, and bumped a television screen. He put his hands to his face, the pistol in one, my only real chance. Then a prod was at my stomach, giving off heat, and he pushed me out the door. "In you room," he said. "Doan tella cops."

"What do you mean?" I said. "Of course not. Hey, we're neighbors, man. Neighbors."

*This struck beams of light from him and he smiled and said,
"Hey, shake me on that."*

*So we went through that whole business again, and then I turned
my back on him and prayed, and the next thing I knew I was on my
bed, the door open. When I heard his close, I tiptoed over, shut mine,
and turned the bolt. I took a can of shaving cream from the medicine
chest, shook it, eased a trembling ball of foam into my palm, and saw
my reflection whiten over its lower half as I imagined myself in a
mustache and goatee, in another city, where I wouldn't be recognized,
now that I had heard his confession. I picked up my razor and
thought, There's the fire escape.*

A one-story drop at the bottom, a possibility.

*Then I saw my eyes bulge at his fluttery knock. I turned to the
door and imagined the splinters as bullets tore through its flimsy
wood. Hanging on to my razor, I opened the door. He was back a
ways under the dangling light bulb, which gave him a blank and
seedy look—one of his hands in a pocket. The hangdog smile started,
as though his safety was insured, as I queerly felt safe, due to the
shaving cream. I poked at it with my razor and said "Cleaning
up!"—which came out with such force his expression changed.*

*He did a wave of embarrassment with his free hand. "Smart
twat."*

*Or so I heard, as his stare caught me head on. "I wanna say I
don't like no whites or black peoples, but you, ayy!" In a couple of
tripping steps he was against me, both hands up, and there was a
dampness over my heart that set me back a year. Shaving cream
streaked his oiled hair. He was hiccupping, and tears came with
such force they flew from his face. "Anybody beat you up," he said,
looking terrible, "you tell you neighbor, okay? I blow his fakking
head off!"*

*With a backward trip, he was gone. His door banged. I shut
mine, bolted it, threw the razor in the sink, and sat on the bed. My
retreat was over, as quickly as it had begun. I was changed, that was
for sure; I wouldn't be the same after that. Getting this down has
ground that in even more. Now I have to figure out how to inform
the police, without Tony and his cohorts knowing about it, or get to
Raul before he gets to me. Whichever way it goes, these pages will
have to serve for now (and for as far into the future as anybody might
need to look at them), as evidence.*

Then I'm rocked farther back, into my center, in this chair between a table and a desk of recording equipment, in the middle of this most Midwestern of cities, and my hearing, extending outward across the silence of the early-morning hour, creates a noise like the fluorescents above, and then the motor of the furnace pump in the basement starts up its song through the arterial pipework that ends at my radiator. I page through these years-old notes, to rearrange and clarify them, and understand that there is no explanation for an event other than the event itself, in its changing impression on memory, besides what it leads to, and not even the Prince of this world himself, Satan—not that hairy chump with horns and a spearhead tail, as he would prefer we picture him, so he can be dismissed, but the genius of malevolence—nor any genius who believes that he or she has evolved beyond him, can give the indisputable explanation, without crossing the boundaries of somebody else's experience. Our memories and words and acts are linked like cells to others, so that no single version is right, and our earliest memories gather in a pattern that informs any other pattern that arrives, adding further density to the original, and that is about all we know.

But I can see the hand of God in it now. And knowing that His ways don't always coincide with mine, within the span of one lifetime, on matters that seem equitable or just or rational to me—which, put simply, are the ways I would personally prefer things to be—I accede to Him. Not to throw Him or the dust of Him, as it might be viewed, in anybody's eyes as I beat my retreat; or because I feel my time is running out, which I feel at times (with only a step between me and death, while the outward world slides down to portions of its end), or because I'm trying to justify the ways of God to anyone. I'm not. I expect to face Him soon, and given my niggardly, hoarding, henlike nature and the knowledge that I'll have to give an account for every idle word, I would rather stay silent or keep my words as unmuddily clear as I can (pasting over certain fears along the way) and still remain complete—an easy open voice improvising as it travels to its end. I want to reveal to at least one brother my side of the tapestry, to confirm any intuitions he might have about the pattern of its weave, and admit that the pattern, though it exists, isn't ours, yet remains our responsibility. If I don't say this now, from the center of myself—since I'm speaking out of so many separate corners—I'm afraid the issues might become confused.

I believe in God, the holy catholic church, the communion of saints, and I believe in *history*. The rock that supplied the Israelites with water in the wilderness, and was struck and abused even then, is the one that offends to this day. You shepherds are loathsome to Pharaoh, Joseph told his father; that's why he has put you out here. And to further the offense, Israel's tribes kept and milked goats, besides eating them and sheep—lowliest of four-footed animals—but were faithful to other dietary laws which could seem finicky, particularly when they were impoverished, since some of the foods were expensive and had to be specially prepared; and besides this, brought offerings for sacrifice, and gave away a portion of their earnings to a priest or rabbi, and tried to hold to all this, even if the world they traveled through tried to tell them they were wrong. Once you've been dismissed as a human being for your beliefs, the next worst form of prejudice, as I've experienced it, is being told you're wrong, often with a shaking finger, and prejudice, whatever form it takes, is a boot in the face. It is greed for the upper position, and it was greed that started the world toward destruction, and greed that now gnaws every good part of it down—a deadly sameness of hate awash.

I'm not as offended by the stability or instability of those who honor God or say they believe in Him—shaking humble piety, or open intellectual acceptance—as I used to be, or envious of it, or try not to be, no matter what the actual face these people or their lives present at the moment they connect with me, although there are times when, seeing some of them, I can't help but wonder, "Now, how does he even . . . Does she think that I . . . How the . . ." And that's the point where I, because of my nature, have to put on the brakes. I have a clearer idea, after the last few years, of the paths that he or she has had to walk, fighting scorn or the amusement of friends, to contain such a commitment, while ordering every aspect of existence every day thereafter, from the moment he or she wakes, until sleep ends a day, until the last day ends. We don't all lead lives that leave others blind by their lyrical blaze.

I've received some pictures of what the end must be like, which I hope to display, although I realize that such an end could be partly like the moments I'm often caught in, when I wake wondering which room it is I've awakened in, with a disjointed incomplete task to straighten out for the final time, before the fire consumes it all, or the executioner knocks, this time with deputies carrying shackles—each minute lengthening into what I imagine, indeed, eternity could be. Then this same sense turns the tables on me, and in a blinding imagistic rush, time picks up so fast that paper shifts into other stacks on top of the note I was looking for, and the room ages down past different shades of paint and patterns of wallpaper, each level growing colder, before I can pick up the only pencil stub left in order to scratch the necessary phrase down on that note I was looking for, fixing it for good this time—while the one voice inside me among the many I hear that I listen to keeps saying, over and over, even at the mere thought of the slightest movement of my hand, No, No, No, No, No! until the room and time I'm in turn so dim I feel murdered.

And so I pray it will soon be the hour when I'll hear her footsteps climbing the stairs in my direction, so I can leave.

DEATH:
HISTORY

"Here," Davey says, and picks up a stick. "I'll show you how he writes his signature. First he makes his beginning C, a fat one, like so, with your J joined up to it, then from there up to your second C, same way, just about, then he goes right on up and fixes this little gizmo on the capital N here, then writes you out the rest of Neumiller this way, big and slow, and then he goes back and puts your periods here and here and here, after the initials. Well, that's about her, for his signature, and she ain't no cottonpickin easy one, I tell you!"

We study the scratchy furrows in the dirt, next to the yellow sign on a metal post that reads STOP, and the leaves of the trees that line the streets in this part of town stir with a breeze that carries heat from the humid country fields, so that the gouged dirt appears to steam beside the blacktop. Jerome and I look up at Davey, who's smiling at us, and a clattering travels through the leaves above and spreads for blocks. I step back for balance and see that the sidewalk behind Davey's legs, with squares of concrete tipped up at different angles by trees, leads in a narrowing band past a grocery store, *Kleinerud's*, whose swinging sign sways in the wind; an alley past that, then the sidewalk humped up in a climb beside a tin-covered building that reaches all the way to the next crossroad, Main Street; across its heat-wavering bulge, a gray woven-wire fence borders both sides of the railroad tracks that run down the center of the parted street; and then the blacktop climbing up the hill beyond, until it's overhung by agitated leaves.

Pettibone, Illinois. Grandma and Grandpa live in Forest Creek, five miles off, and we're staying in their basement, until the rest of their house is finished off, or Dad finds us a place. Davey is showing us the way from the Pettibone grade school to our Aunt Rose Marie's; she lives in Pettibone and Pettibone is the town where we'll live, too, so everybody hopes. Nothing is for certain yet (not like this signature, even secondhand, on the ground in front of us), except that we're here.

+

Jerome and I lie on our bellies on the cement of the new basement, with our faces over the sump-pump hole. It's coolest here. We've never lived like this, in the excited uncertainty of nothing decided, and we've felt that we're on a mission, or lying low, ever since we arrived and Davey draped us with War Surplus equipment. The house rises two stories above us, with the piney smell of Grandpa in every room. He stands with his fists at his belt (a leather loop holding a silver Caterpillar draped from his watch pocket), and stares down at us and smiles, his face set into wrinkled thinness, so that he looks the same age as Dad, and says, "Come with me, boys." Sometimes he takes us in his panel truck to another town where a house is being built, or to a field where a corn crib is going up, but now he motions us into his office.

It's in a corner of the basement, the coolest place besides the sump hole, and if Grandma's not around, he hands us sheets of drafting paper ("The cost, Charles!" she says to him, surprising me with the name that's also mine) to draw our plans on. He lets us pound away on his adding machine, study the nickel-plated pistol with rust spots on it in his desk drawer, a real one. "My dad's," he says, and takes down a leather-covered book about North Dakota, which he says is from the attic of our house in Hyatt, and shows us a paragraph about his father. "You see, Dad was one of the early homesteaders, before North

Dakota was a state." He stares at the book in his lap for a while, as if he'll say more, and then stands to put it away, setting the silver Caterpillar on its leather loop swinging like the pendulum of a speeded-up clock.

"I oversaw the building of shipping crates for the big Cats during the war," he says. "That was in Peoria, after we moved from up north."

He takes us back behind the furnace, near the sump hole, and reaches up to tap—

"Did you ever drive one?"

"What?"

"A Caterpillar, Grandpa."

"Oh, yes. Many times. Nearly every day, then."

"Boy!"

He reaches up to tap a wrinkled certificate in a frame fastened to a set of shelves. "But this means more to me." *Master Boilermaker and Steamfitter*, the certificate reads. "This is the only education beyond high school I got. There was hardly a chance to use it. The switch then was to gasoline. I expect both of you to go through college, like your dad, so you won't have to think about such things."

The shelves are lined with jars of canned fruit and vegetables from their country house in Lishout, where we used to visit in the summers. There are only five houses in Lishout—our Uncle Scott and Aunt Elaine still live in one—with sand roads and sandbanks and sand drifts everywhere, as if sand falls instead of snow, and there's a wooden bench under a roof along the railroad tracks, with a red flag you can stick up on a pole to stop the train. Last summer we took a train to Pettibone, to a carnival set up on Main Street, and the Ferris wheel churned us up past the woven-wire fence toward the sky to the height of the water tower, where we could overlook the black roofs along Main Street, and then stopped, the rocking seat swaying as if to tip us out, and we saw the leafy streets like green borders around the blocks of houses, with a green triangle, a park, at the center of it all, then dropped to the street and climbed up past the water tower again.

Grandpa leans back in his swivel chair on wheels and pushes

up the bill of his basketweave cap, then rests his elbows on the arms of the chair. "Well, boys, it's Saturday. This is my day in the office. Do you want to help with the book work?"

"Oh, yes! What do we do?"

He turns to the desk and hands us pads with his name, phone number, and *Complete Building Service* on them, and gives us newly sharpened pencils stamped with the same information. Then he pushes his hands into the pockets of his suntans and crosses his stretched-out legs at the ankles, a cat in the sun. "First you make out the bills," he says. "Then you make out the receipts."

He lights a Kool cigarette with a lighter that kicks out sparks, and we sit on the cot where Davey sleeps at night, and start writing.

"Or that's the way it should be," he adds. "Then you make out the wages. Then you pay the bills, if there's anything left."

Mr. Man, Jerome writes. *One barn. $50*

Mr. B, I write. *One house. $50*

As Grandpa fidgets at the desk with his own pencil, he smokes more Kools and the room grows blue with an oily smell; I breathe it in and the paper I'm working on develops extra edges that phosphorescent worms weave up through, and then they travel into me and coil inside my stomach. Our Uncle Tom walks in, his face dark below curly hair like Dad's, when Dad was younger, his shirt unbuttoned over his stomach and its tails hanging down, taller through my daze, and gives Jerome and me such a scouring look we put the pads and pencils away.

"I came to talk to you, Dad," Tom says.

"Here I am."

"Yeah, but— Okay, I don't want to work for you anymore. The hours are too doggone long, I never know what time of day we're going to quit, or if I'll have time to go out that night. I'm *dagg*one fed up with it! Plus a few other things around here." He flashes his look on us again.

"Stay, boys. Now, Tom, I don't believe I've ever forced you to work for me. Then again, I might not have had the politeness to ask if you wanted to. If you don't want to, I won't be happy, either, until you find a job you like. Now, I know several people in different situations. Is there anybody you'd like me to get in touch with?"

"I've already decided," Tom says. "I want to be a phone man."

"A phone man?" Grandpa asks.

"It's a clean corporation job, with regular hours and a dang good chance for advancement. I've already talked to Lazy J.B. about it."

"Oh, a *phone* man," Grandpa says, and we follow his look to the wooden wall phone beside the door. "Well, why shouldn't you be?" He stares at it with a finger to his cheek, and murmurs, "Telephone."

And at that moment, as if at his word, it starts to ring.

+

We've never seen so many trees. One has been downed in Grandpa's front yard by the electric company—"A big old boondoggely box elder," Davey says, "deader'n a doornail." The limbs have been sawed off and Davey jumps among them, planning a bunker against the Japs.

"Them little suckers go in for those sneak attacks," he says. "So we got to be able to view the whole circumference of our position from one machine-gun nest. But first we'll put us a machine gun in that big tree out back, so we can cover any action from the south there."

All directions confuse us, without Hawk's Nest, and Davey is older, in high school now, although he's only thirteen. But he understands us—a prodigy, Dad calls him, and that chunky uneasy word is like the blankness behind Davey's eyes when he talks, as if he's moving away from us, as he does now, stepping up on the tree trunk with an ax from Grandpa's shop. "Stand back, Scouts," he says. "That's rule number one in the old manual about the ax." He's wearing khaki shorts, with a felt scapular medal, curled from his sweat, resting higher than the silver one whose chain leaves mustardy streaks along his neck. "I wish I had me a Mohawk," he says, and runs a hand through his hair and sends droplets of sweat bright as the chain flying past the sun. "Then, besides bein cool, I'd be your number-one

Indian lumberjack, no jagging around." He lets the ax slip through his hands to laugh at this, and then his knees give and he sits. "Dammit to hell," he whispers. "I think I just cut off my big toe." A reddish shine slides down the tree bark. "No," he says, "one toe to the good. But, holy balls, does it hurt! And it's pumpin! I hit me an artery! Do either of you guys got a handkerchief?"

Jerome, who's the color of the one he's jerked out, says, "This? Maybe Mom or Grandma will get mad if it's all bloody."

"Hoo!" Davey says. "I got to get me a tourniquet on this. Arterial bleeding!" He wraps the handkerchief above his ankle, and twists its corners with a twig.

"I'll go get Grandma!" Jerome cries.

"Now, just a cottonpickin minute here. I'm not supposed to use Dad's ax, and you know how Grandma can get when she's upset. Let me think this through." He looks toward the highway, turning green under his tan, and then there's an engine sound and the chuckling of gravel as a truck pulls into the other end of the drive.

"Uh-oh," I say. "It's Grandpa."

"Maybe that's the answer," Davey says. "Run and get him."

+

We've never seen Grandpa angry, and we ask Dad if he ever was.

"Huh?" he says. "Oh, Dad. That? Oh, not really."

It's confusing to have all these dads, which most of our uncles also are, and our dad is walking around with a cane; he's hurt a knee, laying tile, but could still join the Army; we saw in the newspaper that he can sign up until he's thirty-six, which is his age now, and we hope he does.

The lot the house sits on is scrub grass and sand, and the front lawn is being terraced, Grandpa says; heat shimmies up from the baking dirt that was dug out for the basement and from black dirt hauled in, and the stepped terraces are perfect for rolling down, if we keep an eye out for prickly pears. Near the house is a Ferris wheel Grandpa built of wood lath, with swinging seats made of juice cans sawed in half and filled with dirt and flowers, which I want to set spinning like the one we rode last summer, but figure Grandma will call out the door about her flowers being ruined, as she did once. On the lowest terrace Grandpa is building an arch of wood lath, a trellis, over the dug-away strip where the front sidewalk will be poured, when the rest of the cement work is ready.

"Come on, boys, let's paint my trellis," he says, and for a whole afternoon we stand beside our Uncle Fred as he works in his white overalls on a paint sprayer hooked behind the Jeep—a real Army Jeep that Davey sometimes gets to drive toward Lishout, to haul the garbage to a dump, and purposely gets stuck in a field or a sandy ditch, so he can shift into four-wheel drive and show us how combat soldiers plow their way through. Finally Grandpa gives Jerome and me paintbrushes and the three of us paint the trellis that day and the next, climbing to the top of the tallest stepladder Grandpa can find, and use up three gallons of white paint—"A horrible cost for such a thing!" Mom whispers to us from the stove in the basement, where she and Grandma cook for the eleven of us, including Davey and Tom, until the kitchen upstairs is finished, and her whisper catches at the binding spots of paint pinching the hair on my arms: "And hardly a job for kids!" But we begged to, and then helped dig holes around the columns of the arch to fill with mulch for Grandma's roses, such an easy job with Grandpa, here where everybody is busy.

Fred rises from the sprayer where he's been working, without even a T-shirt under his overalls—the suspenders a blur across his red-black shoulders—and says past the cigar in a corner of his mouth, "I finally got the blame thing running right, Dad, and ain't she a doozie, ay?"

He lifts a hose with a nozzle on it and a cloud of white spray drifts toward the sand road at the front of the lawn. Past it, railroad tracks rise on a bed of crushed rock, blazing under the sun in streaks that cause us to blink—too hot to step on. Beyond them a vacant lot of weeds, with a clump of osage-orange trees at its edge (I once walked into the trees' smelly shade, and at the sight of the hedge apples, like rubbery green angleworms clustered in balls, I felt I might understand why we moved, but then Jerome called), is like a battlefield to cross. The lot is so thick with sandburrs we had to forge a trail through it with the Army equipment to the state highway, where more trucks slither past in one day than all we ever saw in Hyatt. Across the sticky blacktop is Ferlin's Phillips 66. We go to Ferlin's on K-ration runs, as Davey calls them, for ice cream from the chrome-covered case with fat black doors in its top, or soda from a red case where bottles sit up to their necks in swirling water with a mineral smell and a motor sings in continual service as the case sweats over the concrete—"like a jigaboo stuck in the worst part of Purgatory from his tonsils up," Davey says.

"What do you mean, 'jigaboo,' Uncle Davey?"

"I mean a big ole black one with a wattymelon mouth."

"What's that?"

"Hoo-whee! We're goin to have to get us to Peoria real quick-like for a view. What kind of place you guys come from, anyway, the sticks?"

He holds his arms across our chests at the highway's edge, and a Standard Oil truck goes by in a red-white rush.

+

Night in the basement. Jerome and I sleep on the floor, and Mom and Dad behind a curtain on a foldout couch, the rest of the kids with them. All the sounds of sleeping, instead of sending me under, keep me up; I'm used to matching my breathing to Jerome's. Mom whispers "No!" Then, "I can't understand why the men here can't come straight out and cuss."

"Ha." Dad's voice, as small as hers. "You ought to hear Scott."

"I mean your brothers."

"You know very well that to them it's a sin."

I see my hand on the sheet, a striped paw: my sinful use of it.

"But the intent is there," she whispers. "From the other words they use. It's the same as. Euphemism. If they came right out with it, maybe they'd get things off their chest."

"I'm sorry you've—" A shifting draws this away from me.

"And, oh, this language." This is Mom, faint, hardly there. "This manner of talking like Okies out of Steinbeck. Worse." Fainter still. "It strikes at me like sharp, sharp swords."

The bathroom on the second floor is finally finished enough to use, and Jerome and I have our first Saturday bath in a real tub, where cold and hot water, both, thunder out of one faucet when you turn wheels on the wall. It's so hot out, you wouldn't think it could be hotter, but the room steams. The medicine-chest mirror, with an X of tape on it, fogs over and drips, and we have to breathe in shallow gasps. I soap Jerome's back and he soaps mine, butt between the other's knees, then we slide to different ends of the tub, reversing, to rinse them, waves bucking up, and then soap the sides of the tub and slide around in circles simply to slide, laughing—no hands of hers at us here.

"Don't slop that water out," Davey says from the other side of the door. "The tile and rubber coving ain't down yet, and water'll run through the underlayment and screw up the sheet-rock down in Grandma and Grandpa's bedroom under you, hey! Ain't you about done in there?"

"Just about."

"Balls afire, you're about as slow as a jigaboo in winter honey. It takes me about two minutes in a dang tub. You stand up and soap you all over, and then you sit down and stand up again, and that's it. I'm gettin antsy to get off to that movie show. It starts as soon as it's dark out. I'm going to strip down to my birthday suit, the old bohanger danglin, and if you two ain't done by then, why, I'm gonna come in there and sit on you! Wouldn't that frost your nugents? I weigh a hundred forty-eight pounds now, guys, and that ain't no wattymelon under my belt. That's me!" We hear him slap his stomach. "I *pee* in the tub."

His footsteps flap away. "All I'm gonna be wearin is the Indian moccasins I made out of that craft kit! And I'm only wearin them in case you guys got athlete's foot with that sticky toe jam! Like I do!"

There are twists and shifts to his voice, as if he is undressing, and then the suds widen away and the white tub shines, framing the two of us, and I stand with water falling from me, and think: This is it. I get out in a hurry, hoping Jerome will, too, wrap up in a towel, and step out the door as he says, "Hey, what the . . ."

I tiptoe into a room across the hall, too dark to see in, if sunlight didn't fan in a burning line along a sheet of plywood nailed over the window (only until the right shipment of sashes is in, Grandpa says), and go past the high bed with mattresses at the level of my eyes, stepping over sheetrock and wood scraps to a sewing machine—ours?—with *Singer* printed in the middle of its treadle. Grandma says that Jerome and Tim and I might sleep here soon, so yesterday I climbed up on the bed, higher than a hospital bed, and sank back to the place I came from— or might, I felt, if I ever slept here. Now Davey steps out into the hall toward the bathroom.

"Somebody's *hi*-ding," he says, and sticks his head in the doorway, then steps into the room, naked except for the medal around his neck and the moccasins he's mentioned. He looks taller and darker here, and is so white where his khaki shorts usually ride that I see him in three pieces, divided, and can't keep my eyes from the center: a fringe of hair above a purple-headed lump. "I saw your footprints, chum," he says. "You can't fool the fella who's read the ole Boy Scout manual three times, no siree, Bob! You want to turn my crank for more solid information?" He bucks below his big belly and sends it flopping.

"Hey, maybe that's pretty rough stuff for a youngun like you, huh?" His large eyes begin a search of me, as if he has to pick his way through the blankness in them in order to talk as he feels he should to somebody my age. "My ole mind really forgets sometimes. Well, it won't be long now before you guys can be sleeping here. Were you checkin the room out? We want to make this place of ours as much you guys's as we can. Do you like it? Hey, should I go in there an sit on big brother Jay?"

His eyes are so wide he looks afraid. He backs out and I hear him bang the bathroom door. "Hey, big Jay, I'm comin in to wash the oil and grimy black lines out of the big fat folds in this neck of mine, where I sweat the worst, ready or not!"

There's a louder sloshing and then a cascade of water that settles into points of regular dripping.

And then it comes. "Hey!" Davey says, in a voice that climbs into Grandma's surprise. "Goodness, golly, Jay, you got a Coke-bottle cock!"

+

On the way to the movie, we see a large boy, with a burr cut and a big neck, kneeling next to the road in the twilight shade of a tree, pushing a toy Jeep around on roads he has built as he produces the watery sputtering noises that power a car. "Yo, Davey," he says, and shows big teeth; in the shadow of the tree his skin is black-brown.

"Yo, Leroy. Ain't you gettin a little old for that? You're these guys's age, at the least."

"Who're they?"

"My nephews, bud."

"I didn't know you was married, Davey, tee hee." He gets the sputtering motor going again and a tongue the color of raspberries appears.

I jerk on Davey's arm, to get him to follow me. "I know, I know," he says, "I'm anxious to get to Lunby's too and get us something to eat."

"No," I say, and pull him down, and whisper, "Is he a jigaboo?"

"Leroy?" he whispers. "Naw, he's a regular kid."

"How come he's so dark?"

"Suntan. You'd look like him, too, if you spent all your time in Illinois outdoors."

"You don't look like that."

"Well, I ain't lived here all my life and I don't tan so good. And I spend too much time piddley-dinking around in that gol-blame house, or tryin to find a place where it's cool, so my creative brain can chug along at top speed. Just that machine gun I'm trying to figure out for us would take a scientist!" He looks over to where Jerome stands above Leroy, then whispers, "Well, now, maybe Leroy ain't absolutely normal. Maybe that's what big Jay's trying to figure out. Leroy's a little shy in the brain department, since his parents been divorced. Dee-vorced."

"What's that?"

His eyes enlarge. "Why, it's about the dirtiest kind of sin you can think of. They severed the marriage sacrament."

"What do you mean?"

"I'd draw a picture for you if it wouldn't get me picked up. It means adultery, which is the dirtiest sin of all."

"You mean what old people do in bed?"

"And in a car and in the back yard and on a seesaw. Cripes! Anything else?" His eyes widen as in the bedroom. "Hey, let's get big Jay and go get us something to garbage up on before the movie show, huh?"

+

There's a barricade across the end of Main Street, behind a movie screen like a bed sheet, and another barricade at the other end of the block, where cars turn and go around the business buildings while people walk down the darkening street carrying camp stools and pillows and kitchen chairs. We sit on the blacktop close to the screen, and with an electrical crackling it lights up and an amplified voice echoes between the buildings, speaking words that suddenly appear in print across it: "This evening's entertainment is brought to you compliments of the following local merchants . . . J. B. Lacey."

"Lazy B.J.," Davey whispers, and a man appears walking above us behind a machine like a lawn mower that throws dirt back over his shoes. The handles of the machine jar up and down and then he presses his weight on them and runs around in a half circle, turning the thing in the other direction, and does a skip to catch up.

". . . complete rototilling service. For your garden, your lawn, and those of you starting Christmas-tree farms." The handles of the machine jounce again and Lacey lifts his hands from them and lets it run alone out of the picture as he pulls off his cap and bows. "Your local sales representative for Rototiller, the remarkable, all-purpose lawn-and-garden machine. Phone 94 J."

"Lud Lunby & Son . . ." The colored beams with insects spiraling through them change into a black-and-white picture of the two men in front of their store across the street, in white aprons, with their arms crossed, and I look over and see them, in the dimness, standing the same way. ". . . your local wholesale and retail grocers."

"And tight as a spider's bung," Davey whispers, shaking the box of popcorn he's bought there. "Half old maids."

"Ferlin Johnson's Phillips 66 . . ."

Wearing sunglasses and a visored cap and bow tie, Ferlin steps out the door under the canopy sheltering his pumps and walks with the jerkiness of an old-time movie clown, his usual walk, to a gas pump, sticks its hose in a car, and stands with a hand in one pocket and his head cocked as if whistling, tapping a foot. "Your local Phillips 66 dealer and distributor. Oil changed, lube jobs, and minor auto repairs."

"*Real* minor," Davey says.

"Bud Wumkes . . ." The Standard Oil truck rushes past and is seen from Ferlin's, growing smaller down the street where we now sit, so that I duck, and then the camera swings past the circular grain elevators to a machine shed beside big bulk tanks printed with *Standard Oil.* Enough of the vacant lot, with its osage-orange grove, appears for me to see an empty rise where Grandma and Grandpa's house now stands, and I'm so lost I miss the next words, and then Grandpa is on the screen, gigantic, ballooning until I can't take him in, floating in silent strides toward us in the walk that seems so slow unless you try to keep up with it—moving through a countryside greener than any I've seen in Illinois, and in the blur of his passing I'm heart-struck for home, and then he steps up to a framed-in house, like a harp against the green, and rests his hand on a two-by-four. His face turns up as if he has struck a chord, then he sits on the sill of a framed-in door, pushes up his basketweave cap, looking younger than Dad, and reaches in his shirt pocket and pulls out his cigarettes, puts one between his lips and takes out his lighter, then dives his face toward his cupped hands, the smoke rising in a flat cloud through the house and above the open rafters as the camera draws back and he stares down at a carpenter's rule he folds and unfolds in his lap.

All I hear is the telephone number I know.

+

A black car, with its trunk curved toward the bumper like a turtle's shell, pulls into the crackling drive. Tom goes to the passenger window and all of us hop up on the running board around him. The driver reaches over and a slice of bluish window comes reeling down. J. B. Lacey. "Hey, Thomas," he calls, "are you ready to climb some poles?"

"Can we ride along with you?" Davey asks.

"Sure!" Lacey says, and we rush for the back doors as Tom gets in and kicks the floorboard.

In the back seat, I take hold of Davey and whisper, "I thought he was the Rototiller man." Davey closes his eyes. "I'm about pooped by these questions," he says. "He is. True. He's also the phone man. The switchboard's in his living room. Now are you satisfied? Shhh."

We go down sand roads toward Lishout and across a half-moon bridge of steel whose heavy planking thunders over a tea-colored creek, then through leaf shadow flickering coolly as a refrigerator, and pull off to the side of the road. "Here're some that don't look so bunged up," Lacey says. "You got to watch it so one of those big splinters doesn't sever your manhood. Come ahead, Thomas, I'll show you how to put the spikes on." He reaches back, a skinny man with silver stubble and a beaked cap like the one he wore in the movie, and Davey hands him a pair of leather braces with shiny steel points on them.

We get out in a blasted area as close to a baking desert as I'd care to be, not far from Grandma and Grandpa's old house. Over summer vacations we used to play War here with our cousins, Tommy and Carl, and the idea of this fills me with the loss I felt at the movie. Gray-yellow sand rises in mounds and hills to a rocky roadbed where tracks shine with a brightness that can burn and telephone poles bend and unbend in a mirage.

Jerome and Davey start for the bridge, where we used to fish, and I sit on the running board in the sun, sick to my stomach—erased blank. Jerome's feet come up, powdered by dusty sand, and remain in my shadow. "Are you all right?" he asks, and sits on the running board beside me.

"Ah, hell, you guys," Davey says. "Why don't we have us some fun—go skinny-dipping or gig us some frogs with a stick, or *something*. How come everybody's acting like this lately, like nerds?" He opens the back door and we follow him in; he folds his arms, leans his head on the seat, closes his eyes, and says, "Well, it's cool in here."

There's a billowing cry. We scoot over to the other window, bumping one another to see out, and then Davey pops open the door, and calls in the direction of the men, *"What?"*

Davey runs over the sand toward the railroad tracks where Tom holds Lacey, who is bent over, gripping a leg—all of them wavering and magnified by the ripples of heat. Tom and Davey support Lacey, one on each side, and as they come closer he groans, "Jesus, oh, Jesus me, it hurts." Their heavy breathing and panting enter the car and drive into me *I've caused this.* The driver's door opens and Lacey says, "Sit me down a minute, boys, till I catch my wind." He sinks to the running board where I sat, and I look over the seat and see a rip in his overalls, next to the brace, with a black stain widening from it.

"I'm losing a lotta blood," he says.

"Do you want me to apply a tourniquet?" Davey asks.

"Try."

Tom turns aside with a look of disgust as Jerome hands Davey his handkerchief; Davey has a stick. "You'll have to loosen this every three minutes," Davey says. He bends over Lacey, then Tom bends with him, and something tumbles to the floor of the back seat—the brace, its leather straps caked with blood.

"What happened?" Davey asks.

"I got a little fancy," Lacey says. "I hopped down from too high up and caught myself with the spike when I hit. That muscle'd be torn down to my ankle, the way it hurts. You'll have to drive us, Thomas. I can't clutch with this thing bleeding and bunged up the way it is."

+

Davey tapes two sheets of drafting paper end to end, cuts a neck hole at their hinge, and trims the corners of each sheet round. The three of us rub lengths of Crayola over it until it's green, and then Davey draws yellow embroidery around the ovals we've left on its front and back, and inside prints *IHS.* We've flattened slices of bread and cut out Hosts with a bottle cap. They are in a jelly glass with a cardboard burse on it, draped with a handkerchief, and a sheet is over the planks we've set across sawhorses in Davey's unfinished room. The door to it, now hung, is locked, and Jerome and I have on the cassocks that Grandma has brought home from church to launder for the Altar and Rosary Society.

"I hope you guys know your Latin," Davey says, and opens his missal on one of the beds recently moved up here—one for Davey and one for Tom. "I might flub up on some of the priest's long prayers, since I ain't read them in a while and the priest here kind of mumbles them off, but I know the parts before your responses real good, so you listen up for them. Now, the vesting prayers in this missal ain't in Latin, so I'll just English em through."

His amice is a dish towel with strings tied to two corners, his cincture a length of twine, his alb a nightgown of Grandma's, and his maniple made from another sheet of paper and colored green. He uses a silk scarf of Grandpa's for his stole, and then Jerome and I help him on with the rattly chasuble. He moves his hands below it, straightening things underneath, while he stares down at the missal and reads, "Oh, Lord, who hast said, 'My yoke is sweet and my burden light,' grant that I may so carry it as to merit Thy grace." He glances up and must see my fear; isn't sacrilege the worst sin? "All right, let's procession in," he says, and slams the missal on the planks. He picks up the veiled chalice and backs into a sheetrocked closet, still minus its door, and leans against the wall, his face in dimness, dotted with quivering droplets, and I hear the chasuble rattle as if he's shaking. His eyes are huge.

"Whee," he whispers, "you guys better stay out. It's hotter'n the hinges of hell in here. And my vestments might rip. I'm just going to say me a silent prayer of preparation."

His head bows and I see the dressing room in the Sisters' house, with green light descending and Father's hands directing it over our heads like electricity. Finally Davey steps out, eyelids lowered, and although I'm afraid, I fall in step as if he's Father, the sleeve of my surplice brushing Jerome's, and see fleecy shadow on the floor from the smeared windows, still with purple stickers on them. Davey stands at the altar so long, with drops sliding off his face and striking the chasuble in *thocks*, that I'm sure he'll call it off. Then he raises his arms and moans, "*In nomine Patris, et Filii, et Spiritu Sancti . . .*"

+

No more from Raul. But I'm unable to move because of what he could do. I hear a clack outside the door of something metallic; a machine gun set down. The black hinge in my mind opens on a freeze that sweat slides around. There is whispering in a language I can't understand, and though I've never seen a machine gun set up, I now hear the pieces of one clank into place. The gun is slipped into a tripod with a breathy command, and I feel the barrel turn and train in on me, and then a bolt is pulled back and slams into place. "What did I do?" I want to ask, gagging on acid, and with a sear like a match struck, holes punch through the splintering door and stitch up into a starburst that centers on me, as I think: If this is life, why—

+

Mom is pregnant again. Or must be, since she has started wearing smocks, although there's hardly a bulge. She comes down the basement stairs sideways, one foot down on a step, then the other, *clump*-clump, *clump*-clump—her hand squeaking along the wooden rail, so you always know it's her. The corner of the basement where Jerome and I are lying, playing cribbage, feels crowded, as if she's standing over us. I shove aside the board, no longer interested in this game Grandpa has taught us, even though it's a way of beating Jerome. Everybody gets between the two of us ("We're certainly next door here," Mom has said), and there are days when he doesn't seem my brother, I hate him so much.

Mom goes to the ironing board, in the offset behind the basement stairs where the cupboard, stove, shower, refrigerator, and washing machine are, wets a finger, taps it to the iron with a sizzle, and starts ironing a pair of Grandpa's suntans. No expression—a lack of expression on her face as she bears down so hard on the iron that her hair swings out and strands of it coil and dance with the clumps she causes by setting the iron down firmly with every stroke.

"Darn," she says. "One thing at a time, little Mrs. N." She

grabs a pop bottle with a sprinkler on it from the squared end of the board and shakes out spurting drops that spatter over the pants with a sound like rain on a roof, which reminds me of another room where the three of us once paused to listen like this. In our house in North Dakota? I try to picture that place, and the beginning of a stairway appears.

"I ain't going to play anymore," I say to Jerome, and lie on the cot where we used to sleep, head to feet, until we moved upstairs.

"Don't say 'ain't,' " she says.

"Okay." That stairway. A door swings back from its steps over gray-blue linoleum—a pattern with yellow lines dividing it into diamonds. Is memory a thing I can run? How neat. Then stairs fall into place like cards above the girl with crutches on the Army cot. She smiles at me—

"Don't say 'ain't' and 'yur ole' this and 'yur ole' that, or 'she's a doozie,' and don't let me *ever* hear you say 'jigaboo.' "

She slams the iron down and I sit up.

"Do you hear? Don't say 'ain't' or 'dang' or 'son of a buck,' or fur your Rs till I feel I'm in a cocoon. You're not a couple of hicks!"

From her corner she can't see Davey step from Grandpa's office, where he's been napping, and stand in the doorway dazed and groggy, his face flat and open as the moon.

"I can't stand it anymore! I ain't gonna do this, or that ain't the way we do it in yur ole Ella-noise, until I'm so sick of such uncivilized talk I could puke! This isn't the Medicine Show! Do you *hear*?"

"Well, gee," Davey says, "I—"

And then he runs stomping past her up the stairs.

+

The Standard Oil truck goes by in a backwash of air and chirring tires, growing smaller, and I see it isn't dragging a clanking chain that pops with sparks, like the one in Hyatt. Was it before? Davey lowers his arms and we go in a high-stepping run across the hot blacktop into the shadow of the canopy over Ferlin's pumps. His driveway is as smooth as skin, icy in its oily blackness, and gives off hints of my newest favorite smell: gasoline, when it's freshly pumped and fuming.

We stare into the case of half-buried soda bottles, bloated by the water, and my eyes shy from the Cokes. Not even chocolate soda interests me today, and I decide I'll have a Fudgesicle, or a frozen candy bar with almonds sealed in frigid humps of white; or something unaffected by this heat, from the wooden, glass-fronted case like the one at Sill's.

A faint reflection of me climbs up its glass as I approach, and past my pale and glassy eyes I see varnished shelves holding rock candy, cough drops, and the cigarettes we tell Ferlin Grandpa has sent us for, Chesterfields or Kools—nose-scraping, lung-busting dizzy-makers, both.

"I'll ask your grandpa, boys, next time he's in," Ferlin insists. He's gray-haired and jittery, with a girl's high voice, and whistles to his radio or chews gum as he adjusts the sunglasses under the visor of his cap—like an Army officer's, but the blue of his uniform. "Squirrely Ferly," Davey calls him, because of his busyness, I guess. Then Jerome walks up beside me. It's as if I haven't seen him lately until I see him this way, as a reflection, and there's such soft sadness to his face, I'm ashamed, and turn to him to—

Both of us go flying against the glass and it isn't until we're scrambling back from it, seeing that it isn't broken although there's been a noise of breaking glass, that an explosion goes off like lightning that has barely missed.

"The A-bomb!" Ferlin yells, and starts for the door, then is back and has Davey by an arm. "Was that an A-bomb, or what the hell!"

We hear screams outside and look at one another with frightened smirks. Ferlin runs out the door and runs back in with his hands up.

"Stay right there, boys! Don't move! Don't you dare look out!"

He grabs a copper fire extinguisher and runs out crying, "Bud! Bud! Here! Come this way! Run, Bud, run!"

"Stay there, you guys," Davey says, and goes to the front picture window, which is broken out, and at its edge we see a man stagger into view, wearing a cap like Ferlin's and suspender overalls, his jaw locked open in a scream and his overalls outlined by clinging flames.

"Jesus!" Davey cries, and runs to the door. "Throw him on the ground and roll him around! Where's a blanket? Do you have a jacket? Don't turn that fire extinguisher on him! Throw him on the ground!"

There's a deeper concussion above the man's screams, and in a change of color in the sky, heat drives through the door and broken window. Ferlin yells something about his pumps and Davey unhooks a coat from a wall and throws it out the door. "Use that! Roll him up in it!" Then he runs over and grabs our hands and says, "Let's go!"

Outside, the heat hits worse than the wrestling men on the ground I try not to see, and clumpy black smoke billows in a roar above the bulk tanks. "My gas pumps!" Ferlin screams. "The tanks underneath'll blow!"

Davey runs us to the other side of the hedge-apple trees as a row of explosions, like drums being socked, rise in a sudden heat I feel will take my hair off. Flames storm across the vacant lot. The leaves of the trees crackle and shrivel and some on the far side burst into flame at their tips. Through their noisy burning I see Grandma at the front door waving a towel in the direction of Ferlin's; and then Mom appears behind her, and they grab one another in a hug. Davey yells and leaps. Tears slide from my face and relieve the need to pee that has my groin going elastic, although I manage to keep up with Davey, who still has hold of us, and then a bigger jolt blurs the air and sends us into the weightless plunges of runners in the slow-motion clips of Olympic events, hair raying weightless around— my hearing gone but sight gobbling up every other sense backward to the rubbery-green whirls of fallen hedge apples we leaped; the Standard Oil truck burning in front of a melting shed, its tires circles of blue; one side of the man's face like pink roast, his eyebrows gone; while I wish that I had never wished there would be a war, or Dad would join the Army.

We are at the tracks in such a rush there isn't time to look for trains, across the road and past the front of the house, which gives off heat, to the back. Davey lets us go and runs to the screen door, and calls, "Telephone the San Jose, Mason City, and Havana fire departments! Say it's urgent! A drastic emergency! We need foam! Phone Pekin and Peoria, too! Ferlin thinks his tanks might blow! Call an ambulance!"

It's so cold at the back of the house I'm trembling, about to jiggle into a dance, and I grab my nose, sure that it's bleeding. No, but my feet are—fringed with sandburrs. The screen door opens and Mom comes out, her head down, and has us sit on the steps. She picks off the sandburrs and runs her fingers along scratches and cuts with a touch that soothes. A hose, hooked to a faucet on the house, is coiled beside us. She turns it on and holds a cone of spray over our feet, and I see myself lighting matches at Deke's and sucking up their smoke with leadlike gills (the taste of their salty crust in my mouth now) before I shove them in the dirt and line them up on Deke's sill, and then hear the rustle as she arrives on a run, hair swimming back from her face, and grabs me and the matches so hard my head bangs Deke's door, and yells, "What are you doing?" I start to tell her I was keeping track of them. "Why is it always you! Oh, Lord! Are you trying to burn the poor man's house down! What's he done to you? I'll show you!" There's a sound of matches rattling above her mourning cry as we head for the house, then a trilling through my belly button of a bobby pin digging there as she jerks me around in the porch, and with a *whoesh* there's a smell like a cow horn sawed and I feel fire bite into my fingers and pop their skin like sausages. "How does it feel? Do you know now what it feels like to be burned!"

She stands with her head bowed, letting the water spray straight onto the sidewalk, as if she remembers, too, and then Davey comes up and touches her hand and takes the hose from her and adjusts its nozzle until a single stream rattles out full-length. He walks down the side of the house and directs the water across its front, and then the siren on the tower next to Ferlin's kicks in and thickens the air with its rusty wail.

+

We stand along the road behind the house, where townspeople are gathering, and sometimes walk up the lawn far enough to see, past the rise the house sits on, to the highway. Fire trucks are gathered there, and water fountains up from different directions and falls over the flames with a fluttery rumbling. One truck is parked at the front of the house, with a noisy geyser climbing above the circular grain elevators, and pumpers are down the road at the creek. State Police have blocked the highway and an ambulance has taken Bud Wumkes off.

Ferlin is in the crowd, adjusting his cap and sunglasses as he watches his place get soaked; he says Bud was burned over thirty percent of his body, but a trooper thought he'd pull through. Bud's face won't be the same, though, Ferlin says, and shakes his head. A train hauling foam is on the way from Peoria, he's heard, and some special team is being flown in; they should be here by now. He can't say for sure what happened; the explosions were the truck and the barrels in the warehouse, he thought at first, but those are still going off. A valve on one of the tanks must be open; Bud couldn't say. The thing is to keep the heat in those bulk tanks down until the special team gets here, he says.

There is a dull explosion that everybody moves back from, faces turning away, and then flames climb in orange cataracts with boiling edges flinging off soot, and the round towers of the grain elevators, grouped together in a cluster, turn rose over their silver-painted sides. The truck in front allows its stream to shower for a while on the shingles of the elevators' joined-together roof, and there's a smell like burning bread. Mom steps back with Susan in her arms, her eyes striving to each of us as if to hold us close, while Marie, who's sucking one hand, hangs on to Mom's smock, looking up and blinking her big eyes at the raining ash.

There's a flurry of movement and an airplane comes over low with a noise that sends crisped leaves floating down. It goes into a whining bank over a soybean field, its near wing tip twitching down until it hangs in place, stilled or backing as I suffer a chill about Dad and the war, and then it levels off with a rattly acceleration, and a cry from the people goes up. It comes over lower, its hammering engine vibrating the ground, and in a glide above the flames it's out of sight.

"He must be landing past Main Street!" Ferlin yells with

surprise. "I thought they'd drop a foam bomb on that mess."

"What for?" Davey asks, as if to ask for us about Ferlin and bombs.

"I don't know, son, but I thought they might could do some good that way without anybody having to get in close to the perishing heat of that son of a bitch. The foam from Havana's truck didn't do diddley-poop. I don't want to see another fellow hurt. I've seen enough for today."

A police car with its siren pulsing pulls up to the fire trucks and a figure in white gets out the passenger side with clumsy strokes. Other men run up and pull a white hood with a black square at its front over his head—"An asbestos suit," Davey whispers. The man is helped on with huge gauntlets, and holding his arms out like a monster, he starts across the lake of tar that was once a highway. A hose of foam is played over his back and another goes snaking ahead to lay a frothy path. A foot sticks and then slides as he gets closer to the blossomings rolling through the smoke above the collapsed and glowing shed. A billow engulfs him, and one hand rises to shield his eyes as a message travels through the crowd that he's been paid to risk his life.

There's a sound like squealing brakes and I turn to see Grandpa's oldest vehicle, a battered black panel truck, slide to a stop in the sand road. Its door swings out. "You!" Grandpa cries, and seems out of breath, trying to get out or stand on the running board. *"You!"*

Everybody turns as he gets himself free and jumps down. "You two! *women!* What are—you doing! With these kids here! Are you—!" Clotted anger darkens his face so much his lips bulge. "Get in this truck!"

"But, Charles," Grandma says. "The house—"

"House, hell! Why— All of you! People! Run to the creek! Go!"

Davey has the back doors open, and when we hurry inside, Grandpa's already at the wheel and I see his hands shaking over the broken-out hub. Mom and Grandma get in beside him with the girls in their laps.

"Okay, Dad!" Davey yells. "Everybody present and accounted for!"

"Forgive me," Grandpa says in a hoarse voice. "I was scared to death for you." He gets the truck in gear with a grinding crack, in a jerking that throws us around, and we roll down the road past people heading for the creek. "If those tanks go, I'm afraid our house will. And, oh, these people, what then? We could see the smoke from Canton."

He drives into the sandy countryside to the half-moon iron bridge near Lishout, and everybody gets out and heads for the shade. Jerome and I sit on the edge of the bridge with our feet dangling down, waiting for somebody to complain, and watch the brown water slide past the shadow of the bridge and us far below. Grandpa walks down the bank to the edge of the creek, carrying Marie, and sits her on a sandbar, then lies back next to her, leaning on an elbow, and pushes up his cap. He lights a Kool. His legs are crossed at the ankles and his feet nearly in the water. Marie digs with a stick in the sand beside them.

I look at Jerome, who has his hands up on an angle iron and is leaning one cheek against a girder, and then back down at Grandpa, lying in leisure, a word I understand now, and think: *He reminds me of Jerome.*

"Are you guys out for the exercise, or what?"

Jerome and I are talking about the fireman in white as we walk back from our first week at school. We've turned left at the triangular park and gone past the old gray Opera House, past the corner where Davey drew Grandpa's signature, up to Main Street, then down Main Street, and then right toward Aunt Rose Marie's, where we'll be picked up by whoever is working closest to town on one of Grandpa's carpentry crews. Now a black panel truck crawls up close behind and the window glides down on our side. "I say, are you guys out for the exercise, or what?"

It's Tom, leaning so far toward us that his curly hair droops over his forehead. I look around. How else can we get to Rose Marie's but walk?

"I mean, coming around this way!" he calls out the window, irritated. "I've been following you guys for over a block."

"This is the way we go," I say, when Jerome's face takes on the tight-lipped blankness that means he won't talk.

"Why, you can come right down there!" Tom says, and points to the street at our side, where I see the tip of the triangular park; across from it is a long white house set at an angle to the corner of the block, the place where we turn when we begin our trip around.

"This is the way Davey showed us," I say.

"Oh, hell, he probably wanted you to see the La-mar," Tom says, and laughs. "Where they have the *movie shows*." Davey indeed led us past the Lamar, and we've been reading the posters on its front and red-brick side as we walk past it every day. "Any fool can see this street runs straight through!" Tom cries. "You've been going five blocks around!"

Jerome looks down, ashamed, and I want to turn and keep on walking.

But Tom leans toward us again, and the passenger door gives a crack and swings open, then the panel truck dips at us as he revs its engine. "Come on. Get in. I got a date. Or are you guys so helpless I have to come out there and carry you up here inside and set you down yet, too?"

+

The white house where we've been turning, to go five blocks out of our way, is the place Dad buys. We move in on a weekend. It's a duplex that was once a gasoline station, and a family with two baby boys, the Ebbingers, has been renting the other half. Dad decides to let them stay, for the rent, although they'll cramp us, but he tells them they won't be able to park their car in the double garage. Furniture of ours that won't fit in the house fills one bay, and Jerome and I will be sleeping in the garage until a room for us is finished upstairs; a door leads from the garage into the kitchen. There are tall windows on two sides—for the light, Dad says, when mechanics worked on cars—and the windows look directly onto the road, beside the triangular park, and over a vacant lot behind our yard.

I go out the raised garage door, to the back yard and into the vacant lot, where weeds reach to my ears, with shadowing elms all around, and turn back; inside, Tim is bouncing up and down on the old double bed Dad has set up for us next to the mound of furniture.

"Well," Mom says, when I mention to her how easily I can see in, "I could hang up sheets, I guess."

But she's too busy to. Then she claims it's so filthy in the garage that anything she hangs up will get ruined. "Ask your dad to tack some paper or cardboard up," she says, and tapers the end of a thread between her lips before she spears the eye of a needle.

+

"Where's our train, Mom?"

"I was afraid you'd ask that sooner or later."

"What do you mean?"

"It was supposed to be on that trailer we lugged behind the car all the way here. But your dad said he didn't see it when he unloaded, so we assumed it was with our other things that went ahead of us in the trucks—everything we piled in Grandpa's garage. Now that we've moved in here, we haven't found the train yet."

"Oh, no."

"Are you sure it got taken down from the top shelf of your closet?"

Jerome and I look at each other; we're not sure.

"Personally, I think it was left there. We've been expecting to hear from the Mitchells. Father Schimmelpfennig wrote and said that they're well moved into our house. So they've surely found it by now."

"Will you write and ask them?"

"If I don't hear from them soon, yes, certainly, of course I will."

+

The fourth grade in public school is so far behind the third grade at St. Mary Margaret's (not to mention the fourth- and fifth-grade lessons I've heard) I figure I can sit back and sleep until my sixth year. Except in the afternoon, when Mrs. Corcus, an elderly teacher who lives with her eighty-year-old mother, reads out loud about a ranch in the West, and her voice is like our mother's when she used to read to us at night, and then I picture our bedtime storybook, worn raggedy at its edges, come rustling up as though she's lifted it closer; and then I see the railroad tracks in front of Grandpa's house, and think backward through all the tracks we crossed on our way to Illinois, pulling the trailer, until I'm standing again at the Hyatt depot, waving goodbye to Mom or Grandma Jones and watching farm implements in the vacant lot appear in flashes between cars, and then the implements sway like weeds with the rattling caboose. Another world.

+

I wait under a catalpa at the edge of the schoolyard for Jerome, and when he walks up, with his head down and a book in one hand, we start for home. "What does your teacher talk about?" I ask.

" 'If you had twenty sick sheep and one died, how many would you have left?' "

"Twenty-five. Why?"

"Nineteen. *Sick* sheep."

"Where'd you get that?"

"From her. She talks about a country school she used to teach at. She doesn't say so, but I think she liked it better there."

"I know."

"I never thought I wouldn't like school."

"I know. I learned everything we've had so far in second grade."

"It kind of makes you feel you can pick and choose."

"Pick and choose?"

"Whatever you want to do."

+

"Take them back," Mom says to him.

"But, Mom, I just got them at the beginning of school."

"That's exactly why I say take them back. They're ruined in less than a month. They're beyond wearing anymore."

He lifts a foot and looks at one shoe, turning it from side to side, then at the other. "True," he says.

"I knew I should have come with you to pick them out."

"Why didn't you?" he asks.

This remains in the air so long I'm in the leather-and-denim-smelling store again, watching the gruff man work laces through the shiny eyelets, jerking Jerome's foot around on the stool where it rests; then the man is leaning back, his thick glasses framing bent reflections of fluorescent lights. "Well, it's these or it's those, fella. That's the best I can do for the money you got. These are guaranteed, broke-in, real-leather, long-lasting shoes."

"The sides seem thin and the soles—"

"Pouf! A kid's going to tell me about shoes? I sell them! Do they fit or not?"

"I guess they kind of seem to."

"You guess they kinda seem to, huh? Well, I guess you kinda better take them then, unless one of your folks is going to come by here and kinda shop around with you for a real shoe. I carry Thom McAn, tell them. Where are you boys from? I haven't seen you around. Who's your folks? Do they live in town here? What's your pa do?"

Jerome's lips tighten, and rather than answer all of this (or so it appears to me), he takes the shoes.

Now Mom turns from the back window, where she's been looking out as if watching somebody, and sits at the kitchen table, her favorite spot. She sighs as she rubs her hands over her mounded stomach. She's a hermit here; she hardly leaves the house, except for church, if then. I slip behind her and stare out; only the weedy back yard and the taller weeds of the vacant lot, like a hayfield in the night, and then cloud shadow lifts from it and it looks like a field I've seen before.

"You know very well I'm not in shape to," she says. "I've hardly got the gumption to get up and go."

Whose voice is this, I think as I turn around slowly, and the oiled-down look of her hair from behind is a clue: Grandma Jones.

"Tell the man you want a new pair. Tell him these are made of inferior leather, if leather at all, and the stitching's bad, or rotten, and gone kaput. There's no inner lining and the seams are coming apart at the sides. Tell him the heels are worn down to practically the soles. He can see that. Tell him the insoles buckled up and came out the first week. Tell him any or all of that—all true. Tell him I've seen you wear a pair of shoes for over a year and leave them looking new when you grew out of them, not even worn at the heels, hardly a lick. Tell him I—"

Her hair swings ahead in heavy clumps over her hands, which she lets her face fall into. "Oh, Jerome, Jerome!" she cries. "You were always so good with your shoes!"

+

"Whose are those?" the store owner says to another man after we step through the door that rings a bell; the two are leaning toward one another over a counter and the other man turns.

"Beats me."

"Well!" the owner says, and claps his hands. "What can I do for you? How are those shoes?"

"That's what I came to speak to you about," Jerome says.

The owner turns and strikes the other man's shirtfront with his fingertips. "That's what he came to speak to me about. How do you like that? So what have you got to speak about, huh?"

"I want a new pair of shoes for these you sold me."

"Well, we don't deal in trade-ins at this place or it'd be a losing proposition for me, and a hell of a bargain for you—right, Dick?" He strikes the man's shirt again, and they both laugh.

"I'll pay you extra, maybe, for a good pair," Jerome says. "If you've got a better pair than these."

"Oh, so now you want the others, *now* you want the good pair, now that you've gone and stinkapated these."

"Well, just look," Jerome says, and steps around in the spot where he stands until his back is to them, then tries to look down at the shoes over his shoulder. "These heels are practically worn down to the soles. I've hardly had them—"

"Sure they are, I know they are, I can see that. I know your kind. You drag-ass your heels on the sidewalks and roads all day—I watch you go to school—and wade through mud slop ankle-deep and stomp your feet till the seams bust"—Jerome is turning, slower now, his mouth open—"and then you drag-ass all the way home, and then your folks, or whatever, if you got any—guys at their first factory jobs in Pekin—come in here and wrangle with me about why the hell your shoes wear out! When it's probably the first pair you've had on!"

Later that night, out in bed, watching our frosty breath rise in the dim light from a streetlamp, we hear Dad come in the front door. Something strikes the floor inside and rolls clumsily, as shoes do when tossed, toward the kitchen. "I'll take him to Havana," we hear him say. "Remind me never to shop in that store again."

"Remind you?"

Jerome rolls away and grips the pillow over his head.

"Remind you?" she says again, and a click goes through me as if a switch were thrown, sending a deeper darkness down through the cold of the garage.

+

"Mom, have you heard from the Mitchells yet?"

"What do you mean?"

"Didn't you write to them about our train?"

"Oh. Not yet, no."

"Will you, please?"

"As soon as I get some time, yes, certainly."

+

Jerome and I are serving Mass, after taking turns beside Davey for a while. "I figure I'm old enough to semi-retire," he says, and then glances around as if somebody might be listening, or catch him still in the paper chasuble: "I'm thinking I might be priest material myself."

The church is tiny, with four windows of bubbly ivory glass. There is no organ, not even a piano, and thus no singing, which Mom can hardly bear. It's a mission served by a priest from Havana and the hours of Mass alternate. Sometimes the priest is late but still has to hear confessions before the service, so he drops his hat and briefcase on a chair inside the sacristy door, throws on a purple stole, and goes into the confessional, a kind of janitor's closet across from the sacristy, while Jerome and I get into our cassocks.

There is no locked tabernacle, or sanctuary light, so the Hosts and wine for each Mass, and the priest's private chalice, are in the briefcase. It's of black leather, like Dad's, and opens on a horsey smell that blurs the invisible line between plain bread and wine and Christ's body and blood. We're party to the mystery of this as we open the briefcase and take out the chalice with a linen cloth, careful not to touch its metal or gold-lined interior, which is forbidden, since it has held Christ, and lift out the paten, also untouchable, with the linen cloth. Then we take out the bottle of wine and pour the little bit the priest wants (he says he doesn't like wine) into one cruet, and put it on the glass plate beside the cruet already filled with water and lined with clinging bubbles, and place the finger towel, ironed into accordion folds, between the two. Then we peek out the side altar door to see how many are lined up along the wall to go to confession, trying to gauge the number of communicants; or, if it's a Family Communion Sunday, which falls on the first week of every month, we step out the side door to the altar rail, as Davey has instructed us to, and say, "Will all those who plan to attend Holy Communion today please raise their right hand?"

The shame and discomfort we feel isn't from standing in the front of the congregation, or from seeing the looks of those who don't raise their hands, but from taking part in this awful informality, after Hyatt, and from seeing how Mom bows her head in humiliation. Back in the sacristy, we take a miniature cardboard box from the briefcase, with the Hosts, white wafers, packed in tissue paper like coins, and count out on the paten enough to match the raised hands, and then add five more, in case some people haven't arrived, or others change their minds. Once the Hosts are consecrated, the priest has to eat any extras, since Christ can't be left lying around, and Father doesn't like the sticky dryness of them. He hurries through the Mass, and we kneel so close behind him on the low steps, in the cramped space, that I can see his anklets under the alb and his hairy legs above them. No mystery. No music, no High Mass, no Benediction; no scattering of myrrh and grains of spice from the incense boat over burning charcoal in the censer; not like church.

One Sunday I hold my thumb over the bottle of wine and shake it, sending the wine skating into sparkling explosions inside, and whisper, "I wonder what this tastes like."

Jerome gives me a sour look. "You better keep wondering."

I put the bottle to my mouth and tip it up but stick my tongue in its neck.

"Hey!" he cries, and then covers his mouth as if to stuff the word back; people in the pews have probably heard.

There's a circle of burning on my tongue where the wine has touched, and I feel my blood rushing there.

He grabs my surplice and whispers, "What if Father has gone and poured some back? If there's even a drop in there, it's all consecrated."

"He wouldn't pour it back from the chalice. Any in the cruet isn't consecrated." I try to recall if this is correct.

"It's still a sin. Get out there and confess it to Father."

"I can't. Everybody will wonder what I did."

"That's not the point. Father expects you to receive Communion."

"I can't!"

"What are you going to do when he holds out the Host, shake your head?" Somebody once complained when Davey did exactly this, and then Jerome and I tried to figure out what Davey had been doing in here. What I meant was I couldn't confess this to Father, and let him know that I'd betrayed him—forced my way past his trust to those elements that only a priest is supposed to minister. "You better," Jerome whispers. "Because it's the worst kind of sacrilege there is."

When Father holds out the Host, I shake my head, and later I can't confess the sin, either, although the possibility of piling sacrilege upon sacrilege sends sweat crawling through my hair as Jerome and I lie under our covers in the garage at night. I decide it isn't as bad as he claims, but it bothers me to imagine hearing a story about it from Sister Colette. I don't confess it, but when Dad finally reminds me how long it's been since my last Communion I take the Host again, as Jerome and I serve on a Family Communion Sunday, and I see Jerome glance over at me as we bow our heads to the sandy carpet. I can feel the Host resting over the vinegary circle left by the wine, as if its aftertaste remains on my tongue, and then saliva gathers in a rush and covers the spot.

Afterward, out in the small churchyard enclosed with mossy cement blocks cast to resemble stone, Jerome says, "I hope you finally confessed what you did that other Sunday. Otherwise, you better be ready to say a perfect Act of Contrition. And what if something happens instantly"—his blond eyebrows rise up—"what then?"

Then the chastening of the rest of the day, at home, where even the sunlight looks different, burning idly around faults I haven't noticed before—a board lifting up from the others in the living room, a crack in that off-color wall—as we lie in sleepy postures on the floor and furniture, with the Sunday paper starting its drift and spread, spilling out colored funnies about characters different from the ones we saw in North Dakota, except for the man I keep zeroing in on in my hope of becoming a similar, square-chinned savior: Rex Morgan, M.D. I'll be in a crowd somewhere, maybe at a boxing match, where Joe Louis is redefending his title, and he'll get cut, or knock somebody out, and a man will step to the microphone and say, "Is there a doctor in the house?"

+

JULY 7. *They've taken Raul away. I heard sounds from his room that led me to suspect he'd found someone similar to the sort the fellow in the poncho used to entertain, and then there was a stomping in the hall, in the direction of the bathroom, of too many feet. I knelt at my door and out its keyhole could see down the hall to the bathroom door; from there a sound of scuffling came as hatted shadows moved across its star-imprinted glass. The Mafia? The door swung open and banged the wall, and through the blurry frame of the keyhole, with streaks of outside light burning my eye, I saw two beefy men in overcoats and hats, on each side of Raul, giving him the bum's rush. He was shouting something in Spanish, and looking at my eye. Had they slugged him? They swung him toward the stairs and his fingers, a foot away, flexed from a set of handcuffs. The men were mumbling low—Russian? The KGB? Only the police can use handcuffs, right?*

There was a struggle down the hall, and then the faces of the men appeared, bleached and grim, as they headed down the stairs with Raul between them. I shut off the light, raised a window shade, and looked out on cars that appeared inches high in the narrow street, waiting for them to come out the door, but they didn't. Are there levels of perversity it were best I don't know about?

I went back and put my ear to the keyhole, but could only hear the creak of the building and a wind that originates in the stairwell to the roof. Another noise and I was back to the window, and watched them step outside, foreshortened, Raul like a rag between, and hurry to a black sedan. One opened a door and shoved Raul into the front seat and the other slid behind the wheel, boxing him in. They could be the lowest kind of crooks, I thought, getting away with this. Nobody on the street. I tried to get the license-plate number, but there wasn't a license, and no noise of a police car's fuel injection as they pulled off.

Then, with a metallic clanking, the machine gun slid into its tripod outside my door. I'm afraid if I look out, it'll cut loose, or, worse, nothing will be there. So, before I'm back in bed praying, Oh, my brother, save me, get me out of here, I had to leave some evidence that it wasn't Raul—or can't be, or won't be. He isn't here.

+

I'm waiting under the catalpa for Jerome when a siren starts up in sweeping wails that go through me like water through a screen. Students come running past, and when Jerome shoves through the doors, with their polished hit rails across glass, I think of Ferlin's, and see Jerome's reflection slide away as if he's dividing. We've gone only a few steps when we see smoke rising from somewhere down the street, in the direction of our house. We start into a run, passing students who get older the farther we go, and somebody says, "Is that their place?"

And now I see a fire engine in the street beside our house and a man hopping down from the engine with a hose; and as we pick up speed and the house swings into view on its corner among the elms, smoke appears, rolling over its roof from behind, and my breath, which is coming hard, stops: a silence, then a sound from its center like a stump being struck—my heart—as if all the matches I've lit illicitly, including those at Deke's, have finally set something on fire. From the crossroad I can see volunteer firemen behind our house, beyond the service-station driveway, which we're now past. We run up to the idling fire engine and leap back when the chrome pump on its front bumper kicks in with a groan.

The grass of the vacant lot is on fire, and flames shimmying in their own heat rise over one another in backbends toward the elms. A black char is creeping under our clothesline. The water from the hose hits there first and smoke plunges up with a rumpling sound. The hose coughs and bucks in the hands of two men, then there's a blast of airy spray, and, in the kickback, water rattles off the windows of the garage. I can see the mound of furniture in wavering lines through the panes, then our bed. I notice a crowd of people at the crossroad now, and another crowd in the triangular park, and start for the garage, about to get down in shame and crawl, because everything I do or say has an awful effect—I know that now. I have to go to confession, and then ask Mom and Dad to help me get this to stop.

There's a thundering sound; the firemen are dousing one of the silver-painted oil tanks that feed the floor furnaces in the house's two living rooms—the nearer tank, ours—and, in the window beside the tank, Mom's face, firm-set and white, appears, staring out at the yard as she was staring at it the other day. No, she's staring at us.

We go up the drive and lift the garage door, but only a little, with so many people watching, and Jerome slips down and crawls sideways under it into the garage; then I do, positive that I see black tadpoles of soot floating down over our belongings. He slides the door down from the inside. Piles of boxes everywhere I go, and houses being torn apart or fixed up. Is it me? We go around our belongings to the kitchen door.

Mom is at the window, still staring out, and the sight of her like this, in her smock, with her stomach big beneath, sends a weighty trembling through my tongue where the circle of wine once was, and I have to swallow hard in order to talk. "Mom, are you all right?"

She turns to us in the slowed heaviness of her time, her eyes swollen, her lashes drooping in clinging points. "So," she says, in her voice of a bad cold. "So, the culprits return."

"We got home as fast as we could."

"You mean to tell me you weren't smoking out there?"

"Mom, we were in school!"

"Didn't I see both of you out there as plain as life just now? Oh! Trying to get this damnable phone to work, and then having to run out and grab the clothes off the line, screaming and yelling my head off for you two, with those damn big oil tanks about to blow!"

Jerome and I look at one another, then at her, and she puts her wrists on her hips, her hands dangling, her face blotched with color, and leans over her stomach and wags her head as she says, "Always that smoking, smoking behind my back. You think I don't smell it on you? You think I didn't smell it at your grandparents', where I couldn't discipline you? This place could have burned up with me in it!"

"But, Mom, look at the time. We couldn't be back from school till now."

"I don't need any more of your back talk and I don't want to hear of either of you smoking again, you Smokey Stovers, you! Now straighten up the mess in this house, and then sweep it up, every single room of it! And then get to bed, both of you! I don't care if it is five o'clock and you haven't had your supper yet. Get to bed!"

+

Jerome and I tape up newspaper, as high as we can reach, over the garage windows. At least we have more space than the rest of the family. An enclosure like a closet in the living room (an office for the gas station, Dad thinks) is the girls' and Tim's bedroom, although Susan usually sleeps with Mom and Dad, in the room their double bed nearly fills, just inside the front door. The front-door window is fitted with venetian blinds, left by the family before us, and we have to be careful opening the door, so that its knob doesn't hit the wall and send the blinds into a clashing dance, a sound Mom can't stand.

Fall comes so cold that Dad says at the supper table, "It's worse than North Dakota," and everybody stares down. On a Wednesday night Jerome and I take the old wooden radio out to the garage, so we won't bother her, and as he twists the pointed plastic knob (like the inside of a cathedral arch, as I saw it when I was younger) and the yellow-gold dial comes on, I'm back beside the bookshelves in our house in Hyatt, and to savor the sensation, I turn off the garage lights and narrow in on the glowing dial. There are scratches of music, whines and beeps, and then Jerome finds the right station. We've been looking forward to this night for weeks: Joe Louis is coming out of retirement to defend his title as undefeated heavyweight champion of the world.

Jerome lies back on our bed in the dim light and I sit on a milk crate, with the cold from the concrete rising through my shoes, and wiggle at a loose back tooth that's almost out—barely held at one side by a raw hinge of my gum. I've been in arguments in school, because I insist that Joe Louis is going to win; he's impossible to beat, I've said. So when it becomes clear that he isn't the fighter he once was, and he starts bleeding from the face, according to the screaming announcer, the dark garage floor fades, then reappears as if drawn back on the lines of my dropping tears, and Jerome and I are in a field with Dad and Hank Kauter-Haupt, in a countryside that's flatter than home ground, carrying a bucket across a field where potato vines rustle beyond a picked swath as far as we can see and two tractors, with pickers and trailers attached, throb away from us across the plain. A quonset hut, with potatoes piled higher than its roof, describes, in miniature, the sky's curve as it was on that day near Devils Lake, when I was afraid the water would engulf us, so that when Dad hands a man on a tractor a dollar for four bushels of potatoes, the exchange is so huge against the sky it seems that clouds are pouring through the bill. Then the bucket we lug paired up, grabbing for potatoes missed by the pickers but not gashed, while Dad and Hank move far off, emptying their buckets in a mound we head for, almost full. Hank is coming over, too, black against the sun, and we're almost to him when he stoops and puts his bucket down.

"He's pooped," I whisper to Jerome, and realize how old Hank must be if he was in the First World War, when men Dad's age were in the Second.

"Wie gehts, Hank?" Dad calls.

"Ach, Martin." He lifts a hand and sweeps it in front of him as if wiping a blackboard clean, then raises his other arm, and lets both hands drop at his sides. "Dis lant! So peeoootifull!"

I look out, as an old man who's fought in a war might look, and see hollows of shadow across the picked swath, and the specks of diggers moving only with the motion imagination supplies. Straight ahead the sun is starting to set and a gold sheen, like a raining golden mist, covers the fields. Rows of clouds as regular as ribs arch across the sky—each row in our direction another shade of gold or amber, with the strips of sky between in different blues—as far as I can see by leaning back. I turn. The same rows, but with broader spaces between, going off to that horizon, and nothing else in sight. And then I think, or have impressed on me by the way Jerome touches my arm: *That must be the way home.*

And now as the great black man goes into the ropes, to a roar from the radio, I see him fall and feel he's pulled the sky along, like a tablecloth grabbed going down. In the dislocation, I admire even more the power he wielded as a champion, which has carried him through these rounds, although I know that an end has come to the time when he was the center of my hope and affection. He loses. Jerome flips on the light, and in its flat glaze I realize that the winner, Ezzard Charles, shares my name, and I picture Joe Louis walking up the steps of our snowy porch in Hyatt, pounding on the door with his mitt, freezing in his trunks, streamers of snow from the roof coiling past his shoulders and his oiled skin, and calling for me and getting no answer, the house broken down and deserted, nobody home. Then I see I'm holding a bloody tooth in my hand, its cratered roots yellowish, and rather than say anything to Jerome, or put it under my pillow for maybe a quarter, I throw it across the garage.

When we go in to dress for bed, Mom says, "What's the matter?"

"Joe Louis got beat." Lately I've been our spokesman.

"Is it that bad?"

"Yes."

"You look like you've lost your best friend." She goes down on her haunches, and her eyes, troubled and nervous, travel over our faces to see whether we're withholding anything, or trying to mislead her. She takes me by a wrist. "Tell me. It's not something else? Something you're afraid— Something you don't want your mother to know about?"

And with this I understand that it's our mother who's afraid.

+

It gets so cold in the garage that Dad moves our bed into the kitchen, temporarily, before it's moved to the basement, after a better set of stairs is built down there. But when Mom sees the oil and grease caked on the basement floor, she says, "No, it's too filthy a place to sleep. It's too filthy to have it tracked upstairs. And anyway, I'd never be able to sleep at night with that floor furnace hanging down like it does above their heads."

So the swing-down steps in the ceiling of the hallway to the bathroom are removed, and a new set of stairs to the attic put in at the end of the hall, turning right to climb above the basement stairs beneath, and one cold Saturday Jerome and I are nailing down temporary treads on the risers, while Dad tacks up black-covered insulation to the backs of the same risers, directly below us. There's a half-finished room upstairs, partly covered with sheetrock that has turned a rusty brown and comes crumbling out of its sheath of paper if you bump it. A storeroom? Jerome and I sweep off its walls, caught up in a havoc of sneezing, and then sweep the sootlike dust out of it, between ceiling joists. A path of planks leads to the stairs, and a single bulb on an extension cord hangs above the landing. Dad moves our bed up, plus a cot that Tim is supposed to use but doesn't; he sneaks into their bed, making it four there. I appropriate the cot, because I can't stand sleeping with Jerome anymore; I can't stand touching anybody, or anybody touching me, for fear they'll become involved in whatever it is I'm doing wrong.

Dad also brings up an electric heater and hooks it to the extension cord. Its round copper-colored dish reflector glows orange from coils wrapped around its central core, and reminds me that, beyond the windowless walls of our room, there's a sun. It reminds me of *her*.

+

"Mom, did you hear from the Mitchells about our train yet?"
"No. I haven't even written to them. Forgive me, boys."

+

As Dad tacks up the black-covered insulation beneath us, pushing its woolly fiberglass between the risers and dodging the dust and corruption our banging hammers send down, Susan keeps crying from the living room. Dad's lips, lined with tacks, compress, and then he goes at it with added energy, breathing harder, his eyes rolling to stare at me or Jerome, and I realize I've hardly seen him lately. Then he steps down from the red-painted kitchen stool, which is standing on a plank that reaches across the stairwell from the floor to a stepladder's top, and his heavy strides go through the kitchen to the living room.

"Isn't there anything you can do for her?" we hear him ask.

"I've done everything I know to. She'll have to cry it out."

"The poor thing sounds like she's being tortured."

"Not by me. Maybe all that banging away bothers her."

"Well, isn't there something else you can do?"

"There comes a time when you've done everything you can, dear, as you well know."

"Is it my fault they reneged on their promise of the job?"

Jerome and I sit on the last tread we've nailed in place. The principal's position that Dad was supposed to have when we moved to Illinois didn't come through; he can't find another teaching job; he's been working for Grandpa.

"I didn't intend to be ironic," she says. "You're dear to me, you know that. You've done all you can."

"It doesn't help when I don't know if you'll finish up what you say you will, so that sometimes there's that, too."

"My hands are full. They feel tied."

"I'm only trying to say that that's partly why things are the way they are." Then a new tone. "I'm sorry I don't have that clothes hamper done, or the washstand you asked for. I simply haven't had time."

"That would help. I have to put the tubs on chairs out there."

She means in the garage, where we used to sleep. Jerome and I study one another and miss part of what they're saying. Dad goes on, "Also, it's an entire house to fix up all by myself." Jerome bows his head and takes it in his hands. "The reason there's no order—I didn't get the job. I feel I've failed you in that. And I have to keep up with the job I have, putting in as much overtime as I can, if we want money to redo this place. It's bone-wearying work and a job I don't like."

"I know, dear. I think of you every day at it. I don't know how you keep it up. I'm bone-weary, too."

+

Dad nails a board with coat hooks on it near the bottom of the new stairs to the attic, and she writes a name above each hook, and says, "In this single thing, please obey. Hang your coats and outside clothes up here, instead of scattering them through every room of the house."

We plan to do as she says, but after a week we start to forget, and one afternoon she turns in the middle of the living room, where a coat is lying at her feet, and says, "Everything I do has the opposite effect. I used to keep up and now I can hardly keep from under. One more mess, I feel, is too much." She looks around the room with shining eyes. "And it's times like this when I want to quit for good!"

+

The Ebbingers still rent the other half of our house, and Mrs. Ebbinger starts to visit in the afternoons—or the afternoons are when Jerome and I walk in and find her at the kitchen table with Mom, in sunlight from the window where Mom once looked out at the flames, which still seem partly there. Coffee is on the table and their heads are together like cobblers finishing up a slipper in a rush. They stop talking when we come in or, if we stay in the living room, speak so quietly we're never quite sure what they're saying—though Mom sometimes smiles so that her pearl-gray tooth, outlined in gold, appears, or her head goes back and her throat broadens with her sudden laugh. Often there is the look of a confession taking place, and one day Mom says, "I thank you for your suggestion, Bobby. It could prove to be the best diversion for older children a pregnant mother ever had."

The movies? We've been given the freedom to go to them. A schedule printed on colored poster paper comes in the mail once a month, listing the movies for Monday–Tuesday, Wednesday–Thursday, and the weekend, and we get to circle two features each week we want to see, as long as both don't fall on school nights. On those evenings Mom hands us twenty cents apiece from the greenish sugar bowl in the cupboard, where the colored poster with our circles is tacked to a door. The movies are our reward for helping in the house, Mom says, although we aren't consistent in our help, and Mrs. Ebbinger is always connected in my imagination with our breathless preparations to leave for the Lamar.

She has long black hair and is thinner than I am, though she has two young boys, and her small mouth is always pouting open, while her eyes, moist and brown, slide in a sympathetic, movie-actress way that stirs me most at night on my cot. She keeps moving her cup or the cream and sugar around the table while they talk, as if advancing in a scoring more complicated than cribbage. The coffeepot on the table is often hers. Mom has never had a friend in the house, and their conversations look so personal I'm surprised to hear them talking about the younger children, which is their usual topic, although once Mrs. Ebbinger said, "If you're not getting any more out of it than that, Alpha, why keep it up?"

And one night as I came down the new stairs, barefoot, on my way to the bathroom, I heard Mom say, "Yes, Martin, we do indeed have our coffee every day." I wanted to see her; her voice sounded different. "And I usually manage to have the time to make it, although she sometimes brings her own. Coffee's about all I enjoy nowadays. It runs through me like a sieve and keeps me going. I'm sorry I'm such a miserable failure to you as a wife."

"Alpha, please. You just said you never feel you have time anymore. I was thinking of you."

At the Lamar we slide down in the mildew-smelling seats, with fuzzy velvet arms worn to oily smoothness at their ends, in order to render ourselves even smaller in relation to the giant figures (larger than Grandpa at the end of that open street) who glide across the screen, looming close in vibrating color, and who turn to us as if to speak the word we've been waiting to hear, although when they do speak from those lips that we could lie across, I can hardly hear them, I'm so filled with taking them in—more so in the features than the cartoons, which are like jiggling cutouts of a violence that isn't very funny, and isn't real, although none of the features have anything to do with what we know, either (we whisper about this during our walks home through the towering dark that causes us to feel stunted), since none of the people do the everyday things that normal people do, or even suggest they have to take a pee. So I begin to look beyond the actors to the scenery, particularly when a Western is playing, and learn to see there, in the colors of a hillside or a coulee, wedges of the countryside whose border we've crossed, and feel my emotions pour out so fully they appear to brighten the screen and open tunnels to that country itself, blue above green.

+

We carry home our report cards on the first day of Thanksgiving vacation. Mom is at the table, with Susan in her lap, facing away from the window, and their four hands travel over the tabletop, where sewing materials are spread, as they were spread once over another table Mom cut across with her shears, showering sensations over us. She is finishing a set of curtains for the window behind her. Its roller shade is all the way up, and late fall sunlight—like the last of summer to be burned away before winter begins—is reflected everywhere in the room off a new snow, in powdery light that looks like pollen drifting through the house, and figurines on the center sash across the window, one in the shape of a swan, are silvery-black against the light.

Susan is usually restless when we're around, but now she hardly stirs, except to tap at the report cards we put down. Mom picks them up, one by one, beginning with Tim's, and draws them out of the envelopes, then tilts them in the light as if to catch the smallest notation. She sets them down, puts a hand to her forehead, and leans an elbow on the sheet of light the table has become, and I can smell her hair, freshly washed, as if it's spread through my insides.

"I hardly know what to say. These are nearly perfect, all of them." Her head turns on her hand; she's shaking it.

"But it's so easy here in this school, Mom."

"Yes, and I know how you dislike that. So these mean even more to me." She looks up and blinks at the light. "You've done this without any encouragement from me. What you receive at home usually governs your school grades. You could have rebelled, or been angry, or given up. Even your deportment is good, except for your daydreaming, as your teacher calls it, Charles. Your dad will be so pleased.

"And, Tim, look at you, you who never even went to St. Mary Margaret's, and had to start out here in public school—I haven't been much help to you, either. Your grades are as good as theirs." She places a gold hand over his hair standing up in gold spines. "You've all reaffirmed my faith in the Lord, which hasn't been very apparent lately, I'm afraid. Forgive me. Give thanks for your grades. Pray that I can pull out of whatever this is and be the mother I was. You've blessed me in ways I never expected. Here I am, moved."

+

She isn't feeling well. Jerome and I, at the front door, hear Dad say in their bedroom, "You aren't going again this Sunday?"

"I believe I have a valid enough excuse." Her voice, muffled by covers or a pillow, has the open deepness it does when she's crying.

"Well, of *course*," he whispers. "You're months along."

"One of your sisters-in-law called me 'Fatty' last Sunday, as in 'Fatty, Fatty, two-by-four.' "

"Who?"

"As if the condition I'm in has to do with diet, or what I eat or don't, or how I exercise, or anything of the sort."

"I know who it was."

"Does it make any difference? Pray for me. I need it."

There's a movement from the bed and I picture her dying and asking for me, because I'm the only doctor who can save her, so I talk to her in a whisper others can hardly hear while I blow smoke in her, or lie beside her in the way I know most everything about and hold her hand and do all the rest, the gold window a mirror above these champions of the world, and then Dad comes out and notices us at the door, and through Dad I see our shining gabardine coats, Jerome's a grapy purple and mine bright green, with furry collars and short belts that clip with hooks at our waists like aviators'—the reason we begged Dad to buy them. He draws deeper into the collar of his sheepskin coat, shaking his head in the slow way he used to when he'd come home from school and stand in the door of the room where we were fighting over our toys, and then he reaches for the knob and we step behind him, and I can almost hear the blizzard that must be rising in North Dakota to bring on this sudden cold.

+

Jerome and I are sitting over the floor furnace, side by side, our backs against the wall—shifting on the metal grillwork to keep it from frying our butts like waffles. Dad's installing a central furnace and Jerome and I have been gluing asbestos strips around the joints of the hot-air ducts, but everything has come to a standstill; mold is growing in a pastepot in the basement. The only sound is the sound of the floor furnace forcing hot air between our legs, drying our eyes so it's hard to blink, and the steady clack of needles from the couch, where Grandma knits.

It was dark, as always, in our attic room when Dad came a few steps up the stairs two weeks ago and called to us. From the doorway I could see his hands gripping the floor below the board rail he had added around the stairwell, and his face, in the watery, half-blocked light from the extension cord, appeared to float on a blackness endlessly steep—so that I held to every line of him: the yellowy vessels in his large eyes with their hooded lids, tangled eyebrows rising above his glasses, his upper lip outlined like a woman's, brown in his bloodless face. He raised a hand, and then came up on the plank path to our door and touched us as he said, "I'm afraid I have bad news."

Mom is dead, I thought—because when Dad woke us that morning he told us that she'd been taken to the hospital.

"These things happen and we have to pray it's the Lord's will. The baby died. You would have had a sister. She was baptized right away. We named her Dacey. It's terrible." He took our hands into his, and in that warmth, with his fingers curling around, glimpses of anatomy unfolded in me and I wished I'd never pounded away at myself on the cot.

"But that's not what's bothering me most. Your mother hasn't been well, as you know. Now the doctors say her condition is serious. Pray for her, please."

He turned to leave, then turned back. "Let's not tell the rest of the children for now, okay? We'll say she's away for a while. I felt you two were old enough to know." He started down the stairs, then stopped on the landing and turned, with the light bulb behind shining around the darkness over his face. "Or we'll tell the younger ones she's in the hospital, no more. Rose Marie will take the girls to her house until things are more settled, and Grandma will be here tomorrow when you get home from school. I'll be at the hospital as much as I can."

I heard hammering in the garage the next day and went to the kitchen door and eased its new curtain back. Dad had nailed together the frame of a large box, and now he was sawing across a piece of Masonite whose surface was stamped and painted to look like yellow kitchen tiles. He took the piece and covered one end of the frame, pounding it in place with tacks from his mouth, and I felt as if a pair of hands pulled from cold water had been put to my neck. He was building a coffin. For the baby, I thought, and started to gag—that we were so poor he had to do this, that a baby would be buried in it—and looked around for Jerome, my knees so feeble I couldn't leave the window. Dad worked fast covering the four long sides and then set the box on end, with its top still open, his panting billowing in the freezing air as he stepped back to study it, and then he grabbed up clothes heaped on the floor and started tossing and stuffing them in. Her clothes hamper. I gagged again. He picked up a two-by-four, measured it, and was sawing away in a rush: the washstand.

+

Then Jerome and I step into the cold vestibule of the church on Saturday, after our weekly instructions for Confirmation, and see Uncle Tom standing inside the double doors, clenching and unclenching his fists. He and Fred and Jay have come to the house to plaster its walls, so something visible will be finished when Mom returns, and the house has been a mess of scaffolding and gobs of plaster to step around, until the plaster is set; then Jerome and I scrape it up with broken-down cleaning trowels that bark against the boards in the bare rooms. Tom shuffles his weight, uneasy, and smiles the tight smile that sends dimples into his cheeks, unshaven now. He waits until the half-dozen others have filed out, and then he's at our height, on his haunches. There are bits of plaster in his hair and eyebrows. He starts to reach for us and then laces his fingers over a knee.

"Well!" he says, and his smile trembles. "I suppose you're wondering why I'm here! Your dad says to tell you your ma's been taken to another hospital, a better one, in Peoria. Your dad's there with her now, and he's called your Grandma Jones. She'll be here tomorrow. Your house is in worse shape yet, so I'm taking you to Grandma and Grandpa's for the rest of the day. They have games there, you know, that—"

He stands, and the movement throws moisture from his eyes in spots on the floor. He pushes both double doors wide, and we step under his arms into winter sunlight. "Well!" he says, and slams his hands against his sides as if searching for gloves, the doors still open, then shoves both hands so deep into his jacket pockets that the corners of the jacket stand out in points. Then I see a fine rain of sugar snow ticking over curling leaves as far as I can look, to the mossy cement blocks that enclose the churchyard, where beads of the snow are ricocheting and flying straight up, and hear the ticking grow to a whir like a passing of the years I've spent with Jerome.

"Well!" Tom says again. "Isn't this a fine how-do-you-do?"

I raise my eyes enough to see the blacktop, white, while the sound of snow on the leaves insists that this piecemeal world of white will always remain with me, following after these words of his, to the end of my history, and then I taste the circle like rust on my tongue and see light reflected off the dusty bumper of the black panel truck and sneeze, and sneeze again, and again, until I feel I'm being shot in the head. And wish I were.

+

Jerome and I sit with our shoulders touching, our backs against the wall, on the floor furnace that heats the whole house until the heating ducts to the furnace in the basement are installed and the floor furnace removed and boards put over the hole it leaves. I imagine Tim at the porthole of fire in the basement, but he's on the cot set up beside the kitchen wall, so Grandma Jones will have a place to sleep whenever she arrives here from the hospital to see us, or so Dad can lie near the phone in case it rings. Grandma Neumiller is on the couch, leaning over her knitting of the stitch she has taught to us, and Grandpa is in the kitchen making coffee and, from the sound of his strides, is pouring it out in containers all over the room. Or maybe the stove isn't working and he's checking the wires to see if they're hot, and pulling them out in tangles that smell like our electric train when it heated up. And the floor furnace might be clacking faster than Grandma's knitting needles, because its fan never stops—lifting our hair away from our ears and drying our eyes until they sting, driving in a growing headache. Our heated bluejeans burn our shins, though the line at the edge of being burned is pleasant, like ice. Then Rose Marie, in a tam, looking like Mom, comes through the door with its billowing venetian blinds. Her long gray coat shakes freshness through the room. She tosses the coat through the door to Mom and Dad's bed and stamps her feet in snowy bursts. The phone rings, and Tim, not asleep, is up from the cot.

Grandma answers it. Grandpa doesn't like to. Rose Marie, shaking out her hair, tosses the tam after her coat and comes past in bright slacks as Grandma says, "You want my husband," and hands Grandpa the phone. "It's the hospital," she whispers. "The doctor." Silence, and then Grandpa says, "You don't want me. No, I tell you, you've made a mistake! You don't want to tell me this—you want my son, Martin!"

The phone goes clack. Rose Marie drops on the couch. There are noises in the kitchen like water running, and then Grandpa's legs are at the couch and both pairs of feet, Rose Marie's still wet, go past us into the bedroom. "What!" Rose Marie cries, and reappears, one arm in her coat, her pretty face pulled in all directions—is it a joke? Grandma hurries to her through a heated smell of shoes burning up, and Grandpa looks back at us as they hug and hiccups start, or a laugh, and then Rose Marie is out the door, coughing or crying, with a clash of the blinds.

The furnace fan flutters our pants legs with dusty air that tastes used up—bluejeans burning at a touch, ankles raw, squares of heat printed in us. Grandpa helps Grandma to the couch, and she pushes a handkerchief under her glasses, lifting them high, whispering, "What, oh, what now?" as Grandpa stares at us. A car pulls up, in a noisy slashing of air outside the door, and we hear Grandma Jones's grainy voice. She has been in Peoria since her train from Minneapolis arrived there (I see a shining piston drawing back, the huge wheel chiming on the track in a fan of sparks as implements sway like weeds in the vacant lot), and now the car pulls off, a billowing wave hits the wall—the venetian blinds in their crash—and Grandma Jones is in the door, a suitcase in each hand, no hat, the coiled hair around her head sparkling with snow, her mouth opening, then the thunder of her suitcases dropped. Her arms rise and she starts across the room, hands out—after us with this frozen mask of her face. The cold crush of her clothes and icy hands, her wrinkled cheeks wetly cold, and then her grainy, sifting voice close up: "You mean you haven't told them yet? Oh, Lordy, Lord, Lord, Lord. Boys, your mother—my dear sweet child is dead! Thirty-four years old and stone-cold dead to this world. I can't believe they haven't told you yet!"

Others arrive, stumpy thunder through the floor, the phone ringing again, and Rose Marie is back with the girls. There's a rumbling of feet or the couch being rolled, and we're sitting on it with Susan and Marie and Tim and Grandma, Mrs. Ebbinger leaning against a wall, one hip slung out. Then Davey is in the door, his hands in a satin warm-up jacket with wriggles of reflected light zigzagging down its shiny sleeves, and Tom steps up on the threshold behind him, his head bowed—and I wish I'd never wished that anything would happen to her so I could be a hero. Jerome and I are back on the furnace then, melting through its grille, it feels, and then cold carves our heat in half as Dad steps in, his face waxy-green, moles in Technicolor, his violet-circled eyes on us. His hands under my armpits hurt me as I go above his shoulders like a child, his arms gather me in, and there's a flickering of light like vigil lights while I cling as if he were St. Christopher, bleeding burning blood out of both of my eyes.

A blank comes, then I'm on the furnace again, a headache like brains running down, and there are more wallops of cold, shoes lining up along the couch, a new pair at our end: Dad's. In the kitchen, chairs are being dragged through a smell of coffee and something to eat—a crude sickening thought that drives the rest that is said into me like slivers of bone.

"It was before the coma, before they took her to Peoria," Dad says. "She'd had convulsions. The priest heard her confession, and then said I should talk to her. She said— She prayed the—"

"Even when she was a little girl her kidneys were so poor," Grandma says. "She'd go for days without taking a leak. 'Alpha,' I'd say. 'Alpha, drink some water, please! Get your system going, before you dry up! It could be your life!' I'd say."

"For days she didn't want to see me. She'd stare at me and wouldn't talk. I'd turn to go, time was up, she'd call, 'Wait!' "

There is a restless wobble to Dad's shoes—he can't continue; one floats up to rest on a knee; the white skin of his leg shows; he pulls at his sock to cover it, wipes around the toe of the shoe with a thumb, and if he doesn't jump up and go at somebody soon, I will.

"She asked about—" Grandma Jones's grainy voice is like several together. "She asked about the kids when I first got there—hardly four days now. Oh, so thin even then! Her arms. She said she was tired, and who wouldn't be, with all those contraptions hooked up to her, iron pipes around her bed, and the hell they put her through. Every hour a new test. Who ever heard of uremia, anyway? What kind of sickness is that! Lordy, the last time she asked for Daddy, I couldn't make her understand he wasn't there. 'He isn't well—can't travel,' I said. 'But I just talked to him,' she said. I felt like a damn fool conniving for her attention. 'He's five hundred miles off!' I yelled. 'He's not here! Talk to *me!*' Who knows what she was seeing, or afraid of? So I said, 'I'll get him for you, Alpha. You hang on. It's okay. I'm here.' "

Dad's whisper almost dies. "I couldn't stand . . . wouldn't talk. Said it was her fault, whatever it was, and to forgive her. I knew it was over when she said I should remarry."

"*Martin!*" Grandma Jones cries. "She wouldn't say that! She couldn't have. You wouldn't remarry, Martin. The kids!"

"He may do as he pleases," Grandma Neumiller says. "It's time he had peace."

"Why, why"—Grandma Jones is going from her grainy

intensity into the quavering need for water—"why, Mrs. Neumiller! You have no idea what you're saying. You're in shock!"

"I feel I'm ice." Dad.

"She never looked her*self*! Like my daughter. Till they pulled those damn, miserable tubes out at last! They had a tube up every hole the poor girl had!"

"Mrs. Jones! These children!"

I feel the gold of that day of Thanksgiving vacation widen out behind her at the window as somebody helps me to my feet. Jerome. He leads me out to the kitchen, to the table in the center of the room, its leaves out. Bowls of chicken soup on it, with chunks floating in yellow fat, my tongue turning thick as I see through scorched eyes the wormy splash of noodles slipping off spoons all around the table.

Jerome won't eat. He has his elbows on the tabletop, hands to his forehead, leaning over his bowl, dripping drops into oily pools. Nobody can make him look up. Both Grandmas try. Dad does. And then in a voice climbing to its highest note, Grandma Jones cries, "Jerome, Jerome, you have to eat!"

I feel I'm watched, and feel that if Mom or whoever is watching can see this far, she can see down to where a thought like a snake kicked out of sight lies curled: *If only I'd been different from the start, this never would have happened to her.*

"Yes, you do," I say to Jerome. "You have to. Look. I'm eating. See, Jerome. Watch." I choke a few spoonfuls down, gagging so hard trickles squeeze out my nose and people move back, and then the real thought strikes through my madness: *It'll be one less mouth to feed.*

+

Hands lift me up so I can sign my name in a register beside Jerome's. Then Dad is above us in a dark suit, his face in softer shades of the shocking colors of the other night, and thinner, as he leans to us, his tie slipping out and swinging free, a fatty bulging rawness like liver squeezing from the corners of his eyes, and touches our arms. "Now your mother might look different to you, boys," he says. "She's been very ill." And I feel the person loosed in my madness trying to say, *Ill, Dad? Ill? Isn't she dead?*

He goes to the double doors ahead, and his hands, clenched at his sides, a rosary wrapped around one of them, begin to gesture, his fingers turning out, then curl into fists again, and with his head down he steps into the light of the perfume-and-flower-smelling room, and one hand rises, pale and eloquent, above his chest and cleaves the air as he sails out of sight, and I hear him say in a miniature of the voice he used to use when he was acting, in a room many years removed from this one, "And by a sleep to say we end the heartache and the thousand natural shocks that flesh is heir to."

+

Father Schimmelpfennig, who has driven from North Dakota through a blizzard, assists the missionary priest, Father Hart-Donovan, at her Requiem. Davey serves alone and the priests sing a High Mass without accompaniment. The walls and ceiling of the church are finished in pink and purplish Celotex, and the alcove of the altar is so shallow, and its platform is carpeted in such a dull red, that I think, I've served here? The furnace isn't lit on weekdays, and everybody's breath rises like smoke. After the Gospel in Latin, Father Schimmelpfennig turns from the altar and takes a step to the Communion rail, which wobbles at a touch of his vestments; he steadies it with his fingertips, looks down at her lavender casket, looks out at us, and then lays his hand over the head of the casket and says, "Alpha Neumiller was a saint."

+

On that same cold, sunlit February morning, her casket is carried to the top of a sand hill in the Catholic cemetery at the edge of town, where sections of the iron picket fence are pushed over, and an iron gate is frozen open on rusty hinges. Six uncles carry her under the branches of an oak at the top of the hill, close to a ten-foot concrete cross, the oak leaves lifting brassy lobes through the snow, and here my memory goes. When it's back, I'm beside Jerome, alone, without flapping canvas between us and the sky, at the edge of the football field, on our way to Bendemeers'. I hear sleigh bells and a team of horses appears, pulling a shed mounted on sleigh runners—the stovepipe above its roof trailing a smell of creosote—and the team comes trotting on around us, their hooves muffled in drifts, their backs steaming through burlap stuffed under their harnesses for warmth, and head toward the fields that lie across the plain in frozen winter shapes. Then the near black horse breaks wind and arches its tail in a glistening plume, and a column of smoking chunks comes shaking out to sink and steam in the snow—the smell in winter air like August alfalfa—and then they turn again, the sleigh skimming around behind, and head toward the sun that stains the fields and pastures and the scattered clumps of trees, for as far as we can see, orange-golden, and I think, from this place in the present where I must remain in order to turn from her grave for good: What a world and what a way of life that was and what a way to leave it all behind!

Recorder at right level, proper patches made? my prepared scripts say at the top, since I'm often my own engineer, and then the intro and any musical tracks are added at the New York studio. I read:

> The doorknob now glows. I've cleaned the paint spots and spatters off its surface and dug the paint and grime out of its grooves at last, after being bothered by it for months. It took a pointed tool and emery cloth, to start with, and then steel wool and Brasso, and now, with the door swung in against the left end of this table, as I like it, walling me in on my one open side, the knob shines above the edge of my vision like a miniature sun. First, the radiator in the corner, spattered in the way that fixtures in a ramshackle apartment building get spattered with the near-annual paintings, wasn't to be borne anymore, so I offered my daughter, who's eight, two dollars to repaint it, and since the day that she finished, and stepped back in the smock she wears when she paints at her easel (or was it one of my work shirts?), the haze of the multicolored knob has hovered on and off to my left as if in reproach. She often twists it in a noisy rattle when she visits me here, as if to remind

me of this. It was April when she finished and now cold is rising in the night air again. Fall.

I'm transcribing these notes and tapes for what I believe will be an indisputable proof of the existence of God, at least for me. I say "transcribing," pulling down the word with the closest bearing on this into the slot, because I'm rearranging and copying files of material I've set aside for twenty years, which attempt to deal in a literal way with actual events. I find that I've had different interpretations of their meaning during different recastings of them, which I'd like to get rid of, permitting the events—none of my making—to remain as free of any subjective coloring as on the days they brought me down. Or the opposite. This relief from that might be, then, as I see it, a stock-taking interim.

Lightning has struck here twice. Each time, it's knocked out the power lines to our house. Our kitchen is on the ground floor, at the back of the house, facing east, and a recently installed window above the sink looks out past our fenced-in patch of lawn to the blacktopped parking lot for this place. Directly across the lot is a triple garage of rock-faced cement block which was once a carriage house, or a small barn, maybe (there's a central gable with a door that opens on a mow), since this suburb of Chicago was a rural area not many years ago—anyway, a perfect cupped reflector, all complete, to amplify the effects of such a blast. Power lines swag past the garage and across the alley up to transformers on a pole.

Even before the first blast hit, I'd been sensitized. I'd gone to the Driver's Services Department, to renew my months-expired license, and had passed the written exam and was standing at a counter staring into one of those machines where miniature road signs and rows of numbers are cranked up for you to read in a glow, when its interior went black and my knees gave with the pressure of an impact that seemed to bring in the wall behind. The lights were out. The man who'd been administering the test looked at me with wobbling eyes, as if I were to blame, and the other state employees, perhaps war veterans, were stoical but wore expressions of being at the ready, while applicants scrambled to hide behind counters or find a way out. *It's come*, I thought—that annihilating blast we all anticipate.

A maintenance man in gray twills came running in and cried, "That big baby damn near took my head off! I just stepped out when he hit and he got that pole right outside the door there! You see them sparks come down? They just missed!"

Later, I was at our table facing the kitchen window, guilty about not being at the work I'd set for myself that day—the muscle-bunched physical guilt that I associate with a hangover (indeed, I was probably trying to quit drinking, again, with every day a hangover of sorts)—reading in a magazine whose glossy pages pooled white headaches of light about guerrilla warfare in Palestine, including accounts of bystanders being injured by bombs, which sharpened the guilt in bright obliquenesses I didn't wish to examine. And then did, in spite of myself, as portions of sentences were obliterated by my thought, and then whole paragraphs: it seemed that the psychic disruptions I'd set off in my life had affected at least the well-being of people, I thought, as I looked up, and from those people had been passed on to who knew how many others, because of the ways in which everybody is so obviously interrelated—

And at that point the first bolt hit.

I was underneath the table, and the impact of the report traveling back at the sky, with a force I felt would pull me out the window, before I consciously heard it. Reflex of expecting the worst. The lights were out, and I could hear fizzing and a sound like a whip being cracked out by the barn-garage. The transformers were smoldering, and men arrived in slickers, in the rain the lightning had released, to fix the lines.

It was a matter of months before the next bolt struck, tearing off the upper limbs of our oak and knocking the power lines into the street. The police had to cordon it off until the men in slickers arrived again, and a week or two later there was a cartoon in that same magazine of a pair of angels on a cloud, looking over its edge, one with a bunch of jagged cartoon thunderbolts under an arm, and the other saying, or so the caption went: "Get him again!"

In the space between then and the present, my wife has given birth to a son, our first, here in this house, in the ground-floor apartment where we mostly live (before, when I said "our house," I meant that we rent the entire ground floor and three rooms upstairs, and are given the run of a shoplike room in the basement by our landlord, in acknowledgment of the maintenance and repairs that I do), and our son is already rising from that indrawn center of internal listening—his eyes an unplumbable cobalt blue—that is every infant's retreat, on and off, until about three months. From his vantage we must seem incarnate aspects of gratification that he's at last getting under control, so that now he's more free, finally, to be himself. He's beginning to grab and grasp at objects held up; he's three and a half months.

Unplumbable cobalt blue. This is their essential impact, as if opening onto quirky, inky regions of the brain all the way back to its origin, the moment of being called into matter, a place too appalling to retreat to once common sense has invaded the breathing body around (mostly through its contact with our hands), but for him, for now, still basking within that state and at peace with his source, the only possible place to look out from, toward his frightened elders trying to make their literal sense. It's this look of his that reminds me of my brother Jerome.

The look was in our son's eyes from the moment he was born, here in our bedroom. A doctor presided, standing near the high oak headboard I refinished for the event— and I remembered how, when I had worked it with steel wool in the sunlit yard, discourse with my reconstructed self had appeared like the newly glowing grain beneath my hand. I assisted in the flurry that comes at birth, trying to keep a piece of ice on the point of my wife's back that was causing her the worst pain—she was on her knees with her face in a pillow; back-labor—and I saw only composure in our son's face from the start. A tall skull emerged, and then furrows and wrinkles that frightened me. I wasn't sure what

I was seeing, until I realized it was a form of our daughter as an infant, and then I was able to translate the furrows into a face—blue-plum, lips plum-black—so foreshortened and miniature I was shocked. It was turned to me, with entire calm in it; entirely serene. The doctor's hand was cupped underneath. He turned the face a bit, and then reached out a forefinger and with a rotating motion pulled out what I thought was the cord. An arm.

The composure in the face was like the expression of someone who's traveled through intergalactic space, in limitless patience, I thought, and with this there was a rush of cold in the room, like the black distances between stars, and the presence of my mother hovered near. It came to me that life isn't matter, since matter is so often inert, but an infusion of power from beyond space, a power now forcing this emerging head from the interior of my wife; and I felt that my father's recent death, before nearly unbearable to contemplate, had been vindicated.

Streams of water poured from our son's lips and nostrils, but without a change in his expression, and another force rose in me as if bubbling through liquid toward the surface, and I was overcome by a single word: *Jerome*. It, too, had traveled great distances, I sensed, and immediately knew it was the name we should give our son, and knew as immediately I couldn't live with its connections: the name of our mother's favorite brother, who drowned when he was thirteen, before it passed to my brother.

Then our son was born completely, in a rush, and lay still on the bed, spotted with vernix and blood. His limbs suddenly jerked and he sneezed, and I could see his belly strain, then flatten and bulge as he started to breathe. He hadn't cried yet, and now opened his eyes and began to look around, toward his mother, back up at me, at the doctor, and I could tell he was taking us in by the way his eyes slowed and softened when they came to my wife. Then they moved on with a sober deliberation, as if to pick up details from her point of reference, until it struck me that he was waiting to see who would make the first move.

My wife turned and swung her leg over the cord and

then reached out and covered his chest with her hand. Not one cry.

This evening I did "Rock-a-bye-baby" with him for the first time, and, pretending to drop him in a shaky way, brought out his laugh—a few hearty, open-throated bleats that always seem to take him by surprise, with a gasping intake at the end of absolute delight. He first laughed this way when I threw him toward the ceiling at two months, barely releasing him and then catching him with a cushioning give to my arms—a daily game until my wife walked in on us once and cried out in alarm. After that he was dubious, and clasped his hands as if in prayer as he went up, looking off to the side, instead of directly down at me in exhilaration, as he used to, and once he started to cry.

The end of that.

The next big bursts of laughter came in the bathroom, where all four of us somehow got wedged. The room is only three feet wide, not counting the inset for the tub, with a shredding ceiling I've been meaning to fix but keep putting off, perhaps because of my grim associations with the place, and there we all were, as such things happen in a house with an infant, and especially one who's been waited and prayed for, at large. I was running a tub of water for his bath, and above its thundering my wife held him up to the medicine-chest mirror, drawing me and my daughter, who stepped up on the stool, close, our heads together. He wobbled his from side to side, realizing he could see us on either hand, and then looked straight into the mirror, where our faces also were, and then our daughter, who was leaning so far forward the top of her head was just below his feet, lunged in toward the mirror and cried, "Boo!"

His response, several ringing tones from his belly, with that gasp at the end, was electric. I wouldn't have thought that a child of mine could laugh with such seizures of freedom if our daughter didn't; and then, immediately serious, he was staring into the mirror again, and again she did it, with the same response. We were at this until I felt he was tired of it, as I was, and couldn't take any more.

"Okay," I said. "It's time to stop. Now!"

He's never cried that much, but has a vociferous cry which lets you know it's time he was attended to, and he is fed on demand, regardless of the inconvenience of place or mood or hour, at breasts no longer so accessible to me—a matter that even Freud, rooter among sexual arcana, seems reluctant to bring up. The expression of his face is dependent upon the position he's in (lying, propped up with a pillow, resting over my wife's shoulder), and in each position is different, perhaps due to his face's fleshy mobility, or the rearrangement, in different positions, of his crowded internal organs and their connected systems of exchange, as the members of his family express in separate ways the trial and the gift that he is. By now he seems necessary, in order for us to be complete.

His first sound was *guh*. His babbling is taking on more of the consonants, and he's trying harder to reproduce shades of what I say, watching my eyes and mouth with an open somber look as I talk, and then leaping in with a sudden smile, his upper lip curling as he goes on at length, still observing out of his own pleasure, but now with a look to determine how much pleasure he might be giving me. Though this isn't entirely so recent and has been going on in shorter spells, without so many convolutions, from the time he was six weeks. Then, usually just before dinner, I would get down in front of where he was lying or sitting, in one of those chairs that enable an infant to sit, and have what I called "one of our talks"—the mere mention of which set my daughter howling with hilarity. She's at that age, talking and laughing with her whole body, as if to discover, at the least, the limits of its effects.

She's again in a phase of wearing my clothes, or my wife's. These phases come in regular cycles, at crises in her development, as though she has to put on shadows of us in appropriate ways, to help her through the day to her next plateau. Until, eventually, we'll be abandoned in the way that the clothes are—seldom picked up, left lying where they've been discarded—or so I sense whenever I can forgo my usual anger at this habit of hers. "Dammit!" I'll cry. "Pick this up!" And then I realize that the day will come when she'll indeed be gone, and I sink down in the nearest chair, letting the garment in my hand drop over my knee or into my lap, where she so seldom sits now.

For the first month after our son was born, she would slump in a chair and sulk if she couldn't change his diaper to begin her day (her waking for her long ride to school coincides with his, at six), and I was surprised at her desire to be so involved—but then I was never the oldest. She had to be allotted a certain amount of time with him, alone, to hold him and murmur over him as her mother does, and sometimes after school she would get caught up in a talk with him almost like mine, and after one of these she went to her mother, looking drawn, my wife thought, and said, "Boy, I think he told me all his problems tonight."

"What were they?"

"I wish I knew!"

She's closer to his state than we are, clearly. She might even be able to see into it, and the only jealousy I've been able to detect in her, if it is that, is a certain detached and silent observation of him, her face drawn, as if each were in a separate room, particularly after school, or when she's tired. One recent afternoon she said, and not wistfully, either, "I wish I could be his age again, Mom."

"Whatever for?"

"It's so much fun. There's nothing to do!"

My wife ran a hand through her own yellow-brown hair and then grabbed it in a tail behind, in a gesture that strikes me as especially Scandinavian, and threw it over her back as she laughed with the expansiveness our children have. She's the one whose feet step down firm below these clouds I weave.

She drives our daughter to the pickup point for her early trip to school, picks her up again at night, cooks so many meals there's no need to mention the few times I stir up eggs, or whatever, and no longer has help in the house, as before. She handles our accounts, shops, usually sees to washing the car and taking it in to be serviced, hauls home jugs of water from a well in a city park, so we can drink and cook from an untainted source, and takes the children out for walks and to museums, carrying our son in a sort of sling affair across her front. She does the laundry and the diapers and hangs them out, sometimes in frosty weather, on the lines that I've strung from the oak to hooks at the back of our house like a huge antenna, but of rope. No use attracting trouble that appears attracted to you.

"Even if I can't afford the time to read," I said to her once, "I sometimes have to. But that doesn't mean we can afford a clothes drier."

"Does it mean the opposite?" she asked. Of whatever we both meant, I guess. Look at the energy you would use, I said, in this time when everybody is trying to cut down on it, and she said you sound like President Carter—the same sort of circular excuse. She also keeps up on politics, does the correspondence for our chapel, and on the evenings when we can persuade our pastor to stay after a Bible lesson, she places mats and plates and a couple of the pieces of pottery and silver she's been able to preserve through our many moves (seven geographical states within our daughter's first five years) down on the glowing grain of the oak table I've refinished, and a plain meal takes on the contours, beneath the trembling of candlelight, of an Old World fête or festival of lights.

But about our daughter's jealousy, or lack of it. The other day, as she was coming from her morning bath before her early-hour departure for school, she found me, usually asleep then, sprawled across her bed in my bathrobe with the usurper, the newly loved one (what thoughtlessness! or worse), amusing him before she changed his diaper, and there was a pained and ferocious evasiveness in her that reminded me of the boys next door.

"The boys" is our all-inclusive name for them—three neighbor brothers ranging in age from twelve to seven. There's a gap between the youngest and the older two, and the analogues between them and my own brothers aren't lost on me. Their hair is clipped close to their skulls in burr cuts, as we used to call them—a style from the fifties here at the seventies' end. They threw eggs and tomatoes at our windows and across the windshields of cars in the parking lot, threw clods of dirt and rocks at our daughter and broke windows in our basement and their own garage, tore down part of the rococo stonework of the Italian neighbor across the alley, set fire to ants on the outside of their house with lighter fluid, got a garage wall burning so badly the fire department had to be called, and beat up on one another with a round-the-clock vehemence that sometimes awakened us at 2:00 a.m. Their bedroom window was exactly across from ours, hardly ten feet off, and they slept and spent most of their time there. The beatings drew blood and knocked the youngest one out, and kept me in a kind of fear for their lives, and, in a way, for my family's, too. The unendingness of violence, once set off.

Their house was a rickety, one-story affair, with a room and then another and then a closed-in porch scabbed on to it at different transitional stages, each a bit more temporary than the last. It all telescoped back from a bungalow and was covered with that gray composition sheeting that is supposed to look like brick, but is gray-pink, with black lines for mortar, and its tail end rubbed the branches of our oak. It is owned, as it turns out, by the casket-vault company across the street, where the boys' father works. This was once the far edge of the city, the last stop on the trolley-car line, and cemeteries spread in silence from us for blocks—vistas and tracts of stone angels and mausoleums and olive and black slabs.

Their father is a huge, unsmiling man, with a woman's wide hips and a poor-loser's look in his unsteady eyes. An air of gloom seemed to settle over his GI flattop, so that I wanted to ask him how Korea was—an impulse from the same source that causes me to wonder, whenever I walk a city street, how many of the men I'm passing (if you consider the First and Second World Wars, Korea, Vietnam, and other holding and "police" actions) have been trained to kill. He worked outside nearly every night, a can of beer close at hand, polishing his brand-new van with its bluely translucent windows, or adding a frill to it—or, with barking commands at the boys, wielding a variety of implements in the family's endless efforts to keep the lawn around their deteriorating house in the condition of a golf green, which they did.

Whenever I confronted him with something the boys had done, or might have had a hand in, he would say, "Ah, come on, you got the wrong guy," with a measuring look past my shoulder, and would walk off. He didn't beat them, as I first thought, hearing their cries and the pounding of feet as they were chased, but his wife, who was home all day, did—or tried to, and she also screamed. Seen through their windows, most of which matched one or another of ours, she was magnificently overweight, usually treading around in a shaking bathrobe. I never saw her out of the house more than twice, and then only at night, as if she went by stealth—quick behind the blue windows of the van in an agoraphobia also oversized.

You stop listening closely and then you stop listening at all, in order to live—or so you say to yourself in the city, once you become inured to city life. There are enough troubles in your own attempts to cope with existence hour by hour, you figure. The four of us seemed to form a cove facing away from the chaos battering at us on the other side. We continued to study with the pastor, a former missionary to Ethiopia, who claimed that Chicago is harder to crack than darkest Africa—always with a look at me, I felt. We began to attend the chapel where he preached, which was Reformed and Presbyterian, the proper mix for vigor and inquiry, to my mind. With his firm grasp of the Bible informing my shaky one, and the birth of our son exerting its pressure, while my transcription continued in force (each incident, once down, clustering and accreting around others that grew more rooted as Scripture was revealed to me), my election and calling became sure. We made public profession of our faith in Christ, were received as members into the church, and had our son baptized the same day. So I've become a believer, a fool for Him, as Paul and Pascal say, although I sometimes feel that what I've become adept at is judging, with a bit of the Bible under my belt, and there are times when I'm afraid I'll turn into one of those scrupulous churchgoing unbelievers who know the ropes and so act as if they're entitled to get away with what they can't bear in thee.

We prayed for the boys and their family in general and then began to ignore them—we didn't want further confrontations—and suddenly the boys became friendly. They talked to our daughter across the fence in a way that made me bristle at their youthful innuendos—you could see their suggestiveness simply in the way that they stood. Then they began to come up to me and say hello, spanning the generational superiority I often find myself caught in, even with my daughter, and studied me with such searching looks I had to consider what I might say.

We tried to be more "Christianly neighborly," as I put it, and took them ice cream and cake on our daughter's birthday. I attempted to talk to them when they came up as they did, and tossed back like an uncle the Frisbees and toys of theirs that ended up in our yard. And I tried not to imagine what mischief they'd been up to when I saw them come tearing, breathless, down the alley and pound up the steps to their back porch, or when I saw the police, as I did once, at their front door. Shortly after this, our phone rang one morning at 1:00 a.m.

"Is this the guy next door?" It was a breathless, girlish, teasing voice, perhaps involved in a prank, I thought, as I tried to place it, and Shirley Foster, a friend from high school, came to mind.

"You there?"

"Yes, I—"

"Did you hear that window go?"

"What window?"

"Between our houses here."

"Who is this?"

"Your neighbor."

"Across the street?" I once talked to a woman there about her cat.

"No, no, right next door here." She gave the address, not her name, but I couldn't quite believe her, or connect this voice to the massive, moving presence that filled our window frames.

"You didn't hear it go?"

"I'm not sure I—"

"It's probably one of those kids in your house there, those that've been throwing crap on the windows and busting stuff in the neighborhood up." Did she laugh? Gasp? Intend to make light of her sons? "I hear them down in that basement of yours a lot. A couple weeks ago, they were causing such a racket down there at one in the morning? I had to scream my lungs out from the window here to get them to stop, the creeps." I stepped back and looked out my daughter's bedroom window to their window across from it, where they usually stood when they talked on the phone, but it was dark. "The lights are on down there now," she said. "Will you go see what they're up to?"

I was about to say that there were only two children in the building, ours, and one of them an infant, and that the noise she'd shouted about the other night was me down in the basement, working on a tabletop with an electric sander. Which I'd meant to apologize for at the time, and now, feeling the heat of a blush, intended to, but I heard incoherent sounds, as if the call had become a prank again.

"My husband can't sleep with all this noise! This racket going on! He works odd shifts and has to sleep! You didn't hear a window crash?"

"I haven't heard a thing and I've been sitting right here." At the table, reading again.

"It sounded like it fell from high up. It woke me. I'm alone."

"Maybe it was across the street." The woman with the cat lived there in a three-story, glass-walled apartment building.

"Will you go check, please? Check between the buildings here. I'm afraid. I can't sleep no more. And then check and see what those kids are up to in that basement of yours. The light's still on."

She hung up.

I took a flashlight and went outside, shining it along both houses, and saw that the only broken window was the one to our furnace room. The boys had broken it out weeks ago, and I'd put off replacing it until the winter, when it would be needed and be less likely to get broken again. What was I doing here? Then, beyond the shrubs below my daughter's window, I saw the glowing gold square, greasily dim in the flashlight beam, of the basement window where I do repairs. I must have absent-mindedly left the light on, I thought, and sensed the gray of her bathrobe travel backward into darkness at their window, and was silenced by the strangeness of the night, and the implications of it, closing around my guilt.

I went into the basement and shut off the light.

Anybody with the least bit of good sense, and certainly anybody who'd presume to take on the kind of project that I have—not to mention my own troubles—would know that something other than disorientation or night anxiety was up, you'd think, and get at the cause. I went to bed feeling drugged, and slid down a black ladder into sleep.

We learned that her husband had left her that night, or soon after it, and a week later one of the boys, the middle one, was at our door. I couldn't remember any of them ringing our bell before this, except as a prank, and was surprised to see the boy in our enclosed back porch.

"I'm David," he said. "From next door."

"Sure."

"Mom wants to know if you'll come help move this old refrigerator from down our basement back upstairs. She'll pay you. She's got her own account now. See, our dad left and is getting a divorce, so all our things is being dispodessed. Except this refrigerator is paid for."

"Yeah, and it works good as new," another voice said, and I leaned out the kitchen door and saw the oldest one, who is stouter, at the bottom of the porch stairs to the outside door, as if standing guard.

I followed them to their house, where a neighbor was waiting—a man from down the alley, with the build and comportment of a city policeman. He smiled a gap-toothed grin under his mustache, as if amused that I'd been enlisted for this, too, and pulled open a rickety side door.

"You know Bob?" he asked.

"Not really."

"I've known him and Betty here for twelve years. I guess he's finally had it with her."

We started down the basement to her fluttery cries of paying us, went down a crook in the stairs and through a flowered curtain into the business end of a demolished bowling alley, or so it looked—maybe because the ceiling was so low—and I remembered how I had worked as a pinsetter when I was about the age of these boys, as if stepping into subterranean time. There were boxes of tools and machine parts and paint cans, besides piles of wood that looked like shattered pins, lying around as they had at one of the worst alleys I'd worked, where children and lofters were sent, but all in a dimness that called down damp, without the shining, lighted lanes opening onto the bowlers' side of the world—the kind of clutter you don't want to observe too closely for fear of becoming involved in it in a way that might invade you for good.

The middle boy leaped and pulled himself up on top of a rusting old refrigerator, scrambled across it below the web-woven joists, and, lying there on his stomach, reached inside the refrigerator's open door and pulled down the hinged panel of its freezing compartment.

"See, we defrosted it all," he said. "So it won't be so heavy carrying up. We used to keep all our storage stuff in here. Well, mostly ice cream."

"Yeah, till you put that damn dead mouse in there," the oldest one said.

"He was live when I put him in!"

The policeman was staring down at a pile of dismantled bicycles. "Did your dad get any of these fixed?" he asked.

"Just that one outside we use."

"Yeah, but that one ran before."

The man stood for a while, as if deciding whether to offer to help with these, and then shook his head.

It took the two of us, with help from the boys (and a piece of pipe as a pry), about twenty minutes to get the refrigerator up the switchback stairs. She would call down encouragement, or cry "He's left me!" and cover her face with a smothered noise. When we got the thing into the kitchen where she wanted it, beside a tall tin cupboard of the sort we used to have in our old house, but with the door torn off, she said she would give us checks, because he had run off with her cash. We kept backing away and insisting no, and in the upset of her movement, with the floor creaking under us, I saw into the boys' bedroom and noticed that the blue curtains that faced us, printed with Snow White and the Seven Dwarfs, were tattered and trailing threads along their dirtied hems. A tangle of beds and covers I didn't care to take in.

She ran shaking into the living room, exclaiming something, and I pictured a dimensional form of the curtains, a pillow of Snow White, propped on my daughter's bed—I saw it through her eyes as I sprawled there with my son—and received a sense of how every detail unfolds at every juncture with others into endlessness, and then the woman came running out with a hand-carved leather purse and tried to hand us that. The policeman finally took it, for his wife, he said, but most likely so we could leave. As we stepped outside, with sweat lifting from us in the fresh air, a young woman in a suit as ash-blond and stylish as her hairdo came up the walk in spike heels—a social worker, the man whispered, although in the brilliant summer light, after all that, she seemed an angel.

"Am I too late?" she asked, looking dazed in the brightness that affected even her, blinking her heavily lined eyes as if she expected the worst.

The policeman crushed the purse up under one arm, as a mugger might, and said, "Betty's still there. She's okay."

A few nights later Betty's husband returned, to settle some family matters, or so we heard, urged by the social worker and the police, whom Betty was calling nearly every night, and while he was there she shoved her hands through a window, so we heard, and raked them downward, trying to sever her wrists, in fulfillment of her plea and warning to me.

They're gone now. After she was taken to the hospital, her husband returned to live with the boys. They seemed to carry on in a mutual truce, although his voice would sometimes come thundering down, and for a while they all lugged boxes and broken articles back to their garbage cans in the alley: cleaning house, we thought. Then one day a circular was stuffed into our mailbox about a village meeting in which a vote would be taken to decide whether the casket-vault company could be issued a permit to demolish the house, and put in a parking lot. I couldn't attend the meeting, but my wife did. She said that everybody was so clamorous about the change, because of the boys (they were hated by that many adults?) and the blight of the house, as it was put, that she was embarrassed she'd been concerned about a parking lot.

I tried to visit the woman in the hospital, near this neighborhood, a hospital I'm familiar with, but was told I would need special permission from her psychiatrist, and I couldn't, in my imaginary conversations with him, come up with the credentials for that. So I went to the boys instead, one afternoon when they were playing along the fence, and gave them the Norton paper edition of the Gospel of John that I'd intended to give to her. I said that I'd been in the same place once, and this had helped me out, and they said, Yes, they'd give it to her, thanks. I drew away, unable to mention Christ and the grace of God, as I'd intended to, because the look in their eyes was more than unplumbable.

One evening when we hadn't seen the boys for a while and imagined the house was deserted, we heard heavy feet tramp through it and voices echo in its empty rooms, and then two fire marshals came out the door and got into a van and drove off. Smoke seemed to be building in the house, and just as I was heading for the phone, a fire truck pulled up, its bell clanging and flasher going, and the van followed, lights also busy, along with a growing, bright train of fire-department and police cars. I came upstairs and looked out my front window, leaning over the radiator, and saw a rookie run up a ladder to the slanted roof above their entry, while firemen shouted instructions at him and at other rookies milling past with axes and poles. It was night now, and in the crimson strobing of so many flashers their actions took on an eerie jump and hold as they swung away with splintering sounds and explosions of glass at the windows and doors. Smoke poured out—from smudge pots, we learned—and as I watched their jittering movements, emphasized by fire hats and slickers, the beam of a flashlight went striding through the darkened rooms, and I felt my heart quicken with the fear that a voice would say, "There's a boy in here!"

The day before yesterday, I lay wide awake, with the bed shaking under me as one had shaken and given way only once before, during a California earthquake, and then a crash of noise resounded off the house. A low-throated motor, with a diesel's flat assurance, throttled up, backing away from my bed, and with the clanking sound of Caterpillar treads that came next, I knew the bulldozer had arrived.

I looked through the curtains and saw our daughter at the back of the yard with her box camera, taking pictures before her trip to school. I needn't have worried that the demolition would interfere with our lives. The house was leveled to the ground, and the scraps and timbers of its remains (along with that refrigerator, which went tumbling back down into darkness) were mashed into the basement, and packed there by the bulldozer's treads, in two hours. In the displacing absence, like a tooth removed, I saw that the house one over was built of stone.

Some hauling was done by dump trucks yesterday, a bit more was done this afternoon, and now the lot, skinned of sod from sidewalk to alley, is covered with six inches (I almost said "feet") of packed, crushed rock. Only a scattering of glass is left, lying over our strip of lawn, not from the window she broke out, but where the wall of the boys' bedroom collapsed.

The chill of late night is on now, a chill that comes from both above and below during this season, not just from the ground, as in spring, and since the last cold spell came and then left, our thermostat has never been turned up, as it needs to be at this hour, even taking into account the chill of emptiness where their house once was, and the array of packed, crushed rock at my back. But the thermostat is located on the ground floor, which is where we really live, as I've mentioned, and once I sit here I feel I can't move until a certain amount of work is fixed for good.

The doorknob above intrudes, pulses and glows in its distracting watch, mirroring me and this table, I see, as I look up: a meditative kingbolt. Which side do you open a door from if the door is never really closed, but more a wall that holds you inward? From spring to fall. Six months. The knob is clean even of any fingerprints. So if any of us is really guilty of anything that happened to the people who used to live next door, then most of the evidence, in a certain sense, has been removed.

I listen for any sounds from Jerome through the dormitory wall and Rick Purkeet pulls himself closer and grinds into me from behind, his hot face pressing close, and whispers, "Then what happened?"

"I started to sleep too much. I felt I could reach out and pull death over me like a bed sheet. Jerome and I were sleeping together again—"

"Mmmm."

"From the way we held to one another, you'd think that. But I hardly knew he was there. We were like nothing, like specks in blackness, and from somewhere in that room without a window, I could hear her say, 'Snuggle up, boys.'

" 'What are we going to do?' I would ask.

"And he would say, 'I don't know, I don't know.'

"He had trouble waking me for school. Some days I was late, or didn't go. The teacher said she understood but still sent me to the principal. Dad was at work. He dropped our sisters at our grandparents' on the way. The house was never the same after it was remodeled, and she'd never had a chance to set up order in it, so none ever came. Why wake up, I thought, and dress in that cold, dark room, and go down to a house as messed up as I felt, where building materials were as common as newspapers and toys, and some floors still bare boards, and eat cold breakfast food at a table with dirty dishes stacked on it, and coffee rings all around, like she and Mrs. Ebbinger had just got up?"

+

Even the furniture has the disconnected look it does in dreams. The corner cupboard with embroidery hoops glinting in it, the chrome chairs I used to use to steal my matches, the tall tin cupboard, which reverberates through its length when its door is slammed—now open on shelves of dish towels embroidered by her, cans of spice, an iron that bends the edge of a shelf down, stainless-steel bowls and Fiesta Ware that send out different registers of the colors of her face. Beams of another sort from the couch where she napped, and from its matching chair whose arms are frayed in an open empty density to accept her. The shelves of her books in disarray; the bureau she once painted lime green, whose back revealed, in lumpy, primary lettering, whenever she pulled it away from a wall during one of her angry cleanings: *Jeri is Dum.*

I splash water on my face, rub toothpaste with a finger across my teeth, and head off for school out the blind-clashing door on a run.

+

Dad leaves money in the cupboard, inside the bowl with a sugary green surface sprouting pink glass buds. I put our dishwashing stool next to the electric stove, climb up on the stove top, open the cupboard, and take out change for candy to fortify myself for school.

Jerome is there this morning, at the table, and says, "Are you stealing again?"

Which grates against my black morning mood. "What are we supposed to do? Use this for charity?"

"For what Dad puts it there for. Food and emergencies."

"Candy is food."

"It's sweets. You know you don't buy it when Dad's around."

"So? He doesn't give a shit."

He stares at his breakfast food, his face turning as white as the milk it floats in, at the way I've begun to talk.

"He's told us what to use it for. Look at your teeth."

"Look at your own," I say, and refrain from calling him "Snaggletooth," which might mean another fight—my name for him now that his eyeteeth have come in so large and long they not only square the corners of his upper lip but can be seen, when he holds his mouth a certain way, resting in indentations on his lower lip. "If he cares so much about us, why doesn't he send us to the dentist?"

"He does."

"Right, when you can get your elbow inside a cavity and start running into walls with the pain."

"Maybe he can't afford to send us as often as he'd like to."

"I've heard that one."

"If you wouldn't keep stealing, maybe he could."

"There's money here every time I look. This isn't stealing, it's piddley-dink stuff."

"It all adds up, sneak thief."

"Why don't you give us one of your angel-face smiles about that now, Snaggletooth."

He comes charging across the kitchen and I jump on him from the top of the stove. The change flies across the kitchen and we're back to where we keep promising Dad we'll never end up again, in combat. I'm muscled from running and working to build myself up after my illnesses, and sometimes I have the edge, depending on his temper. He fights in an elbowing, furious way, once he gets going, while I hold back and plot for a particular blow, unless my temper overtakes me. I sit on his chest now and pound his head on the floor and feel clumps of hair come out in my hands as he stares up with the possible end to his life widening in his eyes. He scratches my face, gouges my jewels, and digs at my windpipe as I go over. Then he's hitting me with something I'm afraid to uncover my head to check on, and I think with the joy of revenge of the brick I once threw that hit him so hard in the ribs, when he tried to dodge it, that it sent him arching over backward in a dive. The thump of it hitting, so final, brought up a quick inner vow never to hurt him again, if he was all right, and then he came at me with a moan of homicide and hammered on my back with the brick until I couldn't breathe.

Dad sits us at the table and begs us to stop. The next time he sits us at the table, he asks us to stop for Mom's sake. "Think of her," he says. "Think of how this fighting would affect her."

We promise to stop, and the next time we're in tears before we begin, because we can't stop, and the year seems to narrow to a few sensations: the iciness that enters your sinuses when you're hit in the nose, the smell of crushed grass and raw dirt, and a taste of salt from the sweat of panic, tears of frustration or injury, and swallowed blood; and around that, under the scars added over my head, which he goes for first with whatever he picks up, is a swelling ache from the heated exertion of trying to end it for good and failing at the last moment, out of pity or brotherly bonds, and then being flipped over to land underneath, and giving up hope that this will end at all.

+

I'm being bothered by a bony kid, as tall as our teacher, who has a hawk nose and bright-red lips of the sort you'd expect to find on the business end of a snail. He waits across the street after school, close to his house, a half block off, and cries, "There's the little twerp that lives in a gas station."

"So?" I say. "You live in a one-car garage." Which is true; the garage behind a big house has been sealed up at its front, and he and his mother and younger sister live there.

"You haven't even got a mother, you dink."

"If you had an old man, you might have something to talk about. I'd leave town, too, with a drip like you for a kid."

He rubs one long finger over another, as though sharpening it, and says, "Shame, shame, Mommy's boy. You might act tough, but you go home every night and *boo hoo* over Mommy."

My books hit the ground and I'm off. The few times he doesn't make it to his screen door, I jump him from behind and he turns flailing, with me hanging on, until I kick a leg to bring him down. We're afraid of each other, so whoever has the advantage ends up on top, but I can't light into him the way I light into Jerome, and when I turn shaky because I can't, I say, "Shut up about this or I'll clean your ass."

"Sure, when you get a guy from behind, you chicken."

"Hey!"

It's Jerome. He's picked up my books and is coming over in the slow walk he's developed this year, like an elderly farmer listening to every aching step, which distracts me enough for the kid to get me in a scissors hold with his spindly legs. So Jerome says "Hey" again, drops the books, and pulls him off, and then the kid acts as if he'll go for him, until he sees me on my feet, ready.

"This has got to stop," Jerome says, exactly like Dad, and his look is so sad he must recognize this. "Why don't you settle it for good?"

"How?" I ask, since it might be the solution for us also.

"Why don't you have a boxing match?"

"Sure," the kid says. "With your gloves, I suppose."

He must have seen the two of us going at it in our double garage, with the gloves Dad handed us on Jerome's birthday, saying, "At least use these," as if he knew he couldn't control our fighting but hoped to keep the cuts and bruises down. But we seldom have time to put them on, since our fights are so unpredictable—except when Dad warns us to put them on, or one or the other holds up a hand, an agreed-upon signal that means it's time to put them on, although we've had fights over the signal, before there's any chance to get to the gloves.

"Yes," Jerome says. "Whoever wins three rounds, that's it."

"Okay," the kid says.

"Who'll referee?" I ask.

"Him," the kid says, and points at Jerome and smirks, as if he knows that Jerome and I are enemies, or knows how it angers me that Jerome engenders such trust. The match is set for Saturday. Jerome and I spar all that week in the double garage (cleared now so a car can be parked), in the gritty glitter from the windows, and he keeps saying, "Go under. He's going to have the reach on you. His arms are as long as your legs."

"So what am I supposed to do? Saw them off?"

"Go in under. Don't keep trying to hit him in the face, like me."

"Boy, I'm gonna nail those lips of his, hey!"

"Go in under, I say. Here, let's try this."

He goes to the clothes hamper Dad once built, which has never been used as a hamper and still causes me to cringe with coldness, when I notice it in an unprotected moment, as if it were a coffin. We've taken it over and added hooks and racks inside, and call it our "sports-equipment center." He pulls out a pair of Little League bats, puts the boxing gloves on their ends, and holds them out and pokes at me with them—"What do you think I am," I say, "nuts?"—and this is exactly how the kid holds his arms when we meet in our match. The first round seems a draw, even I must admit, until I catch him with a thump to the chest that glazes his eyes.

"Wait, wait," he says, backing off, and the Mirro-Matic timer dings.

At the beginning of the second round, the kid says, "Here's for your stinking old gas station," surprising me with his voice fake, and gets me on the nose. He has to laugh at this, and all I can see is that mouth I plan to paste, now that I've run the first round Jerome's way, and as I make my move he stiff-arms me off while Jerome, holding the timer above the yellow-tiled sports-equipment center, ducks down and sways when the kid's back is to him, still coaching me. I keep reaching up, looking up, leaping up in a hopping pattern I'm sure will throw the kid off, and then I'm on my butt beside a grease stain, next to a grate where used oil was once drained. Frogs seem to be living in it. They're croaking something about broken oaks, while Jerome counts in clouds of *five, six*—

The timer dings.

"Are you sure you didn't speed it up?" the kid asks.

In round three, the kid acts afraid of what I'll do, now that I've been knocked down, and I'm afraid I'll be knocked down. It's a standoff until I realize the time is almost up and start to wallop him in the stomach with a steadiness that has him gasping as he backpedals away with his arms stuck out.

The timer dings.

Jerome walks over and raises the kid's right hand.

"What!" I cry.

"He won."

"You shit!"

"Well, what can I do? He knocked you down."

"Once, yeah, but for God's sake, I was—"

"Ooo, sorry, little twerp, but you got your own ass cleaned," the kid says, his gloves already off, and he's a half block away on his long legs before I take this in, dumbfounded by Jerome's betrayal. There's a rattly pocking over the gloves and I realize I'm crying.

"How could you do that? How could you say he beat me? I was walloping him all along!"

"I know, but he knocked you down."

"Knocked me—! What about those punches I got in under his guard?"

"I taught you some of that, and then it was so close I thought I had to let him win, to be fair."

"Fair!"

I sock him in the mouth.

He runs for the hamper, to get a bat, I figure, and I jerk off the sticking gloves and head for a garden fork against the wall and then my jaw goes numb and I'm looking somewhere else as a baseball bounces around the echoing garage and I understand I've been struck by it, from the heat of my split lip bleeding a brown song.

I grab the garden fork and throw it like a gig and barely miss. The fight goes flying around the garage, breaking out a window, bringing down a landslide of glass, a long piece of which I go for, to stab him with. I cut my hand in the slithery grappling and have to give this up, and then we're through the door and thumping into the kitchen, where two breakfast bowls miss and erupt like shots on opposite walls. We stop, panting, held in the patchy light through gray windows by her silence at this loss, both about to give in, but unable to with the other in sight, and then we're rolling over the floor of the living room, across the gray-and-pink linoleum with a chromium strip down its center, and onto the bare boards where the floor furnace used to hang. I get into a sitting position on his back and grind his face into the boards' grit and possible slivers of one bowl, and with my other hand grab the back of his shirt collar and jerk up. Something gives and he goes soft. I've done it. There's a gassy smell like rotten library paste.

He lifts his head and cries, "You ripped my shirt, you shit!"

"Big deal." I'm on my feet, in a cold featheriness.

He gets up with a groan through clenched teeth and runs into Dad's bedroom. I hear a door hit the wall and a clashing of hangers in the closet we share with Dad, since our good clothes can't be kept upstairs—and go to see what he's up to. He has taken out my favorite shirt, made for me by Grandma Jones from material I picked out; it lies over me like skin and has such personal value I wear it only once a month. He tears off a sleeve. He rips it up the back. There's an abraded streak down his face, under one eye, like an Indian marking, that gives him a wilder look, along with the collar of his shirt hanging over his shoulder—a hand-me-down from Davey that he hates. He tears off the collar of mine. He stands on it and rips off the other sleeve.

"That's the shirt Grandma made me!"

"Big deal!" he cries, his pouchy eyes bloodshot, and throws the tatters on the bed. "Big deal for—great old Grandma! and you!"

I lie on the bed and pull the pieces of it around my face, as if to catch whatever is on its way out, and then I'm breathing a blood-gargled scream and feel faint. I imagine the kid pointing a skinny finger at me and saying, "Hoo, boy, I beat that little bugger in a boxing match, with his brother trying to help him yet!" Because I've made the agreement, I'll stick to it, no matter how much I might want to shred the kid's mouth, and I imagine the energy it will take to live it down, besides the rags of this shirt in my aching craw on top of that. But I could still forgive Jerome, I feel, if it weren't for the shirt. I see Joe Louis falling toward the ropes, drawing the world after him like cloth, and picture myself in the middle of the schoolyard, at the center of an accident too terrible to name, with everybody shaking their heads and backing off, and Davey, under a catalpa beside the street, saying, "I wonder if I really ever knew the guy."

Then I hear Jerome in the kitchen, sweeping up the broken

bowls, wailing, and wish our mother's spirit would descend and do him in. Her death is worth it if it causes him this.

+

We start to eat too much. I learn to cook and bake, to keep up with our appetites, and sometimes fry eggs before school, standing at the stove on our dishwashing stool, whose legs are getting wobbly, and prodding with a spatula at the eggs in a pan of sizzling grease.

"Do you want these so soft they have snot clots?" I ask. "Or hard as a rhinoceros's nuts?"

"Whatever's eashiest." He's talking through his cereal. "We can't mish shchool."

Or Dad will leave pancake batter from his breakfast, or there is batter in the refrigerator, since pancakes have become our most common meal, and I'll fry a dozen pancakes each, eating away at Wheaties on the stove top while I do, and we'll have pancakes with syrup and jam, or sugar and half-and-half. And after school we hurry home to stuff slices of white bread from a long "family" loaf into the toaster, then smear melting margarine over them, spoon on sugar that sucks the margarine up into gray mounds, sprinkle cinnamon over that, and drop more bread into the toaster while we eat what we've got, saying "Ummm," until the loaf of bread is gone. Or trowel slabs of peanut butter over bread and wrap it around a dill pickle and eat that.

I bake cookies on call, day or night; also pies and cakes, sometimes from mixes, though I can whip them up from scratch—bread, brownies, cinnamon rolls, and cream puffs. Jerome's favorite is Bisquick coffee cake, and we eat a whole pan of it in one sitting, hot, often with coffee, which we've started to drink, at least when Dad isn't home, with flour all over the table and the floor and my clothes (I sometimes have to change after a baking session, slapping at my sagging belly), and then I mix up another batch when we're done, it tastes so good.

"Umm, can't be as good the second time around," Jerome says, sucking a thumb, then his fingers.

"You want to bet? I'm putting in cinnamon hearts this time!"

Mold often grows in the bowls before they're washed. We've given up on the dishes with her gone, and Dad does them now, when they're done, sometimes scraping the stove with a putty knife. He stands at the sink late at night, staring out the black window above it as if he can see whatever she saw when she stared out the other window that now seems hers, and washes and wipes everything we've let go for days.

"I don't mind you doing this," he says once, when I've come into the kitchen to put cold waffles into the toaster and realize that he is looking into the window like a mirror at me. "I don't mind it at all, Charles." His voice sounds as if it's bubbling from underwater, near sleep. "In fact, I think it's wonderful that you want to cook and bake. But when you're done, for God's sake"— he throws a spoon into the sink with a splash—"why in the *hell* don't you clean up!"

He has begun to curse a bit, without the look of tasting alum, which has opened up a hidden part of my inner dictionary. "What the hell," he says one night, throwing the newspaper to the floor, as if a decision has been reached, and for Christmas he buys a television set. It's one of the first in town, a distinction I feel during the cold walk back from school, toward the mast rising from the peak of our house above bare elms. Even with a rotor on the mast, which we can operate with a dial like a timer, sending vibrations through the roof (a spooky feeling of a tent humming above us in the wind when we're in bed, in the blackness of our room, as Dad experiments)—even with this, the picture resembles different shades of smoke in a snowstorm. The sound is clear, even if it doesn't always match the channel where the phantom figures plow through their perpetual blizzard, and I feel that the voices from the radio have turned into fluttering particles that hold me in the hypnosis of those days on the floor beside her bookshelves. We let down the couch, making it into a bed, and lie and stare at the television as if it's a view onto those North Dakota days.

And fall asleep, after eating pastry or Rice Krispies squares I've made, and wake in a darkened room to gray-violet light massaging the ceiling, as soothing as a fireplace and usually as interesting as the programs themselves, and then the room stretches to its length in swift whiteness as the test pattern arrives with an electronic scream. Sometimes we're asleep by then, or pretend to be, and feel darkness fall with a distant click, and then something heavier, a blanket or a coat, is over us, closing in the heat that's been rising from us, and his voice says, "That's all right, boys. It's just Dad. Why don't you sleep downstairs tonight. I need the company."

+

We wake to a bell banging so loudly in the garage it brings down dust in our upstairs room.

"It must be them," Jerome says, and sighs. Three of the members of Dad's basketball team are here for the summer. After work they go out and drink, and then come back and talk about girls, which has taught us a lot. One of them is Dave Mitchell, a member of the family that moved into our house in Hyatt, and we've asked Dad to ask him about our train, and Dad has said he will, but when we check with Dad, he says, "Oh, stop pestering me about that train! You drove your mother wild with that!"

The bell keeps up its iron beating as though it's time for church, and Jerome and I go out of our room, over the planks along its back wall, toward the lit square ahead, with a board ladder leading up to it from below. They're in the garage, looking shrunken from our height, as if the hole is a television screen, with squat shadows of different colors trailing them from overhead bulbs. A double bed, looking low as a mattress, is set up as it once was for us, but now with the Army cot beside it, and two of them bend at the bell Dad has salvaged from a country school that Grandpa turned into a house. They've put the bell back in the yoke that held it, and are swinging it between them with a clanging pulse we have to hold our ears against. The other drops back onto the cot, laughing, from the way his head is thrown back, mouth wide, as if the orange clouds of rust the bell sends up will undo him.

"Time for school, Martin!" Do we hear right? They each have a bottle of beer. Other bottles are standing on the floor, like calf nipples on our high screen. They pause and pass a square bottle around, nipping and slapping one another's shoulders, and then Dave Mitchell throws out his arms and roars, "To pee or not to pee!"

"Right, Martin," the others say in squawking laughter, and one has to lie back on the bed, holding his jumping stomach.

"Toomattow, and toomattow, and toomattow," Dave says, and can't go on for the hawking laugh that has him bending to get his breath.

"Are you going to drink?" Jerome whispers, and his eyes, lit from underneath, stare into the future of his question.

"We have," I say, because we've sampled some of the bottles that aren't empty—a taste like dough left to rise too long.

"No, I mean, when you get older?"

"Yes," I whisper, trying to recapture the numbed dizziness I felt when I found a half-full bottle and drank all of it off without telling him.

He looks back down on them as they settle on the bed in the way they do when they talk about girls. "I'm not," he says. "Look." Their bodies jerk on the bed as they laugh again, and I notice that their shoes have left orange prints of rust. "It makes you talk too much," he says.

+

The only way to keep Jerome quiet about my stealing is to include him. I take him to Kleinerud's and make sure he's standing close when I swipe a candy bar. Wide eyes. I've cased every foot of the store, and know where Rob Kleinerud has to be standing in order to see the candy display. The surest trick is to ask for sliced meat from the case at the back of the store, if I have money for meat, and then fiddle with the scale on the counter beside the meat case, getting Rob so nervous he's glad to see me head toward the cash register, at the front of the store, where the candy is.

Rob has told me that young folks nowadays will steal you blind—a different generation, he says. He had a paper route when he was a boy, he says, and saved up for a store, and that and his service pay did it. He rolls the sleeve of his shirt up to the tattoo of an anchor on his arm, to show me the blue clouds of shrapnel still floating beside it, under his skin. His leg is worse, he says, with sores that open sometimes, and once he lifted a trouser cuff above his polished Army boot, with a top held by two leather straps, then seemed to decide *no*.

Dark-brown eyes stare out from his bifocals, clouded with a sadness that causes me to blush, for his courage when he took a German machine-gun nest and caught the shrapnel, as he's told me, and for shame that I still steal from him.

"You're holding up real well, Charles," he says. "I lost my mom, too, so— I know you boys love your dad so much." He switches around the Life Saver always in his mouth with a clacking against the teeth he says the Army gave him.

I talk to Rob in different parts of the store, never the same, but always in a place that's blind to the candy display. Jerome doesn't feel as bad about stealing as talking to Rob, he claims, though I never really talk, but listen, and the difference between Jerome and me is clear in this, and in what we steal: Bit-O-Honey his favorite, and mine Hershey's, plain, which he takes with almonds; then he'll go for Chuckles, which I can save for last, or if I'm headed that way I'll go for Mason Crows, or, better yet, Jujubes, but Jujubes are available only at the Lamar; then a Heath for him and a Butterfinger for me; Mounds or Almond Joy next, which, in this case, I take with almonds and he takes plain; then Planters peanuts, to cut the sugar so we can eat more; and then I'll take a Tootsie Roll, where he'll go for a Sugar Daddy—down to Snickers and Three Musketeers. Mars for dessert.

Until Rob puts up a display of Tot staplers before the beginning of school. After examining the tiny red nipper in its clear plastic case (staples enclosed) with such a brainful of covetous sparks I feel it's becoming as heavy as lead, I steal one. The next night, when the three of us are watching TV—Dad in his chair, the two of us on the couch—Dad says, "Well, I handed Rob Kleinerud twenty dollars today."

"Twenty dollars!" I say. "What for?"

"Your stealing. Or that's my payment to him this month."

His face is set directly at the TV, as if scorched by its activity of light. "I stopped in for some cigars and he told me this has been going on for a year. I figure I owe him thirty more."

+

October in New York, and a crowd of policemen in the sun
at the corner of Park and the cross street ahead. A tumble
of traffic goes past, the speeding taxis rattling so badly it
seems bumpers will fall off, and then the light turns and the
policemen walk across the avenue and cordon it off, holding
white-gloved hands in solid formation over to a gold-domed
cathedral. Its double doors swing wide, and ranks of men step
out, carrying a flag-draped casket on their shoulders, and start
heavily down the steps, while a crowd in black sweeps past them,
heads down, toward a black hearse flying an American flag
from its aerial. Gray and black limos line up along the curb
behind.

"What is it?" I ask the policeman at my curb, who has a
spiky mustache and a hump in his nose, as if it's been broken,
and looks my age.

"Hoover's funeral," he says, staring ahead as if at attention.

"Hoover?"

"Herbert Hoover. He was President once."

"You mean he's still around?"

"Was."

I turn away and hear my father say as I walk, "There were
times in North Dakota when you'd hear people revile Hoover
as though he caused the Depression. Temporary towns and
camps were called Hoovervilles, after him. Some talked as if
he'd personally sent the grasshoppers and drought that kept
building to the Dust Bowl days. Topsoil blew up in drifts along
the fence lines, and they claimed you could see clouds of dust
all the way to Chicago. Parts of North Dakota ended up on the
East Coast. It was a situation, really, that Hoover had walked
into. The financial crash that came would have come no matter
who was President—it was partly engineered by European
bankers—but Hoover was the culprit. Dad, your grandpa,
understood his predicament, I believe, but Dad was a Social
Democrat, as I am and probably always will be, so he voted for
Roosevelt. I'm not sure Roosevelt had the correct economic
answer, either, with his old New Deal. Other, similar 'deals' had

been tried before, and his weren't much different from some of Hoover's recovery programs. Something had to be done, at least for the farmers who didn't have any land left to farm, it was felt. The Non-Partisan League in North Dakota came up with a few solutions for the state itself, but went to extremes you wouldn't want to see across the country, or we'd be mired in Socialism now, with the kind of state control the man in the street in Communist Russia is groaning under this very day. Hoover had a heart for people, I believe. For some reason, much as I liked F.D.R.'s style, I could never quite trust his political shenanigans, as the folks in North Dakota came not to trust their greatest hero—Wild Bill Langer. Langer got involved in so many back-yard deals he became the bitterest disappointment to the people of any favorite son. He . . ."

But I'm leaning against a wall of brick in New York City, undone by my father's voice, as if I've witnessed his funeral, not Hoover's. This endlessness of betrayal.

+

When I wake up in the sixth grade, the teacher is Enos Clapton. He is also the grade-school principal, and, as Jerome has said, "He's a real disciplinarian. He can make older boys cry. They say when he gets real mad he takes out a piece of garden hose and *whap*. Somebody else said it's a fan belt. Don't contradict him, even if he says weird things."

Clapton has his desk turned sideways at the front of the room, so he can see into the hall to the door of his office, where offenders are sent. In the middle of a workbook exercise, he pedals his wooden swivel chair around and leans back, his hands behind his neck and his elbows out, his big head with yellow-gray hair near the blackboard, which has oily spots along it where he's touched, and says, "Say, class, what do you think of Joseph Stalin?"

He grins and stares around the room with half-closed, gray-green, catlike eyes. "No response? From this usually talkative bunch? Don't you think, class, that Stalin will be classified as one of this century's great heroes?" He grins again, showing broken and tobacco-stained teeth, and all of us look down to our history workbooks, afraid to speak. We're never sure Clapton is serious about these subjects, and if we rat on him to our parents, we figure Clapton will get back at us.

"He's a Communist," Billy Gene Skaggs, a new student who has moved up from Kentucky, says, and I start blinking in fear for him.

"Did I hear mumbling in a Southern accent?" Clapton asks. "Does Skaggs have a contribution he'd like to make to the class?"

"He's a Communist," Billy Gene says, louder. Billy Gene has beaten up everybody two grades ahead of him in playground fights, and Clapton loves to pick on him. "He's a Russian Communist. Everybody knows that."

"I beg to differ with you, Billy Gene. Stalin is a Socialist. The Union of Soviet *Socialist* Republics. Scramble the letters and add *ia* and you've got Russia, right? He's a Socialist, Skaggs."

"However y'all fancy it up, he's still a Communist by me," Billy Gene says. "The Communists are meanin to take over the world. Look what they did in Korea. My daddy fought them bastids there."

"Out!" Clapton says, on his feet, his face flushed, the chair spinning backward till it bangs the blackboard rail. He raises a trembling hand. "Out of this room with that kind of talk! Get in my office! I'll deal with you at recess. Get!"

+

Recess. On the wall of the school beside the rear doors is a row of brick trim eight feet high and just above that a certain dark brick we have to hit with a sponge-rubber ball to make a basket—one of our forms of basketball. There are about ten on each team, since it's mostly a passing game, and Jerome is teamed against Dean Roy Skaggs, Billy Gene's older brother; the Skaggses are exactly the same age and size as Jerome and me, and are taken for twins, but have dark complexions and black hair. Billy Gene comes out a door, holding a middle finger up in front of his jacket, and Clapton glances through the windows at the top of the doors on his way down to the furnace room for a smoke. People ask Billy Gene if he caught the hose, while the game keeps up, and then somebody starts yelling about this year's election. "We need a military man!" Dean Roy cries. "Eisenhower'd clean Korea up. Stevenson's a panny-waist!"

"He's an intellectual!" Jerome says, which is what we've heard from Dad. "We need somebody that can think for a change!"

"Who says Eisenhower can't?" Dean Roy asks, and by now the game has stopped. "He won World War II, din't he? Stevenson's an aighead!"

"He's smart!" Jerome says. "You should read some of his speeches." Which is something else Dad has said.

"Have *you*, Neumiller?" somebody asks.

"He's run the state all right, hasn't he?" I say, and see Stevenson's name and signature on the colored labels pasted across the meat scale at Kleinerud's. "Do you think Eisenhower could do any better?"

"Yeah!" Jerome says, and Dean Roy grabs him.

"Okay," Clapton says from the door. "Can it, Skaggs. All of you! To hear you talk, you'd think the peons from Podunksville—including minors who can't even vote—have some say in our so-called national elections."

+

After school, I see Dean Roy, out by the catalpas, on top of Jerome, who's on his back, and I can tell from the way Jerome's head wobbles that he's hurt. I drop my books and run over, and the kid who beat me in the boxing match grabs an arm and cries, "Hey, that's Dean Roy Skaggs, stupid! He—" I pull Skaggs off and he's at me, fists connecting, and then, perhaps from the kid being there, I get in the blow I'd intended for him, and Dean Roy grabs at a greasy-looking brilliance that I realize is blood. He tilts his head back, gripping his nose.

"You shit-sucker," Billy Gene says, swinging me around by a shoulder. "You know he's got a bad nose."

"No—" I start to say, of course I didn't know that, afraid of what I've done, but Billy Gene is swinging before I can get the words out, and I leap through his fists and get him in a headlock that grates his teeth together. I bang his head on my knee. There must be a crowd, because a cheer goes up. I bang his head again, afraid to let him go, and a kick from behind sends me flying into a somersault. I spring to my feet and turn, ready. It's Clapton. "Do you want to fight me?" he asks, his fists up, and then leans so close I can see the bitter shine in his eyes and smell his awful breath. "Try it! Fight!"

I back away, my arms unhinged and melting, and he grabs both Skaggses by their jackets and heads toward the school with one in each hand.

I pick up my books, and Jerome thanks me as we walk off. "He had me in a choke hold," he says. "I couldn't breathe. He was going to shut me up about Stevenson." He looks back. "What are you going to do when they come after you?"

"Are they coming?"

"They will, sooner or later."

"Run."

"Be serious."

"It'll be one at a time. They fight fair."

"So?"

"If they get me down, I'll cover my head and give up."

+

Grandma Jones has moved to California, so there's no farm in the North to head for. I begin to read too much. My mind moves out on the strings of words into worlds with elbowroom. Or the words slip into a frame that seems patterned to receive them, as if there were waiting slots and shelves in me like the shelves I pull the books from, whether from the tall green cases at the rear of the sixth-grade room, with wire mesh over their doors, like pie coolers; or from the glassed-in bookshelves at home, or Mom's shelves, or the shelves that Dad has built to line his bedroom—now his office, although he still sleeps there in a single bed he's bought, with a headboard of bookshelves.

We ask Dad to enroll us in the Landmark Book Club, and our choices begin to arrive each month. A week before the next is due, we're at the post office every afternoon, standing on a radiator at the window so we can reach the dials to work the combination of our box. Finally, a parcel-post reminder is among the bills, the pink card as frayed and worn as a dollar bill, with a hint of our own feathery lightness as we carry it to the window. There's the cardboard of the book box to deal with first, then the jacket to study and stroke, and lift free to smell the cover and binding and pages inside, and then the sparkling print that leads down brighter levels to the clear-cut world of Paul Revere or John Paul Jones or Robert E. Lee (the only problem, now, being who will read it first, and sometimes we take turns and sometimes lie upstairs on our bed and read side by side) or Abraham Lincoln—all dedicated to ideals beyond mere fighting.

We don't take the books to school, or even mention them there, and in my homeroom I find others that attract me on the pie-cooler shelves. I read them at recess time, when nobody stays inside but girls.

"What's he reading now?" Jeannie Ebner whispers in a low voice, as low as most boys'; when she raises a hand in class, she places the other over her underarm to cover blond fuzz. She's the daughter of a wealthy farmer, and the most recent female focus of my attention; she wears huge crinolines, and shining harlequin glasses on a long nose with knobs that seem perfect for those little squeezers of glasses to rest on.

Her hanger-on, Willa Petey, a poor town girl, swishes over, brave in her affection for Jeannie, and says, "It looks like monkeys to me."

It's on evolution, Clapton's favorite subject after the U.S.S.R., and I'm looking for particular behavior—my family!—or comments I can wedge in below the point of being punished, since I've secretly sided with Billy Gene.

"Eeep! Eeep!" I cry, forcing my lips into a muscular, monkeylike mouth. I hop on top of my desk, hunched over, arms dangling, and start scratching, then leap to the floor, helping myself along on my knuckles in a sideways shamble that causes the girls to shriek so loud my hair tingles. I scurry past them and, at the back of the room, scramble up on the counter of one of the pie-cooler bookshelves, emitting my noises, and then all that's left is the cabinet above, with a surface of wire mesh before there's a top to get hold of, and with the extra-human agility that comes to me in such states, I'm suddenly up on its top, dancing sideways along its narrow dusty ledge, close to the ceiling, which I'd hit if I weren't in my crouch, feeling the whole thing wobble and give as I pretend I'm about to leap down on them. I can't see them through my crossed eyes, but they sound so frightened I turn into a true monkey. "I'm not crazy!" I cry, hopping up and down. "I'm ape!"

"Ape-man!" It's Clapton, up from the furnace room. "Get your fat butt down from there! Now!"

I grab hold of the trim on top and ease my legs down and paw around to find a foothold, until finally he grabs me at the waist and wrenches me free. I clasp and wring my wood-scraped hands in what must look like begging, and Clapton extends an arm toward his office and walks on the backs of my shoes as I head there, saying "January, February, March!" and slapping the back of my head with each *"March!"*

In his office he reaches behind his roll-top desk, then flops back in a wooden swivel chair and starts whacking the palm of one hand with—it's a length of red rubber hose, is what it is.

"I've about had it with you lately, Neumiller, and then—" He hits the hose on the desktop and I jump. "Then up on those cases like a damn orangoutang! Did those giggle-britches put you up to it? Answer me!"

"No."

"Oh?" This goes up in a high womanish way and his bushy eyebrows rise. He leans forward in the chair and there's a reek as the tobacco-stained teeth appear in his crazed smile and his eyes mist. "Perhaps you are a dumb-ass, huh?" He pokes at my hanging shirtfront—the way I wear shirts now to cover my gut—with the hose.

"Is that true? Are you a dumb-ass?"

I'm not sure what to do; I shake my head.

He treadles backward and turns to stare out the window, and in the leaf-tinted light his face looks green. "No, we know that's not true, don't we," he says to himself. "You could be a rather bright boy, I believe. I mean, I never had trouble with your brother." He turns back to me. "Is it the situation at home?"

My chin feels socked and wrinkles so tightly it keeps quivering.

"Oh, good God!" he says. "Not that, now." His eyelids close, pebbly-orange in his wrinkled face, and he sighs. "So far this semester you've handed in thirty-six book reports. The requirement is four. If the reading is doing you good, and not getting you into trouble like today, keep it up, I encourage you, but please please please do not hand in any more book reports. Now get out."

I can't move.

He swings around and slams his desk with the hose. "Get out!"

+

I read whatever I can about Abraham Lincoln, who is everywhere in this state. The license plates have *Land of Lincoln* on them, and when we travel from Havana to Lincoln on old Highway 29 into 10, and there are odd angles of right and left turns, some of them at ninety degrees on the open prairie, and I ask why the road does this, Dad says, "Well, it follows the route Lincoln took when he made the circuit of the local courts on horseback. It follows his route religiously. Now, these sudden turns, I understand"—he swings our old Hudson on a tire-screeching slide around one—"these turns are where Lincoln hitched his horse and went off into the bushes to take a leak."

Jerome and I turn to one another, surprised, although he played Looter once, and I look out over the green land, with elms rising here and there among the bristling fields of corn and soybeans, and feel that Illinois might be bearable, if Lincoln walked here.

All the affection that I can't express for my father (as I lately sometimes think of him) pours into Lincoln. I've read every book on him in the pie-cooler library, and the last one, in its final chapter, described the blood dripping from Lincoln's hair onto oak leaves as he was carried across the street from Ford's Theater to the Peterson house, and I relived the wounded stickiness of my own head. It was criminal, unbelievable, that a person existed who once hated Lincoln—that face I've studied so closely in pictures I know the pattern of lines under each eye. Lincoln is the point where history turned; I can see the purpled swelling of his right eye, where the derringer ball is lodged, as I imagine myself at his catafalque in the Capitol rotunda, with lines of people winding past with echoing foot-steps, and think: If a President was shot, everybody is fair game.

Dad has started teaching again, at seventh-grade level, in another building, and the first time I go to meet him and he comes down the dark hall in the suit he bought for the state basketball tournament, now loose-fitting, with a tie twisted between its lapels, I see that he is like Lincoln, and a chill of fear encloses me. Dad has black hair and is tall, with bony expressive hands, and shoulders that seem to graze the classroom doorways when he steps through them, checking each one like a watchman, and then he stops in front of me and I sense the sunlight from the basement of the high school in Hyatt on us, and stare up at a face as sorrowing as Lincoln's—that distant, rocklike look of the photographs.

"Yes," Dad says. "Time to go home."

There, at night, he sits at the fold-down desk he's built into his wall of bookshelves, with rows of books above him, and grades papers by the light of a single-bulb lamp with a tiny shade scorched brown, or pages through one of the catalogues from which he orders his clothes for school. The living room is always darkened, for watching TV, and television light lies over his shoulders when he leans back at the desk, wearing the gray twills that he changes into at home, and above his large ears I can see where his hair is turning silver, and think: If he had joined the Army, he could have been shot there.

On a night like this, Clapton comes to our door. Dad turns on all the lights and asks him in, and Jerome and I sit up at attention on the couch, as if we're back in Clapton's room. He has a heavy briefcase in one hand, and he and Dad talk inside the door for a while. Then Dad pulls out the chair from his office for Clapton, and pulls up another for himself from the kitchen, and they sit. I'm so frightened I can hardly listen, and as Clapton talks he stares at Jerome, then at me, and smiles his wolfish smile, with that glittery look in his eyes of a dirty secret, and says, "You certainly have two there who'll use them."

He reaches into his briefcase and hands us a heavy book, bound in white, with slick pages that smell better than any I've sampled—an encyclopedia. The set, he says, can be bought in monthly payments. He rubs the knees of his slacks, and in the light of our house a shine appears. His gray sweater, with buttons down its front, the only one he wears in class, has ragged cuffs. There are spots on it. Dad, beside him in twills, with his shirt out and unbuttoned, and a T-shirt with the name of our school printed across it, pulls at his chin as if it's a beard. My feelings cross and recross, with Clapton's catlike eyes on us, his lips so tight it seems he's swallowing something down, and my love for Lincoln takes a different turn as I realize I'm staring at the two men most like Lincoln in our Illinois town.

+

The stories that finally affect me the most are by Edgar Allan Poe. A razor-sharp pendulum swinging closer while rats scrabble away, the yowling man walled up behind bricks by a friend, the heart of a murdered landlord beating under the floor when the police arrive, and worse, what the words and stories stir up; catalepsy, waking in coffins, mausoleums, the unendingness of death, mossy tresses growing underground, our helplessness to escape an awful end—the way the world appears to me now.

+

I'm in our bed upstairs, reading a new piece by Poe, "Imp of the Perverse," in a book from Dad's shelves. Poe says that science should classify man by what he does; then it would have to admit to one of the most primitive principles: perverseness. I look up and the light bulb dims, and a fear, as fragile as the coils in the bulb, frazzles me. We stand on a cliff, he writes, and look over, sick at the height, and the imp takes shape, "and yet it is but a thought, although a fearful one, and one which chills the very marrow of our bones with the fierceness of the delight of its horror. It is merely the idea of what would be our sensations during the sweeping precipitancy of a fall from such a height. And this fall—this rushing annihilation—for the very reason that it involves that one most ghastly and loathsome of all the most ghastly and loathsome images of death and suffering which have ever presented themselves to our imagination—for this very cause do we now the most vividly desire it . . . To indulge for a moment, in any attempt at *thought*, is to be inevitably lost; for reflection but urges us to forbear, and *therefore* it is, I say, that we *cannot*. If there be no friendly arm to check us, or if we fail in a sudden effort to prostrate ourselves backward from the abyss, we plunge, and are destroyed."

I close the book, feeling the light bulb has gone out, afraid to look up. "Jerome?"

There's only the coolness of the house, with no stir of

noise—Saturday—and I remember that he and the rest have gone to Forest Creek. With Dad. *Our father*, I almost think, in my state. I go to the door, past the end of the stairwell, and my legs turn so numb I have to sit on a board placed across the joists. There's a drop to the ceiling over the Ebbingers' half of the house, and my feet hang over the drop like weights drawing me into their rooms. Boxes are piled on a platform ahead, and I can see a white-yellow glow above the top of one. I ease myself onto the joists, like nerves drawn tight, and step from one to the next to the platform, then dodge my head around the yellow glow. I pick it up. The plaque we bought for Mom, on that awful Mother's Day. I hold it against me, and step back to where I was, our upstairs floor at the level of my waist, and notice open gaps between the studs below. I drop the plaque into a gap and it rumbles down inside the wall and hits with a splash.

Then I scramble up on the boards and go down the stairs and out the blind-clashing door on a run.

+

Our blue Hiawatha's chain guard and fenders are removed—stripped. I ride it around the concrete drive, and the point, it develops as I ride, is to keep on the outer section of the concrete, and to never allow the front tire to cross the joint into the next section, which takes some maneuvering, since the central part of our house sticks out beyond the garages on both sides (the Ebbingers' double garage sided over, however, since it's where they live), and as I come around the central part, past our front door, the drive pinches in to meet an island of cement that held the gasoline pumps. I ride counterclockwise, along our garage, take a left at the center wing, a right past the front door, another right along the other side, a quick left along Ebbingers', an angled left along the curb at the edge of the drive, a hard left along the street, another along the lawn, flaring up to the concrete island, a left around this end of the island, a right around the other end, and then, down a ways, a left where the drive angles to the street; a difficult left at the other outer curb, and then along our garage again, on and on, the concrete starting to blur and jiggle with turns that tug at my insides, as I go as fast as I can and still remain within the lines, pumping on the longer stretches, leaning into turns, growing dizzy from the same direction and inward tilt, retracing the same contours on slightly different lines, and feel if I can keep up this pace for a dozen laps, my family will be safe, wherever they are, because I imagine them in danger—captured by an evil force, Hitler, and my riding here, without crossing the lines, is the only way to save them. A giddy dizziness starts to climb my throat at the thought of failing, now that I'm caught up in this, the house flashing past, a window, air, a tree above, grass, a curb, sometimes almost crossing a line, sometimes a bit over one, but so close it doesn't count (does it?), losing track of the number of times by now, or the exact amount required to save them, and then thinking of my grandparents, aunts, uncles, faces blurring in the concrete, and then a patch of sand brings me down with a crash.

I hop away, crying "Hoo hoo hoo," and make it to the concrete island, massaging my knee against a swelling heat, and notice, out on the lawn, a coil of hose, and think, I could start a car wash to— Oh! I see myself in the medicine-chest mirror, using Mom's metal-backed mirror (the mate to the brush she used on us, now hidden on the shelves above the toilet stool) to check the scar at the back of my head, and catching, in an angle of the mirrors, the apelike mug of Carl Sandburg, the Illinois poet who wrote "The frog comes on little cat feet"—or so I misread it; lately I've been misreading so often there must be something wrong with me—and wonder why Jerome never mentioned this deformity. I've told him about his teeth.

A black motorcycle pulls up to the edge of the lawn, a German one that runs on belts instead of a chain and belongs to Skip Wangsdorf, a student who stops at our house when he's exercising the boxers his family raises, to talk to Dad, as other students do—while Dad stands at his workbench in the garage and the boxers struggle against their leashes, clawing at the concrete—and then Wangsdorf comes out and asks for my latest story. The only stories he's interested in are the kind I've heard from the Skaggs brothers, and I've learned by now that I can't remember anything unless I see it in print, so I have to invent a new story each time, elaborating on the same theme, drawing from my sisters' anatomies, and now, in my hurt and dazed state, with my eyes trying to cross, I see that a girl from Jerome's class, Diane Naughton, is on the saddle seat behind Skip, pulling herself against him in a bear hug.

"You see that kid there?" Skip asks, and juts his chin at me, then revs his motorcycle to make sure I don't hear, but the noise broadcasts his voice. "He knows the dirtiest stories I've ever heard."

+

On the night of the national elections, Dad stares at the TV and says, "That party has moved so far from what Lincoln believed in they have no right to mention his name." When it's clear that Stevenson has been defeated, Jerome and I go up to bed and lie in the blackness, and then both roll away and start sobbing at the same time, and I see my turtle, grown huge, moving across the continent toward California and Grandma Jones.

+

Jerome and I run to the post office after school, to help an older boy, Don Nelson, with his paper route, and go at the papers, bound in their bundles by wire and smelling of cold air and ink, with pliers borrowed from the postmaster. Once the papers are free, we fold each one three times, lengthwise, the last fold tucked inside the first, and slip on snickering rubber bands. When Don pulls up to the post office, on a bike he's stripped down to ease the load, with a deep basket at the front, we load him up.

Winter is beginning, and Don rolls one pants leg up on his thin calf, where black hairs lie coiled, and as he pedals we run on either side—"This ice is a bitch, boys; grab me if I go"—and at his command fire papers at porches and doors. Sometimes Don lets us collect, since people are easier on kids, he says, and in the darkening winter afternoon, or in the dark of evening, he stands with his bike beyond the slice of gold that falls over us from an open door, where heat pours from around the grouchy offender who hasn't paid his bill for a month.

On Saturdays, when the post office is closed, we go to his house on the hill at the other side of town to collate the funnies into the Sunday paper, then fold it and apply the rubber bands.

This paper is thicker, so we have to make several trips back, "to replenish our supply," Don says, and sometimes he lets us sit in the big basket as he pumps up the hill, panting and gritting his teeth at our ears. His mother has popcorn waiting, in cones she has rolled from the brown sheets the papers come packed in, and cocoa ready, which she lets us spike with coffee. She hovers close and forms the tented space I used to feel from Mom, with a scent of hair past her face and further tented curves to the floor, and I wonder whether Dad couldn't marry her.

One afternoon Dean Roy Skaggs walks into the post office just as the wires Jerome has snipped on a paper bundle go into a scrabbly clawing over the floor, and says, "Hey, Nelson, you still got them two conned into doin that? I'm going to have me that there paper route from you yet, buddy, you wait and see. Maybe I can even get me some action at the *Pekin Times* itself on this here child labor you got. Hail, man, down in Kentucky we don't even treat our darkies like that."

So we turn again to our books, and Mrs. Nelson is removed from us like a sheet our mother drew from a clothesline, snapped into shape, folded, then laid inside a drawer, and slammed the drawer closed—gone along with Mrs. Ebbinger; her husband has found a better job and they've moved: the whole empty house now ours.

+

Jerome befriends a classmate, Carly Sanderson, and the two devise a form of basketball they play in Carly's basement, employing a tennis ball and tiny hoops—fashioned from clothes hangers, with nets crocheted by Carly's mother—six feet high. The school purchases a trampoline, and I find I can perform forward and back flips not only on it but nearly as well on a pair of mattresses I place on the floor of our basement. I practice here for the time I'll have on the trampoline, then carry our portable record player down and improvise dances to "Turkey in the Straw" and "The Sunny Side of the Street," working flips on the mattresses into the steps. I join the tumbling team. Jerome goes out for basketball. I collect stamps, inhaling carbon tetrachloride until I see Lincoln nodding at me from the door in his stovepipe hat, and keep a card table set up in the living room for these experiments. Then Jerome starts to use the table for his homework. He and Carly have vowed to be co-valedictorians of their high-school class, and Jerome is already working toward that.

+

Using a handsaw, Jerome and I cut out, from measurements in *Boys' Life*, a plywood backboard, and paint it with white house paint. It won't dry well because of the cold, but we can't wait; we beg Dad to buy us a hoop and attach that, and then we have him fasten the backboard between the doors of our garage. "Why, the paint's still wet on this," Dad says, from the top of the stepladder, looking at his hands and his gray twills (unable to see his hair), and has to bolt it in at just under ten feet, because of the overhang of the roof. Then he has to buy us a basketball.

There are games after school and on weekends, with high schoolers often joining in, and I practice for hours every evening, by the dim outside lights, to perfect a set shot at a guard's distance. I get good enough so that Jerome will stand on my spot during a game, or will call to the person guarding me, "Don't let him shoot from there! He's dead!" But by then my shot is off, and when it goes through, he says, "Damn. See?" I work on a jump shot to one side, for variety, and get nearly as good at it, but can never duplicate my shots on a real basketball court, without the open sky to arch the ball across in a parabola as fine as the trails of jets that sometimes appear (a different sky, now, too) above our slightly-less-than-ten-feet, slightly-forward-tilting backboard.

There's a popular song with the refrain "Oh, I discovered a *bomp bomp bomp* right before my eyes!" and a local radio station offers a prize to the person who invents the best phrase to fill the *bomp bomp bomp* blanks. A "pair of skunks," I figure, has a chance, but decide "A-tom Bomb" would probably win, when I think of how our classes dive below windows or pile into crawl spaces under stairways for A-bomb drills.

When I'm in church, or in a crowd at school or at a restaurant, I anticipate the bomb's impact, and keep glancing around to see if an opportunity will develop to save somebody's life, which is how I figure I'll make my mark. And almost every day I imagine Abraham Lincoln returning to present-day life. I'll be delegated to show him around, and I can picture how surprised he will be at superhighways, automobiles (I'll show him how a car heater works), telephones, electric lights, and how he'll say, in amazement, "Why, this is a miracle, son."

"President Lincoln," I'll say, "it's the modern world."

Fall, and Jerome and I lay out one half of a football field in the back yard and mark its boundaries with lime and plaster from the half-full bags stored in our garage. We alternate football with basketball, but don't draw a football crowd unless we play touch, which both of us dislike. The only ones who appreciate tackle as much as we do are the Skaggs brothers, and in the formal rules and battering of the game, Billy Gene and I become friends, although I've apparently made a bad choice. One day Dad turns from the workbench where he gives advice, and says, "Your Grandpa Neumiller used to say to me—and in my experience I've found this to be true, so I believe it bears repeating—'You are judged not by who you are or what you are but by the company you keep.'"

+

"And?" Rick Purkeet says. He moves a hand to my chest and pinches over it, trying to locate a nipple, and I see the football field as it was, with the cocoa-brown box of a milk truck at its far end, and the belfry from which the bell (now in our garage) used to swing, bearing a flagpole that leaned toward the milk truck— Then I'm in a curving alley, lined with hedges, behind Dr. Sprunk's office (a building of imitation brick across the corner from our house), holding a bow and arrow I've made of sticks and twine. It's late spring, a frog is hopping beside a budding hedge over veiny, threadbare leaves, and I release an arrow at it, then grab my hand and howl. The arrow has scraped a raw gouge across an oval blister below my thumb that I got when I was devising a seal for a letter by melting a crayon with a match, and hot wax dripped there, sizzling, in my final foolish act, I figure, as I throw down the bow and head for home, extricated from the last alley of childhood.

"This Billy Gene must have been some butch, huh?" Purkeet whispers, and I wonder again where I am. Then he moves, and from his heat behind I know he has a high color of arousal in his vein-brindled cheeks.

"I guess."

"Your dad sounds like a Marvin."

"Marvin?" I turn, surprised at this, and wonder if I've mentioned Dad's name. "What do you mean?"

"You know, dependable, steady. Patriarchal."

"A Marvin doesn't seem too bright to me. He is."

"Oh, I bet! I'd like to meet him."

"What do you mean?"

"Oh, ho. Just to meet him."

"You probably will."

"I'm sure I shall." He's trying to unbutton my shirt.

"I got a terrible case of athlete's foot about then," I say.

+

It begins with itching and blisters, and then crevices open between my toes. I sit in the bathroom, on the edge of the tub, with the medicine-chest fluorescents and overhead light on, and examine the shiny blisters, the chains and clumps of bulges, smelly seams and open creases, and the deep craters of water under tough skin. These I get with a needle I heat under the faucet—or with a match, if Dad's not home. Then I soak my feet in hot water in the tub and whine at the pain.

The bathroom door creaks open: freckle-faced Tim.

"Are you taking a bath?" he asks.

"Not quite."

"I got to use the whistling seat. My moosekaylies—the old

butt muscles—hurt from holding her in." Tim has been acting so crazy lately it seems that he is. "Are you scraping the scales off, brig bave blubber, in the middle of the week?"

Was it possible that I didn't bathe as often as I should?

"Or getting the crust and jam off your ackalicker feet? Scrape! Scrape!"

I throw a smelly washcloth that connects with the door in a *whap*. Gone. The blisters enlarge, and I sit for a half hour each night on the edge of the bed, popping them, and if spray hits a lip or my eye, I jerk back startled, wondering, Can you get athlete's foot of the face? The blisters become infected, yellowish-green, and a few swell to the size of my thumb. Shoes are a cramping pain, but I have to wear them, to cover it up, and I start to limp on both feet. I put toilet paper between my toes, and wrap them with it to absorb the fluid, but my socks get soaked and sometimes the dampness seeps through the seams of my shoes. The sight and stench of my blanched and wrinkled skin as I unwind the paper causes my stomach to buckle. It's too awful to see a doctor about. "Good God!" he'll cry. "What did you do to those? *Pinch* them?"

There's a weekly ad in the funnies, delivered now by Dean Roy, as he predicted, showing the feet of a man on a stretcher, with words below that go something like "Will you let your feet go without using *bomp bomp bomp*, our new Athlete's Foot Compound, until you, like this man, need an operation?"

One day during a football game, Tim's round and freckled face pokes forward as I'm dropping back for a pass, and he cries, "Chase him! He can't run! He's got the ackalicker-foot limp! Rot toe!"

I take after him, my hobbling diminishing as the need to catch him displaces the pain, and get in a clout that sends him out of sight again.

"For God's sake, why don't you see a doctor?" Dad asks.

I'm stumping across the living room, where he's watching TV.

"Do you hear me?" he says. "I'm talking to you. Old Doc Sprunk is right across the street, you know."

"What would I see Doc Sprunk for?"

"What for? Those feet!"

I was sure I had hidden the affliction from him. "He'd just paint them purple," I say, because he seems to use a purple compound on every sore and complaint.

"Well, it might help. Good Lord, you make mine hurt to see you!"

One night as I sit on the bed, spraying the area, convinced that the reek will do me in before the pain, Jerome comes through the door and socks my back so hard it feels a shoulder is out of place.

"Now *I've* got it," he cries. "Now my feet are going to rot off, you rotten scab! You, you"—I see him struggle not to curse, and urge on the temptation by giving him the finger—"you dog among dogs, you!"

He stomps out, not limping yet, and my head hangs so low I could roll it between my feet, if it weren't for the shape that they're in.

+

"Enaid Yewed Nothguan," I call her.

"Oh, backwards!" she says. "Oh, how neat!" She is in Jerome's class, a friend of Carly's, and has bigger breasts than many older women ("She's had knockers on her since she was eight," Carly says), which gets her bra strap snapped a lot, especially by Don Nelson, who sits behind her in study hall and whispers things that cause her downy cheeks to turn the slapdash red of a peach. Now her brimming gray eyes swim at me beneath glasses of a cat's-eye shape with multicolored frames.

"Oh," I say, and look aside. I'm lying with Jerome and Carly and their friends on her lawn, where black-barked elms border the street, and a pasture, lined with barbwire, rises like a golf green beyond the elms—the edge of town. Pulsing lightning bugs gather at the line of the last evening light that hovers several feet above the lawn. We're all pulling at the grass of the lawn with a squeaking, grazing noise, adding to its scented heaviness, and suddenly she stretches, lifting both arms above her head, a sight that makes my ears ring, and then lies on her back on the grass, her breasts pooling, and curls her fingers around mine. Small, thin, damply warm—heated parts of a person I can barely take in, out of awe. I'm sure she thinks she has hold of Buck Tiedke, a skinny classmate whose black hair grows down to frame his face, and I let my fingers slither free. But she looks at my hand, takes it in hers, and turns her deeply-lying gray eyes on me, and her lashes, silky and curled as a child's, wiggle.

Everybody starts to leave, struggling up like my centerpiece, which is pulling such thick sap through my limbs it seems it's shortening the trees. She passes her hands over her hair, grips it at her neck, and says, "Oh, Charles, why don't at least *you* stay and talk. These guys are such bores!"

They groan—for me, it seems, and go off.

I stay but the sap is thickening in my head, which is about to leaf, and within its interior branchings there is no room for speech.

"Why don't you lie down, too, Charles, and put your head by mine. Here." She flips her hair out backward and I notice stems in it I want to pick free. But I lay my head down on it—the top of my head against the top of hers, my feet as far away from her as I can get them: those shoes.

"Well, you could come here." She pats the ground beside her.

I don't move.

A hand comes over my hair from behind, and her tiny fingers are at the side of my face. "You have real neat lips," she says.

I lick my lips, then chew on them to see what they're like.

"Your voice is so deep for your size. Wouldn't you like to kiss me?"

I manage a croaking note.

Her hair squeals out from under my head, and then she's at my side and lowers her face in its canopy of hair until her lips are over mine. Their trembling but muscular pressure enters my blindness like a lamp carried to a familiar footfall from another part of the house into the room where I lie, dazed and ill, and a smell, like hot milk and honey, saturates my mind. Two heavy-moving circles lower onto my chest and widen, and I blink out like the fireflies.

"Unnn," she says, without removing her lips, and her licorice breath travels into me. "They ur neat. Doan hold'n stiff like that, like kissin beddie-bye." The pecks of the Bs go so deep I experience the jolt that came when I bit through an electrical cord, and there's a brush of lightning over my feet as if the swollen pods on my toes have popped, which I'm afraid she'll smell on my breath. Then I feel, behind her active softness, teeth, and understand how people accomplish this in movies with noses in the way.

She rises and the night widens into a scattering of stars above her face, which is cratered from German measles (a pimple stands in the center of a crater), though its fine-skinned texture is more delicate than baby skin, and I want for her sake to heal it smooth.

"Wouldn't you like to do that more?" she asks. "Or are you young and silly like the rest of them?"

"I don't think so. I mean—"

With her lips over mine, she lowers her weight along the length of my body, and I feel the front of my pants will rip. There's no knowledge of the separate parts of me, and no control of them.

"Why don't you call me Dewey instead of Diane," she whispers. "Nobody else does. It's more romantic, isn't it?"

"Yes."

"Diane!" It's her mother, calling from the back of the house. "Are you still out there, dear? Time to hit the rack!"

"Come back tomorrow after dark," she whispers, and runs off with her long skirt shaking above white anklets—all I can see as she rounds the corner of her house—and then I hear the thumps of her feet on wooden steps that seem as hollow as my chest, and a screen door slaps.

Back home, sitting on the edge of the bed beside Jerome, who is busy with the affliction caught from me, I unwrap my toes and discover that the athlete's foot is clearing up.

In two days it's gone.

+

I exist in a state where everybody but Dewey is invisible—ghosts at the fringe of life. She asks me to go on a hayrack ride with a youth group from her church, and I tell her Catholics can't.

"You don't have to *join*," she says. "It's just a real neat ride out under the stars, and later we stop and have a luscious feast of marshmallows and weinies, mmm!"

So Dad shakes out the drooping wings of his newspaper and appears, his brushy eyebrows in half-moons above his eyeglass frames, and says, "Aren't you a bit young for that sort of relationship?"

"Relationship? It's just for a ride. To get out of town."

"Is Jerome going?"

"Yes." Dewey has arranged for her friend Della, who has moved into town recently, to go with Jerome, as insurance. "Carly, too."

Dad shakes the paper out and is gone again.

"Well?" I say. "Can I?"

"May I. Not 'Kin I.' "

"I know, I know."

His head goes back and he holds the newspaper farther out, as if his sight is failing, and his eyes appear to travel too far to be covering merely columns. "Oh, ho," I believe I hear, or it could be one of his nightly groaning yawnings that come at this hour, the exact time to attack him with requests.

"What?"

"Oh, I *suppose*," he says, and then folds the paper up, throws it on the floor, and turns back to the television, his lips parted and a finger probing the mole like Lincoln's beside his nose.

+

We burrow under her blanket into the broken bales as the hayrack creaks and tilts over a gravel road, rocking us in a trembling blackness that's shot with sparks when our teeth clash. The droning of the tractor overpowers all sound but her breathing and a few faint voices singing "Ninety-nine Bottles of Beer on the Wall." Jerome's monotone buzzes among them, and the chilly early summer brings out a smell, above the unbundled alfalfa, of tractor exhaust mingled with lemony hedge apples, a combination that assures me this has happened before, although there were no locked lips opening wetly, I believe, and I have a sudden scare that I've called Dewey (as I almost have a couple of times) Mom.

"You have such neat arms," she answers. What is it I've

said? "They have such long silky black hair on them, mmm!" She grabs my wrist as if in anger and presses my knuckles so deep into one breast I gasp at how giving it is without causing her pain.

"Hey, you guys down there," Della, a noisy tomboy, yells and pushes on my back with a foot. "You ought to see this night." She lowers her voice and sings " 'Ghost riders in the sky-ay!' " like Frankie Laine; she's always adding sung and half-sung lines from songs to everything she says. "Hey! Ain't you two ever comin up for air? 'Clippety-clop, hi-yawp!' "

"Yeah," Jerome says, and from his voice I can tell he's smiling, his eyeteeth indenting his lower lip. "Yeah, give her hell!"

+

Now at the Lamar my focus is on the foreground as Alan Ladd looks up from the bottoms of his eyes toward a woman, his mouth moving into the one-sided smile (also used by Richard Widmark) I'm trying to imitate. Or John Wayne comes blazing toward the center of the screen with his yellow bandanna and the tassel on his hat streaming backward in a wind as steady as from a furnace fan, and Dewey, not Jerome, sits beside me, our arms on an armrest worn as smooth as animal skin. She holds my hand until hers is so damp she has to wipe it on her skirt or my jeans, and usually, later in the movie, takes the hand in her dry one, ducking her head underneath, and draws it over her shoulder. Then Jerome and Carly and Buck Tiedke, sitting farther back, say in squeaky voices, "Oh, kiss me, gopher teeth, my tonsils need scratching" or "Ooo, it hurts so good, 'don't' me some more!" or make smacking noises on their hands until the theater manager starts down the aisle with his flashlight. In the darkest scenes Dewey slides below the seat back, pulls my hand around to the front of her blouse, and presses our twined fingers deep.

"Jagitchasumskin yet?" The weird word comes from above and I turn to see Don Nelson and Dean Roy Skaggs slumped down in the seats behind us, looking like gnomes, both showing their teeth.

"I say—" Dean Roy swallows down some popcorn and I

smell its salted butteriness on his breath, wishing I could buy some. "I say, did you get you some skin yet, ole buddy?"

He winks through the Technicolor patchwork shifting over his face and Dewey swings around as if she'll climb the seat and whispers in a hiss to Nelson, "Shut up, you *fish*, you geek, or I'll claw your face up!"

I'm about to tell her she's made a mistake, it was Dean Roy, but Nelson says, "Aw, Dewey, you wouldn't do anything like that to me, now, would you? Especially with your kid here. He might go pee-pee."

"Don't you dare use 'Dewey' to me! Get out, you beast!"

"Right-o," he says, and pushes up from his seat, leaving Dean Roy shaking his popcorn, and walks up the slanted aisle to the stub wall at the back where the manager usually stands, and then I see the upper half of the double doors swing open on the lobby's orange light and slap back and forth together like somebody brushing his hands.

"Oh, I hope he *chokes* on blowing his two-bits," Dewey says, and flounces down in the seat and grabs my hand and presses it into the middle of her skirt and pushes up. An accident, I figure. In her anger. It's how angry she can get.

+

She and I ride a summer-school bus to a neighboring town's swimming pool, and sometimes she kisses me in broad daylight, which silences Jerome and his friends. When she and I are alone, I feel I could do more than rest my hands over her blouse, though she sometimes pushes them away, whispering, "I'm weak!" But if I did more, as I want to, I'm afraid of where it might lead. I would like our relationship, as much as it's able, to remain pure, as long as I can run home, or drop into a ditch along the way, and get relief. On the other hand, as it were, my mind is often filled with a phrase I'm not sure I haven't read in a book: "Big tits in their prisonage."

My idea of romance, up until now, has been to lie in bed and imagine I'm standing in line (I see a line for this; it leads up a gangway to an open airplane door) for my turn to kiss Leslie Caron, the star of *Lili*, on the lips. But on certain nights I'm sure I'll have a heart attack in Dewey's arms if our kissing doesn't move ahead, and occasionally her hand will travel toward my center, as though she would like matters to move there, and I have to undertake to edge her heated fingers aside with an elbow—seeing the inside of our church during a service in hot summer, with people paddling the air in front of their faces with paper fans (a picture of Christ in Gethsemane on one side and the name of the funeral home on the other) stapled to handles like oversized Popsicle sticks: the shame. Because if matters did indeed move ahead, or I got under her blouse and kissed her there, as Dean Roy has suggested in the post office, everything could fly out of control, or "go all the way," and then she might discover a little finger rattling in her sleeve.

So what really keeps me from it, I'm sure, is the notion that a hairless Coke-bottle cock might arouse her glee (I've noticed some of the hairy ropes slapping thighs in the locker room, and even Jerome has straggly blond coils above his), since, from my vantage point, looking down, it's miniscule. And when well-meaning relatives like Fred or Grandma say to me, "Say, Charlie, when are you going to grow," the end of the thing itself throbs, and then plunges in grief. Public urinals are taboo. I never knew they existed until we moved to Illinois; in North Dakota, even at basketball games away, there were stools in booths. With doors on them. That locked from the inside. It removes a bit of the starch from my starting masculinity to have to sit to pee, so the deformity's not seen, and, what's more, one's whang whistles, with that flap of skin.

On top of it all, I'm not sure how everything fits, if it would, so for a staying maneuver I've developed an awful secret worse than my athlete's foot. Before we leave on the swimming trips, I go down to the basement, where I've started to sleep this summer, in a big iron bed next to the cold furnace, and take out my swimming suit and jockstrap plus a woolen sock I've wadded up, and stuff it deep. Into the jock. Jerk the suit on, then my pants, blowing a breath of relief that Jerome hasn't thundered down the stairs, as he did once, and almost caught me with the sock hanging down. In the dressing room at the pool, trying to keep my back turned and step out of my pants when no one is looking, I feel beads of perspiration spring between the hairs on my head, the only place I have hairs, for fear somebody will say I should shower first, or will pop down my trunks, a common trick. Nelson and Dean Roy are usually along on these trips, and once when Jerome isn't there, Nelson says loud enough for everybody to hear, "Did anybody ever notice how little Neumiller always comes with his panties on? I wonder why?"

They are maroon, with gray laces down the sides, and I keep the drawstring pulled so tight it would be like ripping off skin to pull them free. I grab my towel and wade through the medicinal footbath, no longer necessary, since Dewey has banished my affliction, out into sun on painted concrete, my sense of things as awry as colors in this light. She arrives with her glasses off, looking older, her hair stuffed inside a rubber cap, a pink clip on an elastic neckband over her nose, the front of her suit bulking low, wearing her big-toothed grin, and says, "Don't you love to swim? Don't you love these summer days?" Then she gives a closed-mouth, lip-wrinkling smile as she glances down in smug approval.

+

"Do you still love me as much?" she asks.

"Sure."

"You don't act it, Charles."

I tug at the grass under their badminton net, as we all tugged at it summers ago, it seems. I miss Jerome, and wish she wouldn't always chew Blackjack gum, although there's something almost dirty about the licorice taste on her tongue.

"You hardly say anything to me anymore."

"I didn't at first."

Her skirt is spread in a circle around her, and now she grabs it in a rising whirl, and walks up the three wooden steps to their screen door. How short she looks, I think, and receive an awful sense of myself; I'm shorter. She steps down one step and sits with her chin in her hands, then throws her glasses off onto the grass, and starts sobbing. If I leave now, I can crawl away behind the garage, I think, and make it to the alley before she knows I'm gone. But I stand and go up the steps, helplessness hung from a hook, and put a hand on her back.

"Hee! hee!" she sobs. "I feel so vacant! I wish I could die!"

Then through a movement of her head and hands she's running my mouth over the wetness of the textured skin of her face and kissing me in a fevered press. She twines fingers with mine and presses my hand over a breast, where I feel ribbed circles widening as far as I can reach, into a givingness that makes her gasp—I can hardly wait to run home—and then she moves my hand to the middle of her skirt, grips it with her legs and leans back, and I'm afraid to move, except to hold the kiss until it feels my teeth will fold backward.

+

"Hunh?" Jerome, sitting on the edge of our bed, looks up at me from the blank deafness of childhood.

"I said, 'Is there a cookout at Carly's tonight,' or what?"

"Uh. I think we're going to play some croquet."

"At Dewey's?"

"Uh, Della's, I think."

"Let's go, then."

He lies back on the bed. "I don't think I want to."

"I do."

He sits up. "Maybe you should stay here."

"Why?" But his pronouncement forces me to sit.

"Maybe they wouldn't want you there."

"Who do you mean?"

His look enters with a gentleness that sets his eyes trembling, and I remember him saying last week that he'd never get serious about a girl, with all there is to do, and me saying that he would if he was in love, and then there's an impact like the trailing boom of a jet and I'm up on caving legs with the news he's trying to communicate: Dewey and Carly.

+

The pup tent is pegged down in the moist grass of Carly's yard, and a smell of oily canvas that's been baked in the sun seems to form a wedge against the weight of the stars. I listen for voices, keeping Dewey's back door, straight across the street, in sight. First there was no cookout, and then no croquet, because Della was having cousins in from the country, so I've come alone to the tent. Voices rise from the direction of Della's, but none of them carries across the night with Dewey's inflections. I hear the beaded whir of a bicycle chain and clattering fenders—Carly's bike—and close my eyes and hear it stop in the street between the tent and Dewey's with a screech. The bike is wheeled and I can picture footprints appearing in the damp grass.

"Hey, Chuck, are you awake?" It's Carly.

I settle my breathing and send up a snore.

He lingers, and then, in an action too stealthy to reconstruct, he's past the gravel at the edge of the street, and his chain whirs. I open my eyes and see him turn the corner and pedal toward Dewey's house, and then he glances back in my direction and stands, bearing down to pump, and I take off on a sprint across the street. I tear into the alley behind Dewey's, run along the hedge behind the next place, and hit the dirt at a skimpy lower hedge that borders the next house. Della's. I can see through the hedge to a picnic table, glowing under spotlights mounted on her house. No one in sight. A kickstand grates down on the other side of the garage, and Carly says, "I guess he's asleep."

Voices rise in a murmur, as if they've been holding their breaths, and Della says, "Well, why don't we go back and enjoy it, hey?"

I crawl along the line of hedge running toward the garage, keeping next to the hedge so I can't be seen, and in spears of splintered light through its stems, I notice that my arms are bleeding from the dive.

Della is talking about her country cousins and how her parents thought they would never understand that they were supposed to leave: "We had to keep cluing them in about that."

"Sounds about like mine," the voice of Buck Tiedke prints across the night.

I feel unsafe and snake-crawl down the line of hedge to the back of the garage, concentrating so hard on being quiet I can't hear what it is that they're saying. Then I feel their voices pass between the house and garage, and laughter canopies over me like an umbrella popped open above the hedge. Then Della says, "Suck a hotchee, ding a ding dong."

"Della!" Dewey says. "Do you realize what you just *said*?" The umbrella closes down to lighter laughter, and they gather at the picnic table in the artificial light. I crawl along the garage and see that the drive is clear, with Della's new bike under a spotlight, and then, in a double-or-nothing shot, I stand and dash past the front of the garage, then across the space between it and the house. Silence. I scurry in a crouch under windows to the house's front corner, and come to a leg-quaking halt. I get on my stomach and peek around the corner of the foundation. It's a new house and there are a dozen tiny Christmas trees at its far end. I crawl down into them, over the raspy crush of needles, my heart sending up waves of pine scent, it seems, in its shocks and trips of release against the ground. Then I ease up far enough to look out.

Carly and Jerome and Della are sitting at the table, on the bench facing me, and a bit farther off, where the light starts collapsing into blackness, Dewey and Buck stand together, swinging their held hands back and forth as they stare at one another and smile, and through the pine comes a scent of August alfalfa that assures me this is my imagination. But she keeps swinging their arms, pivoting a little on her toes—so that her glasses shine blank, then black—and when somebody mumbles something, she says toward the table, "Oh, I still like him a lot, honestly! But every time us guys want to do something by ourselves he walks up with that look like he expects to be alone with me."

"Right," Buck says. "Like a sick old dog. Yipe! Yipe!"

Laughter goes off at his barking noise, and I see Jerome's face pale to stone in the light. "So I think somebody ought to tell him," Jerome says.

"You," Dewey says. "I've tried *hundreds* of times."

What?

"Me, too," Carly says, and hits the table with a fist. "I was going to tell him when he asked me to sleep out. Dewey, this ain't good!"

"So why didn't you?" Dewey asks.

"La di-di-da, sh boom, sh boom," Della sings, and punches Carly's shoulder. "Old Carly's a chicken like the rest, hey?"

Jerome says, "I told him once."

What!

I feel I've screamed. In the aftermath of silence, blind to

them, I hear their questioning sounds, and then his voice: "I said, 'I'm positive Dewey wants a different relationship.' He just walked away."

Why, that dirty— I thought he meant she wanted to be planked, as we put it, and I couldn't face the technicalities of that.

"Well, what do you think of the new table?" Della asks. " 'Mule tra-ain!' Come on, Dewey, say something, hey?" She knocks on its top. "We got it for tonight, with the cousins all here, but we sure hope we get to use it from now till the end of our lives. 'Sin*cere*-ily.' "

Dewey comes to the table in her swirling walk and runs a finger along its edge, turning at the table's end, her skirt swinging out, and Buck, with a hand on the tabletop, too, begins to follow behind—poor old dog himself already, I think, and it's more than I can take.

"How much did it cost?" Dewey asks Della. "Do you know?"

I stand up from the trees and say in my loudest voice, through a complication that feels like geysers and lava going out my head: *"I'd say about nineteen ninety-nine!"*

The girls scream and run to the house, with Buck and Carly behind. Then Jerome stands, shoves his hands into his pockets, and comes over in his slowed farmer's walk, staring down. I'd like to take him by the throat and— He looks up and his eyes, trembling as they did on the bed, enter me and travel down to a point where I realize that he knows I've heard everything, and then to a remoter point I wasn't aware of, where I'm helpless and afloat, held only by his look, which informs me that he's the closest I'll come anymore to a mother.

"Come on," he says, and puts an arm around me that arrives from her height, and has me halfway to her place in heaven. "Come on, Chuck, let's go home."

+

So it's Buck Tiedke, for a while. Then it's Skip Wangsdorf, again, and then it's Don Nelson, of course, and later in the summer it's Davey, for God's sake, back home from college. I avoid him at church, even when we go to Grandma and Grandpa's for a meal, but one night he walks up to me in the basement, where Jerome and I are playing Ping-Pong, and says, with his eyes widening as they did once in the upstairs bedroom, "Chuck, I'm sorry." And just the thought of her, the beginning of an apology about her, has me bellowing the way I feel I should about Mom. "Chuck, please. It was her idea. And think of all the guys in between. It's not like I stole her."

But she's mine! I want to scream, and throw myself on the couch, to muffle my noise. Steps go up the stairs; Davey's, then Jerome's. I must miss a stretch of time, or else they shut off the lights, because when I look up, it's dark in the room. I lower myself to the floor and crawl to the sump hole, run into a box, feel around in it, and discover toys. A cap pistol. I pull it out. Until a few months ago I was playing with this. I pull the trigger and it bangs with a flash; caps still in it. I stick the barrel in my mouth, close my eyes against the flying gunpowder, and pull the trigger. *Wham.* I suck the smoke into my lungs, coughing against its complicating snarl, hold it down, and *Wham!*

I keep this up until my head dims and both lungs feel scraped raw. It hurts too much to take air in—only slightly worse than the sick emptiness left by Dewey, which I feel when I walk across town, keeping hidden, and stare at her house, hoping my state will call her out, or I can give her the one look that will call her back; I keep up my vigil, if she goes out, until she's back inside at night, feeling that as long as she's there she's mine. But no, this is worse, I can't breathe, my cells vibrating at triple speed, a blue bulge swelling against my forehead from inside. I cough but can't suck air in, lungs crushed, and start in a crawl to the couch. I'll die. Her fault. And Davey's. I get up on the couch, faint, the front of my head riveted to the bulge, and hear footsteps start down the stairs. Grandpa. He sits down near my head, and the giving cushion drops some sense into me. I smell his cigarette, cough, and can barely squeeze air back in. He sighs as he smokes, and I figure Davey has told him. Or Jerome. A hand comes over my head and rests there, the blue bulge rising toward it in language, and I'm out. Back in this room. A boomp boomp against the door. It doesn't give, but broken images of its frame unfold across the room, and the men in hats who removed Raul are double-timing toward me and in a sudden weighty rush shake the floor as they stomp around the bed, one checking the windows while the other says with borscht-beety breath, "Yess, iss KGB." He throws the corners of the grape chenille cover over me as the other jerks down the roller shades—one shooting up and clattering—and then they unholster their pistols, heavy with silencers, and as the tips of both buck and spout flashes, I hear, "Iss caught at hiss dorty tricks."

+

I'm fixing the shredding bathroom ceiling, at the top of a stepladder, in a strip of heat. Apparently the tub upstairs overflowed, leaving brown-edged stains, and now a lumpy rain falls onto a tarp on the floor as I slide a trowel under the plaster in a widening hole which seems to open onto the room above. Half the ceiling will have to come down, I see, and when I work like this with my hands, there are other accompanying sights and seizures of words. Now the face of the woman who was my stepmother for five years, when our father finally remarried, appears, and from this perspective I see his attraction to her, which arouses me, no matter how uncongenial I found her then, and by this I'm led to understand my attraction to my mother, wholly physical. —Which is why sons don't like stepmothers, a voice in me says. —It's not that the stepmother is an interloper. She arouses that forbidden love.

 —This is the way workmen keep sane, the voice says, in reference to my inner monologue, as a section of plaster falls in spatters to the tarp.

 —Another way is television.

 —But as an escape. There's a sameness to television fantasies.

 —Goodness, the world is too complex for simplistic commentary.

 —There. You mimic the dimension of television when you even mention it. Or the characters on it.

 I pause with the trowel, wondering if I can use this in my show, and imagine a pair of brothers lying on the floor in a sunlit house, beside a set of bookshelves, below a cloth-covered speaker: my ideal listeners.

 —If you can't reel off a pat answer, like a character or a

newsman on TV, or if you give an answer that addresses two or three sides of the same question, or give answers that branch from there into different possibilities as you talk, then people tend to mistrust you, or act as if you've evaded the question by not giving a direct answer, or any answer at all, when what you want to say is . . .

I'm in front of Sister Benedict's desk, in a primary-size chair, serving as a dictionary for the rest of the class; they're reading at their desks and when they reach a word they don't know, or don't know how to pronounce, they walk up in the varnished light of the room, with its wire-mesh windows in shadow, and ask me. Mary Angelica Schoenbeck does, blond hair sticking to her face, which has a blush climbing it like a filling cup, and as she turns away I reach out with a foot and kick her skirt high—red-blue material going up to a shock of underpants, like the sudden contraction in my sight as I watch the splintered end of a yardstick go spinning down between the narrow boards the desks are fastened to, and realize that Sister has connected with such a wallop to the back of my head that she's snapped her disciplining tool. Where is Jerome?

—You see how hard my head is, I want to say to Sister.

—I see you can't be trusted, she might answer me.

There is room for any variation, weightless and displaced from working overhead so long, and then I look down to see a single foot, shod, in the medicine-chest mirror, enough to allow me to enter the room in another state, naked, stumbling on giving ankles, panting, to the sink, the mirror reflecting ambiguous eyes into the back of my head, ready to open the first incision, and feel the funneling of the experience of that night send scattering sensations across the scars over my wrists. Because the death of my mother left my attachment to life so tenuous it was a cord I could cut!

Then I see myself in bed on another night, grinding my head so hard into the headboard that its tall oak panel bends backward, until I feel I'll have to cry, "Help, dammit! How can I—" And in the frosty silence the room seems to enlarge with every breath I take while needlelike beams of red project from my eyes, and then the numerals 10:33 appear as if I'm staring at a digital clock, and through its face I see a passenger jet crash into the cupola of a house, and think, *It will happen then*—as the film over reality breaks like the boys' window next door and a freezing lens appears over that inner eye that is the focus of the mind, and I see outside myself, under a spotlight, a pair of legs as thin as Dad's at the last shake and quiver on a cake of ice—sufficient for me. This remains now with such power that my legs on the stepladder feel stiff, tumescent, rigid as a teenager's, and the rain of plaster seems to be me spattering over the canvas.

There's a squeak below and I look down on my daughter, foreshortened and wide from my height, staring up at me. "What?" I say.

"It looks so nice!"

"Nice?" I say, half crazed. "I haven't even got started yet!"

+

I go out for basketball and get to suit up, due to my demonic pursuit of dribblers (tall sloppy ones the best targets) and to the moves and tricks I've learned, after weeks of practice under the garage lights, from the Harlem Globetrotter Marques Haynes. I can be counted on, if given the chance, to stall a game for as long as the opposition can take the dribbling in conjunction with my height, about five feet, before they pile on. I shoot my foul shot a bit to the left of the center of the free-throw lane, along the path of my dead set shot, but as it goes through, sewing up a close game, I'm underneath to seize it in another form, and I rock back on my flexed right leg, swinging the weight around behind, so my knuckles touch at my waist on the other side, and then go into the arm-extended double spin with its sudden leap at the last to send the discus off on the arc I can follow only after the dizzying recovering spin at the edge of the ring. Then the flat flop of it on turf. I place in meets in the discus, and in long dashes at top speed, and one day the coach, who has persuaded me to join the tumbling team, walks up and says, "Chuck, if you could grow a couple inches, you'd be the best 220 man we have. Your legs've got to go twice as fast as some of these guys, so you got some kind of remarkable speed."

"So what should I do?"

"Well, get more protein in your diet. Drink a lot of milk." His eyes roll up. "Pray."

+

Jeannie Ebner's skinny, unattractive hanger-on, Willa Petey, comes up as I'm practicing during lunch hour in the discus ring, using the sun as a focus for my toss, and says, "Hey, I got a message for you."

"Oh?"

"Bobbie Gilette says to say she likes you."

"Oh?" I look and see Bobbie over under the flagpole, and assess her through Dewey's image: her skinny height, her breasts, about the biggest in our class, standing in points like Dixie cups; her candylike curly close-cut hair, and then her face that begins so well, with a perfect nose that ends in nostrils pointed and thin, and below that a gapped set of teeth splayed out on her lower lip.

"Well," I say to Willa, "I don't know if I could get close enough to do much good with those god-awful big buck teeth she's got."

+

The bishop of the diocese appears that spring in the Pettibone chapel in gold-embroidered robes, holding a golden crozier in a heavily ringed hand, and stands so close I can see the elastic at the sides of the gold miter that rises into a peak above his head. He's here to catechize our Confirmation class, before confirming us in the faith, and for the first time since our move here the church is packed. I've memorized the Ten Commandments again, and know the catechism fairly well, and understand how much sin I can bear, according to the stated limits, deep in my bones. For my confirmed name I've chosen Sebastian, because of a picture of St. Sebastian—pierced with arrows like a pincushion—which Sister Colette once showed me, but also because the name of the trapeze team in *The Greatest Show on Earth*, my favorite movie, is the Great Sebastians. The bishop is new, installed only this year, and in the sweep and majesty of his handling of his crozier and robes he emanates an awful authority. So I'm surprised at his lighthearted teasing, and the personal questions he asks, seldom from the catechism.

"And you," he says, and I rise on weak legs, a husk around the grief over Dewey, and say, as I've been instructed to, "Yes, your Excellency."

"Goodness, I guess it's you speaking in so deep a voice."

"Yes, your Excellency."

"In a tone not so unlike an old nocturnal bullfrog. When did your voice change, my son?"

"It's been this way as long as I can remember, your Excellency."

"My, what an extraordinary infant you must have been!"

The congregation laughs out loud, the first time I've heard laughing in church. I'm shocked, and when I manage to get out, to remain correct, "Yes, your Excellency," the laughter gets worse. I stare down a rising dam of tears at Jerome, and hear, "I imagine you and your twin, then, must be in demand for your harmony. You may be seated, son."

In the rustle of Jerome's rising, I'm released and sit, and if the Holy Spirit enters me, it's then, as the reminder of the two of us as twins opens up that closed-off time, with her alive again, at the center of us, and then Jerome settles beside me, already done, and I'm almost back to myself when holy water hits in a spray across my face. I turn to one side, trying to keep from raising a hand to protect myself, holding trembling liquid freckles over most of my face, and it's as if I've turned aside to see her. She's moving away from me through the lighted, colored arches of our North Dakota years, her back to me, hair streaming behind, and I put a hand to my frightened eyes to stop a streak of salt speeding through the trembling drops at this unexpected consolation after the losses of these last years.

LOSING

I walk under the schoolyard trees alone, across the road to the football field, and walk to the end of it, then turn back. The water tower stands highest, silver-gray; the high school with its bell cupola against the clouds is next; then the steeple of the church, with a cross on top; the bulks of houses, mostly white, below the puffed-out colonnades of trees. I can't place myself. I turn toward the countryside, in the direction of the Savitskys', and the swoops of the plain seem movement underneath me. I sway between blue and green, and then the wind that's always present rises, parting the grass and weeds, and my eyes go up, into the near-blinding sky and *No* registers in me, back again to the plain, where I see a single far tractor shimmer in a field dark with cloud shadow, and then up into blue again, *Yes*, startling me.

History repeats itself, Dad says. He and I are back, along with the girls. Tim is in Wisconsin with a great-uncle and aunt, and Jerome is at the house in Pettibone, with two Mitchells from the basketball team. The Mitchell family here has taken the girls into our old house. No Lionel train. Dad is on a year's leave of absence from Pettibone, to serve as the superintendent in Hyatt, and he says he doesn't feel right (to use his words) trusting me away from him, so I figure he trusts Jerome.

I look back toward town. Dad and I used to live near school, in that tan house, but extra work kept him so busy I was never sure when we would eat, and the house felt emptier than an actual empty house, with only one in it. The spiderwebs we knocked down were doubled the next day, and mice gnawed in the wall beside our bed like hardheaded old men chewing on raw carrots. I stayed home from school too much, on the bed in a daze of shame, and when I looked out from the daze, Dad was teaching, a shock. Or I was in Mr. Weiler's early-morning science class, at a lab table sealed in varnish, enervated from the effort to stay awake, holding my notebook over an erection, a further shame—new growth and straggly hairs to deal with. Or in Rimsky's Market after school, with Brian and Leo and Arno Litwak and Douglas Kuntz, drinking pop—Kuntz and Leo perched on the top of the cooler against a front window, saying that the members of the former state basketball team were drinkers, and some of them drunks now.

"They sit around talking about the games like they're movies," Leo claims, and sunlight glints off his new glasses. "Some of them guys couldn't make it from one end of a court to the other from the booze." Brian studies me with a smile, nodding his big head, then takes a slug of Coke and says, "Yeah, but don't tell your dad, Lids"—my old nickname.

"Hell," Leo says, "some of the guys got loaded the night they won that last game."

"But he don't know they're stumblebums with sewer-gas poots!" Kuntz cries, and grips his big nose. "Fwee!"

Dad and I live with the Kauter-Haupts now, in a bedroom with an adjoining bathroom (there was an outhouse at the other place), and Mrs. Hank cooks for us. The dresser in our room has to be organized just so, to conserve on space. There's a mantel along one wall, enameled green, but the fireplace is bricked up, and a Kauter-Haupt daughter arrives at home one afternoon and stands in our room with an arm on the mantel and sings:

> *Show me the way to go home,*
> *I'm tired and I want to go to bed*

and unpins her gold-red hair and shakes it down her back, the sun from the windows igniting ends of it like wire in flame.

I had a little drink about an hour ago
And it went right to my head

Her parents come to the door and listen—her mother half as tall as Hank, her hands clasped over the mounded apron at her waist—and when the song is over, the girl says huskily, shrugging the shifting outline of her hair, "A drinking song." She looks around, then at us, and says, "I used to sleep here. This was my room." I'm charged with such a sense of her in the bed I can hardly lie still. Dad can't figure where the entire family slept, since there are only two bedrooms, and seven lived in the house at once. I study him from my daze; he's in a chair at the fireplace, staring at the bricked opening as if staring into flames.

"Hank, you know, was in the First World War—an officer, I believe. Maybe you could get him to talk about it." His elbows are on his knees, and he rubs his hands at the imaginary fire. "The war to end all wars, they said. Ha. All it did was pave the way for madmen like Hitler."

He shakes his head, the end of this thought, and from the way he rises I know it's time for bed. He paces around the room with his hands in his pockets, the bottom of his suit jacket bunched up, as he sometimes paces in front of a class, or as he might have once paced for Mom. He pulls down the knot of his tie, jingles the change in one pocket, takes out a handful and places it, as he does each night, on the mantel. He lays his billfold beside it. He studies himself in the mirror above the dresser as he removes the tie. He hangs his jacket and shirt on the chair back. He tilts his head, sticks an index finger into an ear, and wobbles his fist in such a vigorous way it sounds sexual. He sits on the chair, pulls off his shoes, pulls his pajamas from under the pillow, and goes to the door, nodding, to say he'll be in the bathroom. I hear him gargle with mouthwash, and he comes back with his glasses off. He places them on the dresser, picks up his rosary, and wraps it around his right hand—a reminder of my habit, enriched by the red-haired daughter.

The light goes off and he crawls into bed beside me, smelling of the mouthwash and his gamy hair, and groans. Some nights I wake to him pulling me close. Once when I thought I was alone in the house, I went for the couch and was so hard at my habit I didn't hear Mrs. Hank walk in. She went right by, into her bedroom, and since then she has figured, fitted up with her daughter's hair, as my partner—worse shame. She's not much taller than I am, but broad, with hands that dangle below her waist, and frizzy silver hair drawn back from her bulging forehead; she speaks a German dialect Hank teases her about. Wide-spaced teeth sprawl from her mouth, and there's a constant chipmunk movement to her upper lip, which has coiled whiskers on it, as if to bathe the teeth before she speaks. "Fleischkopf!" she calls Hank. "Kluna"—not *kleiner*—"Fleischkopf!"

She seems to sense the shame that forces me through each day at a remove, and bakes a new dessert every evening and watches me eat, bathing her teeth, to see if this will call me back. While she washes dishes, Hank and I play checkers in the dining room, Hank sitting at attention after all his years out of uniform. I never ask about the war.

"Ach," he says, jumping with a checker. "It vas hardest on da horses, poor tings. I vas in d'artillray." He puts a hand around a cuff of his white shirt and looks toward the window, and the sun forms gold coins of his glasses, one with the artificial eye beneath. "Ven ve set up to schoot, ven ve travel, alvays ve vatch for dem horses. Dey get schot, ve're done. You see det horses all along da fiels. Ach! Sometimes, at de end uf da vahr, ve dun't get no food. If ve see a det horse, den, ve—ha!" He breaks into laughter so loud Dad steps out of our room. "Sometimes, ve—ha!" The helpless laughter keeps up until his lips draw above the gums of his dentures, and the dentures tremble and dance. "Ve hide da horse, da leg or vhatvegot, ha! in da barrel of d'artillray piece. Hee! Oh, ha, ach!" Tears run from his good eye down his cheek, and he touches them with an ironed handkerchief. "Vunce ve vas eating und a captain come. Soup iss cooking. 'Chentelmen,' he sess, 'smells goot. Vas iss?' Dis vas vurse, I—dis, hee! Times vas vurse now. *Ve* pull da gun around instead uf horses. 'Chentelmen, I choin you,' he sess. He's da captain; nobody sess no. He's starving too, we tink.

'Chentelmen'—ha!—'is goot!'—ach, ha-ha!—'is goot,' he sess. Ach, ooo, *Christmas!*" Hank cries, and Dad starts in on the wheezing laugh that means he's lost control, which affects Hank so much his shoulders start jumping and he doesn't bother with the eye. " 'Dis fleish in da soup, iss,' he sess, ha!"—and now Mrs. Kauter-Haupt starts braying in the kitchen—" 'iss beef, no?' 'No,' ve say. 'Iss goat?' 'No,' ve say. 'Horse?' Now ve're afrait! 'Chentelmen, iss fleish, no?' 'Jawohl,' ve say. 'Den vas iss?' 'Captain,' I say, 'iss—iss *dog!*' "

That night, from his chair at the fireplace, Dad says, "When you think of the poets and philosophers Germany has produced, and then see that same culture give birth to, well, a Hitler . . . There were people in the forties who would rather you didn't know they were German. Even now, I'm sometimes ashamed of the German blood in me. It went that deep."

Our box at the post office is a drawer of the sort that businesses have, and I shuffle through the mail before I hand it to Dad, looking for a letter from Jerome. Few arrive, and most are about school, or a speech contest Jerome is preparing for, or the carpentry business; he's keeping books for Grandpa now. I've sent off for free mailings, and finally receive a catalogue from Douglas Magicland in Texas, and feel my face burn from the descriptions of magic. I discover a kit of tricks for $5.95, and figure that, separately, the tricks would cost $12.80. I have to make a special case, I'm sure, because our car didn't run for a month and Dad couldn't afford to have it fixed. I show him the kit of tricks.

"May I, please?" I say. "They're actually worth $13.00."

"You've written $12.80 here on the page."

"Yes, $12.80."

"Are you sure your math is right?" he asks, and looks down at me in amusement. He always teases me about my ineptness in math, so this year I'm taking not only math but general business, plus the science course that is mostly math—besides English and history from him. When I read the science text, its principles enter those slots and shelves that I discovered in myself in Clapton's room (entered also by material from the set of encyclopedias Dad bought from him), and each entry opens onto such a further infinitude of exactness I know that science is my love. It's the cause of my morning arousal as much as any girl, although three girls sit at the varnished lab table with me each morning, in this school where girls outnumber boys two to one. One of Dad's goals is to reduce the number of boys who quit school.

I'm too small for six-man football, he says, but I go out anyway, and when Mr. Weiler notices my speed and urge to tackle (the teams here play both offense and defense), he makes me quarterback of the fresh-soph team. "Not suck," Leo says to me in the locker room, where everybody can hear, "but because your old man's boss, not?"

"He hasn't got a thing to say about this!" I insist.

Kuntz says, "Ask him not to have a thing to say about me, huh?"

In the first game I attempt some runs, but the other team's bulky quarterback keeps punching through and creaming me. Kuntz, my fullback, can't do any better. I ache all over, and on one play, when they have possession, the quarterback comes toward me at full throttle, in a dare to take him down, and I dive as if he's Jerome and hit his knees. My neck feels snapped; I can't walk straight. But he's limping and it's our ball. I call a pass ("In this wind?" Kuntz asks), and it connects. I try a draw around an end, then lateral off to Kuntz, but the quarterback, recovering now, takes him down. I fake a handoff and fade back to pass.

"Hey! What's wrong, you fool, did that tackle affect your *brain*!" It's Dad, shouting from the sidelines, and I get so rattled I'm dumped behind the line. "You!" Dad calls. "Don't you know you don't pass in a wind! Are you afraid that guy's going to hurt you? Run with the ball!"

In the huddle Kuntz says, "What's with Pop?" I look up and see Dad pacing the sideline, his fists clenched, and notice Mr. Weiler, with his hands deep in his trench coat, look aside at him in surprise.

"He's not the coach," I say. "Six-oh, that first pass that worked."

"Pop's right," Kuntz says. "You can't pass in this!"

"We've got to gain that yardage back. Six-oh."

As I fade back, Dad yells, "Stop him! Stop the game! Yank

that lunkhead out of there! You hear me, yank him out of the game!"

Just as I release the ball, the quarterback connects, and when I get up, partially knocked out, I see that the rest of their team was drawn in so far that Kuntz has made it to our five-yard line. Arno Litwak comes charging in to substitute for me.

"I'm okay," I say at the sideline to Weiler, who looks alarmed, and then Dad grabs my shoulder and swings me around. "Can't you hear?" he says. "Don't you understand plain English?"

"It worked."

"Worked? You're supposed to take orders! You're part of a team!"

I squint down the field, to the next play taking place, and see Kuntz dive over for a touchdown. "See?" I say.

"See, hell! You're not going back in this game!"

I look at Mr. Weiler, and he flaps his trench coat around himself with his pocketed hands and turns away. Arno stays in. There are no more passes, and we lose by six points. I take off ahead of the others to the locker room, holding myself in control, and when the rest appear, I wait for somebody to say, "So who's the boss?" I'm ready to sock whoever says it. Not a word; everybody undresses in silence. I sit with my helmet in my lap, afraid that if I move everything will spill, and then Kuntz comes over and puts a hand on my shoulder.

"Some nice passes today, Lids," he says.

Everybody in the locker room murmurs approval.

"That's why I don't coach anymore," Dad says at the fireplace, with the clotted look of shame from the hotel in Valley City. "I should keep my big mouth shut." For the next two months he does; there are no more talks. I leave the Magicland catalogue on the dresser, to say that I expect restitution, and he orders the kit. When it comes, I'm not as taken with it as I thought I'd be, but I have a skill for manipulating the tricks, and my patter arrives from the air, it seems, effortless. I organize a performance for the Kauter-Haupts in the living room, and Mrs. Hank squeals like a child, clapping both hands over her teeth. Afterward, Hank wants to know how each trick works. A magician never reveals his secrets, I say—a part of the instructions in the kit. No, but how does the water and rice-bowl trick work, he asks, just between us; he won't tell anybody else. I don't give in, and over the next weeks, whenever he's sitting at the dining-room table and I walk up, he snaps his newspaper out at arm's length and sets his chin.

We don't go home at Christmas, because of the car, and in February a letter arrives from Jerome; he won fourth place in Original Oration in the speech contest, a disappointment, he writes; and it looks as if he won't get to come and see us at Easter, because of Grandpa's income-tax reports; Grandpa has bought Ferlin's service station, for an office and shop—an investment. "Sunday we (Grandma, Tom, I) drove to Peru, to St. Bede's, to see Uncle Davey"—Davey is now studying to be a priest—"and ate at Kiyokos (the cafe so dark you have trouble seeing each other). Hope you are all OK. We are." He signs himself "Yours, Jerry."

I sit in bed with the letter on my lap. Outside light, reflected off snow, dissolves the wall between the windows—Grandma Jones's kitchen—and I think that there is no shame worse than sexual shame, a shame that has brought me to the moment with this letter in this bed.

Dad walks into the room, jingling the change in his pocket, and goes to a window—black against its light, except for those nearly invisible worms weaving in and out at the edges of his shirt, as if even the present is being consumed by a former life. "Homesick?" he asks.

I shake my head. How can I tell him that this is home, although it can't be, now, and the effect of this on me?

"History is death," he says. "Once it was life in full stride, but not now. We're always in the middle of things that aren't quite history, and as much as I love the subject I often want to say, lately, 'Let it go! Let it be!' "

When the snow is gone, he drives me to the farm where he used to work, and says to Mr. Savitsky, "Evan, I'm afraid I'm too tied up to help you this season. How would you like to break in my son?"

Mr. Savitsky, who's broader than Dad and seems taller because he leans back when he looks at you, steps up and lays a hand on my head. "So," he says. "Now you're a farmer, ay? Now you're farming with me."

The next day I'm driving a tractor, and next the tractor is hooked to a plow and packer and pony drill, and I'm seeding the width of three furrows in one pass. The wheat and the barley must be planted, a demand of the season that is like a promise I knew existed—this aroma rising from an eighty-acre field more powerful than a hundred gardens. If Dad isn't able to drive me to the Savitskys', I walk five miles down section lines, noticing the varieties of gumbo and loam, each with its special tint, while meadowlarks unravel their calls from fence posts and barbwire, rocking the golden vests under their throats at the sun, and I feel I only have to float a bit farther, or call in the right inflection, and I'll come over the next rise and meet Jerome.

Now I turn, and start back across the football field for town. The school year is over—today I took my last exam—and unless I'm able to stay with the Savitskys, we'll be leaving in a week for Illinois.

+

My son walks into my workplace, an old granary I've appropriated on this farm in the semi-Badlands of western North Dakota, and I wait with my back to him as he pauses at the recording equipment on my other desk (he's not to fiddle with it), and then I turn and find him at my elbow, staring down. He's six, and has traveled with me from the East, to help me prepare the farm for the rest of the family. For two days he's been busy on the riding mower, trying to level the two acres of yard that have grown up as high as his ears. He's nearly four feet tall; yesterday we inscribed his height on the mudroom doorway where the rest of the children's measurements rise in laddering pencil marks.

He looks up, and I understand why people mention his beauty—these huge enigmatic eyes, with his mother's many-hued depths of empathy, and her blond hair, which since last summer is darkening from white-blond—but what I see in him is Jerome. My son is the only one who looks into me as Jerome did, to assess my hour-by-hour attitude, and his eyes are the same backlit blue. His features are Jerome's or mine—a doubled mirror effect—and there are moments when he is a brother as much as a son, so that I feel a shaky inconsistency as his father. Once before a meal, when I was mentioning the rest of our family in a prayer, I said, "Lord, you know I love the family dearly, but I must confess that this time together as father and son has been so important to me I'll miss moments like this when the rest arrive." There was a psychic stirring from him and I glanced up, as I've told him not to do when I'm praying, and saw beginning tears bulge through his black eyelashes.

"Dad," he says, and looks down again, and I realize with a pang of being trapped that it isn't going to be a simple question; he knows I don't like him to disturb me here, although I've said that he may, since we're alone. I've been a parent long enough to know that whatever looks like order from the child's side is usually improvised on the other one.

I have to restrain myself from saying, "Come on, what is it?" and instead say simply, as a parent should, "Yes?"

"I think you have to help me. Come and see."

He walks out the door, assuming I'll follow, so I have to. I step out under a billowing blue that grips every horizon and dizzies me when I've been away awhile, go around a corner of the garage, grateful for anything that ameliorates the sky, and find that he has our second riding tractor (of an aged pair that came with the place), with a tiller mounted behind, backed up to the riding mower, the two connected with a chain. There is only one battery between the tractors, which has to be switched back and forth, and he's already done this. From one and a half to three and a half, his attitude went from "Daddy can do it with his big hands" to "I'll drive the tractor soon so you can work all day in your shed, Dad."

"So you're tired of mowing and want to till," I say.

"Can't I till the garden?"

It's lying fallow this summer; I've run the disc over it with the field tractor, but there are areas that are difficult to catch with larger equipment. "All right. You can get the places I missed."

"First let's pull the mower in the barn, in case it rains."

"I'm supposed to sit on it and steer while you pull it, right?"

"Yes," he says, and looks down again, afraid I won't approve of his plan; he could have driven it there himself before switching the battery.

"All right," I say, and sit on it.

He starts up the tiller tractor and pops the clutch so badly that the chain, which is hooked over a center probe that regulates the depth of the tiller tines, snaps loose. "I was afraid of that," he says.

I find another way to hook up the piece of chain and say, "Now ease out on the clutch," and he does, a good apprentice. It's working; he's pulling me. He turns back and grins. "Give it some gas," I cry. The sky everywhere exerts such pressure on my shoulders I'm anxious to be back at work. I try to shrug this off, and relax for the time I have with him, but as we near the door of the barn, which he has slid back on its rollers, I cry over the noisy engine, "Pull it in to the left!"

"Left," I see him say, then frown as he considers. He knows he has to get left and right correct if he's going to drive, and he wants to drive more than a garden tractor. He has a good memory for mechanical things. When he wasn't quite three he climbed up on a self-propelled swather in the yard, threw two switches that had to be thrown, and then turned the key in the right direction to start it, and it started. He can't remember the actual act anymore, perhaps because of my fear and anger, although he remembers riding with me on the swather, and could probably start it today if he stepped up on it cold.

When he was younger, I used to get down on the floor and play with him at the level where he spent his days, and being that low, on my stomach, with my ribs giving in a way that approached the pain that patient memory brings, I saw the room as he did: the furniture bulking in protectiveness, as it bulked once for me, with my parents sitting above; and the walls themselves, their windows high up, containing them where they sat—and I sensed how important biblical standards are to a settled family life (in its covenantal aspects), and how as a father I felt the same protection, containing me in a further family, as I'd once felt when I was lying half asleep on another living-room floor and the pastor from Ethiopia who used to visit us stepped into the room so quietly I wasn't aware of him until he spoke my name, and then I looked up and saw him in the easy chair above me, with sunlight over one half of his face, sitting as my father once sat, with both hands over the chair arms: Lincoln in his Memorial.

I used to lift my son above my head in joy, though with a tug of uneasiness, not only because of my wife's reaction to tossing him toward the ceiling, or his response to that, but because I felt I was "exalting him," a phrase that flooded my mind each time: "For not from the east, nor from the west, nor from the desert comes exaltation"—nor from lifting your son above your head—"but God is the Judge; he puts down one, and exalts another."

We are in the cool dark otherworld of the barn now, dim ghosts, and as I bend to undo the chain I slip into the evening at the medicine-chest mirror when I saw my father staring out at me, and then realized I was seeing myself, dusty after working till dark to seed oats in wet spots that couldn't be planted when the rest of the fields were sown (my son on the tractor beside me then, strapped into the seat with a belt)—I stood at the sink and, at the shock of seeing my father, thought of my daughter in town with her friends, and realized I was protective of her in a way that could be viewed as overprotective, as she viewed it, and then a thought came as clearly as if printed across the mirror: *I have to understand myself before I'll understand him*, meaning my father, and then in a more general internal tumble: *You can't understand the son without understanding the father*. And in an intuition swifter than thought I knew that this might be the most far-reaching personal insight I would ever have. I was forty at the time.

Now, back in my granary, in yet another of these rooms, light-headed from the sun, hearing the tiller start to pull down in the garden, I see dimly, on a pile of blank paper, a scrap that reads "My son——," as if he has left it. I bolt shut the soundproofed door, and register a chill of age—when experience overlaps experience until it seems life is a reliving of the same dozen experiences. So we press and are pressed forward through each day, borne on the currents of memory and regret, leaving in our wakes bright bubbles, vacuoles of peace, the still points of the beginnings of our children's memories.

+

I watch the toes of my cowboy boots from North Dakota, which have inlays of Thunderbirds set into their uppers in white and turquoise leather, travel among loafers down the corridor between the gymnasium and the high school—hardly hearing the noise of the students, and thinking that I'll have to get something other than boots, when somebody nudges me. Billy Gene. He's a head taller, at a height that seems to participate in the coolness of the gray-enameled corridor, the back of his collar turned up and his dark hair greased back in a DA. "When'd y'all get back?" he asks.

And then, "I dig that fancy footgear, cowboy."

That settles it; tonight I ask Dad for a new pair of shoes. Billy Gene slides across the crowd to the gymnasium rest room, plucks a comb from his rear pocket, and uses the glass of the door as a mirror to primp, and suddenly his greeting settles with me better than anything since I've been back. Certainly better than Jerome; I hardly know him. Carly has moved to Peoria—"There goes our co-valedictorian deal!"—and has promised to keep in touch with Jerome, but the group around them has disbanded, and Jerome has developed a new gabby cheerfulness, or picked it up from the Mitchells, so that I feel he's deserted me, or driven my daze of shame into a lobotomy—a word I've learned from him.

+

Dad says, about the fourth place Jerome received in Original Oration, "Your ideas are good, and you use fine examples to make your points, but you need more work on your delivery."

True, I think, because even I can tell that he's stiff, from the performance he has staged for us of last year's speech.

"I'll tell you what," Dad says. "I'll work with you. Let's set our goal for this spring as getting to the Sectional. Then you have your senior year to place in the State."

They both grin with the excitement that seems to be animating everybody but me.

+

I perform my magic tricks for the family, and afterward, up in
our bedroom, Jerome goes on about how "amazingly good" I
am and how my "skill stunned and overwhelmed" him, while I
stare blankly into his eyes, trying to stop or at least slow him
with my look, and then he says, "If I was that good at something,
by golly, I'd do it professionally!"

"All right," I say. "You be my assistant."

"Great!" he says. "Good going! You're on!"

+

On the platform that holds boxes still unpacked from our
original move, I find a formal jacket with tails, moth-eaten and
rusty, and sew it up to fit me. I dig out Dad's black leather
briefcase, filled with old insurance policies, and discover that
the leathery smell of its interior has turned musty, so I rub it
with vinegar and black shoe polish, and then print across it, in
a printing even I recognize as terrible, *Screwdini,* a television
name. If a trick fails, I can blame it on the dizzy ineptness I'll
adopt, and the tricks that do work should have a greater effect.
I set the briefcase on my lap: perfect, except for the printing
—yellow, ill-shaped letters, none the same size, all running
downhill. I shove my head inside, and in that black magician's
world I hear its metal studs striking down in the hall, and
observe it unfold with gifts, like colored silks that never stop,
and then see the fields outside Hyatt open overland to the
Savitskys', with a meadowlark rocking on wire as I go by at the
speed of sight, and hear my mother's voice, which I've never
been able to recapture, say from a closed space, "I'm a girl of
the Plains, boys, and I'm riding the Soo Line."

My first job as Screwdini is for a rural PTA. Jerome macks
down his hair with water and Vitalis, combs it down to his
eyebrows, folds his upper eyelids back (which he can do with a
pressure of his fingers) in fleshy strips, with his lashes pointing
upward, and steps around the stage like a sleepwalking Frankenstein, toting off debris as I crazily perform my tricks. When
I threaten to make him disappear, and he ad-libs a growl, I cry,
"You wait! I'll get you yet!"

He studies the speeches of Adlai Stevenson, watches politicians on TV, and begins listening to tape recordings of the winners of the Optimist International Oratorical Contest. He decides to enter that contest next year, too, if the local Optimist Club will sponsor him.

"Of course!" Dad says. "I'm the president!" Elected this month; I feel the two could form a club themselves, optimists that they are.

Jerome turns to me from the tape recorder, where a reel of flapping tape is slowing down, and smiles the smile that squares his upper lip. "That way," he says, "I figure I can kill two goals with one speech."

Why have I become more silent under his talkativeness? I have. I look out at him with a straight dead face and figure that this can't last very long; I'll subdue this in him, too.

"My second goal would be perhaps too presumptuous to mention, no? Or might it take some of the internal pressure off? I don't think I'm superstitious about it, though—I don't think I'm that far gone, hey? No, there's something about this speech itself that threatens to be . . . scintillating!" He pauses to check my response; the same dead stare. "All of course due, you know, to my unique, innate, inner sagacity."

He lowers his eyelids to half-mast and purses his mouth in a perfect anal pinch. If only he could be like this in a speech!

+

I could remain in the biology lab all day, staring at this glowing feat in the microscope: mitosis. Yellow-blue bands outline a shape in speckled light, now trembling with a shimmer of tension at its attempt to divide, which I can't imagine taking place apart from me. Then I picture, like an overlay, Bobbie Gilette under the flagpole as I assess her height, her breasts, her poodle-cut hair, and her nose that begins so well and flares into nostrils above the buck teeth on her lip. I look up from the microscope and see her, across the varnished table, staring at me from dark-brown eyes, and my scientific interest is up again.

Jerome and I walk in and discover Dad home early from school, with a clipboard on his easy-chair arm, keeping score of a televised baseball game, as he does when he's withdrawn. He starts a supper of pancakes, and then removes his plate from the table and puts it back in the cupboard. "I don't believe I can take pancakes tonight," he says.

Should we cheer? Has he, too, had his fill of these over the years?

"My stomach, I guess," he says, and goes into his bedroom. We hear a groan as he lies down. He is so generally healthy, he hasn't missed a day of school, and because of this and his Shakespearean acting voice, he's been chosen to boom out announcements to the morning assembly hall. Jerome goes to his room, and then returns with a puzzled look. "He says there's a catch in his stomach. Maybe he lifted too much, he said."

"When?"

I wait for a wordy explanation but he flops back in the easy chair, glances at the clipboard, and sets it on the floor. A heavily made-up woman is cackling on the television. "Let's go for a ride," he says.

We get into our turtle-backed Hudson, with a step-down doorsill that makes it difficult to sweep out, and he tools around town while we have a smoke. "If you're going to smoke," Dad has said, "smoke in front of me!"

At Dewey's edge of town, Jerome takes the sharp curve out past the Protestant cemetery, where twin brick buttresses inset with *Meadowlane* stand at each side of the drive and a length of thick chain, with a reflector attached to it, is strung between the buttresses—swaying slightly in our back draft, I see, as I glance toward the gravestones. Holy God, I think, don't let Dad be sick, please. What would we do?

Jerome drives out the road, the local drag strip, and I imagine people cheering from bleachers on either side, although no fantasies of myself as a savior occur. There's a snarl from the engine as Jerome smacks up the ivory bulb of the gearshift, with a dark cross inlaid into its end, and then the binding revolutions of a downshift as we're tossed in the low-centered, gripping sway the Hudson has when it decelerates. At the crossroad, as he begins to back around, I say, "My turn to drive."

"Bull. Not after that last trick."

He has had his license since the summer, but I won't be of age until next fall, and my need to drive, after farming for the Savitskys, is becoming consuming—even though I can hardly see over the wheel, or the dash, either, unless I have a cushion underneath (and then it's difficult to reach the pedals properly)—and whenever he lets me practice it seems necessary to pack as much into each session as I can. The last time, I was so tired of his careful driving, I said, "Let's see this old Hoosie bark," and popped the clutch. "Stop that!" he cried. We were in town and could pass for one another if the new city policeman happened by, at the bottom of a rise that led to a cluster of grain elevators, and I let the car coast back at a good speed, and then again popped the clutch. There was a whistle of rubber and a sudden sound like a complicated clap of backfiring. The car wouldn't move. "It must be a universal," I said.

"Universals!" he cried. "What do you know about universals!"

It was the differential—the spider gears in it, the mechanic said, which had chewed up the gearing on the axles, a major expense. A steady series of problems have developed since then, as if I'd disrupted the car's nervous system, and recent repairs have run higher than the car originally cost.

Now Jerome backs around to face the way we've come, when a U-turn would have been easier, and cruises down the strip, past orchards and pastures, and then the curve, a hard left, the twin buttresses with their chain, and I figure it's the car bills that have set Dad back.

Lord, I think, don't let him get an ulcer because of me.

+

The cramp, as Dad calls it, is present the next day, and on Sunday he stands in church stooped, holding his hand over it. He serves us dinner and goes to his room without eating, and finally Jerome gets up and follows him. Their voices travel back and forth in reasonable tones, and then Jerome's rises: "But, Dad, you've got to eat!"—like Grandma Jones.

Jerome and I watch TV as if chained—he's chewing his nails and I'm twirling and tugging at my hair—but as if it might deliver the word we've been waiting to hear. The weatherman seems to be standing at a replica of intestines, and then he jabs his pointer into a mass at their center and says, "And here is the storm center moving toward us tonight."

When we go in to say good night, Dad is lying in bed with his knees drawn up, and he asks us to wedge a pillow under his back. When I wonder how he can sleep that way, he says, "I'm not sure, but I have. It's the only thing that feels good." Upstairs we hear him groan, and Jerome whispers that he's worried about appendicitis.

"Should we call a doctor?"

"Appendicitis is supposed to be tremendously painful, Dad said. He says this isn't so bad, and claims he'd know if he had to see a doctor. I'm not sure where he gets that, since he never sees one. I figure . . ."

Go on, I want to say, sorry for my growing hate of his talkativeness.

In the morning Dad's face is gray and glazed, with drops of sweat trembling on it, and his eyes, deep in their sockets, stare far off. He asks us to help him stand, and his pajamas and the sheets are wet, we discover, when he sinks back and drags us down with him. He places a hand over his stomach. "Yes," he whispers. "Take me to a doctor."

Sprunk has retired and the nearest doctor, a recently arrived young man, is twenty miles off. Dad rides in the front seat between us, his knees up, leaning against me, and I understand how he must have felt about my injuries, and then he leans harder into me, groaning, and the smell of illness in his hair tightens my groin.

By the time we pull into the town, he says he is better, and sits up as if something has eased, holding to the dash with one hand. He has brought along the cane he used years ago when he injured his knee, and he walks with it, less stooped over, into the doctor's office. He is taken right in, and comes out soon with the cane over an arm, smiling. He takes a packet of pills out of his pocket and shakes them: The Medicine Show. His temperature isn't high enough for appendicitis, he says, and the doctor couldn't find the pain that should be associated with it. He's scheduled to come back in two days.

+

The superintendent calls us out of the study hall the next day and hands Jerome a note that says Dad has been taken to the hospital. In Lincoln. By Grandma and Grandpa. "I'm sorry, that's all the information I have," the superintendent says, with a look that implies he has more.

"Lincoln!" I say, as we go clattering down the metal-edged treads of the stairs. "That's fifty miles!"

"It must be where the doctor practices."

Together we hit the brass bars of the double entrance doors and step into fall sunlight, and with the metallic ratchet of the doors behind, as brassy as this light, I feel we're Westerners setting off for trouble, then look down and see cowboy boots. Jerome drives as fast as he can on Highway 29 leading into 10, swinging into the curves on the open prairie, two-handedly shuffling the wheel back again, while I flinch at the groan that starts up when he shifts down—the rear end?—and stare out from under the dome of the Hudson at the pink-gold, picked beanfields and cut corn, with a catch like anguish for Savitskys'.

Dad is in the operating room when we arrive. A specialist told Grandma and Grandpa that he had to be taken to surgery— immediately, they say—and Grandpa signed the papers. I'm afraid to ask, What papers? We wait on an imitation-leather couch for an hour, and then Jerome produces his cigarette pack, shakes one out to me, and lights us up, and Grandma, who's never seen us smoke, puts a handkerchief over her glasses.

"Dad knows," I say, but I put it out, as if this might affect him. I'm dizzy. Light seems to extend only a few inches from my face and I see, as if through shaded window screen, a boy go wobbling along on crutches at the back of the lobby, where a corridor leads to a pair of glass doors with backward printing across them that reads *Emergency*. Through the doors I see the cause of the light; it has started to drizzle, and it seems that it's thick darkness that is raining down.

A sudden tangle of reflected red in the drive is cast by a limousine station wagon backing toward the building, and then two men in suits and hats get out and wheel a stretcher covered with purple velvet through the doors. They turn and push through a pair of solid swinging doors, and Grandpa says he has to go for a walk.

He helps Grandma up, and I watch as they go toward the door, to see if Grandma is as weak as she seems—a gauge—and Jerome stands up. Dad's doctor is coming toward us, tall and thin, in a white shirt with red suspenders over it, and I'm suddenly afraid that he looks so young.

"It seems days since I saw you boys," he says, glancing at me, and I remember that I kept to the corners of his office, evaluating it. "I'm sorry I couldn't get to you sooner, but the specialist—I was sure he was best for your dad—said we had to take him right to surgery, and I didn't want to compromise that decision. Your dad made me promise I'd stay with him through it all. He'd gone into shock. I've been in the operating room"—he glances at his downy wrist—"for three hours now."

"How is he?"

"He's in a room. We're doing all we can. It was his appendix after all, which was my first hunch. But with no sickness to his stomach, and his temperature so low, well . . . It's been ruptured for days, sometime before he saw me. Didn't he mention any sickness, or the pain?"

"Well, yes, sure," Jerome says. "But not that bad, he said."

"A constitution like iron, I guess. At the point we are now, it's difficult to say how extensive the damage is, since his appendix ruptured some days ago, but he does have peritonitis. That's serious, boys."

He glances at us with a professional excitement, or terrible secret. "Do you want to hear this?"

We nod.

"He's very strong, as you know. Most anybody else's system, at the point his was, couldn't have taken the shock of an operation. It was a risk, but our only route, and he came through with flying colors. He was talking nearly right away—an amazing recovery. 'I made it, didn't I, Doc?' he said. 'I wasn't sure there for a while.' Goodness!"

"So he's all right?"

"Well, there's his strength, and that's what we'll have to

bank on. I'm sure he has religious faith, and this might be the key to him pulling through—we see this over and over. I stopped in his room on the way here, and he was already completely conscious. He seems lucid. His major worry seems to be you—and the rest of your family, of course. But he suspects that you two were probably called out of school. Now, normally, I wouldn't let you see him at this point, but the surgeon and I agree that it might do him more good than harm. We're dealing more with a spirit than a body at this point."

My concentration is so fixed on him he's nearly absent, although I'd like him to keep on talking so we don't have to move from here, or scream—but I say, "Considering everything, then, he'll be all right?"

"I don't want to get you boys' hopes up and I don't want to lie to you. You'd probably hate me the rest of your lives, and rightfully so, if I did. I'm thinking of your home situation. Let your brothers and sisters know you have a wonderful father. Taking everything into account, I'd say he has a fifty-fifty chance of pulling through. If it were anybody else, I wouldn't give you that, boys."

+

He's lying on a high bed with a bottle on the floor beneath. A tube runs from under the sheets into the bottle and the *plik plik* of the drops that strike its bottom are the only sounds. Two other bottles, one of blood, the other yellow, hang from a stand beside the bed, and tubes lead from them to his arm, strapped into a plastic splint that holds it extended full-length—waxy fingers curled. His hair looks longer against the pillow, and his face, or what I can see of it for fear of moving too close, shines against its bones.

His lids lift and his eyes, shades lighter, go on a vague search above him. The lids close.

Jerome takes my arm, as if he can't advance alone, and I'm over Dad's arm lying in the splint, grayish skin glittering with miniature beads of perspiration, the curled hand calloused yellow-orange. Jerome takes the hand in his and folds the fingers over his own hand. "Dad?"

His eyes roll beneath closed lids, and he sighs. I feel my

own body has been cut open like his, but over its entire area, at every joint, and is held from head to toe with stitching at each turn; if I move, everything will rip; Jerome's, which is joined at the same seams, will too; Dad's will; we're held together by giving threads.

"Dad?"

His lids are open and his eyes, glazed but with a gathering intensity of focus, study the ceiling. "You're here," he says, and clears his throat to free his voice, rough at its edges.

"How do you feel?"

"Better. Pain's gone. If I don't cough. Charles?"

"Yes," I say.

"All right?"

"Well, yes. Are you?"

"Bet-ter." This goes down a long slide. "Doctor says I made it." His eyes close as if he's examining himself to gauge the truth in this, and then his lips part, and his tongue searches over them.

"Are you thirsty?"

"Mmm," he says, and as Jerome reaches for a beaded water glass with a bent straw in it on the bedside table, I know why the doctor has said Dad is worried about us. His lids open as if he senses my fear. "You know, they don't give me shots. They give them to that." He signals toward the yellow bottle with his eyes. "I saw the nurse— The bottle has a rubber top. She stuck the needle in it. I said, 'Better that way. Doesn't hurt—' " His face draws inward on a pain that seems to center in his nose. "Probably figures I'm a goner."

I hold myself unmoving against the giving threads, and then my eyes go to the gray hair above his ear as the *plik plik* arrives like the pocket watch ticking in Lincoln's vest after his death, and I understand how it feels to be John Wilkes Booth. I've done it for good.

"The doctor says you'll be all right," Jerome says.

"Pleasant young—" He swallows hard and his Adam's apple, with a spray of whiskers on it, disappears into the hollow below his chin. "I will," he whispers. "I have to. You children . . ." There are further trembling words.

"What?" We both move close and my nostrils fill with rank fumes that must come from him.

"Don't be afraid, you—" His eyes flutter and close. "I'm tired."

"Do you want us to go?"

"Charles?"

"Yes," I say, and seem to glide closer on rolling wheels.

"Do you know I'll be all right?"

"Yes."

"I'll sleep, then." He turns his face away and is asleep.

+

The headlights aren't right, and the car is pulling to one side, Jerome says. I sit up and look out the windshield, narrow and airplane-like, with a post down its center, and in the yellowish probes of the lights the pavement seems dim, gray as cardboard, and from the contained and strumming capsule of the car, with the dash lights covering us like warmth, we seem to be standing still while the highway revolves underneath us. *No*, I think. Night. No moon. So it's a relief when lights heave up in the dark and stagger out across the prairie in the pattern of the lights of Pettibone.

Earl Stuttlemeyer, an old acquaintance, waves us down on Main Street and leans in at my window, neon light rising like fibers from his head. We decide to drive around and have a smoke—three pairs of legs in bluejeans under the dash. He asks about Dad. We tell him part of it, holding in reserve what we've seen, and then there's only the sound of the engine as we travel the back streets, toward the south and out the drag strip we traveled another night, and then again Jerome's slow process of backing around to turn.

Which angers me so much, now, I feel as I did when I took off on the bike to get free of him.

"Did you ever floor this thing?" Earl asks.

"Many's the time," Jerome says.

Right, when I'm driving, I start to say, and then gravel is tearing away underneath us, and in a leap we're on the blacktop with a dancing skid and a floorboarded groan, then a jammed shift into second, a new whining in a higher key, and then third, that leap, and the windup to its highest register. There's a sudden backing off that causes us to slump forward as the pocketed density of inner air eases in its compression, and I glimpse the speedometer, sixty, and shove my foot into the floor as Earl says, "Hey, the curve."

I catch fifty as the gravel band at the edge of the curve sways into view. There's a sudden lunge as Jerome jams the gearshift into second, a frazzle of tires sliding over the graveled shoulder and then thudding into ruts that send up exclamations from him. Brick buttresses widen in the dim probes as he swings right, and I throw myself back on the seat in relief as I see that the chain is down and that he isn't going to try to complete the curve he probably couldn't make anyway but go down the drive into the cemetery, which we're roaring toward in our growing slide, and just as I let go of the breath it feels I've held from the time we walked into Dad's room, Jerome cries, "Open up those gates! Here we come!"

A finger of light penetrates to me. I rise and swing away, tumbling in a line down a graph, out. Then beside him, over frying heat, with objects magnified and floating off. An amplified weeping inside a metal room. Forehead and teeth outside the numbed lens light enters through. The car, too huge, swelling with pressure into space—dashboard going, the heater at my knees releasing steam—and I'm out. My hip on fire, the bent seat forcing me into a melting heater. Then I see that the room I'm trying to identify is a shattered mirror in my lap shivering with clotted blood.

"Jerome!" The name goes out in endlessness, above the echoed weeping in a metal room. "Jerome! Where am I?"

"I don't know, I don't know."

"I can't move!"

"Steering wheel's—"

"Are we dead?"

"I don't know, I don't know."

"This is Hell!"

"Don't!" In the echoing, a chuffing train starts up and gathers speed.

"I have to move or I'll burn up!"

"Accident."

"Can you move?"

"A litter," he says from the radio. "A car. We're in it."

"I can't move. Help me!"

"Can't reach."

"Earl, oh, dammit, oh, help me!"

"Yes, help."

"Oh, it hurts, it hurts! Oh, Jesus, why does it hurt so bad?"

"I don't know, I don't know."

The heater louvers melt to rubber and I'm out.

The dashboard, clearer, dented in. A windshield, up too high to see out of, spangled into diamonds. Other lights down.

"Turn off the key!"

No noise now.

"Jerome, turn off the key!"

"Key, ah, chee, a—"

"Turn off the key!"

"Oh."

"Ahhh, God!"

Down the front of my shirt, soaked black, pinchers of crackling heat grip my skin—a tickling excellence leaving me in streaks. "My throat's cut! The blood's running down! Jerome!"

"Somebody comes."

"Oh, help me, please, oh, Jesus, this is killing me!" The clotted mirror in my lap flies aside—out. Then my jeans, black, with puddles seeping out, one leg so huge the seam is split, the skin beneath blue.

A balloon like my head is blowing up in swelling loops of rain—screaming like me?—then an explosion brighter than searchlights.

Dean Roy and Don Nelson squeak: "Key off?"

"Smoke."

"Steam."

"Is he?"

"I don't know."

I don't know. A face close up. "Jesus!" Gagging backing off. Another moving in. "Holy Jesus H, man!"

The gagging fading to a powdery wheeze; more lights, a prod at metal, clacking and prying over the floating space above my seams—clump of claws. A car speeding up and its screech.

"No, it's steam."

Heated hard breathing. "Dear Jesus, be with them. Charlie?" A refolded shift of years. "Charles, can you hear me?"

Voices carom in from behind:

"Can he?"

"Get back!"

"No, Neumillers."

"Mean, man, mean."

"Get that jack."

"No, doors are jammed."

"Earl called."

"Out the window, I guess."

"That house down the road."

"No, it's steam."

"Charlie, can you hear me?" The near one's breath, his eye's heat.

"Yes, I believe."

"Hey!" Other voices spreading farther until they begin again, a black-and-white jumping of faces in a rush back to the source: *Hey, ey ey, ey.* Shoulder clamped in a freeze, the black and white sending flakes of faces into a sudden curve of gravel soaring up. "No!"

"Charlie, please!"

This near one's heat. I roll. Sleeve in to me, white head lit from behind, a radiance clipped to it, bugged eyes wobbling behind wire rims. Elmer Reed—funeral director's assistant.

"Charlie?"

"We're dead." Crowley, the director?

"Mr. Crowley couldn't come. It's me."

"Gaaaw—" The bubbling out my craw drops heated clots over a leg. Jerome gone. Reed reaches across, bugging eyes shying in retreat: "Now, Charlie, this might hurt." He shakes the shoulder in his gloved grip, then the glove sinks deep. All the voices gather to cry *Hoooeeeeee!*

+

Don Nelson's face is above, under a ceiling, and I must remember not to hit him in it while we're on the route, rolling together, the pink around his eyes part of the sickening hum that's bleeding me. I vibrate close as he holds my hand in a hardness like rice.

"What are you *doing*?" I say.

"You were trying to get at your throat."

I jerk away into the blankness of night—out?

"Charles, please."

"Is a jugular cut?" A gargle.

"I don't know."

"Dad's in a damn hospital."

"Hush."

"I'll bleed to death!"

"Lie still."

"Jerome?"

"He's here."

"Are you here?"

"Over here." Past Don, only his head, with a strap beneath, on a squeezed cot, bloody sheets. The lines I've been rising awake on are the reeling sounds of an ambulance siren.

"Where are we?"

"I don't know, I don't know."

"At the bridge." Nelson's squeak. "The Mackinaw."

"Don't tell Dad."

"We're going to Pekin."

"Fast?"

"Sixty."

"Is that all the faster that damn—"

Rumble of the shadowy bridge, then the blackness that takes me out tumbles down from a distance—the pain below arching up to connect with it—and my jaws go wide with a scream.

No sound.

Don is saying, "If I was dumb or mean to you guys, you know, like I've been a couple times, I really—"

+

Hard ice underneath, shoulders pinned, spotlights and a hum beaming out of a glassy square above, my jaw shuddering below my eyes to get free of the zero hardness crushing me.

"We got him waiting, can't you see?" Nelson.

"Sorry, no doctor yet."

"At least give this kid here a shot, you Frankenstein."

"I'm an X-ray technician."

"Well, get him off this table. Help me! He's going to fall."

A searing glare erupts. I struggle to free my head and see, on a black slab, a tipped-up shrunken body, clothes red-black, a thigh like a chest below my caked belt, bluejeans split over it. Down there, a cowboy boot twisted backward, the pointed toe reversed, wobbling on its outside edge on the slab, and in a jolt like electricity I'm out.

Another voice says, "Here, I can do this," and glittering shears enter the boot. Out.

A surge of energy hurts my returning mouth, and the lights come up, my head to one side, footsteps pouring cleats down the hall and then Crowley, the funeral director, bangs inside, bald dome alight, eyes dull beams, and steps up: It. But Uncle Jay floats in, or a balloon of him, face gray-green, bleeding dollars, and leans on a wall. He cries with swelling heat, "Good Lord, isn't there anything you can do for him!"

"Who's he?"

"Their uncle. Jay Neumiller. We were at a Knights of Columbus meeting here in Pekin when Elmer called. Goodness."

"Will he assume responsibility for a surgeon?"

"Of course. Jay, have them call Holcomb. He's the best."

"Haven't you called a priest yet?" Jay's heated cry.

"We didn't know."

"Well, call one, now." Gone, drawing the others and the room out after him. Night, where stars spatter my face like water and one dot glows on its way through the arches where she disappeared.

+

A pursed and puffy face sets my tongue buzzing at the frequency that has called it up—gray-blue eyes at mine, and lips which say, without a voice, *He's up.* His jacket comes off and swivels out sweet perfume.

"Start the blood right now. Take right tibia, right fibula, better take the femur on that side, too. Left femur, poor lad. That entire leg. The hip. Spine, all of it. Skull." Heavy prodding walking up an arm, then a breezy hinging of it, the gray-blue eyes at mine again. "Does this hurt?" The other arm. "These seem okay. Now this." Where the shears glittered through bloody leather. "Is the uncle available?"

"Here."

"Does this boy have any deformities?"

"Goodness no."

"I was afraid of that."

By now the growling buzzing in my teeth, tastier than Novocain, swings me to the top of a lopsided swell, and I cry, "Bullshit! I'm pigeontoed! *Ahhh!* God!"

"How long has he been here?"

"About an hour, Dr. Holcomb."

"On this table?" There are clucks of a tongue, somebody on a tractor a mile off. "Give him another hundred cc's of that. Hold him here somebody. Gently, please. Left femur impacted, radial twist of—"

Gently, they disappear. A shaft of blue lowers through the tumbling darknesses and I see Dad's arm, with a tube in it, strapped to a white-plastic sheath. No. Mine.

The pale face purses coolly above. "See these?" He holds up small scissors and snicks them. A rumble from a distance underneath comes out in a ringing miss at yes: *Eeessip.*

"I'm going to use these under your chin."

"Jugular?" My eyes pull toward one another and seem to touch.

"No, your jugular is okay. A quarter inch one way or the other . . . But there's a mess underneath. I can't deaden it all. Bear with me. This will hurt, but not like your other hurt—more a chilly pinch."

From the buzzing vibrations a lighted mirror arrives and bends in behind, then jiggles tilting to a hairline peeled back from an oozing skull like a melon skinned.

"No, don't touch. It's not as bad as it looks, but we have to watch for infection. It's the other, underneath, that's rough."

"Me?" There is a hole with cords and bloody flaps down on a chest, and I slide backward onto the lowering beam that lifted me.

Frozen ponies riding knives are punching holes, a creak of

scissors speeding a searing line across my throat—eyes bleeding silver heat. His gray-blue ones, with a mask beneath, swim too close. "These are stitches now. Near the last. I apologize. I have to know where the feeling is. I'm not quite a plastic surgeon, but from the looks of this so far, the young ladies will still admire you."

A crimped pulling at a point of pain so deep it's warm, and something snaps like a rubber band from there to my chest. "You son of a bitch," I say, and go for him, but there are binding straps—then gold is descending from windows in wedges newly discovered, just in time.

"Charles?"

A fragile pose. Turtles? The wedges break apart at the unexpected freshness of the name, arriving from a different part of me, and I turn, afraid of how it has learned to speak: a puffy tuber with the look of Jerome lies inside angles of lighted heat. We're at the stove, it seems, to roast this potato that sings above the gold in a strident key.

"Charles, can you hear me?" A hole in the tuber opens and leaves.

"What's wrong. Can't we eat? Dad?"

"Your legs are broken. You're in traction. We're in the hospital."

"My throat."

"It's okay. Both are broke—oh, jeez!"

"Yours?"

"No!"

"You still hurt?"

"It's hard to breathe."

"Where are we?"

"The third-floor solarium. Three east. You're on sedatives."

"Everything that happened wasn't in the car?"

"What do you mean? We had an accident."

"Why's your face that way?"

"My cheek hit the window post. I hurt my ribs and a knee. The emergency brake. But my leg's not broken. Oh, I wish—"

The swollen tuber turns, struck down its side by a shining line, and I participate in caravans of music moving from the wedges into sections of countryside like beams of wheat. Grass in bottled light. Then a sudden plunging at my center like a washing machine drops me below a diving board—a sea thrown up in a slow wave while the overbed table comes gliding up, flapping a wing. Eat? There's a heat-poached place beyond my eyes, legs frying, into which I'll be sick, and pinpoints of light scream to another angle and gather in a noise like speech: "For tonight we'll tell your dad it's because of school, or you had to stay late. We'll make something up." The granular darkness of a cheek with a white brush cut above echoes under a canopy like Grandpa's voice. A movie of him. He says, "The doctor doesn't think your dad should have to take the shock of it now." Me? "Tomorrow we'll say something about you two staying with the younger kids, and after that I'm sure he'll know something is wrong. Let's pray he's better by then."

"It's all my fault." A bubbling from the tuber beneath.

"Don't torture yourself. It's over, you're young, you'll be okay. Keep your strength up for him. I'll be back and forth with news."

"He's awake." The moving hole of the tuber forms speech.

The granular face turns on its screen and its glasses come off to peer through the heat beaming out of me, then something rustles over the sheets and a hand is on mine. "Now, Charles," he says, in a voice aimed so exactly at me I'm sent back under the sea. In the heated confusion there, another face, or his changed and doubling on the screen, unfolds to say, "See a sleep?"

Amber ampules at an open door. "Can chee have more? Can't chleep?"

"One more tonight. I'll cheat."

"Can't chleep."

"I know, poor guy. This shift's worst. Here, see?"

"Can't chleep, can . . ."

+

I open my eyes, on my back on this bed, the inked squiggles of wood grain on the wardrobe an oracular discovery. I rise on an elbow. New York: home. I touch the scar under my chin and fluttery sensations enter my throat, branching into ticklish runners, and then I sit and the sensation spreads down my chest like the blood of lives over me. My ribs lift—strummed. The headache is gone but an afterimage of it persists in a knucklish knot at the back of my neck, and I recall, before everything disperses under rationality, that some of the images from the morphine were of Indians, dancing and carrying bows, and that one of our roommates in the solarium, where we were put because of overcrowding, was an archer we'd met at a Boy Scout camp, who on the last day of camp couldn't compete for our team because he was confined to his tent after being caught dancing in front of a fire after curfew, naked, his parts painted with Merthiolate—now in the hospital for surgery on a cyst: "Right next to my butthole and twice as big." He was in the far bed, beside the door, and Earl in the bed next to him, with a cut on his forehead like the gash he gave me on a basketball court once when I dribbled past him and scored with a wise remark—punching me so hard my upper lip split over my teeth (the tip of my tongue goes to the scar drooping from that point); and then Jerome beside me, the bed on my left empty, so that when I woke sometimes, facing that way, I would think Jerome was gone. He stayed through my term of traction, ten days, and beyond the operation.

The right tibia was broken down its center at an angle that should have broken the bone behind, but didn't, and my left femur so smashed that traction didn't help. An orthopedic surgeon, called in from Peoria, appeared in a segment of the lucidity that sometimes came, a heavy shadow of beard on his face and black hair frothing from his nostrils and ears, and explained that he would "open" my thigh, "open" a place at the back of my hip, start a pin "back there," at the center of my femur, "send" it down the marrow, threading the pieces of bone along it, and insert the end of the pin in the stump above my knee. He was built like a fullback, with a Polish or Russian name, and at my drugged fascination he exhibited X-rays. His big hands molded the air as they might mold me, and then he sketched on a pad it seemed his hairy fingers would devour, and I looked into the brown eyes of Hogelvode; the drugs. I couldn't ask what I wanted to. So as he took out a metal tape and ran it in an icy strip over my good thigh, I said I wanted to see the pin before he put it in.

"It's probably psychological," I said.

He laughed, and a smell of lawns came from the square green gum that shook inside a box in his pocket. "All right, we can do that."

Then: "Doctor?" Cottony warps woofed through fear. "Will I be able to walk?"

"I don't see why not."

"The same as before?"

"Well, we haven't gotten in there yet, to see what's up."

"Will I run?"

"It could be different. You'll be in a wheelchair first. It's possible for your walk to be affected, yes."

That was enough.

"But don't worry, Chuck," he said. "I'm going to make you my very special patient." A big hairy paw came down on my good thigh and I yelled as if he had squeezed the mangled one.

"Oops," he said. "Fooled me there."

Before surgery, through the haze of the drug taking on dimensions yet to be disclosed (if I sleep), Jerome's head on its hump of pillow rolled to me. A crystalline line hit his nose and pinged in dotting chips over the pillow as he sighed something I had heard in her voice. "Legs. I wish mine were broken, or at least one, and not both of yours, oh . . ."

I pulled his look with me to the bottom, as I went under again, and fixed on its burning blue—Mom's eyes, from the Scott Haig house, I saw, with a cold clack of consideration my tongue sent up—fixed on me with longing, a lover's plea. I have the look here, and even in the aftermath of this interfering present—the shelf across that door, these wood-papered walls, the bedsprings erupting under my hams, the trailing drone of a jet going over and drawing off in the thunder of its wake a blurred portion of the one thought that seemed important—

In spite of this, I know that I was loved by somebody who would have given a leg for me.

+

The stainless-steel pin, with four ribs down its length, a star bit, turns in silver light that drips through my sheets. A set of barbs, stepping down in bites from the sharpened tips at each end, sends overlappings of language down to the original language rooted in my navel.

"Bones have no feeling," the hairy Russian says, and presses a big thumb to a sharpened tip. "About this much will penetrate above your knee and this much stick out at the other end—but next to your pelvis, as I've said, and we'll put a rubber cap on it, so you won't even know it's there. If all goes well, we can pull it out in about a year." He lays it on my overbed table with a ringing sound, and the pursed and passive face with gray-blue eyes treadles up and nods at me. "I'll be there to keep an eye on him and do the stitching up, so you'll have an example of what I can do, given the right conditions."

They look at one another and laugh and I madly join in, and then the Russian is around painting Merthiolate over the thigh as though to tickle me further, with a sensation like a tongue moving over the numbed vacancy of a pulled tooth, while at the same moment a voice says in a familiar mellow tone, "Can't I see him, if he's awake?"

She turns in a red coat, tall, frothed with curls, the Grecian purity of her face pushed out below her nose by the row of spaced teeth, and then sails off Grandpa's screen, blurring into pink patches, her lips over mine impossibly giving, as if several women are wetly entering me, and I have the sense to make sure the shrunken remains of my parts, down to a candle tip from this ordeal, are covered, and encounter something under the sheet like a concrete stove. What's up, I want to say, and then Holcomb and the Russian appear, above green dresses, and by sudden seizures of their mouths enter the echoing tunnel I'm trying to escape from.

"You fared well, lad."

"What I thought would be worst isn't. It's that tibia we'll have to watch. I had to put a full-length cast on that leg."

"Yes. Here's your guest."

A face like Bobbie's parts into patches of pink entry, sending eroding channels through the concrete, and a cavern opens where blue breath blew. Her voice: "I love you. I always have."

This reechoes as the rest subsides, and then the resonating of a bell begins, and I see the doctors in their dresses rock back, uprooted, and want to ask about the woman, but she draws away, a handkerchief out, and turns so only shoulders support a red coat. This waggles and then burns in, locked in place like a door, and with a resonating note draws me into a tension where each ear faintly remains, with a single phrase strung thinly between: *Permanently hurt.*

+

The mangled car has been towed to our back yard, and a ghost of Dad, thirty pounds lighter, with the skin of its neck slack, wanders from room to room on the resurrected cane. I'm on the flopped-down couch, where I can see the television and the kitchen table, and I try to raise the full-length cast—a solid ghost, immovable, though attached to my hip—from the pillow where it rests, but can't. If I manage to begin to, the foot at its far end, with only the tips of toes showing, starts to slip down the dull swag of pain parting my shin. A pain of another kind rises from a coiled knot at the center of my restrung thigh, so naked and vulnerable-looking, with its bubble-gum-colored scar, with such perfectly spaced nicks left by the stitches, from hip to knee, it's like a zipper that might burst. The most painful point (without drugs to help now) is the scar on the cheek of my butt, perhaps because I know that the rod of arrowed metal with its barbs protrudes beneath.

But none of this is comparable to the "realigning" the Russian performed on my tibia, after exhibiting an X-ray and then wheeling me up to the cast room himself, wearing a smock askew. He got out an electric drill fitted with a circular blade and started sawing into the cast, until I yelled with fear that he'd cut my leg. "Oh, this only vibrates," he said, and held the blade against a hairy paw, grinning, then went back to cutting at the cast with a tingling strum that stirred up an erection, and then I saw that he'd removed a window from the cast. He was studying the X-ray hung on a lighted frame, and then he took hold of the cast with both hands, put a knee in the window, the way you'd break a stick, I thought, and I heard the beginning of a scream as my back arched and I went out—oh, these rooms that I've been in and out in!—and when I came to, battering at him with profanity, he said, "Gee, I didn't know it had knit that much. It shouldn't have hurt. We really are going to have to watch that bugger like a little baby."

Worst of all, though, is being off the drugs, and having to relive the accident over backward, each detail slowed and viewed through the lens at that tunnel's end—the worst in clearest focus: clots of blood plopping over my fly, the twisted foot in spasms on the X-ray table. Then again the squalling hop of the tires out of the gravel, knowing each time how it will end, seen from this side, but never knowing how I'll emerge—broken over the shattered rearview mirror in my lap, or on this side, whole, aware that it will arrive again, with no drugs to dim its effects—until the afternoon when I wake in our old house in Hyatt, parched, and watch the cast attempt to jack me out of the couch, my brain partly gone, scraped away by an implement left inside.

+

Jerome, still limping, travels from me to Dad, who has a draining wound in his stomach which has to be dressed twice a day. A slack fold rolls out from Dad's stomach where the incision was made. It's a corner of this that is draining, and is supposed to, but the continual lumpy infected look of it has the doctors worried, Jerome says.

Dad can empty my milk-bottle urinal, but not the bedpan; he can't bear any upheaval of his stomach, and my system is sending out segments of its wordless hell, with a stench of the dirtiest depths. Jerome is home at noon to help with this, and to change Dad's dressing, but I seem to be attacked with an urge whenever they all sit down for a meal. Jerome comes limping through the arch—no door between—to handle things, and Tim cries, "This is it! I've had it!" while Dad pushes back from the table, white, to head for the other side of the house. "It's all right," Jerome says, propping me up with pillows, instead of leaving me flat on my back, as they did in the hospital, which made things tough to manage, and then holds up a bed sheet for privacy—or as a baffle, perhaps. Then he carries in a basin with a cloth floating in it and washes my crack.

+

Grandpa finds a wheelchair, a wobbly wooden one of Spanish–
American War vintage, in the Legion Hall, and Jerome builds
a plywood ramp from the kitchen door into the garage. I won't
wheel down it; I'm sure it will collapse, or the chair tip. My cast
sticks straight out on a hinged, extended wooden leg-rest,
causing the chair to feel off-center, and I grip the wooden rail
around its wheels—as big as bicycle tires—when Jerome tries to
push me out. "No!" I cry. "Leave me alone!"

+

He moves me to Dad's office, onto the single bed, which I'm
afraid I'll fall out of, and to get me into the wheelchair (which
Dad can't do), he has to lift me at the armpits and drag me
backward, trying meanwhile to keep the chair from rolling off.

"No," I say. "It'll never work." He has both arms around
me and is straining behind in an amplified dimension, more
substantial than mine, where real people move—as I've noticed
whenever I'm able to rise from the brain-blackened, truly
lobotomized state I now reside in.

"Try," he pants.

"Maybe if we didn't have this antique. No, not that way!"

A flap of skin and flesh is pinched between the top of the
cast and the wheelchair seat, although he has placed a pillow
there for me to sit on. "Dammit! I've told you—" I haven't, but
I want to say, "You'll never know what it is to have broken legs!
A bumped knee and a scratch on the cheek and you bitched
about it for two weeks! And it's your fault in the first place!
Driving a broken-down car like—" But with his arms encircling
me, a cheek at my ear, I know he knows what I mean.

+

One afternoon when he isn't handy and I'm feeling trapped in
my chair, I hear a cry come from the kitchen. I roll gingerly
out, still getting the knack of matching the heft of each hand's
push on a wheel, and see Dad at the kitchen window, his back

to me, staring toward the car. Sunlight shifts at the edges of his shirt in lengthening beams, and his elbows are at his sides, as if both hands are covering his stomach. His incision has opened, I think, and the dulled state enters my brain with a force that I feel will put me to sleep.

"I don't understand," he whispers, so that I'm not sure if he knows I'm there. "How could anybody come out of that alive?" He looks over his shoulder with shining eyes, then draws a handkerchief from his hip pocket and blows his nose. "Great God Almighty in heaven. We're all here."

+

I get outdoors, finally, by backing down the ramp, which feels safer than going down it headlong. I've asked Jerome to leave the garage door open, and I wheel down the incline at its base, to the drive, and trundle around on the concrete, restless, remembering my circuits here on a bike. I roll over the sidewalk and out to the street, then down it, and soon I'm rocking over the uneven grass of our back yard. I stop a few feet from the car, out of breath. The crease of a V, where we struck the brick upright, indents the center of the grille and continues up the center of the hood, which is jackknifed higher than the roof, and for the first time I hear the *crump* of the impact, metal raining, then the radiator and air from the tires blowing in high-pitched screams. Light clipped to magnified surfaces, the breathing heat of a face at my ear: "Charlie, can you hear me?"

The headlights, turned in toward each other on either side of the crease, bugged eyes, send a glancing flash off a brick column, webbing the windshield gold. I shake my head. Both corners of the bumper are bent out like horns. The front end is lifted off the frame, the driver's door ajar, and somebody has soaped its window in a pre-Halloween prank. I wheel up and look inside. A fish smell, fall's drugged flies in orbit there. Rusted blood on the seat cover, the seat back folded forward, as it felt. No rearview mirror in sight. Beginning cracks at each side of the windshield—Earl and Jerome—and then closer to Jerome than I thought, near the center bar that restrained me, webbed glass bulged out, with pieces of hair in it. The radio speaker that raked the bottom of my chin. The rear of the engine heaved through the floorboard, forcing the heater back. No space between it and the seat.

A glove, a wrench, a doll, clumps of homemade soap go springing past, and I'm on scorched ground pocked with lumpy anthills, the turreted gables of the house at her shoulders as she raises her face, with reflections of the sky dividing it in jagged streaks. Her warning to us. I feel the car slide on the curve with a frazzling sound of gravel, a lit fuse headed toward its end, then the realignment as Jerome starts down the drive, the breath of relief as I fall back in the seat, ablaze with peace at the moment of impact (the cords in her neck as she cries, *Perished here!*), and know that this is what saved me.

+

There are leaves under my wheels, the crush and scent of them and their crablike scrape across the concrete drive. The season's lengthened sunlight over my arms, now dark with silky hair, my muscles hard as the wooden armrests. I stop in the street on my tour of our corner to watch the wind sway the top of an oak beside our house; its upper limbs nod and chatter while its remaining lower leaves stand motionless. I wheel to my spot, as it's become, at the far side of the second garage door, where the curb of the drive forms an angle with the corner of the house, and stare into the triangular park.

The tops of the trees there sway away from me, then bend farther, and loose leaves lift off in the high wind like stylized streaks of rain. In the space of silence before their clatter to the blacktop, I understand that I don't have to worry about what I'll do when I grow up. I don't know what it is, but it's clear that it isn't a matter of concern or of my choosing, yet suits me. Another flight of leaves travels off, and a portion of the darkness in me lifts like a swirl of smoke into the wind, and as I examine my hand on the armrest, the darkness is invaded with light that renders me alien, on a route to recovery.

A man who's been walking up the street stops at the edge of our drive. Elmer Reed. He says, "Do you remember me, Charlie?"

"Sure. Thank you."

He walks up, his shoes gritting over sand on the concrete, and stops beside me, his face a deep pink and his eyes evasive behind wire-rim spectacles. "You know, I've thought of that time a lot."

"Me, too."

"I expect so. I don't usually handle accidents, and I hope I never have to see one again."

"I'm sorry I wasn't very nice."

"You were in awful pain. Are you now?"

"Not really." I sit as stiffly upright as Grandpa.

"You're looking well. You know, I've thought since, if it hadn't been for that car, those frames—I mean, that unibody or whatever it is Hudsons have, welded, with that low box in them, well . . . I saw your Uncle Kev out at the cemetery the other day. He was re-laying the bricks of that column, and I stopped and asked how you could have come out of it. You know how quiet he is. He worked away, whistling under his breath, and then said, 'Beats me. Because this thing sure didn't give.' "

He takes off his hat and looks up at the swaying trees.

"We were lucky, I guess."

His eyes come back to that window again, light clipped around, his sleeve shoved in, and the moment enters us both. "It was the hand of the Lord. I know that. From the car down to every detail." He pulls his hat back on, and goes off with his hands in his overcoat pockets, across our drive and across the street, under the shedding elms at the back of the old Opera House, toward the funeral home.

+

"And that's the story of the beginning of my accident, Justin," I say, as if I'm speaking to my son, and turn off the microphone— only the open electronic pitch it would take a professional to detect coming from the equipment in this soundproofed granary. A segment for my show?

I shut the recorder off and treadle backward in my soundless chair.

The first time the wheelchair tips, as I'm trying to raise the garage door Jerome has neglected to leave up, I go clattering into the center of the accident, hearing a trace of the gargled cry that came from the flap of my throat. I'm sure I've rebroken both legs, but when my heart stops sending out shocks that redden my vision, I realize I can hand-walk backward. I make it to the ramp, up it, through the open door, through the kitchen and living room, into Dad's office, and pull myself onto the bed. I drag one leg up and then lift the other in place beside it. Then I slide back, shoulders down, out of bed, hand-walk to the bathroom, and crawl up on the stool for an hour-long cleansing squat.

+

Dad has switched to a pipe, so I use his tobacco and toilet paper to roll cigarettes—a mess, but something to smoke. I sit in the wheelchair and watch TV, whose reception has improved, from the time I wake until Jack Paar and his Cuban compatriots end their personal jokes, and then "The Star-Spangled Banner" begins and the unfurled flag beats in the wind in such an earnest way I feel I'm a veteran watching my country go under, too feeble to do anything but permit myself also to be drawn down.

There's a thread of story in the soap operas, however, that ties one day to the next, especially in *The Edge of Night*, and I wear Mom's gold wristwatch, which I've found in a drawer of Dad's desk, to make sure I don't miss any of the episodes I'm sure she would want to see. I get out my stamp collection and discover that the carbon tetrachloride returns me to the visions of the hospital, and then Lincoln steps through splintered light from the solarium windows, removing his hat, and says, "Charles, it's time we made peace."

+

I feel I'm five. I assemble an airport scene that includes baggage carts, fuel trucks, and a passenger plane with a ramp on wheels. I arrange the pieces on a plywood base I've asked Jerome to cut out and paint for me. I run baggage trucks to the plane, as engrossed as I've ever been, then set the ramp in place, and in a stunned moment of thick thought I see my missal on the floor and imagine it's a hangar and I'm a person on its scale—a ballpoint on the plywood like a sewer pipe. The books above Dad's desk are cities, and my window opens on gold haze. Below, through my pajama fly, hair springs up in coiling profusion, and my Coke bottle rolls over onto the top of the cast. Now that I know I can go to pieces in an instant, or be bent into another shape, I wonder how it would feel to be a woman (a glimpse of the gold around my wrist) and have a hole to fill. I pick up the ballpoint as a pressurized shimmer from the hospital reduces me further, and imagine I'm Leslie Caron in the open airplane door, with a line hurrying up the ramp toward me, and see fluid rise from the eye I move the pen toward—sicker than I thought—and then a voice says, "Be a doctor, Charles."

+

"Well, I don't see why you couldn't be," Jerome says. He plucks a single cigarette from the pack in his shirt pocket with the nails of a thumb and index finger, lights it up, and sits and fans the smoke away with one hand. "I mean, sure you could, if you set your mind to it. It takes a lot of study, though, even past college level. Let's see. You'd probably need a good scholarship."

He's thinking of our doctor bills, I'm sure, which we figure will run into the thousands, not counting Dad's, since the bill from my bone specialist, for the operation alone, is six hundred. Jerome hands me the cigarette, then leans forward with his elbows on his knees as if he's a doctor himself, thinking this through, and I can picture him in glasses.

"You'd really have to hit the books," he says, and looks up. His eyelids have the reddened outlines of emotion, as if he's pleased that I've found my future occupation.

+

The red coat is off, over my toes, dense with her and her perfume, and she comes in a courtly country way that can go gangly, in her tight skirt, to me in bed and takes my hands, her splayed teeth shining in her smile, and, in a move no man could accomplish, is sitting on the bed, out of reach, still holding my hands. She was stupid to kiss me with the doctors there, she says, and winks an eye, but thought she should carry out her whole plan—"Kinda lay my claws on you, ha!"—since she'd skipped school and hitchhiked there, and couldn't restrain herself, she says, seeing me in bed. She blushes and laughs. A pimple is ripening between her plucked eyebrows, and one such flaw in her white skin, when my eye catches at it, sends her hand there as if she's received pain.

She talks about her father, a farmer who does factory work in the winter to pay off their mortgage "after drinking away the calf-and-egg money, the old guzzle-gut—and I raise the calves!" she says. A pin on her sweater, above one breast—representing a prize from a fair—shudders in trembling suspension above the curve of cashmere at her cries. She talks until her father makes his presence known by tooting his car horn outside. She unfurls long legs from under her skirt and extends them straight, as if inviting me to gawk, taking her time, or crosses them and swings one, sending bars of light glancing from her polished shin, below the hem she holds in a line across both knees, and I clench my teeth, not about to be taken in, as I was by Dewey.

"You probably wouldn't even like me," she says from her height, as my toes cool from her coat coming away, "if I hadn't of caught you on your back, ahhahaha!"

Her father's laugh, which reminds me of the high-speed exit I now take down the ramp into the sun. Honk! honkety honk!-honk!

Or Jerome appears, working the zipper of his jacket up and down, a dark head near his arm, in time to drive Bobbie home. He has started to date a girl from our church, Lynette, who is Bobbie's neighbor—from the turtle-raising area near Kyle Lake, where girls have a reputation for being fast—and is now grinning at me from behind Jerome's arm. They might as well be going steady, Dad has said, the way they talk after church, but Jerome hasn't mentioned the prospect of this, except to say that if things remain about the same, once I'm up and around, it'll sure make it handy for dating double. Then slapped his forehead with the heel of his hand as we both laughed.

+

Stainless-steel tables, autoclaves, and steel shelves stacked with tools and rolled towels. The modern metal wheelchair I'm in, the hospital's, lightweight and easy to maneuver on its pneumatic tires, doesn't have the stout substantiality of mine, or its broad-wheeled inertia, like overdrive, which I've come to like, feeling as if I'm rolling up into the present from the Civil War. I rock a wheel close to Jerome's scuffed shoe, breathless about seeing the X-rays—too many of which, I've read in a book, can neuter you. The Russian flips a switch and there's the plik and stutter of several fluorescents, then with a hum my bones hang gray-pale from a wall. The Russian rumbles. "You haven't put any weight on that cast, have you?"

"No." I think of the chair toppling, of hand-walking around the house, being dragged and carried, and of Bobbie on top of it one night.

"I'm not entirely satisfied with the tibia. It might have slipped a bit. Well, maybe not. It's straight yet." He holds a measuring rod to the X-ray. "If we get more than a half inch either way, at this point, there could be trouble with the displacement of your hips. You're at an age when you're going to grow."

I strike the armrest of the chair as if his word insures this.

"Any particular problems?"

"That itch."

"It comes with a cast. It's probably psychological." He wiggles his eyebrows to see if I recall this. "You can't get at it, that's why."

"But it's awful."

He glances at his wristwatch, crosses his arms, and leans his shoulders against my illuminated bones. "Can you describe it for me?"

I've been preparing for this. "Well, it's like a little pinpoint is shot straight in, and then right where it hits it kind of mushrooms out, real warm, with feelers spreading down from it, or *up* into my calf here—wiggly things covered with itching powder. They wiggle in and get a grip, and then the whole area around that first little point is one great big itch. Then another one shoots in."

He laughs so hard his big head rubs the bones behind, stimulating my itch. "That's about as good as I've heard it described," he says, and ruffles my hair. "Good for you, Charles. Fine. Okay, you can go."

+

She's talking about taking aspirin with a carbonated drink, to get a "buzz on," and as she tries to explain how she felt, at my urging, she laughs and takes hold of her head and flings her hands from it like flinging shampoo, and I get a glimpse, beneath her sweater, of the conical cups of her bra trembling with fleshy weight held restrained. "You wise-ass," she says, and reaches out, her splayed teeth clamped on her lip, and slaps my face. "Egging me on!"

+

The speckles in the tile floor rise, shifting under my bent-down head, then rock and take on a molecular rush that has me grappling at the handgrips as I stab through this new altitude and try to get my breath.

"Good!" the Russian cries. "Now swing out with the other crutch!"

+

We're in a copper-colored Hudson a couple of years older than the one we wrecked, with Jerome at the wheel, on the way to Forest Creek, to demonstrate my walk. It's a swing-one-leg-out-with-the-crutch-on-that-side, swing-the-other-leg-out-with-its-crutch rock, not a double-swing-of-both-crutches, pulling-the-legs-up-after hobble, as I'd thought.

"The proper technique," the Russian said, "so you won't put all your weight on either. And don't. Only barely enough for balance, as I've warned, or you'll shorten one or the other up. And don't fall for the temptation everybody falls for when they get up on crutches: *Don't try to walk.* How have you bunged this cast up so much?" By tipping over on a fast run down the ramp, I want to say, though I don't dare mention this, after his anger when I insisted the itch wasn't a usual one. "Jerome, make sure he doesn't use coat hangers down this, huh," he said, wrapping soaked plaster gauze over the grayish and gummy conjunction of the cast with my crotch: "Let's just hope he hasn't already messed things up."

"Hey!" I cry now, from the sidesaddle position I'm forced to adopt, in order to rest the length of the cast on the front seat, with my back near the cigarette Jerome holds in one hand. "Slow down, will you!"

"What?"

"Are you asleep again, or what? Slow this car down!"

"What for?" He glances at me, dreamily debonair over the angle of his cigarette, in his new manner of striking poses. "I'm hardly doing fifty-five."

Slamming trees are flashing past the blackened strip half as wide as it should be, with gravel shoulders narrowing ahead and a tremor in the car blurring my sight. "Slow down, you ass!"

"Well, you have to go at least fifty-five or the front end on this thing shakes like the dickens. Can't you feel that? Listen, ur-urrr. Sixty and above is the best."

"Slow down or I'll get out and walk!"

We creep into Forest Creek at forty—about our speed of impact, I figure, fighting to keep from crying. "I'm just getting on my feet again," I say, leaning into him. "I finally have a girlfriend!"

Bobbie's parents are in bed by eleven, unless there's a cowboy movie on TV. These her father stays up to watch, and often her mother, too, from under the covers, through the open door of their bedroom—at one corner of the living room. Her father sits beside the bedroom door in his chair, next to an oil heater, in a cowboy hat, staring over the top of a dining table whose surface shimmers like a swimming pool in television light. Even when he's out on the town, or in bed, I can picture his great veined face with its wet eyes like a bull's, his teeth splayed out over his lip, the model for hers on a grander scale, like his braying laugh; then the hard belly hanging over his belt that he keeps slapping and hugging with both hands, a dear friend. Her mother is an insomniac, and used to nap on the couch whenever he was in town, until Bobbie told her (she whispers this to me now) that we appreciate our privacy.

"How could you say that?" I whisper. "Did you say what for?"

"You think they don't know? You think they didn't get their jollies when they were our age? You think they still don't? Listen."

I figure this is pretty disrespectful, but stimulating. I glance at the glow of their closed white door in the snowstorm of television light: no noise that I can hear, but we keep the volume on the set up, for camouflage. Our maneuvering begins in the kitchen, after Jerome drops me off; quick wet kisses in a corner where winter clothes hang, while her parents watch the evening news. Then a talkative time at the kitchen table, over cookies and milk, as they prepare for bed, to illustrate the youthful ease of our relationship, then some grinding against my hip at a counter that holds a sink pump, whose candy-red handle seems a representation of my tongue—until I can't take it, standing on the cast. Then in to an easy chair, fevered and out of breath, where she reclines over a chair arm, to keep her weight off me, yet remain frontally exposed.

Occasionally a knock comes from inside the bedroom, then the wisp of a voice. "Bobbie? You up?"

"Ma?" Getting untangled. "What did you think?" Pulling

down her sweater and skirt. "We fell asleep?" By now she's slumped in the other chair, an elbow on its arm, a hand up to shield her flushed face. "Come on out." If I can grab my crutches meanwhile, and have them both in a hand, held upright, in declaration of my injury, I do so.

The creak of the door, her mother padding around the oil heater, birdlike legs below her robe, without a glance at us, into the bathroom at the other corner, and then the crush of its door like a clutch that allows us to pause, going at the speed we are, and breathe a bit. Her mother turns on faucets and shuffles her feet, and Bobbie grimaces like a baby on a potty at the release, and once, after her mother is done and has brushed her teeth, which she brushes every time she enters a bathroom (as Bobbie, who carries a toothbrush in her purse, also does), and is on her way back to the bedroom, she says, "Bobbie, your hair and sweater is mussed."

My crutches feel rubbery as the arm supporting them.

If we miss the double spear of headlights through the fog enveloping their farm at night, or don't hear the chatter of the front-end linkage on their country road or the peculiar whine of the Hudson engine off the levee, Jerome taps the horn, which is partly emasculated, missing one trumpet—a mooing wheeze. There's a procedure in order to leave: a last few attacks in the chair, advancing into territory I couldn't take if Jerome weren't there, which I'll be able to regain the next time; Bobbie straightening herself while I slip the foam-padded curve of the crutches under my armpits; then my wade in the swing-walk out to the kitchen where the coats are hung—Jerome visible through the pane in the kitchen door, against his window, sometimes rubied by a cigarette. Jerome can see us only from the waist up, and it's here a hand first travels down her hip; out to the porch for a bit, then to the car, her breath breaking over my cheek in the cold, igniting its fuzz with frost, and then her run back, which I have to turn to watch, to see her legs swinging out against each side of her tight skirt.

"Can't you ever hang it up?" he asks.

"What?" I'm lowering myself, backward, into the seat.

"When I say it's good night, that's that."

"Yeah, but what do you manage to work in before then?"

"What kind of crap—"

"Now that you're going steady, Bobbie wants to go steady with me."

"It's not necessarily the solution you might think it is."

As he goes for the keys, I say, "You mean, you're not copping as much as you thought you'd be?"

The steering wheel wobbles from the sock of his fist. "You're about the crudest, low-life scrounge I know! You figure you can say anything, because I still feel guilty about that car wreck!"

+

At home I thump into the bathroom and he heads upstairs, his chin so far forward it forces his Adam's apple out and draws the cords in his neck taut. I lower myself onto the edge of the tub, the cast slipping but the sink handy to get a grip on if I start to fall, heading in a beeline back to the closest I came to the borderline tonight, sure that Jerome is up to the same upstairs, the bup bup bup of Satan's hot beat, a fishy stink like his breath, and the grip of his anonymous pussylike paw.

+

Sunday. I've recovered enough from college to attend church, but I sit here with my leg extended as if it's still in a cast, while bells in the neighborhood go off—the way I used to sit in a pew back then, with my leg out in the aisle, listening for a reading from Luke, the Physician.

+

"No, now, when you make that point," Dad says, "you should bring your hand around and open it, to indicate how obvious it is that this is the conclusion your audience should reach. Like this." In a fluid sweep he unfurls the gesture for Jerome.

Jerome is standing beside the TV, which is going at a low growl, his head in front of the pinup lamp that was once in our bedroom. He steps back, his darkened face grim, and leaps into the oration again. The moment for the gesture arrives, he attempts it, and I glance at Dad in his easy chair, his elbows on its arms, steepled fingers to his lips, and notice that he doesn't flinch. I twiddle my standing crutches beside the couch and think, Boy, if I couldn't make a simple gesture like that when it's needed, in a more natural way, I'd quit.

+

Bobbie and I are in the back of the Hudson. In order to extend my cast across the seat I lean against her, then slip a hand inside her coat. The engine is amplified in the night by a bad muffler, and Jerome's and Lynette's heads are like one lumpy one they're so close—the pointer of Jerome's held cigarette at two o'clock. Already I wish we were back from the basketball game, my first outing on crutches, and in Bobbie's house. Banks of snow, speared by cattails, go past to the right, and behind Bobbie's head is a levee so dark it seems half the world is gone. Then along a "ditch," one of many canals draining Kyle Lake for irrigation. The road follows one side of the canal—picked cornstalks shuttling past—and then takes a ninety-degree turn across a wooden bridge without railings, and then another ninety along the canal's other side, the dark levee now high above us, and I discover a humid atmosphere sheathing Bobbie inside her coat. She stops the upward journey of my hand with an elbow, but her stomach sucks in, and then she gets hold of my hand and bends my fingers back until they crack in the cold. "Not here," she whispers, her breath distorting my hearing so much I almost miss the promise: *Not here.* Suddenly she's up with her hands on the front seat: "The bridge, Jerome."

"Jerome!" Lynette cries. "The bridge! Swing left!"

I hear clumps from the grabbing brakes as I hit the front seat, then the frazzled slide of locked wheels, gravel hitting the heated floor I've tumbled to, and finally a leap to a stunned stop.

Bobbie pulls me up onto the seat.

"Back up," Lynette says. "Real slow. I think my wheel on this side's gone off. I wouldn't want to swim tonight."

"Rock it," Bobbie says, as the wheels claw and resound over planks. "No! Don't! You'll drive a big sliver in one of these old baldies!" She lays her hands on the front seat and says, "Lynette."

Lynette crawls over the seat and they get out Bobbie's door and step in front of the headlights, dark shadow bulking up from their backs, and with their pushing we come free with a backward leap.

I lie against the door, trying to find my voice, and think: Oh, my brother, what are you trying to do, kill me?

For Christmas, Grandma Jones sends us each a pair of suntans and a floral-patterned Hawaiian shirt that she's made. Jerome and I go to my room, pull off what we have on, and get my suntans on by wriggles up the cast; then he pulls on his and I swing-walk beside him out to the living room, and there's a flash: in the picture the tops of our heads show best, bent down, his with a shining oval at its center from his recent crew cut, mine with hair hanging long from one side, the other half still growing in, evidence preserved; our eyes are on the cuffs of the trousers at the tops of three socks, with a white stovepipe between. We've grown.

+

Now the intensity of our maneuvering is speeded up, her face to the coats inside the door, the sleeve of one sometimes gripped in her teeth, a gun rack above with shotguns about to blow, her height a boon here, since I have to keep on the crutches if I don't want to end up a freak. And Jerome arrives later now, so that after one o'clock, when her parents are snoring, we circle around the end of the table, past the jiggling TV, to the couch, where her skirt, with a studied wriggling beside the cast, comes up, ghosts of electronic light down her legs, until she suddenly grips a wrist with such force I feel she'll crush my bones in her squeeze. One night I sit up and cry, "Ah, gahh!"

My pinned thigh sticks straight out, unbending, and I hold it in both hands, knowing as surely as if I'm seeing it on an X-ray that the capped end of the pin is hooked in a muscle of my thigh, stretching it like piano wire. "Ah, God!" I cry.

Tap, tap. "Bobbie?" The clawing wisp from behind the glowing door. "Bobbie, you okay?"

"Ma?" "Oh, sure." "What do you think?" "He just bumped one of his legs." Then in a whisper to me, "What is it?"

With both hands under my knee, I try to sway the thigh back and forth, to unhook the pin from a pain like the arch of a foot cramped, but gouge the muscle worse. "Where's Jerome?" I say. "Why is he so late? Oh, Jerome!"

"What's the matter?"

"This damn thing—" In my anger I jerk the leg higher, swinging it to one side, free, and my foot strikes the floor with a clump. I massage the bruised muscle, feeling oily sweat crawl around my eyebrows, and figure I've learned my lesson. "Maybe we're getting too serious," I say.

+

"The reason I asked you guys over here tonight is this," Dad says, and places his clasped hands on our dining-room table, now in the other side of the house. "You've asked me for the car to go see Lynette and Bobbie again. So far, that's been fine. I like them both. They aren't the most intellectual students I know, but they have good minds, and over the years I've come to respect them." I gulp as if taking down a cup of cottage cheese at one go. Teachers seem to hear of student goings-on, perhaps through a network of parents, before students do, and I decide that if it comes down to a direct question, I'll lie. "Each has an easygoing disposition that's probably good for you. Now, I don't know about the motivations behind your relationships, and I'm not sure if that's entirely my business. I don't know whether you have questions you'd like to ask, or, if you did, if I could offer any advice you'd take to heart. I've had experience," he says, laying his spread hands flat, so that the authority of a high-school administrator emanates from him. "I've had experience with this situation, and I've had experience along these lines myself, at a certain point in my life, and I thank God that although I had all the answers then, I'm not so sure I do now. But there's one thing I want to say." He raps the edge of the table with an index finger. "You can fool me, maybe, but not the Lord. I've learned that. I don't want to hear about these girls getting hurt, or into any kind of trouble—of any sort, you name it—because of either of you, do you hear?" He pushes away his chair, irritated, and says, "Isn't there some wholesome, public entertainment you can think of to take them to? Meanwhile, for God's sake, watch it with the car on those untrustworthy, back-country roads!"

I stare down at the tips of my crutches, which I've been twiddling, and realize he's heard about our accident on the bridge. Untrustworthy? I turn to Jerome, and his face, like Uncle Jay's, is gray-green.

+

I'm in a former storeroom, on the landing down from the study hall, in a green easy chair—a stage prop—with my cast up on a matching footstool, working on a lap desk Dad has built. When he returned to school he stopped on this landing, resting on his way to the study hall, he said, and wondered what was behind the door; not much, he discovered, when the janitor opened it for him. He had the janitor move out old books and set up a long table and a wooden file at one end, and then had him build bookshelves over the wall behind my chair, and the janitor still stops in to see how we're doing, gnawing on an unlit pipe.

Dad does his grading and class preparations here: his new office. It's my office, too—a busy place; teachers hand me assignments on slips of paper, and I have a folder for each subject, which, when done, I dispatch back to them through Jerome or Bobbie, or somebody who's stuck in his head to say hello, on this busy thoroughfare to the study hall. There's still a smell of aged book bindings, along with cut pine, in the room, muddied by a newly opened radiator giving off too much painty heat, and I'm just inside the door, close to the crowd. Dad works at his table along the opposite wall, his back to me, and now and then turns to look out the triple windows at the winter air, his hands down flat on the tabletop, as if he'll rise. Then he sighs and turns back to his work, and sometimes shakes his head, and says, "Say, how do you spell—" And I spell it from out of the glittering shapes that have replaced the dark locus of my lobotomy. "That's what I thought," he says. "But when you see it in this student's writing, and then stop to think how it's spelled, it sure doesn't look right."

+

Jerome drives me to school, where Skip Wangsdorf and Earl usually stand at the double doors and take me under my arms ("You're not much to manage," Wangsdorf says, and I am down to mostly muscle), and carry me up to the green chair. I can handle the flights of stairs, but it's a slow journey, and Dad's afraid I'll fall backward. The maze of steps through the rest of the school, into the hallway where I first saw Billy Gene, and then up another flight of gymnasium bleachers to the cafeteria, I'm not up to. Jerome brings me lunch on a tray.

I miss cigarettes. I miss the shaggy versions I rolled, I miss Jerome shaking out tailor-mades, and I miss television. I keep looking for the wristwatch, now back in its drawer, and worry so much about my favorite characters, and whether they'll survive their predicaments, that sweat squeezes out my scalp— I'm breathless, panting. No clock in the room. As bad as on drugs—free-floating, the worst yet to come. Finally the janitor installs a wooden school clock above Dad's desk, so at least I can tell when I'm missing a show, and the knowledge that another one is over helps me to withdraw.

Jerome is hitting the books even harder, to "sew up," as he puts it, his chances for a scholarship. His oration is better; he took second in the District, and will go to the Sectional. He stops to talk, and people wave behind his back as they go by. Dad turns in his chair, spanning the moles beside his nose and eyebrow with a thumb and forefinger, and Jerome goes on in a new garrulousness, now with a rural burr to it that causes my senses to perk up, abraded—he's saying something about wowing some critturs or creatturs with a new line he has for the end of his oration. He gives 'a sample (Dad smiles, still fingering a mole), and looks at me; I turn the line over on the lathe of my growing skepticism, then shrug. Bobbie steps up, her books over her breasts, and the bell rings. No, no dispatches. She runs off, throwing her legs out from the sides of her skirt, and Jerome says, "Keep chipper, fella, huh?" and goes off in his jaunty walk, tapping the banister.

Is it Lynette, I wonder, who has him talking this rot?

+

He and I are in the basement in Forest Creek, with Lynette and Bobbie, playing Ping-Pong. I work this by standing at a corner of the table and leaning my weight on both crutches, one gripped under an arm, so my paddle hand is free—although I sometimes have to fling myself around on the crutches for balance. This is the public recreation we've decided to seek, but the game gets as serious as anything we might do in a car, and Jerome starts slamming kills with Dad's coaching fervor, once he and Lynette are behind. Bobbie is a poor player, goofily off-balance, who pounces to punch at shots, or spins in a circle with one leg up when she attempts to slam, either missing the ball or connecting with my back as she completes her pirouette. I can't stand people who are physically inept, I realize, and throw my paddle down, weakened, and go in a wobbly swing-walk to the couch. I ease myself onto it, and have to go through a half dozen separate actions simply to lie down.

No wonder I loathe myself. What if I end up a gimp?

"Worn out?" Jerome asks, out of breath, and lights a cigarette.

"Light one for me," I say. And to Bobbie, who's hovering near, "Would you pass that to me, please?"

"Who was your slave last year at this time?" she asks, arching the eyebrows she now plucks into pencil lines of perpetual astonishment.

"Well?" she says, holding the cigarette out of reach.

"Well, what?"

"I said, 'Who was your slave last year at this time?' "

A real sharp intellectual girl, I want to say. One who could play Ping-Pong. The lousy saying is Willa Petey's—the same Willa who got me to be a monkey in Clapton's room, and is now Bobbie's hanger-on. Willa affects a prissy distance, though nobody would want to get near, and calls lepers "leapers," panthers "painters," and the gums around her teeth (as if to distinguish them from the gum she chews, which she's constantly chompily chawing and snapping) *"gooms."* Even Dad, who can generally set aside prejudice for a student, says, "Oh, Willa Petey," and looks off in the distance and sighs.

Bobbie hands me the smoke, then goes at her gum like Willa.

"Thanks," I say, trembling at my ironic insincerity, which I hate. When I suggested that maybe Bobbie shouldn't let Willa hang around, she said, "You mean I'm supposed to give up all my friends for you, too." What else has she given up? I once heard Dean Roy say on the stairs to the study hall, for my benefit or not, "One thing about skags, since they cain't get no guy, is they grab hold of a girl and make her stay loyal, see. It's always a girl who's good-lookin and half intelligent, but she don't realize a skag's a skag, no matter whose tree she's up."

Bobbie tries to take the cigarette from my mouth, and I grab her wrists and wrestle with her from where I lie. I could kill her. I want to tell Jerome to take her home—what's he doing at the other end of the room, anyway? Suddenly the lights go out, and in one of those movements Bobbie is so adept at, she's on top of me. "Gotcha," she says, in her gum-and-toothpaste-smelling breath, and I picture myself here the night Davey apologized about Dewey, the pistol in my mouth, about to pass out, and suffer the shortness of breath that comes when I think of my television shows, the grip of Mom's wristwatch gone, and then see Mom and Dad on this couch, after we moved here, blankets hanging up, and hear her say, "Like sharp, sharp swords!" and feel pinned by them.

"Are you hot?" Bobbie whispers, burying me deeper under layers I feel I'll never rise from.

+

I used to think that your internal territory could never be abused, but it can be—by invasion, insomnia, misuse—mostly by lying dormant and falling into deeper silence. A rock down a well. The impact that's faintly heard, finally, is death. Not just that it feels that it is, in its

slow upward drift to your ears. It is. The highest any speculation can
reach is sanctified silence. No bones or meat or sack of baggy skin to
rub against. Yet the initial substance at the center of the greatest
thought is me. Out of silence, cells form until there's a fingerprint,
then the fig leaf of identity—being born, family, society; then
community, or communion, though the time it takes for some to feel
ready for these is a life. I have two friends in the city I've promised to
see, whether a week or a month ago, I'm not sure, but it's time.

One of them, Marco, an actor, the more delicate of the two, has
been smoking marijuana, and everything has become unmoored,
unstuck for him, so that his reality, as real to him as mine is to me, or
as real to him as I am, takes place within the world we both negotiate,
but is in opposition to it—a fence of inner fantasies to buck. He's
caught up in a running commentary on a life that baffles him. "Do
you like my hair poufed up like this?" he asks, pressing one side of it.
"I used to like it kind of slicked back, but I think it's nicer poufed up
like this."

The other, Al, also an actor, is consumed by silence and the
maneuverings within that silence of his ambition. The silence draws
you into his aura like a vacuum you feel will collapse, or implode, if
he doesn't soon find work equal to his ambition—with his inviting,
Mona Lisa smile—when he isn't acting foolish in order to conceal his
seriousness, or to cover the fury that can break from him like a bucket
of bolts through a window. An unsparing camoufleur—all learned on
these city streets.

I sit back. Black night, or as near to black as it can be with
the corona of incandescence always over the city—that building
downtown, with a ladder of lights up its center, out my window.
Curtains back, admitting city noise like grit over the sill. I look
toward the doorway and faint dots project from my eyes in the
dimness, and I begin to move from one to the next, divided at
my center, giving off a note that seems to rise through resisting
liquid, as if there's a hesitating quaver at my source. Too late
to leave? Could Marco and Al be waiting for me with the same
faith with which I wait, believing Jerome will appear?

I lower my bare feet to the linoleum, not sure I can move.

+

The next time the pin catches, igniting pain from my hip to my toes, I stay home. I can catch up on my television characters, and perhaps settle for good the itch in the cast. I get into the wooden wheelchair and trundle around the house, trying to recapture my days of mindless immobility, but I'm past that, plus the ten years I've outstripped the dwarf in cowboy boots. Bobbie. I want to respect her as a person yet also plank her, and the ease with which I've come to hope for this sin frightens me. Hell's gates have fur.

I bang my cast on the hinged-out leg-rest—the itch again, which has heated whirlpools in it. The banging usually helps, but now stirs things up so badly I call Jerome at school and lie on my stomach and have him rap over the back of the cast with the handle of a table knife. Every time he pauses I cry, "Don't stop! Please! I can't take it!"

Finally he sits back and sighs. "I think we better call Holcomb. I can't keep this up forever, and you can't go on like this. There are a couple of brown-looking spots on the back of your cast."

"Probably from banging it on that crappy wheelchair."

"I don't know. They seem damp, and when I hit them you sound as if it feels twice as good. I'll call right now, if you want me to."

"The other guy put it on. Call him. He's the specialist."

"Yes, but Holcomb's head resident where it was done. He seems more approachable to me. The specialist, well, he's pretty rigid about times and procedures. You know"—he bends the fingers of a hand backward—"the old bone-crusher type."

We both laugh; I called him "Bone Crusher" after he re-broke my leg.

"And it's about time you mentioned the pin catching in your hip."

"Yeah. Right."

He goes into the kitchen, and while he's on the phone with Holcomb I bellow out a reminder about how bad the itch has been.

"He also says— Oh, you heard him."

I turn to the airport scene, ashamed, trying to find my place in it again, but Bobbie seems to hold me away. Finally

Jerome walks up and says, "He wants to talk to the specialist to make sure, but figures you can probably come in next Wednesday, when the guy is there."

I almost roll off the bed. "Next Wednesday!"

"All right." He pulls out the chair from Dad's desk and sits, his elbows on his knees, and looks up at me. "He said if you're that concerned, he'll try to arrange it sooner. He's not positive the specialist will concur, since you aren't scheduled to have the cast off, but this trouble might merit having a look at, he said. Now . . ."

As he talks, a spot at the center of my calf starts taking a pee.

+

The wheel shrieks down one side of my foot, plaster dust rising, then curves and whines up my calf, sending such a flurry of hornetlike itching across the back of my leg I feel I'll have to let the load of itching pain blow loose—which would send me, from the strength of it, flying backward out of the cast against a wall. The Russian holds aside my bag, squinting through goggles (Don't flub up here!), and the machine shifts into a faltering scream through the soft and greenish clothlike edge of the cast that smells of my crotch. Burned turkey meat. He goes back to my foot and starts down the other side and with the loosening of pressure and entering air the cast starts to rumble on the stainless-steel table. I'm falling apart.

"Hold this, would you, Jack," he says, and Dr. Holcomb steps up, a prim rubber apron over his suit, and grips my toes with one hand and slides the other down the sole of my foot, and with the first touch of flesh there in months, cool and gentle, I cry, "Oh, Christ!"

Jerome, again the color of Jay, stares at the floor.

The Russian clicks off his saw. "What's that smell?" He shoves the rubber swimming goggles to his forehead and wiggles his hair-stuffed nostrils in a kind of hula. "Curious. See what I mean, Jack?"

"The sloughing off?"

"Meatier. I should mention, Charlie, that your leg might look like hell, to use your language. You're normally wearing away skin every day." He rubs the back of a hairy arm and roughs up flakes. "See? But here, inside a cast, it can't wash off, so there might be big scales—ugly, brown, wrinkled things, as thick as scabs sometimes, and some casts have a god-awful stink. We're getting some of that. Bear up. I know it's kind of scary having it come off—like losing the support of an old friend, or waking up without an arm or, in your case here, aha, a leg." He pulls his goggles down and applies the screaming wheel again.

The only way to go is backward, out of myself, and in that oracular realm a distant continent is sending wormlike streams along islands of itching. I feel a pressure at my back, as if Jerome has moved there to help me sit, but no hands support me, and I receive a picture of us sitting back to back. The sawing stops. They're prying at the cast with tools, and then its top, like a casket lid, pops off, and in the white freeze Elmer Reed is on my other side, his pink face lit through the honeycombed windshield, the glove sinking into my shoulder: "Charlie, this might hurt." The bloodied heater, with hooded louvers that draw my consciousness down in lines like marching men, to the center of a rending worse than the splits, a burning force that attracts my face in its slow fall, then the clarity of air parting over it at the jolt of its stop. All of me past the edge, graph out. Then the probe entering in a shuddering, a hovering of—

"Light."

"Lights you have, Jack."

"And hold that penlight here, too, Doctor, if you would, please. There, see, in the lower part of the cast. It does appear to be blood. Peroxide, please."

The dark and shriveled stick of what is left of my leg, as bushy as a chimpanzee's, lies on white towels, on a shining table that reflects my bloated head. Holcomb steps up, with a spotlight wobbling in behind his head as my throat constricts. "Now, Charles, I'm going to take you by the shoulders here and turn you, and Dr. Zabotschernitsky will very carefully raise and turn your leg, so you needn't worry about it. Ready, Doctor? Now, lean back and go slowly with me, Charles, on your side here first—good. Now all the way to your stomach. There."

"My God, I don't believe it!" the Russian cries. "What is this?"

"Now, what we're seeing, Charles, looks like a serious infection to me. It's difficult to say, though, because the cotton binding from the cast is still clinging to it. Could I bother you for those tweezers, Doctor, please? Thank you. Charles, do you feel this?"

"No."

"I'm lifting some of the cotton free. Do you feel this— here?"

"Ah, God!" It's the lance of pain the itching started with.

"Sorry. I tested a particular spot with a probe. It's a positive sign that you felt it. Now, I'll just keep lifting this away, as I was before, and you let me know at any time if it hurts."

I can hear their separate breathing, then hear the Russian adding faint words underneath, and I look over at Jerome. He's gone.

"I'm afraid what we're dealing with here, Charles, from what I can see of it so far, is a massive infection. Your follicles have opened for some reason and deep pits have formed inside them—very pustulant—across the back of your calf. Some of these have migrated into larger areas of infection, and they look awfully deep."

"I don't understand," the Russian says. "I've put on hundreds of casts and never seen this! Chuck, did you stick something down there?"

"Nothing would reach!"

"That's it. You went and screwed this up."

"I'm not sure a scratch would have opened his follicles in this way, Doctor. It looks to me like a reaction of some sort, perhaps an allergy. There's even ulceration. A sensitivity to something in the plaster, perhaps. The lime, maybe."

"I hate plaster," I cry, recalling its touchy dryness on my whitened skin, and spots of it on Dad after Mom's death.

"I'm going to have to do some scraping and pruning away, I'm afraid, Charles, to clear this up, and find out what we actually have. It would be best if you were awake, so I'd know for sure where the line on some of this is, but I wouldn't expect to ask that of you. For some of it, I'll have to use the scalpel. Would you want to be awake?"

"No."

"We'll check you into the hospital, then, and—"

"I'll stay awake!" Jerome and I have a double date planned for the weekend, and I can't bear the idea of dealing with drugs again.

"I'm afraid we'll have to check you in in any case, Charles. You'll have to be on antibiotics for some time, and I'd like to keep an eye on this. We have to get to it this afternoon. Now, if you don't mind."

"What the hell have I got? *Gangrene!*" I crane my head around and see ribbons and pools of pus over raw meat. No wonder Jerome is gone and the Russian has a hand over his mouth.

"As far as I'm able to tell, it doesn't appear to have reached that stage yet, Charles," Holcomb says. "We can be grateful for that."

+

There is a metal triangle above my bed and through it a stream of tasty anesthesia carries past an edge of the operating room, where a voice is saying, It'll never stop, it'll only get worse, it'll never stop. The sweet squeeze of drugs, my mouth gulping for more from the triangular stream. Bobbie? A booted version of her cheeks go out the door. "Yahwell," a man in the bed beside me says. *Jawohl?* Or the television screen on the wall, higher than I've seen one hung, says it, about to fall on him. "Yeah, well, your girl was in for a while, too, but you was asleep. Is she nice stuff?"

This is actually happening, I realize, and I'm out.

+

My leg, swathed in bandages, has to be elevated, they say, and then the Russian stops in and tells me how to use the "trapeze" to move in bed. I try not to look toward the television that the man in the bed beside me swings out on an arm, because he takes this as an invitation to talk, and goes on in his coarse way about his wife, or "the handful of hamburger they cut out of my ass."

The first time Holcomb arrives to change the dressing, I

discover that my knee, swollen like a grassy coconut on the monkeylike stick of my leg, won't bend. "Now what's the matter?" I ask.

"It's cartilage and fluid built up from no exercise. It'll work free, don't worry."

Then it's the Russian, smiling again: "Can you bend it?"

"Just a tiny bit, and then it gets real shaky."

"Here." He lifts it under the knee and has me lower my foot until the whole leg wobbles and then pops stiff. "Let's see what flex we have in it." He takes hold of the foot, with one hand still under my knee, and presses down until I yell and kick with my other foot at his face.

"Hey!" he cries. "I'm just trying to help you here!"

"Well, it's not going to help to break the son of a bitch again!"

His face sags into an expression it might take on years from now, and he says, "All right, let's be friends. I'll do this a few more times, gently, and then give you some exercises to follow each day, okay?"

"I'm sorry," I say, clearly no longer his special patient.

+

I'm in our upstairs room with Jerome. It's so long since I've been here that Dad's oak desk, once in the hallway in Hyatt, now flush against the wall at the foot of our bed, surprises me. Dad hasn't used it since he built the desk in his office, and I had forgotten that we carried this one up in the fall and covered its top with a skin of special material Dad ordered and squeegeed on, meant to emulate marble. I can pull the swirls in its pattern into points of concentration as Jerome goes over my prescribed exercises with me, or changes the dressing as he's been taught to; he squeezes pink paste from a tube over gauze pads, pats them in place down the back of my calf, wraps the calf with gauze from a roll, and then wraps an Ace bandage around that, with just the right tension in each turn so the itching is contained but my foot doesn't go numb or turn blue. I lie back on the bed, and he holds the leg on his shoulder, to keep it from quaking as it does if my knee bends, or I sit on the bed with the leg held straight out, staring at the desktop, and he gets down on the floor. His breathing here, in its amplified warmth as the bandages enwrap me, reminds me of being helped into clothes to go outdoors, and I'm transported from the stairway in Hyatt where notes once arrived on a string around a knob of this desk to the kitchen, and see around the edges of his bandaging the shine of sunlight on the linoleum next to the oil heater, the ribbed vents in the heater's rounded top sending up simmering slices of heat thick as toast, the brown of its porcelainized enamel bearing miniatures of the kitchen windows embedded in it; puddles of water on its base where tinny spots are worn through its wood-grain paint, the pendulum of her dress and the pertinent crinkling her heels send through the metal base, then the smell of her hair under my nose, like his now, until I'm crying as I used to at the pain of feeling returning to my frozen feet. It isn't the sight of the craters and gouges or the valleys that I could place a pencil in that causes this, as he must think, it's— No matter how many losses, loss also never remains. He sits back on the floor, finished, revolving his knuckles over his eyes as he did when he was the age that I've returned from, and says, "Well, yes, I guess I'm responsible for this, too."

"Oh, be quiet."

"Well, I was the one who—"

"Shut up! Can't you get off this! Is it all you can think about?"

+

Marco is actually modest about his achievements. "I haven't really done anything yet so far as acting goes." And "I taught my friend Bill how to cook and I taught Les"—his girlfriend. "Now they both cook better than I do. Isn't that something?" His baffled openness. Nor is he secretive about his life and affairs; he tells Les everything, who he sees while she's away, what he does with them (sometimes when I'm there), and although he's not immodest about himself, he's so matter-of-fact in his running commentary, it's disconcerting. "Don't I look good like this? When my hair's poufed up this way, right after I've shampooed it, I'm handsomer, no? I feel more vulnerable, too, like a whole new person. See how much better I look?"

How does one answer this? "Uh-huh." More important, to get to the point at which every friendship flounders, can I trust him? Which leads with equal (or greater) weight to: Can I trust Al?

+

I'm on top of her, hardly a crutch length from her parents' phosphorescent door, and I put my ear to her lips, and my lips to her ear's shapely polished whorl, and whisper, "What?"

"You know what your Uncle Fred said to Dad in the bar last night?"

Fred is the only Neumiller who is ever in a bar, and I've begun to admire him for this. "What?" I whisper.

"He said—this is what Dad said he said: 'Hey, Chris the pisser'—that's what those guzzle-guts call Dad—'Chris the pisser, I hear we might be related yet.' "

The stifled hurry of her laughter, as if to make it upstairs, sears out an area of my hearing, and my face falls to the couch. I picture, past its nubbly weave, wavering lines of smoke lit by whirligigging neon signs, and the two huge men, with their bellies on a bar, braying at one another across a smelly room.

"Oh, no," I say to the couch, and her skirt comes down as she sits.

+

"Let's organize our life," Jerome says.

"What?" I'm at the end of the bed, holding my crutches, with my leg as straight out as if the cast were still on.

"Let's get organized so we can hit that good academic stuff. What about this?" He walks over and raps the desk's marbleized top. "Let's start with it." He pulls open the drawer above the kneehole, and papers spring up. "How much of this do you want to keep?" He grabs a wastebasket, wads up some papers, and tosses them in. "Let's make some decisions here, like we planned to in the fall. We'll share the top drawer, mostly for supplies and school stuff and stationery. These drawers on the side, well, I'll take the second one, and you can have the top, okay?"

I poke the big binlike bottom drawer with the rubber tip of a crutch. "What about this?"

"We'll share it, too. Use it for files and such—bigger things."

"What's in it now?"

He squats at it, braces a hand against the desk, and tugs it out. "Oh, God. Clothes. Real old stuff. *'Worn and need-ing patched.'*" He mouths this like one of Dad's Shakespeare lines. "Way outgrown."

"Happy anniversary."

"What?" he says, and pivots quick, still on his haunches.

"Happy anniversary. We're about where we were when school began."

"Oh." His eyes appear to take in all the corners of the room in a second, and then he sits on the floor. "Yes, I guess it must seem to you that a lot of time's been lost. I've tried to imagine what it would be like if it happened to me, but it's not the same. We're different people, obviously." To soften this he adds, *"Odd-viously,"* as we pronounced it once. He lights a cigarette and draws on it with his chin jutted out at an angle that stretches the cords in his neck, and I try to think of one of the ways in which he imagines we're different. He turns to the desk and starts to empty everything from its drawers, including the clothes, into the wastebasket.

"No," I say.

"What?" His back is to me, with a smoky cloud clinging to his hair in blue prongs.

"I don't feel so much time has passed, really. It's been like a dream."

+

I still use the crutches, but with one half of me ominously lighter minus the cast, and I can now negotiate well enough to get to the school cafeteria. I'm at a crowded table, with Bobbie beside me, and Jerome is at the table behind us, holding forth in a mock-professional voice about the distinctions between moron, imbecile, and idiot, his latest discovery. As if in answer, Earl, at the head of our table, crosses his eyes and lets milk drip from his straw onto Willa Petey's plate and says in a cooing voice, "Cat drool."

"Can it!" Willa cries, acting offended enough for five.

Everybody at the table starts belching, except the girls, of course; and me, when I catch Bobbie's glare.

"Dig the cat's eyes in the Jell-O, girls," Don Nelson says, poking into a grape with a fork. "Suck up that juice when they pop, mmmm!"

"I'll barf on you, you sick freak," Bobbie says.

"I'd love it," he says, and shows his long teeth in a smile.

A girl gets up to leave.

"Speaking of which," Dean Roy says, stirring his turkey tetrazzini, "I find to my taste you cain't beat this here warm monkey diddle with maggots in it, all blended in good old hawked-up Kentucky donkey snot."

Chocolate milk blows from my nose over the table—"Colored pissin!" Dean Roy cries—and drips over my shirt as I laugh. The rest of the girls, including Bobbie, get up and go to the garbage cans where leftovers are scraped, a couple of them dipping with gags at the sight of the can's contents. Dean Roy leans to me and whispers, "Jagitcha that sweet slim thang yet?"

My eyes levitate, and I brush over my shirt with a napkin.

"Ah, God, it's so tough when you go on and on, and getcha so close ever night, usin all the tricks you got, an you just never quite. And you come home a-draggin them lover's nuts, Lord!— like a couple bowlin balls bangin around on rubber bands. Blueballs, the doc said to me once when I went truckin in with a pair about to bust in a wheelbarra I got. *Blueballs*, he says. These's way hell and gone beyond lover's nuts, and there's only one solution, he says. Let her get a hold on your meat. So now you take my advice, boy"—he looks aside at me from under the single eyebrow that grows above his nose, and raps the edge of his cafeteria tray with a table knife—"you let her get a hold on that meat."

+

"Were you grittin the ole teeth last night," Jerome says, "or what!"

"Oh?" Since the accident, my eyeteeth feel shorter and worn away.

"What's up?"

We're sitting on the edge of the bed together, dressing for school, or I'm dressing as much as I'm able to, until he has to slide my jeans up the unbendable leg. I try to remember any dreams, but my mind is a mass of such tightly wound thread no strand gives. In the confessional last Sunday, a young priest substituting for Father Hart-Donovan questioned me about the occasions of my "heavy petting," the extent of it, the areas of her body, and I wondered, Do I have a Jesuit?—the order Davey speaks of with pride when he's home from the seminary, pacing around Grandpa and Grandma's house in a full-length cassock, smoking filter cigarettes. Then, back in the pew, I couldn't remember what I'd been assigned for penance, because the priest said I had to say no to my desires, or stop seeing Bobbie, and I wondered if the absolution would be effectual if my numbers were off, and when I looked up, after adding ten Our Fathers and ten Hail Marys, to be sure, I saw that Jerome was down on the kneeler, still praying, although Mass had begun.

"Should something be?" I ask, in my black morning mood.

"You don't usually get the grits that way, fella. I thought it was your knee, but you didn't seem to be lying on it wrong, so when you kept it up I finally gave a look-see, then a touch: no effect. Your sores didn't seem to be suppurating, as they say, through the wrappings, that I could see. Then I couldn't get back to sleep. I've been up all night."

Talking? I want to say—this rural note in his rolling talkativeness I can never place. "What, watching me?"

"No, no, no, I was working on my oration. Say, do I have a doozie of a line to draw the end up neat, now, or what, is all I can say! I'm going to win first place in the State with this baby, yet, you wait and see!"

+

He's at the wheel, with the family in the car, driving to Havana, where we plan to attend late Mass, since we couldn't wake in time for church in Pettibone. We got home at three in the morning from a double date, and found Dad waiting up for us: "This must stop!" he said, and I was sure he could see me speeding in a hobble past the end of the table—Bobbie in a crouch, one hand to her stomach as if in pain, the other over mine on a crutch's handgrip, as if to guide me to our narrowing point, where my mind forks. This must stop, too, I think, as if the priest has installed a conscience, because it can't be endured, simply physically, although I'm not sure how I want it to end. On the other fork, I'm beginning to resent her insistence that I hourly affirm our "going steady," since we haven't exchanged rings, besides her sullenness about the way my head keeps cranking around at other girls who appear to be going by in an endless procession for my approval—the thought of which stimulates my need to take it out, which means exposing it, although that now is maybe all right, since I've measured it against a dollar bill, so the final delicate lever seems to rest . . . From my sidesaddle position in the cockpit I see, down the road, a big white boat come wobbling into our lane from behind the car towing it.

"Hey!" I cry. "That boat!"

"Where?" Jerome says, and looks on either side, as if the boat I mean is in one of the sloughs along the highway.

"There!" I say, and point straight ahead just as the approaching car, caught by the boat's weave, heads out over the centerline for us, shaking in the angle of a skid, and suddenly the seat gives—Dad pulls himself forward—and I'm about to dive for the floor, if I didn't know the havoc a Hudson heater can work, while the ghost of a brick upright printed with *Meadowlane* sails toward the hood.

"Hey!" Dad yells, and reaches for the wheel, knocking his hat off, but we're already thudding onto the graveled shoulder, Jerome's feet stabbing at pedals. The other car squalls past in a blur outside our windows, bringing the boat around in another jackknife, and there's a screech and thump at our rear fender.

"Jesus!" I cry, and we go rumbling down the shoulder into the ditch, tilting so steeply Dad leans the opposite way. "Get his number!" he cries. "His license, I mean! Ach, that gol-blame boat's behind!"

Be still, I think, out of the calm that comes when a train opens the night behind your bumper the moment after you've crossed a set of tracks, flying boxcars shaking the ground while your bones melt, and it's Dad who finally speaks. "You," he says, and grabs my shoulder and gives a shake. "I don't care what happens, there's no excuse to use language like that!"

In church, at the end of a pew, with my leg out in the aisle like a reminder of Bobbie, I repent. At the one time in my life when I should have made a perfect Act of Contrition, waking from that accident, I was using the worst language I've used. And I've continued to. How can I change? *Begin with Bobbie* bubbles up in me in the voice of the Jesuit. Yes, I must, I think, and at that point Father Hart-Donovan, who moves in a more slowed and stately pace in his home church, turns from the altar, and looks from my leg in the aisle to my face in surprise, and then raises his arm and whispers, *"Dominus vobiscum."*

+

I finally find Jerome, after searching through the house for a half hour—or rather I see him, at the bottom of the basement stairs, his chin in his hands, staring away from the antiquated console radio I've begged from an uncle and plan to revamp, and I have to sway back on my crutches from the pull of the stairwell. He has dragged the radio away from the wall, and has plugged it into an overhead socket where a bulb dimly glows. He holds an ear close to the metallic cloth behind the wood grille of the speaker, and is playing the radio at such a low volume I can hardly hear "Red Sails in the Sunset" from where I stand.

"Hey," I say in a soft whisper of surprise—as surprised to see the radio out and going as him in this attitude. "Hey, what's up?"

He turns to me with misted eyes that sails indeed seem to be crossing behind, and then turns back to the radio and shakes his head.

+

I lean my crutches against the automatic washer, keeping my hands on its top to support my weight. I pull away, knees flexed, and turn to one side, wobbling to find my new center of gravity, and my hips begin to rock as if the bones below are driving into mush. With my hands paddling I try to take a step on my suddenly numb left leg, then dive back onto the top of the washer, and lie panting into my dim reflection on its top.

+

There are pairs and groups of girls outside the drugstore, and others sitting on car hoods and fenders up and down the main street of Havana, which is known for its women. Jerome tools around and taps the Hudson's steering wheel in time to "Honeycomb," and then his Adam's apple protrudes as his head comes around.

"Hey, there's that Frieling and her friend."

"Who?"

"The one I was talking to that Sunday after church."

"You mean the time the boat trailer took a bite out of our fender?"

His lips compress, and I want to say, Are you going to pretend it didn't happen? He parks the car, gets out and slams the door, and goes to the front of the drugstore, where a blond girl in a white dress is sitting on the hood of a car, her arms behind her and her head tilted back, so that her hair hangs nearly to the hood. My ideal is still Leslie Caron, whom Bobbie bears a resemblance to, but there's something about this blonde that weakens me like the image of the brick upright closing in: fate met. A stocky girl with her hair cut short, like a pudgy Doris Day, leans both elbows on the fender, beside the one in white as if in attendance. Mine, I suppose. Jerome talks to them both. The blonde dips her head to one side, reaching behind to take the fall of her hair in her hand, and draws it over a shoulder as she sits up straight.

Jerome smiles and his hands rise, crossing, and grip his arms at his shirtsleeves.

+

By mistake I pull open his drawer in the desk and see drafts of a letter that begins "Dear Lynette, This might be the hardest thing I've ever had to write," and slam it shut. So, I think, he's planked her. A day later, when I can't understand why I didn't continue reading, I hobble back up and find that the drafts are gone. I pull open the top drawer we share. A good deal of stationery is gone, too.

+

After church, I stand back and watch him and Lynette talk as usual, although she looks paler and perhaps more pimply and mature, and decide I was right; he's had her. But when we get home and he sits on the couch, pulling loose his tie and collar, and opens the Sunday paper in front of his face like Dad, I notice he's wearing his class ring.

That night as I lie in bed and he sits at the desk working, I assume, on his oration, I say, "Is something wrong with you and Lynette?"

"How do you mean 'wrong'?" He doesn't turn.

"Aren't you going together anymore, or what?"

He raises his hand with the ring on it, fingers outspread, and lets it drop, his back still to me. "We probably won't be seeing each other as often. We felt it was getting too serious. I mean, going steady." He holds the pencil almost horizontal, at the eraser, and rubs it crosswise on the paper—shading a drawing, it seems.

"Are you seeing her this weekend?" I ask, worried about my ride.

"Probably. We'll probably still see each other. We still feel essentially the same. You know." He looks over a shoulder, presenting only one eye, a distant planet retreating from me. "It just couldn't go on. We're too young."

+

Bobbie says, "Oh, sure, as if supposedly feeling the same about each other will make a shit of a bit of difference in two weeks." She's on her stomach in the grass at the center of the turnabout at her house, staring toward a rust-gray barn whose roof is being scratched by branches of a nodding tree.

"What did Lynette say to you?"

"Not a damn word—are you naïve? Our problem is my old man."

I look up from where I sit, and the trees running in a line

below the levee—which stands darkly above their crowns—
shudder in the wind, and then lean toward us in the evening
light. "Well," I begin, and feel pulled by another wind that
passes over and moves on. She's told me that her father has
said she has to work this summer, to help pay for her clothes,
on a detasseling crew, when she isn't working for him, which
means working weekends, and as Jerome and I were driving
up, her father came barreling past us on the gravel road, leaning
on his horn and fishtailing, spreading plumes of dust that
farther on lay like mist, lit gold by the sun, above his fields of
corn—after an argument, I learned, that ended with Bobbie
and her mother in tears. Now this darkness filling the farmyard
as fast as the water held by the levee probably would. My
crutches, one on top of the other, lie in the blackish grass as if
it's grown up around them. "Won't you have to do what he
says?"

"Some help you are! After telling me this has been going
on with those two, so you probably won't be out!"

"Sure I will. He'll drive me out even if he isn't seeing her."

"My ass. This is it. Everything at once."

"I love you a lot," I say, and flinch at the words.

"Shit!" She puts her face in her hands, and I slide around
on my rear and lie beside her, then look at the house: the lights
are out. Even with my hand on her back, she seems at a distance,
yet more solidly fleshy on the ground, and I rub the material
of her blouse between my thumb and fingers—the texture of
her clothes, even, dear to me now. She cries, "How'd you like
it if your dad was a dip like him, the old fart!"

I kiss her neck, and she comes at me with such headlong
fervor I speed my zipper open, and then it takes five minutes,
it seems, to jerk it free of the complications of underwear and
find a way to work it past the copper teeth. I draw her hand
down, and she grips and pulls at it with such force, like milking
a cow, that I have to say, "Hey, easy."

Later, when it's as dark as midnight, and there are still no
lights on at the house, she says this has to stop.

"Sure," I say, and put the shrunken counterfeit back. "We're
too young, right? Younger than Jerome and Lynette, right?
Naïve."

We go together to the house, which is cooler inside in its silence, and she walks straight to the couch and sits, her elbows on her knees and her chin in her hands, her upper lip drawn down in distress over her teeth.

I ease myself beside her, and lay my crutches on the floor. She stands as if she's upset, takes two jerky steps, and turns on the TV.

+

I roll away, gasping, onto my back, and the white ceiling hovers at several levels until my middle-aged eyes fix its height. "Goodness!" I say. "Now I know why I do it in such silence."

My wife pulls herself onto me, her breasts widening over my waist, and I see that this ceiling, like the one in the bathroom, will have to be patched and repainted, too. "Why?" she asks, genuinely interested.

"Oh." I sift through those nights on the living-room couch, close to the glowing door, trying to discover a way of approach that won't cause offense to the girl, or the two of us then, or my wife, and I'm about to strike off "Adolescent conditioning" and let her take it from there, but instead I say, "The first girl I really went with, in high school, lived in the country . . ."

+

I push myself up from our TV, from a drama where "Love Is a Many-Splendored Thing" keeps playing in the background whenever the teenage lovers get free of their parents, and go swing-walking toward the door.

"Where are you headed?" Dad asks.

I turn and his eyes, in the television light, are like caves beneath the miniature screens reflected in a curve across his glasses.

"For a walk."

"At this hour? Alone?"

"I guess."

"Aren't you seeing Bobbie anymore?"

This is it, I think. Jerome has gone to see Lynette, and I've decided I can't face Bobbie right now; after she turned on the TV and got her hand on it again, she guided it toward what felt like a curly-metal copper scrubber and shoved against me until I felt cut up, raw and bleeding, deboned. She whispered, "We did it for real!" And I thought, We did?

"She's working," I say. "Detasseling corn."

"I see." He draws his chin against his chest and puts a finger to the mole on his cheek, as if to point it out, and taps there.

"I also thought we might be getting too serious."

"Mmm," he says. "Like Jerome and Lynette?" He seems to be merely seeking information.

"Sort of like them," I say, and would like to add: Also, I didn't want to get her into any trouble, you know, because of anything I might do, and I've done it. But I'm not that far gone—or I am, to have even thought this, so I turn away. "Sort of, I guess," I say, and pull open the door, glad for the clatter of the venetian blinds, for once, and the way they slash apart my emotion at his concern.

I push off on my crutches into the night.

LEARNING

Night, with the ladder of lights outside climbing toward its summit, time to go—and I'm off, afloat over lighted windows forming tiers down the sides of blocks in this city that is home enough for the disaffected youth from half of the heart of the country, to Cooper Union, the parting of ways. Left to Marco's, right to Al's, the pull in each direction visceral, my bowels upset at the dislocation from bed. A bronze plaque is fastened to the building, something about Lincoln giving a speech. I try to concentrate and take in the strength of bronze to keep my sphincter sealed, but gas shifts, with the weight of Lincoln added, and the pressure builds until I feel I'll send a slug of pennies blowholing over concrete. A bookstore around the corner, a plea for their stall—illness, I say—and after a cannonade like a shotgun down a culvert, I'm off, my direction set, toward Al's. He's in Jimmy's, near his apartment, talking to the bartender about an air conditioner.

He turns to me with his indecipherable look, and orders two steins. He has a new girlfriend, he says—French. All he needs now in his new apartment is an air conditioner, he says, whether in a logical connection or not; his mother has given him one, but it's at her place, a few blocks downtown. The beer is numbing my nerve centers too soon. I order wine, and

Jimmy's, with its booths and hardwood dividers between mirrors above the back bar, achieves a new buoyancy, as if appearing out of its place in time. I say that we'll carry the air conditioner up. He says it weighs a ton. A quarter ton, I say, and his foolish grin appears. I feel I'm talking out of the emptied hollow of my innards, not my mouth, into this cavern of wood and stamped tin, to figments of us in a mirror.

But soon we're carrying the air conditioner up, after waddling with it between us for blocks, still in our suit jackets. We get it up the first flight, the exertion causing us to cackle like crystal-ringing guinea hens, and finally it's in his apartment. No, no more tonight, he begs, and points to the accordion grille over his only window.

A narrow studio with a shining parquet floor. I pace around and utter appreciative noises. There's a round oak table, stripped and rubbed to a gloss—the only furniture, other than a cot with a cover on it, and two chairs we draw up to the table. And now an air conditioner. He laughs as if he's read my thought, and then he draws back, into shadow, and stares at me until I'm uneasy. He leans forward with his elbows on the table, his hands clasped to one side of his face. It's a single shaded bulb suspended above us that casts such eerie shadow. His face is pale and grainy. He grins, and lines spring into the corners of his eyes and along his cheeks, although he's only twenty. There's a mole on his cheek that he'll have to decide to remove, or else retain as his facial signature. He raises an eyebrow and sighs, as if giving himself over to me, and then he strikes the table and holds a finger up.

He hurries to a pint-sized refrigerator under the sink, his coat flaring back, and for a moment is only an outline against its open door. It crushes shut. He has a bottle, forefinger around its neck, that he sets at the center of the table, and is back in his chair as if he hasn't moved, or altered his smile a centimeter. But the perspiring bottle of wine is between us.

"I was going to save it for Vera. My girl. Housewarming. When she didn't come, I tasted it. Seven bucks."

He's back at the sink above the refrigerator and then a pair of heavy crystal glasses come down on the table in two plocks.

He leans out of the light and his hands, pale lamps, unfold and open to me.

"You pour," I say.

"Da host," he says, in the next-to-lowest of his lowlife accents, and I realize that Jerome's rural garrulousness was an ironic heightening of the Illinois accent that everybody in Pettibone had: sharp swords.

Al pours with a hand below the neck like a guillotine, watery blood.

Great wine, I indicate, with my sip, and he raises his glass: "To the place." A dusky tenor with the wheeze of an older man in it.

He stares at his glass on the table, and a far-reaching solitude in him takes on the shape of the room. I'm permitted to observe entire solitude. He'll achieve what he wants with this ability to give himself over entirely to himself, and that is the way to know what somebody will amount to: by the quality of unselfconscious silence he keeps. The room is purged of everything but his mood, an instrument struck—the accordion gate across the window like a snag in his thought. His eyes remain on the wine, his face gold, and the table seems to revolve until the bottle of wine is back in front of me, empty.

He pulls a plastic bag and fixings from his pocket, and rolls a torpedo, letting shreds lie where they fall. He begins a gesture, a turn of one hand, almost of impatience, and I move my chair up. He has me light it, and we pass it back and forth until our sensibilities fill the room, no borders, the city listening at the edges with a crackling like electronic equipment. A stir in him resonates through my cells, and he assesses me with half-closed eyes: *Really?*

He demonstrates with a passive face and a few gestures how he'll serve Vera here. They're eating. He leans to her to talk, smiling in a way that arrows out wrinkles of stress as he grips a napkin in his lap. She approves. There's an internal backing of relief, and the stress disappears from the wrinkles, although his smile remains unchanged.

He holds up a finger, reaches into his lap and lifts a strand of spaghetti from it, and drops it onto his plate, plik. I laugh, appalled at the noise of my horsey barnyard "Heee!" and he reveals himself twenty years from now, smoking a pipe, with a winking leer at somebody not Vera. He shows me how he sanded the table, and I'm so absorbed I don't notice at first the perspiration falling from his face onto it. In two quick steps, he's to the cot. He stretches out on his back and shows me how he sleeps. He wakes and turns to the light from the window, aging again—the first glimmer of apprehension appearing in him—and when he lies back down, he shows me how he'll die.

In a hurried movement that I miss in my involvement, he's in front of the air conditioner, taking a shower in the morning, and his gestures suggest how refreshing it will be with the air conditioner going. Goose bumps form on him and he has to slap at himself, and then he saws a towel across his back to warm up. In another movement I miss, he's in front of me. I rise and he takes my hands. Another mole above an eyebrow is like a truer eye staring into me. His lips tremble. He takes me in his arms and I hug him as I would— Could I hug Jerome like this? He slaps my back, a broad hand, and I feel only affection for him, and understand at the same moment that it's time to leave.

I'm off.

+

Jerome is taking the back road to Havana, driving through the wildlife refuge, over curves and bridges threading marshy sloughs. A worse-than-usual shaking begins in the Hudson's front end, with a clatter like steel being beat, and the car nosedives so hard that I hurt my hand trying to keep away from the dash in the uproar of tearing rubber.

"Jesus!" I cry. "What did you do now?"

He gets out, walks around to my side, and looks down with his hands at his hips. I crane in the seat and can see, behind, a furrow plowed by the front wheel through the sand of the shoulder. The green flatlands of the marsh, with blue ponds lined with cattails and connected by water wandering in paths, settle into place beyond the furrow. I wrench open the door, panting, and get out on my crutches, above dead grass combed back like hair over the sand.

"The wheel seems off," he says. "Look."

The tire, scraped and bruised bright-black, is wedged into the rear of the wheel well at an angle. The car is resting on it.

"The axle must have snapped," I say, out of breath. "Look how it's swung back. Jack it up."

"Why?"

"Why? To see what the hell's wrong, what do you think!" I turn and swing-walk away, the crutch tips sinking unevenly, and see, over the shoulder, after a ten-foot drop, blackish whirlpools turning beneath the water. No, reflections of gnats, swaying and thinning near me in a whining thread of song. My eyes go up —a mound of dirt ahead, huge, with weeds straggling down its sides as they did within another moment like this, my legs weak and ruined, fluid leaking from a hole above an ankle.

What have you done, Charles?

The metallic ratcheting of the jack echoes across a deserted farm where Dad comes trotting past, rolling the tire, heading down the road out of sight. Streamers of ants over a demolished car, then her face at the pinup lamp, lit gold at one side: "And the kingdom shall be the Lord's"—gone, icy fingers from that night at the nape of my neck.

I turn; he's bent at the front of the car, elbow working, as the bumper and chrome bars of the grille—arched like an open mouth—inch up. I step near, disturbed, and see that his blond hair is pink at its roots, as if stained by blood. He reaches out and his fingers, spidery-bunched, open and flex as if reluctant to get a grip on the tire. A car is coming from Havana toward us, swaying on its shocks, packed with a family, it looks, and then the windows glide down and arms poke out with middle fingers standing up from each fist, and somebody in the back seat cups his hands below his slicked-back hair and hollers, "Get a horse!"

Jerome doesn't look up. He pulls at the tire, gets it loose, and rolls it out, a clashing sound swirling in its hubcap, and shoves on it with both hands. "It doesn't seem flat," he says.

"Bastards," I say, meaning the hoods. "It probably saved our lives. The tire." He leans it against the car and looks up, afraid or surprised—a streak of grease down his cheek in a wild line. I hit the hubcap with a crutch tip. "Take that off."

He pries it loose with a tinny shriek and greasy nuts scatter over the grass-combed sand.

"I knew it! The lugs from the wheel came off! Good God! Who in the hell ever has this crap happen to them!"

He straightens, hefting the tire tool as if weighing it, and Dad's pained smile appears on his face. "Who?" he asks, and the tire tool clunks against his chest as he puts his hands there. "Me."

+

We're cruising up the hill toward the root-beer stand, to see if Lynette is working tonight, when Bobbie and Willa come walking down the sidewalk toward us. "Should I stop?" Jerome asks.

"Why not?" Perhaps he can see in Bobbie's manner, as I can, that something is wrong.

He pulls over, gravel cackling against the curb, and they walk on past, laughing or pretending to laugh. I unlatch the door, prop it open with a crutch, and slide out. "I'll meet you at the root-beer stand."

He takes off and sways, slamming the door shut, a new trick, and I realize that I'll have to negotiate a high curb and then an embankment of grass above it to get to the sidewalk. "Hey, Bobbie!"

They stop, their backs to me, and Bobbie says, "Did I hear my name?"

"Maybe you might have," Willa says, and turns to me, then slaps a hand over her gooms and goes into a widow's hump at her giggle.

"Oh, come on, Bobbie," I say, nearing the sidewalk. "What's up?"

She turns, her face as red as the pump in her kitchen, and says, "You're asking me? How's Havana, you shit?"

"Oh, come on, can't we talk?"

"Sure. Why don't we go on over and make ourselves comfy in one of those?" She juts her chin toward the used cars in the lot we're near, and the buckled front of one off to the side seems for a second to be ours. "Maybe we can discuss the situation of Havana gash."

"Hey!" I whisper, and rock back on my crutches.

She pokes Willa in the ribs with her clutch purse and they force out another laugh; then she turns on me with eyes that appear black. "So what have you got to say for yourself, wise-ass?"

"We went there once. You know about Jerome and Lynette. He's scouting around. I didn't even get out of the car."

"How about Saturday?"

"What have you got, a local network? We stopped at Lishout." She knows we have cousins there, near the wildlife refuge, and I'm ashamed to say how the tire came off; after Jerome bolted it on, we drove back home.

She looks down and says to Willa, from inside the shadow her curls cast over her face, "I'll meet you at the restaurant."

Willa goes trotting off, and I work past a gravelly pothole, closer to Bobbie, into the veil of her perfume, and realize that she's wearing my favorite sweater, one of black cashmere that enhances her color, with a heart-shaped pin above a breast—the highest I'm able to look—and then splashes strike the rhinestones encircling the heart, and blacker spots scatter over her breasts. "You ass, you *shit*!" she cries, her fists over her face and her purse turned out. "I feel like cutting my wrists!"

"Please, I—"

"Don't come near me!"

"All right, fine, I—"

She flings her hands away, and I maneuver back. She steps up and seems to look down to where I hang from my crutches, and whispers, "Are you the kind that fucks and runs?" Tears darkened with mascara spill in fattened paths down her face. "You think you're pretty smart, don't you? You think you're real cool, right, some kind of damn—intellectual, or something! Well, I think you're a lying little geek. You're a dumb-ass!"

"Hey, Bobbie—"

She shoves her purse in my face, and I go stumbling backward, trying to get my balance. "I only went to Havana once, and I—"

"Shut up! So now you've got the strut of the guy who got his! You mealymouthed chickenshit! *I hope you rot in hell!*"

Her scream turns me aside, and I look around to see who's heard, but in every direction the street is deserted—only our car, on the hill at the root-beer stand. She's running off, already at the railroad tracks, her legs swinging out from her skirt, and I start after her but turn again; a waitress is walking toward our car with a tray. Lynette.

Have she and Bobbie talked?

I stab out both crutches and step off on my pinned leg, a technique I've adopted for speed, and head up the hill to the car.

"What did Lynette say?" I ask.

Jerome is slouched down in the seat, under the orange lights of the root-beer stand, slowly chewing a chili dog. "She said Bobbie said she's going to slash her wrists."

"That's what she said to me!"

"So talk to her."

"She doesn't want to talk."

"Sure she does. Give her a chance."

"All right, finish up. Drive me down there, okay."

"Take it easy. Give her a chance to catch her breath."

I crawl in and press against the seat back, testing my shaking knees, and attempt to be casual. "I wonder what brought this on?"

He glances over at me, then back at his chili dog, taking down a swallow it seems he'll choke on, and his eyes, in the orange light, appear to redden. "Save it for Bobbie, okay?"

+

AUG 8. *A mistake which might seem worse if I believed that the measure of life is self-improvement. I visited the wrong friend. I know them well enough; I've acted with them both. Marco at the moment has the most developed talent of the three of us, and has come as close to adapting his classical training to an everyday tone as any actor who's been trained that way (as Al hasn't), but Al, who's younger, can open up an energy that sets you back from him onstage, as you check whether his senses have snapped. Both are on a downhill course, in that fragile time of first beginnings, when you have to learn to shape what you are before it takes your life. I was weak-kneed but could walk, and with my first step floated. Evening of ambiguity.*

+

We drive the blonde and her friend from Havana's Main Street to a house they direct us to, and they perch on the back seat as if it's soiled, so formal I want to hurry back to Bobbie, who, when I walked into the restaurant that night, was gone—home with her dad, Willa said, and then added, "She figures maybe she'll probably be too busy working to talk to you for a couple of weeks, ha!" Now the blond girl pulls back the fall of hair that covers one eye, and whispers, "Is that Mel?"

The chunky one looks out the rear window. "Yup."

"Oh, Jeez, he isn't supposed to drive while he's on probation."

"What?" Jerome and I say at the same time.

A hardtop with rumbling mufflers rolls past, fists rising out the windows, and the burr-headed hood at the wheel, on my side, says, "You're going to catch yours, buddy."

"Tell him you just drove us home!" the blonde says, and both scramble out and run toward the house, leaving the back door ajar.

"Roll up your window," Jerome says. "Get that door!" But they're already piling out of the hardtop ahead, some in black leather jackets, and heading for us. I lock my door as Jerome starts off, the car going into the bucking coughs that usually signify a kill, and somebody grabs the handle of the door left open. "You dirty—" he begins, and tries to get a foot up on the high sill as I raise a crutch, and then goes spinning off as the engine catches with a roar.

"I hope you tore his finger off!" I cry.

"I don't. It looks like they're getting back in the car."

I look around; indeed. I turn and get up on the seat with my good knee, and close the back door, then push its lock; the one across the car, I punch with my crutch tip. Jerome floors the car, in second gear, all the way up the bridge over the railroad tracks, and, once at its top, hits a hard third. Their car comes over the crest, in a leap, it looks, toward us, and I hear our gas pedal thump the floor. We shimmy around the corners of Quiver Beach with them at our bumper, their car sliding outside us when the force of the turning permits them to, as if to come around, and I yell, "Don't let them pass!"

"What if a car comes?"

"Don't let— Dammit!"

They pull up even with us on a straightaway, and I see, when I glance up from the road, where I feel I have to stare to hold the car in place, iron pipes and a waving baseball bat, and then somebody leans out, his hair going crazy at our speed, and swings at Jerome's window.

"Hey!" Jerome cries, and ducks, our tires screeching.

"Watch the road!"

"They're crowding me off!" He puts on the brakes and there's a double squalling as both cars grind closer to one another at the edge of the blacktop, and I hit the dash as I see them slide into our lane, their rear end tailing around, and then Jerome grapples at the wheel with a growling in his throat, and we slither around their passing side; then I'm pressed back in the seat as he floors it again.

By the time they catch up, he's had to turn on our headlights in order to see, which causes me to wonder if anybody has ever checked the rest of the wheel nuts. They start around and I say, "Now don't let them pass!" and he swings into their lane, then weaves back and forth as they try both sides. Headlights appear ahead. "Now what?" he asks, and when the lights are too close to bear in the wrong lane, he swings into ours, climbing to top speed, and in a rattling burst of their mufflers they climb up even to us, the lights ahead jerking bright and dim, big as plates, then looping aside as Jerome hits the brakes and in a blaring of horns and rubber all three cars fly past one another without a crash.

"Sonsabitches!" he screams. "Don't you care what you *do!*"

By now their car is far ahead, and the one behind us appears off the road, its headlights skewed skyward.

"They're going on," he says. "They're afraid that guy will call the cops." He slows. They slow even more, going into maneuvers to keep us from coming around, and as we start into a curve I see that we're doing only thirty. "Keep up your speed!" I cry.

"How?"

Their rattling suddenly resounds out of the curve, and they pull off out of sight. "What's this?" he asks.

"Is there any turnoff along here?"

"Not that I know of. Why?"

He coasts over a stretch with no sign of taillights, up a dip, then down it, and a ways ahead their car sits crosswise in our lane, doors thrown open, the group of them fanned across the road in front of it.

"That's why," I say.

"Should I stop?"

"Stop? They aren't going to beat in a window and quit. Floor it! Head to the left!"

The group looks looser there, and must see our car buck or hear its roar as he hits second, because they leap aside at the last instant and we rub past their bumper along a shoulder that's a drop-off—where the tire came loose?—and there's a clattering of pipes and bats on our fenders.

"Now kick it! Get to the Lishout turnoff! We'll go to Scott and Elaine's!" Our relatives. Scott is an ex-Navy man, who keeps firearms handy in his house, and I picture us blazing away at them from a sand dune. We get to the turnoff without seeing lights behind, skid around onto it, thump off the approach onto the sand road, and go through the trees, over the tracks where Davey used to put up a flag for the train, and I see that the house is dark: not a light. I work down my window to breathe, and hear a screeching of tires beyond the turnoff, down the long grade known as Lishout Hill, and then an engine revving as a car backs.

"Shut off the lights," I say, and look out on a blasted, moonlit landscape like the one where J. B. Lacey spiked his leg. "They've got two choices at the crossroad. Maybe they know we have relatives here."

"Which way should I go?"

"Past the house."

He eases along a bank of sand out my side of the car, and I imagine us stuck. "Chickens," I say.

"Right, they could have had three carloads of us back there."

"No, I mean, attacking a guy in a cast—I mean, on crutches."

"Right," he says, and drives deeper into the darkness of the dunes in rigid silence.

The Russian sets my crutches aside, takes my hands, and walks backward, encouraging me with wagging eyebrows, and I go into the choppy shuffles of a ninety-year-old, my butt stuck out. The pinned hip quakes as if about to pop, and the bone of my other leg, with the knee above still stiff, feels it will buckle and spear my foot. I lean against a wall.

"Okay?" he asks.

I shrug.

"You can still use your crutches when you need to, but I want your brother to walk you a bit like this every day—okay, Jerome? I guess that's about it, then." His eyebrows form a solemn ribbon as he shakes my hand. "If you need anything, call. Keep your chin up."

He's off in such a rush his jacket billows at his back like a filling sail, as if he wants to be across the ocean when I collapse.

"Are you okay?" Jerome asks.

I remember us parking in the shadow of the hospital, earlier, while I craned to look up through the windshield, aware of my dependence on this place of brick and steel (the canopy over the entry, the solarium above), which has become a part of me—literally, in a way: the pin.

I nod and grab the crutches. "Let's get home," I say.

+

Summer, and here I waddle like a baby with a full diaper if I'm not on the crutches. After all I've been through, this is the point where I want off. Then one evening Uncle Jay sticks his head in the front door and says, "Come on, Martin, we're going to get you a car."

"A car?"

"We're going to buy you a new car."

"But I can't—"

"Get up! Come on!"

+

It's an American Motors Rambler hardtop, the first new car we've owned, and we take it on a vacation to North Dakota. We visit the Savitskys, who are harvesting, and the Kauter-Haupts, where we're served Mrs. Hank's finest strudel. We stand on the corner of Main Street with Kuntz and the Rimskys, smoking and talking about our accident, and then Arno Litwak walks up with a girl he introduces as his sister; she's been living in Montana with their dad, he says. She looks at me with a pout, and although I still navigate in my stiff-legged waddle, she permits me, that night on the Litwaks' steps, to get almost as far as I have with Bobbie. We promise to write twice a week, which I do, for a while, once I get back, and a letter finally arrives from her. Is this what became of Jerome and Carly's vow to keep in touch? If she and I, strangers, did what we did in one night, what might lie ahead? And Bobbie is behind, I think, with a catch of remorse at this trend in my thought, and stand up.

All I really want to do, I think, is walk.

+

One late summer evening, when Jerome and I are out driving, we see Bobbie and Willa walking along the highway. "Stop," I say. I get out and learn that Bobbie doesn't want to talk to me alone. "Nice car," she says, and I finally persuade her to go for a ride. She gets into the back seat beside me, and then Willa climbs in the other door, wedging me between.

"No crutches," Bobbie says.

"Right."

"How is it? I mean, without crutches?"

I turn to check for irony, and find her studying her skirt.

"We were on vacation," I say, as if to explain everything.

"I heard." Then it sounds as if she says, "Run into any strange?"

"What?" I say.

"Thanks for the postcard."

And then she sits in silence, running her finger down the seam that opens in a pleated flare at the hem of her skirt.

+

She doesn't return to school. Willa says she's working in another town, and a month later says she's home again. "She doesn't talk to me no more," Willa admits. "I heard she was dating this guy, he was married once? Two kids? Now he's divorced?"

I figure if the guy was married, there is one thing he must know about.

"It's too bad about Bobbie," Dad says one night, when he and I are alone in the living room. "She had potential as a student. Some don't."

Cigar smoke coils above the hand hidden from me as he stares at the television—he is speaking more and more out of shadow, it seems. "I wonder if the possibility exists that you'll ever see this as part of your effect on her. Anyway, I hope you've learned."

+

My favorite shirt, black, has vertical white stripes like a prisoner's. The junior class manages concessions during basketball games, which means counting the take afterward, and one night, when the crowd is piling down the bleachers, Earl, who sometimes acts like my trustee since the accident, takes me aside and says uneasily, "Bobbie's here. Somebody said she wants to talk to you. I'll count up."

She's on the highest bleacher, on the cafeteria side of the gymnasium, in her black sweater, sitting alone. I climb the stairs in half steps, still unbalanced on my creaking legs, and walk over under the close ceiling and stand beside her. In the aura of her perfume, I begin to give, but she stares straight ahead with her arms crossed, busily chewing gum, and finally says, "You could have got me pregnant."

"How?"

" 'How?' I'd like to kick your teeth down your throat."

"You're not pregnant."

"How would you know, wise-ass!"

"You couldn't be, not from me." I'm almost ashamed to admit this.

She turns, furious, her lips gliding up her teeth. "You mean you're one of those guys that says he's sterile?"

"A lot say that?"

She blushes and stares down; her lips are chapped, with lipstick-stained shingles of skin curling up from them. "I might have got an abortion," she says, and the gym resounds with the word, one of the worst in my vocabulary, as she knows, since we've discussed the Catholic view on this: murder one. Worse, when you consider that the victim is helpless. I can't go much lower, I figure, so I say it: "I didn't come."

"You didn't come!"

"Hey, Bobbie, hold it down." I glance around the gym, which looks deserted, but voices are crawling through corridors off it.

"You didn't *come*! Oh, God, after all that, you didn't come, too?"

She covers her face, pulled into jerking seizures by sobs; I hesitate, then put a hand on her back.

"Don't touch me!" she cries. "Get away, you cripple, you!"

+

Jerome and Lynette start dating again, but soon they aren't talking. He starts to work on his Original Oration—"Getting a jump on the herd!" he says—sure that he'll go to the State. I want to try out for Original Monologue, so I sit at our desk, always surprised at the squeegeed-on marble, and try to think of something funny; the monologue is supposed to be humorous. It would be interesting, I think, to have a radio here. I dismantle the console in the basement and carry its innards up, cut a hole in the cardboard of our wardrobe, fasten the speaker inside, run wire from there to the tuning equipment, sitting bare at the back of the desk, and have a working radio.

I keep it tuned low, with cigarettes and an ashtray close, and begin to write through a man who has been selected by his club to give a speech on ladies' night, to explain away the rumor of a drunken bus trip from a baseball game. The man makes such a muddle of things it's obvious that the rumor is a veneer over something worse, and finally he backs from the podium, his hands up, fending off the ladies. Or men. I saw something similar on TV. After everybody is in bed, I slip down and watch it for possible jokes I might use—who'd be taking note of them at this hour? Jerome is asleep by the time I return to our room and scratch down salvageable lines, reworked, beside the glow of the radio bulbs, with only the whisper of a voice rising from the speaker, and then I sit back and smoke until I can sense the last consciousness in town go out.

One night, as if resuming a conversation, Jerome says, "You know"—startling me—"I think I might join your team."

"My team?" My head cranks around to place him, and I start to put out my pencil in the ashtray.

There's a cascade of covers as he sits, and then he says, in no logical sequence I can discern, out of the darkness, "I'd give most anything for a drag on that."

I start to hand him the pencil, then double back to the ashtray and pass on my smoking stub, and a bright orange mesh centers over his mouth, then projects his nose at me.

"What do you mean, join my team?"

"Maybe I'll enroll in pre-med."

I try to translate his expression as he takes another drag. My plan to be a doctor is such common knowledge that even when I'm in the pool hall, playing a game of rotation or sitting in a tall shoeshine chair, with a sack of Planters peanuts poured into a bottle of Coke, surveying the lawns of the tables below, where Jerome takes shots with crow fingers—even in this place where we now spend noon hours—everybody, including the paunchy owner, calls me "Doc."

"I thought you were going into speech," I say. "Or English lit." Why does this sound hollow now?

"I haven't sent off my applications yet."

"So enroll in pre-med. We'll go to medical school together and start up a clinic."

"Let's see about my oration first," he says. "That's the key."

Dad casts us in the Contest play. "Well, both of you are going to the District, anyway," he explains. "The Borghum boys can be understudies. One claims he wants to try Radio Speaking, and the other After-Dinner Speaking, so I have to take them seriously." He twists up his lips and wobbles a hand back and forth in the air; the two are brothers our ages, athletes who have never registered any interest in speech or theater, probably out for the release time. "You four can help with the set and the lights. Junie Sisco is playing the lead."

Our play is about the homecoming of a runaway son. I'm

the son and Jerome the father, since we look alike, and Junie, who is developed like Dewey, the mother. The older Borghum, a basketball star, is now dating Dewey, and rumor has it that the younger one dates Bobbie; the brothers live in the vicinity of Kyle Lake, and the way they understudy us leads me to suspect that they're spies. My part isn't that big, but I get to lay my head in Junie's lap. Jerome is dating her, or has been, and one night when I'm taking the car on my first solo tour of town, I see a Hudson parked at Junie's house. Jerome, I think. Then it occurs to me that we don't have a Hudson anymore, we have the car I'm driving, and finally it hits home: Don Nelson. After our accident, he bought a Hudson like ours.

And with this I've had enough coupling up to want to remain alone for good.

+

Jerome wins second in the District, and when I hear that I've won first, I think: It was wrong to be so critical of him. The play places also, and in a few weeks we're riding to Lincoln, where the Sectional is held, in the superintendent's station wagon—so that all of the contestants, whether competing or not, can attend—with Jerome at the wheel. The play doesn't go over well, since he and Junie aren't speaking offstage, and I fluff some of my lines before I get to her lap. He wins third with his oration, and I'm disqualified.

"Disqualified?" I say, feverish that my jokes have been discovered.

"Disqualified!" Dad cries, and roughly grabs me by a shoulder and manhandles me upstairs to the contest office and shouts, "What is this!" All of the people there turn to us. "How can he be disqualified?"

"What was he in, Mr. Neumiller?" a woman in a suit asks.

"Original Monologue."

She leafs through some sheets. "He used an introduction, the judge says. There can be no introductions, according to the rules."

"All he did was give a setting! He did exactly the same thing at the District and won first! Before he went onstage there,

I took the judge aside and asked if giving a setting could be taken as an introduction, and she said, 'No! Absolutely not!' Now what is this?"

"I'm sorry, but our judge, at this level, has taken exception to that. He views this contestant's remarks before the monologue as an introduction." She holds up the page, with a red X across it, then sighs and gives Dad a wounded look. "Mr. Neumiller."

"Yes," he says, and swallows—a rooster with its ruffles up.

"You've judged for us at these contests yourself."

"I have indeed."

"You know a judge's decision is final. We can't countermand that."

"But the judge at the District said—!"

+

Junie won't ride back with Jerome; she crawls into our car with Dad and the props, and it's a long trip home in the station wagon, with everybody gloomily silent. A contestant who advanced to the Sectional, a girl in Oral Interpretation, didn't place. The play didn't place. With his third, Jerome won't go to the State. Dad has asked Jerome to drop the girl off at her farmhouse, between Lishout and Forest Creek, and as we come down the steep grade of the Lishout Hill, I say to Jerome from the passenger seat, "You better slow up. I think her turn is soon." He's dreamily nursing a cigarette and his jaw muscles bunch as he clamps down so hard it looks as if he's bitten through. The girl leans between us from the seat behind and says, "Here, Jerome!"

"Hey, there's—" somebody begins as Jerome brakes hard at a reflector on a post and we nod forward, and then in a spangled shrieking fly backward in our seats. "Hit the brakes!" I cry, as we sail so far to one side it feels we'll roll in the ditch, past her lane, where we eventually land.

"What the hell!" a Borghum cries.

"Why didn't you brake!" I say.

"What do you think I was doing?"

"That ugly sonunna—ugh!—hit us!" a Borghum says. "I think my neck's broke!"

"Oh, goodness, I hurt!" the girl cries. "Oh, me!"

"Oh, God," Jerome says. He embraces the wheel and lays his head down on it, and the horn goes off, blaring beneath the steaming hood.

Nobody is seriously hurt, except perhaps the older Borghum, and cars gather at the sight of us in suits and Sunday clothes in the ditch. The rear of the station wagon is ruined, crushed forward two feet, where the Borghums were sitting. It was a fellow student, Henry Kubitz, and not the carload of hoods from Havana, as I first feared, who rammed us from behind. "Guess I was kind of daydreaming," Kubitz says, and looks like he still is, standing at the front of his car beside a crumpled fender, gripping his bleeding nose with bloody fingers. The sight of blood and sheared metal sends me back into the ditch, feeling sick to my stomach. I turn and see Jerome in the station wagon, with the door open and his feet on the ground, his head in his hands, and for a moment I can't walk.

+

He and Dad and I are in the living room with the TV off and the lights out, as if hiding. Parthenogenesis. Something reproducing out of itself in the dark. The springs of the couch tremble and Jerome socks it, and cries, "That station wagon is ruined!"

"I'm sure DeMaster has insurance that covers you, or he wouldn't have loaned it," Dad says. He inserts his pipe in his mouth as if he hopes this is true, and appears to swallow part of it in the darkness.

"I can't do anything right!" Jerome cries, and runs upstairs.

The silence revolves me toward a mirror of clotted blood over my thigh where a—

"It is terribly unfortunate," Dad says, with the slur of a pipe smoker with a stem in the way. I go into the bathroom, throw cold water on my face, then creak upstairs, and at the sight of Jerome slumped on the bed, revelation comes. We're too old to be sleeping together.

"I can't take it!" he cries. "I can't face anybody! I can't—"

"Stop."

"Did you hear what Ted Remington said?" This is the father of the girl he's dating now; Remington's was the first car that pulled up. "He said, 'That's the second time for him.' "

"He meant Kubitz. A few weeks ago Kubitz was driving his dad's pickup back in the hills, I heard, and rolled it. Remington said, 'It's the second time for that guy in a month.' He meant Kubitz."

"He did not! He meant me!"

"Hey, come on, don't—"

"I can't take it! This is it! I give up!"

I turn to the stripped-down radio to conceal my smile; melodrama doesn't become him. Next week he'll be going on about the State Contest and how— I hear a sonic boom from an actual passing jet as my thought is ordered into reality's lines: That's not true. He's graduating.

+

He and another senior drive to Peoria to take their physicals; they've been accepted into NROTC, which means a four-year scholarship. Jerome returns from Peoria with the bent look of an old man; he's failed the physical. His eyesight. Soon he's wearing glasses with gray-silver earpieces and silver wire under the lenses, and I start squinting and looking at things sideways, until I decide to have my eyes tested, too. One is slightly weaker, the optometrist says, though still 20–20, and suggests that I might use glasses for reading, if I want to.

Whenever Jerome is about to say something important, he puts a hand to his face and pushes up on the silver centerpiece of his glasses with his middle finger—as he does now, sitting on the edge of the bed. He says, "A *low blow* all around. Now I really do need a scholarship."

"Yes," I say, and push up on my glasses, with frames exactly like his, and sigh. "That sure does seem so."

+

We all have recovered from the accident, although the older Borghum is seeing a chiropractor, or "chiro-chopper," as I call him, in my loyalty to medicine—a quack who plays on people's fears with no recourse to science, and is probably taking Borghum for a ride. Then Borghum says that a lawyer has talked to the chiropractor, and they've decided he has whiplash, something nobody's heard of, which Borghum might never recover from.

He's going to sue. "People are doing that now," Dad says. "A way to get even." He shakes his head; it's not clear whether Borghum intends to sue the superintendent, or Kubitz, or Jerome or Dad, or everybody. Then we hear that it's been settled out of court, and the superintendent allows Borghum, who has missed a month of school, to finish his senior year next fall, which means he'll be eligible for basketball for another season. He buys Dewey a big diamond engagement ring.

+

The week of Jerome's graduation, we drive out to the State Forest with his friend who is entering NROTC and drink a gallon of Mogen David under a bulging moon. With a few sips, my arms turn as weak as my legs, and my stomach feels it's scraping ribs. Jerome shouts, "Best class of the fifties, hey!" into the woods, and then his friend grabs the empty bottle and throws it toward a stand of trees whose trunks appear as crystalline as the glass of the shattered bottle flying past them.

At home, bucking like a badly springy Hudson over the toilet bowl, retasting the wine with such force it feels the bottom of my stomach will strangle me, I finally bark on an emptiness that leaves lines like cuts up my esophagus, and my glasses fall in. *Never again*, I vow, as I fish for the glasses, *never another drink*, and then a voice like Jerome's murmurs a question from the other side of the door.

"Go away!" I yell.

"I'm afraid you can't render me invisible," Dad says. "I'm not sure what you've been up to, although I can guess from the smell, and all I can say, Charles— And you up there! Jerome! Are you up there?"

"Ahhk." Or so I hear the burr of sound from our bedroom.

"All I can say is I hope you two have learned!"

Jerome is at the state university, enrolled in liberal arts, and I'm working on a new monologue. A German scientist like Wernher von Braun (who has been explaining rocketry on television) is explaining rocketry on television—a first paragraph of gobbledygook I figure will get me a laugh right off. I pick up my glasses, hold them at arm's length, and sight at the radio through them: lenses like windowpanes. The scientist goes into a spiel—Screwdini on a rampage—about a rocket that had to be lit with a match after the countdown ("And dere vas our herro, und back dere vas our herro, und ober dere . . ."), and gets so tangled up he finally switches to an advertisement for a cereal whose box contains a miniature rocket, which he launches by lighting a match—pantomime! sound effects!—and then watches it descend—fisssh!—at his feet. The outline. Which I develop without stealing any jokes, except a variation on the hero, which I heard on the *Tonight Show*. Dad and I both watch it now, although lately it irritates us to be in the same room together, and Dad sometimes says, "If Castro's Cuba is as great as he claims, how come all those Cubans on his show left it, and never go back?"

We eat cookies and crackers that we pile beside us, or popcorn I've popped, and one night he turns, just before he pushes up from his chair for bed, nods at a bowl of peanuts, and says, "You won't be satisfied, I suppose, until you finish those, right?"

Which is exactly what he does: finishes everything within reach. I stomp across the room, upstairs, and vow to stay away from the television, and him, too.

+

Jerome arrives for Thanksgiving, and tells me, up in our room, that he's been cast in a one-act play. I ask him what it's about, and he says, "Oh, this teenager—that's me—breaks into an old man's shop and the man catches him and ends up instructing him in a kind of humanistic approach to basic values." He pushes up his glasses.

"I see," I say. "Is it a good part?"

"Fair. One of two leads."

On top of the pile of books he's brought home is a paperback with an Army-green cover and printing across it like the Baltimore Catechism. "Is this about a painter?" I ask.

"Portrait," he says, pushing up his glasses, "is one of the more profound and perhaps seminal novels of this century."

I open it up, and my glowing radio tubes seem to lend a tangled crispness to the words that at first appear to be in another language, but before I've finished the first page somebody has peed a bed, and I think: This is it! This is the real thing!

I hand him my monologue, and he reads it through and then looks up from the bed where he's lying. "This has potential," he says. He did not laugh once, however, during his entire read-through. He shoves up his glasses, and I decide to resurrect mine from the desk drawer where they're buried. "It might even turn out to be quite good," he says.

"It's going to be in this German accent, see, sort of like Hank Kauter-Haupt's—or his wife's, actually—and that should really help."

"Yes, I caught that. I'm taking oral interp this semester."

"I mean, I think the accent itself is going to bring it off."

"Yes," he says, and hikes his glasses higher. "You'll have to develop a real flexibility and flair in your delivery."

I tune my radio farther out into the night—Chicago, Quebec, New Orleans—and on some nights, dizzy from coffee and cigarettes, I sense the caricature of the German scientist extending through the house, so that it seems I'm shaping his speech to fit its rooms, and one night there is nothing left to alter or shape; I'm done.

I miss the work so much I wonder to Dad what I should do. "Well," he says, "I suppose a person could do most anything, if he put his mind to it." So I start a piece about a jet pilot shot down over Korea; his canopy jams ("cockpit of falling freedom gone"), and as he heads down he thinks of his wife and children. I can't decide if the canopy will eventually release—have him wet his pants? crap them?—and after a while he sounds like Jerome saying, "I give up!" I leave him suspended, and start an article about two men on Main Street talking about Orval Faubus. They make a mockery of him, and the piece ends with one saying, "You can't find diamonds if you don't pay attention to the coal!"

I'll publish it in the local newspaper, I decide, and then tomorrow finish the story about the jet pilot, plus a poem or two, and publish those—suddenly capable, with one thing done, of ensnaring the world.

"Well," Dad says, straightening the pages in his lap. "Some of it's pretty extreme, I think, but the end"—he holds a hand out in the air and wobbles it—"is sort of interesting."

"Extreme?"

"I don't agree with Faubus, either. He holds views antithetical—well, opposed to my way of thinking. 'A man's a man for a' that' and 'You're a better man than I am, Gunga Din,' and so forth. You have one of these fellows calling him a 'mealymouthed geek.' And other names. Somebody might get the idea that you have a problem, too. Now, I'll admit that men on the street might talk like that, but this is on paper."

He goes out to the kitchen and pours himself a cup of coffee and sits at the table with the pages. So I pour myself a cup and sit, wishing I had the guts to light up in front of him.

"I still think about the Second World War," he says.

What's this?

"The school board in Hyatt came to me and said they might try to have my draft deferred. I don't know if they did; I was never called up, and I never asked. I'm pretty much anti-war, but never felt I could say it in so many words, since I'm a teacher. With the First World War, the ethics got worse, until nothing was sure. Before, there seemed to be a purpose, or a right and wrong, even in war. Then came Hitler. People who complain about the atrocities in Germany—which were inexcusable, true— often seem the first to forget what took place in Russia, and is going on there to this day. And what about Hiroshima? I maintain that the atomic bomb would never have been dropped on Europe, no matter how bad it got there, and the reason it was dropped where it was is partly racial. How many times did I hear, during the war, 'Those dirty little Nips,' or worse, as if they were a subhuman race. How it used to grieve your mother when you two talked that way, 'playing war,' as you called it.

"So, you see, there are many different types of prejudice, from large to small, and we often continue to be blind to our own."

+

I tone down the piece and the newspaper editor takes it, and asks me to do a weekly column about the two men talking. Quemoy and Matsu, Nixon and Eisenhower, and the town itself get included, with overtones of local events, and as I write I see Dad in his chair, or in the rocker on the other side of the house, staring ahead as he talks: "The Dirty Thirties, as we called them, seem the turning point of present history. It became apparent then that our economy is based on farming; even steelworkers have to eat. During those dust storms that darkened the sky from the Dakotas to New York, we sat in our closed-up house, knowing that those were crops going up. The dirtiness wasn't limited to the air. There were sharp practices at the elevators and in the grain market itself, along with farm foreclosures that seemed unjust. Your grandpa was so affected by what happened to him and his father, he can't talk about it to this day. I'm still not sure what all was involved.

"The downhill slide began even before Hoover, who was probably better trained for the situation than anybody. He had spent most of his life feeding starving people in China, Belgium, Russia—most of Western Europe after the First World War. Both his parents had died before he was nine, and it seemed to me that he spent the rest of his life, in a sense, taking care of his sisters and brothers. He organized the most efficient lines of food supply the world has seen.

"His managerial skills were what the country needed when he was elected President. You have to call it Providence. I believe he was willing to take the blame, as long as an organization for the recovery of the country was set in place, without imposing Socialism. I still think that he and Harry Truman—certainly a great President—will eclipse F.D.R. when history puts them in perspective. F.D.R.'s programs couldn't have worked without the machinery Hoover had set in place, and Roosevelt's conservation projects were poor, pale copies of Teddy's. But, oh, what an actor! How colorful and persuasive he was, and how he relished the office! I voted for him twice, maybe on that basis, so there you are.

"In another sense, I'm still back in those years, inside that house, and there are days when I feel I spend half my time trying to escape. Yet here I am, telling this years later to my son, who's nearly the age I was then, in the hope that it won't be forgotten."

+

The character of the German scientist broadens as I practice the monologue aloud—first alone, then for Dad, and then for one of his classes. I'm also producing my weekly columns, and one evening as I work a thunderstorm erupts, sending tinselly flashes through my radio, and congregates above the roof. I write about the noise of the storm, thinking of Poe, and then admit that I'm afraid of it, as if singled out.

I take the poem down and hand it to Dad, and he reads it in his easy chair and then gets up and goes to the kitchen window. The storm is still in progress, and ignitions of lightning silhouette him in stuttering brilliance. He glances at the sheet of paper and then puts a hand on the sash, and I can picture him here with his cane, staring out at the car, and understand that he's as affected as he was then. I'll write a book of poetry, I decide, dedicated to him, and give it to him on his birthday, and by then I'll have enough columns . . .

He turns, blinking as if sightless from the lightning, and says, "I'm not sure all the lines are right, but this is whole. It works."

+

The stench of bats and rags has
Not overcome my mind, or bathroom.
Voices cry at midnight, variously,
Because arms have heavy hands to carry . . .

The lines of this poem, which appeared in my column today, tumble through my unrest, unnerving me further. The poem was intended to be humorous, but changed under my hands. Then at noon I had to give my monologue to the assembly hall, and now my hands shake as I fit a pipette and rubber tubing together for a chemistry experiment. Billy Gene Skaggs sidles close, with his belt buckle to one side, collar turned up, and slicked-back hair shining in the light of the botany greenhouse beside us. "Hey," he says, "that speech of yours, man—crazy!"

His lab partner, a former Little League catcher who's turning into a boozer, I've heard, grins and says, "Chucker, baby? Way out!"

"And that pome thing you wrote about bats?" Billy Gene says. "I got my clucks out of that, too. Funny freaky stuff, man!"

Well, I think, as the two return to their experiment and I stand with sunlight gripping my shoulders: That's it. That's all I need. I've got it made.

+

In a movement that feels imaginary, I turn in this chair as my daughter walks into the room. Or basement, actually, with cartons and boxes piled behind the deep freeze, and recording equipment on a table in this cement-block offset that I've lined with perforated soundboard.

"Well, what are you going to do?" she asks. She's twelve, with ripe Tartar cheekbones padded with a youthful fullness her body is beginning to assume, and violet shades of a newborn still in her eyes, or so I see it. For a week she's been after me to respond to a publication that claimed, for the second time around, that I used actors for the voices on my show. After the first article appeared, without any support or ground in truth, I asked the writer to visit me, and gave a day over to him and his assistant, recording several different voices on my equipment, and then playing them back. They started an interview and I told them (with the recorder running) how I began doing the usual sort of interview show, with actors and writers and celebrities, as voluntary labor, over Public Radio, while I made my living recording the voice-overs I had done for years. The interviews were live, with a seven-second lag, and one day when an interviewee, an elderly actor who'd been having problems with alcohol, didn't show, I took his role and another, inventing both voices, and it turned into something of the sort I'd once written in my columns. The real interest was in the second person, who, it turned out, was an analogue of Jerome. My knowledge of him permitted me to cover any topic in character, and to allow my father, also, to speak through him, because the attraction of the show lay in the people of the small town "we" spoke about (which took the shape of Hyatt), rather than in impinging current events—as if present politics is the ultimate truth, when it seldom touches on it, as anybody with any sense can see.

I said all this, and added that for years the other character seemed my servant, leading me to the subjects I wished to talk about, until I understood that I was *his* servant, since it was out of his silence that avenues of interest opened, often surprising me. With the advances in technology, I said, pointing at my equipment, it became possible to record the show wherever I went, as I'd always claimed I could do.

Their publication printed a truncated version of parts of the interview, although I gave them a copy of the tape, and said again that I used actors for the voices.

My daughter is restless, twisting her fingers as if in pain, and I recall her saying at the edge of another conversation I was involved in: "It takes my dad about ten minutes to answer any question I ask."

"What do you think I should do?" I say to her now.

"Oh, Dad!" She stomps a foot, and I'm engulfed by the aroma of a flushed young woman, which I'd nearly forgotten: the young do burn. The new article also took issue with the content of the show ("small-town opinions with the reek of prejudice of small-town America, unable to be smoothed over by the host's grandfatherly jocularity"), and then me. I wasn't inventing the voices, it claimed; witnesses had seen me try, and it wasn't the same, and of course it wasn't, without the dimming confines of a speaker, an absence that permits the imagination to work: radio's power. I had noticed their looks when I played back the tape, and I realized it was like watching a ventriloquist close-up—that rubbery dummy is never quite the same—and remembered an early lesson: "A magician never reveals his secrets."

They had questioned me about a church I was attending, and the finale of the article, homing in on this, went: "He claims to hear other voices he matches to his and with his recent professed spiritualism perhaps we can next expect him to be speaking in tongues."

So uninformed they don't know the difference between Christianity and the occult? How can intelligent discourse be carried on? I scoot down in the chair, shove my hands into my pockets, and try to look relaxed, as I was in the dining room of that other house when I heard my daughter, in the next room, whisper to one of the host's children about the time lapse before my replies. Caused because I sort through voices, or images that assault me?—now of that dining room, whose walls were decorated with "Joy" and "Peace" posters that I associate with Holy-Spirited Protestants, although this couple is Catholic, perhaps charismatic.

I was there to pick up my daughter, and as I had coffee and cookies at a table that looked hand-hewn, my host mentioned that not so many years ago, when the winter turned bad in this part of the state, children from the country often stayed with a family in town, usually a church family, so they wouldn't miss school, and then said, "I was staying with friends in town when

I received my First Communion." I looked out the window to a broad plain green with moving crops, where tree rows rocked into the distance, and had to press my tongue against the roof of my mouth to cover the rusty circle where saliva once poured. Oh, Jerome.

"It's probably best to forget it," I say to my daughter.

"Dad!"

She's seen me angry—the element that, to her, is probably least fair: that I'm not angry, as I have been with her, over less.

"I didn't say it was easy."

"Then let them have it! Say they were lying!"

"You could spend the rest of your life doing that. Is it really the proper response?" I find it impossible to say to her, as I have before, that we are commanded to love our enemies. I try. "We're com—"

"Oh, I know," she says, and waves this aside. "These people are wrong, though. They're liars. They're perverse. Nerds!"

"Then it's best to forget about it."

"How can you do that?"

Eat shit, tempts my tongue, and I look down to a pair of hands in my lap, with raised veins and stringy cords, wrinkled as my grandfather's—mine. "It will be difficult," I finally manage to say, but she's already stomping out with that rounded rear power of a woman.

These partings. I'm surprised by emotion at the pain my passivity might bring her, considering the ways in which it permits her to be taken advantage of— No. The only hope, a covenantal hope, is for her to be so well instructed that she responds out of truth firmly rooted and numbered by verse, not nostalgia. I swivel around. Perhaps this jolt is what's needed, perhaps I've been too settled here, in this house and this phase of our lives; or am I afraid we'll have to leave soon, to atone for this time of peace—that sweeping fatalistic vision I must curb? Suddenly I'm alert. I never pull out of my anxious torpor, or semiparalysis of self-control, unless a disaster intervenes, reaffirming my apocalyptic, or fatalistic (since there's hope in apocalypse), vision of things; and in the midst of disaster I'm able to make quick decisions under the worst stress, not sure whether this is coldheartedness or an actual gift that would perfectly suit a doctor embattled against the odds in an emergency room. Until the dailiness of it paled, perhaps, or tortured me into true insanity—and then I imagine Jerome saying, "Why do you keep at it, if it bothers you so?"

"There's no hope for her if I don't, or in the life she has left."

"Plenary hope?"

I'm not sure where this has come from, and I imagine Jerome—have I imagined this? is it possible to imagine anything that experience can't fashion into an image?—I imagine him saying:

"So what's the effect of this commitment on you?"

Something about being afraid? Free? Fearing God? Obeying His— "It could be summed up in one of Dad's favorite sayings."

"Which one?"

"Be grateful for what you get and don't expect to get one thing more." I recite this in Dad's voice, and turn to Jerome from the black window of the room where our reflections shine.

"That sounds familiar," he says. "I can identify with that."

+

The monologue receives first in the District and second in the Sectional, which means the State, and the State is held on the campus where Jerome is enrolled. He has arranged for me to sleep in his dorm room on the weekend of the competition. It's pleasant living alone, but it will be good to see him, I think, and pull the cigarette from above my ear, where it's resting like a pencil, and light up. I'm driving to the contest in our car; Dad says he doesn't want to go through the tension of semifinals, and plans to bring some students down on Saturday.

I come to a complete halt at the four-way stop on Highway 136, and look at my watch; I have to register a half hour before my event, which begins at 2:00. It's now 10:30—plenty of time. I look both ways, my cigarette dangling, and wonder if the Rambler can get rubber; in the year or more that I've driven it, I've never tried.

I rev it up and pop the clutch—ah, yes!—and check in the rearview mirror to see how much I've laid, bucking as I hit the clutch for the slam into second, and the gearshift sticks. "Vas iss!" I cry, the German scientist, and pull over to the side of the road and attempt to work the lever free. It won't budge. Buildings lie down a crossroad, so I head in their direction, groaning along in low, and suffer a rush of the first fear of being late. Or worse. I press the car up to forty, and it sounds like the engine will blow. The buildings are like a mirage moving farther off, but then I pass a sign, EMDEN, and a man at a service station raises the hood and has me try to work the gearshift lever while he fiddles down below with a pry. "Nope," he says. "You can't manipulate the yoke?" I ask, something I've heard from Mr. Savitsky.

"Son, this is jammed to-hell-and-gone beyond that. What'd you do?"

Pick at it? I drive in low back to the four-way stop, and try to achieve a rational state as the smoking engine cools; about sixty miles that way to the university, at thirty miles an hour, at best, would put me there in two hours. It's close to 11:00 now. I might make it, provided the car held up. Thirty miles the other way to Pettibone, less to Forest Creek—but what then? I turn toward home.

I don't meet anybody I recognize along the way, and come rumbling down the right-hand shoulder, with cars going past like jets, into Forest Creek, and see Grandpa step from the door of his shop—Ferlin's old service station—to locate the roar I'm sending up.

I pull screeching over and scramble from behind the wheel.

"I thought you were going to that speech thing," he says.

"I was but—" I can't go into it. "Our car shift's stuck."

"What?"

"It's stuck in first! I'm late!"

He looks older and confused, and then his face is suffused with sudden energy. "Ours," he says, and takes a step in the direction of their house, then turns back. "Ach! Grandma has it!" He's out of breath, and these pivots of his, quick and jerky, have him agitated, red-faced, his throat as swollen as the day of the fire. He raises a hand and points: "Tom's!"

A '55 Pontiac convertible with a torn gray-canvas top that doesn't convert. I open our trunk for my suitcase, which I remember because of the graduation suit Dad has bought me, weeks early, to wear for the contest, and see Grandpa crawling out of Tom's car, now fired up, as I run over with the suitcase swaying. I throw it into the back seat.

"Gas, three-quarters," he pants. "You can make it."

"But I only have about an hour, and it's almost a hundred miles!"

"Drive!" he yells, his lips trembling, and points in the proper direction. I'm already spinning off, throwing gravel back at him, when he bellows *"Pray!"*

I'm hardly past the Forest Creek bridge when the needle sways to a hundred, a hotter car than I supposed an uncle would have, and then I'm afraid to check, for the concentration it takes to keep on the road. I don't slow for the four-way stop, checking in both directions as I blast through it at a hundred (a quick glance), and then feel my speed pick up as I press the accelerator into the mushy floorboard. If a cop comes? He'll have to catch me. I'm afloat, when I don't let my eyes drift to the sides, and there are hardly any cars, a help, since I don't feel safe unless I'm straddling the center line. I see a railroad crossing ahead in time, the X crossbars on posts striped with black, and do such a late zigzag check for a train I hardly notice the approach—a huge hump, I realize, as the car rises and remains aloft, airborne, and I remember Billy Gene in a pink shirt saying in the pool hall, "If your front wheels ever leave the road, man, like up over a hill when you're flyin, you better keep them babies straight aligned as you know how when you hit down, be—" I'm not sure when I hit, because my head wallops the bulging canvas above so hard I'm unconscious a second—a squalling, a wobble to the steering wheel, and then I take my foot from the brake—the final warning of Billy Gene's speech, I realize, and find myself straightening on the other side of the road, the tail end sliding forward, the center line V-ing less with each correction, and then I pour the gas to it again.

Pray? It feels constant in my freeze. Dear God, you wouldn't let me miss this, would you? The answer, if any, isn't clear, and my foot jumps in tension on the accelerator pedal. I don't let up until I'm in the neighborhood of the campus, where I slew over to a curb and yell at somebody who looks like a student, "Hey, where's 215 Illini Union?"

He points behind me and says, "Well, there's the Union."

Out the rear window of plastic, across a stretch of bright lawn, next to a rusty-stone hall, is a brick building with a white cupola that roofs a blue-faced clock; I can't read the time. I park where I am and run in and register just under the deadline, and think, as I step out of the office and lean against a wall: Okay, Grandpa, I made it.

But I have only a half hour before I go on, and the plan was to stop at Jerome's first, so he's probably worried that I never got here. I run out and grab my suitcase, then stand in the street with it; I'll have to change in a rest room, but what about the suitcase then? I get into the back seat of the car and start to undress (no makeup needed for this!), and when I get to my socks I remember Grandma Jones saying, "Always wear clean underwear and socks that match, in case, God forbid, you're in an accident and they haul you to the hospital and pull off your clothes and say, 'Ugh, what a shameful sloppy mess!' "— which has happened, I realize, although I can't recall anything but jeans and a bloody boot, and then I'm laughing so hard it feels I'm heaving my monologue into the jumbled-up suitcase.

The first contestant has begun when I step into the room— a lounge with couches and easy chairs at its edges, plus metal chairs set across it in rows. A girl in a formal is speaking in front of a white-brick fireplace, and as I sit down I have to pant to get my breath, afraid, but about to cackle. After the third speaker, a discussion begins between one of the judges and a university student, a young woman overseeing the event, and I hear her say, "He didn't respond to roll call."

"No," I say, and stand up. "But I'm here now. Here."

Who? My name is checked, and I'm allowed to step up in front of the fireplace, so anxious I rush into the speech and find I have to cross my eyes to keep from the audience the blurred countryside I'm still flying through. I pause at the sudden laughter, surprised, and receive a shock at the sight of Jerome near the back, beside a post, smiling as if I'm a stranger on TV, which is what I'm supposed to be. I'm inserted into the monologue, and play the tension of its language against a growing ease that rises from the audience. Then I'm sobbing over the toy rocket that has crashed into the carpet at my feet, aware as I've never been of my failure as a scientist, and suddenly scales tear from my shoulders with a ripping sound that I realize is applause.

I go to my chair and sit, afraid to look at Jerome.

+

There's a ticket on the car. Jerome has to run to his next class before there's a chance to talk. I straighten out my suitcase and move the car—it still runs—to another street. Late that afternoon, I watch a university student post the names of the finalists outside the office where I registered, and I turn away and sit down in a phone booth. I don't want to know. The girl who posed in front of the fireplace in her formal runs past in tears. I should call Dad. But he'll ask for the results. There are whoops and cheers from the vicinity of the office, and a contestant hurries past and punches me and cries, "Good goin, buddy!"— so easy to be magnanimous when you've won. I get up, wishing I were in disguise, and walk over to the list. My name is at the bottom.

+

Jerome is under the covers but has his pillow propped against the cement-block wall, leaning back, his hands clasped behind his head and his elbows out, and I'm on his roommate's bed in my undershorts. I've been talking so fast about my monologue and the history of how I put it together, it feels my jaw will fall off. "Mmm," he says. "Good."

Then, "It sounds like you've been a sedulous worker."

"Sedulous, huh? Well, now one judge says it would be 'helpful if the contestant established more eye contact.' I told you I had to hold everybody off so I could get through it, after that drive. And the other guy says, 'Can this broad German accent perhaps be interpreted as prejudicial parody of all such dedicated scientists as Wernher von Braun?' Good God, I'm— I mean, *we're* German. At least part."

"Right," he says, and reaches up and hits the light switch

above his pillow. A boulevard of streetlamps, out the window that occupies one half of the far wall, sparkles like the sight of my name on that list, and I feel I've seen these rows of light before. "I think you ought to get some rest now, though. Tomorrow's going to roll around mighty fast."

"I'd like to know why Original Monologue is scheduled at such an ungodly hour—nine. I mean, I'm lousy in the morning. I won't have eye contact due to the sleep gluing them both shut. Sheesh!"

"Sleep, then. I have an eight o'clock. I'll wake you in time."

Images of other contests, and then the girl in the formal at the fireplace, enfold me like covers pulling tighter than the ones I roll beneath, and with an awakening jolt I see the Pontiac, huge and slowed, climb into its leap above the tracks. I turn to the cement blocks, yellow-green from the outside lamps, and run a finger down a mortar joint—a nice job of pointing, nearly as good as Kev, I think, and see Kev in the distance, whistling under his breath while I mix mortar in a mud box for the bricks he's laying on a new house, then picture him at the brick upright, which gives me a surge of energy sufficient to last a day. I sit on the edge of the bed, dizzy, and step over and open the door: slash ablaze, a hall I enter. The dorm is rectangular, four stories, with a courtyard in the center, this hall circumscribing it, and only a pair of swinging fire doors at the center of each long side—an indoor track. I take off in a trot, figuring fatigue will help me sleep, and after a circuit I start to run at top speed, slowing only for corners, and taking the double doors at full stride, finally feeling shortness of breath when I head down Jerome's side on the next lap. Then a head pokes out an open door in the distance, and I slow with slapping feet, and stop: a stranger with mussed hair and chunky glasses that magnify blood-speckled eyes. "What's this?" he asks.

"Well, you see—" Now I'm out of breath. "Well, whew! my brother lives down there, see, and I'm in this speech contest event that—"

"What?"

"Right, the State speech contest. You see, I was—"

"I don't care if you're the friggin Easter bunny! You can't

do this with people trying to sleep. Quiet hours start at ten. It's 2 a.m.!"

"Gee, I'm really sorry, I—" I'm panting. "You see, I—"

"Oh, for God's sake, shut it off! Go to sleep!" He slams the door.

+

In the morning, I walk to the fireplace with fewer in the room, groggy from the faces that assaulted me with such cumbered wakefulness last night I was never sure I slept until Jerome shook me and said, "It's time." I'm the last contestant, and I've been nodding off. Modify the accent, maybe? There's a single judge for the finals, sitting in shirtsleeves at a small table, looking skeptical, and I let him bear the brunt of my eye contact as the monologue rattles in its rhythms to the end.

Again Jerome has arrived, I see as I finish; he's at the back of the room, and starts the applause, which has a scratchy lag.

"Great!" he says, and hugs me with the arm that isn't holding books as people file out.

"Great? I didn't think they were even going to clap."

"They were so moved, they were so surprised, so taken aback—"

"Oh, come off it."

"Really!" In the sunlit room his eyes have a glint as bright as his glasses, on whose lenses windows lie reflected like sidewise ladders. "You overwhelmed them folk! Or, well, whelmed them, anyhow, ay?"

+

At an auditorium on the campus, where the awards program is held, Dad arrives with every student who's competed in anything, it appears, plus Grandma. I sit at the edge of our group, near a wall of the auditorium, next to Jerome, and keep sliding down in my padded velvet seat, like the best of the ones at the Lamar— closed now because of television, I think with a pang. There are six finalists in each event and the names of the five who have placed are called off at a microphone by a master of ceremonies, sending up whoops from the audience. These five then file through a door to a wing of the stage, and their places are read off, beginning with fifth. "A poor man's Academy Awards," Dad whispers to us behind his hand. Each winner has to perform his speech, or read her poem—a lengthy process that sets those endless electronic worms in action, vibrating from their home in my stomach up into my wrists.

A slinky man in black glasses, with earphones on, is in the orchestra pit, in a wooden chair, hunched over a tape recorder, and as each performer begins he sets the reels revolving and I focus on them, to hypnotize myself. Please, I pray, let it end. A fifth, that's enough, for Dad, so our school will be listed in the results, and— The man at the microphone has announced another category and I hear my name.

"See," Jerome says, under the attempts of our group to cheer like the gatherings from cities. "I told you!"

I stand and my eyes roll down the aisle into the orchestra pit. Feet? I'm up a set of steps, so certain that the swaying of a curtain is me swaying that it's difficult to stand straight. The white-haired man at the microphone, under a spotlight, is like a pulsing star with feet. Two of our group have walked out to him. Another. Holy shit, I think, and almost do in the Robert Hall suit Dad has bought ahead of graduation, am I in the wrong bunch? Second place is announced and I still remain, or my heart does, ending in an explosion above my belt. My arms are absent or frozen. I shake and flex them to find if they work, and now I'm supposed to give a speech I wrote a year ago? A brittle clatter like a shelling begins as the pale star recedes from the microphone. My timing is off, I realize, as the reels on the recorder below spin like platters on a speeded-up phonograph, the man in black earmuffs grinning up. I wade through a molasses of words that hinder my speech, eyes at my nose tip, about to start bucking over a toilet bowl—unable to catch up to the beginning I've already lost.

And by some process I can't reclaim, I'm in the lighted auditorium, walking up the aisle toward our group, a pin in a gold box numbing my hand, and then arms rise. They're standing. Dad is down in his seat still, glasses up on his forehead, a hand over his face, and Jerome shakes both fists. I've lost half my brain, I feel, and when I start to sit Grandma reaches over and grabs an arm so hard I have to take hold of the back of her seat so I don't fall. She pulls me down to where she can grip my neck and presses my face against chilled cheeks and kisses me on the lips—with strangers here!—and then slides her mouth along my cheek to an ear; a harsh whisper: "I wish I was your mother, not me!"

+

Our class has organized a drama club, and the speaker at our first banquet is the county superintendent. He's also a preacher and a popular after-dinner speaker, and we're fortunate to have him, we feel, seated with Dad and other faculty members at the speaker's table. Except for sideburns and a bit of silver fringe above his ears, his broad head is entirely bald, and tapered at its top to a ridge that reflects light off both sides as he turns to people at the table to talk. It's rumored that when he hears of a student who has become involved in delinquency, he befriends him and takes him along on his speaking tours, and tries to convert him, an apparently shameful process I've been spared in the Catholic Church. One such student, who has appeared in juvenile court—from our class, in fact—is at the end of the speaker's table, in an ill-fitting suit jacket, stirring his food as he stares at his plate.

The superintendent begins his talk with jokes that nobody seems to have heard; or I haven't, in my research, and people laugh and loosen up. Then he tucks in his chin against his tie—a radio announcer's voice—and looks up out of pale eyes as he mentions something from the Scriptures: a parable? My mind goes off, and I picture myself receiving the year-end award, from my accumulated points . . . A microphone? It seems the man is speaking into one connected to my hearing. His eyes are on me, high in his bald skull, staring from under bushy eyebrows as he holds his chin against his shirt. I can't unhook myself, and hear him mention a man who worked on a painting for years, toward the end of his life. "There were brilliant colors in it, in hues that people had never seen, but what caught the attention of everyone was his use of red. The painting grew in dimension and brilliance and the red continued to stand out in an unearthly way. It was then that the painter's friends noticed that his health was failing. They urged him to stop, and take the rest he so clearly needed, but he could not or would not, and never once left his painting. His cleaning lady came in early one morning and found him at his easel, dead. Those who knew him weren't surprised. They'd somehow expected this. He couldn't have gone on the way he was, at his age, they said, and lived. Yet they were hesitant to step into the garret where he had worked; his painting was that overpowering.

"It was his masterwork, there was no doubt about it, but it was the quality of color—never seen by anyone before—which held them in awe. Then it was discovered that he had been painting with his own blood."

He tucks in his chin, his eyes still on me, and his left eyebrow tips like a wand. "Students, it is this kind of dedication that I call you to. We are given specific, individual gifts, each of us, which we are to exercise stewardship over. These gifts are given by God as surely as those inalienable rights, mentioned in our Constitution, derive from Him. The world might say there's more to it than this, or more to be made at another occupation, but we recognize in our hearts whether an occupation suits our gifts or not. To disregard these gifts is in a way to disregard Him, whatever our outcome might be. The painter I spoke of died in poverty. It was only then that his friends noticed he'd long ago run out of materials to paint with—all materials, that is, but one: his life's blood. He died in poverty, but surely he ended in joy. Not one drop of his blood was shed in vain. His masterwork stands to this day.

"Now, all of you have special gifts that are quite evident as we gather tonight in celebration of them. But I say this, for the benefit of that one person who is perhaps not making full use of his talents—another name for the gifts distributed to us." He pauses and holds up an index finger: "I say this for that person, and I say, 'Trust in the Lord with all thine heart, and lean not on thine own understanding!'"

I feel set down in my wheelchair on the driveway, where the last of warm fall sunlight lies in gauntlets over my arms as leaves start down and scatter across the triangular park in stylized streaks of rain, and I experience again the tumbling downward into darkness, to that place where I come to rest, on a solid plateau, alive, and then I see my hand move from the armrest of the wheelchair to my college application and change my choice of curriculum from Pre-Med to Speech and Theater, and then, in a more practical afterthought, change this to a category in the catalogue that attracted me: Teacher Training for Speech.

"I've hidden, I think," I say.

"How do you mean?" She's in a chair facing mine, and now she crosses her hands in the lap of her skirt, as if she intends to touch opposite knees—a real *femme*, as Purkeet would say—then shakes back her heavy blond hair. It's rough and uncombed, gilded by late-afternoon light from the window behind (beyond her are pale trembling leaves), and whenever she punishes its loops and strands with parted fingers, or scratches at it, I feel she's trying to cast it off. Does her job as counselor cause this, or tire her so much? There are violet streaks under her eyes that sometimes spread to the hollows of her cheeks as we talk. This is our third meeting; the psychological part of my entrance exam suggested I see a counselor—that is, this is required.

"I hide behind times I misrepresent." I'm making this up.

"How do you mean?"

"I pretend they were good once they're gone."

A hand is to her hair, digging in it, then tossing it back toward the leaves. A falling, or feeling of fullness present in me lately, deepens, as if I'm neglecting the single matter that needs attention, which I can never define. I say, "I think it's my mother. Her death. At that age. I—" My hands start up, and I stare at them as if unable to speak, knowing I can arouse her sympathy with this.

"Yes, loss," she says, and sighs. "I'm afraid we have to end our session for today, Charles." She rises and goes to the coatrack, the only furniture in the room besides a bookshelf and our chairs, and takes her long, unfashionable coat, like an old woman's, and shrugs it on.

"I'll give you a ride to campus, if you like."

I'd like to take her in my arms and kiss her tired mouth. The way she stares at me, and then relaxes on one leg, I'm sure I could. But we seem to turn in circles toward the hallway, and then we're outside, in her car. I ask her to drop me off at the library (she's concerned about my study habits), and the deep fall sky is darkening by the time she pulls into the shade of the twelve-story building: winter soon.

"I realize how wrenching this might be," she says, staring out the windshield. "I can't be your mother, even if I wanted to. You'll be okay." A hand comes off the steering wheel, as if she'll reassure me by touching my thigh, but then she grips the wheel and turns to me with a troubled stare. "Look, I'm willing to call next week our last visit, if you'll show up on time."

I get out and slam the door. I won't be there, I realize. Does she? I walk in and out of the library and sit on its steps, then on a stub stone post at the edge of the walk, linked to others by swags of chain—a child again, unwanted except by the dean. The neglected matter presses me into the pediment. It's not my classes, or Purkeet. At the end of the State speech contest, the finalists lined up onstage for a photograph, and I saw Jerome at the apron, with his elbows up on it, and reached down as he reached up, to haul him aboard, but instead he gave my hand a hard shake. "Well, you made the big time," he said. A fellow behind him, with thick pursed lips and a red shaving irritation, rolled his eyes, and appeared to be kneeing the back of Jerome's knees with a gentle rocking of his weight. "Oh," Jerome said, and ushered him up. "This is Rick Purkeet. He lives next door in the dorm. He was in that play with me. Rick, this—" Purkeet waved Jerome away. "Please," he said. "I feel I know him already. This guy is fabulous. He ought to be working for WILL—the radio station that was recording this. Hey, I'll get you a job, guy."

A football player lopes past where I sit, and I recall saying once to Jerome, "Do you think smoking might have affected our growth?" and he said, "We'll never know now." He has switched to pre-med, as I expected, and for the first time I recognize, as clearly as if it's Jerome who has loped past, that we've taken each other's path. I haven't acknowledged this, stupidly, until now; and on those days when he ministered to Dad and me after the hospital, or the night I passed him the cigarette, when he gave up speech and theater for medicine (knowing I needed the freedom he was seeking more than he did?), I missed it. Our paths have not only crossed; they're traveling in opposite directions.

Still the pressure remains, as if it's rendered me blind to this but doesn't alleviate it. Rooted here. Hungry. But I won't go back to the dorm, where a student with no arms will be using his feet to eat with, and Jerome will be in our room studying chemistry or physiology toward his five-point, while the pile driver preparing the basement of the new dormitory next door keeps going ka-*lang*, ka-*lang*, ka-*lang* until it's dark. Hold me here, I want to say to the counselor, and then I see, above the campus elms, the first stars send down lancelike beams.

+

Purkeet's roommate, a senior, is away on weekends—"after the whores in Danville," Purkeet says one night when he invites me to a party, and I walk into a dark room, with only Purkeet there. "What's your pleasure, mate?" he asks in a voice like Popeye's, narrowing one eye.

"Isn't that illegal," I ask, nodding at the liquor on his desk.

"Oh, I slip the floor director a five every other week for the privilege. I'm a senior. We theater people have a way about us."

I refuse a drink, and go back to our room uneasy about the way he's said, "I lost my mommy when I was your age, too, you know."

+

"I've found the most fantastic word!" Jerome says, with the exuberance that irritates me. He takes two steps to his desk, behind mine (we study back to back), drops his books on it, and turns and sits on its top.

"Okay," I say, and shove my psychology text aside. "What?"

"S-O-U-G-H, pronounced 'suff.' The sound of trees. 'A sough of southerly wind in the uppermost boughs.' Bee-*you*-tee-full, no?"

"Not bad," I say, and blush, thinking of the time when I asked Purkeet what *sudo* meant, since everybody in rhetoric class was saying *sudo* this and *sudo* that, and I couldn't find it in the dictionary. "Because it's P-S-E-U-D-O, you fool," Purkeet said. "But how dear! You probably have no concept of it. You're straight you! Deception doesn't enter your makeup, or those beady little eyes. Oh, you!"

That night, as Jerome and I lie in our beds under the covers with the lights out, I picture us here the night of the speech contest, before I was a student, and think I hear him say "sough" again and ask, "What?"

"It's tough."

"What is?"

"Another way to state it would be: It's easier to think if you don't have to put it in words."

+

Purkeet says, "My father used to tell me, before he turned suspect, that all you could do with a woman was love her, and hope she loved you. You couldn't even think of a woman being faithful, he said—but he might have picked that up from the other woman, my stepmom."

"He turned suspect?"

"By marrying her. After only a year. I didn't like her, and still don't, to tell you a secret you might have surmised. I never trusted him after that. He was away a lot, filming for TV, and I had to stay at home and put up with her, a real bitch. *Steaming.* One summer I was his schlep when Mommy wanted me out of the house. I learned I liked the lights and excitement and theatrical ambience. Milieu."

"Schlep?"

"I toted his suitcases of cameras and equipment. Ed Murrow was always there saying 'Hup! Hup!' and combing his eyebrows. 'Tonight we visit a family in East Wooster, Mass.,' " he says, exactly like Edward R. Murrow, and when I laugh he puts a hand, tentative, on my shoulder. "Did your dad remarry?"

"No."

"Lucky boy, saved that bitchery!" He takes my hand in both of his and kisses it.

Jerome is studying when I return to our room, with an amber innocence out of childhood on his face from his lamp as he turns to me with blurred eyes. "Oh, hi," he says. "Did you have a good talk with Rick?"

+

This pressure of the neglected task I can't define. On the way to a class, with my hands in the pockets of my trench coat, and gripping each other through its material as if I have to hang on to keep from coming apart, I push through a gap in a hedge, my face down, and out the other side almost run into a black convertible. It accelerates, and a man above me, hardly an arm's length away, sitting on the tonneau above the back seat, puts a hand up in panic over his face. Then smiles, relieved, and leans to speak to somebody in the seat below him, his pinstriped jacket bowing across his shoulders, and the afterimage of his smile registers on me: the Democratic candidate for President, John F. Kennedy.

+

"Okay, go to the office of your college and ask for Dean Richel," Purkeet says. "He'll be wearing these cute little half eyeglasses, and he'll check you out over their tops. Tell him this counselor, this messy broad, is bothering you. Describe her. Say you don't need counseling anyhow. Tell him it's just that you're a lonely boy in this big world. Act sad. When you get up to walk out, swing your ass a bit."

I enact an approximation of this for the dean, and in a week I receive notice that I won't have to see the counselor again.

+

The television room is filled for the final Kennedy–Nixon debate. Kennedy's jaunty staccato returns me to the moment I stepped through the hedge and his hand went up (a memory I shy from when I picture his fear), and I recognize, from his jauntiness, why he was accused of printing up a flyer, a picture of Richard Nixon with his heavy beard and jowly evasive look, with the caption underneath: "Would you buy a used car from this man?" The caption could go under Nixon at the end of the debate, he looks so unwell, and I know Kennedy will be our next President.

Mike Rosen, the only pre-med on our floor besides Jerome, turns off the television and flops back in his chair to a hiss of escaping air from its cushion. "He can't be elected," he says.

"Why?" Neal Pritzger asks, and Jerome leans back into darkness; Neal is Jerome's friend, a mechanical engineer with carroty-red, crewcut hair, who usually has a slide rule banging in a case at his belt. They met in a rhetoric class, and Neal keeps saying to Jerome with a grin, "All animals are equal but some animals are more equal than others, right, Jay?"

"He'll listen to the Pope," Rosen says. "The Pope'll run the country."

"Haven't you heard what Kennedy said when—"

"Oh, hell, you can't believe a politician. Or a Catholic."

"Hey," several people say at once.

Purkeet turns to me with a questioning look, then scuffs with his knuckles at his curly widow's peak. The discussion moves to religion, and then to Christ; just the mention of His name angers Rosen, whose girlish face goes red. "Jesus Christ is a myth," he says. "He was invented by a bunch of Jews that went nuts!"

"Did you ever read Josephus?" Neal asks.

"He was probably paid to lie like the rest of them. Jesus Christ was about as much the Messiah as my big toe. He didn't even own a donkey. Anybody who'd say 'I am God' has got to be insane."

"That's your opinion," Neal says.

"Right, Pritzger, my medical one. Shit, he was in debtors' prison till he was thirty and it warped his mind. He got delusions of grandeur. They finally caught up with him, and he got what he deserved. Then some crazy Jews in his cult snuck his dead body out of the tomb."

"That's what Matthew says you'll say!" Neal insists. He's angry, but I don't hear any more; Purkeet is studying me with solemn eyes, and then Jerome, who's been sitting back in silence, stands up and leaves.

+

"So?" Purkeet says. "How'd you hear about Jews in your church?"

"In the reading of the Gospel."

"There wasn't ever a sermon about them?"

"No. There was a song they sang at Lent, in one church we went to, with a line 'While soldiers scoff and Jews deride.' "

"See."

"But I didn't think Jews were any more real than Roman soldiers or Pharisees. There aren't any of those around, are there?"

"Well . . ."

"Maybe in the way you'd call somebody a Pharisee, true."

"Didn't you ever call anybody a Jew? Or say 'Jew-boy' or 'kike'?"

"No."

"What are you, Swedish? Scandinavian?"

"Partly."

"Not German."

"Some."

"Oy vay."

"I'm sorry."

"You can't help it! Don't always be saying you're sorry—just like an old Cherman! So that's why your brother is studying German, huh?"

"Why are you?"

"It's supposed to be easy for me, like Yiddish. Six semesters and I'm still trying to finish! Are you going to take it?"

"Not if they pay me."

He hugs my neck. "You're a loyal little squirt, aren't you?"

+

Purkeet and I do a reading of T. S. Eliot ("And three trees on the low sky," I intone, and he says afterward, "You know something, Cholly, that I don't") on WILL, and perform in radio plays together. Until the week when I'm given the lead in a version of "The Telltale Heart"—too large a role too soon, with speeches pages long. Purkeet is the old man I murder, and my last line, "It's the beating of his hideous heart!" comes out in such a screech it causes him and the director, the slinky man in black glasses who ran the tape recorder, to laugh out loud ("We'll leave it," he says. "It's eerie"), and from that time, whenever Purkeet wants to indicate that something is especially awful, he clutches his chest and cries, in the squeaky voice that came from me, " 'It. is. the.'—watch the vocal periods, Cholly— 'beating! of hi-is hideous! *haart!*' "

+

"Look with pity upon this medical guinea pig for a Yiddishe surgeon. I was eleven when my mother, God rest her, went to sing with the angels—I talk this way so I can take it, understand?—and in a few months my dad took me to this evil-minded little man with a scheme to further free the Jews. He would chop off their noses. As if I wasn't traumatized enough by my schnozz! Later, I figured it was Dad's wedding gift for Stepmom, so she wouldn't have to live with a grotesque. So Doc chiseled mine down to this ski snoot. 'Ve dunt have da procedure, quite,' he would say, when he took me around to plastic-surgeon conventions, which he did—his proud little product. They'd run their fingers down the bridge here, looking at Doc's pics of before and after, and—"

He takes my hand in his, bends out a finger, and runs it down his nose. "See? Feel the bumps and knobs on it? Chips. He was picking chips out for a year afterward. Dr. Gruesome didn't sharpen his chisel so well that day; now they turn the Skokie girls loose in an hour. A salutary gent. He made me a shiksa. You wouldn't know about my dark Semitic roots if I hadn't told you, would you? Nobody does. Except members of the tribe, with bumpy bridges of their own. I pass.

"I think it's the nose job that got me off— Hammered

on like that right after she died, you know. Then Dad married to this harridan who was never a Yiddishe mama to me. 'Oh, mein Pa-pa,' " he sings in a falsetto. " 'So gen-tile, so a-dorable!' She ran a tighter ship than any Swiss. Neo-Nazi? Oh, she'll forgive me. She's forgiven me all my foibles—grudgingly, grudgingly, over long grudging years, until they've all gone away. Except the one she can't get rid of."

I know he wants me to ask what, and when I don't, he looks away.

"I would say she has a strong suspicion. A good sense of smell. Suddenly I was an acceptable beauty, and old enough to go out on my own, so I'd go to Lincoln Park and say, 'Hey, mistah! wanna rub my nose?' And this obscure, unseemly, quaint and curious, gaunt old bird of yore—if you get the idea—yet somehow courtly vagabond, well, wino or *tramp*, he'd say"—his roughest voice—" 'Naw, little fella'—oh, how they like little boys!—'but I bet you got sumpin else I'd like to rub, a heh heh.' "

"Please. I know you couldn't stand that."

"Stand? Oh, you should have seen me, down on my knees in a dirty, crappy stall, where a cop might walk in, working away at something that wasn't washed in maybe a week, holding my new nose like this with one hand and with the other also playing the bagpipes, and looking up out of my big baby-blue eyes to see if he'd knife me. Afterward."

He takes hold of me and then pushes away, shaking, and covers his face with his hands. "Oh, I was a go-getter! From the start! Oh, God, Cholly, please let me have you!"

+

Over Thanksgiving vacation, at home, Dad ushers me to the other side of the house, sits me down, and then sits across from me, sucking noisily on an empty pipe. "You once asked me why we moved to Illinois," he says.

I can't remember ever asking him this.

"I suppose your mother wondered why we moved, too, I've thought since you asked. I always saw the move as the next step in our plans. When Grandpa and Grandma and the rest of the family moved to Illinois, in '38, your mother and I moved here, too, you know. Then a friend in North Dakota found a teaching job for me in Hyatt, and since jobs were scarce, we went there for the year. We stayed on. I kept trying to find a way back and maybe she, in her way, kept settling in more. If you wanted to be psychological about it, I suppose you could say it was part of the general unrest at the time. The end of the twenties, and then the Second World War, had undone so much of what we thought was normal, or what we had grown up with, that there was a sense of wanting to consolidate, or recoup some of the losses, and establish old bonds again. I wanted to be close to your grandma and grandpa, for that reason. I thought your mother did, too. Now I don't know."

+

"I missed you," Purkeet says. "You and your beady little eyes. Oh, the way your tush sticks out like a Wa-Watusi's, whoo!"

"It probably happened on one of my falls."

"Falls?"

"From high up down to the ground. Or on the original one."

"The first time you stood up to waddle to Daddy?"

"With Adam. In Original Sin."

"You know, not everybody appreciates your humor. You throw people off, because you never smile. Laugh, yes, but never smile. People expect a joker to have a devilish, witty grin, no?"

"So what's there to smile about?"

"Ah, sweetie, you're a Yiddishe baby after all!"

+

Semester's end: the basement of a campus beer hall where Jerome and Neal and I have gone is so crowded that any movement causes other bodies to jar like molecules, and now the collision of them rocks back and forth with the song everybody is singing—"My eyes are blind, I cannot see ee ee, I have *hey!* not *ho!* brought my specs with me!" Jerome has found a table and sits wedged against a wall, staring down his nose through his pushed-down glasses from red-rimmed eyes, as if the song is meant for him, and now he wipes a knuckle under an eye. About his 4.5, although all he does is study? The shouted singing rocks the basement, or the bodies rock, and suddenly my stomach feels injected with yeast. I find the stairs and crawl up them, swallowing back explosions of foam, and see, at the top, a door partly open, and taste cold air. I butt it wide with my head and crawl out into falling snow and start bucking like a mounted dog and see on the snow, in a slab of light from behind, the blood-red wieners and slimy beans Jerome and I woke to in another light, humping me up further, with a force that will have me gargling my balls if this keeps up, and then I realize I cannot drink again, ever. Must not.

+

At home, at Christmas, all is calm, all is bright, and one evening Dad turns off the television and the three of us sit in the silence of winter. Then he says, "I've never rejoiced over anybody's death. I know what death is, and what it can do to a family. But I must admit I didn't feel much remorse when Ed Finley, the dry-goods-store owner, died last week, after the grief he gave your mother about that pair of shoes."

I move our typewriter, the one Dad gave us both for graduation, out to the landing of the stairwell, so I won't keep Jerome awake, and sit cross-legged at it on the floor. In a letter today Dad mentioned another death: the county superintendent. "Is there something you can do?" he wrote, and I saw the boys in our garage, from the height where we once watched, clang the old bell and track a circle of orange footprints. I sense the bell swinging in a rhythm I have to match to this memorial, as I've called it, and letters clatter onto the paper in a ragged order.

i
Just that the day was cold, a chilled day,
Or that the wings of birds
Stiffened, feathers crisp in the wind, beaks
Empaled in frosty breath, just
Permanently, this. The rest will remain,
However vivid, impermanent as an icicle sword.

How many days the same bell tolls
Orange with rust in the shrouded garage,
Belling out its same chill sound, will these

Boys stop, hold their breath in resistance,
Shut their ears to its sound?

Silence in the stairwell that's become the garage with beds in it.

ii
Just that these boys, our boys, fear the
Ordered chill of steel
Sealing the bell's orange mouth, fear the
Energy of ice and rust, the engagement of
Pallor with fire; just that they fear and that
He did not, that is much to remember.

The irregular rattle of the typewriter echoing flatly in the stairwell joins a sliding grit of feet climbing up the stairs.

How many days from a season's death,
Orange of autumn, green of spring, will the
Breath of its going catch in our lungs; and we,
Breathing a picture of its presence on glass,
Suddenly remember how frost will melt.

Purkeet's curly head appears through the bars of the stair rail at my side, rising, and then he turns and comes up the final flight, smiling his slight covert smile of affection. "Busy boy, huh?" he says. "I thought I heard a beaver up here."

"Beaver?" I say, and turn back to the typewriter. "Scared?"

He comes across the landing and stands behind where I sit—uncomfortable, conscious of my crossed legs starting to cramp—then leans his knees into my back. "Don't," I say.

"Scared? That somebody will see?"

"I'm busy."

"You're touchy." There's a silence as he reads the page I'm marking with a ballpoint. "Who's this? Me?"

I pale, I'm sure, from a sensation like the downward slide of blood.

"Is this me?"

"He gave a speech when I graduated. It changed my mind. I mean, about what I finally decided to go into in school."

"So you've taken up with the nice old auntie?"

"He just died of cancer."

"I'm sorry. Really."

iii   three thocks

Just that the season's

"I can't finish with you standing here."

"Okay," he says. There's a gritty sound of a pivot and I turn to see him stepping high, swinging his butt and banging it with a book as he sings, "Keep up that rhy-thm and I'll dance for you!"

bell has rung

Over the crust of
Snow and caught in ridges and pools of ice,
Every flake and crystal filled; and that the crystals,
Pools, will melt in spring and send flowers and grain
Hurtling through soil. For that we will never forget.

How many days we live in the
Orbit of the moon, we never know,
But hope for the calendar till the day we
Break. Then, eyes to the stars, we will, perhaps,
See them as crystals we lost one day in January.

+

Jerome and his friend Neal attend the intramural fencing matches—a clashing of foils and handguards in the brassy light from the high windows of Men's Old Gym—and seem surprised when I work my way into the semifinals. They move to the front of the crowd at the central piste. My tumbling background helps, along with the skills picked up in fencing class, besides a vocal roar I've developed to accompany my flèche—sometimes merely a roar to throw my opponent off, followed by a quick thrust under his guard. If I can't run as fast as I once could, I can still move fast. I'm sweating behind the screened beehive of my mask as I take on my next-to-last opponent, a skinny, squarish redhead, and with my first touch Neal jumps as if I've stabbed him.

What's this? Then Jerome steps back, and my equilibrium goes as if he's removed his support, a deserter, and it occurs to me that he knows about Purkeet. Does he imagine I'm a fag? I've been quiet so far into the match, and prepare to bawl into my noisy flèche, when the redhead performs a mirror image of it, roaring, and scores a touch on me. Back down the piste, and then a quick jab from this squarish ungainly rooster that the referee calls a touch. It has slid past under my armpit.

"Hey!" Jerome cries, to the referee, I assume, but the cry affects my timing so badly I'm touched again: three. "Dammit!" I say, and tear off my mask and throw it on the floor. I walk over to them with my foil up, shaking its tip; Neal's face is red-pink to his carroty hair, and Jerome raises a hand as if he expects me to run him through.

"What is this?" I say. "What are you up to? Do you realize you probably lost this championship for me?"

+

Purkeet buys a blue convertible a few years old. "Why?" I ask.

"I've always wanted to use the last of my bar-mitzvah money on sweet number one, and I had to reward myself for passing German. My instructor says I will. I can graduate. Home free."

"Why didn't you take me along?"

"My roomie's a whiz with automobiles."

"I know something about cars. I could have helped you."

"He's great when it comes to mechanics. He said it's sound as sound can be." Purkeet knocks on his closet door.

"Why did you have to get it right away?"

"I couldn't wait to reward myself, and roomie tells me the flyboys from Rantoul have been flocking into the bars in his part of Danville."

"You bastard."

"Beware, my lord—"

He holds up a hand for one of our routines, a shared

imitation of a bad actor, and I say: "—the green-eyed monster—"

"—*Jealousy!*" he cries.

"Okay, you got me there."

+

One Sunday Neal comes into our room after lunch, and wonders
why I haven't been to Mass. "What are you," I ask, "the priest?"
And then Neal, the pious sort of fellow who probably once
considered the priesthood, goes on to Jerome about how the
monsignor on campus has managed to buy a new Cadillac again
this year, in spite of all the problems in the world, and I decide
to quit going to church for good.

+

Dad arrives the next Sunday, as if alerted. "It just struck me to
drive down," he says, spinning the car keys on an index finger,
uneasy.

"Jerome's somewhere in the library," I say, "studying for
finals."

"Well, can't we talk?" His easy smile disarms me. We're in
a parking lot beside the dorm, on a giving melt of tar. It's a hot
spring day, and the reflections off cars present an image of a
closed space with bars of light burning through. Dad runs a
finger under his glasses, as if to catch a tear, and I see a
snakeskin shimmer in his watery eyes, set deeper in their sockets,
as if to say *This is killing me.*

"I suppose you heard that Davey got married," he says.

"Married!"

"He was back from the seminary, you know, putting off his
ordination. He spent a couple restless months at home. The
next thing I knew, he was dating Junie, or Rosa, as she calls
herself now—her real name, I guess—Rosa Sisco. They were
married last week."

"Good afternoon, Charles." It's Purkeet, using his cultivated
upperclassman voice. He remains a ways off, in a tentative
stance, as if he'll retreat in shame from the ruses he employs.
"Is this your dad?"

"We just had lunch." As though this would explain things. I stare at my shoes to signify he should leave.

"Mr. Neumiller, I'm Rick Purkeet. Charles admires you a lot." This hokey normalcy is what Purkeet would call the social graces.

Dad steps over and takes his hand. "Rick, I'm pleased to meet you." He looks pleased, although there's a bleached grip at the center of his face as if a flashbulb has gone off. His smile is so easygoing he can't suspect anything, I figure, and a strand of hair falls onto his forehead with the firmness of his handshake. "Charles has mentioned you."

"I hope he wasn't too unsparing."

"Oh, no. He appreciates how you've helped him, or shown him the ropes, at the theater and radio station. I've heard you on the radio."

"Oh, good," Purkeet says, and gives a breathy, clucking laugh of blushing pleasure. It means this much to him to hear about himself? "Well, now *I've* got to eat." He places both hands, spread wide, over his shirt, and then appears to catch himself; he waves. "See you."

Dad, whose face is grayed by a further effect of the light, watches over my head as he walks off, and says, "He seems a fine young fellow."

+

Later, when Dad is leaving, Purkeet follows us out and stands at my side instead of Jerome, who is studying still. As I watch Dad go across the blacktop toward the Rambler whose transmission I once ruined, I'm so upset by his ingenuousness and the way I've aged beyond it (so that it seems we'll never coincide again in the present), I almost run after him.

"He reminds me of a Sabra," Purkeet says in his room. "You've got a honey of an old man there." He grabs my arms and kisses me on the mouth, and in my guilt I hardly resist— though I know that if there was ever a chance that he could have me, it's gone now, as surely as I know that the streak like blood running down my chin is his saliva.

+

I've only sipped at his liquor before, but this Saturday, as I spill out angry swatches about my mother, I drink too much. I kneel on the floor with my head on his cot, my arms out, and cry, "I don't want to live! I can't stand it!"

"Hush, your brother will hear you."

"I'm sick! You've done this stuff to me!"

"I've never forced anything on you."

"Bullshit! You get me drinking and start acting lonely, then try to pull this kissy-face shit and I—I'm embarrassed for you!"

"That's not true. Be quiet."

"I'm not going to! I'm going to do every damn thing you tell me not to!" I'm on my feet, in my fencing stance, and then I swing to the side of him and sock his closet door.

"Stop this!" He has his hands on my shoulders, shaking me so hard my vision blurs. "You'll have to leave. I'll never ask you back."

"Good!" I say, and in a half-dive I slam my head into his door.

"Charles, *please*." His voice is so shaky I realize I can't see. "Let's get some fresh air. I'll take you for a ride."

"I'm not going to ride in your buggermobile!"

I take hold of the doorknob and with a twist of my butt send him stumbling backward, jerk open the door, and step into a tilting hall, where bars and yellow globes of lights resound. "Buggermobile!" I cry, and feel the echo rush from the ends of the hall to clap at my face.

"Quiet hours!" somebody yells from inside a room.

Something leaps over me, blocking the light, and I paw at it: my trench coat. "Ass!" I yell, and get it off, down on the floor. Somebody grabs an arm and spins me—Purkeet. He squeezes my shoulders and shakes me, furious. "You shit!" he whispers. "Another word and I'll kill you!"

A door at my side opens: Jerome, wiry bed-sheet wrinkles imprinted in a cheek, his glasses off, in an old T-shirt and bluejeans, barefoot, his eyes out of focus and as pouched and watery as Dad's.

"He's had two too many," Purkeet says, and tries to get a sleeve of the trench coat up my arm. I slap at him and waddle off balance. "I thought it would help if he got some fresh air."

"Liar!" I say.

"Quiet hours!"

("I'll kill you.")

"You okay?" Jerome asks. His face bows and bleeds into rivulets as I open my mouth and hear a bellow echo back. "I didn't want to do that crap!"

"Yeah, heh heh, I shouldn't have bought him that last drink," Purkeet says, fiddling with the coat again. A sleeve slides up my arm.

"That's not it!" I say, trying to shake it off.

"Shhhh. We'll get you some fresh air."

The other sleeve slides up, and Jerome takes that arm; my ribs lift and strain to ease my stomach, and when I take his hand, it's trembling. "You're overworked or something," he says. They hold my arms too hard, like policemen, fingertips digging in, as they lead me down the hall on floating feet. "I'm going," I say, as they stop somewhere. Sliding doors roll closed, and my legs give as an elevator falls. The stench on my breath is a hole my consciousness clings to. A clatter of doors, fingers pinching my arms again, and I'm in dark night. They whisper above me as if standing on a column that the pile driver has slammed to the bottom of the basement next door, ka-*lang*, urgent, and then Jerome holds me, alone, one arm around my back, and the night opens like a door swung wide on snow— stars frozen in blurred formations.

"Something is crazy," I say.

"School?"

This wakes me up. "What did I say?"

"It's making you crazy."

Those are Jerome's bare toes on concrete. "What?" I ask, and gag.

"You were upset."

I try to stand straight, and remove his arm, but he won't let go. "Where's Purkeet?"

"He went to get his car. He's taking you for a ride. You'll feel better once you get away from here. The end of the first year's the worst. You're *all right*." He shakes me. There's a crunching of gravel and Purkeet's convertible, with two tires up on the curb, eases toward the sidewalk where we stand.

"Look," I say. "He can't drive!"

"He's pulling up next to us so you won't have to walk. Be nice to him. He's trying to help. He's sorry he got you that drink."

The car door beside me cracks open, with Purkeet lying across the seat under the interior light, his arm out, and then he's back at the wheel. Jerome helps me in. "I'll roll your window down," he says. "The fresh air will help." He slams the door.

"He'll improve," Purkeet says, ducking his head to see Jerome, and then we pull off. Silence. Slabs of lighted buildings turning on every side—tombs lit. Then the pulse of streetlamps picking up as the automatic transmission glides through its gears, and a silver net of branches spins down in the air close to us, past.

"Nice scene, Chuck," he finally says, in a quavering voice. "Now the whole fucking building knows I'm queer." The stubble on his pouting chin is white, and his curly widow's peak a lid I could lift off.

"Why didn't you let me help pick out your car?"

"Can the shit, okay?"

"If you really liked me, you would have."

"That could be, Charlie."

"Stop!" I pull the handle and pop open the door.

"Charles!"

"Stop the car! I want out!"

"Damn it, you'll hurt yourself!"

"Stop! I have to puke!"

He slams on the brakes, and I jump out under a dim lamp in an older neighborhood and take off down a side street in a sprint. "Charles," I hear faintly. A door slam? I hit top speed, the trench coat straight out from my arms, and head for a fence hung with stars. Which town? I slip off balance, staggering as if a foot's gone, and slow enough to see a swoop of cable before it catches my waist.

Out flat. No body. Only its warm electrical outline in death. Then the battle to take in air, Kuntz quacking above on a blue bar. An explosion of vomit sprays the back of my teeth as I return, sprawled on a mound of dirt—straggling weeds on it. A downed reflectorized sawhorse, lumber scraps, lights strung across the beams of a half-finished building, divided into diamonds by protective wire mesh.

"Jesus, Cholly, are you okay? I'll never forgive myself—" His hands grip my shoulders and more vomit flies, splashing rubble and cinder blocks, or I'm on the floor with my head on the cover of his cot, dead from the waist down, reaching out to hit with my fists. Dirt, the ground; a cable above, beams strung with lights sending a scattering of sparks through my eyelashes. A cyclone fence a few feet away parts at the edge of a black basement.

"I'm going to kill myself!" I cry. "I'm going to kill myself!"

+

I see myself walk into this farmhouse for the first time, through square and tilting rooms like the fields outside, past bookshelves and boxes that form a path to the desk ahead where Inez Berg, wearing a sweater as red as the suit she wore one winter night, with hair silver as snow, rests her hand on a file folder, smiling in a pressure of light from a large window which appears to extend her into another dimension—a byproduct of my medication, in this long period of recovery after my hospital stay. She nods for me to sit in a hand-made chair, at the desk her father built, and opens the file. I assume it holds the original deed to this farm, homesteaded by her parents, which we intend to buy, but I'm staring at a letter written in my mother's hand.

"I've kept all their correspondence," Inez says, her mellow but deepened schoolteacher's voice slowing me. "They both wrote so well."

In my stunned, drugged state I'm unable to read the page in front of me, and a grip of stitches tightens across both wrists.

Inez moves the letter, and there are my father's measured, slanting strokes down through pages I set aside one by one, able to understand, at least, that this was written the winter our mother died, and then in a trick of light one portion looks outlined: "The complications of this life are a misery. No wife, five growing children to attend to, and who knows how deeply in debt. It's Christ alone that keeps me on my feet."

+

Purkeet hardly speaks to me in the remaining month of school, and is away each weekend in his car. So this whirlwind courtship, this testing of the other side, is done. I sit with my back to Jerome to catch up on the semester, my missal from Dad on a shelf above, the ka-*lang* going on daylong until dark, and figure I can salvage three courses. Then I'm in a city park in the old part of town, with Purkeet and three friends from the theater, including a strawberry blonde who has a narrow face that streams backward from her pointed nose as her body streams back from her breasts, so that I want to nail her streaming to the spot. We all join hands, form a circle, and sing, "Wherever we go, whatever we do, we always will do it together!" Purkeet's eyes brighten with emotion, and I think, He means this. They're serious. I feel so old my college days might as well be over, when they've actually just begun: the end of my first year.

+

My wife is at the other end of a log I'm trying to swing around to a position where it can be sawed. We're newly married, in the woods, in snow to our knees, and damp flakes are falling in clinging clumps between us. "Are you even lifting?" I ask.

"Yes," she gets out, a word all pluming steam.

"Then help me swing it! Work together!" She has on a red stocking cap and looks up out of wide blue eyes, her nose reddened and starting to run, and the shape and set of her lips, her faint eyebrows, the features of her entire face, are Jerome's. My God, is this why I married her, I wonder, and in the midst of our precarious dance, I let the log drop.

+

Jerome is in the hospital, and I'm in tights and a flared skirt of motley, watching a gray-blue stage flat go trembling away from me. The hands of the person carrying it become visible at its edges as it goes out the door, and altered light enters the stage carpentry room. I go to a worktable and study miniature models of sets, a project for a scene-design class, and adjust my beret, of maroon velvet, which has slipped during my energetic last scene. The tingling atmosphere of someone seeking my attention covers me, and I turn as a girl from the makeup crew, her blond hair sparkling in the stage lights, comes through the door where the flat disappeared; she puts her hands on my shoulders, says, "You're my Feste," and kisses me on the mouth. Then leans into me with her breasts and rubs, observing her effect with frank pale eyes.

"What's the matter?" she says. "Aren't you my usual happy Feste?"

Her Feste? "My brother is sick. He's in the hospital."

"That bad?"

"He might have to have his appendix removed."

"We'll go see him after the performance. It's your last. Do well!"

"He can't see anybody until tomorrow."

"We'll sneak in." She smiles and her teeth, sparkling in the light, appear pointed.

I hear a familiar line onstage and the prompter sticks his head in the carpentry-room door. "Neumiller? That's your cue."

"Tomorrow morning!" the girl says, and grips my fingers so hard they crack. "I'll go with you to see him!"

"Hey, I have to—"

"This is like a kilt," she says, running a hand under the skirt, up my tights. She hands me a Kleenex. "You better wipe your mouth first."

+

In the early morning I feel drunken on the street with her beside me. She hasn't slept, either, she says, and grips my arm with both hands above the elbow, keeping up a rub with her near arm. In the stirring spring light, her hair looks bleached, corn-yellow, with white and gold flossy strands among the loose waves edging her rose-pink face. She's laughing at something, her plump lips crimson, and I realize that I have trouble taking in half of what she says. Something about light? "It's like syrup," she says, and I assume she means the layer of sunlight that appears to be burning the top of the hedge we walk beside.

"Oh, look," she says, and is off the sidewalk, in mulch beneath the hedge. The plump white bell of a mushroom has pushed up through the mulch, and beside it a spiderweb beaded with dew sends down guy lines. She presses it with a fingertip and it gives like a trampoline, shedding dew, and then a spider sails along a filament toward her finger. "Bitch," she whispers. "I wouldn't put it past you to try to poison me."

+

Jerome's hospital room is hushed and the blinds pulled, projecting separated sheets of light in bars across the ceiling. A beaded glass of water, with a bent straw in it, sits on a wooden table beside his bed. His face, turned aside, looks formless as putty without his glasses, and as gray. She leans her breasts into me and tickles my ribs. "Don't!" I say, jerking my elbows around, and see myself from another height, in traction, thrashing beside Jerome. His lids lift, his head rolls, and he looks up through gelatinous eyes.

"Oh, God, it *hurts!*" he cries. "Oh, Jeez, help! Give me a shot!"

Her tickle to my ribs has caught up, and causes a coughing buck about to become a laugh.

"Jerome. I'm here. You had an operation. Are you okay?"

"You. Oh, God, it hurts!"

I'm ashamed I almost laughed, although I still might, which makes it worse. I take his hand and our connection of giving threads, which I first felt when Dad was in the hospital, reappears.

"I'm sorry it hurts," I say, and there's a shimmer of recognition.

Jill, at the other side of the bed now, takes his hand. "I'm Jill," she says, in the husky tone her voice takes on when she's solemn. "I'm his new girlfriend. I was—" She takes her plump lip in her teeth, and a tear rolls from one eye down the powdered plane of her cheek. Can she do this at will? "I hope you heal soon. I have a gift for you."

She leans over and kisses him on the lips.

He looks at her, then at me, unsure, and licks at the lipstick on his lips, which I can taste on mine. "Jill," he says. "I, ah, I've be . . ." This arrives in a blur, as if he's rushed, and then he's asleep.

+

"When I was young, not a teenager yet, we lived in a suburb of Chicago." She's lying on her back on the ground and I'm lying beside her, staring into swaying leaves that part and admit sudden shafts of light. "People still farmed in the suburbs then. One man's field came to the edge of our back yard. I used to walk there. He had chickens. The land there was strangely level, even for Illinois, except for this rise in the center of his field. I believed it was an Indian mound. I used to lie on it, staring up like this, and dream that someday I'd be rich and famous, and feel clouds pull me toward that day. Somehow the chickens were part of it. I was never quite alone. I told this to the minister's son, that boy I said I dated, hoping he'd have some cosmological answer, and he— He was lying beside me like you are, only on his stomach, with his eyes shut. Do you know what he said?"

"I can imagine." She has said that for a while he was her "only love, but too young—furious with passion," and once climbed up their porch to her bedroom window, and wouldn't go away until she promised to perform a certain act on him, which she says she didn't.

"He said, 'I see you there with your clothes off.' I had them off."

"The bastard," I say, and sit and feel sunlight enter my eyes and expect to see, under its blaze, her bare expanse, but instead picture her leaning over Jerome's hospital bed. "He ought to be shot."

+

There's a problem of money with her; I have too little. I'm embarrassed when we go out—even to the Union, like now. We sit at a table against one wall, with our heads doubled in a mirror, in a representation of the jealousy I surround her with, able to endure such times only because I know we'll soon be alone. The cup of coffee in front of me is a torture in this context, and I try to recall the number of sweaters of hers I've seen monogrammed *jj*. I've borrowed a dollar from Jerome, but if she orders a cheeseburger, which she usually does, turning it and licking ketchup from the bun as she squints at me and grins, what then?

She's saying something I can't hear; I must learn to concentrate. She laughs, tossing back her flossy hair on both sides with quick flips of her hands, and her short sharp teeth, with saliva shining over them, look needlelike at the ends. *The better to eat you with,* I hear in Purkeet's voice, and blush and reach for my coffee.

"What?" she asks. "Oh, Charles, look, you're dripping that all over you. When you have coffee in your saucer, you should take a napkin, like this"—she jerks one from the dispenser beside our mirrored twins, checking herself there—"and place it in the saucer, under your cup, like so." Which she does. "It absorbs the mess."

"Where's the ticket?" I ask, wild. "I'll pay. Let's go."

"Ticket? Oh, how amusing!" Again she laughs, and takes her throaty time about it. "You make it sound like a traffic violation!" She gives me a narrow look, and I notice that her eyelids are fatty, which helps. " 'Check, sir,' you say, in a gruff voice, bored with it all."

She draws a cigarette from the pack in her purse—now this; she's learning to smoke—and when she lights up, then draws on it, she stares down her nose, which is broadly healthy, so that her eyes cross. I could teach her something there, I figure, but decide not to speak, and become so nervous with abstraction I'm gone. "What?" I ask.

+

"Oh! another hospital bill," Jerome says, and holds his head above the book on his desk. He still seems in pain, and stoops a bit when he walks. "Besides that butcher who hacked me up, on top of it all."

I turn back to my text on psychology, a subject I love, and think: Some way for a future doctor to talk.

+

Jill pledges a sorority, although I don't want her to, and after Easter vacation she asks me to come to her sorority house at six in the morning for a gift—a ring, I assume, for some reason. I have to wake Jerome at 5:30 to borrow a couple of dollars in case she wants a cheeseburger. "That's it," he says, and falls back in bed. "That's the end of the money. I'm out."

Jill steps from the mock-Southern mansion looking aged from sleep, or lack of it, and takes my hand and leads me in silence all the way across the campus. "Where are we going?" I finally ask.

"To a special place."

We pass the pale, sun-bleached brick façade of Men's Old Gym, and after some playing fields and a few more residential blocks, we're on the open prairie, with trees scattered in fields like puffs of breath, and through my aching legs I sense the former ease of my overland walks to Savitskys'. "Okay," I say, limping. "This is far enough. What is it?"

She leads me into a field of picked corn not yet replowed, as if looking for a particular row, and just as I feel a shock of concern about her sanity, she throws herself on the ground and starts wailing.

"What is it?" I ask, and ease down beside her, scared.

"I wanted to give you my virginity! But it's cold here!"

She rolls over and unbuttons her coat, to show she's wearing only shorty pajamas, her face frail as smoke against the lumpy clods and tangled roots. "I was going to give you my ring! I even brought you these!" She throws a shiny packet a row away, and I see a brand name that is discussed in the dorm: Trojans.

"I wouldn't use one," I say.

"How can that be!"

"It's against my religion."

"I didn't know you were religious," she says, and sits, her eyes wide, with tears dark from dirt down her cheeks. "It could make all the difference," she whispers, taking my hand. "Carry me home."

I pick her up and manage to make it, panting, to the edge of the highway on my weak legs, and then she wriggles loose and drops to her feet. "That's enough," she says. "I had to make sure you love me."

On the way back, we stop to see a friend of mine from an acting class, who says, "You two are bonkers," and goes back to bed, and it happens so fast on his couch I'm not sure that it has.

+

I look for a job, necessary now, although the school year is almost over. I'll have to live away from the dorm; I assume she'll want to marry me. During the last week of school, when she is nervously checking a Hallmark Cards calendar she carries in her purse, I'm hired as the caretaker of two apartment buildings; part of my wage is the manager's apartment in the basement of one. Jill leaves for Chicago, promising to visit often, and Jerome helps me move in—the airy humid space of three rooms of my own, with only a bed and table and couch, and books. We discover a door off my living room that leads to a large adjoining apartment, and he walks around it for a while, and says, "I'm tired of the dorm. I bet Neal would rent this with me." He and Neal sign a lease with the landlady, and Jerome leaves to spend the summer at home.

On Jill's first visit, she says, "Pretend you're a doctor examining me." The next time she brings a book on Eastern arts, and by Saturday I'm crawling around on raw elbows and knees, sad that she's not a real blonde, when she cries, "Don't you love to experiment!"

+

Dad is marrying a widow from Chicago, too fast, I feel, without consulting any of us, and my only consolation as I pack is that I'll be spending the weekend with Jill. "My dad's funny," she says, in a dark rear room of their suburban house, exactly like all the others along the street—no open field in sight. "Once when I was sunbathing out in the yard, he walked up and said, 'Why do you lie on your back like this, thinking of boys?' I was. He's anxious to meet you."

He sits in a recliner in his suit, chain-smoking as he stares at a TV with a nearly round screen and flicks his cigarettes toward an ashtray like Grandpa's—a bowl with a circular trap-door at its center that sends butts spinning down inside when you press a plunger. He turns the liquidy, romantic gaze of Jill on me: "How old are you?"

"Nineteen."

"College is a necessity," he says, then back to the TV.

At dinner he sits in silence while his wife, as thickly plump as the younger daughter, Sis, carries on a dizzying conversation.

"If our name weren't Jarvis," she says, fixing her skewed stare on Jill, "but Marvis or Munro, we surely would have named you Marilyn!" Jill lifts a hank of flossy hair out horizontal from her head, laughing so hard pinpoints of light appear on her teeth, and then pushes her chair back and stands and curtsies. She wants to act but hasn't received a role in any production.

I can't sleep in the bed I'm given in the basement, at the thought of her above me, but I must drop off toward morning, because I wake to something scrabbling under the sheets, at my privates, and fling back the covers to find Jill, in a robe, grinning and holding up a tape measure.

"Just checking," she says. "Time to dress for church."

We sit in a back pew. I don't want to hear the vows Dad repeats; don't they violate everything we've lived by? His new wife, Laura, is as tall as he is, bulky through the hips, and at the thought of them in bed I'm so ill that when we file into the church basement for a wedding feast of mixed Italian food, I feel I'm eating my mother's insides.

+

I'm back to painting, cleaning, and scraping grease out of broilers and burner wells. I've reached a point where nothing anybody says or does surprises me—a new height of reality, I adjudge. I read *Crime and Punishment* over a day of terror, and find Raskolnikov the model for my redefined reality. Jill has a job in telephone sales, and claims that her boss is making advances, but won't elaborate on the phone. She doesn't visit that weekend. Jerome arrives the next, with a carload of furniture for his apartment, the first apartment I painted—all white, as he requested. I give him a black-wire record stand, left behind by a renter, which the landlady gave me, and after we've walked a few times through the pair of doors between our apartments, which I've freed up with oil, he says, "Isn't there something you could do about those?"

"I already fixed them."

"I mean, for Neal and me. You know, so things are more private."

When he leaves, I nail the door shut on his side, walk

around to my apartment, and slam mine. At the end of summer, after a musical production, I throw a cast party for Jill's benefit, but she doesn't appear, and sometime after midnight, when everybody has had too much to drink, I say, "How awful to lose my brother." What do I mean, I wonder. "Death is the worst loophole," I say. "Hideous how his hair and nails continue to grow." I've slipped into the character from Poe I mismanaged over the radio. "This is the most hideous aspect of death. That they grow. I check on him each day. Yes, you've wondered about that peculiar stench, haven't you?" I stand, conscious of a smell I haven't been able to purge the apartment of. "It's my brother, and on nights like this, with him so near, I sense it grow! He's here! Yes, I confess—see!" I leap to the door between our apartments, feeling needles of sensation pass through my back, and yell, *"Here!"* I jerk the knob, wondering if this is the door I nailed shut, when it flies back with such a bang, revealing the other, dark, closed door, that I scare myself. In the dim light their faces turn to me with blanched looks, and real fear enters me in a backwash.

In the morning, I wake to a vision of their faces, and wonder, How did I do that? They are all actors, but were held: my best role. A sign of my heightened reality? I have a hangover, but no body is in bed with me, in confirmation of my worst nightmare—only a jacket, left in last night's general hasty exodus. It lies over my bare feet, dark on the bedspread in morning light through the window shade.

+

It's difficult to keep up my grades, since Jill and I aren't getting along. She has never explained what her boss was up to, and assumes a distant look when I ask. Once she says, "Well, he was older." We make the rounds of parties and drink too much, and for a while it seems that whenever she wanders away in the midst of the din and drinking and I find her, at last, in a hallway or a darkened bedroom off to the edge of the activity, she's in somebody else's arms. "Just experimenting," she'll say, then fall onto my chest and cry, "It's you I love!"

If I sing one of Feste's songs:

Fly away, fly away, breath,
I am slain by a fair cruel maid

tears roll so easily down her cheeks, I'm sure I've been monu-
mentally betrayed. One night I leave my apartment, walk along
the house to Jerome's, then down the steps to his room—narrow
as a corridor, off the entrance. He sits in a blaze of light from
the gooseneck lamp on his worktable, like an interrogator, I
think, as I try to explain my problems with Jill. He keeps
glancing at a glossy textbook open at his elbow, revolving an
unopened pack of Luckies and hammering its top, then its
bottom, on the table—patience, I figure, is what I need to
learn—and finally says, "Maybe you're getting too serious."

+

Grandpa Neumiller dies, of a sudden heart attack, and at home
I can hardly speak—grief and anger, compounded by Laura.
Every time I look up, she's staring at me as if it's her fault,
which is how I feel. Why did they marry? Just the sight of her
sends currents of sexual pain through my thighs. I couldn't live
here, but I'm not sure I want to go back to school, either, until
in a sudden inner rearrangement I see Grandpa in a rearview
mirror, waving goodbye as convertible canvas fills like a sail
above my head, as if in the next moment we'll both lift off.

+

Rootless. The friend from the acting class, Stu, asks me to move
with him into an old house at the other end of town. My landlady
understands, she says, and admits that there won't be much
work, anyway, until spring. Jerome helps me pack my books
and a few boxes, and it occurs to me that I'm moving, partly
anyway, to get away from him. The discovery exerts a pull to
remain, but he and I finish loading Stu's car, and Jerome walks
away to his apartment with his hands in his pockets, the way
Dad once walked from me in the parking lot, and I sense myself
age beyond my family again, but this time in the form of a
lasting goodbye.

+

Is that my wife calling from the bottom of the stairs in the tones of euphony and youthful freshness of my name? Each time the call comes for me in that name, now, it's for a person I never expected to be.

+

I place a napkin under my cup, although my inclination is to throw it all at her. She has talked before about dating others, besides the fraternity dates she is required to solicit, but over the vacation she has decided she must. "I can't be exclusively yours anymore," she says.

"You must have forgotten your boss, and those guys I keep dragging off you at parties."

"Don't be petty."

"Petty? I'm talking about reality."

"As of the moment, reality's changed," she says, and stands and hikes her purse strap over her shoulder and walks off.

Yet she's at our run-down house nearly every weekend, sitting on the edge of my bed, nervously paging through her Hallmark calendar before she accedes, if she does. I can permit her most any abuse, I suspect, as long as she stays, and one night she jerks down Grandpa Jones's goatskin chaps, which I've removed Mom's hems from and tacked, spraddle-legged, above the bed, and tries them on, and then has me get into them without anything underneath, drags me to the room where Stu is engaged with a woman friend, cries "Ride 'em, cowboy!" and shoves me in on their bed.

+

"Meet me on the steps to Lincoln Hall Theater," she says a week later, over the phone, and I figure: This is it; she's pregnant. Why else ask to meet where she met me as Feste? I throw on my coat and run to campus through the cold. She's inside the building, on the landing of the first flight of stairs to the theater, where wide limestone steps part and curve on two sides around a marble wall with a niche that holds a bust of Abraham Lincoln. She's leaning next to the bust, holding a cigarette with theatrical expertise, though she looks pale and puffy, with the strained myopic cast that comes when she isn't wearing her contacts, and before she notices me I see that her face is stripped of makeup—even the usual powder that gives it the luminous wholeness of a Kabuki face: the source of her beauty that's eluded me. Oriental. I take her hand, and she drops the cigarette and twists it under a tennis shoe—tennis shoes in this cold.

"Charles, I'm afraid that, well . . ."

"Don't worry! I understand, I'm ready to—"

"We have to break it off."

"What do you mean?"

She pulls back her trench coat to reveal a pin, with a gold chain trembling from it at another point of attachment—a jewel that might be a diamond—above her breast. "I'm pinned."

"You dirty bitch!" My voice echoes and rebounds up the stairwell, and we both look around quick to see if anybody's heard. I lean in close and whisper to her reddening face, "You mean you're exclusively his?"

"Don't be so hurt. I still love you, really. I do. Maybe we can still work it out."

"Work it out!" I roar, past any consideration of others now. "You just said we had to break it off!"

"For everybody's sake. Maybe someday you'll settle down."

"*I'll* settle down! What about you?"

"Be mature," she says, and her lower lip tugs sideways and trembles.

I stab with my tongue at tears going past my mouth as if to taste the bitter end of this, and then wipe at my face and see grease spots and mustard on the sleeve of the coat I've been wearing since I pressed from the hedge and frightened Kennedy—its cuff frayed, with black threads dangling from it. I'm so shocked I go into the jumpy furtive looks of Raskolnikov, as if I've turned into this dreaded character from Russia.

Jill steps back, trying to assess the power of the wildness in me.

"Let me show you what I feel," I say, my whole face shaking with the effort to restrain myself, and jerk off the gold band she has given me—her grandmother's, she said—and fling it so hard I hear it go in chiming hops down the steps.

"Charles!"

"I'm sorry!" I say, afraid of myself; and the hallway, as if activated by the sound of her ring, resounds with the class bell. I run down the stairs as the ring rolls into the marble entry (glass doors and columns), where a plaque of the Gettysburg Address is fastened to a wall, and grab it as the first rank of footsteps comes around the bend. I feel my face melting as I work back through the crowd to her, and see her eyes brimming and running with the tears that pour as easily from her as water. Then her mouth opens, saliva spanning her teeth, and she howls. I kneel among the students climbing the stairs or hurrying down, pressing in from both sides, and slip the ring on her finger. "You *ba*-by!" she wails. "You spoiled shit! I just wanted time to *think*! Screw you! Screw, screw—!"

People have paused, and when I stand, their movement continues, but she is running up through the crowd, and I find I'm facing a greenish bust of Lincoln, rubbed brassy over his nose. My fist comes up, and I shake it in his face—as long as anybody feels like this, Abe, there's slavery you never freed! I plunge my hands into my pockets and grip them through the material of the coat as I walk through the beginning of a blizzard to Jerome's.

+

I pace and sleep and wake in a daze. Spring arrives through the daze, but it must be false spring, because it's winter again. I'm lying on a black-plaid mattress on Jerome's floor, when he says, "Shouldn't you be thinking about class?" I reach for my chin, as if to recall if this was what I was thinking, and feel a beard. I walk across town to the house I've rented with Stu. He isn't there. I try a switch and no lights come on. Then I realize I can see my breath, and stare down at a note on the table in the dimness, reluctant to discover anything further:

"Electricity and phone out. Also fuel. Got any dough?" There's a number where I can reach Stu, "Where it's warm," he adds.

I pull a butcher knife from the heap of dirty dishes on the drainboard, and sit at the table with it. I lay my head down to think.

+

"Charles, aren't you cold?"

There's a hand on my shoulder, and Stu's face, huge and rose-colored, with spirally hair growing low over his forehead and out from his temples as if taking advantage of this dream to invade his face, is above me in mist. "I mean, gee," he says, "the heat's been off three days."

"It's over."

"How's that."

"Jill broke up with me."

"Good. I always said she wasn't worth you."

I look away, to the window across the room—a fuzzy slab of crystals overlapping crystals in blue light.

"Look, you got an intellect, Charles, and she— Well, you know. *No!*" he cries, and backpedals away from me, holding a hand over his coat in a vow, "No, I've never been near her! When she comes up at a party, I run!" I turn back to the window, and my thigh starts to quiver from the cold, as if the pin has frozen at its center. "If I was forced into it with her, like that sorority widow friend of hers you introduced me to, I'd have to shut my eyes and think of something sexy, like basketball. Hey!" he says, and grabs an arm and pulls me so I'm sitting, faint with dizziness. "Let's go to the diner. I'll get us breakfast—corned-beef hash and poached eggs. I saw your brother. He's worried. He said for you to call him. Today's the last day of tryouts for *Taming of the Shrew*—no reflection on Jill—scheduled for weeks. You better shave first. Use a piece of ice from the sink there. Or the butcher knife in your coat pocket you forgot to stab yourself with."

+

I'm cast as Grumio, Stu as Curtis, and we sit up at night and rehearse or talk, his chatter setting off the sort of laughter that hurts. One afternoon I hurry through the underground sanctuary of the Theater Department, and somebody takes my arm: the chairman. He leads me to the inner cubicle of his office and sits across his desk from me.

"Charles," he says, "I've just received some wonderful news. You're the recipient of our undergraduate fellowship this year."

He smiles and hands over an envelope. "Here's a check for three hundred and fifty dollars. Congratulations. And, oh—" He leans back in his creaking wooden chair and turns toward the wall, where Noh masks are mounted—a pudgy gray-blond man like Jill's father. "I've heard about a job opening at the library. It might be just the thing for you."

I work as a page in the stacks, and one evening stare down from the tenth floor to the stone post where I sat during my freshman year, and saw for the first time how Jerome and I had switched directions. I raise a dusty book in my hand, weighing it, and think: Now we're farther apart.

The weekend after the final performance of *The Taming of the Shrew*, I wander through the basement of the theater, dazed by another end, and start for the green room to check the urns for coffee. The costumiere, a petite beauty who usually costumes herself in black, steps out of a lighted doorway down the hall in red, with glittery prongs of pins in her mouth, and gives me a look of concern. She removes the pins.

"Charles," she says, "what are you doing here?"

"Nosing around."

"You're being inducted into Alpha Psi Omega tonight, aren't you?"

"Me? Oh, no. No fraternities for me."

She clacks over in the cold light reflected off polished concrete and stares up at me from clear brown eyes. "It's an honor, Charles! It's an honorary theater fraternity. Didn't you get your invitation?"

I sigh, unsure, but unwilling to lie; I no longer check my mail.

"The festivities start in a lamb's shake. I was on my way out. You come along. It's just across the street at the Pi Phi house."

I do a stagey downward gesture to indicate my clothes.

"The bluejeans are fine. Here." She jerks open the doors of a metal wardrobe, one of many lined up to hold costumes, then the door of the next, and tosses me a suit jacket. "This should be your size, if I remember right. Here's a tie." I catch it. "And a white shirt. Now somewhere here—" She keeps flinging open doors on another row of wardrobes, down the opposite wall. "Ah, here." She tosses me a can of shoe polish. "Change in the green room. You can walk me there."

I step up the stone stairs of the sorority house, with her on my arm, and in the entry she says, "On time! They're just finishing up the punch. Good." Across the room, the flossy head I was afraid I'd see turns: Jill. She walks over, smiling as if we talked yesterday, and I want to paw the wood-paneled reception hall, but stand as chastened as if this were her house. She puts a hand on my sleeve and her eyes sparkle with the aqua-blue of her contacts. "You were beautiful as Grumio, love. You were so, well, unconscious of self you truly were him. Masterful!"

"You don't think I was a whining, selfish babyface?"

"Please." She looks down in her geisha luminousness and I notice that she's not wearing the pin. "Can't you ever forgive me?"

"Haven't I, a few dozen times?"

"I like your clothes," she whispers.

"You would."

"I believe I could love you again. Could you me?"

The costumiere is banging on her drinking glass with a spoon; the seating arrangement has me far down the banquet table from Jill. How these young sophisticates eat! I feel like an interloper, Raskolnikov in borrowed clothes, and sit back from the table as Jill's father sat back with the family so noisy. The costumiere has been speaking; she's president of the local chapter of Alpha Psi Omega, I learn, and Mistress of Ceremonies, as she says, and goes on: ". . . an induction that gives me special pleasure. I'm not sure he knows this, but I was one of the judges of Original Monologue at a State speech contest some years back, and I recognized his talents then. Charles, would you stand?"

+

Afterward I work through the crowd, noticing that pointed-toe shoes are in fashion again, and sneak down to the basement of the theater. The costumiere has left the wardrobes unlocked, and I open the one for my jacket and see a row of capes. I take one of black wool, lined with scarlet, and go down a concrete corridor to the property room, through its heavy, weighted, fireproof metal door, and throw a switch that fires a single bulb above in a cage like an egg basket. I go to a leather couch, with a rolled leather pillow at one end, and sit with the cape in my lap. This would be stealing. Have I sunk so low, after this evening? I find a cigarette in the crumpled pack in my pocket and light it up.

Every imaginable chair or dresser from any century, or its replica, is here, along with carpets, dress forms, saddles and birdbaths, armor— The weighted door creaks inward and I grind out the cigarette and stand, prepared to apologize to the costumiere. It's Jill.

I sit with the cape to my face, aware of her perfume before I sense her near. "Are you still my Feste?" she asks. "Or are you Grumio now?"

I'm fairly sure she doesn't expect me to answer this.

"Which of the dozen parts you've played?"

Her voice, deadened by the furniture, is so uncanny I look up; she's squatting on her heels in front of me, inches away. She stands and hikes up her skirt on each side, until the tops of her nylons appear, gripped by a garter belt, and then sits on my lap, her elbows on my shoulders and her hands at the back of my hair. "Could you make love to me?"

"Just a minute," I whisper, and raise a finger, and she leaps up and wriggles down her skirt as she studies the door, startled, her lips parted. "Let me think about it," I say, and walk off.

+

I'm halfway to Jerome's before I remember I don't live there. I'm carrying the cape, and still have on the coat from the costumiere. How did I manage to do the opposite of everything I've imagined with Jill? I'm not sure where I am, and see Mrs. Glick's street corner, alight with lilac leaves, then feel that the bone of my right leg will part along the angle of its break—a sensation I've had before, but never this strongly—and plunge through my foot. I sit on the curb, weak, then lie back on the grass below the stars, overfilled. On a blanket in the corner of our lawn, next to Mrs. Glick's, I shrink inside the coat until I'm miniature. *Jerome?* His name so strange, like a car taking off.

The stars nail us inside one another's identity, this hand below a cuff like a paw pulling us onto the opposite shore, our lives spilling like water—gone. God, don't let me think that. If I'm here, he is, and You have us both.

+

I rise from this life textured like a chenille spread and see that there is no place I've been where Jerome hasn't appeared, through the door or an opening on memory, and then pressed near, and at his presence now I know it's time to keep watch through the night to our end.

+

Neal invites Stu and me to a year-end graduation party he's holding for Jerome. Jerome has been accepted to the university's medical school, and Neal will be going to Georgia Tech. When Stu and I step down the stairs to their apartment, carrying our bottles of Chianti, I see Jill across the room, on the black-plaid mattress on the floor, sitting with one leg out, as if dropped there.

"I hope you don't mind," Jerome says, hurrying up. "I ran into her on campus, and thought, Hey, why not? I thought you'd like to see each other again." He pushes up his glasses and a seedy scent of gin that seems to match his T-shirt with holes in it surprises me; his widening eyes say, *I thought you would appreciate this.*

Stu hands his bottle to Jerome, and says, "This is for you. I have to go, really. There are sixteen subjects I have to study for. I just wanted to stop in and say 'Congratulations—goodbye.'"

Jerome raises and lowers the bottle with the look of a child at a birthday party, and says, "Hey, thanks."

Jill stares down her nose at the drink she's turning in her lap, as she used to stare at cigarettes, and I feel as sorry for her as I feel attracted, but attracted. A hand comes down on my shoulder and Stu leans in close, blinking in anger, and whispers, "Chuck. Kick her in the nuts for me, okay?" Then he goes out and up the stairs with the clattering chromium trim on their treads that I should have fixed.

Jerome, with his bottle of Chianti, waltzes *one*-two-three, *one*-two-three, into the kitchen, and now I notice the dark crowd parting to let him through. I go over and sit on the mattress beside Jill.

"A dud, that guy," she says, still staring at her drink. "A real jock. A mistake. It's you I love. Can't you forgive me?"

I sit back against the wall and decide not to talk, or try to interpret "It's you I love"—this formal comedy of her speech. Jerome hands me a glass of wine, and soon the room seems to tip and funnel its volume toward the mattress. Jill swings out her legs and lays her head in my lap, but I don't touch her. A worse weight than the undefined feeling of fullness has started in me again. I rise with the rising decibels of music, within separate slatted darknesses spotlit in between: drinking from a bottle in the kitchen while Jill stands with her back against a refrigerator; focusing on the teeth of a man talking about a motorcycle; examining the motorcycle in starlight; then lying on the drive beside a heated blonde, whose springy curly hair shines in the moonlight in a shade I've always imagined. She says, "It's way past curfew. You're just doing this because everybody knows I'm the only woman here."

I hurry back to the basement, and the room bends inward on its frame. Jill isn't in sight. I run into Jerome's bedroom. Empty. I stumble to the kitchen, and receive a shy grin from Neal, who's emptying bottles into a cup. I step into his back bedroom—coats and one couple on a bed—and go to the door to my old apartment, then jerk open the bathroom door beside it. Jerome and Jill push back from one another but remain linked by a string of saliva bowing between their lips.

"You son of a bitch!" I yell.

"Chuck," he says. "See, I—"

I'm in the bathroom with him behind me, and in the same motion connect with a slap that sends Jill stumbling backward, hands going up, and in a billowy uproar she takes down the plastic shower curtain as she falls. I turn on the cold water, and she cries out in such anguish I wonder why it isn't him. Through her spread fingers, the side of her face is taking color in the shape of my handprint; her sweater is soaked and shedding flying drops, her flossy hair plastered in strings to her head where blue streaks of scalp show. I reach down in an explosion like ice over my back, the water still going, and pick her up as I did in the cornfield, and say, "I'm sorry. Please."

But she hops down, elbowing me in the neck, and by the time my eyes have adjusted from the bathroom's glare, she's at the other end of the apartment, jerking open the door, gone. I see the wire record stand I gave him as a gift, at the door to the living room, piled with books, the bastard. I kick and shake it free of books, lift it above my head, and slam it to the floor, then leap on it. The shower goes off. In the silence I hear a noise like a dog being kicked. Me? How could you, I try to say, and rock on the stand as the howl keeps up, fighting for breath— a rope pulled winding from my stomach out my eyeholes, ah!

"You don't understand," he's saying under this, on the floor beside me. "She walked in while I was taking a leak. Yes, I went along with it, and that was wrong, and I'm sorry, really, sorrier than I can say. But it was her idea, you have to understand that."

As if I didn't, as if he had to tell me, as if—

In the shuttle of dark that earlier opened on spotlit scenes, I hear Neal's voice like the rawness in my own throat, from a direction I can't place: "I'm worried. Maybe we should call somebody. He needs help." And then Jerome, farther off than Neal: "No, it's all my fault. I'll take care of him."

Now my howling opens the pile of gravel we're sifting beside the outhouse when Grandma Jones arrives, and then enters the outhouse, where echoing boards, weathered so much you can see the entire yard, are draped with cobwebs, in the corners, over splintered rafters and studs, besides those webs spanning the holes, which you have to push past with a sticky breaking. The dark mounds below, marbleized by sprinklings of lime, with catalogue pages sticking from them in tufts, increase in substance until they have to be pushed back with poles, except in winter when they freeze and rise close enough to resurrect stories of rats and snakes living in them. Crickets chirr from there, a bat once went flapping around, and worms in summer give off a smacking sound like a loose screen in the windowed porch of that other house, where I'm in a chair with handgrips, straining to her sounds of encouragement until I

shake, and then turning to see in the white pot the glistening
stick and buttery chocolate wads it feels I've coughed up, out
of this moment, from my craw, as she takes me in her arms and
cries, "What a good boy you are!"

I'm dangling, being lifted in a dark room, above a wire
stand flat on the floor, and then I find my feet and jerk both
elbows free. Footsteps go off from the force of her voice, which
has silenced everybody.

I'm in another room with Jerome coming at me, besides
another face, and I shove past them both with the power of the
offended, free.

+

I turn on my tape recorder and hear "No!" and then, past a
hiss and creaking of reels:

> There is no magic but the magic I imagine,
> Tampering with the natural world to transform
> It, out of ambition, into a world that it's not.
> The magic that was magic has left me bare.
> Why not permit a tree to stand as a tree?
> What perversity of spirit compels
> Me to claim it as a projection of me?
> Not magic but avarice, hate, my mortality;
> It transforms all it falls upon, transforming me.
> Standing at night, hatless, in Tompkins Square,
> I stare upward and feel foliage stir within
> Me, feel roots send down branching roots
> And sense the imminence of fall, and then,
> Seeing that leaf descend, undo myself, claiming
> It as a death (this deceit, this conceit) in me.

+

At the house, which is empty, I pull the chaps off the wall,
throw them into a suitcase, toss in underwear and socks, close
the lid, and walk out. The sidewalk and trees, disjunct from the
night, roll by as if on wheels, but with an offside jarring that
grows as I tire, the side of the suitcase tipping sliding lights at
me if I look down. By the time I reach the campus, then its

tree-lined quadrangle, deserted and lit along its walks by lamps, I have to sit. The closest bench is concrete, semicircular, like the miniature ruins of an amphitheater, with a column rising from its center ten feet into the air, capped by a round lilac agate the size of a bowling ball. I drop the suitcase and sit, and at the far corner of the quad, along the side of the Chemistry Building, a single figure comes walking through the dark, and I know it's Jerome.

He passes under a lamp without looking up, and then cuts across the grass of the quad and up to me. He puts a hand on the back of the bench, as if out of breath, then sits at that end and lights a cigarette—a sudden bronzing of his cheek and lips—and leans with his elbows on his knees. "I can't tell you how sorry I am."

The concrete column is as rough as stucco, with triangular shadows curling back from peaks and pebbles toward its dark side, where I sit.

"I don't know if you were listening before, but she was—"

"I don't want to hear about it."

The bells in the tower of the rusty-stone building behind us chime out the four notes of the quarter hour.

"What can I do?" he asks.

"Nothing."

"What are your plans?"

"Nothing."

"You have a suitcase."

"Go to California." This now occurs to me. "See Grandma Jones."

"You have money?"

I hadn't thought of that. "I'll hitchhike."

"You have to eat!"

His voice is Grandma's, saying, *Jerome, you have to eat!*

"Why don't you sleep on it," he says. "Come back to my place."

"Not there!" All the buildings on the quad echo this back.

"People will wonder why you're here."

"I'll tell them."

"I mean, you know— People will worry about you."

"Who?"

His cigarette climbs in a curve and his face caves into lit streaks as he draws on it. "Me." Then his face and the cigarette part and fall from sight. "Neal. Stu. He called. Jill called, too."

"Did you have a pleasant talk?"

He leans back, a portion of his face lit, and his lips compress. "She's upset. She's at a friend's. She wanted to know what happened."

"What did you say?"

"Not much. None of her business."

"Ha!"

"I said I was going to look for you."

"How did you know where I was?"

"I didn't. I took off walking."

"Who told you I was here?"

"I said, I took off walking."

"Shit!"

He sits back, and a gold skin of light on his glasses slides away over tunnels of blue. "Charles, what do you want?"

"I want justice. I want something out of this!"

His eyes enlarge as if to say: You mean you actually expect justice? He says, "Shouldn't you call Dad, if you're going to California?"

At Dad's name I grab my nose to keep silent, but tears spill over the backs of my fingers. There's a rustle and Jerome's hand comes down on my shoulder; he shakes it. "Don't take this on yourself. It's my fault."

"*No!*" The buildings return this in a clapping report.

A hand glides across my back and he takes hold of my arm. "Please, I feel awful. Think this through. Think of yourself. Think about school. Rest, then decide. If you really want to go, all right." He raises me to my feet within the grip of his arm, then grabs the suitcase with his other hand. "Come back home with me, will you? Is that okay?"

LAST LIGHT

Now after twenty years of exile, the unbroken blue of a frontier I can breathe. North Dakota. I start across the fields of our farm and feel my bones, as giving as chocolate, compress, until I seem only inches tall, on wide weak legs about to give altogether. Everywhere in sight the countryside is dusted with snow, and I recall the first time I walked here, weeks after we'd moved in, when I had reached the inner adjustment that seemed necessary. My existence often seems a walk, yet for weeks I put off walking these acres covered by our deed. The land of the farm is deceptive; it lies at the base of surrounding hills, and appears to be flat. Hogback buttes rise, gray-green, to the south, and three buttes stand on the north horizon like tepees—to my left now as I dip and lift on transformed legs, the way I did during my first walk here, over levels I never expect, in the midst of unaccountable hollows that bury the farm buildings and then bring them up in swoops at another spot, confusing my sense of direction, until I come to this end of the waterway, where high broom grass, applauding in the wind in winter sunlight, assaults my senses and I see, on a height enclosed by trees, the house and outbuildings with their roofs like wings in downbeat, alighted where they'll remain. During that first walk, I felt suspended at the sight of them, treading water, and then a flash came from the house, the storm door catching the sun as someone opened it, and I realized that the door could be considered mine: the house and farm too much to contemplate.

I'm out of breath now, the snow a better rinse of air than rain, stubble crushing underfoot as if sugared—sensations from that reservoir where everything is a reminder of something else: age. The more age permits my imagination to extend under this sky, the more details register and lead me to understand that imagination is, indeed, memory—*what is* more profound than any fantasy. Crystals are clipped to yellow stems in overlapping conjunction. A spear of grass thrusts through a cap of snow on a tuft of stubble, the gold carcass of a grasshopper attached to the green wobbling blade. If the land is like a woman, it's a woman no one can tame. "And my spirit cannot be tamed by life," I hear my mother say, in one of those echoes that arrive with greater force the further I move from her death, down the corridors of memory.

I know now why academic technicians, out of a sacred kind of fear, resort to programs and chemicals to slap the land into shape; it has the power to undo anyone who depends on it in a single turn. Beyond control. Stewardship is another story. The original covenant commanded not only dominion but fruitfulness, multiplication, replenishment, filling out—all of which imply a relationship. Down on your knees like the most dedicated gardener. At a time when mobility in America is viewed as a birthright, we've settled here, unmoving, to establish that relationship. Not near the place where I was born, where memories contend with one another over every square centimeter, but two hundred miles west, in this rugged southern corner of the state adjacent to the Little Badlands.

In a dream I woke to this morning, I saw that certain of us will travel at the speed of light and be frozen at its speed in glory. But under this, like a supporting structure, was the darker dream that has remained for years and rises when it wishes, unbidden, as if to set in place the single pitfall along the way— an image that first appeared with such assurance I woke fighting for breath in a blank dark room that tasted of sulphur: a Central or South American, in sunglasses and a cap shapeless as a cloche, is staring over a battlement above the clouds, an arm lying on the rough stone, with an expression of intent in his face of the sort you see in people of terrible ambition and temper, who at last have the temper under control. The sight of his blank, cold look chills me, communicating the greatest stumbling block to anyone of intellect: neutrality. To suggest that thought can be drawn from the air, or straddle every fence, is to deny thought, or original thought, at least, and the face of this watchman is blank for a purpose: not to warn.

Now faint islands of drifting snow allow me to walk easily across the depressions they've filled among these rough, freeze-hardened furrows and clods. I feel I've been in hiding for the months that we've lived here, although my hiding hasn't been purposeful, and I need fresh air. A bent-winged killdeer goes whistling up from underfoot, and I stop at the thought of my daughter. How will she be affected by our move? Or my son? He is one and a half, but by the time he is reading it will seem I'm still recovering from that killdeer, given my foreshortened sense of time, which this downhill side of life keeps tipping me toward.

"Why go back to North Dakota?" my brother has asked.

"Because I'm North Dakotan," I wanted to say, and laugh. Because of—wherever I would look or point a finger. The plain details of each day, which are everybody's province, are the most important, it turns out, since everybody must contend with them. When I think of how I've resisted learning from experience, I want to hide in a corner of the granary I'm soundproofing, and howl with the vow that I'll never again be that way; never drink, never lie, give pat answers, point out anybody's weaknesses, or fly apart like a ship torpedoed on its home run. As I have. A newspaper headline last week stated 11 DIE AS STORM BLIZZARDS PLAINS, and I misread it as I DIE AS STORM BLIZZARDS PLAINS, trying to place the point of reference, when this had happened, and why a blizzard.

The only indisputable proof of the existence of God (a study I've set aside) is God's existence in you for eternity.

I walk off the edge of the field. In a swale where the waterway deepens so much you could bury part of a city block here, houses and all, I go down a slide. Impossible to mow this. Not just because of the slope, but these stones—red-yellow, with half-circle indentations down their edges, as if holes had been bored in layers of these, dynamite inserted, and whole sheets of them blown apart. But this is how they occur in their natural state. The grasses here, frosted at their tips, or bearing caps of snow, flay my clothes and nip at my elbows, though I raise them nearly to my neck. This undaunted production of the land when it's permitted to return to a state halfway natural.

Up the other slope, slipping on snow stained brown from blown sand, and I'm on a plateau, a small hayfield in the far corner of the farm, a half mile from the house. A creek the waterway empties into has eroded away the other side of the field, years ago, and there are pools down in a marshy corner where the fence lines meet and deer lie. Square bales stand in the field in pyramids of six, the bottom three with their cut sides down, so the twines won't decay or get gnawed by mice, the next two flat on top of those, and the sixth crowning these— the last of the hay, eighteen bales we couldn't get on the hayrack the final evening of hauling, and haven't been back to pick up. The top bale of one has been knocked off—by the wind, I assume, since the wind has been that strong.

The dislodged bale lies on the ground at an angle to the pyramid, fine snow packed in fibers tight as a broom, and I push on it with my foot to tip it up. The grass underneath, crushed flat and dry, nearly as green as on the day this was baled, is preserved in a rectangle like an opening onto the actual world of that October afternoon—late for haying, but the month we arrived, and we couldn't let this go to waste. I've brought a Bible along, a heavy one with a leather cover, and I set it out of the way below the pyramid, test the twines of the fallen bale, find that they're sound, and heave it to its place on top. I sit on the lowest bale, my back against the others, facing south, out of the wind, my feet stretched out, and place the Bible in the lap of my heavy wool pants. No buildings visible here, only the tilt and buckle of land dim with snow—blue below blue with such a range of unpolluted yellows and browns and brown-purples and blonds and tans and every shade of gray rubbed through the surface that I could be in the center of a nineteenth-century painting, the palette for contemplation.

I flop open the Bible and its pages peel back in the wind

as if tearing, a chatter I allow to continue, although it's noisy enough to— But who would hear? I flip pages back and forth until I arrive at Ephesians. I've decided to memorize the book, as an elderly woman suggested the early Church must have done, but I haven't been able to manage even the first chapter. The verse I should by now have moved beyond, which has been revolving in my mind as I walk, is: "In whom also we have obtained an inheritance, being predestinated according to the purpose of him who works all things after the counsel of his own will."

The verse lies raw on the sun-bright page beneath my memory of it, dusted with crystals of snow that cast hooded shadows over the print, and then travels down past physical and psychic barriers in application. The sun has already warmed me, I realize—always present, even on the coldest days, even during snowstorms, when steel-gray beams of it shuttle through a swirl of flakes and seem to hold them in suspension. I close my eyes and picture such a snow, with sun penetrating it at glancing angles, like the snow that arrived earlier and was gone before this sugar-snow fell in its weighted dusting. The picture spreads cold over my back, although I'm out of the wind, and without vision the wind is white and smells of sage from the rectangle at my feet, and then the image of my dream returns to me: traveling at the speed of light yet stilled in glory.

I'm used to being alone, and so not deceived by the sensations that can come when one is alone, but now I feel as if I'm a rower who has been working single-mindedly and looks out from the body of the boat to see it propelled by dozens of other oars, and in the silence I give thanks for the Reformed principles that have set my life in order.

I open my eyes. Stinging light. Rises and hummocks of dimness that swell in the distance, the tall grass I waded through swaying to one side with a new onslaught of wind—what my ancestors saw when they crossed the sea and then half of this continent: waves to the horizon. That hogback butte to the south is like a creased blue island rising from this sea underfoot, in more upheaval than one of water, though with the same wallop of sound when a wind like this works up, the grasses clamoring as if to get out of the way and then parting like fur as they lie flat; the sizzle up a beach of the foremost wave, which keeps curling ahead of the others though they're more massive, extensive, taller, weighted with an impact that can crush, and keep rolling in from farther out, like the waves behind waves of wind on this countryside of grass. Or so I see as long as I'm removed from the struggle with the wind, and have leisure to watch: the tented shelter imagination provides to the free. Reality's incarnate application of each detail to the space each has been allotted. Fantasy a prisoner's urge to escape a cell you can't see.

There's no possibility of engaging reality in the endlessness to which it corresponds without understanding the life at the center of it, for its own glory; the snowflake on my eyelash blurs the beauty of its attenuated precision. Perfection. Unalloyed perfection, I think, and slip into one of those moments when infinity invades the present with such power the future is past, so that I know that in many ways I'll never move beyond this point in my life. I look up, composed enough to let my eyes rest on the roof above the snow, our new home, and the memorized verse prints itself out across its shingled roof.

Oh, my brother, this dear and persevering realm of memory . . . Which wasn't how I intended to begin this. I wanted to tell you how our house looks overlaid with snow, how we are settling in here, and to let you know that as many degrees from the epicenter as two hundred miles are, I've come home again. It can be done. If one can sustain the impact of the move, and survive these times of helpless return to the condition of a worm on whom the whole is lost in his crawl across magnified detail, clod on clod, it can be done. New beginnings sink down and wash off across the tided caverns of the original loss.

I have survived, and I will live on.

+

In the very dead of winter, with Jerome at medical school, I stand in the stage-left wing, near the carpentry room, staring into a hand mirror a makeup girl holds up for me—late because of the note I lingered over from the one person I hope is in the house tonight—and hear applause as the lights come up on the set. The makeup girl pats water over my face to set my powder, and there is more applause, building, for the costumes, as the procession of the court begins onstage, thinning the ranks in my wing. I jerk on white gloves, shove a pearl ring in place on a finger, my back to the set, and bend for the girl to place the crown on my head, as a prop man runs up and claps the scepter I've forgotten into one hand. I turn with a swirl of my full-length cape overlapping in a tumble of folds on the floor, its weight tugging at my shoulders, then catch it up in my free hand as the royal retinue walks into stage light, and then I tread with Richard's regal liveliness out to the edge of the apron, until my cape washes up against the retaining rail, seeing the blur of faces layered in rows up the raked auditorium to the filled balcony, like rising tiers of my inner agitation, and cry, "Old John of Gaunt! time-honored Lancaster!"

+

She is in the basement afterward, leaning on a strip of wall between a pair of full-length mirrors outside the men's dressing room, in her rust-brown suit with suede trim, gripping a package over her breasts. Her curly, whitish hair adds a widening aura to her beauty, and dozens of people travel in and out of the mirrors on either side, as if emerging from her—Katherine, not Kate, possessor of every Katherine's easy nobility, though not a Katherine either, entirely, with her hearty laugh and sunny, disjointed jollity that paves my path like light. She laughs now, coloring with an emotion I once assumed to be coy (after that night when I first lay beside her in Jerome's driveway), and says, "I have two surprises for you. This." She hands me the package she's been holding, the size of a phonograph record but too thick, and reveals the white field of her healthy teeth, then glances behind me. "And him."

I see the familiar face and graduation suit in the mirror before I turn to Jerome coming at me, a new tie pulled loose at his throat, his hands going out, and take him in my arms.

"Great show, good brother," he says, and pounds my back. "It's the best I've seen here, really. You could come up to Chicago and teach them folk a thing or two. Hey, good to see you, fella, good to be here. I wouldn't have missed it for my life!"

+

Then it's 6 a.m. and the three of us are slipping down a sparkling street, recovering from an all-night cast party—during most of which it must have poured this freezing rain. I lean against a car for balance and slide along the glossy varnish it's encased in. Each branch and twig of every tree is sheathed in ice and clacking in the breeze for blocks—agitated pendulums. Katherine gingerly trots a few steps and slides up, laughing, and I grab her with an impact that cracks some of the skin from the car and sends it crashing to the street, where the breeze sets pieces of it off in a tinkling slide. Jerome is down on his gloves, with his rump raised, churning slipping feet like a spinning sprinter. "If I make it to that there tire by you guys," he says in a voice so loud in the empty morning street it seems it will bring down all this ice, "I think I'm going to have to lift my leg! Them folk didn't have enough bathrooms for the thirty-six-hundred-some people there!"

Katherine and I laugh, flattered, since the faculty couple held the party partly in our honor, and she grips my arm. Jerome fell asleep in a captain's chair in the middle of the living room before midnight, and an hour later Katherine was asleep on the floor beside him. Jill was present, of course, and led me into a library and through a wall of books, where only she would have known there was a door, into a darkened narrow hall where she kissed and tugged at me as she used to tug at others, and begged me to take her back, making vows I knew she wouldn't keep, but with such fervor I was prepared,. half loaded, to believe her. She made a proposition it might have been difficult to resist, if I hadn't retained a clear picture of the sleeping head on the floor near a couch, her whitish hair in disarray over the flat package (a recording of Verdi's *Otello* which I now grip in a freezing paw), and of Jerome asleep above her like the guardian of the room.

Now she brushes her lips over mine and takes hold of my trench coat, the same ragged one, and says, "I love your wrists." I flip the cape I've taken to wearing over a shoulder, exposing one half of its scarlet lining, and adjust the astrakhan cap she's given me—"to complete your outfitting," she said, in her quirky way of speaking. She leans into me and whispers, "There's never a major moment without accompanying squalor. I learned that from *Esmé*. It's squalor that puts an edge on every aristocratic nibble of mousse, and squalor that gives the dimension to this day."

Jerome, down flat, is pulling himself toward us with his elbows, a swimmer, and I can see the two of us going to him on either side, leaning as one, and lifting him to his feet. But for now her eyes, the blue of his, are so close they send their color through me into the ice. No, it's the sun. It's rising now. Everything is stilled yet adazzle.

+

We ease open the armorlike doors at the rear of the law auditorium, late. The man is on a lit platform, behind a podium, saying, "I named the goose for Marianne Moore." In the light laughter, the three of us find seats and sit. "Who is, though, a dear friend," he goes on, "and whom I nonetheless admire as a poet." Then he begins to read. Across the abundance of ruffles frothing from Katherine's blouse, I see Jerome put his chin in his palm, fingertips to his mouth, and bite a nail. He's on spring break and is worried, I know, about his grades.

The spotlit poet reads in a driving, disjointed lilt, holding the spread fingers of a hand near his broad bald head, which is tucked into the squarish shoulders his suit jacket hangs loosely from. He appears top-heavy, swaying with the words, now twiddling both hands as he takes a few quick steps for balance, his eyes focusing beyond us in a blank, visionary glare. His mouth reminds me of Jerome's, I think, and look at Jerome again, then slide down in my seat, not sure whether I care for this man. The first book of his I picked up fell open to a poem about an office where dust settles over pencils—ordinary, I felt—and with the fixed blankness now in his face, he resembles a businessman. In the afternoon he spoke like one, to the dozen of us who interpreted his poems for an audience, when he commented on our readings, and then he raised his head and cried out a poem of such power that Katherine took my hand.

He has finished reading, and is talking about another poem. Or is he? His voice has a declamatory lilt, and the spotlights pick up a shine of moisture on his reddening skull. "Oh, the hours it takes to reconstruct a second that is past!" he says. Then, "Oh, the whiskey on your breath!"—sounding out of breath himself—"could make a small boy *dizzy*."

In a blur the word whizzes by, an object, and his hands rise and orchestrate the next lines as they arrive, like a conductor working a tiny baton in close quarters, and then he dips and sways so far to one side it seems that he'll fall and his body, big and bearlike, comes from behind the podium in a glide, rocking with quick light steps that have a look of springing away from pain, as if his feet are injured and barely able to support his bulk—yet he's on tiptoes, dancing with a fussy delicacy, his fingers fluttering a tremolo over imaginary piano keys, his eyes ablaze and engaging all the audience now: "Then *waltzed* me off to bed!" His fingers run an uphill glissando to one side, an arm across his face, his emotional power above the peak of this afternoon, and then he adds in a weak, broken voice, taking hold of his meaty front with both hands, "Still *clinging* to your shirt."

In one movement the audience is on its feet in applause. Jerome flips his tie over a shoulder and raises his clapping hands above his head. He whistles and stamps his feet, and then turns and shakes me an OK sign, closing an eye in a wink that draws up his jaw so far it looks dislocated, and I cry crazily into the noise, "Yes! Yes, of course!"

+

The party, at an administrator's fancy house, moves at the pace of an underwater ballet. There's a buffet of hors d'oeuvres next to a bar the administrator works behind, mixing drinks. Roethke, alone on a couch set awkwardly in the center of the room, tests the balance of a drink on a knee, then sways from the waist as his eyes roll from wall to wall—a beached sea lion everybody evades. A few of the faculty pause in front of him on their revolutions of the room, and say a few words, or reach down to shake his hand. Jerome has had four drinks, and is displaying for an acquaintance, a graduate student, the book of poems

Roethke inscribed for me this afternoon—"For C.N., who reads them better than I"—and the grad student says, "Huh, he makes his 'I' like a backward C."

I down my drink and turn to Jerome, "Come on," I say. "Let's go see to him." I sit at one end of Roethke's couch, leaving room for Jerome in the middle, but he walks around and stands at my back. Roethke's big head revolves and his hooded eyes scour me in mistrust. "Aren't you afraid you'll catch it?" he asks, in his lilting reading voice.

"What's that?"

"Nobody's sat." He stares straight ahead, his knees high and parted and his drink gripped in both hands between them, glum. "I might've come over, if I could stand easier. Gout. The gentleman's disease. I admire the way you read. I didn't want to broadcast it to the academic goons."

"You remember me?"

"I wrote in that oily book you gave me—was it a library copy?—that you read them better than I do. A hell of a set of pipes. Do you want to make a record with me?"

"You're kidding."

His eyes, watery blue, bore flatly in on me, although a circular area of his upper forehead seems to bulge beyond them. "I don't kid anybody under forty, except publishers. They take your work and scrub your can and say you owe them. I'm selling my next book to three, so they can fight it out while I cut with the money and run. Caedmon asked me to do a new recording. Last year I was outré, now I'm in. They have a studio date set up for the fall. Put some poems you like on a tape and send it to me. I'll try to talk them into you doing half, me half."

Jerome prods my back and I look across the room at Katherine, whom I've been asking lately to marry me, it seems, every hour.

"Is that your girl?" Roethke asks. "The blonde you were with, the one watching you now with such affection?"

"Yes."

"Lovely eyes. And her smile— Who's that beside her? There on that barstool, that fidgety brunette you had a word with."

I tell him the name of the girl, an exchange student in theater who's been on campus for a year, and say, "She's British."

"The Limey's failing. No gams. She'd be quite, quite, otherwise."

"Pardon?"

"Those calves. Like Yorkshire hams."

I notice through the mist of drink that her lower legs, hitched up on the barstool, do look bloated, deformed.

"Poor thing," he says, and stares down at his glass of melting ice, then shakes it as if it's a dice cup.

"Would you like another drink?"

"Our host has kept up. I've had my quota. Who's that at your shoulder, your shadow?"

"My brother."

"He reads poems, too?"

"Nope," Jerome says, before I can answer.

Roethke swings his head as if he'll rear up. "I bet you write them."

"I memorize bones," Jerome says. "In about a decade I'll be a doctor, or that's the general idea."

"Good business! Fine wage!"

"That's what I've heard," Jerome says.

The party has shifted into a higher gear; soon they'll want Roethke, I figure, and I don't want to give up the chance to do a recording. I plant my heels in the spongy carpet, and say, "What's your favorite poem?"

"The present dozen."

"In the book you read from?"

"Yes, and 'Meditations of an Old Woman.' Those are from my grandmother. They still surprise me. I can see them; mine I can't."

"The new poems must be difficult."

"To do? I'm going full bore."

"Right at the edge."

"Just over, a few have suggested."

"Like finally making it to the top of some high stairs, and then you realize you're falling down the other side."

He sits back with the glass on a knee. "Where'd you get that?"

"What?"

"What you just said." His eyes narrow in his mistrust.

"I just said it."

"You're pretty smart, huh?"

"Not that I know of."

"For your age." He rocks and heaves his weight back and forth on the couch, then pushes himself to his feet and heads toward the door, left open for circulation, in his soft-footed, slow-rolling gait, limping on one leg. He bumps into the doorjamb with a shoulder and leans there, his jacket bunched at his back, as if staring through the screen door at the night, and then pushes it open and steps outside. After a pause he goes lumbering past a large window, still carrying his glass.

"What did you say?" Jerome asks. "I missed that."

"I don't know. It came out."

Through the window we can see him stop at a car, his back to the house, settling himself as if to take a leak, but his head turns up. In the afternoon, at the reading, he mentioned his young wife and read poems for her, and I'm sure he's looking in her direction, west. I go over to Katherine and tell her about the recording, so giddy I feel I've downed several drinks, and then do down most of the one she's holding. Behind us Jerome insists to the grad student, "Yeah, Roethke asked him, it's true, I heard it, be*lieve* me." The speed again has picked up, and when I look around, a quirky flickering of light presents features of the people in staccato poses as they talk, although I can't make out any words, and the room starts into a tilt that funnels me toward another time.

Roethke, back inside with an outdoor breeze trailing him, treads toward a nook at the other end of the room, with three-quarter-high walls of hardwood cabinets, where crashers who have carried in bottles of their own are gathered, and is gone. Katherine whispers that we should leave, but I need confirmation about the recording. I go into the nook and see Roethke at a counter, pouring another drink. I sway at this, after his mention of a quota, and have to set a foot to one side for balance as the room darkens and narrows to the passageway behind books where Jill led me that earlier, winter night. A proposition of that magnitude? The only light appears to rest over Roethke's ridged forehead, and then he leans his rump against a stove, drawing the light with him.

"What were you looking at outside?" I ask, surprised at my prying.

"To see if my lucky star is still there."

"Was it?"

He swirls the ice in his drink. "Not so absolutely as I'd like it to be. Maybe it's the latitude. But I have my nervous button on." A finger glides to his lapel, where a circular disk, bright scarlet, the size of a cigarette end, shines like a drop of fresh enamel. "I wear it when I travel. From my mother. I believe it commemorates her taking out a half mill in insurance." His eyes swing in a pattern of inward search. "Your mind tends two ways at such news from your mother: that she'll be okay, and that you're the beneficiary. Personal history of a black sheep. All I have to do is press it, like this"—I follow his finger, one-minded, nearly hypnotized, and watch it make contact—"and everything goes away."

I step back for balance, and see one half of a face, porous, with light gathered across an eye staring down at me. "Don't forget your stairs," he says. "And the abyss." He holds up a hand, fingers spread, as if to shove this into me, and rocks in his bearlike dance. "The abyss? The abyss? The abyss you can't miss. It's right where you are—a step down the stair."

Then I'm outside, in the night, on a blackly gleaming street, with Katherine supporting me on one side and Jerome on the other.

+

Jerome is in Chicago for the summer, working in an emergency room, and I'm at home, fighting an academic backwash. I've switched curricula so many times (now to radio-television) that it will be another year before I graduate. Grandma Jones has died. I was handed the news before the final performance of a play I now wish I never had tried out for, *Waiting for Godot*. A policeman rang my doorbell at 2:00 a.m. with a telephone message from California: "Grandma died. Will you come to her funeral?"

Laura and I use the large house to evade each other. Katherine is on a summer-long tour of the East Coast with her father, and whenever I step into the closet where I keep Dad's tape recorder, a pressure like a hand holds me from Roethke's words, so that my readings are like random sounds striving to make sense. And now this:

> *Hi Love!*
>
> *I'm strangely distressed as never before or perhaps oftentimes before. I want to become a monkess and live alone in this white apartment and sit out on my fire escape and eat raw unwashed carrots and become* me *. . .*

I fold up the letter, my hands shaking so badly my knuckles knock together, and pick up a pencil.

A DRY YEAR

> *Grandmother: unable*
> *Footsteps on tufted stairs, unable*
> *Stir up whirlwinds   dust?*
> *Stairs flatten. A*
> *Wrinkled sister rolls them up,*
> *Sends letters, her tears*
> *Mine I count.*
> *Bitter stuff to admit. I lie too much.*
> *Unable to   I*
> *Rain these—what?—over empty—*
> *Pen going dry. One last thing:*
> *Though I hear your voice above*
> *The jays crying "Drink your fill!"*
> *I see my brother*

I see him at this kitchen table, coughing up his soup the night our mother died. The telephone rings. I'm close enough to reach it, but let it ring. Dad grabs it at last, then hands it to me.

"Yes?" I say.

"Guess who, sweetie?"

"Purkeet."

"On the button!"

"Where are you?"

"About thirty-six miles away, according to my map." He hums a pitch and then sings, from the theme of a local radio station, "*Pee*-oh! re-ah!"

"Peoria? Why, for God's sake?" I stand and turn, and there is Dad, at the window, with his back to me, staring into the night over the back yard.

"I've got a job at the radio station that sings this ditty into your home dozens of times a day, I bet. I knew it couldn't be so bad down here if it was where you're from, and— Surprise! I like the job! They have me doing everything, even on-the-air stuff." Then he says, as if covering the receiver, "Some of these guys are gay. Erase that. We'll make a tape. Come down and spend the day, or, better, a night. We'll make a wild tape, in this fabulous studio, on A-number-one equipment."

I try not to offend him, but won't make any promises, and finally he says, "You shouldn't forget old friends. Are you suffering a terminal case of central Illinois torpor, or what?"

"What."

"Come see me! Come by me! We'll reminisce and have fun!"

I sense that Dad is listening with his entire back. Finally I take down the phone number Purkeet gives me, and hang up.

"Who was that?" Dad asks. He doesn't turn, but can perhaps see me in the window, where I'm able to dimly make out his reflected face.

"Somebody from school. You met him."

"Rick Purkeet?"

"Yes. He's in Peoria—working at a radio or television station."

"Did you know that?"

"No. But he always said his dad could get him a job in TV."

"You should go see him."

"He asked me to."

"Maybe he'd have a lead on a job for you. Did he mention a day?"

"This weekend."

"Well?" He turns with a smile, shaking the change in his pocket, and I realize that he has been worried I won't find work of the sort I want. He says, "Go ahead, go, why don't you? Use the car."

+

Purkeet inserts a cartridge tape into a console at the radio station, then looks off through a glass window of the studio as if to listen more closely. I can't see any change in him, except that he's wearing a tie. It's difficult to understand the hurried voices that arrive over a speaker, but I recognize one as Purkeet's, imitating an old man; he's talking to somebody about a car. Music comes up, and with the tag line I understand that it's an advertisement for a car dealer.

The tape beeps at a cue dot and pops out of the console. "That's just one thing I've done," he says. "I'm both voices, did you notice? A bit like Second City, eh? I have artistic freedom here. I can be *creative*." He opens his hands beside his face. "Surprise! I like it!"

+

In the same convertible his roommate picked out, Purkeet says, "You're not prone to jumping out of cars anymore, are you?" the moment the thought occurs to me. "Just kidding," he says, and then punches on his radio and sings, "Pee-oh! re-ah, deep in the *hard* of Illinois!"

I was afraid it was going to be like this, I nearly say.

"Should we try Szechwan?"

"Pardon?"

"Oliental. Dinner. Or do you prefer Italian? Mexican, hombre? Greek? There are some surprisingly good restaurants here—a new French one, fairly authentic, opened last week."

"It doesn't make any difference to me."

He slaps my thigh, and says, "Haven't changed a bit, have you?"

+

In a foldout couch in his apartment, Purkeet rolls in greenish light from a pair of windows fitted with gauzy curtains, giving off heat like a radiator in the humidity, and says, "Come on, come here," and I sit back, with my trousers on, in an old chair draped with rough cloth.

"Are you still stuck with that Jill?"

"No."

"Oh?" There's a note of surprise. "You told me there couldn't be anybody dearer than the sweet darling bitch."

"Then I met—" I resist mentioning her name. "Somebody else."

"He? She?"

"Please. In her case, there isn't anybody . . ."

"Dearer? Bitchier? How about giving me a try—just once."

"No."

"Where's the spirit? This moping's enough to get me, well, down."

I could tell him how Katherine's father arrived with a woman friend for a performance of *Waiting for Godot*, the night after I'd heard about Grandma Jones, and how the woman was so appalled at my onstage character she wouldn't speak to me. "She was sure I was a true horny, beaten-down, unshaven wino or, well, *tramp*," I could say, and he'd probably say, "You're a damn good actor." Katherine's father, though civil, apparently thought worse; he ordered Katherine not to see me again, and at the end of school he took her on his tour of the East. Now he wanted her to enroll in an Eastern school.

But none of this could convey any sense of the succeeding levels of darkness I'd been descending into since that performance. Back home, I worked on a carpentry crew, in a daze, always tired, unable to sleep at night, and one morning was told to wet down the inside of a double garage attached to a new house, in order to settle the sandy soil before a slab for the garage was poured. Halfway through this, I was told to take a truck and pick up a load of cement blocks in a city forty miles off. I kept fighting sleep on the way back, and then woke to find myself headed for the guardrail of a curve at seventy miles an hour and discovered that the brakes wouldn't work, with the weight of the cement blocks added, and just missed the end of the rail, barreling straight ahead, and hit the roof of the cab as I had in the convertible, dimly aware that a gravel road had appeared in a straightaway off the curve, and came down on it with an impact that broke several cement blocks, as it turned out. Finally I got the truck slowed, turned and drove back, and discovered a crowd at the house. Uncle Fred stood with a cigar in his mouth, shaking his head as I walked up. The water I'd left running had created such pressure, mixed with sand, that it had caved in a wall of the basement; the muddy slide, mixed with blocks, sprawled halfway across the floor, and had crushed a new furnace and water heater. Then there was the sound of an air horn, and two ready-mix trucks pulled up with cement for the garage. So I've been working on a plastering crew, and my shaking fingers feel they're sandpapering one another with the dry erosion of my skin from lime.

I could tell him how, when I step into the closet . . . Ah, no. A vision of that morning with Katherine and Jerome returns, in its dazzle of impossibility, and the gauzy curtains near Purkeet's bed seem the same I've seen in every room I've entered since. If there were a hammer handy, like the one I use at work, I'd start in on his windows.

"Can't you talk to an old friend?" he asks, busy under the sheet.

"Your talk leads to one thing."

"Is that what your girls say?"

I think about this until it seems another season, and the green-tinted wall appears as leaf shadow, then the curtains sway in over a leg.

"Don't leave," he says in a shaky voice, as if he's crying or pretending to, or merely moving his beat up a notch. "I need you!"

What day is it? Which year? Soon it seems that the boy in bed, below the chair where I sit, is asleep. This regular sound of breathing that once carried me off. How difficult to sit up with a child helpless from fever, when his sickness seems the result of your own indecent behavior. You go to the kitchen to get him ice cream, and find it at last in a snowbank outside, where you stored it, the carton still intact inside the chilly film that gathers over life, once separated from its source. Lord, you know how I put on my shoes and rose from that chair, and walked out the door down the street through that humid Illinois night. But before I return to my son inside, I have to admit to my astonishment at the crystalline mass of the Milky Way at this latitude, gathered like a wave about to break over me, and I offer this prayer before it does. Amen.

+

Sitting in a passenger jet, looking through its oval porthole across the sunstruck aluminum wing at baggage carts and forklifts busy under the bellies of planes down the oil-stained and rose-gray concrete of the airport, I seem to be seeing over a grainy bedcover the miniature vehicles of the model airport I built, of a dimensional stability that permitted me to enter the plane imaginatively, to this seat where I sit, above the activity of pieces being pushed beyond the porthole by younger hands, inside prophecy given form, a nylon strap over my thighs.

I travel to the East to record, and twice a year from city to city, to conduct interviews for the shows that are aired when I'm on vacation, or ill. I vowed to pursue Katherine everywhere I could, projecting my voice from as many stations as possible, and leaned on every show with the pressure of courtship. I wasn't perhaps grateful enough when it worked and she returned and married me, so I've lost her again.

The whistle of the turbines has increased and we're backing—little access to these thoughts unless the coming minutes might be the last. Too often, lately. If I disregard the shaking that sets every bolt and screw abuzz, the takeoff is smooth. Then the first hard bank that comes so soon I'm hanging sideways over industrial rooftops and a pale-lime water tower that seems our pivot and so will be the point of impact if we fall. The desired angle of perspective, or trajectory, is at last achieved, with some wobbles and tilts of the wings, and the engines begin to back down. The misty landscape has right-angled connections except where irregular tufts of hills and loops of streams connect—fields everywhere else: green-gold tinged with brown and red before the onset of fall, with blank black squares between like the impact of heat from a register. Then past a curling wrinkle of shore outlined in white, over Lake Michigan, into early morning still partly under a phase of night—the sky above the lake lying in low flat straight bands of color, beginning with brown-black at the bottom, then an orange band, then gold, then yellow, fraying into brightness where rays of sun take hold, so that a greenish-aqua haze disperses, higher up, into baby-blue. Then dark-blue opaque stormy night above that. One star. Or planet, perhaps, in its morning shine, and I picture Katherine as the wing goes down on my side.

Will I ever face her free of myself before I'm gone from this life for good?

College has no power over me, with Jerome and Katherine gone, and I keep stopping in the street to think, This is life? I call Jerome, but can't explain my disaffection, so I quit school and take a job at a television station, producing used-car ads. When I graduate to booth announcing, which I enjoy, and then appear on camera, my sole consolation is passing on my walk to work each day (in a used-car lot managed by a dealer other than the one I work for) a 1958 Jaguar, and knowing I could buy it, like that. And although it's a matter of months, it seems the mere flash of a reflection, a shifting of weight, before I'm traveling toward Jerome, rocked by the rhythm our Lionel train used to take, with everything I ever owned left behind, except what I can carry in a pair of suitcases. Plus a guitar. I've learned to play two folk songs on it.

I'm rocked to sleep, and awaken within the period between the six o'clock news and the nightly preparation for the news at ten, when a colleague from the station and I would go across the street for a drink. I push myself up into the swaying aisle and use the backs of seats for balance as the train chatters over a raised roadbed with its listing hula-twitches. There's hardly anybody in the bar car, and I sit alone at a table with my beer, feeling aged and wealthy with the fatness of five hundred dollars in my breast pocket. Then a faggy-looking Okie with hair slicked back like Elvis is across from me, saying, "Da y'all mind?"

He's drinking the same beer but from the bottle, I see in the blackened glass, where distant lights pulse and then a red flasher whisks by, clanging, leaving only our faces projected over the speeding landscape—milk-white, rippling ghosts.

"Whach'all up to?" he asks, and before I have a chance to consider this, he modifies the question: "Whatcha do?"

If you're not in a trade or business, how do you answer? I say I've relieved myself of a television job for another assignment, keeping this formal.

"Yeah, I figured y'all was in show business or one of them entertainment fields."

I look directly at him but can't discover any irony—although it's difficult to detect malice in a Southerner, with those layered manners from far before even Reconstruction.

"Or maybe politics, I'se thinkin, like the Kennedy-type boys, with that there hair down past your ears."

I get a glimpse of our reflections as my neck muscles gather in a grip; since I've let my hair grow, people mention this resemblance, and when they do, I feel those branches clawing my back as I break through the hedge and Kennedy's hand goes to his face—an image I had to contend with at the station on the afternoon when the network broke into a show with the announcement that Kennedy had been shot. Two days later, as my colleague and I were coming back from the bar we'd been visiting more frequently since the assassination, into the studio's lobby, I ducked and threw an arm around him as, on the monitor, a man stepped from a crowd and shot Lee Harvey Oswald in the guts. The world as it was now.

"I was thinking you might even be one of them Beatle-creature guys, you know, like the singers Ed Sullivan had on his show a while back?" He turns the end of his cigarette in the ashtray, his lips pursed, then raps it, while I try to decide what it is, other than his resemblance to Elvis Presley, that holds me. Then I have it; his accent is Billy Gene's—and with this I sense threads from my past unreeling over a landscape suddenly blank, and I understand that the North and the South divide America against itself, as Lincoln saw.

"You see them guys and you got to wonder if they're one-hundred-percent stud stock, or maybe ain't got a little female in em, ya dig?"

+

At Jerome's green-painted rooms off Washington, he leads me to a dented refrigerator, hands me a can of beer, and says, "What happened?"

"I quit my job."

"I mean, with you? Let's go out to the other room."

A room with two chairs, a worn couch, and a wobbly-looking table, where a three-legged lamp with an orange plastic shade, pleated like a Chinese lantern, gives off colored light. Jerome sits in a chair with a bean-bag ashtray on his knee, and I settle on the couch, where he has said I'll sleep. "Joe, you know," he says, pointing with his beer can toward a room off the kitchen— his roommate's: a tidy Japanese in a golf shirt and shorts who shook my hand at the door and then went bowing back to his desk. "Joe apparently wants to study for a change. Did you tell Dad you quit?"

"No."

"You plan to?"

"Yes. Could you tell him? I don't want to talk to him right now."

He sets the can on the floor and places both hands on the arms of the chair, cottony under his fingers, and the room seems to fill, beyond the lamp, with dark-green light. "Sure, I could, I suppose." He studies me and places a hand over his stomach and slides it toward his ribs as he taps its top with the fingertips of the other, up a ragged T-shirt with the same holes as the gin-soaked one he wore the night of his party.

"What are you doing there?" I ask, nodding at his hand.

"A habit, I guess. Percussing. Listening through the old layer of meat. The only person you can really practice on is yourself. Occasionally Joe and I cooperate, but he's so damn ugly." He smiles at a meaning beyond me. "I'm at a point where I'm developing all the symptoms."

"Of what?"

"Whatever we're studying. Diverticulitis. Lung cancer. Did

you hear about the Surgeon General's report? Pinworms. Scabies. Tapeworms. Tinea capitis, characterized by scaly patches penetrated by a few dry brittle hairs." He keeps up the tapping.

"How do you feel about school, or what you're doing now?"

"There are days when I'd as soon be pushing a lawn mower," he says, and gives Dad's look of tasting alum. "I guess I'm second-guessing the wisdom of the medical profession. Disillusioned?"

"Are you?"

"I'm wondering. Isn't this the disillusioned era? I'd rather be Gandhi. It isn't necessarily the brilliant ones who make it as doctors. Quite a few of those, in fact, give in from the pressure. It helps if you're smart, but as long as you have a kind of sheer, dumb, dogged will to make it, you can. That's both disillusioning and an encouragement, I guess." His smile now is almost like the Okie's on the train.

"Hmm," I say, convinced that if I were able to listen closely, I might understand what he's saying, but I can't translate his new semaphore.

"You soon realize that doctors aren't necessarily a special breed, or the saviors of the world. We've got a few real clunkers, even, teaching us." He cranes his head. "Right, Joe?"

"Right" comes muffled from the room off the kitchen.

"Of course, some professors are probably here because they couldn't hack it as doctors. Two, anyway." He leans forward, urgent, with his elbows on his knees. "You have to hear this. I was in the emergency room the other night when they brought a guy in, get this, with a Coke bottle up his butt hole. 'Goodness,' I said, 'how did this happen?' 'I was naked, I was painting my room, I was up on a ladder,' he said, 'I fell on it.' He wouldn't change his story. 'Good thing it didn't break,' I said, and he started groaning. I examined him and the bottle was not only past that first curved bulge, you know, but all the way up, with his sphincter closed over the bottom—no way I was going to get that out. Then I noticed. 'A good thing, too, it had Vaseline on it, huh?' I said. 'I used that trying to get it out!' he yelled. Would not change his story, or admit he'd been diddling. There must be a moral there, such as, Fess up, or it'll get worse. The encouragement to me about school, a heh-heh"—this is a new laugh, with his teeth clenched in a smile and the cigarette jutting up from a corner of his mouth, F.D.R.—"is that I'll make it, I'd say. I got that old tenacity or sheer plod. If I survive this year, I'm in like Flynn."

Beneath the lesson of this, which applies to my schooling in a downward tumble past Purkeet, I sense an insistence on the hickdom of our background, or the platitudinous parts of it. He revolves his cigarette end on the ashtray as if screwing its pale pointed coal into a sphere.

"Just so I don't end up a Cyclops," he adds.

"How's that?"

"That big round mirror at the center of my forehead my only eye." I notice with this that he's wearing the glasses with gray-silver frames he wore in high school. "And that eye focused only on medicine. I've started reading some other things this year." From the raggedy chair he produces a paperback with a huge V across it. "Have you read this?"

"No."

"Not bad, for a novel about paranoia. I like some of that German writer Grass's stuff. I'd like to read him in the original. I figure a lot of his humor is probably verbal. Mailer and Updike are running a weird race. I liked the *Rabbit* book. *Balthazar* isn't bad if you can take persimmon marmalade. I like all I've read of Kawabata. Actually, the whole Oriental culture interests me. Joe's influence, I guess." He cranes his head back again and yells, "Ain't that right, Joe?"

"Whatever you say, big J," the dim voice replies.

"I'm talkin about your *hair*-a-tage, boy!"

The voice says, "I told them, 'Don't sign the Sino-Soviet pact, guys. You can't trust the little stinkers.' Did they listen? No."

Still with his head thrown back, so that his Adam's apple protrudes like a curled knuckle, rising and throbbing as he talks, Jerome calls, "Should we extemporize for our guest on the sub-sub-culture of Chicago? Shall we let him in on the secrets of the best spots for Chink food?"

"Big J, I have this test."

"Come out and have a beer! Don't be a grind!"

"Big J, buddy, we have this anatomy practical tomorrow, remember?"

"Do you have to study?" I ask in a sudden whisper, surprised that his head is still thrown back as if to provoke his roommate further.

"Naw. I'll flunk it." He turns to me, alert to something, and his smile alters. "No, I'm ready. I know my bones. You have to realize that Joe's the one who usually doesn't study." I can tell that he knows I'm uneasy about the way he talks to his roommate. "It's probably one of the reasons we've decided we're perfectly matched. I get too serious in my plod. We both do. We've picked up a grotesque brand of Dad's seriousness." He rubs his cigarette around in the bottom of the ashtray, as if writing there, then looks up quick, like Dad. "I say grotesque, because it's way overblown, without his forgiveness underneath." He draws on the cigarette and one half of his face streaks yellow as if in a net of pain. "I should speak for myself. I've learned a lot living with Joe. Something about him and his culture keeps nagging at me. Buddhism, the whole bit."

"Do you go to church?"

"I tried a few places for a while, when I first came to Chicago, but I couldn't pretend my heart was in it."

"I know what you mean," I say, angry, positive that it is the Church, primarily, that's the source of my problems.

"I figured you were back."

"In the Church?" I ask as he says, "In the Church"—an echo.

"No."

The room, already too dark in its dark greens, takes on the darker atmosphere of being the last shelter in the city, with a last lamp going, when late-night conversation lifts loose from even this single mooring.

He says, "If it's not at the center of your life, it can't be called religion, and religion comes in all varieties. Dad has it as much as anyone I know. Joe has a touch of something, which I'm still trying to figure out. It would be condescending to call it 'inner serenity.' A lot of the guys here—well, medicine is their religion. For me right now, the Church itself—'Holy Mother

Church,' within quotes, as it were—or the Church as an institution, isn't it."

I look past him, toward something about to rise from the orangy shadow in a corner.

"At this point, I guess I'd have to call myself agnostic," he says. "I'm not insensitive to different kinds of belief, I don't think—that's why I felt you were somewhere new—and I'm not hardened against it, or angry about it, like some I run across in school. Or the emergency room. There's something science can't classify. God? I have a sense of a central sort of mystery, especially in healing. Some of the things you see are scary, and a lot of it is swept to the side. So, *something*. But that's about as far as it goes for me. Not too intellectual, eh? If it isn't at the center of your life, and you admit that, things fade fast."

The shadowy corner has yielded its substance, and I stare into a vision of Katherine. My feelings for her are as close to religion as anything I've felt in the Church, and our relationship, or my dedication to it, existed in a realm like religion, as she displaced Jill and Bobbie and Dewey back to *her* and became, not like *her*, but *her* equal in the individuality of her womanhood, so that each setting where I was with her took on the dazzle of that ice-covered morning; and she hasn't faded.

"What about Katherine?" he asks.

I tell him, trembling, that she is now living in a semi-Southern city, where she has re-enrolled in school. "I still have hope," I say.

"Don't give up."

"I won't."

"Sheer plod."

"I know."

"It'll work out. It's clear she loves you."

I look up, surprised at a sear in my lungs and eyes like ammonia, and see a dim miniature of my face, reflected in his glasses, staring wide-eyed back at me.

"How did the Army finally classify you?" he asks.

"1-Y. National emergency."

"Your legs?"

"I'm assuming that. I didn't ask."

He turns to the side to evade smoke as he draws so hard

on his cigarette that it juts up again like F.D.R's, and then plucks it free. "I kind of figured that. Someday I'd like to see the X-rays."

What's this, I wonder, and picture steam rising from under our jackknifed hood through the glare of turned-up headlights on *Meadowlane*, and say, uneasy, "You're sure you don't have to study?"

"Yes," he says, and looks down.

I wonder how often he thinks of the accident, and he remains so long in silence, with his head lowered, that I'm sure he's fallen asleep.

"Oh," he says at last, and looks up through a mist of anger. "Oh, yes. Well, I could always review. A good review never hurt a plodder."

+

I sleep through the day, waking as he and Joe revolve in and out of the apartment for classes, and toward evening I feel a hand grip my shoulder from behind.

"Is there anything you'd like to do in this city, boy?"

"Hn?"

"While you're in Chicago? Do you want to go out, or order in a pizza?"

"Sleep."

"Well, you can do that. You're in the perfect position for that."

Absolved from work? I wonder. Lying on his couch?

"Sleep, then," he says, and his hand draws away.

+

When I wake, it's to the darkness of that last shelter in the city coming unmoored. My hands are shaking so badly I have to hurry to the refrigerator for a beer, and in the search for an opener I start to pant. Letter to Dad, I think, and shift the orange-plastic lamp to one side of the scarred-up table. My first impulse is to mention Katherine, so I take my time getting paper and a ballpoint from my suitcase, then I pull up a chair and arrange everything until the impulse has passed.

April 17, 1964

Dear Dad,

A few days ago I quit my job at the television station. I worked there long enough to pay most of the bills I owed, including some due with the university, and when the work started having no return other than a paycheck—no inner joy or even satisfaction—I quit. At the moment I'm in Chicago with Jerome. In a day or two I'll be leaving for New York. Perhaps you think I've executed another inconceivable, harebrained, asinine blunder.

I'm not certain he'll think this, but I'm sure it will be the interpretation my stepmother puts on it, so I let it stand.

I hope not. I'd rather starve and feel a small amount of peace and inner joy than be financially secure and suffer constant restlessness. I have to do what brings me peace, and what I believe I was meant to do. Anything else is painful compromise.

I sit back. The words have appeared like a fall down a stairway, and feel that abrupt. I try to formulate the final direction and encounter such a swirl of images, most of them connected to Katherine, that I have to lean through them to reach the page.

Perhaps you think I've ruined what was working for me— quitting school, quitting a job that paid fairly well—or that I've wrenched and interrupted an enviable security. I think not. I believe, like Hamlet, "There's a divinity that shapes our ends, rough-hew them how we will." I go to a future of endless possibility—including every conceivable kind of failure. But I cannot lose, because by doing what I feel driven to do, I won't fail myself. And that, after all has fallen away, is what I have to live with.

My hand is trembling so much I have to go to the refrigerator again, and when I take a side step to balance a swirl of thought, like a line of fizzy bubbles in my favorite agate, I figure it's the beer—it has me afloat, detached, held within a morbid disinterest that numbs my arms.

*As long as I, in my deepest despair and hopelessness, can fall
back into myself without being repulsed because of a compromise
at the center of my heart, the loneliness that might come won't
affect me. All my work can be honest, unfettered, and loving,
because I know I'm engaged in what means the most to me. If
I'm capable of satisfying myself, I'm sure someday I'll be able to
satisfy others. It will only take a lot of work and perhaps a little
suffering. I'm prepared for both. Though I'm not headed toward
the most lucrative use of my potential, perhaps, I believe I'm
doing what is most unselfish. Because from this point there will
be no compromises, no sense of doing merely out of duty, and,
what is most important, no possibility of disappointing anyone.*

Charles

I glance over the pages and discover that I'm unable to
read them. I imagine Dad opening them at the fold-down desk
in the room where I used to lie on the cot in my cast, his
troubled and intelligent eyes trying to take them in, and sense
the molecules of that blizzard from the kitchen in Hyatt open
inside me. A hand grips the back of my neck—Jerome—in what
feels like a professional manner, and then doesn't feel like one.

"What's that?" he asks.

"A letter to Dad."

"I'm glad you decided to write. He'd feel bad if you didn't.
I was going to call as soon as you left, but I wouldn't ever be
able to say it in the right way—I mean, so he'll understand."

"You think he will?"

"At least it won't come as a surprise from somebody else."
He grips my neck harder, then releases it. "Do you want to go
out now? We could go to some all-night place."

"No."

"Another beer, then?"

There are three empty cans in front of me. "No, I'll sleep."

But when I close my eyes, I start to picture all the rooms
I've slept in, and don't know where I'll wake. Or worse, who I'll
wake as. Then the imagistic rush of sleep begins, and I have to
fight to keep the people from turning into marionettes, which
will mean my mind is gone. I wake to the sound of bells tolling
in the neighborhood, and sit up on the couch with my face in

my hands, as if returning from a serious illness. *Or just at the start of one*, a new quick voice inside me suggests.

"You're up," Jerome says from the lighted doorway across the room.

"What day is it?"

"Sunday. Late."

"Could you take me to the airport?"

"Today? You have a flight out?"

"I'll make a reservation."

"Well, it's a good day to borrow Joe's car," he says.

I pack, then see the letter in its envelope, addressed, on the table, and a stir of last night's illness starts in me. "Will you mail that?"

"Sure," he says.

Joe goes backing toward his door again, bowing, after shaking my hand goodbye, and I see Neal retreating from me as I rise from the wire record stand. Jerome and I grab my luggage and get into the car at the curb, a Renault with holes in the floor that open onto the street. Now we're going to be cramped to make my check-in time. He hurries through the gears of the floor shift, taking side streets to the Expressway, hands jumping at a racing speed, and the sight of them in their rush reminds me of Grandma Jones. There's such a straining in my own hands to leap like his I feel I'll have to sit on them. Grandma. These communions of loss he and I can never express in grief.

Once we're on the Expressway, going at a faster tilt, I say, "What did you think about Grandma—"

"It was awful!" he yells above the noisy engine, before I can say "dying." "It hit me as bad as Mom's! I was just thinking about her!"

I look at his face, firm, his eyes fixed on the road—the complications of his response set in stone.

"Even when we don't talk," I say, "I feel we understand each other."

He gives an OK sign in my direction, then a quick glance like a peek. "I've felt that." A single firm nod. "Well, we're almost there."

He insists on coming in and standing beside me as I get my

ticket; I check the guitar and one suitcase, and he carries the other down a long corridor of glass, through a darkened hub, down a narrower corridor to my gate. Now that we've made it, I have a half hour before the flight, I notice, terrified that neither of us will have anything to say, and he sets down my suitcase, claps his hands, and cries, "Astound them fellas!"

"I guess."

"The theater people in New York."

"Dad."

"Make em love your butt!" He takes me in his arms and pounds my back as if hitting a series of spots in a certain sequence, and cough balls of unresolved conflict fly out my mouth. "Remember, we love you," he says, blurred by a sudden movement, his glasses striking light, and with a slam to my shoulder, his back is turned, and he becomes miniature as he walks off with his hands in his pockets, gone in the crowd.

+

Even in the airplane, where I look out on sun-fried clouds that close over every connection below, the Church has followed. On the plastic tray of food in front of me, a place card grants Catholic passengers a special dispensation from fasting, via the Bishop of Kansas City. I stare down at the creamy clouds tinged silver along their edges, and an anxiety, drumming with the pressure of the near-deafening engines, starts at my feet like electrified water and rises. I've failed my father, I think. I'll die before I've kept one promise to him. And then: This time, I've hurt him so badly he'll never recover.

+

I come banging with my luggage up the tilting stairs and cheesy hallways to this room. I circle the bed, I raise a window shade: the fire escape. Green-painted bars divide the street five stories below, and off in the distance, a tower with an illuminated clock; a gold dome bathed in spotlights; and a tall apartment building lit at its center on every floor, like a ladder of light leading to a sky so starless it could be a ceiling where the ladder ends. Home.

Blank darkness, as the full reel revolves on the arm of the projector, a loose strip of film clacking with increasing speed. Lights up. Only a few reels, scattered out of order, from that dividing moment in time to our end.

+

SEPT 13. *For the record, my name is Charles Neumiller. I'm—*

A cop's rapping seems to originate at the door with the shelf across it, but the other one trembles from the force of a knock. "Yes," I say.

"The super. I got a letter you ain't seen."

+

A bright space opens through a dislocation of drunkenness, and I waver, unsure of where I stand, and discover that I'm on the phone with Jerome, who's in Okinawa. I say, "Why'd you pick the Air Force?"

"I didn't. At the end of the senior year they put our names in a hat and went by threes: Army, Navy, Air Force. Democratic."

"Where did Joe end up?"

"The Marines."

I laugh, and the barks bounce back in concentric bursts, ringing and re-entering one another. "Hey, this is like talking down a culbert."

"Pardon?"

"A culbert. You know, like a culbert unner a road—Midwesternese."

"Oh." There's the prim concision his voice has before he puts a cigarette to his lips.

"Hey, are you smoking?"

"Yes, I am."

"The Surgeon General didn't scare you, huh?"

"Oh . . ."

"Hey, what time is it there?"

"About 0500, Okinawa time. It must be late afternoon, stateside."

"I'm not sure. It all looks the same to me. What's 0500?"

"Five in the morning."

"Did I wake you?"

"Oh . . ." I can imagine him shrugging.

"Sorry! Do you have a cold?"

"Not yet. But I'm standing in a tin BOQ shaking in my undies."

"BOQ?"

"Bachelor officers' quarters."

"A lot of initials, huh?"

"Oh . . ." Another offhand shrug.

I want to say down the culvert, "This is a transoceanic call, these 'Ohs' of yours are costing me a buck apiece," but meanwhile I'm trying to figure out the reason I called. He's been in Okinawa a year, although at the moment it seems we're in his green-painted room again. "What's going on there?"

"I guess we might be leaving for Korea."

"Korea?"

"We're being issued sub-zero fatigues and Naha is in the tropics."

"*Korea?* I thought that was over in the fifties."

"That's what some people thought about Vietnam, no?"

"Oh, right," I say, although it seems something is askew, or perhaps incriminatory in his response, and then, just as I'm wondering whether it's proper for him to mention this on the phone, I hear a sound like a racing car crossing the culvert. "Jesus!" I cry. "What was that?"

"Beats me."

"Did they erase that?"

A silence pulses closer, with a breath from him, and then reverses back over the distance. "How long have you been up?" he asks.

"I don't know. A day or two."

". . . wondered . . ."

Is this electrical static? "Hey, the new show is doing fantastic. We've been syndicated."

"Great."

The silence is like a rock in its drop down a deep well. "Can you get the show there?"

"A guy here with an international transceiver taped one last month."

"What'd you think?"

"Tops . . ." The rock hits water. ". . . high"—a squawk— ". . . better."

"Is that static on the line, or reservations?"

There's a long breath through his nostrils that practically warms my ear, then he says, "How's Dad?"

"Dad?" I look up and see Dad centered in a cameo of mist; then he swings away and is pacing down a hall, and I understand I'm in the house he's moved to in northern Illinois; Katherine and I are living with him until we find a place; this is his phone. "Oh, he's fine. Fine."

"Can I talk to him?"

"Sure."

The receiver is grappled away before I have a chance to offer it, and I turn my back on the awful irritation Dad inspires in me. Laura has died, of breast cancer—I had barely begun to become acquainted with her when I was staring down at her rouged face in a casket—and now Katherine is under Dad's rule, which at times seems noxious, as if he's bent on bringing womanhood down.

"Jerome!" he cries, and I flinch at the thunder of this down the culvert. "By golly, how good it is to hear your voice!"

Then Katherine's face floats up, her whitish hair streaming back in a futuristic frizz as her features narrow to the unattractive set they have when she's angry about my drinking. She whispers, "You must get off. This is costing us a mint!"

I wave her away, and hear Dad cry, "Congratulations! Yes, we got the note," and remember why I called. In his letter Jerome said we shouldn't be surprised if we heard soon that he wasn't single, because he was "trying to tie the knot, and if that works out, when you meet her, you'll know why I'm so smitten. She's black. But more Yankee and American than I'll ever be. Her family has lived in Boston for a hundred years."

"Oh, fine," Dad says, and I know I'm being talked about. "No, it's okay. I'm going to put him right back on, and not take up more time."

The receiver is returned to my hand, heated and moist, as if he could squeeze something further from it with his grip.

"So," I say. "You plan to get married."

"You'll like Julie. She teaches English on the base. When I met her, I discovered I was developing all these problems with grammar."

"Not like 'car' and 'cow'?"

"I hadn't thought of that. I'll bring that up. She appreciates a challenge. That's why she's teaching military brats. That, and she wanted to travel. She and her friend. *Her* and her friend? See?"

"Male or female?"

"What?"

"Her friend."

In the pause, I picture him reaching over, in a T-shirt and the aviator glasses with smoky lenses he was wearing when I last saw him, to grind out his cigarette. "Female. Also from Massachusetts."

"Hey, there's one thing I want to know, and this is really important. I mean, this is why I called, okay?"

"Yes?" He sounds evasive, tentative.

"I mean, is it really true about *Olientals*"—I warble this—"and some of the other darker races, maybe, you know, that it's split sideways, like they say, and not up the middle?"

I hear Katherine cry "Oh, God!" above Dad's groan, and

then see Dad go striding down the hall away from me, shaking his head, and the room deflates, a sack of darkness. There's a catch in Jerome's breath, then a sigh. "How have you been?" he asks, as if beginning all over.

"Oh, fine. Fine, fine. Didn't I just say that? Fine."

"Katherine?"

"Great! Fine."

"Could I talk to her?"

"Katherine?" I glance around but she's not in sight.

"Just say hello." Is that him or me? I? The deflating room keeps darkening—no lights. What is it? "Charles?" a tiny voice says. I sink down as the phone is grabbed from me, and I'm out.

+

"Are we rolling, Jack?" I ask, and my engineer, from the other side of the glass partition, points a finger at me to say, *You're on!*

I turn to her, without the formality of an introduction, and say, "Now, Miss Odenthal. Or Katherine, if I may call you that?" I pause, alert to the possibilities of each intonation.

"Um," she says, and even this is given grudgingly. I've lured her here for this interview, and now she appears stricken, her face the yellow of cream beneath her bulky, oversized shades.

"I'd like our listeners to know something about Manhattan's Audubon Club. You're an officer of it, right? Isn't it strange, to begin with, to imagine Audubon in Manhattan? Isn't it?" Silence. "Katherine?"

She pulls off her shades and says, over the open airwaves, "Pardon me, have I met you?"

+

"Jerome, do you hear that?" Julie asks. She hasn't sat since we've arrived, and now she strides from the bay window to the fireplace and stands on the red-tiled hearth, tense, her face to me, taller than Jerome in her heels—her hair clipped short and smoothed back over her skull, so that her bones and features, and especially her eyes, stand out from the bluish underlighting of her skin.

She revolves her hands as if washing them, and the hoops on her wrists clash and ring.

"Julie, honey, I've told you: *N. O.*" He's slumped in an easy chair across from us, with his shoes off and shirt unbuttoned, sipping a beer after an evening of rounds at the hospital, following a day at a clinic.

"It's eerie," she says, and her eyes draw inward to listen. "I've heard it since you two got in." She looks at me, then at Katherine, on the couch, as if we're to blame. "It's coming from the fireplace. Like a mouse in the chimney bricks. Ooo!" She runs her hands over the graying gooseflesh on her upper arms.

Katherine studies me in remorse. We've flown here on a credit card, with our daughter, on a late-night impulse, after too much to drink, and I'm so appalled at this, and its eventual cost, I've had Jerome write me a prescription for Valium, blue, which I take each hour with gin. Julie's insistence about this noise shoves me deeper into the maze that's been at my nerves since we knocked on the door and she said, "Oh, my God, you."

It doesn't help that I hear the noise also—so high-pitched it's like a needle at my inner ear. "I'll check it out," I say, a way of getting through this, for tonight.

"Honey," Jerome says to her, "it's your hypersensitive imagination."

"No, I think I heard it," I say as she exclaims, "The heck!"

A silver heel of hers rings on the hearth. "It's this place," she says. Not the house, which is fine, she has said, but this Southern city where Jerome was offered a residency in the specialty he wanted to pursue after the Air Force: family practice. "There's nothing worse than being an Okie from Muskogee," she said at lunch, and Jerome, home then, said, "Honey, this isn't quite Muskogee, it's—" "Oh," she said, "have y'all listened to that there accent?" in such a perfect imitation of the way he once spoke, I had to laugh. Then she raised her fist with a twisting motion, sending the hoops crashing to her elbow—a clearing gesture, as she called it; she's a student of body language, and said to me an hour after we arrived, "Are you resisting me, holding your arms crossed over you like that? Jerome reacts the same damn way. You two are born brothers—some pair." So

Katherine and I have felt the added uneasiness of having walked into a marital dispute, in the midst of one of our own.

Shaky as a blind man who has lost his bearings, I run my fingers over the fireplace, then I hold an ear so close to the bricks I'm sure something will enter it—but I know that the best way to handle fear, for me, is to pretend I'm not afraid until I'm not. I remove the fireplace screen and lean it against the bricks, then get down on my hands and knees and crane my head up toward the flue.

"Does this have a damper?"

"Yup."

Impossible to see for blackness. "When did you use it last?"

"Julie?"

"Oh, late in the winter, if you can call that cold rain winter."

I glimpse a curve of metal and grab a handle that gives, letting down light over my face, along with raining soot.

"That?" Jerome says. "I checked that last night."

"When, Jerome?" Julie says. "You didn't tell me."

"Well, if not then, the first night you got so disturbed."

"You mean upset," she says.

There's a faint scrabble above. A bat? I paw over a crumbly ledge above the damper and duck as something hits at my feet with a plop.

"A nestling!" Katherine cries.

"Oh, my God," Julie says, and I hear jangling as if her hands are shaking above her head.

I back out of the fireplace and see a wing twitch free from a clot of feathers, a rubbery yellow beak opening back to a globelike eye.

"Jerome, do something!"

He brushes past me to corner the bird on the fireplace floor.

"Don't touch it!" she cries.

"Julie, what is this?" he says. "I'm sure it doesn't have anything communicable—goodness!" He holds it near his face, one hand curled around its wings, and its head wobbles back and forth, membranes closing on both eyes. "I'm afraid it's past help," he says.

"Two days!" Julie cries. "I can't bear to think of it!"

"Did you have to, Charles?" Katherine asks, and I turn from the hearth, surprised, to find her standing above me, her face white within the newly straightened fringe of her hair. "Did you have to do that?"

"What?"

"Couldn't you leave well enough alone?"

"I didn't put it there. I didn't build a nest in the chimney!"

"There aren't more, are there?" Julie asks, in a breathlessness of fear.

"Maybe you didn't, but—" Katherine is so angry she can't speak. She tries to: "You came here and . . . I'm sure it means something!"

She grabs up our daughter and strides out of the room and into the echoing entry, grappling with the door handle, and our daughter's head appears over her shoulder, staring at me with wide, startled eyes.

+

Jerome is on the phone from the city in New Mexico where he's opened his own clinic, and I'm in a chair at the center of a dismantled dining room I'm trying to convert into a recording studio, staring down at the way in which the ribs of my sweater part over the potbelly I've grown. "Anxiety," I've said to Katherine, since my impulse is to bury anxiety under food. I can't be an alcoholic, I've said, because I don't like liquor or drinking; drinking is only a means of getting by.

"In this day and age," I say to Jerome, "can it be that bad?"

"Again, I hate to sound like the Grim Reaper, but I think we have to look at this realistically. Actually, he's tremendously strong, simply physically, and that's in his favor. But the prognosis isn't good. It's melanoma. You know those moles he has . . ."

"Well, of course!"

"It's a cancer of them. Or the pigment in them. One on his stomach became irritated. He had it removed. It turned up positive. The unhappy part of this cancer is that it can be carried by the bloodstream."

"Oh, no."

He sighs, and a pair of hands press on my knees. Katherine

lowers herself to the floor between my legs, and stares up in concern. Then I'm taken by surprise, as I have been at every juncture of this year, to see such a striking replication of Katherine—our daughter, now five—come running up on tiptoe, trying to be quiet when I'm on the phone, her white-blond hair lifting away from her shoulders, and then stand looking over Katherine's crown with Katherine's same gravity of concern.

"Yes, I know, I've been through this myself," Jerome says, and the strangeness in his voice might be the clogging abrasion after tears. "We should look at the positive side—that they got it all—until there's a reason not to. This cancer doesn't always move fast, and if he can make it through, oh, the next year or so, I'd say the outlook is good."

"That's it?"

"It's about all I can give you now. If it metastasizes, then it's probably pretty much downhill. I'm sure they would try chemotherapy, which with his constitution he could take, but—" I can see him shrug, and I picture again, as if in close-up in that room in Valley City, the dots and clumps and growths over Dad, and imagine a hundred places the cancer could reappear. "Ach!" I say. "Some comfort."

"Right. That's how I feel. On the other hand, we have some time to think this through, in its relationship to everything else, and prepare ourselves. Not everybody's given that."

"I was just starting to get myself straightened out!" I cry, and the pressure of Katherine leaves my legs.

"I know that. Believe me, we all appreciate that. I know Katherine does. This should give you even more incentive to hang in there. For her sake. For Becky's, too."

I look up and see the two at a greater distance than I expected, nearly at the door, holding hands and backing from me as if already on their retreat—dismembered parts of my anatomy.

+

Feb 28

Double Valentine's Day. I see that trying to be explicit, as I talk to Katherine, is a form of being dramatic: what will hold her attention most? Should I then be more refined on my show—the planning? Hell, I'm not that interested in myself, Katherine— this record book you gave me. See how drunkenness makes me trail off from what was well begun to impotence.

Mar 14

Purged at last—is it so?—of this little woman pierced and trapped at my center like the lady in the box a magician runs swords through. A dream of my mother, the second since her death, last night. She was on a couch with her grandfather or father or uncle on the left and her sister on the right. She was out of a mental hospital after 16 years and was sitting on a pillow—only half her real size, doll-like, and I laid my head on her shoulder, though it was a manikin's, and cried. No words. Her hair was gray, in three tufts on her head—the top and each side. Then into an 18-dimensional dope dream.

+

"It's late to be calling," Katherine says.

"I've had a sort of mystical experience."

"I've had some recently, too." This seems a challenge.

"I couldn't find the end to your last letter, you know? It was written on a separate scrap of paper, remember?" No response. "I knew it was here and I searched every cranny I could think of—" I look up, and a strange room restricts my vision, as if fogging its edges. "Then it seemed so important to find it, I felt the actual world might end if I didn't. Or I might. Totally fragmented anxious desperation. Suddenly I parted at the middle, and my legs left me and went to the kitchen counter—that's the only way I can describe it—out of body. There was a gray haze or rain falling through me that felt like the end, and then I was over my legs again, ka-whoosh, and leaned over and reached behind a toaster where the scrap had fallen. I know I looked there once before, but there it was. I keep this place neat. I have the scrap here now."

"Huh."

"What was yours?"

"Oh, they're kind of difficult to explain."

Silence.

This is the way our conversations go now.

+

"Jerome called."

"Oh," she says, so faint I look down my nose into the perforations of the mouthpiece as if to check whether she's there.

"The cancer has reappeared in Dad."

"Oh."

"It's almost two years but— He's already had one chemo-therapy treatment. Apparently it was so awful he doesn't want another. I didn't know about it until after Dad was back from the hospital. Then Jerome called." Silence. "Not one word about it until now. I don't know why."

The gentle-breathing silence from her suggests that she does.

"Do you?" In the silence I look up, out the sliding-glass doors of a high-rise apartment, the first of many temporary ones, at a gray-green slab of late-August lake sliding toward a curve of shore, and suffer such a dislocation I have to step back for balance. There's a measured sigh from her, not quite of weariness, and I say, "What are you thinking? Can't you talk?"

"What can I possibly say?"

"That you're sorry?"

"I am, for him. But it's not my fault."

"Who suggested that?"

"Maybe I'm still that close to the edge. It's difficult to iden-tify my feelings. I have to rebuild myself from my feet up."

Let me know when you get to your waist, a voice inside rasps, and I move my lips to savor the words, though I don't speak them.

"I haven't been drinking," I say, to reassure her. "I haven't had a drink since you left. Almost three months." This is true, but I've been squeezing every sedative I can from a therapist I'm seeing, and chain-smoking marijuana, so when I sit at a microphone I feel I'm broadcasting in the clinical sense of sending coded messages into the universe.

"Good," she says.

A muscular widening in my ear, like an openmouthed yawn, allows static to spill through the earpiece of the phone in her direction, as during my moments of "broadcasting."

"What do you want me to do?" she asks, surprising me.

"I'm just telling you what Jerome said."

Silence.

"Well, you could tell Becky. She liked him."

"See what you imply?"

"He's her grandfather. She should know."

"I'm not sure now is the right time."

I think of the letters that arrive from my daughter, in irregular printing—DAD I LOV YOU—like shouts, and feel raw across my lap. A piercing connection strikes my back, below a shoulder blade, as if a hypodermic has been thrust there—a sensation I feel whenever I pace the apartment, convinced that an outside, invisible power is shooting me up, and think, They can't do this! It isn't fair!

"Maybe later," a dim voice says, "if he gets worse," and I realize I'm on the phone with Katherine.

"You know best," I say. I wonder at this, and when I retrace the words, I see that she's interpreted them as irony—ah! a cat trying to scale a stone wall from the inside! "I've been reading the Bible," I say.

"I have, too." This again takes the tone of a challenge.

"Could you write more? I've written almost every day for the last few weeks, but I've only got a couple letters from you. Becky writes."

"Your letters to her aren't the soundest."

"What does that mean?"

"It's been difficult. I'll write to your dad."

This is so much like the person with bodies pouring from each side of her at the mirror, I feel jerky sprays of tears head toward the mouthpiece, afraid they'll enter it and shock her.

"What have you told him?" she asks.

"That you left"—I swallow like Grandma Jones, anxious for a glass of water—"and we're trying to work things out."

"*I left.*" This is a flat whisper of surprise.

"You did."

"You forced me to."

"I was at the edge, too! It was all going—!"

She has hung up.

+

In yet another apartment I reach for the ringing phone, mounted so high on a wall that whenever I finish a conversation, I have an image of talking on tiptoe. Before I can settle the receiver, it says, "Charles?"

"Jerome!"

He sighs, his signal to me to prepare myself. "He's here."

"How did you get me at this number? Who do you mean— Dad?"

"Yes. It was the shock of my life."

I turn and see through the tall windows, above the buildings across the courtyard, an orange-pink sky, and wish the woman who reminded me of my daughter were here, staring out at a counterturbulence of snow, as on that dark Christmas Eve when my father was so present.

"When was it, again, that we talked?" Jerome asks, in a voice unlike his own, and I imagine him bowing his head and gripping the bridge of his nose, as he does when he removes his glasses. "A week or so ago, now? He'd just taken the second series of chemotherapy treatments. He claimed they almost killed him, so we figured we'd soon hear that it was time to go back, he sounded so weak. But two days ago he called and said he was on the way out. Did I call you then? No, that's right, I just got this number from the radio station. He told me the date and the flight he'd be arriving on—seemed lucid and real cheerful. So I probably wasn't as prepared as I should have been. When I saw him at the airport, I'm sure he noticed my shock. He'd lost fifty pounds and was so pale I couldn't help saying, 'Dad, you're anemic!' Then I gave him a bear hug and he went 'Ouf!' and stepped back, hurt bad, from the way a hand went there. It's metastasized so badly on one side of his chest he can't zip up his jacket! Why in the hell I was never told this, I don't know. It makes you wonder what kind of jerks are running these supposedly famous clinics! I'm not one for treating the family, as you know, but I got him to our clinic right away and got him typed and pumped two quarts of blood into him. They didn't bring his red count up to normal! So I turned him over to a colleague, who put him in the hospital. He's been there for a couple of days, getting more blood, and the attention he should have had before. We've asked him to stay at the house, with us, when he's discharged tomorrow. This is stopgap, of course, and my colleague—a fine fellow, a great guy—told him quite directly what his odds are."

"You mean, he told him he's going to die?"

"He's been told that his chances are slim—short of a miracle. He wants to spend Thanksgiving with us. That's, let's see, four days off."

"You want me there."

"It would give us a chance to talk, and maybe settle a few things."

"I'll make a reservation when I hang up."

"I hope I haven't shocked you by the way I've gone into this, huh? Laid too much on you? I guess I needed somebody to talk to."

"No. I mean, that's okay."

"We can't give up. Even in a case like this, we have to keep our hopes up. And, Charles? Please don't take this the wrong way, I mean, I've had a few tonight myself, but for the duration, as long as you're in our house, with everything that's going on—considering the pressures—Julie and I have to ask you not to drink. Do you understand?"

I nod, already turning from the conversation, unable to speak, about to hang up, when I see, on a shelf beside the door at my back, a three-by-five card set upright as if for me, covered with careful printing: "Beloved, think it not strange concerning the fiery trial which is to try you, as though some strange thing happened unto you. —I Peter 4:12"

+

Down on my knees, I lift my head from Katherine's lap, and her face, at this uncommon angle, after months of absence, looks enormous, weighty as stone, with elongated shadow from a lamp darkening half of it with further weight. She sits in the only piece of furniture, a green-velvet-covered chair, in a large living room. There are two chairs and a table in the kitchen, single beds in two bedrooms, and a bottle of Stolichnaya, half full, above the sink. A pair of crystal goblets, near her bare toes on the carpet, are green against its pale-beige plush. She is trying to establish their home in this Chicago suburb—Becky already asleep when I called from the airport, changing planes for New Mexico.

"Can we?" I ask.

She stares beyond me, her eyes empty of their many-hued depths of concern, and if it weren't for the magnified shadows of her silver-bleached curls, I might not recognize the slight headshake: no.

"Couldn't we try?"

"It seems too late, doesn't it?"

In our lives? at night? "You can have all the furniture."

"You want to buy me?"

"No, for you to use. Most of it's still stored at Dad's. You need it. Get it. Have it shipped. I'll ship it for you."

"Whatever would I do with it all?"

"Fill these empty rooms. You and Becky use it."

She puts her chin in her palm, with an index finger next to one eye, and stares down her chenille robe, which she has on over a nightgown, with pajamas or underwear under that, from the elastic I've probed. I slip my hands under her thighs, fuller from the weight that she's gained, and rock her legs from side to side. "Could we get together *this* way?"

"Isn't that what you meant?"

"I meant for good. Start all over again. Could we?"

She pauses enough to think, her fingertip pressing and altering her eye's symmetry, and says, "The furniture, okay. That, definitely not."

"We're still married."

"On paper."

"Legally."

"As of now," she says. Her lawyer has filed for divorce, on grounds of mental cruelty, and has warned my lawyer not to contest this.

"According to the letter of the law," I say.

"How many have there been, recently—this month?"

"Please." I rock her harder. "Please?"

"Don't."

"Just some comfort," I say, rolling my head in her lap, and I'm amazed when her hand comes over it, tentative, exploring my hair, then presses. But as I slide my hands free she grabs them at the wrists.

"Don't we all need that," she says, into the darkness where I kneel.

+

"It's been a real struggle to manage alone," Jerome says, and places his glasses on the counter where we sit, on stools like barstools, and massages his eyes with his fists. "For both of us. With work, and then the children. Vita is six now. She's all right, but scared by it all. 'Why doesn't Grampa give me a balloon,' she said last night—Dad always had balloons handy for her—'and be well?' Marty turned three last week. Real active. If you hadn't come, we would have had to hire a nurse. I'm being straight-out with you. Dad takes that much care."

He looks toward a window set horizontally above a stainless-steel sink, at the greenish false dawn gathering over the desert, and I'm so disfranchised from the flight, after Katherine's refusal in spite of her encouragement, that his metal-rimmed aviator glasses on the counter seem to be staring at me, and I don't know how I'll manage without a drink.

"I hope you aren't hurting for a drink," he says.

I shrug.

"One or the other of us is with him whenever he's awake."

"How is he?"

"It's difficult to say. Sometimes he acts so much himself I forget why he's here. Then— He's usually lucid, but some confusion has started. At this point, things are going so fast it's probably not healthy to think about it."

I notice that his shirt bulges above his belt, and he looks shorter, with thinning brown-blond hair receding from a fore-head like Dad's—my attention brings his eyes on me; he swivels to the counter and picks up his glasses by the earpieces. "Our procedure is to sit in the room with him as long as he's awake, and encourage him to move around. He needs a hand now and then, and we generally help him into the bathroom. He's in some pain. His joints or muscles have tightened up. Again, the speed of this. He needs somebody to grab on to, to steady him. He fell off the can once and gashed his head. We're supposed to record his temperature every two hours, and his bowel movements, and we give him a light sedative, codeine. This is what Jim, the doctor friend I mentioned, has asked us to do. Dad's under his care, not mine, which is best, as far as I'm concerned. I'm a son in this.

"Here, let me get your suitcase. You can keep it in Marty's room—Dad's now. Marty's in the guest room, because his bedroom is bigger. Let's see if Dad's awake. He's been looking forward to seeing you."

He's lying on a low bed, and I realize I'm listening for a *plik plik*, as if he's been cut open again, while the three of us are held at our seams with giving threads. But he's not that man. This new man sleeps with his knees up under a comforter, and his face, turned to the side on pillows propped against the headboard, is as lean and handsome as in his youth. There's a rustle and I realize it's Julie, ghostly invisible in the dark, rising from the chair beside his bed. She walks over, and then hands are on my shoulders, smelling delicately of the desert, and she kisses my cheek. "God bless you," she whispers.

+

I'm studying the youthful austere thinness of his face, free of his glasses, when he opens his eyes.

"Dad."

"Charles. You're here."

I take his hand, and his lips compress as he turns his face to a pair of sliding-glass doors whose curtains are parted on a lawn brilliant as a golf green. "Was I a fool to say that truth is most important?"

"When?"

"All my life."

"No." I'm not sure that he's heard me, so I shake my head. He's asleep.

+

I draw the curtains open over the wall of glass, on a brilliance so otherworldly it seems that miles of desert light are focused on this patch of green, isolated by a plank fence. "Close those," he says, startling me. Narrow horizontal windows along the ceiling admit a pale-lime version of the emerald light, and he lies back, studying the currents of heat waves and shadow in this lighter upper level, as if watching a flowing river upside down, and then he's asleep, his knees drawn up. A lump large as a fist beneath his pajama top, like a breast developing on his left side, trembles as he breathes. The youth of his face is partly due to its copper color, and a Band-Aid rests at an angle high on his forehead, where thinning hair, combed sideways, begins. His fall. He's sweating so heavily when Jerome comes in that we place towels over the pillows under his back. "He says he's more comfortable this way, high up," Jerome whispers, and then has to leave for work.

I sit in a director's chair beside the sliding-glass doors, and in the semi-dark I picture Dad turn in snow-reflected light under the roof of our old Chevy and say, "Do you two always have to shoot at one another?"

Was I asleep? He wakes and talks to me as if I've just arrived, the same question about truth, but in a high, weak voice, all its resonance gone. I ask if there's anything I can do, and he appears to think this through in larger terms than I intended, and then looks up from eyes that have enlarged since I arrived, and whispers, "Could you pay that note?"

"Note? The loan, you mean?"

He nods. Money I borrowed from him to set up a studio on one of our many moves, which I've never repaid.

"I'm sorry it's bothered you. I'll pay you back right away."

"It's not me," he says, his voice like a child's, and raises long thin steady hands, then lets them fall on the comforter. "The *bank*."

I realize he means a note he co-signed with me, after Katherine and I separated and stored our things at his house, which is coming due the second time around. "I'll get it to you, canceled, as soon as I can."

"Thank you." He's still looking away, and this is so faint I feel metal currents enter my mouth as if to seal it; I must keep my word.

+

Jerome comes in from work and whispers that he and Julie have a dinner date they should keep, with a sitter set up, and I tell him, Yes, go. He sits on the edge of the bed and takes Dad's hand, tests the Band-Aid, then smooths back Dad's hair. "You're looking good," he says, and Dad purses his lips with the look of tasting alum, and turns away.

Jerome bows his head, abashed, then checks the recorded temperatures on a pad on the bedside table, and gives me a look of longing as he leaves. When it's dark, I draw back the curtains from the glass wall, and Dad says, "How many times I've probably said this, yet it nonetheless remains true . . ." He sighs as if overtired. "The nights I used to lie awake waiting for one or the other of your second shoes to drop. Why do people wait the whole day to do their serious thinking over a shoe, undressing?" He looks at me as if he expects an answer, and I shake my head. "Jerome was worse. Slowest. I'd fall asleep in the middle of waiting for the second one." He sighs again. "The first has hit. *Listen.*"

Soon he's asleep.

+

I volunteer for the late-night shift when Jerome and Julie return.

"Get some sleep," Jerome says. "I'm used to this."

"No."

Dad wakes coughing. He has been coughing more, and having to spit up in a handkerchief he keeps clenched in one hand. "This medicine junk," he says. "I think it's binding me up. Let's try." In the bathroom he coughs and spits up so much I have to support him over the toilet bowl, and on the way back to bed he pulls away from me, wobbling on unsteady legs to a dresser, and jerks open a drawer on a three-year-old's jumble of clothing and socks.

"Do you need something?" I ask.

"To change my T-shirt." He plucks at the pajama top.

His suitcase lies open, a transient's, on the floor beside the dresser.

"I'll get it for you."

He plucks at the pajama top again. "This one's all pukey."

It's clean, but I change it, wary of the swelling tumor on his chest, swathed in bandages and pungent of oily burning protein—or even worse: the stink of a filter when a reversed cigarette is lit.

Back in bed, he says in the childish voice, "Did we forget?" and I help him in his unsteady walk back to the bathroom, to perform this most personal function. I've noticed that after each visit, no matter how cursory, he washes up, as if years of teaching have rendered him finicky, and then after he has washed, he combs his thinning hair, studying himself in the mirror. This time when I help him onto the throne, as he calls it, and then stand outside, staring through the crack between the hinges of the partly opened door, sensitive to his privacy, yet near enough so I can get to him if he slips, there's a series of such percussive explosions in the bowl I don't know how to react.

"All this talk," he says in his old voice. "How about some action?"

+

The cough starts, jarring me to the soles of my feet at its dryness and the way the tumor trembles, and then Jerome walks in after a night on duty. "Can't that be removed?" I whisper.

"It would just be cosmetic," he whispers. "At this point, anyway. It might stir things up worse, Jim has said, and be a further blow to his system. I asked Dad if he wanted it removed when he was in the hospital, without going into any of this, and he gave me that half smile of his—you know, partly pained— and waved me off, and said, 'Forget it.'"

After Jerome has gone to bed, his son Marty, who looks like Jerome but with ginger skin and hair curly as Katherine's, appears in the room as if sleepwalking, comes up to me, crawls into my lap, and falls asleep.

"Thanks," Julie whispers, before I see her, and lifts his heated weight, a further loss to me over the rawness left by Becky.

"You're becoming an all-purpose hand," Julie whispers, and grips my shoulder. "You're doing real well. I know you miss your family."

+

I've nodded asleep, and wake to an empty bed. Codeine? I turn and see Dad in the bathroom, standing at the sink, his face to the mirror. I feel fear and a dimensional slippage, as if I'm watching the character in the movie *2001* age past death to a fetus, and hear, *Three gray tufts, one on each side*, and rush to the door, out of breath: "Dad?"

He slowly turns and stares out of whatever age or realm it is that he's reached, and says in his new high voice, "You forgot the note!"

+

"4:00 a.m., bowel movement black as grease," I write, and he sits up in bed, alert, as if readied for breakfast by this. I try to arrange an afghan, which he seems to favor, over the comforter across his knees, and he pats it and says, "Like an old lady recovering from a safari."

We both laugh and I'm surprised at the thought that he's trying to entertain me. "Did Grandma knit it?" I ask.

He looks down in shame, then plucks at a loose strand of yarn curling up from it.

+

The canceled note arrives in the mail, and I hand it to him. He studies it, then lets it fall to the comforter, in an airy tumble down his raised knees, and says, "Wilson, Hoover, F.D.R., Truman, Eisenhower, Nixon, Ford—all those Presidents I lived through and their endless documents. How they seem manipulated now! Only Kennedy stood up to whatever group it is that runs things. Or tried to. And him they shot."

+

He sits at the dining-room table for Thanksgiving dinner, black-silver against another set of sliding-glass doors only inches above the lawn. "Our grampa is ill," Vita, the six-year-old, says in the tone of an adult. "But not so ill he can't have Thanksgiving dinner with us." I hear the tense precision of Julie in her voice, and with her pronouncement she and Marty sit and stare at the glazed-brown, half-carved turkey. They won't eat.

"Children!" Julie cries, and then the whole table is silent.

"Are you going to open that, Dad?" Jerome asks, about a telegram that sits propped against the stem of Dad's drinking glass.

He picks it up but doesn't seem to understand how to manage the envelope, so finally Jerome reaches over and slits it open with the carving knife. "Can you read it, Dad?"

He holds it up to the sunlight, and says in his high voice ("It could be at his vocal cords," Jerome has said, turning up a corner of his lips in distaste): "We are with you in spirit. And you are in our prayers. Love." He lays it on his lap, over the knitted afghan, and stares down as if studying its placement on the weave, and in the silence there's a *plok* as a tear hard as bird shot hits it.

"Who's it from?" I ask, trying to distract him. I assume Tim or Marie, and turn to Jerome, who looks gravely at the knife he's revolving beside his plate, sending bars of light glancing across his face, like a miniature spotlight searching out his tired eyes and tan-blue lids.

"Katherine and Becky," he says.

We clear the table, and Jerome and I move to a couch in front of a curved fireplace of adobe, as if to be alone to think, and Dad says behind us in his childlike treble, with a querulous tremor of surprise, "Oh, look! It's from Forest Creek!"

Jerome glances at me, and I realize that either the address on the telegram is misprinted or Dad has misread the name of the suburb—one of many in Chicago with Forest in it—where I saw Katherine on my way here.

"Are they living in Forest Creek now?" the eager child's voice asks.

+

"Is there a Bible handy?" I ask Jerome.

"I think we got one for a wedding gift. Let me see."

He rummages through bookshelves on the walls at each side of the fireplace, and then with Julie's help covers several rooms of the house I haven't seen yet, and finally comes back to the couch. "Nope," he says.

In the arch to the dining room, Julie puts her hands, pale at their edges, to her temples, and says, "My daddy would be cha*grined* to hear this—all those Reformed Presbyterians and Unitarians so nice to him!"

"Did you want to read it?" Jerome asks, and I can see the veil of control he sets in front of his surprise.

"I thought I might read it to Dad."

"Jim and I are going to have a priest start coming in every day."

I can't mention that I'm beginning to believe that a priest in himself isn't sufficient, or anyway isn't the real priest we're given access to through Scriptures, and Julie, behind his back, points a finger skyward, and nods.

"Goodness," I say, confused, "isn't there something I can *do*?"

"You've done more than anybody could ask," Jerome says, and glances at Julie. "All of us have. We're doing all we humanly can."

"I mean, some chore or job around here—something physical I can do before I go nuts."

This last word registers in him with impact—his eyes swerving to their corners like a horse about to rear, dark with apprehension. In the slowed pause, as my statement and his look unfold, it's as if he's said, *There's a lot more to get through.* Then with a new eagerness, he says, "Hey, I know. This huge branch broke off an old tree out in the back yard. I've been meaning to cut it up for firewood, but haven't even cranked up the new chain saw Julie got me for my birthday. How about that?"

"Lead me to it."

+

In a deafened cocoon, I watch the whirling blurred blade glide into black bark and then heartwood, sending reddening spray back over my shoes, shattered fragrance, and imagine its entry into flesh. I slow to the speed the glittering sun seems to take in its trajectory, and locate a rhythm that corresponds to each sectional cut down the limb. When I start to feel perspiration —which has been popping out on my face but disappearing into the air—curve around my eyes, I straighten and see that the limb is nearly done, still retaining its original shape, but with bright cut bands every two feet. The pieces have buckled and hug the contours of the lawn, which, from my upright perspective, looks pale silver in the overhead sun. I shut off the saw, drawn into a thick silence, off-balance, and in a shuffle of sensations I alter.

This light everywhere—that it exists, that it is present each day. That it was imagined, and within it is warmth. Sprays of sawdust widen from a limb in its intensity on emerald grass. I raise my hand, numb from the saw, and it appears out of a sleeve, separate from me, a creation from antediluvian time— miraculous in its placement above silver grass that a limb grips like a larger paw. The cold sensation of outside eyes passes over me, and I turn and see, past gold glare on glass, Dad sitting on the edge of the bed, staring out at me. He raises a hand.

I walk over, panting, and slide back a door—a growling rumble. "I'm sorry. Was I—?" I indicate the branch. "Did it bother you?"

"Bother me?" His smile is so broad the skin pulls back tight on his skull, himself again, and he says in his own voice, "You ought to know by now that anything that sounds like work is music to my ears."

+

He stares into the mirror too long, leaning past the sink, turning his face from side to side as I observe him through the crack in the door. When he comes out, he says, "I need to walk."

"Walk?"

"I need some comfort. If you don't have that, what's left?"

I walk him around the room, until his tottering steps grow worse, and then he turns away to the bed, drops to its edge, sitting, and arranges the pillows. He falls back, immediately asleep, and then stirs and says, with half-lidded eyes, "You've got the wrong man."

"Who?"

"Oh, something about being young."

I pour three codeine tablets out in my palm and wash them down, then sneak into the dining room, to the cabinet of liquor I noticed during Thanksgiving dinner, and fill a tumbler with vodka. I tiptoe back to the director's chair, and sit and sip the vodka straight, setting the tumbler under Dad's bed whenever I think I hear someone. The liquor and codeine begin to work at the same time, one rising from below, the other suffusing warmth downward, and then they make contact. Suddenly I'm sniffling about breaking my word to Jerome, in his house, and then a side current draws my consciousness down to a dot. Through it I see Dad in a chair beside a potbellied stove in his garage, his chin in his hands, listening to his radio, alone, as he used to sit when Katherine and I lived with him, and I want to approach him, as I wanted to then but couldn't: the irritation he aroused in me. When Katherine left and it seemed there wouldn't be an end to our separation, I showed up in Pettibone with a secretary, as I called her, at Grandma's new house—Doc Sprunk's offices, remodeled by Tom, across the corner from our old place—and Grandma ordered us to leave. "Doesn't she fancy herself a Christian?" the woman said. "What's she keep those statues and crucifixes around for, if she can't be civil?" Most of the relatives wouldn't speak to me ("The prodigal son, eh?" one said on the street), and then I heard from my sister Marie that Dad was coming down from up north to see me. I sat in Marie's house with the shades drawn, waiting for darkness in order to make my escape, as I saw it, when Dad's car pulled up. I didn't want him to see the woman, so I went out the door, into a spring-warm street that widened with light until he and I seemed miniature figures in a landscape like Hyatt's, and he took me in his arms and pressed a rush of static out my ears, and then stepped back and put a hand to his chest as if in a vow (was the tumor beginning to grow even then?), and I said, buckling with surprise at the importance of this to me, "You're a true Christian."

What I need now is that forgiveness, I think. *The Lord is my shepherd. I shall not want. He leadeth me beside the still waters. He maketh me to lie down*— There's an internal emptying as my memory goes. "Oh, God, forgive me," I whisper.

"Yes," he says, and I look up and see his eyes closed, their lids trembling over exposed wedges of whites with a dream.

+

I wake to the sound of his voice: "Darkness. Resting. Darkness. Resting. Don't want to go. Darkness. Resting . . ."

+

I rise from a dream of books and scrolls beneath me—that drafting paper from Grandpa's office. Dad is thrashing under the sheets in pain. I give him three codeine tablets roughly, in a hurry, and pull out the pillows so he's flat on his back. When the pain keeps up, I say, "Would it be better if you were sitting higher again?"

"What was that?"

"If you were sitting higher, like you were before, do you think it would help?"

"I thought you said *singing* higher." This is spoken in his child's treble, and I picture Jerome behind me on the gray risers beside the piano at St. Mary Margaret's, reaching so hard for a high note I have to—

"Well, it can't last long now," Dad says.

I'm afraid to respond to this.

"Before it's time to get up," he says.

I help him rearrange his pillows as they were, and discover that the sheets are damp again—the air drenched with the oily, scorched-protein smell, its taste at the tip of my tongue like a burn.

"I guess the time has about come," he says.

"To get up?"

"To form the board."

"Board?" Bunched cold nerves give way down my back.

"Oh, just there." He waves his hand toward the wall where the bathroom light burns in a yellow strip along the nearly closed door.

"You mean in the bathroom?" I say, suspecting that "forming the board" might be a euphemism for a difficult bowel movement.

"Hardly. But I'd sure hate to get tangled up with those dogs."

We both laugh, in a gentle scattering of release, and he sighs. Earlier in the evening, something aroused the neighborhood dogs and they were barking so loud they seemed to surround the bedroom.

"I don't think I know what I'm going to say next," he says. "This dope."

"Do you understand that you might die, Dad?"

He turns from me and his chin wrinkles and trembles as mine did in front of Clapton. Then he nods, and from beneath a black wave I see myself leap from a loft door and flip into a green world heading toward me faster than light.

+

In the morning, Dad says he wants to talk to Jerome alone. I go into the kitchen to wash my tumbler at the sink, and find water over its bottom, as if somebody has been there. I sit at the counter and have a cigarette from a pack lying open, then another. I'm having my third when Jerome walks in, lips set, and grabs up the cigarettes and lights one.

"He said he wanted to die on Thanksgiving, but couldn't."

"What!"

"He was just about there, he said, but was afraid to."

"How could that be? I mean, how could he? Hold his breath?" I'm angry I was excluded from their talk.

He looks out from a mist that once contained crossing sails, and says, "Oh, I've heard stranger things. He says he wants to go home."

"Home?"

"Actually, to Grandma's. He wants it to end, as he put it, at her place—in that back room of hers, I guess, where he's been staying when he's in Pettibone."

"What did you say?"

"That's what we were talking about—the details. He seems clear as a bell, as if he understands this might be his last time this way. I could fly him back in an air ambulance."

"I thought you didn't— You know."

"If it's what he wants, I'll do it. He seems set on it. His insurance will cover some—but that's not important." He sits at the counter and grinds out his cigarette. "He wants to be buried beside Mom, he said. God, I couldn't help thinking through it all, from his tone—" He shoves his hands under his glasses, shoves the glasses up, and leans his elbows on the counter. "It's probably one of those crazy thoughts that come at these times. I kept thinking he wants to *see*—" His voice cracks as it used to in high school. "He wants one more look at that god-awful gas station we used to live in!"

+

The door is trembling with the force of the knock. "Super! I got a letter you ain't picked up. You ain't been down in a while."

"Yes."

"I'm puttin it down by your door here, okay?"

I press my ear to the flimsy panel until I hear a pad of footsteps, then open it in time to see his bare bread-brown back, with suspenders over the Brillo-like hair on his shoulders, go rocking down the hall.

+

I have to fly back to New York, to tape some shows, and Jerome says he will charter an air ambulance a day later. He tells me not to worry, while he drives me to the airport at the racing speed I've shied from before; he'll be in touch. "Thank you for keeping your promise about not drinking in the house," he says, and I struggle, as if in the chair beside Dad's bed, to restrain the whimpering sniffling that began when I broke my vow. At the airport, as we clomp toward the plane that's already boarding, he slips twenty dollars into my pocket. Then he hugs me, as if to say: Have one on me. Which I do. And more, but make it to New York, to the studio, on time, able to carry out the interview I've scheduled with an actor. Jerome calls later to say, "The trip went wonderfully! More medical equipment in that Cessna than most hospitals have!" He says not to worry. Dad seems improved, being in Pettibone.

"I'm going to stay on a few days, in case anything comes

up. I'll call if it does. Marie and her husband are here to help
—besides the ten dozen cousins or uncles I can enlist if I have
to, and Grandma, who seems angry, by the way, as I read her.
She hardly talks. Tim and Cheri are coming in from Wisconsin
tomorrow. So don't worry, okay? Charles?"

I'm rumbling down the Chesro's steps on a run, with a suitcase in each hand, one bumping the wall my shoulder used to brush and the other resounding off newel posts below the banister. This is it, I think. My retreat is over. Done. With all the noise, Tony is at his door, looking as he did on the day I met him, except for his fireman's suspenders, and there is his daughter, peeking at me with her smile from behind his butt again. There's a seizure of joy like a contraction of pain in my chest, and I laugh so hard that both of them laugh, too, in a way that brings his wife up from behind, wiping her hands on a towel while she manages to hold the big diapered baby in the crook of one arm, to see what's up.

What would be the quickest way to say it?

+

As the super's suspendered back retreats, I grab the letter and shut and lock the door. The envelope is full. From Jerome. I rip it open on the way to the dresser, and hold a thin deck of three-by-five cards.

> *Dear Charles,*
>
> *Forgive the stationery. I'm hurrying this off in the X-ray room. The New York excursion is on. By the time this gets to you,*

*in fact, it's possible that generous Joe and I will be there. We
figure it's about a 20 hour*

*drive and are going to beat ourselves blue. Joe suddenly got a
wild hair and decided now was the time. We're leaving tomorrow
evening after we get a few things in order and get packed and in
the car. We expect to be there Thurs,*

*the 24th, probably late afternoon. We'll go to the Village or
wherever you are, or better yet, if you were at the actor friend's
where you said I could leave a phone message, I could call you
there and we could set up specifics about where to*

*meet. You see how improvised this is going to be—no real game
plan. I have to go now and unless you hear somehow otherwise,
expect us there Thurs aft. Sorry I can't be more precise. I'll call
your friend—Marco, is that the right name?*

Love, J

The improvised quality of the cards exerts such a negative
pull, I think: Don't you care? Then I realize that this is Thursday.
Today! He could be here! A fractured factuality keeps denting
my brainpan with all I should do—but there's nothing about
him I can contain, as he leaps and crosses and enters the places
he already populates with an authority only he can claim. Who
would want to contain him, I think, working fast, already
dressing. So he's here!—I reach for the keys and the doorknob
at the same time—my brother!

+

Footsteps come running down a hospital corridor. A nurse is
removing an intravenous needle from his arm. This is the
nearest hospital to Grandma's, in Emden, where he's lasted into
the next year, January of the Bicentennial. Katherine holds me
as footsteps pour rapid cleats down the hall in an old pattern—
both of us here for his final days, both here at the hospital
tonight, on one of the rotating shifts Jerome has set up, when
Dad began fading so fast we called all the others. Except for
Tim and Cheri, who were leaving their shift when this began,

and now Tim leans against the far wall with his eyes closed in the concentration of prayer, Cheri moves from that side of the bed, holding Dad's hand, to this side, and takes hold of the other hand, as the nurse tidies the pillow around the haggard sunken face of brown bone, and Marie and her husband complete the pattern of cleats and appear in the room. Marie stops and draws herself up and cries, "I knew it! We were in such a hurry we hit a rabbit, and I knew it happened that second! It was seven after two, and it happened then, didn't it?"

She peels strands of hair from her face with trembling fingers, then goes to the bed and picks up the hand Tim's wife has left free and rubs Dad's arm. "Oh, he's still warm yet," she says in her throaty voice. "Did you know that?" She puts a hand over his forehead. "Dad, you're still warm. Dad?"

+

In Marie's house, Marie is telling Jerome, who flew back once from New Mexico after his flight in the air ambulance, and now is back again for the funeral, how she and her husband were hurrying to the hospital and hit the rabbit: "And I knew it was exactly when Dad died. I had Ben look at his watch, and it was 2:07, and I knew that was the exact moment he died—when we hit that poor rabbit, I told Ben."

"You couldn't help it," Jerome says.

"You think it's possible to know things like that, then?"

"Anything's possible," he says, and turns and starts walking down the hall in a harried retreat.

"Do you believe in reincarnation?" she calls after him.

He continues to the end of the hall, looking cornered, and then flings up his hands and cries, "I believe in *everything*!"

+

Jerome and Julie have decided that she will stay in New Mexico with the children, so the two will remember their Grandpa as they saw him last. Jerome and I have the duty of greeting people at the "viewing." My daughter Becky runs up and clings to my waist and Katherine, as if to relieve me of her, leads her off. These partings from them. None easier than the last. Sight giving on the most cherished features. Sometimes a mismanaged, last-minute kiss, no more. Now an elderly man shakes Jerome's hand, giving off a stink of gasoline, and says he hurried right over from the service station. He puts both hands to his kinky, yellow-gray bush of hair that looks electrified—it's Enos Clapton—and cries, "God, this is awful! just awful, boys!" He takes my hand, his eyes brimming with the wild glitter of a cat's, and says, "I know I'm next!" Then he goes to the casket, set against a brick wall of the new church, and looks down at Dad, or at his head lying sunken in a tufted pillow—face somehow filled out, lips so unnaturally tight they look sewn shut. A girl begins to climb the set of steps placed at the head of the casket by the funeral director, to permit children to see inside, and I realize it's Becky, with Katherine there, and through Becky's eyes I register the severity of his features, unlike this in life, and picture Lincoln jolting forward at the derringer blast, Joe Louis grabbing the sky as he topples flat, and Dad's face is imprinted in me in this final manifestation, yellow-bronze, insupportable— a monument at last.

+

Davey, an ordained deacon, portly and with a full bushy graying beard, stands in white vestments at the lectern of the new church and delivers the homily for the Funeral Mass, "An Older Brother's Love." The ragged edges of his voice close my hearing down with his first words. Four members of the Knights of Columbus, two of whom are Mitchells, members of Dad's state basketball team, march up the center aisle to the closed casket and pass something among themselves, and then, stepping back, pop an American flag open in the air between them, and lower it toward its trembling reflection rising from polished wood.

"As a doe longs for running streams, so longs my soul for you, my God," Davey reads, and tugs at his beard as if to tame it. "I have no food but tears, day and night; and all day long men say to me, 'Where is your God?'" Indeed, I think, and when he reads on about going with the multitude to the house of God, I hear a rustle of clothes, the voices of children, and past the white blur of the carnation pinned like gauze to Jerome's former First Communion jacket, I see Dad in sunlight lift a camera to his face, pointing it in my direction, his wavy hair falling over his forehead, and feel the nudges of Brian and others lining up for our procession as Dad sails in and reveals drops pattering over my tie from both eyes melting.

+

Then I'm walking down a cross street in my springy, buoyant walk, putting into each step the deliberation of youth, of giving all to every act in order to fill each to its edge, wearing the suit jacket I had on when I arrived in the city, bristling with the kinky jubilation too much nervous pride can bring at the thought of Jerome in the city, and feel my brain continue to shunt and spurt sparks at every juncture of thought with the promise of seeing him again.

+

We're at Mom's grave, where we once stood as if at the edge of the football field, seeing a team of horses heading forever toward a clump of trees on the orange-red horizon. But now we stand beside a cherrywood casket, with an apparatus like an accordion window gate beneath it, the metal hinges partly concealed by artificial grass that looks like the waxed grass in Easter baskets. The oak is gone, cut down, a bare stump, but the ten-foot concrete cross is here, beyond the canvas shelter over the grave, and the canvas above our heads bows and then cracks in the wind like a whipped thick sheet as Jerome takes Grandma's hand. Becky and three other grandchildren step up and insert red roses into the corner handles of the casket, and the sounds of the canvas pick up like gunshots going off. I turn to Jerome. He shakes his head.

"Where?" I say in a tiny voice, to the one at my other side, Katherine, meaning where did the roses come from.

"I asked the children to do it," she whispers.

"Where—?" I say, and hear Dad's voice at the end—high, querulous, imploring. "Where—"

"At a florist's," she whispers, as though this is the answer to the question I can't formulate, my whole self divided and impaneled against its animal insistence on autonomy.

Jerome and I look level into the same eyes at the same height, and then give inward against one another, without Dad there, between us as he had been between from our births.

+

Another rush to board a jet. Banging down the narrow aisle where passengers draw back from the pair of heavy suitcases I'm unable to entrust to anyone. No more traveling light—the need merely to arrive, equipped to the teeth, now the point. Bismarck this time, for a Bicentennial celebration, scheduled months ago, by contract, before Dad— Fumes of fuel penetrate the cabin, as if a tank is leaking, and then the thunder crack and winching groan of the landing gear drawing inside at the instant of lift-off, too soon, a wing tipping in a bank above warehouses with printing on their gables: AIR SERV— *Stop. I want off!* No carnival ride of revolutions from a base on earth, but this final upswing that will end in death. No! We pull into a climb that seems to leave froth behind in its power, and above ten thousand feet, the double vodkas I knocked back in a stand-up airport bar bring on a stratospheric blackout.

I wake on a downhill glide of growing silence that will end at our point of impact. A freeze in the cabin tightens my doubly belted bladder in a grip I can barely take in the arctic cold, and out the porthole the fields of different sizes take on tones of off-white, white-gray, blue-ivory, with yellow-gold at subtle intervals—all in squares called patchwork, though there are Orientally carved ponds and pastures, outlined by fence, and farmsteads with windbreaks like shakos, crazed networks of sand blown into featherings over snow-blanketed fields, which lie in strips as often as in oblongs or squares, and with the regular pattern of section lines thrown awry by a road or stream or body of water larger than a pond but less than a lake and, farther west, sand-ridged and -ringed hills and buttes—North Dakota.

Mid-March. No green.

Then Dad's face arrives as it was at the last, in the hospital, its waxy sheen overlaid by scaly dryness, lines grooved deep, graying hair dead dry from the carnivorousness of the disease, his lips parted in pain, stuck to yellowing dry teeth, the bones of his head bulging from the gravitational force of going off from us for good; and I hear myself say, "Do you understand that you might die, Dad?"

A desire to prepare him for the end, or crassness?—a self-styled perfectionist's need to coerce him into accepting a perfectionist's absolutes?

It could be the North Pole below, with converging Mercator lines about to touch, and then another thunder crack brings on the vibrating resistance of descending landing gear—quick hills swelling up, bearing the shadow of the plane in sharp dips, and then the green-gold curls of a river, rumpled, ice-crusted, shadowed on both sides by valleys blackly populated with staggering collections of trees. A drop, a lowering braking turn around a hill that sends me forward to see, on its bare summit, a pale building like a pillar of ice, or the Infant of Prague hurrying near, and then Dad's mouth drops open as it did at the end.

+

I head away from the airport in a cab, sliding from the windows on one side to the windows on the other, trying to keep the building, visible from nearly every street, in view, and suffer a panic of dislocation. It's not the North Dakota I knew—its flatness tugging the sky tight at every horizon, as if it were tied there, a tent. This landscape has the abrupt tilt and surprise of the levees and flats near the farm where Bobbie lived, and more. Flat-topped and conical hills and buttes pile at the edges of the city, with further buttes beyond in a blue dimension, and dark crevasses and coulees leading from their heights down to the Missouri—the river we're crossing, according to a sign. Is my resistance to it due to its place in my father's history?—"my father," as he has become: for good now? His insurance trips here. Dad? Already his fast fade from the living. Dead. That thick weight on the tongue. Then in a sudden reversal, he has Jerome's hand in one of his and mine in the other as he leads us over a rectangle of lawn like a pool to a sculpture of an immigrant family, monstrous above him in its bulk under the cold-tinged, caustic sun of early July—about to erupt into the fireworks we'll light from his cigar. His springy, sunstruck hair

dives in curly shadow over his forehead in the wind as he points
down a wide lawn to the tall pale building ahead. "The state
capitol," he says, stepping into the shadow of the sculpture to
shade his eyes. "Nineteen stories high—the skyscraper of the
Plains, they call it. Actually, it's fairly impressive seeing it this
way, don't you think, boys?"

+

"Hoo, wow," Charlie Witherspoon, my contact at the capitol
building, says, and his straight, glossy-black hair, which he keeps
pushing back, whisks the yoke of his flowered cowboy shirt as
he shakes his head. The shirt barely reaches inside his low-slung
Levi's, cinched with a tooled belt that reads CHUCK at the back.
He shoves up his horn-rimmed glasses with a thumb, and tucks
in his chin above the file folder he holds propped open against
his chest—the man whose official stationery bears the heading
State Director of Tourism and Publicity.

"Let's see, tonight's North Dakota Greats Night. Shoot, it
ought to be about the best thing the state's seen." Low laughter
emerges from him with the smile that folds his upper lip over
his lower at the corners. Jerome? "It might go down in history.
I'm a history buff, too. In a setup this size, you get to be Jack-
of-it-all."

"What's up?"

He stares over the folder above the tops of his glasses,
studying me with deep-brown eyes as if to decide whether I can
be trusted.

"I mean, is it the state's anniversary, besides the Bicentennial, or what?" I ask, and realize I've revealed how little I
understand about the state, although I refer to it on my
show.

"Nuu, it's the eighty-seventh year of statehood." He tosses
the folder onto the hardwood desk he hasn't yet sat behind.
"But there were trappers here before the *Mayflower*, so if you're
talking white settlers, hey, we're older than the East! Also, those
trappers didn't subdue any Indian nations—read 'destroy' for
'subdue'—but cooperated with them, as they damn well better've
out here in the sticks."

"Are you Sioux?"

"You mean this?" He lifts a swatch of his hair as if it's a wig. "Shoot no, I'm a Communist." He laughs so heartily I'm sure he's trying to pass. "The NPLers got hold of my dad. Naw, I'm probably as Kraut as you. Then again, you never know what Great-granny did, right?"

My cold stone face won't register the slightest response—every vestige of humor emptied by an extra gravity pulling me down in surges, causing my cells to fibrillate within a separate system of their own. To try to cover my freeze, I say, "I'm thinking of a Bicentennial show on the state. Could you recommend a book?" Then I notice that all the shelves around the room are loaded with history volumes.

"I'll do you one better. I'll send you a carton of required reading. Perks. What's your address?"

I give Katherine's, since she and I decided, after the funeral, to attempt to live together again. He picks up the file from his desk and makes a note: "Sooo, the 'greats' tonight. Eric Sevareid turned out to be the hardest to get. Roger Maris, Peggy Lee, Louis L'Amour, Era Bell Thompson—the black woman who was editor at *Ebony*? *No problem*. Harold Schafer is here in Bismarck now, of course. Lawrence Welk is booked for years, he said, ah-vun-*two*. Only Teddy Roosevelt and that poet of tedium, Robert Foley, couldn't be here, for the obvious reason. We plan on reincarnations of them soon."

"Come off it."

"Nuu, we have a local-heritage actor who's doing them both for the History Center opening next year. Or the year after that, depending on our legislature. Citizenry are already complaining about its cost. With the phased-in stages of state history they've got planned for the Center, they'll probably keep cranking things up until our hundredth, in 1989. It looks like some politician's dream of hog heaven. Sock it to the people till they choke! Let's see, then tomorrow night we have the Heritage Festival—Scandinavian folk crafts, German polka bands, Ukrainian egg painting, Native American dancing and—"

"It's a stampede!"

"Come on, now, Chuck, don't pull any of those characters from your show on me. Hey, you're the greatest! I'm the guy that got you here!"

Now get me out, I want to say, and feel the surge of cells in a panic like anger weighting my feet.

"You'll be on the next night, right before our local-heritage actor and raconteur. He's top-notch—doing a skit on a Mandan cowboy. He even borrowed the guy's six-gun from an Indian granddaughter down Standing Rock way! God, we'd love to grab that sucker for the History Center! The gun, I mean."

"But my contract calls for me to be here three days!"

"Right, today, tomorrow, and the next. Mingle with the folk. Tell em North Dakota's great! Attend the parties. Do some interviewing. We're informal here. We'd like you to do live interviews with all the 'greats.' Well, tape it and say it's live when you play it on your show, huh? Some of our 'greats,' well—" Holding an imaginary glass, he throws his head back, glossy hair flying as if from a punch, and then peers over his thick glasses and winks. "Give em hell, Chuck."

+

On the roof of the capitol building, where I've gone to breathe, I find iron bars set into a limestone ledge, with Cyclone fence strung between, to restrain my Imp of the Perverse. I stare through the diamonds of wire with a strain like sun blindness, afraid that anything I take in will add to my specific gravity, and settle on the slow swell and double curve of the Missouri, with its rugged breaks rising to a plateau and, above that, hogbacked and rounded buttes repeating range after range in gray-blue winter mist until a final range tucks itself into the edge of the sky at infinity—alien as a seascape. I sway with the wind that arrives in buffeting gusts, setting the bulky winter clothes of sightseers vibrating and snapping like flags as it drives granular snow from the ledge into my eyes. I blink against it, then set down the heaviest suitcase, with the recorder in it—the other at my room in the semi-seedy downtown hotel where I, along with the rest of the second-raters, as I take it, have been booked—and grab the bars set into the battlement.

"Don't jump, Chuckie," a voice says. I turn, still blinking, to a tall man with a Mennonite beard, dressed in a three-piece dark suit, without an overcoat or parka like the others here, his hands in his trouser pockets and his suit jacket bunched in folds. He rocks with the wind that lifts and flattens his layered haircut into a blue part at one side of his skull. "I figured I'd find you sooner or later, but—" A gust of wind rips the rest of this away. "You don't know me, I guess. I'm Arno Litwak." He reaches out a hand, then draws it back and sucks in his trembling lips. "You and your brother's best friend." A shadow of unpleasantness, like the shadow of his beard shaved back to where it rises in curly sprigs, settles coldly over his face. "Well, second-best, maybe. I guess the Rimskys were your favorites, huh?"

"What are you doing here?" I ask, too loud—like a nighttime threat delivered in a house where a door has slammed.

"What about you—planning a tightrope walk? I don't know, what's your schedule?"

I pick up my suitcase and it floats, weightless, to shoulder level, where I hold it as if I had intended this. "Live interviewing certain 'greats.' Tomorrow the dog acts. Nothing until the day after that."

"Let's have a drink."

+

"Let's see," he says, and revolves a gold-crystal ashtray as if it's a steering wheel on the surface of the circular oak table. "You're what, two years younger than your brother?"

"Closer to one."

"He was in my grade. He went to college?"

"He's a doctor."

"Gadzooks! as we used to say, ay?" He grabs his glass and empties it; he drinks as fast as I do, and has a spray of whiskers under his nose that he missed in a shaky or careless morning shave. "I mean, here I sit, a lowly dentist from North Dakota *Moo*, the agriculture center. No, Jerome was always a decent fellow, I thought."

In comparison?

He signals for another round, then revolves the ashtray in the opposite direction. "I suppose he's seen the bills—mortgages, the whole bit. True, a dentist is lower down the ladder, but my practice is good." He holds up a hand for viewing, his fingers spread wide. "When the bills get too bad, I hop in my Piper Comanche and head for Canada. To hell with farmers' teeth. And their wives'. Fwee!" He holds his nose.

"You fly?"

"Till the Credit Union repos my plane. No, I go up at least twice a year for the fishing. Say, someday let's throw us a few cases of beer in the Piper, and head up. Give me a call. Call collect, what the hell."

"Is it safe—wilderness flying?" What I mean to ask is if he can be trusted.

"Safer than driving a tin can down the Eisenhower Expressway!"

I suffer a jolt of apprehension about Katherine and Becky at this.

"I interned in Chicago. Ran into Buddy Schoenbeck in a bar. 'Biggest little city in the world,' he yelled, 'ain't it?' Buddy. Huh. He was a sales rep for a powerboat company. Both the Rimskys are in Missoula. Leo opened a pie franchise and got Brian to do the baking—no head in the oven for Leo with Brian handy. Kuntz is a career Navy man."

"I always believed that I'd run into Kuntz, in Navy blues, in a New York bar."

"He's above the Navy, as he'd see it—the Marine Corps." Another jolt. "Who else of the infamous crew? Your girlfriends are all married."

"Girlfriends?"

"You seemed to grab off a few," he says, and narrows an eye, and I recall his cousin—sister?—on porch steps after the year with Bobbie.

"Father Schimmelpfennig died, I guess you know, of lung cancer."

"No."

"He wasn't a priest to me, but I liked the old gent well enough to quit smoking when I heard. I figured it was costing us—I and my wife—seven hundred bucks a year. When we got the Piper, I told her quitting covered the payments on it. Hell, not even the annual, now. No, little planes are real safe. Well, every once in a while somebody augers one in."

"Pardon?"

"Oh, you get in a storm, or a weird cloud cover, and the next thing you know you're upside down or flying for terra firma when you think you're headed east. I'm fairly good with instruments. My trade. You hit Ma Earth under throttle, and we call it augering it in, if you get the picture. It happened to a friend this year—nobody knows why. He powered his Cessna into a desert, flat as this table, out in New Mexico."

"Who was he?" I ask, through a clog like chocolate in my throat.

"An old buddy—the flying dentist from Pembina. You wouldn't know him. Not famous." He wrinkles his nose and appears to take a measure of my anxious fear. "He left a wife and daughter. Too bad."

I look at my watch and he says, "You cowboys—always in a rush."

"Cowboys?"

From his wild look, eyebrows rolling, he hadn't meant this to be pejorative, or didn't understand I'd know it was, and is off-balance. "You know, people out on the roundup, always busy. Public sorts of types. Me, I'm just a slip-em-a-shot-of-novocaine, Dentist Joe type."

"What would you do if you weren't?" This has emerged as if I might grant his wish—confirmed between us by his wavering look—and I see through to another exchange of this sort, with Purkeet, in a Broadway restaurant where he'd asked to meet me and sat nibbling at a Kaiser roll as he studied my face, and then said, "You can't desert your friends, Charles. Friends are important." "Have I deserted you?" I asked, and looked up and saw an elderly dapper man in a natty suit and tie at a distant table, entirely bald, his head a healthy rose-color, with a mischievous rodentlike wriggling to his face as he leaned to speak to an elegant woman who wore a floor-length white dress and a broad-brimmed hat draped with a black veil, the veil gathered under a choker holding a cameo at its center: a pact. "Well, you haven't kept in touch; you haven't kept up with me," Purkeet said, and I started to say I was married, and then I understood; since he moved to New York, he had been in a play off Broadway. "You mean you want me to interview you?" I asked. "Since you put it that way, Cholly, a heh heh, why not?"

"Create custom jewelery," Arno says. He points to a twist of silver on a finger. "I made a mate for the Frau. You know." He holds up his hands again, fingers outspread, and I see the corded delicacy of them, and it finally penetrates: fillings and bridges and caps—jewelry. "There's money in it! Say, do you have a broad for the duration?"

"I'm married!" I say in such a rough, sharp rasp he sits back.

+

In the lower level of the capitol building, Roger Maris, in a Yankee uniform, swings a baseball bat in a roped-off corner. Eric Sevareid stands at a square, antiquated NBC floor mike (Wrong network, I think; unplugged, I see) and says in his on-the-air voice, to a short woman in tweeds, who holds a pad at her breasts like a reporter, "But as I said in my memoirs, in prose as clear as I could summon . . ." Era Bell Thompson sits between Tom McGrath and Louis L'Amour at a table in an alcove, where all three are autographing copies of their books, McGrath and L'Amour like coppery wrinkled petals of a triptych unfolding from Era Bell's blackness at the center, and in a legislative caucus room named the Blue Room, according to the brass plate above its doors, tables are being set up in cabaret fashion for Peggy Lee to perform tonight. On the last day of the festival, after my appearance, and then the cowboy's, she's to sing in the House of Representatives, already sold out. The only one who looks free to interview is Harold Schafer, sitting on a couch in tailored Western wear, in an area marked off with velvet ropes of the sort used in movie theaters, looking down at a table and rubbing his fingertips over his forehead as if over a knot in one of the many millions made by his Gold Seal products (the pink glass-wax in a pink can with a seal in a circle at its center, which Jerome and I once smeared on the dishes), or the growing bill for this bash, which he's probably footing. Crowds are moving down the echoing marble lobby past the celebrities as if they're exhibits, and then, back in a corner, a group of people speed into the clatter of marionettes, and enter my terrible headache.

+

"Jerome! Did I wake you?"

"Yes."

"Sorry."

"That's all right, I'm up now." A brisk voice and a wash of sheets as he sits in the oversized bed I once sneaked a look at, and there saw, on its far side as across a snowy plain, a dark, wrapped body—Julie asleep.

"Hey, I made it to this festival in Bismarck, you know, the one I mentioned I had to, ah, attend?"

"How is it?"

"Oh, fine, fine, fine. Say, how are things with you there?"

"Fine."

"Fine! Great! Hey, you know what I did?"

There's the sigh of a relocation for a long stay. "No."

"I went and left without my tranks. Quillizers. No prescription." Actually I haven't had a prescription since the therapist, a summer ago.

"Oh."

"Right. I'm in pretty bad shape. Besides about Dad, of course. The worst. I was wondering if maybe you couldn't send a prescription."

"You mean, mail it?"

"I was thinking by telegram."

"Telegram!"

"Not common practice, huh?"

"I don't know that I've ever even heard of that."

"That's what I was afraid of. I've had it." I grab the quart of whiskey I've ordered up from room service.

"Get some rest. At least lie down. Prepare ahead for whatever you have to, and *do it well*, for—"

I'm afraid he's heard the bubbling glug of percolating whiskey or its whistle at my lips from the way that he's paused.

"Right, I will," I say, licking at its sting on my cracked lips.

"Gather your resources and hang in there. What is it, a day?"

"Three. Two now."

"For Katherine and Becky. You've got to think of them."

"Right, I know. I will, right, sure. Yeah, okay."

+

Then I'm waking, sweaty and naked, to a telephone receiver at my face. *Her?*

"What? Are you there? Listen, I'm really sorry if I've been what I shouldn't have— You know, whatever I shouldn't be. Or do. It took all I've got to hang on. Bear with me, okay? It can't be long now."

Silence, then a sea wash of static connects me to two men in flashy clothes in the hall to whom I hand bills in large denominations out of a suitcase I didn't know I had, which I call my Folding Bill. Then Al, my actor friend, wearing specially constructed shoes, walks to a hotel door (I'm on the other side, unable to move from bed) carrying a costume that has expended the resources of hundreds, on a hanger that will permit me to escape— Who would he be helping me to escape from? Or is it Marco, my other friend, made up to look like Al? Jerome?

"Hello, are you there?"

+

What's going on, I think, trying to disentangle my senses from a chant some Indians from Fort Yates are sending up near the Blue Room.

"Are you Charles?" It's a woman like the interviewer of Sevareid, and I have to deliberate before I'm able to answer, simply, "Yes."

"Hi, I'm Sandy Pinkerton."

There's a spangling like bicycle spokes in her voice, and I see a washboarded road with wheels turning reflecting tines over it as if driving its surface along under the sun. "I'm sorry. I mean, pardon?"

"Sandy Pinkerton. I used to play with you and Jerome, remember?"

"You had a great big trike."

"I believe it was about standard."

"What happened?"

"How do you mean?"

The radiating streaks in her eyes hover, held down, and then part to admit me. "You used to be so tall."

"Maybe that's how it seemed to you. I was, what, twelve to your four? When we moved. Nothing, now. My age probably enlarged my trike, as far as that goes. For you." Her tongue travels around her upper lip as if to aid mine, cracked from alcohol, and I see through to her creamy firmness, with translucent freckles in clotted bouquets on her cheeks: the sculpted lids of a Swede. A few inches shorter, even in the high boots I've taken in in a quick sweep; a tooled-leather purse.

"That's right, you moved to Bismarck."

"Here. My mother still has her house here. I live in it with her." This seems difficult for her to get out. "I've been a model till now—a Miss this or that or Queen Cream Cheddar. Then in New York. I did some political writing there. Have you seen anything of mine?"

"No."

Her eyelids lower to half-mast to excuse her blush, and an eyetooth nicks one corner of her lip. "Mother got ill, so I came back. This music wasn't meant for echoing marble halls, would you say? Or this ceiling. *Any* ceiling. Anyways, somebody said, Why don't you go into politics? I knew so many people from the Miss–Queen events, and then anybody who's been to New York City, *and made it back*, is a hero. The first time I ran for the Senate I was elected. I've been a state senator two terms. The legislature meets every other year, and it's an off year. That's why this." She swings toward the crowd—a fragile fine profile—then back. "So sometimes I still model. Not much else to do, right?"

My neck swells with blood as if growing gills, and my voice locks, at cross-purposes to its autonomy.

"Anyways"—she glances toward the Indians, showing another profile, of a pale matron, with a swag of flesh below her chin, and the dancers, stripped and trimmed with feathers, glistening from sweat, the shaking bells around their ankles double-timing in the silence, begin to slow—"I thought I'd see what my playmate's little brother is up to. I've heard your show. It was often funny, earlier on. Damn serious now, with that family stuff. I helped vote this in. Are you enjoying it?"

If I were able to talk, should I lie?

"Ah, I see," she says, and takes my arm. "Where'd they put you up?"

+

A hand mike is lying on the apron, as I requested, I see as I walk onstage, in a spotlight that causes specks in the maple boards to glitter silver. I'm trembling so badly I have to hold the mike in both hands, and my voice, my means of income, will hardly work. "I feel I've gargled some hail," I say into the mike. Silence. Then somebody in the wings, a dark bulk from where I stand, laughs so hard he has to slap his hams, from the sound, and I sense the audience's attention shift to him. "Well, if that's the case, let me just rattle some random words around by way of *preface!*"—the word cascades into the resounding auditorium, and I try to find a face I can address in the staggered tiers above—"until my voice stops caroming around at the back of my throat and settles down in my mouth as it should, like a nice snug pair of dentures." Arno? I clack my teeth into the microphone. Silence. A bead of sweat streaks down my ribs, and I start to ad-lib a parody of my flight here, but discover I'm in a deeper tangle than when I was bumping with my suitcases past shying faces down the narrow airplane aisle.

I step back, one eye burning from the spotlight, take some panting breaths, and begin the standby I hold in reserve, a threnody on the passing cowboy, then remember that a cowboy is coming on next, and the further I get into the threnody, with no response, the faster I go, to get it over with—although I know I should slow down. For some reason I break into the speeded-up gobbledygook of the German scientist, straight from my high-school monologue, not sure if I ever finished with the cowboy, and say, "So vass? Ve fint ve not unly have to relinkvish da produtrid, but ambulate." I give a quick bow, setting the mike on the apron at my feet, spraying it and the boards with the perspiration bursting from me in the absence of applause, and walk off. There is silence until a man next to me in the wings starts pounding his hands—the same one, I'm sure, who first guffawed—and then the scattered staccato beyond of polite applause.

This fellow, who has tufts of gray hanging from a ten-gallon hat, stands bent and bowed in thin chaps, with zebra wrinkles of an African drawing down his face, bypassing a bandito mustache. He puts a heated hand on my shoulder, and says, "Chuck. Are you all right?"

The tufted hair and seamy wrinkles are makeup, I see, as alarm for me deepens in his amber eyes. "The cowboy bit was good," he says. "I think I heard most of it on your show. Maybe you went too fast. But that's them." He juts his real unwrinkled chin toward the auditorium.

I'm afraid to ask what he means, and realize that the pattering I hear, which seemed a round of feebler applause, comes from the feet of people dressed in black, arranging props on the stage.

"They've got the Dakota syndrome. If you're a native, you're nothing, like they're nothing, because nothing good can come from here—their view of it. You're unreal unless you've been on TV or made six million. Better, like Welk, to be on TV. Then they won't stop talking you up. It's the love-hate syndrome these sonsabitches were born with."

"I feel awful."

"At least you can admit it. If you can't, you can't change, or repent, as our granddaddies put it, and there's something to that. Guilt is the first sign you've done something you probably shouldn't have." The curtain beside us gathers in folds to the faint thrumming of a motor, drawing aside on a stage where dim lights come up. He pulls a rolled cigarette from a shirt pocket—"Not a joint," he whispers, "a prop"—and lights it. "I've tried Buddhism, TM, the works. Guilt's healthy in the proper perspective. I shit barrels of it every day without blinking, due to"—he pulls a pistol from a resonant holster and points it at the audience—"those syndromistes."

"So what do you do?" I ask, desperate.

"Let em have it." A burst of fire lengthens the barrel of the pistol a second before the stunning report sends me backward. "Sorry," he whispers. "Part of the act." He raises it and fires again and my ear aches, deafened. He cries "Hoo-*whee!*" in a high voice, and fires overhead with an impact that could bring down a traveling drape, then sways onstage as the lights come up and creaks across to a log-rail fence at the center of his set and leans on it and says in an old man's wheedling voice, "You ain't heard of me, except you read some North Dakota history. Turkey Track Bill. Wail, that's *me*."

+

I try to sneak out the building down a side hall that opens onto another lobby, and see Sandy Pinkerton leaning against a marble column, under light fixtures that are heads of wheat eight feet long. She leads me to a cab, and then comes up to my room and sits in a chair so worn out that its fibrous stuffing shows, and when I say again that I haven't read her articles, which she claims appeared in the *Partisan Review* and on the Op-Ed page of *The New York Times*, she kicks up a leg and crosses it over the other as if she'd like to have my head between and crush it.

There's a knock at the rattly door. Friends of hers, probably, she says, and then somebody is on the floor in front of me, playing a guitar that I ask for in order to sing my way back to the first night at the Chesro, Dylan again, not thinking twice, while a young man does something with a mirror, and then rolls up a hundred-dollar bill to the size of a drinking straw, and motions me over. More people arrive, until the crowd seems it will push out a window, and then she's in the chair again, alone now, the din absent, her legs crossed, smoking a cigarette, her face reddening and her mouth open strangely sideways as she talks. These tailings off of thought, muscular apostrophes, folding freckled skin, and then, close up, an appearance like snot on cornsilk as my high-school friends step down from the cooler in front of Rimsky's window and start into a dance suggestive of hacking with mallets, nodding their heads like people in speeded-up newsreel clips as they chant, "It might look like an oyster! it might cook like an oyster! but it's *not*!"

+

I wake on the floor, naked, next to a vodka jug so dry it could have cobwebs in it. Arno Litwak here, a beard? Lights like gooseneck lamps were trained in. All videotaped? One sock is on but twisted backward. There's a rush of rustling clothes down a stairs, and then a voice: *You can't destroy the evidence this time, flyboy.* I pack and in a minute I'm in the identical cab, with drill holes in the panel beneath a window in the shape of a

cross. The mud flap of a semitrailer ahead reads *Beaver Check,*
50 Feet, and then we rush under his rearview mirror, as large
as a medicine chest, across the bridge, where a turtle in our
lane, head lifted, is straddled by our squalling tires, the state
itself going blank, no longer there—this melanoma of the soul,
bloodstream-run.

Pushing into the plane's boxy rest room, I bump the door
against a man pulling on a hairnet, my beginning thoughts
blowing out into fragrant, exploded views, then stinking of oil.
Once we're airborne, an Indian girl Becky's age, with slick black
hair clinging in points to her shiny warm-up jacket, begins a
formulated jumping around, from one seat to the next, aisle to
window to aisle, and then a jump to the row ahead, a chess
move, keeping up the racing speed of Jerome, and it feels my
skull will give unless she slows. I say, "Are you afraid?"

"Oh, no," she says, and jumps ahead to another seat,
terrified now.

No wonder, I think, because I can make out red and green
dots in rows beneath the carpeted aisle, as if landing lights or
lighted city streets are glowing through the fuselage—and aren't
these films being beamed into the plastic portholes as they
throttle up the jets and hold them there to simulate the throes
of flight until a further scene is set in place? Then drop us off
at another entrance or exit in this endless labyrinth of illusion
we're manipulated through for some observer's bored amusement—fodder for a laugh. No, no drink!

+

Down the gangway, into the glass corridor of the airport.
Katherine isn't at the gate. People turn to bleached images
passing me, while I walk at the convergence of such weighty
color streaming in from every side it feels I'm carrying everyone
I pass, helpless, until a slow and killing heaviness gathers in my
leaden legs—impossible to get to the river, to throw myself in.

Then Katherine comes striding slowly up.

We go into a restaurant of plaid walls, my suitcases banging
down like blocks of ice, and I say, "I can't take it. It's the—"

"Oh, stop."

"No, I—" I attempt to confess, as I vowed I would if I saw

her again—in pawing bursts that ride a fretwork of images. "With Jerome's friend," I say.

She swings to me, tears forming dripping fans from her jaw, and cries in a whisper, "You shit!" She shoves at something on her head, a knitted headband, as if to tear it off, and her hair swells within it. "I knew it the minute I got that drunken call!"

A grip of shackles fastens at my wrists with the news that I called.

"I'd like to kill you," she whispers, and shoves back her chair and walks off, swaying. She leans into a wall of glass in the walkway to the terminal, a fist to her face, and I start for her with the suitcases, startled at the sight of her profile against a jet's tail fin in the raining sun. "I'll leave," I say, but she hurries on, an arm up as if to ward off blows, striding with the unsteady weighty power of the betrayed.

+

In her car, her face set, the bulge of hair inside the knitted band like a headdress, she drives across the median, into the far lane of the Expressway, where a man in a denim jacket is running down the shoulder in front of a semitrailer, one hand back as if to fend it off. "What?" I cry, and turn to straighten this out, but two motorcyclists gun ahead and park on a bridge, and one resembling Skip Wangsdorf raises an arm toward the orange-pink sky to point out the approach of Armageddon, while the other unbuckles his helmet and pulls it off, cradling it under his arm like a fetus as they watch for a figure to appear from the roiling orange like a nuclear blast, while behind the radio grille a concentration of media equipment keeps squawking my name. Her stony face is the only one able to guide us through this to the other side, not Jerome.

I have on a hat, and pull it over my eyes, unable to watch anymore, my heart tripping with a force that hurts my tongue, a fast-socking fist that will knock me out. We stop. She leads me down dark halls, into spaces unlit except by a streetlamp outdoors, her house, and in every room are boxes and belongings piled in haste—truckloads I had forgotten I'd carted here for her: disorder from every former life.

On her single bed, piled with suitcases, *in sin I was conceived*, I can't lie still or quit saying, "Hoo-hoo-hoo," with each breath. Can't smoke, cigarettes like feelers of metal from fillings down my throat, and I imagine my head in a metal safe, with three mice also inside, under drinking glasses smoke is pumped into, slowly gagging and dying with opened needlelike snouts, and then cigarettes are stuck in every hole and smoke is forced into me until I'm blue. I'm up out of bed, pacing in double-time high as a horse as I picture my mother like a planet out of orbit hurry past the moon, and understand that the wedge of womanliness at my center is the tip of her heart that has passed into a cavity of me and now is beating out of control. "No-no-no!"

On a wall like a screen I see a soaked doper banging at the door with a pistol, convinced I'm the cause of his psychosis: *You'll be pounded down and every bone in your body crushed, you—*

A thumping then on an inside door, mine. Katherine opens it up.

"This can't go on," she says. "You have to get out."

"Where—" This feeble thread through noisy breathing is Dad's.

"For a walk?"

No-no-no! But the hat and a coat on. A hand. Feet. Out this door, another, down a glassed-in porch reflecting half of me, across a street where two cars start at us, backing, and are foiled by sudden traffic. We go under piles of stacked apartment buildings, where another car comes speeding up from behind, down a concrete ramp, and just as I'm ready to give myself up or dive beneath, it's past us, a pickup. A man leaps out and hurries off, looking over his shoulder with reddish eyes, carrying a six-pack of Coke—real coke for snorting, part of a bet on how long I'll be able to last, broadcasting.

She leads me through a chain-link fence, its diamonds severed and sliding over her in shadow, the headband catching and her hair twisting like flying flame over the wire. Then through brushy hedge to a cemetery with stones like sails to the horizon. No!

"Come." A tug. Time for judgment on this buzzing clump

of flesh that can't be stopped except by a sword—no place to hide among these obelisks and stones, the present gone into a future burned up by the past.

A bulky boulder rises from a mound of grass, taking contours of a face—is one, an Indian's, carved into rock, a projection his nose; eyelids and lips notched in beading grooves, Dad. Dead.

"See?" she says.

Beneath stylized feathers that form a headdress:

AN ANCIENT INDIAN TRAIL
ONCE PASSED THIS BOULDER
SKIRTING THE FOREST ALONG THE
DES PLAINES RIVER . . .

No more. The ranks of notched-in print are barbs, continuing in a heavy dozen lines I can't take—him at the last, with his magnetic pull of rock drawing everything in range down in death.

+

Back home, she undresses and lies down in the beauty of her skin, so dim to me I can't experience even the surge of possible death. She undresses me. A bath? No, no cells dissolving down the drain, among slops in pipes pouring over babies' heads, maniacs slamming radiators with hammers—like this banging at a door with panes of glass.

She leaves the room in her robe, and is far off, faint, at the door, saying he'll have to wait—who?—and I'm up and stomping again.

"UPS," she says, and floats in with a box, cardboard smelling of rain, and drops it with the tumbled thump of a body onto the floor.

"Where—?" This childish plaint of Dad in his tremolo like fear.

She slashes it wide. Books, every book I might need to trace the history of the state that is now a blank, excised from me for good.

"I have to get Becky from school."

Don't! A smell of autumn light from the armrest of my wheelchair at the click of the door. Closes. Fall? Oilcloth odor of a satchel and cedar pencils in my brain—intolerable to leave, too, or leave this behind.

Sleep? A door bumps and bangs, Becky's voice, her feet thumping, muffled. "Oh, here's Dad's suitcase!"

"Yes, he's here, he's not feeling well, he's resting."

Face into my pillow to muffle the oh-ho-ho, no-ho-ho under a sound of pans, bangs of an evening meal. Then Becky's voice, low. Listening?

Water running in the tub that will take her down. *Wait!*

+

I've stepped up the speed of my springy walk that served until I developed Dad's heel-hitting tread—each step taken in a deliberation that might be his last—but no thought for me at this age of any end, or even a direction toward one, every step a new start, past a man in Bowery dress whispering to a parking meter. He gives a sidelong wave to somebody like Al crossing the street ahead, at the corner, who steps behind a building, gone. I pick up speed and start to run, unable to hold down the anxious heat of seeing Jerome, and meet the cleaning lady coming toward me in her sorority hobble, crying hello as I trot by and pick up speed, passing Tony so fast I almost miss him. At Cooper Union a spindly kid in a velveteen shirt turns on me the Caribbean cool of Raul, and the narrow street beyond, with its strip of chilly sky, is like running down a dark corridor—past a window of recording equipment, where they're trying to clear me for a hookup to a satellite that will broadcast the one vow I must not break.

I'm up from the heat of Katherine beside me, moving so fast in my bathrobe in the high-prancing pace that I step through its hem and bottom half, shredding it. I throw it off, and go past piles of belongings giving off purple edges from the streetlamp, into the kitchen. The door on this side, the one my daughter sleeps behind, closed, the light on on the kitchen stove for her, the hands of its clock at a time I can't decipher—bending back from my magnetic need to translate them. The sink. A window above it. Car-door slam. A garage across the parking lot, where a man turns with eyes that send blue beams into me. Undertaker's manikin. Death's carpenter bearing bodies away.

No! I'm to my daughter's door and fling it wide, in flight, and hover there. Safe? Alone? A stir under silver light like loss, my teeth chattering above her breathing, and then the door shut quick. A faint naked form starts the high-prancing in the refrigerator's front. Into the alcove of the linen closet—her pistol here? the .22 acquired for the city?—the bathroom abattoir across from it, a swinging door flapping its coughing flops. I lock it back. The dim dining room, awash with sensations that send my hair up, more articles added to the piles, it looks, surfaces askew, this plush pale, *pale plush carpet* to soften my prance. The membranous part of the brain that sorts memories ruptured—everything bleeding into other cells. Into the bedroom, where her sleeping heat sends tripping warnings up. *Thou shalt not commit adultery*, a single sheet over her center like a sarong.

The box of books—a newspaper tossed in on top, with scribbling on it: "Caught this by Sandy." I try to steady it in my prance, and see: "Figure Neumiller's fee and the deadly time he spent after 'gargling hell out of his throat,' in his words, and it's 75 smackeroos a minute."

I had to be there *three days*, I think in Dad's voice, and fling it to the floor. The headline reads: 7 DEAD, 27 INJURED IN HOTEL FIRE.

This, too? The revving engine stalls, with a catch and cough that could be regret, then picks up at a higher speed, the prance now a run—shadows blurring past as I get to the linen closet, and dismantle it in a dozen jerks. No .22. A toppling stumble of a gallop to the bed where she steams beneath the sheet, to her closet. A chain saw on the floor, below hanging clothes. Taken from Dad's place with our furniture. The sight of it shifts me to the slowed weight of underwater strides. This house buried beneath a flood, cakes of ice overhead, and only this saw to use to cut a hole through the closet into the closet above, the only escape, out through the ceiling with the saw, through the roof, Katherine and Becky hurrying after, holding to the sheet, swinging up and pulling them onto the colliding ice—

Beside the saw, a metal safe of papers and policies, with three mice under glass tumblers inside, where my head will soon be crushed and smoke pumped through bleeding tubes until the last of hacking death is in my throat, and I'm guillotined—chicken flop and thump of a body blowing blood over ice. Hell not heat but freezing cold. Naked in it. Skin stretched over arctic snow, every nerve bare for jeeps and snowmobiles to barrel across. The one above you, in this stratified state of endless perdition, your worst enemy, kicking you in the face; the one below, the one you love, trapped under your flailings to break free.

Out to the dining room, into sensations breaking like waves that toss my hair in swirls, into the living room. Only the green chair available, still, with all this furniture—worse piles present, more surfaces askew, every inch of the room a jiggling scale weighing the objects in their placement and my wild stomping, so that any milligram of change will have to be accounted for. Heat like needles down my palms, and each turn a juncture of right angles I've walked before within the larger angles traced so often by Dad that I can never move beyond them or keep up—step 715, 714, 713, his face the yellow-gold of winter light, brown lip lifting over dry teeth, the trembling tumor pulling up the incline of pain toward his neck.

I turn and through the shadowed walls of foliage see myself in a suit jacket slow for the walk through Washington Square, but with an inertia that causes me to hop and trot—happy at my nearness to Jerome, at Marco's, his phone. I pass a park bench and see the same carving I saw when I opened a $\diagdown\diagup$ letter from a lawyer in California and read it here in $\diagup\diagdown$ autumn light through the bare branches of a ginkgo, the first to shed, and found that my one-fifth share in our mother's one-fifth portion of Grandma Jones's estate was also enclosed: a check for four hundred dollars. An amazement. That she had saved this. And now I had more months free.

+

I bump into a box, and a group of booted feet go rumbling across the room overhead like animal hooves. Out in the street, cars gun past in a life-and-death race—and Enos Clapton, rising to point at me, sends his chair spinning aside to slam into the blackboard tray.

"What—?" in that tiny dead voice of Dad's.

Secretive to the point of flippancy. The battered sermon-maker adopting his noxious distance to preach. I wish you were dead!

I bang into a bronze umbrella stand holding fencing foils, a walking stick, a battered black umbrella—this racing engine, in its clattering howl of floorboarding, about to come to a halt. A foil out, its point at my stomach, and then a dive to the floor on top of it, hough!—flying so far free of Jerome I feel him fly equally in the opposite direction in his will to live, and pull me after, bloody intestines gritting on rust.

Cut the act! And your— At the circular dining table, in a gliding shuffle of sensation like ocean beams, the bearded man from the parapet above the clouds appears. *—your goddamned ghostly covenantal grotesquerie and bloody internal violence, you pimp!*

"Who-oo?" I say, rising from the sprung foil, tearing it free.

"I am goddamned Satan, Jack. How does that grab you? Makes you almost have to hide a grin of self-importance, huh?"

"No no no."

"I got your balls and left foot in a sling and you go *no* in shaky triplicate? Come on, you can do better than that, Jack. Speak up!"

In a stink like a struck wet match he's gone. The table remains, round as my raw gut, burning at its center like a swallowed live cigarette. I go into the living room in my highest prancing run, the booted feet following above to aim their equipment down—*save my darling from the dogs*—into the entry, to the front door I push back and lock, too late: the machine gun. With a clatter the window gives like a sheet of water cascading to the floor. There's a metallic *thuk* through thick teeth, and I'm down before the pane completes its cascade and erupts in spangles around my face swimming off. Cratered pockets are seeping down an arm. Burns in my belly from the foil or machine-gun slugs. A *thwup-thut* of a .38 or bigger bore, and then a figure like Bobbie's father appears and lowers a shotgun, and in its stunning blow to my head there's no sound. *Unbelievable shit!*

A scream. Fingers broken or bleeding, studded with metal

and nuggets of glass. Not over yet, this state of never knowing if the imaginary is real or the real imagined—as I go in an elbow-scraping crawl to the bathroom, the sink—*ding! ding! ding! Time's up!*

+

I push and lock the door or swing it aside and kick out the stop to send it *kaluck-coughing* both ways, and it opens wide on Marco. He's sitting tailor-fashion in undershorts on his foldout couch. Across the narrow room his girlfriend, Les, squats against a paneled wall with her knees up, in bluejeans, between the windows that look on the angled flight of a fire escape, staring from close-set tremulous eyes—soft fox.

"Did he call yet?" I ask.

"Just did!" Marco cries, and I receive a noise like a rush of static through my ears as the phone on the bed beside him rings.

"He said he'd check if you were in, and call back," Les whispers.

"Marco's," Marco says.

But the static is growing, and when I step from the door into the apartment I hear equipment on and running, generating the oily, yellowed-Scotch-tape smell of electronics, so that as I go around the end of the bed where covers are trailing, the wall behind gives in sliding reflections over soundproof glass on a studio engineer at his board, finger pointing. There's a crackle of magnetic receptiveness, a microphone, as Marco hands me the receiver.

"Jerome!" This reverberates at the edge of feedback through equipment being adjusted to the proper level.

"Hey! I'm in this little Polish or Russian bar beside your place."

"My place! You're in the city?"

"Ukrainian, Joe just said."

"He's right, Ukrainian."

"So I hope we're in the city," he says.

"You mean, it isn't easy to tell."

"As I see it, in my state."

"You made it! How'd you work it?"

"We drove. Long. I'm in waking sleep. I think I better pull a shave job at your place—when you get back here, if you do."

"I'll be right there!"

"Now that we're here, there's no hurry."

"Have a beer on me!"

"Will do."

"I'll run!"

+

Glass. Glass shelf. Clack. Where? The straight razor here before I left, now gone. No, there. The clump of its box on the floor. Too dull, spots of rust on its reflecting blade like blood. A double-edge next to it, new. Bang of the mirror. My huffing breathing speeding up until I'm too dizzy to feel, a husk. Cold even eyes of murdering blue that I avoid, gagging—a current like ice water up my arms, worse than tinfoil on fillings, at the sight of the dropped razor box. My face rocking in reflected gags from water in the encrusted bowl.

Flush it! Was this before?—*a murderer from the beginning!*

A new razor blade, sticky from its wrapper, gripped at a corner so it won't break, quivering in spasms in my hurry to find the spot. I drive it deep, in a gouge and twist to say that I'm never coming back, down any early-morning light—*Let it out like air!*

I switch to the other hand, and thrust harder, dragging it deep, feeling a catch on cords—jittering elastic now in both legs, medicine chest open on the infinite space I'm twirling through.

Back to the first wrist, its bleeding clogged, I dig in, faint, everything slowed—the last black bile about to blow out my throat, the faucet running over the parting sting, spilling rusty strips and pink streams in bloody spatters. Cold? Hot? Which? Steaming.

"God, that hurts! Oh, it *burns*! Ow!"

I tilt in a stumble to the dining room, trailing scattering loops over the carpet and cartons, in a clatter over newspaper, to the fencing foil—its handle propped against the floor, point to my stomach, a dive! Flat clump on the floor and flying snapped steel sprung whistling free.

"Mom! It's Dad! Dad! Dad! Mom, come here!"

A bang, a door, a furring of clothes as I pull myself on elbows in sexual panting to the bathroom, over the sill, time up. Hide from her here—her seeing. Wheezing engine dying out. Phonings dialed. "Police?" I paw farther into the bathroom, get a sticky greased grip on the sink trap, still warm. A spatter from numb wrists onto the floor in a pool. Oh, breath. Dark, down to a blue dot—miniature sun I rose and woke to. Now gone. A jolt. Cold hall bleached light. A jolt. Then something hits at an outer layer in a pounding rush.

"Let go of that pipe!"

A prying at the shadows left of my fingers clutched.

"Come on, buddy, be nice."

"God, get a towel on those."

More prying at a distance, where currents hum inside chrome.

"This guy has got that grip they get."

"I'll get—" Steps going out of the room, out the kitchen door, the porch, into a cold my feet follow. "Hand me those." A warm wrap around my wrists, parting the incisions in them in pains that streak to my chest. Then my ankles grabbed, and suddenly jerked and tugged until my wrists rip and my body stretches out the door and down the stairs to the porch—the slashes parting at the cords where a pipe trap shakes from their jerking. "Okay, he won't give up. Hand me it." A wallop to a buttock. "That'll have him in about two shakes."

+

A slow time to strap or bolt the remains of me onto this rock, and then a turn toward blinking blue that is the direction I must remember, in order to travel back—set in dots under an airplane rug. A slide beneath a red signal, flashing in black-and-white blips—"and lock him up for good."

"I'd like to."

"Did you see that kid."

"How about his wife? He's the kind that—" A smell of leather, a holster. Motor sounds rock us under the sway of a fuzzy ceiling, windows of wire mesh on both sides, my arms gripped in tongs. The faces above in shaded visors, then a turn that might be my end, to hear my daughter say before I went, "He's the one that should have to clean it up!"

A jolt into interstellar space, freezing hell, and then a slow-packed rhythm, with me awash in it, and I'm gasping light. A white room in which a man in a white smock, wearing a mask, says, "Jesus."

"What's that, Jerry?"

"He meant it. Both wrists. Start the blood. Two. Get one in a leg there."

A wheel revolves my body and I see in a slide from its height, through quadrants of the rooms it's divided into, that I have to live through every scene in every room (Raskolnikov with the ax, the widow getting hers) of every book there is, from the Inferno to mathematical madness—my shaking body strapped naked to a rocket taking off, and then I see, over the sheet on my toes as I lift off, down the last dim corridor left, Katherine and Becky afloat, pinned to the air, staring at me, and can't rise or respond. "I—"

Pinned to the air at every edge of her clothes, her headband holding the sign I should have deciphered: Eternity.

+

Ready to go. Numb body rumbling on wheels, police at each side—a turn and bump along a shelf of concrete, nearing stars above my toes in prisms of blue. Horses, coming unstuck from the stellar freeze, thunder down a ramp tilted to receive the blows of their hooves. Columns reach to another ramp overhead, a scrape of the feet trundling these sections of me along an icy field, the landscape rolling back to the room where the endless-ness of reliving it all begins again. I drift on sections of stretchers, my pilgrimage here, then bump through double doors, held open by a bar, to another set of doors—the noise of an audience in an auditorium beyond. Operating theater? Jerome at a podium, to oversee me wheeled in, then serve as judge—or the fiery eyes of Christ himself appear from bronze? Police whisper, "Late"—too late, and I'm drifting down narrowing ribs, deeper than I've gone before to a whir of wings, the bump of a stretcher against an inner door nailed shut. It gives a ways, releasing

shocks of heat and voices from inside, while my head struggles
to remain, in spite of the jolts of travel starting from underneath,
and I give the secret nod to start the recording I've hidden
away, and then all doors slam shut on us in the consuming light
of our end:

> Oh, my brother, remember North Dakota,
> The nights of angular snow, the drift of snow
> That rose until it reached our windowsill
> And then rose slowly up the glass; below
> Its fuming surface, visible through the glass,
> The quiet crystals, glittering, blue, serene.
> Remember the trough of ice that guided
> Our sled down past roots, stumps, stones,
> A culvert, bumping—you on the bottom, me on the top,
> Knocking your breath out—down the steep bank
> To the uneven flatlands of the frozen lake below,
> Skimming across its ripples, the sled slapping
> Down like the hull of a light boat, taking us far
> Out onto the lake, farther out than we should have gone, then
> Slowly slowing to a stop. In its white center,
>   Silence
>
>
>   Spring
> The dry and transparent air. The buffalo grass
> We pulled up from around the rabbit pens, the way
> It squeaked in our hands, the green sound. Remember
> Mary Liffert, the widow who made us pray
> The Hail Mary, the dignified rock she adopted while we did;
> The lodge we made by tunneling under the pile of brush:
> Our talks beneath the network of limbs, then silence—
> Your backlit eyes absorbed in a conversation beyond me,
> Wordless, serene. Oh, my brother, remember North Dakota,
> The glacial boulders piled up in the shape of a boat,
> Visible above the waves of wheat, sailing . . . Where?
> Out of North Dakota, out of that country, out
> Of childhood, to now. But, oh, my brother, above
> All, remember these small beginnings, these
> Crystals, remember, or I might have invented our love.